WHERE LOVE RULES

"Satisfying . . . with plenty of romantic intrigue and suspense."

—Publishers Weekly

"Readers wanting a good family saga will enjoy this!"

—Library Journal

"A fast-paced novel that covers a broad swath of modern history."

—Fort Worth Star-Telegram

"Beautifully blends politics, heritage, romance, honor, and history."

—Pensacola News Journal

Charter books by Elizabeth Nell Dubus

CAJUN
WHERE LOVE RULES

ELIZABETH NELL DUBUS

WHERE LOVE RULES

CHARTER BOOKS, NEW YORK

The author gratefully acknowledges permission from
the following sources to reprint material in their
control:
Irving Berlin Music Corporation for excerpts
from lyrics of "A Pretty Girl Is Like a Melody"
by Irving Berlin on pages 175 and 176, © copyright 1919
Irving Berlin, © copyright renewed 1946 Irving
Berlin.
The Edna St. Vincent Millay Estate for lines
from "First Fig," from *Collected Poems* published
by Harper & Row, copyright 1922, 1950 by
Edna St. Vincent Millay.

This Charter book contains the complete
text of the original hardcover edition.
It has been completely reset in a typeface
designed for easy reading, and was printed
from new film.

WHERE LOVE RULES

A Charter Book/published by arrangement with
G. P. Putnam's Sons

PRINTING HISTORY
G. P. Putnam's edition/July 1985
Charter edition/January 1987

ISBN: 0-441-88279-X

Charter Books are published by The Berkley Publishing Group,
200 Madison Avenue, New York, New York 10016.
PRINTED IN THE UNITED STATES OF AMERICA

This novel is dedicated to the many friends whose presence in my life, and in the lives of my daughters, during a long and rough passage, made all the difference in the world. Your faith in our ability to survive, your support in tangible and intangible ways, your shared laughter and shared tears—but most of all, your love—were and are proof to all of us that human beings can continually challenge adversity with hope, and sorrow with compassion. Special gratitude is given to my editor, Roger Scholl, without whose encouragement and belief this novel would not have been written.

I would like to acknowledge the Reference Department of the East Baton Rouge Parish Library, whose aid in the research for this novel was invaluable, and also recognize the Flora Levy Endowment in the Humanities and the Katherine duQuesnay Endowment for the English Department of the University of Southwestern Louisiana for a grant supporting this work.

Where love rules, there is no will to power;
and where power predominates, there love is lacking.
The one is the shadow of the other.

—Carl Jung,
The Psychology of the Unconscious

PART ONE

1

December 28, 1916

The mallard dropped from the sky, morning sun bouncing off
the green feathers that capped its head. At the edge of the
pond, a lean yellow dog watched it fall, head lifted, body
ready. Then, just before the bird hit the water, the dog leapt
forward, entering the water with legs already pumping in long
glides toward the floating duck.

Claude Langlinais stood in the blind, his shotgun broken
open and ready to reload. He looked at his son, Beau, whose
eyes followed each move of the swimming dog. "Makes you
wonder why anyone ever wants to do anything else, doesn't
it?" His free arm made a long possessive sweep that took in the
marsh around them, the pond formed by a creeping inlet of
water, the morning sky. "I tell your mother that there's a better
show out here than in any of those New Orleans theaters she's
always taking me to."

Beau's gaze made the same long possessive sweep. The
marsh grass was brown, its tall dun-colored spikes brittle under
their feet. The soft sponge of earth, fed by water from below,
drenched by the rains of December, would not be dry again
until high summer. The rustling, chirping, slithering life of the
swamp was still, quiet, nesting against winter chill. Only
the explosion of squadrons of ducks beating their way across
the sky, calling their long, cold cry, broke the winter sleep. He
shook himself, took a deep breath of air. It was seasoned with
the salt of the Gulf of Mexico, some thirty miles to the south.
He felt, suddenly, that he understood why, when his father and
his grandfather spoke of their land, their voices had a note
heard only one other time—when they spoke of their God.

The yellow dog came toward the blind, the mallard
cushioned between his jaws. He trotted over to Claude, who

3

took the duck and added it to the ones already crowding his canvas game bag. "Good boy," Claude said, rubbing the wet head. "You'll outdo your daddy yet."

"Looks like he got into something," Beau said. He bent over and rubbed the dark patches that stood out against the deep yellow fur.

Claude glanced down, then leaned closer. "What's that, Beau? Mud?"

"Something sticky," Beau said.

Claude's hand reached out, rubbed at the matted fur, then went to his nose. His eyes swept the horizon again, settling on the path the yellow dog had taken from the marsh to the pond's edge. He left the blind, hip boots sucking against the sponge of mud with each step he took. Something in the way his body was held made Beau follow him, carefully setting his own feet away from his father's already water-filled footprints. "What are you looking for?"

"What Duke found," Claude said. "See that?"

Beau looked where the finger pointed. Large bubbles broke the surface of the pond; they formed, grew, burst, and were succeeded by others so that the water seemed alive, taking breaths of the same cold air that filled Beau's lungs. "What's making them?"

"Gas," Claude said. "Remember when Solange Sorrel flooded his rice fields last spring? Saw the same thing."

"But that means there's oil here, doesn't it?" His mind cast the picture of Duke's dark-patched fur before him. "On Duke's coat—is that oil?"

"Let's find out."

They moved in small opposing circles, gradually covering the area near the pond. Beau saw his father bend forward, reach down to the earth. Claude straightened, a hand held in front of his face. Even from where he stood, Beau could see that it was black. "Papa. It's oil?"

Something of the brilliance of the hard winter sun was in Claude Langlinais' face. "It is." Then he went to Beau, moving as quickly as the heavy boots allowed. He daubed oil on Beau's forehead, his cheeks, with a grin as wide as the horizon, a laugh as tall as the sky. "It is, Beau." Claude laughed again. "Mais, I don't know anybody but a Langlinais can go out to get ducks for supper and find oil besides!"

Beau stared down at the dark puddle that crouched at his

father's feet. He remembered the stir Solange's find had caused last spring; everyone in neighboring New Iberia and here in St. Martinville had expected to outstrip Spindletop, and though so far most of the activity was on paper only, with exploration companies being formed locally and a few of the big oil companies leasing land, still, there was no question that there were oil deposits beneath the familiar fields and marshes, waiting to bring a rush of prosperity that would have nothing to do with spring plowing and summer droughts and anxious harvests.

"If there is oil here—I mean a lot of oil—what would that mean, Papa?"

"Money," Claude said. "Lots and lots of money." He slapped Beau's back. "Now, let's scout around some more, see what else we can find." He looked around him, squinting against the sun, which blazed higher now in the gray-blue sky. "Need some landmarks, so we're sure to find this corner of the swamp again. All right—see those trees? The three cypresses over there? Pace off the distance between this spot and them, Beau."

Just before he moved off, Beau turned to Claude. "We have money now, Papa. Lots of money, don't we?"

A quiet, watchful look crossed Claude's face. "Depends on what you mean by a lot, I guess, Beau." He thought of the many fingers in local economic pies that were controlled by Langlinais hands. "The money we have—it comes from things we've built up, like the sash and door factory, or the automobile agency. Or the furs and lumber." He waved a hand, again the long possessive sweep. "Making money from what's on top of the land—that's one kind of money. Making money from what's under the land—that's the best kind of little extra, the best kind of lagniappe." He gave Beau a gentle push. "So, Beau, go do what I said. So we don't misplace this lagniappe."

With even, rhythmic strides, Beau marked off a line from the pool of oil to the base of the triangle formed by the three cypresses. Counting off the paces as he walked, he had almost reached the near tree when his leading toe struck something hard.

A stake, red cloth fluttering from it, had been driven into the ground, and leaned at a slight angle toward those same three trees. The wood was still raw, yellow, not yet weathered. "What in the world . . . ?" He turned, saw Claude moving carefully over the ground, eyes cast earthward. Cupping his hands around his mouth, Beau called, "Papa! There's something here—a stake."

They stood together, looking at the slim length of wood that was as incongruous amidst the underbrush and fallen branches as though it were a finished piece of furniture. "It's a surveyor's marker," Claude said. He grasped the stake, began to pull it from the ground. Then his arm stopped. He stood a moment more, hand still holding the stake, then slowly let it go. "Somebody's read a map wrong. Probably whoever surveyed Beau Chêne for Marthe de Clouet before she sold most of her land off."

"There's another one over there," Beau said. The second stake made a line away from the first, a line that marched further from the pond. "Damn!" Claude said. "Who'd they have doing this job? Somebody either blind or blind drunk. That one's even further off the mark."

"But where does Beau Chêne begin?"

"Not here," Claude said. He straightened, looked at Beau with eyes hot enough to help the sun warm the day. "I don't hunt on another man's land, Beau."

Something had entered the morning, something foreign to the marsh, to the hunt. His father was using a voice Beau hardly ever heard; sometimes, if men from the legislature were down to meet with Claude, snatches of such voices could be heard from Claude's study, or from the front porch where they sat on hot summer nights. Hard voices, voices heavy with knowledge.

"I guess people do make mistakes," Beau said. He didn't quite understand what the stakes meant, or why finding them brought that hard note to his father's voice.

"This is a pretty big mistake, Beau." Claude's voice was still hard, but it had a smoothness now that made the hardness a weapon, not a shield. "Whoever put these stakes here put a hell of a lot of Langlinais land inside Beau Chêne's boundaries." He looked along the line the two stakes made. "We'll find more of them, I'll bet you anything you like." Claude walked toward the second stake. "Come on, let's see."

Jumie Langlinais leaned back in the rocking chair pulled close to the fireplace, his eyes locked on Claude's face. They were to have spent the afternoon of this twenty-eighth day of December, 1916, completing their review of their books; for a long time now, this had been a pleasant task, a time for the two of them to look back over what a year of work had added to their security, and to lay plans for an even better future. But today Claude had returned from his hunt with his mind full of the surveyor's stakes he had found, stakes that had, apparently, lopped off a long, narrow line of Langlinais land and added it, like another strand on a heavy chain of beads, to that belonging to the de Clouets.

"It's hard to see how a surveyor could have made such a mistake," Jumie said. "Of course, back in the swamp like that, on land we've never plowed—still, it's hard to understand."

Claude stood, moved with restless, angry energy. "Damn! It's never over, is it? The fighting for what's ours." He looked around the room that had been an office for some years now, but which originally was the cabin built by the first Claude Louis Langlinais when he had finally reached Louisiana, with his wife and children, after their hard exile from Nova Scotia over a hundred and fifty years before. "I'll bet when the first Langlinaises got here, they never thought we'd have to keep winning this land over and over again."

"A mistake, Claude. Mistakes can be corrected."

"But if they've already passed the act of sale for Beau Chêne, it'll take a hell of a lot of work to do it. Papa, that could drag out for years. And in the meantime . . . in the meantime, the oil just sits there! No one will take a lease on land with a clouded title."

Jumie reached forward and took a pot of coffee from the trivet set over the coals. He gestured toward Claude's empty cup, and, at Claude's assenting nod, filled it, and then his own. "Your mama made crullers this morning. Come sit, Claude. Drink your coffee, eat a cruller. I'll talk to Marthe." He spooned sugar into his cup, stirred. "I don't think they were really going to sign the papers until the thirtieth. The representative of the sugar refinery couldn't get down here until then. So there's still time."

Claude shot a glance at his father. "You make it sound so simple. You and Marthe will sit down, have a drink together—and between you settle the fate of the world."

"Does being in the legislature make you talk like that, Claude?" Jumie's voice was soft, but the words still threw a challenge between them.

"Hell, Papa," Claude said. "How can you see what goes on in Baton Rouge and not get just a little less trusting, a little more cynical?"

"Claude. I can see that you would not trust men who have shown you they don't know how to speak the truth. What's that you say to me? That a lot of those politicians lie when the truth would serve them better?" Jumie leaned toward Claude, stretched out a hand. "But, Claude. This is Marthe de Clouet we're talking about. You know how far back Marthe and I go. When I tell her that the men surveying her land made a mistake, she'll have it surveyed again. She may not be a Langlinais, but Marthe, she doesn't steal land!"

"Let's just hope she hasn't let her son-in-law have a piece of this pie, Papa." Claude thought of Charles Livaudais, the New Orleans lawyer Marthe's daughter Hélène had married. Livaudais' legal skills were less used in the courtroom than in the back room of state and city politics—rumor had it that he was privy to darker secrets there than if he defended the most blatant criminals. Claude sighed. "Trusting Marthe de Clouet de Gravelle is one thing—trusting Charles Livaudais is another."

"Because Livaudais backed Ruffin Pleasant for governor, you think he's a thief too?" Something in Jumie's voice, a kind of detachment from what his words meant, hit Claude, hard. For the first time, he saw that his father was getting old, that the ins and outs of politics, the machinations of those wresting power wherever they could find it, had no interest for Jumie. It had not been always thus. In fact, thought Claude wryly, he himself would never have run for the House of Representatives in 1912 if Jumie had not convinced him that as the heir to the Langlinais holdings, he must carry their flag into the field where lasting decisions were made. How he had fought the idea, how he had argued that managing their land and their businesses was more than enough for any man! "We've survived the British twice, we've overcome sickness and flood and Yankee occupation, and Reconstruction—our own politicians won't get us," he had said, knowing all the time that he would have to leave his beloved marsh, his rich land, to sit at committee hearings and long sessions in the House chambers in Baton Rouge.

He remembered what had made him say yes. A hunting trip with his son, Beau, the same weekend the men from New

Orleans had come for his final decision. A young face, greeting the dawn with the same eagerness as the dog bounding at his feet. Young arms hefting a gun, swinging it against a sky that covered Langlinais land with a blanket of blue. A young voice, shouting across the crisp air. "Papa! Papa! Isn't this the best place in the whole world? The very, very best?"

The assurance in that voice, the confidence that this land was theirs to keep, to love, made Claude leave it. His hand drifted across the open ledger book. A long row of similar books told the Langlinais story, recounted the diligence and dedication of generation after generation of Langlinais men, each of whom had dropped his mantle on the shoulders of the eldest son. That mantle had grown both richer and heavier as the years went by. The early fur trade had expanded, the lumber mill boomed. So many details, so much responsibility! Zut, that oil would be good, yes! Let it flow from the ground, flowing money! And goddammit if that puny little line of stakes was going to hold him down!

He went to Jumie, put a hand on his father's shoulder. That shoulder had borne the mantle well, had carried the Langlinais flag into the twentieth century, and had steered them through all the changes that had brought. If Papa were tired now . . . His muscles, still lean and wiry despite long hours at the desk in his office, the desk in the legislature, tensed. If Papa were tired, he must rest. Claude had a strange sensation, a feeling of something different. Then he realized that in that quiet moment, the mantle had been passed. "Of course, a man can be on the other side of the fence and still know how to make a straight path, Papa. Livaudais—he knows only one kind of path. The one that gets him to what he wants. And if it takes him over another man's land . . ." Claude's shoulders lifted, a shrug that meant that although he could read Livaudais' method, he could not comprehend it. "Well. Anyway, let's hope one little visit with Marthe will straighten it all out."

"There may not even be much oil there, Claude. One little pool—"

"But that one little pool—if that's all there is—is ours, Papa. Ours." For the first time since entering the office an hour ago, Claude laughed. "Mais, I tell you what, Papa. With the kind of luck the Langlinaises have, I don't think that's going to be just one little pool, no!"

2

The age-softened pink brick walls of Beau Chêne, gleaming in the rose light of sunset, seemed to bask in the calm air trapped beneath the tall oaks that formed the alley to the road and that clustered around the house itself. Jumie, riding through the high double gates that fronted the road, reined in his mare for a moment and sat in that stillness. How many years had he been making the path between the Langlinais farm and Beau Chêne part of his life? The sun ducked behind a low streak of cloud and the light went out of the sky. The house before him seemed to shrink too, pulling its proud façade close around it, gathering its forces as though against assault. He thought of the sale of Beau Chêne's fields, those rich squares of land that had been granted to the first de Clouet when he and his wife and children had fled just ahead of the blade of the Revolutionists' guillotine. For long, long years those fields had been part of one of the finest sugar plantations in the state. Now they were being sold off to a large sugar concern; if it had not been for his intervention . . . Here Jumie smiled, thinking of Marthe de Clouet de Gravelle's reaction to that word. Well, if it had not been for his suggestion, gracefully taken, Marthe would not have kept the fifty acres immediately surrounding the house, nor the mineral rights to the rest of the land. Mineral rights! Damn the oil. He was getting old. Maybe there was something to Claude's charge about the surveying. But not because of Marthe. He tightened his knees against the horse, whistled softly, put the mare into gentle forward motion.

A figure rose up before him, one arm waving. "Jumie! For heaven's sake, what are you doing coming in the front way like company?" Marthe de Gravelle had a scar of mud on one cheek, where a hand had brushed against it. She held a pair of long-bladed clippers in one hand, and though the December twilight was chilled, sweat dotted her forehead. "I've about worn myself out pruning these roses. Nat said he'd do it, but gracious, Jumie, if I've reached the point where fooling with a few rosebushes is beyond me . . ."

"Nothing is ever beyond you," Jumie said, swinging down beside her. He took his handkerchief from his pocket and rubbed at her face. "You've got mud all over your face, Marthe." Then he picked up her free hand, inspected it. "And blisters on your hand. Let Nat do the pruning—you do the picking and sniffing."

Marthe tucked an arm through Jumie's. "Sounds like a lovely life. Oh, Lord, Jumie, I'll be so glad when this sale is finished. I've got an ache in my neck that won't go away until that money is safe in the Teche Bank."

"When will it be finished?"

"The thirtieth. Day after tomorrow."

They were nearing the house; Jumie had a sudden wish not to take his questions and Claude's doubts inside. "Will you be too cold if we sit here a minute?" he asked, gesturing to a stone bench set beneath one of the massive oaks that gave the place its name.

"Jumie, what is it? What have you come to tell me?" He could see Marthe mentally counting—René, Nanette, Hélène, Caroline. Her children and her granddaughter—the names on the beads of worry she carried in her hand.

He sat facing her. The sun was making a last appearance in the sky, throwing its energy into a splendid display of rose and purple and deep gold lights. The rays took the gray from Marthe's hair, shone only on the waves that looked like molded gold. "Marthe." He took her hand. "As far as I know, I don't have anything to tell you. Nothing to worry you, I mean." His fingers were playing with hers; even with the blisters, Marthe's hands felt soft in his. "Who did the surveying? For the sale?"

Marthe had been staring down at their two hands as though they belonged to two other people entirely. "Surveying?" She moved the hand he held away, brushed at a strand of hair that swept across her forehead. "Well, I had gotten the Landry brothers to do it. Then Charles was down hunting, and he said he'd send someone out from New Orleans. I couldn't see going to all that trouble, but he said something about utility company rights-of-way and, I don't know, you know how Charles is when he sets his mind on something." Marthe laughed. "I've learned to save my objections for really important things."

He couldn't have known about the oil, Jumie thought. No one ever goes back to that part of our land, only to hunt. Then it struck him—Marthe had said Charles was down hunting. "Looks like they should have taken one of the Landrys with them," he said, trying to keep his voice easy. "Those city folk, one bit of swamp looks like another."

"What are you saying, Jumie?"

He looked into her dark blue eyes, eyes that would never admit to the almost sixty years Marthe had. This was Marthe, the woman who had hoed corn when she had to, run Beau Chêne when she had to, sold her fields when she had to. No pussyfooting around her, thank God. "Well, they got some of our land mixed in with yours, Marthe. Back in the marsh." The eyes made a question. "Claude and Beau found the stakes this morning. They were out getting some ducks and they found the stakes."

"But, Jumie, how in the world could they make a mistake like that? Is it much land?"

Jumie shrugged. "Not a very wide piece. But long."

Without warning, Marthe began to cry. Her face went down behind the cover of her hands, her shoulders shook, and a sound that almost broke Jumie's heart filled the space between them.

"Marthe . . ." He pulled her against him, held her. "Marthe, now look, it's nothing that can't be fixed, Marthe . . ."

She leaned away, looked up at him. "I'm sorry. I know you can't stand crying. It's just—oh, Jumie, I've counted so on this sale, if anything goes wrong—"

"Nothing's going to go wrong. For God's sake, they can't plant sugar back there in the marsh. Only reason that part of your land is in the sale is that there was no point leaving it out, long as you kept the mineral rights. It can be resurveyed, just that part of it."

"Before the thirtieth?" She stood, and the normal Marthe, the Marthe who had begun running Beau Chêne when her father died, and who had taken on all the hard burdens her husband's death had left her, stood before him. "Maybe the Landrys could do it. There's not time to get those people back from New Orleans. Will I have to tell Alcide LeBlanc? You know what an idiot he is to deal with!"

Jumie rose too. He felt better now. It was out in the open, where he and Marthe could deal with it, as they had dealt with everything for years and years. "I've always told you, one of the luckiest things is Alcide being the agent in all this. He thinks he knows everything all the time—act like you thought he'd caught it too, just from looking at the plat plan. Don't worry about Alcide."

Marthe looked at her watch. "I don't think Paul Landry would mind if I called him at home. It's not that much land, they should be able to do it in the time we have." She caught at Jumie's arm. "Could Claude or Beau show them where it is, do you think? To save time?"

Jumie thought of the way Claude had described the seeping pool of oil, the gas bubbles breaking upon the water's soft face. "Claude will want to go, I think. Call and tell me what Paul says."

She was all business now, intent on the task ahead. "I will." She stood on tiptoe, kissed Jumie's cheek. "But I'll give you time to eat Geneviève's supper first. I happen to know you're having duck and oyster gumbo."

"You got people for supper?" He looked at the house. The lights in the upstairs parlor were lit now, but the dining room on the ground floor was dark.

"Charles and Hélène won't be here until New Year's Eve morning. And Caroline spent the day in New Iberia; the Favrots will bring her home around nine."

"So come eat gumbo with us," he said. "The telephone works from our house, too."

Marthe, in her turn, looked at the house before them. The tall white columns, the jalousied lower and upper galleries, the delicate outside staircase, made it a showplace—but showplaces could be just as empty and lonely as less magnificent houses. "That sounds wonderful," she said.

Beau watched the yellow flash of fur as Duke darted into the undergrowth crowding the clearing and then backed out, the short length of stick grasped firmly in his jaws. He turned, ran to his master, and put the stick in Beau's outstretched hand. Beau buried his fingers in the thick-haired mat of fur, stroking gently. "Sticks aren't nearly the fun that ducks are, are they, old boy?" Beau said. Duke wasn't the only one disappointed that the daily hunt had been called off; when Beau had joined his father in the big kitchen for early breakfast, Claude had

been dressed not in hunting gear, but in work pants and shirt.
"No hunting today," Claude had said, sipping on his first cup
of fragrant black coffee. "I'm meeting with the Landrys' surveying team out at Papa's in an hour. Going to walk over the
land with them, make sure that this time those stakes go where
they damn well belong."

Beau felt a jolt in his plans for the day. During the Christmas
holidays, he'd come to love the early mornings, the quiet cups
of coffee with his father in the bright kitchen, the taste of ham
or bacon or boudin lingering in his mouth as he and Claude and
Duke drove out to the farm. Then the bustle of getting the guns
and shot and game bags out of the car, the long walk through
the dawn to the blind, the settling in against the damp chill of a
persistent night, the hush just before the sun woke up—the
quick throb of the marsh as every creature in it responded to the
sun's rising, and its promise of life for another day.

"Can Duke and I ride out with you anyway?" Beau had
glanced at the big yellow hound settled in his corner of the
kitchen, anxiously watching for a morsel of ham or a forgotten
biscuit. "Duke needs his exercise and I . . . well, I'd kind of
like some myself."

"Just so you stay away from where they'll be working,"
Claude said. Since Jumie had called Claude the night before,
telling him that Marthe had gotten hold of the Landrys, and
that they would have a team at the Langlinais farm first thing in
the morning, he had felt somewhat, but not much, easier. It
was like being on a committee in the legislature, a committee
where an important bill was being considered. Even if the early
sessions went well, you could never let up until the bill had
been reported out favorably. And even if a man said he would
support you all the way through, if someone else offered him a
better deal, it was amazing how quickly yesterday's promises
became today's denials. No, until the correct survey had been
filed, he would not let up his watch. It was one thing for
Marthe de Clouet de Gravelle to believe a casual error, a little
mistake, had been made. The test, like the committee vote,
would be when Charles Livaudais arrived in a couple of days
and found out what had happened. Claude smiled, a light
tracing of humor across the grimness of his face. Committee
opponents, and those on the floor of the House of Representatives, knew what that smile meant. Not that Claude found the
situation funny—but that he found it winnable.

And so they had driven out to the farm in the new Buick, looking, as Claude's mother Geneviève would say, "like two chicks from the same egg." They did look alike, both with compact, wiry bodies whose easy grace and swift movement belied the strength beneath. Beau had his father's hair, the brown mixed with blond that his people called "chatin." His features were like Claude's, too. A smooth line of cheek that curved down to a firm, rounded chin. A broad forehead framed by one curving lock of hair. The nose, not the beak that proudly crowned many a strong face in this part of Louisiana, but smaller, straighter, with the slightest break that took it back in time to Roman conquerors. A smile that began as one quick curve, breaking the still smoothness of the face, then broke into a wide grin. Girls watching Beau Langlinais smile found themselves smiling back; they also noticed that they remembered the way Beau smiled long after they were no longer with him. Only the eyes were different. Claude's were brown, the brown of his father's. But Beau's were gray, like those of his mother, Alice de Blanc Langlinais. And like his mother, Beau had heavy, dark lashes that his two sisters envied, complaining they were wasted on a boy. "Nothing is wasted on Beau," his grandmother Geneviève said, bending her head low over her crochet work to hide the look of pride whenever she thought of her handsome grandson. And though she used to say to Beau, as she did to his sisters, Marie and Francie, that pretty is as pretty does, she could find no fault with Beau's manners. "He loves life," she said to Claude once, watching Beau dance with Marie. "But he loves people, too, and that will keep him balanced."

As for Beau, he paid little attention to his looks, only being careful to comb his hair properly before appearing at his mother's table, and scraping the new fuzz from his chin and cheeks several times a week with the razor his father had ceremoniously presented him. He paid far more attention to his body, testing it against the fields and swamps, developing its agility, its tough strength. Out in the swamp with Duke, he had played a hard game, running ahead of the big dog, tossing the stick further still, racing to beat Duke to the goal. Now he looked at the height of the sun in the sky, measuring it against the path it must travel to reach noon. "Let's go get Grandmama to give us goûter," he said. "And think about how many more ducks there'll be tomorrow since we didn't hunt today." The dog fell in beside him, and they began picking their way over the water-marked marsh toward the fenced grounds of the Langlinais farm.

They had gone several hundred yards, could, in fact, see the first fences, the first signs of cultivation in the midst of the wild land, when Duke began to growl deep at the back of his throat. Beau's hand went swiftly to the dog's collar. "What is it, Duke?" His eyes tried to penetrate the grasses, the shrubs, to find a rabbit or coon. Then he saw something moving in the trees just ahead of them, a bit of blue that broke out of the screening greenery, a blue that in a moment became Caroline de Gravelle Livaudais.

She had not seen them yet; her eyes were on something in her hand, something which Beau could see, as she neared them, was a small bunch of wild violets. Then she looked up, and he saw the startled look on Caroline's face, replaced in a moment by fear. "Miss Livaudais—it's Beau Langlinais, Jumie Langlinais' grandson. Don't be afraid." For just a moment, the fear stayed in place. "Christmas Eve—at church? We met outside, afterward."

He could see her remembering, and watched her eyes lighten with the reassurance of that meeting. He had watched her all during midnight Mass, his eyes taking quick sideways glances at her shining curls, the way her cheek curved so sweetly, the way her lips caught in a small, open round of softness when she sang the responses to the prayers. He remembered another feeling stirring in him afterward when he was introduced to her. "My granddaughter, Caroline Livaudais, come to keep me company this Christmas," Marthe de Gravelle had said, one arm hugging Caroline close. "You two haven't seen each other since you were both about four years old and you played on the upper gallery all one afternoon," she said, drawing Beau in with her other hand.

"I hope it's not twelve years between meetings again," Beau had said, taking the gloved hand Caroline held out to him. Her hand had been small, light, feeling in the smooth kid glove like a perfectly formed model of a hand with no life of its own. Then the hand had moved, had clasped his quite firmly, before letting go.

"For goodness' sake! Beau Langlinais!" Caroline said, the fear gone, flying high toward the tops of the giant old cypress trees with Caroline's laughter. "But you look different, you know!" she said, laughing again.

Beau laughed too, looking down at his khaki pants, the knee-high leather boots laced tightly beneath them. "I guess!" He looked at the flowers in her hand. "Wild violets. A little early for those. You wouldn't have found them if the weather hadn't been so mild."

Caroline's cheeks were pinker now, flags of color. "Will they last, do you think? If I put them in water right away?"

Beau shrugged. "I don't know. My sisters—Francie and Marie, you met them outside of church—are always bringing stuff back to the house after they've been out here. And Mama. She goes out in the fields and gets cattails and goldenrod. Grandmama Geneviève has a fit—asks why they're always bringing weeds into the house." The flowers were already dying, stems becoming limp, petals wilting. "Where did you find them?"

Caroline pointed to the woods behind them. "Show me," Beau said. He followed her into the cool damp, his feet covering the small prints her shoes made in the wet earth. She led him to the clump of violets, lavender flowers almost hidden beneath the deep green leaves. Beau knelt and took his hunting knife from its sheath. Carefully he loosened the earth around a clump of violets, digging a circle around the plants so that, when he lifted them, their roots were still in the soil. He found several broad sycamore leaves nearby and wrapped them beneath the plants. "Here," he said, handing them to Caroline. "You can put these in a pot, or even in one of Mrs. de Gravelle's flowerbeds."

"But how lovely of you!" she said. The wilted flowers dropped from her hand as she took the plants. "I'd never have thought of doing that. Beau, thank you!"

"Look, I'm on my way up to my grandmama's house for goûter—would you like to come?" He guessed the reason for the frown that crossed her forehead. "Goûter is—well, a little taste of something nice. I guess that's how it translates."

Caroline laughed again, a laugh that moved across her face until all her features were in motion. Lord, he could listen to Caroline Livaudais laugh forever and not get tired of it. "I do study French, at Sacred Heart in New Orleans," she said, skipping a step to make her pace match his. "But we don't use it outside the classroom—not like you all do down here."

"I guess the country is pretty dull, after New Orleans," he said.

"Oh, no, it's not!" Her eyes were very much like her grand-mother's, Beau thought. They were the same deep blue, had that same way of getting very wide when you said something she liked, or something she didn't quite understand. "I adore the country. And the luckiest thing, I'm going to be here all during Lent. Mama's going on a trip to rest up after all those balls, and I'm going to stay with my grandmother at Beau Chêne."

He had almost forgotten who she was. Caroline de Gravelle Livaudais, whose mother grew up on Beau Chêne, and whose father was on the other side of the political fence drawn between the New Orleans political machine and those who would break it down. He thought of the surveyors, even now restoring to the Langlinaises that which had been engulfed by the de Clouet lands. He felt something pulling, a kind of thread that would tie him to the Langlinaises, and would bind him away from any dealings with those who might oppose them. He moved, a kind of twisting movement, a subconscious breaking free of those clinging strands. "That's good. I come out to my grandparents' a lot." He paused, waited for those wide, deep eyes to meet his. "We can . . . spend some time together. There'll be all kinds of flowers out then. You'll need a big basket." The sun had found a hole through which it could send its rays. They were caught in it as though in a spotlight; Caroline's hair shone brilliantly and there was fire in her eyes. Beau felt a vague stirring, something he'd never felt before. It was like the time in history class when the teacher was lecturing about the Justinian Code, and all of a sudden he understood what law really was, what it was supposed to do, and tried to do—and had, in that minute, decided he would become a lawyer.

"That sounds . . . very nice," Caroline said. Her voice was composed, the words light, but her eyes were not. She looked down at the plants in her hand. "I'll take these back to New Orleans," she said. "To . . . remember you by." As they approached Geneviève Langlinais' kitchen garden, Beau saw a group of men moving toward the house from the fields on the other side, clustered with his father in the center. The survey-ing team must be finished, he thought. If that were so, why did he still feel that everything was up in the air, that nothing had been really settled? He looked at the girl beside him, who had paused, watching the surveyors. Maybe Caroline was shy.

He led the way to the back steps of his grandparents' home. "Grandmama!" he called from the back door. "Grandmama, it's Beau." He ushered Caroline ahead of him into the big square kitchen just as Geneviève came in from the hall. "We've been out walking, we're starved, Grandmama."

A look Beau couldn't define came over his grandmother's face as she looked at the two of them together. Then, with a quick shake of her head, she came toward them, smiling, hands outstretched. "Well, listen, I have a whole tin of those good little cakes I made for your mama's big party on New Year's Eve, only she said they taste good but they don't look pretty on the plate!" She turned to Caroline. "Now, I ask you, do you eat with your stomach or your eyes?"

"You're coming, aren't you?" Beau said to Caroline as they sat at the table. "To our New Year's Eve party."

"Am I invited?" She put out a hand, touched his with one fleeting stroke. "I don't mean to be rude. I really don't know— I mean, no one's said."

"Your grandmother is certainly invited," Beau said. "And that always means all houseguests, too."

"Oh, good. Mama and Papa will be down, so we'll all come." She took a bite of cake. "Mrs. Langlinais, I agree with you—we eat with our stomachs," she said. "These are delicious."

"Have some milk," Geneviève said. She had fixed coffee for herself and now sat down across from them, studying Caroline. "You're the image of your grandmother," she said. "Marthe de Clouet de Gravelle, she's what my Jumie calls true blue."

Caroline flushed with pleasure and bent her head over her plate. But while Beau's hand automatically reached for a cake, automatically brought a brimming glass of milk to his lips, his thoughts were back in the swamp, when he had first seen the stakes, each with its bright bit of red cloth like a drop of blood trailing across the marsh. The line they'd made had followed the line small pools of seeping oil had made; had that line not been changed, the oil find would have been on Beau Chêne. He shifted in his chair. His father had not said in actual words that Caroline's father's surveyors had been acting on orders. But Beau knew that was what his father thought. The thread that had seemed to pull at him earlier, trying to tie him to the Langlinais view, had not, after all, lost its strength. He felt it in this kitchen, felt it weaving itself around them, between Beau and his grandmother, stretching out to where his father walked with the surveyors. Was there room within the circle the thread made for Caroline? And if there were not, could he duck beneath the circle's limits and still leave it intact?

3

Alice Langlinais picked up the necklace that glittered up at her from its velvet bed, held it against her neck, and leaned closer to her dressing-table mirror. "Claude, what do you think? With my new necklace, will the Spanish combs be too much?"

"It's your party. Wear every damn jewel you've got if you want to." He went to her, bent and kissed her shoulder, then let his lips follow the curving line down to her breast. "Here's another party for you to think about." He pulled a square envelope from his breast pocket and handed it to her.

Alice rose, smoothing her cream-colored crêpe-de-chine skirt over her hips. "What is it?" She took the envelope, a look on her face like that of a child gazing into a window filled with sugar confections. Claude watched as she removed the card from the envelope, read it. "Oh, Claude!" Her eyes glowed. "An invitation to dinner at the governor's mansion!" Her arms went around his neck, her lips came up to meet his.

"And here you've been worrying since last May you'd never see the inside of the mansion again," he teased.

"I wasn't really worried," Alice said, leaning back in his arms. Her face now was relaxed, the child whose father owned the confectionery shop. "You did fight Ruffin Pleasant tooth and nail, though. I keep thinking he's going to want to get even."

Claude laughed, the big laugh that boomed against their bedroom ceiling, splitting against the branches of the crystal-dropped chandelier. "He might want to. He'll have a hell of a time doing it."

"Charles Livaudais is in the governor's pocket, isn't he?"

"Or the other way around," Claude said, releasing her. He thought of the evening ahead. They had had to include Charles and Hélène Livaudais in the invitation to the party; he hoped they would find themselves otherwise engaged. Although the sale of Beau Chêne had been successfully completed the morning before, although the line of stakes now marched obediently along its proper course, he had an uneasy feeling that they had not heard the last of the episode.

"You've got powder all over your coat and rouge all over your mouth," Alice said, brushing at his shoulder. Then she looked up at him. "I wish Charles and Hélène weren't coming."

"Now, Alice. You're not going to let a silly woman like Hélène spoil your evening, are you?" He rubbed her rouge from his mouth, took her arm, tucked it under his, and led her out into the wide upper hall that ended at the landing of the curved staircase.

"Nooo. No, of course not. It's just I want everyone who comes to a party here to have fun—and you know Hélène never looks as though she is having a good time!"

From below, a high, sweet wail came to them, followed by the rapid beat of drumsticks. "That doesn't sound like that little band from New Iberia," Alice said.

"It's not. It's one of those new jazz groups from New Orleans." He could see Alice's eyes widen again; color pulsed in her cheeks, her entire body quickened with pleasure, as it did when they were in bed. "Oh, Claude! A jazz band from New Orleans! Well, if Hélène doesn't have a good time tonight, she never will!"

Claude patted Alice's hand and moved forward. The jewels in her tall combs caught at sparkles of light from the chandelier, sent them bouncing off the brilliance of the diamonds at her throat. He knew her war with the Livaudaises was a personal one, that she had little real interest in his political differences with Charles Livaudais. Nor had he told her about the surveying stakes. Let her go on thinking the main field of battle was in drawing rooms and front parlors. Claude sighed. The smell of ham baking, of milk and eggs heating for eggnog, of hardwood fires burning, surrounded him, floating up from the reception rooms below. A rich smell, an almost palpable smell. A smell that went with all those leather-bound, gilt-edged engagement books in Alice's writing desk, books that

held enough luncheons, teas, receptions, dinners, theater parties, and balls to wear out any three women. A richness that
went with the rich leather of her address book, whose pages
were filled with the names of shops in New Orleans where
Alice bought shoes and gloves and handbags, the names of
dressmakers, tailors, bartenders and hairdressers, the names of
an ever-widening circle of friends, all of whose lives matched
Alice's own. And yet . . . and yet he could not help but feel
that Alice did not quite believe in their life. That she saw
Hélène Livaudais as belonging to those people who had always
lived, and would always live, in just that rich way—and herself as belonging to people whose late arrival caused a tenuous
hold. He thought of the pools of oil, gleaming now under the
moon. If they were in fact the surface showing of a deep well,
Alice would never have to look back again.

Below them, the doorbell chimed. "What do you bet that's
Miss Bessie?" Claude said. "I've never known her to miss
being first at a party so she can watch everyone else come in."

Alice gave him a little push toward the door. "So open it, see
who it is." She glanced through the double doors into the
dining room at the long walnut table, centered with dark green
magnolia leaves tied with velvet bows. The heavy lace cloth
fell in folds to the rug, the gold and crystal serving plates
gleamed. The new French wallpaper, one of the last shipments
to leave before the start of the war, had made the room elegant,
imposing. Her hands closed together in an almost prayerful
gesture. The rest of her house was wonderful, too. When she
and Claude had built it nine years ago, moving in from the
farm to live in this tall frame house, bay windows and round
towers breaking the symmetry of its lines, the elder Langlinaises had behaved as though they were colonizing barbaric
territory. Alice ran a hand over the smooth millwork that
framed the double door into the dining room. They hadn't
understood, Jumie and Geneviève, that she had wanted something that was hers, something generation upon generation
hadn't already left a mark on. Inheriting businesses is one
thing, she thought, glancing into the front parlor with its
heavily carved Signouret love seats and chairs. Inheriting
farmhouses is another. And by the time they had moved in,
even Geneviève had had to admit that Alice had a flair for
houses. Lots of tall windows, an array of light colors, green
plants to offset the dark woods and Persian rugs. The house

was like Alice herself—bright, charming—uniquely itself. Alice sighed, happiness going through her with every beat of music from the back parlor, with every new aroma from the kitchen. And now she had dinner at the governor's mansion to think about and plan for. As she went forward to greet Miss Bessie, she made a mental note to call her dressmaker the very first thing when these holidays were over.

Miss Bessie was followed by a crowd of people; as one guest said, "If you needed to decide something by public vote right this minute, you could do it here in Claude's house." And by the time the group from Beau Chêne arrived, Charles Livaudais guiding his wife, his mother-in-law, and his daughter into the hall where Claude and Alice were receiving their guests, the party had worked its usual magic: Alice's eyes shone, her cheeks glowed, and her tongue chattered happily with every new arrival. Borne on that crest of gaiety, she sailed forward to greet her new guests. "But come in out of the cold! Yesterday like spring, today it's winter all over! Caroline, you're as tall as your mama, we're going to have to put bricks on you girls' heads, you're growing up too fast." She beckoned to Marie and Francie, who hovered near the table, watching to see that the serving plates were continually filled. "Marie, Francie, you remember meeting Caroline Livaudais after Mass on Christmas Eve?"

"And Beau has met you since, hasn't he?" Francie said, her eyes full on Caroline's face.

"Yes, the other morning," Caroline said. She didn't see the look her mother shot her and went on. "He was so kind; he dug some wild violets for me when the ones I picked wilted."

Alice felt a tension charging the space between her family and their guests from Beau Chêne, and moved forward. "Now, let the girls take your coats. Francie, you carry them upstairs, Marie, take our guests into the dining room, and be sure Caroline meets the young people." She bustled around them, gently maneuvering them away from the door and into the mainstream of the party. From down the hall, she saw Beau coming toward them, darting through the crowd of guests that filled it. She stepped toward him, a hand out to take his arm. But he seemed not to see her; he moved past, in a line that took him directly in front of Caroline. "I'm so glad you came," he said. "I . . . I was afraid maybe you wouldn't."

Now what? Alice thought. She could see a frown forming on

Hélène's face, could see one thin hand going almost automatically to the tiny gold watch that hung from a diamond bow pinned to the lace frills at Hélène's throat. "I was afraid maybe we wouldn't, too," she heard Caroline say. "Mama said she had a frightful headache. But Grandmama must have given her something for it, because after a while she said it was better, and we could come."

Alice glanced at Hélène. Their eyes met in a look that pushed aside the rich smells, the vibrant music, the elaborate food, the chattering, laughing guests. "I'm glad you're feeling better," Alice said across the space that look made. "It would have been a shame if you were too ill to come."

"Yes," Hélène said. She took Charles's arm, said something Alice could not hear, and moved toward the entrance to the dining room. She'll make her manners and leave, Alice thought. She felt a frown pulling at her lips, creasing her forehead, and made herself smile. Then the doorbell rang again, the hall was filled with another swell of guests, and in the happy ceremony of greeting them, Alice forgot that small jarring moment.

By eleven o'clock, the young people had taken over the back parlor, filling its cleared floor with bodies swinging to the high sweet cry of the trumpet, the low echo of the saxophone. Beau had not let Caroline out of his sight, and though he allowed other boys to dance with her, he saw to it that he had two dances for every one of theirs. "She's your spit," Jumie said to Marthe as they stood in the doorway watching. "She's going to be a great belle."

"Oh, Lord," Marthe said. And when Jumie looked at her: "I know, it's supposed to be the nicest thing in the world to be a belle, to have so many men after you all the time. But, Jumie, it's a terrible responsibility! Now, don't laugh at me, it is! If a girl has any honor at all—all those broken hearts!" She looked at Beau and Caroline, dancing past them. "There are some hearts that just don't ever recover."

Jumie took her arm. "Let's hope Caroline never breaks one of those, then." He said it lightly, but his eyes went back to his grandson and Marthe's granddaughter, standing now in a corner of the room, heads close. "Claude suggested gathering in his study for supper—get out of this crush." He led her down the hall, opened a heavy paneled door under the stairway, ushered her ahead of him. "Now, you sit, Marthe. I'll get plates for both of us."

"You spoil me, Jumie," she said. But she sank into one of Claude's tall leather wingback chairs. She was surprised that they were still at the party. Hélène had finally agreed to come, but clinging to her "headache," had said they would stay thirty minutes and no more. "We'll stay only as long as we have to," she had announced. Charles had not replied, and Marthe had thought he agreed. Until Hélène came up to her and said, petulance turning her voice into a thin whine, that Charles was having a good time, and intended to stay until they had rung the new year in. "How *can* he be having a good time?" Hélène had said. She had raised the lorgnette she carried to evening parties and peered through it, the curved glass reflecting the sulky look in her pale blue eyes.

"I don't know," Marthe had answered. "This isn't his usual kind of party, is it?" Marthe's voice was cold, and Hélène had quickly changed the subject. There was no good arguing with Mama about Charles; Mama preferred to think the world was run as it had been when her beloved father was alive, though God knew he had made himself blind to its many faults and failings! Hélène herself didn't really like to watch Charles when he got a certain look on his face, a look that reminded her of nothing so much as the way her mama's black cook looked when she was fixing to wring a chicken's neck. Not cruel, not really. Just kind of mindless—as though nothing he was seeing had much value except to him. Bother! She always got queer ideas when she came down to Beau Chêne; it was all that fresh air—it made her brain think of all kinds of crazy things. Watching Charles move through the crowd with that look on his face made her restless—and thirsty. By the time Charles took her into Claude's study for supper, Hélène had had four glasses of sherry and two cups of eggnog well-laced with bourbon, and was more than ready to start in on Claude's Bordeaux.

Charles was in excellent spirits. Nothing stimulated him quite so much as being in what he saw as an adversary situation; he was fond of saying that if there were not something faintly disreputable about being a criminal lawyer, he would have enjoyed just such a practice. Being on Claude Langlinais' home turf had excited him, although he had also been disturbed to see how many of the area's prominent people thronged to Claude's house—and seemed damn glad to be there. One other thing had stimulated him. As Alice Langlinais moved through the crowd, speaking now with one group, now with another, his eyes had followed her. It had pleased him to watch the way the silk crêpe clung to her breasts, and caressed the line of her hips and thighs. He had let his eyes wander over her, toy with her—and once, her eyes had met his, and he had had the infinite pleasure of watching her blush. So she is not unaware, he had thought. Tall, with a body he kept just this side of being fit with disciplined rounds in his club's boxing ring, Charles Livaudais still had the looks which had made him such a catch when Hélène de Gravelle, ignoring the depleted Livaudais fortune, had married him. "There's enough left," she had told her parents. "Charles is bright, the head of his law class. Money isn't everything. Anyway, he'll make more. Lots more." As he had. Looks, charm, brains. And that mindless look that made Hélène nervous. If Marthe wondered how Charles made so much money, and so quickly, she kept her mouth shut. As for Hélène, she had long ago regretted the impulse that made her choose green-eyed, black-haired Charles Livaudais, with nothing but the family home on Fourth Street and a position in an old and solid law firm to offer her, over the less exciting, but more constant, beaux. The charm her husband dispensed so lavishly on other women, Hélène found, was taken out of the account that should have been paid to her.

Filling Charles's glass with wine, Claude studied him carefully. He was forking ham into his mouth with the same gusto with which he joined a political fight or took a new woman to bed; Claude, watching that vitality, knew that here was an opponent closer to his mettle than any other man he knew. He must not know about the stakes, Claude thought. He's not eating like a man with a secret to defend.

Marthe was watching Charles, too. "I forgot to tell you, Charles. Those surveyors you sent out from New Orleans? They made a mistake."

Claude's eyes, like sentinels still alert after a long watch, fastened on Charles's face. Was that a flicker of movement? "What sort of mistake?" Charles said. He sounded mildly curious, slightly interested.

"It's all right now," Marthe said. "I had the land resurveyed. Well, just the part of it they'd managed to get mixed up!" She laughed. "Jumie was right, one piece of swamp looks the same as another to city folk!"

"I'm not sure I'm following you," Charles said. He smiled at Alice, who sat across from him. "This wine jelly is wonderful,

Alice. I wonder if you'd give me a little more, please." She rose and brought the bowl to him, ladled a spoon of the clear, roseate jelly onto his plate. They seemed caught in a hush, a space only the two of them occupied. Her eyes felt drawn to his fingers, holding his wineglass carelessly. It's his power, she thought. Claude has it, too. They can put a wall around you, make you forget everything else.

"I'll set it here," she said, putting the bowl on a low table by his chair. "In case you want more."

"I usually do," he said. He dipped a piece of venison into the jelly, ate it. Then he turned back to Marthe. "Are you saying that my surveyors didn't make a good job of it?" The curiosity and interest were still controlled, but there was another note in his voice, a watchfulness that matched Claude's own.

"They got some of Jumie's land mixed up with mine, Charles," Marthe said. And Claude, seeing the way she looked at her son-in-law, knew that Marthe had not been fooled. Like Claude himself, she believed the mistake to be deliberate.

Charles sipped wine. "That seems almost . . . impossible, Marthe. How did you decide that?"

"I told her so," Claude said. Charles's eyes swung in Claude's direction. "At least, I told my father and he told Marthe." Claude sipped wine in his turn. "It was quite a big piece of land, Livaudais. And not . . . perhaps not worthless."

Hélène, who had been sulking ever since she had been herded into this room, stood up. "Wait a minute. Just wait a minute. What's going on here?" Boredom had made her drink more wine than she should have; she was not drunk, but the reins that sobriety would have put on her tongue had gone slack. "How did the Langlinaises get themselves involved with that survey?"

Claude had risen when Hélène did; he faced her now, wineglass in hand. "We didn't get ourselves involved, Hélène. Beau and I were out hunting. We saw stakes where they shouldn't have been—"

"How could you possibly *tell*," Hélène said. Hélène's face, whose lines showed the long hours in New Orleans' drawing rooms, lingering over black coffee and sweet liqueurs with the ladies until the men came in trailing fumes of cigars and scents of brandy, lost its smooth control. Her voice, tired by those same long hours, no longer country-fresh, cracked on her words. "Isn't one stretch of desolate swamp just exactly like any other? God, do you Langlinaises really carry a map of your precious land around in your *heads?*"

Marthe's hands tightened on the arms of the big chair. "Your headache has obviously returned, Hélène." She pushed against the chair, began to rise. "I think we had better go home."

"In a minute, Marthe," Charles said. He had moved slightly, his body blocking the door, its bulk a shadowed mass against the oak panels. He turned to Claude. "Hélène's thought intrigues me. Do you have a map of your land in your head, Langlinais?" He put a careless emphasis on that name, setting it apart, somehow, from names which came more easily to his tongue.

"It's our land, Livaudais. Been ours for over a hundred and fifty years. And I've been walking that land for almost forty years, since I was old enough to toddle after my papa. Been hunting it, marking trees on it for lumbering, trapping on it—do you think I don't know my own land?" Claude's voice made a separation, too, separating Livaudais from men who understood land and put him with those who did not; the voice said plainly that men who did not know how another man knew his own land had much work to do before others took them seriously.

Charles was conscious of Alice Langlinais leaning forward in her chair, her eyes large, fastened on her husband. He wanted those eyes on him, wanted the look that now belonged only to Claude to turn, to be caught on his own face, to be diverted. He took a step closer to Claude and laughed. Like Claude's smile, the laugh had something more than humor in it. "A lot of trouble over a piece of swamp, Langlinais." Again the faint distortion of the sounds, the wrongly placed emphasis on the syllables. "I imagine the sugar company would've let you hunt over it."

Claude also stepped forward, the space between the two men narrowing so that their presence made a tight, tense force. "No one *lets* me do anything, Livaudais. Particularly not on my own land." He reached out to the lowboy that held the decanters, picked one up, and filled his glass. "Besides, it is more than ducks this land is good for." He set the decanter down, and for a moment the light gathered in its cut-crystal bowl made him blink. Then he lifted his glass to his lips, his eyes meeting Charles's over the rim. "There is oil on that land, Livaudais. Pools of oil even a city-slicker surveyor can see when he puts the stakes along a line that put those pools very neatly inside the boundaries of Beau Chêne."

The tension that filled the space between Claude and Charles ballooned, pushed out over the rest of the room, so that they were all caught in its tight cover. "Claude . . ." Jumie was beside his son, a hand pulling at Claude's arm. "Now, look, Claude, it's New Year's Eve, a party . . ." Marthe, too, rose, moving helplessly toward where the two men stood.

"Are you saying my men deliberately stole your land?" Charles watched something flare in Claude's eyes—admiration? His eyes slid past Claude's to search Alice's face. And, yes, it had turned to him, she was watching him with those huge gray eyes, a dark fascination fighting to possess her.

"I wouldn't say behind your back what I wouldn't say to your face, Livaudais," Claude said.

Charles laughed. He was really enjoying himself now; the somewhat walk-on part he had played throughout the evening, spear-carrier to Claude's leading role, was gone. Now he occupied the position he played best—antagonist, adversary, opponent—enemy. "Is this your famous Cajun hospitality?" he said. "Invite a man to a party and then call him a thief?"

"I didn't invite you," Claude said. "You are a houseguest of someone who was invited. It is she, not I, who is responsible for your behavior."

Now Hélène had had enough. She had borne Alice's beauty, the way Charles had not let her out of his sight all evening. She had borne the way the Langlinais boy had taken Caroline over, had borne hearing Claude Langlinais praised by every mouth that ate his ham and drank his eggnog, had borne watching her mother flirt with Jumie Langlinais, but, by heaven, she would not bear hearing her family insulted by the likes of Claude. She sprang out of her chair, the sudden movement making her lurch. "Are you saying we would not have been invited here if we had not been staying with Mama?" Her face was flushed, the several glasses of red wine having combined with the earlier drinks to color her skin with dissipation. "Because if you flatter yourself for one minute that we wanted to come here—if you think I *want* to be obligated to you and your wife—if you think that—"

"No one thinks anything of the kind," Alice said. She stood at Claude's side, her hand thrust through his arm, her eyes flashing anger. "I've no idea why you did come tonight—when you had a headache that would have excused you. But I know very well it was not because you wanted to."

If Charles had not been looking at Alice with all the pleasure he took in watching her clearly showing in his face, Hélène might yet have collected herself and her coat and gone home quietly. But as she turned to tell her husband that it was time to go, she saw his face. The look there was one she had never seen directed at her, not even on their wedding night when she yielded to his wishes and stripped herself bare for him. And yet Alice Langlinais earned such a look fully clothed, standing at her husband's side as though she were the most virtuous of women.

"I suppose I came to see the show," Hélène drawled. Her eyes glinted in a way that made Marthe want to weep. "I'd heard how skillfully you use your charms to attract men—I wanted to see for myself if it were true." She swept Alice with a long, ugly look, beginning with the softly waving black hair caught at the nape of the neck in a Psyche knot, continuing down the slender figure to the neatly shod feet. "It looks like a lady," she said, again in that slow, bored drawl. "Isn't it too bad it doesn't act like one."

As though springs had suddenly broken the bands holding them, Marthe and Alice both moved toward Hélène. Marthe's hands were stretched out, ready to take Hélène's shoulders and force her from the room. But Alice's hand was younger, quicker. It raised high, moved forward, slapped against Hélène's cheek. In the instant of stillness that followed, the sound of flesh on flesh echoed, seemed to grow louder.

Then Claude spoke. His lips were white, his fists clenched, the knuckles bloodless. "It is one thing for me to catch you out in a piece of bad business, Livaudais. It is another for your wife to insult Mrs. Langlinais."

"She slapped me," Hélène said. Her hand had gone to her cheek, clung there as though fused. "She slapped me. Charles, do something. Charles . . ."

Charles looked at Alice. She was breathing hard, her breasts rising and pushing against the clinging fabric of her dress. Her eyes were proud, filled with a passion he knew he must make his. She raised her eyes to meet Charles's gaze; he saw the challenge in them. "What we will do is go home," he said. He slipped an arm around Hélène's waist. "Come, Hélène, you're not yourself." It was then he did the final, unforgivable thing. He smiled at Alice.

The rage that boiled up in Hélène was an old one, one she lived with daily. It took little to loose it; Charles's smile to Alice, seeming to imply that this entire disgusting exhibition was her fault, ended any control she might still have had. "You seem to have forgotten that you have been called a thief and I have been slapped," she said, breaking away from him. She gave him the same kind of look she had given Alice, a contemptuous, measuring stare. "If you will not defend your . . . honor, I at least will defend mine." Then she stepped forward, raised her hand with slow deliberation, and slapped Alice smartly on first one cheek and then the other.

Before her hand had found its second target, Claude's hand was on Hélène's arm. The instant she slapped Alice again, his fingers closed over her flesh, squeezing the flabby skin, almost crushing the bone. He spun her away from Alice, pushed her toward her chair. He turned to find Charles on him, one fist already jabbing its way toward his chin. "Mon Dieu, so it comes to this!" he said, kicking a small rug away and dancing out of Charles's range.

Against the firelight, beneath the bright light of the brass chandelier, the two men squared off, taking little testing jabs, throwing measuring punches. "Oh, Jumie, stop them, for God's sake, stop them!" Marthe cried. But the moving figures ignored her cry, ignored the pleading gesture with which Jumie held out her hands to them. Claude saw an opening, ducked under Charles's long reach, and landed his fist on the taunting chin, noting with satisfaction the blood which flowed onto Charles's high starched collar.

"Claude, what . . .!" His mother's voice behind him made Claude miss a step; Charles's fist crashed through his defenses, landed a heavy blow on the side of Claude's head, a blow that made him stagger and throw punches blindly until he could get his balance. Out of the corner of his eye he saw Geneviève, a plate of biscuits in her hand, dart through the door and close it quickly behind her. "Jumie! Jumie, are they crazy? Jumie, make them stop!"

Jumie moved toward the men, who were locked now in a wrestler's grip, each searching for a way to break from the other. "Claude! Charles! Enough—stop, I say."

"Livaudais. You ready to stop?" Claude grunted, his hands solid on Charles's arms.

"Never." Charles spat the word out, sucked in air. With one strong push he broke from Claude's grasp and aimed a blow at

Claude's face. Suddenly, inches from Claude's head, Jumie's face loomed. The fist found a mark, and Jumie fell, his body crumpling in the space between their feet.

"Jumie! Claude, your father!" Geneviève rushed to Jumie, kneeling and cushioning his head in her lap. "Alice, get some brandy. In the cellarette, behind you."

Claude looked stunned. He glanced at Charles, who stood, still poised in a boxer's stance, fists high, head low. "You hit old men?" He lunged forward and grabbed Charles's shoulders, began shaking him violently. "You hit old men, you canaille?"

Charles's hands came up, tried to break the hold. "An accident—he got too close. Come on, Langlinais, it's enough."

Geneviève appeared beside them, one hand on Claude's shoulder, another pulling at Charles's arm. "I'm telling you, stop this nonsense this instant, this instant, do you hear me?" Her voice was climbing out of control. Claude looked again at his father, stretched out now on the hearth rug, and came to his senses.

"I'll get Dr. Jaubert," he said. "He was still here a while ago." He hurried toward the door, then looked back at Charles. "And, Livaudais—pray he is all right. If you know how to pray."

Alice held the brandy glass to Jumie's lips, her eyes still filled with those two powerful faces confronting each other, bent on hurting each other. And one, at least, doing it for her. Behind her Marthe and Hélène were talking, Marthe giving Hélène a stern-enough talking-to to last her through Lent. She heard the door open again, then Dr. Jaubert and Geneviève were bending over Jumie. She stood, wondering where Claude was. Charles Livaudais came in with coats in his arms, and gave one to Marthe, who wrapped it around Hélène.

Then the door burst open and Beau came tumbling through. "What happened? What's wrong?" He saw Jumie and pushed past Alice. "Grandpapa—what happened?" His eyes found Marthe. "Mrs. de Gravelle—"

"There was a fight," Marthe said, her voice flat. She was putting her own coat on, carefully avoiding Charles's offer to help her. "Your grandfather got hit."

"But who . . . ?" He moved toward Charles. "It had to be you."

"Now, look, sonny, don't make things worse than they already are," Charles said. He reached out and tapped Beau's shoulder. "This has nothing to do with you."

"It has everything to do with me," Beau said. "And if no one else will call you to account, I will." With the last words, his fist came up and caught Livaudais' chin. But Charles had learned enough about the Langlinais method of fighting. He knew better than to stay within the range of those punishing short jabs, and danced backward, sending a long arm toward Beau's out-thrust chin. He had finally gotten angry, had finally responded to the successive failures of the evening, rage pulsing through every nerve in his body. The young man opposite him was six inches shorter and at least forty pounds lighter than Charles—if he had taken on such an opponent in his club ring, he'd have been called down in short order. But there were no rules here, none that mattered. What mattered was that this was a Langlinais, and that at least one Langlinais face would bleed before the night was through.

Charles danced backward into the hall with Beau following him, ducking and weaving to stay clear of that long reach. Around them came the cries of the other guests, who watched in disbelief as Charles kicked one of the runners that spread its multicolored length along the polished hall floor out of their way and then took advantage of Beau's momentary distraction to land a blow solidly to his cheek. "Stand back, give them room!" someone cried, and the crowd pushed back toward the doors leading into the front parlor and the dining room, making a ground on which they could meet. Beau, reeling from yet another blow, fell against a small whatnot, its shelves full of Alice's Chinese porcelain. He watched it shake, tremble, and then fall heavily forward, the sound of breaking china mingling with the screams of the women, the shouts of the men, that surrounded them. There seemed to be nothing in the world but those two heavy fists which were able to get through any defense he could muster. Once he felt his fist connect with Livaudais' arm, another time he managed to hit the white-shirted chest. He needed something to distract Charles, needed an ally who would get that murderous attention on something other than Beau. Then, from just behind him, he heard Caroline's voice. "Papa! Beau! Oh, Papa, what are you doing?" He forced himself not to turn, and saw Charles Livaudais' eyes shift toward his daughter's face. That split instant was enough—leaping toward him, Beau put all his energy behind a

blow that landed on Charles's chin, and made it spurt brightly
red again. Then Livaudais turned once again to Beau, his lips
set, his eyes blank; his heavy fist connected, and Beau fell into
darkness on the long, sliding sound of Caroline's scream. Over
the noise that filled the hall, the clock on the landing began to
strike twelve. And though Beau and Caroline were at the same
spot, Charles's blow made it impossible for Beau either to
carry out or to remember his cherished plan, the thing he had
been looking forward to all evening—the last stroke of midnight, when it would be the new year, and he would have an
excuse to kiss Caroline.

4

Dawn had come, was already lifting the fog which clung to the
branches of the huge oaks and trailed from the azaleas and
camellias between them, when Marthe, followed closely by
Charles, wearily let herself into the house and sank into a low
chair in the front hall. "See if Berthe is up," she said. She tried
to smile. "I'm dead for a cup of her good coffee." She watched
Charles stride down the hall toward the kitchen, seeming as
filled with energy as he had been at midnight when he had been
using it to fell every Langlinais in sight. She heard voices,
knew Berthe would be with her in a moment, bearing a tray
with the strong coffee and hot milk that would act like a tonic
to her blood—and her nerves.

She sank back, rested her head on the chair's brocade back.
When Charles had walked into the waiting room at the hospital, she had thought she had lost her mind with worry over
Jumie. Marthe had insisted on going in to New Iberia to the
Dauterive Hospital while Charles took Hélène and Caroline
home; certainly, he was the last person she expected to see that
night. But in he had come, his eyes clear, his voice steady, his
purpose firm. He had taken the chair next to hers and fixed his
gaze on her. "Now, listen to me, Marthe. Don't go all shocked

on me and ask me what I'm doing here. How is Jumie Langlinais?"

She had shrugged her shoulders, a helpless gesture that said everything and nothing. "Dr. Jaubert says it was a heart attack." She looked away from those green eyes that seemed to bore into her and know everything she was thinking, whether she said it or not. "Whether the fight—being hit—had anything to do with it . . . well, we'll never know that."

"It couldn't have helped," Charles said. He took her hand. "I behaved like a damn fool, Marthe, and I hope I'm man enough to say so." She looked at him quickly, started to say something, and then was quiet. A smile flickered on Charles's face. "Even a man like me has his limits, Marthe." Now the smile came back, derisive, bitter. "I may rape widows and orphans, but I don't usually hit old men."

"Charles—"

Claude had come upon them then. His own anxious fatigue made it impossible for him to conceal his feelings when he saw Charles Livaudais. He had stopped, turned on heel, and begun to stride back down the hall. Marthe had risen, gone after him. "Claude! Your father—is he . . . ?"

"He's finally conscious," Claude had said. "That's what I came to tell you."

Charles had moved forward. "Believe me, I'm glad to hear that." Then he had held out a hand. "These two families go too far back to let the stupid behavior of an in-law make a break. I've come to say I'm sorry."

Claude had looked at the hand as though he did not know what it was. "And for what are you sorry?" he said.

"For not controlling myself," Charles said. "For not telling the truth."

"What truth is that?" Charles's hand was still extended, still a forgotten object.

"The surveyors did make a mistake, but it wasn't on purpose. There are pools of oil on Beau Chêne, too, it's why Enterprise Oil has signed leases." Charles's shoulders raised, the extended hand made a small gesture. "They saw pools of oil, thought they were where they should be. If I'd said so in the first place, a lot could have been avoided." He moved his hand closer to Claude. "As for my wife—"

"Hélène always has been a silly fool," Marthe said. Her voice seemed to break something that was building between the two men; they both looked at her and then at each other, and at the same moment, moved to shake hands. "Now, can I go see Jumie?" Marthe said, with such anxiety that Claude put his hand under her elbow and steered her down the hall, pausing only long enough to say to Charles, "You understand that on the night my father has almost died I am in a mood to forgive almost anything."

Well, at least an apology had been offered and accepted, at least they had shaken hands on it, at least when she entered Jumie's room she had not felt as though she were from an enemy camp. There was one other apology still to be made, but whether she was up to dealing with Hélène, she just didn't know.

"Miz de Gravelle, you going to make yourself sick staying up all night," Berthe said, approaching her with a tray. "Now, you go and sit at the table like a Christian and eat this food and then you are going to get in bed and sleep." Berthe set the tray on the dining-room table and fussed over Marthe, making her butter two biscuits, standing over her until she finished her egg. "Mr. Charles says Mr. Jumie's going to be all right," Berthe said, her eyes on Marthe's tired face.

Marthe smiled, and a light came back into her deep blue eyes. "Oh, Berthe, yes, he is! Dr. Jaubert says it will be a long recovery, but he really will be all right." She sipped her coffee and then smiled again. "And do you know what he said when he finally did wake up? He looked at Miss Geneviève and he reached for her hand and he said, 'Did you think I was going to go off and leave you?'" Suddenly Marthe burst into tears. Berthe nodded to herself and then took Marthe in her arms.

"Now, you just cry it all out, Miz Marthe, you just have a good cry, and then you go up and take a nap and when you wake up you'll feel all fresh again." She held the graying head against her bosom, patting Marthe as though she were a nursling. Hummph, Berthe thought, no wonder she's all wore out. Miz Geneviève almost lost her husband last night, and Miz Marthe, she almost lost her rescue-man. When the tears hesitated, paused, then stopped, Berthe helped Marthe rise. "I'm coming up with you, make sure you behave yourself and go to bed," she said.

"I have to wake up in time for noon Mass," Marthe said.

Berthe laughed. "Now, don't worry about that. St. Martinville done had one shock already—if you didn't get to noon Mass, they'd think the whole world done come to an end."

Marthe leaned against Berthe, feeling the comfortable strength of that broad body. "It just about did," she said, thinking of that terrible moment when Charles's fist had slammed into Jumie's face. "It just about did." And as she slipped into sleep, she wondered if the bridge two hands had made was strong enough to hold.

Beau stood on a slight rise in the long field that began just below the farm's kitchen garden and ended at the boundary line of Beau Chêne, looking toward the great house, which was still faintly misted with the morning's fog. He had gone out to the farm from the hospital, refusing to go home, explaining to his parents that he had promised Geneviève, who would not leave the hospital under any circumstances, that he would see to the chores. He went about those duties in a daze that was not completely the result of little sleep and a forceful blow to his jaw. 'Tit Nonc, the helper who lived on the place, worked alongside Beau silently, content to let the good God take care of this crisis, as He could be depended upon to take care of every other. "Your grandfather, he's a good man," 'Tit Nonc said. "God takes care of good men."

"He's not . . . not over the worst yet," Beau said. He heard the waver in his voice, felt his eyes, which seemed twisted in their sockets from the pull of fatigue.

'Tit Nonc shrugged. "So. So he gets well and takes up his good life here—or he goes to God. Either way, God takes care of good men."

Now Beau thought: But we're not ready for God to have Grandpapa. A sense of his grandfather, of his presence in this field, surrounded Beau. Here he had learned to shoot, here he had learned to train his dogs. Here he had listened to his grandfather's stories, those stories which were always ready, always there to make Beau laugh, or to teach him something about the way men—Langlinais men—lived.

He wished his grandfather were here now, could tell him a story which would make sense of all that had happened last night. One moment he had been flirting with Caroline, telling himself that if he could continue to make her laugh, she would surely let him kiss her at midnight; the next moment his grandfather was unconscious and he was fighting Caroline's father. Beau rubbed his chin. It still ached, but not nearly so much as his spirits did. He looked again toward Beau Chêne. A figure came from the back of the house, began walking up and down the paths of the garden. Seeing Caroline made the ache in his jaw manageable, and, perhaps, his spirits were not beyond healing. Smiling, Beau began walking rapidly across the field, eyes locked on Caroline as though on a channel marker. And as he walked, he hoped she had inherited not only her grandmother's beauty, but her independence as well.

Caroline saw him coming and veered her course so that she walked to meet him. She had fled her mother, fled that line-marked morning face that had begun the day with a stubborn refusal to apologize to Alice Langlinais. Caroline had heard them arguing, her grandmother and her mother, the two voices fueling each other as the lines were drawn between them. Finally she had heard her grandmother say, her voice stiff with suppressed anger: "You will not write to Alice to please me, Hélène, if you do indeed decide to do it. I am not the one to be satisfied. You must satisfy yourself, live up to your own standards of what proper conduct is, and what it demands." And she had heard her mother's answer, spoken in that cold voice Caroline knew so well.

"Thus far, my standards demand that I apologize only to people I respect," she said. There had been a silence then, and then her grandmother had appeared in the hall, and found Caroline holding her book as she sat in the window seat on the landing, eyes mirroring the emotion in Marthe's own.

"Well," Marthe had said, bending to kiss Caroline's cheek. "A good sleep does not seem to have made your mother feel better at all. She won't go to Mass, she says, so we shall have to represent the family alone." She had looked at her watch. "Meet me downstairs in an hour, darling, Nat will drive us in."

Caroline had heard her mother calling her and had run down the stairs, making her feet carry her quickly beyond its range. She had run through the French doors that led from the dining room out onto the broad front gallery, and had then settled down to a more dignified pace that carried her around the house and into the back garden. As she met Beau, a hand outstretched to him, she involuntarily looked over her shoulder at the window of her mother's room. The draperies were still drawn; good, Mama was probably sleeping or sulking or having her maid mix up one of those potions she used to hide the ravages late evenings made on her face.

"Oh, Beau, isn't it the strangest kind of morning? It doesn't feel like the new year one bit." She sighed. "If we were at home, people would be coming to visit already, and to wish us a Bonne Année."

"Do you wish you were home?" He had taken the hand she offered, and held it still, willing himself not to hold it too tightly, not to remind her to take it away.

"Of course not! I'd rather be here at Beau Chêne than anyplace in the world."

They fell into step, taking the path that led to a stone bench placed near a marble statue. Caroline tucked her hand through Beau's arm and looked up at him. "It's just . . . last night was so . . . well, so upsetting, Beau." He saw her lip tremble. God, was she going to cry? What in the world would he do if she cried? "I mean, everyone . . . you and Papa . . . fighting . . . your grandfather getting sick . . . Mama being so—"

"Don't think about it," he said. "It's over, really it is. My grandfather is better, your father and mine made it up—it's over, Caroline, we don't ever have to think about any of it again."

She gave him one of her long, clear looks that said they both knew he was wrong. "Well, we don't have to think about it *today*," she said. "Oh, Beau, tell me something funny, will you? I feel as though if I don't find something to cheer me up I'll just cry all over the place!"

"I'm no good when girls cry," Beau said, "so don't you dare do it." He brushed the leaves and twigs from the bench and sat beside her. "A funny story—let's see—well, did I ever tell you about the time Duke and I went hunting and it was so cold he wouldn't go in the water after the ducks?"

Her eyes were light again, ready to be filled with laughter. "Silly, we just met. You haven't had time to tell me much at all."

"Did we really?" he said. "Just meet?"

"Yes," she said, and the single word slid out on a long, happy sigh. "And maybe that's the strangest thing about this strange day, Beau Langlinais. That I keep feeling I've known you forever."

"Since we were four," he said, reminding her.

"Oh, that doesn't count, because I don't remember," she said. She looked around the garden as though she were memorizing the setting, the way the sky looked like pearl-colored silk stretched high above them, the way the scarlet and white and purple camellias starred the deep green bushes, the way the great pink house looked, drowsing in the January light. "I'll remember this," she said.

"And me," he said. "And me."

Marthe, sitting at her desk, had watched them meet. She could see them sitting on the bench, see the intense pose of their young bodies, the serious looks on their faces. For the first time since late last evening, she really smiled. The bridge Charles and Claude had made might not be strong enough to hold. But the one those two were making might be.

Jumie Langlinais came home from the hospital the day before Claude and Alice left for Baton Rouge and the dinner at the governor's mansion. Geneviève settled him in a rocking chair near the hearth, where a small fire blossomed, its petals of flame softening the slight chill in the February noon. "Don't think I'm going to stay here very long," he told Geneviève. He lifted his arms while she tucked a quilt around his waist. "I'll let you play this little game awhile longer—then it's all over, all right?" He thumped his chest. "It's in there, beating as good as ever."

Geneviève went to him, a glass of wine in her hand. "Drink this, it's good for you." She placed a hand on either of his shoulders, bent toward him. "Jumie, you listen to me. This is no little game. As for your heart—it played a trick once, it doesn't get a chance to do that again. Me, I'm going to take care of you—and, Jumie, I'm going to do it whether you like it or not!"

Jumie remembered the pain that had closed around him, his surprised thought: It's my face that's hit, why does my chest hurt? He remembered sinking beneath the waves of black pain, gasping for air that was no longer there. The pain had gone, but its memory had great force, greater, perhaps, than he had. He felt the small stir of rebellion die, somewhere just beneath that slowly beating heart. He settled back against the high back of the chair, pulled the quilt up toward his chest. His big hand, hardened by all the years of hard work for Geneviève, for the children, stroked Geneviève's cheek. "Geneviève. A man would be crazy, I think, not to like being spoiled by you." He drew her into his arms, felt her cheek nestle against the place in his chest where that devilish heart played its games. He could see through the back windows the long stretch of land that ran from Bayou Teche through woods and swamp, ran for three

square leagues until it met fingers of water reaching inward
from the Atchafalaya River. That land had been like a person
in his life, an intimate, sometimes closer to him than Geneviève herself. He opened his hands, let the land go. He turned
his eyes from the window to Geneviève's face. "Mais, anyhow, there are other Langlinais men. Claude—and Beau." He
felt lightened. Maybe you could accept dying when you knew
the living would carry on. Jumie smiled. "That Beau! Now,
there's a Langlinais for you, clear through."

"I'm frightened for him, though, Jumie. That war in Europe.
It's getting worse."

"He's just sixteen, Geneviève. Even if we did get in . . ." He
measured her worry, decided she already knew what he meant to
say. "And I have to say, it looks like we will—but even if we
did, he's much too young to go." He willed his own eyes to
remain calm, sure. "We don't send babies to fight the Boche!"

"Wars and boys get older, Jumie," Geneviève said.

"True. But even so, it wouldn't be the first time a Langlinais
fought in a war, Geneviève. And lived to tell his grandsons
about it." But he knew what she was thinking. Wars you could
march to in a few days, a week, were one thing. Wars that
began and ended with one battle—the Langlinais who had
fought with Lafitte's pirates at the Battle of New Orleans had
had such a war. But this was far across the ocean, seemed to
have little to do with them, or with their land.

"Those wars were different," Geneviève said. She looked
past Jumie, at their land sleeping through the winter. "Before
we fought for our own land. Beau—he'd be fighting for land
belonging to the English and the French. Jumie, that French
king was no better to the Acadians who made it back to France
than the English king who drove them out. Now they want us
to drop everything, send our boys over to fight for them." Her
hands closed into tight fists. She jabbed at the air. "Let them
that took land from others, and hung onto it, fight for it. Me, I
fight only for what belongs to me."

"Heavens, Geneviève, you sound so fierce!" Marthe exclaimed, entering the room, a large bowl in her hands.

"Geneviève doesn't have enough to worry about," Jumie
said. "So she's worrying about Beau going to fight a war we're
not in yet and that he's too young for anyhow."

Geneviève got up. "Jumie, I'm going to heat up some nice
soup, make some toast. And then you can have some of Mar-

the's good floating island." She took her apron from a hook near the stove, tied it around her waist.

"I meant to tell you the other day, Jumie," Marthe said, going to sit beside him. "Enterprise Oil is talking about starting a well very soon—they must really think they'll make a strike!" She leaned back in her chair, her eyes fixed on Jumie's face. "But, Jumie—I feel sort of funny about that first well. The lease covers acres—but they want to drill very near the property line, back near the part I had resurveyed." Her hand moved restlessly. "Between the pools of oil on your land—and the ones Charles saw on mine. I don't know—they say it's all right to drill right up to the line . . . but, Jumie . . . lines don't go underground. They might hit your pool."

"Maybe we'll get there first," Jumie said. "Claude's formed an exploration company, they'll be drilling soon." He reached a hand toward her, took the one she gave him and held it tightly. "Don't worry about it, Marthe." He smiled. "One thing about what happened to me—it taught me to let the young ones do the fussing. And the fighting, if it comes to that." He leaned back, began to rock. "Me, I'm going to sit by this fire until good weather comes. And then I'll show your granddaughter where to watch for spring." He looked at Marthe sharply. "She's still coming?"

Marthe squeezed his hand. "She's still coming."

"Good," Jumie said. "Be nice to have a pretty young face around the place." He closed his eyes, slipped away from them behind a mask of sleep.

Marthe looked at Geneviève, and saw her own thoughts mirrored on Geneviève's face. The Jumie they had known and loved for all these years was gone. In his place was this old man, slipping toward death.

5

The road Claude and Alice Langlinais took to reach Baton Rouge curved through the swamps stretching between St. Martinville and the Atchafalaya River, and then past more marshland until it broke out between the fields of plantations lining the west bank of the Mississippi River. In the clear gray light of the February morning, the branches were still stark, traced with a fine Oriental brush across the gray of the sky and the dun-colored earth. The waters in the bayous and ponds were still, a leaden color that was like the cover of a coffin. Beneath that cover, seeds burrowed deep, taking the last bit of nurture from the soil before beginning their burst to the greening world of the coming spring. Yards and yards of cypress growing beside the road were owned by Langlinais Lumber; even now, trees marked last autumn were being felled, to be floated out on the high waters of summer. Beneath those tall trees lived the small animals, the nutrias and raccoon whose pelts formed a great part of the inventory of Langlinais Fur and Hide. And in the still waters slept the alligators, whose hides would appear as shoes and belts and handbags on some of the wealthiest women in the world.

The automobile Claude drove had come from a new subsidiary of Langlinais Motors, the firm in Abbeville that sent a steady stream of Ford vehicles to the backyards and converted stables of the region. The new place sold Buicks; Claude had bought a big touring car for them to use "in town," and that endorsement was responsible for a growing trend toward Buicks in his part of the state. There was something about the way Claude handled that Buick, something about the solidity of man and motor as he drove to a meeting of the directors of the bank in New Iberia, or to a meeting with his factor or stockbroker, that made Claude Langlinais more than just known. That solidity made him respected.

And if when Claude and Alice were first married they had been invited everywhere because he was the heir of a rising native family and she was a beautiful and charming bride, they were invited now because it would be folly not to. A knowledgeable eye, reading the names on the backs of the invitations that arrived in the mail or were hand-carried to the Langlinais door by servants, could have put the precise value on each one, and could therefore put a precise value on Claude and Alice themselves. Depending upon the source of the invitation, that value might be social, political, or economic. But at this point in their lives, their value on any of these measures was the same—high and rising higher.

The fact that Claude's funny stories and Alice's warm manner had not changed, but only become richer over the years, made their popularity complete. The men of the parish, the region, and, increasingly, the state, might speak first of Claude Langlinais' holdings, of his power. But they ended any discussion with a reminder of Claude the man. "That Claude," someone would say, smiling. "That Claude. One thing, he's still like he always was. His money hasn't gotten into his head and made it big, no." The women might yearn over Alice's jewels, resolve to copy her clothes, feel a slight nudge of envy at the richness of her social calendar, the variety of her days. But they, too, had to admit, if fairness were to be served, that when it came down to it, Alice Langlinais remembered well that French saying "Ce sont les hommes qui font l'argent, ce n'est pas l'argent qui fait les hommes"—It's the men who make the money, 'tisn't the money that makes the men.

Claude lounged on the bed, watching Alice dress. They had arrived at the Heidelberg Hotel with plenty of time for Alice to rest before dinner. And with plenty of time for making love. His eyes followed the curve of his wife's throat, the way her breasts thrust against the smooth silk of her camisole. He reached toward his dinner jacket, hanging on a chair near the bed, and drew a small green velvet box from a pocket. "Catch," he said, tossing it across the room to Alice.

Her hand automatically came up, grabbed at the flying object, closed around it. He watched her open it. "Claude!" The light in the diamond earrings might take back seat to no other jewels, but it would have to take back seat to the light in Alice's eyes. "Oh, Claude!" She paused, earrings raised toward her ears, half-turned to the mirror at the dressing table, half-facing Claude.

"Go on," he said. "Put them on. Then if you like them you can thank me."

"Like them!" Quickly Alice removed the plain gold earrings and replaced them with the long diamond drops. "Like them! Oh, Claude, they're splendid!"

She pressed herself against him, her lips soft against his, and Claude thought, not for the first time, how lucky he was to have this woman waiting for him at the end of all his days. He held her close and then released her, gave her a teasing push. "Now hurry up, Alice. We can't keep the Pleasants waiting."

"I'm almost done," she said, going back to the dressing table. She leaned forward, turned her head to watch the fire-light in the diamonds that swung gently from her ears. Her own color was up under her rouge, and her eyes glowed like her jewels. She rose and stood while Claude put a mink-trimmed peach velvet evening cape around her shoulders. "Charles and Hélène will be there tonight, Claude, did you know that? I saw his name in the book at the desk when we checked in this afternoon." Her mouth curved in a satisfied smile. "Hélène will probably have on those old sapphires—and I've got my wonderful new earrings!"

Hélène Livaudais picked up the heavy necklace from its bed of velvet and held it out to her husband. "Here, fasten this for me, will you?"

Charles moved toward her, took the gold-and-sapphire circlet from her hand and bent to clasp it around her tilted neck. The forward motion of her head made the loose skin beneath her chin fold evenly like a small roll of flesh-colored cloth; Charles knew that when Hélène looked up again, the looseness would move up into her face, a face marked with fine lines and dropping flesh, hooded eyelids that were the legacy of too many late evenings, too much rich food, too much wine—too much indulgence.

She caught his eyes in the mirror, shrugged. "This necklace is really outdated, isn't it? As for the tiara—well, the earrings are lovely, anyway." She inserted them into her ears, the small gold wires penetrating that globular pink flesh. She clasped the matching sapphire-set bands on one arm, held it out before her. "Should I wear both on one arm, Charles? Or one on each?"

"For God sakes, Hélène, do what you want." All the jewels in the world weren't going to make her young again, nor give her the fragile beauty she'd had when he married her for those rich fields of sugarcane that stretched out around Beau Chêne. Fields that had been sold not two months ago, thereby making the de Gravelle fortunes dependent on one thing—the flow of oil from the well Enterprise Oil had begun to drill.

Hélène stood and motioned for Charles to hand her her wrap, a deeper blue than the French blue of her silk gown. She shouldn't wear those straight lines anymore, Charles thought, seeing the gentle sag of Hélène's breasts, the small round

stomach pushing against the silk. A memory of Alice Langlinais as she had looked on New Year's Eve came before him.
The soft fabric of her dress had clung to her breasts, which still
rose firm and high. Damn Claude Langlinais! As they left the
room, Charles glimpsed his own image in the mirror. Well, he
had not lost his looks—nor his figure. And women like Alice
Langlinais were, after all, another breed. There was a certain
tension, a certain awareness, in her eyes when she looked at
him, a tension that seemed promising. In a much happier frame
of mind, Charles offered Hélène his arm and led her out into
the hall.

"The Langlinaises will be there tonight, Hélène," he said.
He watched a frown crisscross the lines in her face into a quilt
of anger.

"Honestly, Charles," Hélène said, her head giving its quick
automatic tilt, her thin nostrils closing in an arrogant sniff. "If
even a governor like Ruffin Pleasant invites such people—"

"Shh," Charles said. "There they are." Claude and Alice
stood waiting for the elevator to come, something in the pose
of their bodies making them seem soft, tender, redolent of
some emotion long foreign to Charles.

Claude moved forward, extended a hand. "Hélène. How are
you?"

Hélène blinked, felt a nudge from Charles, and put her own
hand forward. "Good evening, Claude. Alice."

The elevator doors opened, and Claude stood aside, ushered
Alice and Hélène in ahead of him. "Well, Charles," he said as
they followed the women into the small gold interior. "Think
the food will be as rich as the politics tonight?"

"Will be if the governor spices it up the way he did the guest
list," Charles said.

The operator, half-slumbering his way through the length of
the evening, jerked awake at the sound of Claude's laughter. It
bounced around the small golden walls, boomed against the
heavy doors. He looked at his passengers for the first time, and
remembered who Claude was. Langlinais, that Cajun fellow
from St. Martinville who cut his own way through the morass
of the legislature as he was said to cut his own way through the
swamps of his home parish. And the other one was Charles
Livaudais, who wasn't in the legislature, but who nonetheless
had as much power or more than if he had been. He was in with
the Ring, that fancy New Orleans crowd that slipped around

and twisted first one way and then the other so that if you didn't keep a good eye on them, you might almost believe them when they said they cared about the people and the state, except that the people and the state didn't seem to get quite as rich quite as fast as Livaudais and his friends did.

The operator turned to Claude. "Mr. Langlinais, sir. I just want to tell you. I sure do admire what you do in the legislature. Yes, sir. Me and my friends. We think real well of you." He made a bow in Alice's direction. "And ma'am, I want to tell you. That picture of you in the *Advocate* a while back? Some fine-looking young ones. Must have a really nice mama."

A flash at the back of Claude Langlinais' eyes, a sudden stiffening of Charles Livaudais' shoulders. The operator smiled. The evening did not seem so long now. Something in Claude Langlinais' face said that he knew what it was like to be passed over, to be treated as though you were not quite there. And though he had long since reached the place where that did not happen to him, still, he cared about those still bearing that burden. With a flourish, the operator opened the heavy brass grille and then the heavy doors. "Lobby, ladies and gentlemen." He bowed to Claude. "Mr. Langlinais, sir, you all be wanting a taxi?"

There was a feeling of gradually heightened excitement in the Langlinais automobile as they drove to the mansion on North Boulevard. Claude was preparing himself for the evening ahead, an evening that would be filled with all the almost invisible displays of force, the almost unnoticeable signals of rank and privilege that characterized any such evening which masked political dealings with fine food and civilized behavior. He knew why he, one of Governor Pleasant's strongest opponents, had been invited. "How better keep watch on an enemy than have him under your nose once in a while?" he had said to Alice. Besides, Claude thought, pulling up in the mansion drive where a servant waited to park the automobile, Pleasant's victory wasn't all that clear-cut. He had led John Parker by thirty-two thousand votes—but ten thousand of those votes were from New Orleans, cooked and served up by the Ring. John Parker beat Pleasant in sixteen parishes, and in ten others he did better than the 37-percent average he had across the state. It didn't take a mathematical genius to figure that out of the sixty-four parishes in the state, twenty-six could hardly be considered Pleasant strongholds. Which meant the representatives of those parishes, himself included, could put any number of spokes in Pleasant's wheels.

Alice's excitement had another base. One glance at Hélène Livaudais and her own self-confidence had soared. There was a challenge in going to a party given by a governor who would gladly see her husband out of the legislature and out of power. And touching her new earrings for luck, Alice Langlinais felt ready for it. On Claude's arm, she sailed into the large reception room where Governor and Mrs. Pleasant stood, the color in her cheeks almost the exact peach of her peau de soie dress.

The guests who gathered there represented an expert balance of men solidly behind Pleasant, those who were supposedly neutral, and one or two who, like Claude, were acknowledged opponents. Lieutenant Governor and Mrs. Fernand Mouton and Assistant Attorney General A. V. Coco, Jr. and his wife were talking with Chief Justice of the State Supreme Court Frank A. Monroe, the man who had administered the oath of office to Pleasant the previous May. John Overton, a man with strength in central Louisiana, was in a deep discussion with J. Walker Rose, managing editor of the New Orleans *States* newspaper. The rest of the guests were a mixture of sugar planters, lawyers, and upstate legislators—a mixture that was a microcosm of Pleasant's support group. Only a novice at politics could not have interpreted the nuances of power demonstrated in the protocol of who spoke first, who deferred to whom. "The louder people laugh at a man's jokes, the more power he has," Claude was fond of observing. Then, with a wink—"Unless he's a Cajun, and his jokes are really funny." The group he was with laughed now at one of his stories, a laugh that made Alice, talking with Mrs. Pleasant across the room, look up and smile. Claude smiled back at her, took another glass of champagne from a waiter's tray, and walked over to where the governor stood talking to the cluster of men that included Overton and Rose.

"Overton's telling us about a young lawyer up in his neck of the woods who's beginning to make a name for himself," Pleasant said. "Took on the Bank of Winnfield for a poor widow a while back and flat cleaned their plow." He turned to John Overton. "What's his name again?"

"Long," Overton said. "Huey P. Long." He laughed. "His own uncle's an officer of the bank. He sent word to Long that he couldn't understand Huey's denunciation of the bank—didn't Huey know how much his uncle had done for the Long family?" Overton laughed again. "Huey told Harley Bozeman to go back and tell his Uncle George and the other bank officers that he had no personal feeling against them—but that they should feel complimented he considered them big enough fish to be good targets."

"Got any of his father's leanings?" Rose asked. "Old Huey was pretty strong in the Farmer Alliance up that way."

"Right now he's busy building up a practice," Overton said. "Rate he's going, he'll do that pretty quick. Whether he's got any other ideas—"

Claude knew he was not the only man making a note of Huey P. Long's name. Four years might seem like a long time, but they'd be ready to start campaigning for the next election, at least the underneath part, within the next few months. Parker could hold his support in southwest Louisiana; give them a strong man in the central parishes, and a crack at the Ring in New Orleans, and they just might elect themselves a governor in 1920.

"It's like we say at home," Claude said. "Le cochon sait bien sur quel bois il va se frotter.'" Yes indeed, Claude thought, the hog does know well what sort of tree to rub himself against.

"How are things down your way, Langlinais?" Pleasant said. A small hush fell over the group.

Claude shrugged. "Oh, a little of this and a little of that. Plenty to keep me busy."

"Some of the this and that wouldn't be gubernatorial politics, would it?" Rose said. His voice was genial but his eyes were not. His publisher, Robert Ewing, wanted to be a force in Louisiana politics, and men like Claude Langlinais were nothing but obstacles to that ambition.

Claude grinned. "Long about now what I'm worrying about is whether this year's crop of crawfish are going to be fat and fine and good for boiling." He touched Rose lightly on the shoulder. "Tell you what. I'll put on a big potful and you come on down from New Orleans, see what kind of serious cooking we do."

"Long as the only thing in your pot is crawfish, Claude,

we'll get along real well," Rose said as they followed Pleasant in to dinner.

The evening had been going well for Alice, as Claude could see by the flags of color in her cheeks. Her dinner partner found her amusing and charming; a number of times, he laughed so delightedly at something she said that she had to repeat the remark so others could enjoy it. It was impossible not to be aware that she was both the youngest and the most attractive woman at the governor's table. And when Alice felt sure of her charm and beauty, her other qualities were enhanced.

So when the musicians playing in the drawing room after dinner swung into a quick two-step with some of the rhythms of the new jazz, she gave herself over to the pleasure of it. In another forty minutes or so, they would be back in the hotel, and the best part of every party, lying in Claude's arms talking about it, could begin.

"That music is meant to be danced to, don't you agree, Alice?" a voice behind her said. She turned to find Charles Livaudais at her elbow.

"It is good," she said. One foot had begun to tap in time to the beat of the drum, and almost unconsciously her body had begun to sway slightly. She had been aware of Charles all evening, though she had not been part of any group that also contained him. He had been seated diagonally across from her at dinner, far enough down so that he was out of speaking range, but near enough so that he could hear the amused response to Alice's wit. By the time dessert had been served, Alice had felt as though there were a thin, taut ribbon tying her to that presence.

"Then may I have the pleasure of this dance?" he said. The formal words mocked the light in his eyes. Alice's eyes flew to Claude, standing with Governor and Mrs. Pleasant across the room. There was space in front of the musicians, but whether it was intended for dancing, she did not know.

"No one else is dancing," she said, looking into those challenging eyes.

His hand was on her arm. "Are you afraid?" he asked.

Something flared inside her—anger that this man thought himself so attractive that she was afraid to trust herself with him, anger that he thought she was afraid to do what no one else was doing. Her eyes flashed, and she stepped forward. "All right," she said. "Yes, let's dance."

She felt Livaudais' arm come around her waist, felt his hand firmly on her back. And from the corner of her eye she saw the look on Hélène's face. Alice smiled. Let Miss Hélène put on all the airs she wished. Let her think her money and her social position put her out of Alice's retaliatory reach. Alice could still make Hélène's husband interested, she could still make his eyes follow her, make him seek her out. As they had followed her at dinner. And if she had sent him enough glances from under her long lashes to give him every reason to believe she was aware of him too, well, tant pis. Women fought with what weapons they had. Tonight, hers were working very, very well.

"You dance marvelously," Charles said. A few other couples joined them on the floor; Claude danced by with Mrs. Mouton, and John Overton had Mrs. Pleasant in his arms.

"It's one of my favorite things to do," Alice said. Then, because it was true, "You dance very well yourself."

"I do other things well, also," Charles said. His lips were nearer her ear now, and he had drawn her slightly closer to him. "As I imagine you do, Alice."

The words seemed to be picked up by the beat of the drum so that they repeated themselves in Alice's head, a low, steady tattoo of meaning. She felt the strength in the arm that held her, the impossibility of getting further from him without struggling. "Oh, yes, I like to swim—and to ride a little," she said. "A little tennis, even, when it isn't too hot."

"I don't mean outdoor exercise, Alice," he said. He drew his head back so that he could look down at her face. He had steered them away from the center of the floor; they were near a small alcove hung with heavy portieres. He turned so that their backs were to the room, their faces hidden. "I was referring to the most pleasurable sort of indoor exercise. I think you like that, too."

He was holding her right hand tightly in his, and her left hand, circling his neck, could not get free to slap that insolent face. "Let me go," she said. "Now."

"But the music hasn't ended," he said. They were still dancing, her body touching his as they moved, his hand pressing her close. "I expected you to pretend to be insulted—at first." He smiled down at her. "I'm willing to wait."

"That will be a long wait," Alice said. She stiffened her spine, made her body go rigid in his arms. "You have forgotten yourself. Don't do it again."

"Forgotten myself?" He laughed, throwing his head back and almost shouting. "It is you who have forgotten yourself, forgotten who you are. The wife of a man who has barely crawled up from out of the swamps, pushing himself forward with his money and his Cajun jokes. You should be flattered I pay attention to you, under the circumstances."

She felt herself reeling under the contempt in Livaudais' voice. She felt abused, made foolish, and tried once again to break from him. "I shall have to tell Claude if you do not release me," she said. Her voice was low, tense, barely covering the small space between them.

His voice became cold, distant. "Do you think I am afraid of him? Of course he impresses people in his own district, fools others. But believe me, if he continues this stupid opposition to those who have real power in this state—we will break him." His arm tightened around her for one last emphatic squeeze. His eyes bored into her soul. "And who then will stand between us when I want you, Alice?"

Something's happening over there, Claude thought, watching the scene over Mrs. Mouton's head. Alice's face, seen in profile, had hardly changed the last few minutes; it was still, still and almost frightened. Livaudais looked as he did when he was lobbying, making a point he felt invincible. Claude heard the last sweet note of the trumpet with relief. "Thank you," he said to Mrs. Mouton. He looked at his watch. "We have a long drive back home tomorrow. I'd better collect Alice."

"She is so lovely," Mrs. Mouton said. "Here she is—my dear, dancing becomes you, you and Charles made a striking couple."

"Thank you," Alice said. In the small time between the end of the dance and going to meet Claude she had been able to gain her control. She would not tell Claude what had happened, though he had certainly noticed something. She would tell him that Charles Livaudais had been telling her a story that seemed unlike something a lady should hear, that she had not known whether she should laugh or not. And then she would talk about something else, and never, never let Claude think about it again.

But she would think about it again. She had flirted with Charles, she had to admit that. Because the knowledge that Hélène Livaudais' husband found her, Alice Langlinais, more attractive than he did his own wife had been a balance on her side of the scale. Who would have thought he would take the game so far! She felt again the way his eyes had looked, the deep cold in them. He said he would break Claude. She felt something crack, a fissure in the wall Claude had built around them. A kind of helplessness came over her—how could even her Claude take on men whose money and positions stretched back for generations? Then the poker she had put down her spine while dancing made itself felt again. Whatever else he was, Charles Livaudais was no gentleman. That made a crack in his armor, one her weapons could penetrate.

As she crossed the room on her husband's arm to thank the Pleasants for their hospitality, her head was high. The battle between Claude and Charles might be political and economic. The battle between her and Hélène might be social. But the battle between Charles and herself was purely a battle between a man and a woman, fought on the oldest ground of all. She smiled, feeling her beauty draw close around her. On that kind of ground, she was sure of winning.

6

Claude stepped onto the plank walkway laid between the storage tank and the derrick, and looked up at the derrick tower, which reached thirty feet into the air, the long poles forming its corners making a twelve-foot-square base. Latticed against the marsh sky, it seemed strange, alien. Forty feet away, its twin rose from the land on Beau Chêne, already pumping oil. Claude's arm swept forward, pointing. "With any luck, Beau, ours'll be doing that soon."

A man moved from behind the derrick, approached Claude. "Morning, Mr. Langlinais. This your boy?"

"Brought him to see the drilling start," Claude said, roughing Beau's hair with his big hand. "Beau, this is Dusty Hawkins, the best damn drilling-crew foreman between here and Dallas."

Hawkins shoved a hand at Beau, grinned at Claude. "Not much to see so far," he said. "Just the bit chopping up the ground for a while. But, hell, Mr. Langlinais, that bit may just start you up an empire." He laughed. "You and your boy here might be hobnobbing with the Mellons. Or the Rockefellers, if you think you can stand 'em."

"Acadiana Oil's got a long way to go before it takes on Enterprise Oil and Standard Oil and the others," Claude said. He nodded toward the derrick on the de Gravelle land. "Enterprise Oil's got that well, and drilling more."

"Which is why this is the place to start," Hawkins said. "No way of knowing whose side is on the deepest part of the pool—so the only thing to do is get in there and get out what we can while the getting's good."

"I don't want any trouble," Claude said.

Beau looked up at his father. Since they'd arrived at the rig, he had sensed excitement building in him; though his father's voice remained even, as calm as the still water in the marsh ponds, his eyes, going from Dusty Hawkins' face to the rig and then to the drilling crew assembling around the derrick, were alive with anticipation. "What kind of trouble?" Beau asked.

"This patch of oil's been . . . disputed before," Claude answered. And Beau remembered the line of stakes, those objects so defiantly holding land they did not belong on.

"But that's settled—isn't it?"

He saw his father and Dusty look at each other over his head. "Sure," Claude said. "Sure. Just want to make sure it stays that way." He jumped from the platform onto the soft earth, water-marked by early-spring rains like a throw of brown velvet shot with silver.

"And me," Dusty said. "I don't want any more trouble than an ornery well gives me anyway." He stared across the way to the pumping well on Beau Chêne. "But I don't see any. Got a good team here, they know what they're doing. If there's oil on this side, we'll hit it."

Claude turned away from the derrick, motioned Dusty to jump down beside him. He jerked a thumb toward the men moving about the Beau Chêne rig. "That well's been producing for six weeks, Dusty—they might not take kindly to another pig at the trough." He leaned closer, making a tight triangle of their three heads. "Trouble I'm talking about is what you read about from time to time—fights between crews, and worse."

Dusty spat into the marsh grass that sprinkled dew over his boots at every step. "Hell, Mr. Langlinais, you don't need to worry about these boys starting anything. When you hire Dusty Hawkins, you get oil, not trouble."

Claude laughed. "That's what I was told, Dusty." He slapped him on the shoulder, then looked back toward Beau Chêne and shrugged. "What they'll do . . ." An arm came around Beau. "That's what a working well is like, son. That's what we want a whole damn forest of."

The mist was clearing, pulled from the sky by the finger rays of the rising sun. Across the marsh, the steady sound of Beau Chêne No. 1 pump came. With each thrust, more oil bubbled up from the salt dome below, flowing into the storage tank— money to refill the dwindling supply in Marthe de Gravelle's accounts. It was not that he didn't want Marthe to do well. But she'd not live forever, and then Beau Chêne would change hands. The son, René, was the obvious heir. But René kept losing himself—and as much money as he could get his hands on—in one European escapade after the other, while the youngest girl, Nanette, lost herself in medicine and missionary work. That left Hélène—and that meant Charles Livaudais. Claude thought of that flow of money filling Livaudais' cavernous pockets. Hell, given that kind of base, Livaudais would dig in so deep they could never get rid of him.

He turned to Hawkins. "Beau and I are going to watch you all begin. Then we're going up to my mama's for a second breakfast. If you've never had boudin, you'd better come."

"I'm not going to be able to get my belt around my britches," Hawkins said, "way these ladies keep coming on with the grub." Then he lifted his head, attention fixed on the rig across the way. The Beau Chêne crew was lined up close to the boundary line, chanting words which were at first carried away on the marsh air, but which then took shape and became clear. "Dry hole, dry hole," the sounds came. The volume mounted, the chant became a cry. "Dry hole, dry hole."

Hawkins turned to Claude. "On the other hand, Mr. Langlinais, my crew won't run from a fight. If someone else just has to have one."

"Neither will I," Claude said. He moved with Hawkins to the edge of the derrick, motioning Beau to follow them. They watched the men put the drill bit into place, watched them fire the boiler that would provide the steam to drive the engine.

And in spite of his own resolve not to put much faith, or hope, in this well, Claude felt his own spirits building within him, like the steam that built up in the boiler. If they did strike oil, with this well, with others . . . Sugar had made a river of white gold, was making it still for big producers. The war in Europe had sent sugar prices soaring. It was Marthe's bad luck she'd had so many bills called she'd had to sell the fields that might have seen her out of debt. The Langlinaises had never done much with sugar; they'd put a lot of eggs from different kind of fowl together and come up with a pretty fine basket. But if they struck oil—everything else they did, the furs, the lumber, the automobile agency, the bank stock, the sash-and-door factory, all of it, would be just so much extra, so much lagniappe. Claude put his hand on Hawkins' shoulder. "Tell you what. Any fighting needs to be done, you call on me. You just tend to the drilling."

The steam in the engine boiler was ready; the pistons began to move, slowly at first, then steadying into a rhythm that would be maintained day and night until oil was struck or the hole abandoned. The pulsing beat overlaid the scurrying sounds of the marsh animals and startled a red-winged black-bird, which erupted from a nearby bush, rising almost straight into the air, the sun highlighting the scarlet markings on his wings. The metal bit glinted in the sunlight, too, as the crew guided it toward the place Dusty had marked. Beau watched that shining piece of metal, hanging above the earth like some giant's fishhook. He watched it drop, make contact with the spongy earth, and begin cutting through it. Dirt was thrown up around it; a man stood near the casing pipe, ready to follow the path the bit made.

"Like going through a piece of your ma's chocolate cake now," Dusty said. "But we'll hit something worse soon enough, get slowed down some."

"How far do you have to drill, Mr. Hawkins?" Beau said. It seemed to him that there was enough casing pipe to line a hole to China.

"If I knew that, I wouldn't be working for someone else," Dusty said, and grinned. "Tell you what, I wouldn't have built that big storage tank if I hadn't expected to fill it up."

Beau looked at the earth-walled tank, basking in the cool May air. The sound of the steam engine seemed familiar now, part of the marsh, part of its life. "Gosh," he said. "To look at this marsh, you'd never think there was anything much under it, would you?"

Dusty pulled out tobacco and paper and rolled a cigarette. "Never mind what's underneath. On top you and your pa got some of the prettiest land I ever saw."

Beau looked at his father and saw that look—that special look he got when anyone talked about his land—cover his face. He felt a oneness with his father, with the land. The raccoons washing their breakfast at the pond, the birds swaying on the tall grasses—all one. And all his. "That's for sure," he told Dusty. "But like my grandmother would say—I hope the beauty's not just skin deep, all the same."

Claude, staring past his own rig to Beau Chêne No. 1, heard his son and smiled to himself. There was that rig over there, pumping money. He felt a sudden pull inside, a grabbing deep in his belly. God, how he wanted to hit oil! From nothing, his forebears had built a small empire. Along with the lumber and the furs, the businesses, they had handed down another legacy—the ability to meet every challenge. No matter what, they had always prevailed, the Langlinaises. Sometimes by craft and cunning, sometimes by bold and open strokes—once or twice, with swift grace decimating the enemy. Prevailing was all, prevailing was everything. Increasingly, though, such efforts took time, took energy. Men prowled the halls of the legislature, out for an easy way to wealth. Judges were purchased, and made decisions in the darkness of someone's pocket. To prevail now would take more time, more energy, and more money than even Claude had. Unless he struck oil. Then he could turn his attention away from the lumberyards, away from the fur trade, away from stock deals—and face those men in New Orleans and Baton Rouge who would, if allowed, with one stroke of a legislative or judicial pen, rob him and his of everything they had earned over the past one hundred and sixty-five years.

He took a deep breath. They would hit oil. They had to. Another deep breath, willing himself to be calm. Then, to Dusty and Beau: "Let's go on up to Mama's." He smiled at Dusty. "You like fig preserves?"

When the United States declared war on Germany on April 6, 1917, war stories pushed everything else from the front pages.

Even an incipient oil boom seemed insignificant to eyes turned across the ocean—especially to young men still at home who wanted very much to be with their compatriots "making the world safe for democracy."

"You'd do better to be studying your Latin," Alice said, coming upon Beau poring over the war news in the *Times-Picayune*. "When you get to college, they're not going to give you a test on that old war."

"Somebody else might," Beau said.

"Now, what does that mean?" Alice said. Then she went to him, pulled his head forward, and kissed the soft brown hair. "Listen, just because that crazy Bonin boy went off and joined the army, don't get ideas. You're too young, Beau, they'd never take you in one minute."

"They took Étienne."

"Because he's so big who would believe he's still just twenty? Anyway, he has a birthday in September, and he'll be twenty-one. What's the use of sending him home?"

"Mama . . . Mama, there're some things a . . . a man feels he just has to do."

Alice felt laughter rising from the place inside where mothers see their children as always young, always innocent. Then the darkness in Beau's eyes capped it. She hugged him, feeling the same astonishment as always at the length of him, the strength of this tall young man she could once hold in one curving arm. "That's true, Beau. There are." She held him away from her, looked into his eyes. "But, Beau, feelings aren't enough. We have to think, too." Briskly, she let him go. "You're only seventeen years old." She measured his resolution against her knowledge of him. "Beau, you wouldn't want them to send you home? Like a dog not disciplined enough for the hunt?"

His face fired with his angry blush. "I'd like to see them try!"

"Well," Alice said. "You've worked up a lot of excitement. My rosebushes need weeding, go take it out on them."

"Mama—"

"Go!" she said, giving him a little push. "But, listen, your Aunt Claudine wrote, they want you to come visit in a few weeks." Watching Beau's face become excited at the prospect of going to New Orleans, Alice smiled. These children! Thank heaven she knew enough to keep one step ahead of them. Though with that Francie, even three steps wouldn't be far

enough. It would be a long time, a very long time, before Miss
Francie would be trusted to visit in New Orleans. Well, with
Beau off at LSU in the fall, with Marie going to Miss Louise
Taylor's school in New Iberia, she would have more time with
Francie. How funny that she was two years younger than
Marie, and already so much more grown-up. If she could just
put Francie in a box, sit on her until she was old enough to get
married! Alice sighed. Boys you wanted to hold back so they
wouldn't have to go to war, girls you wanted to push so you
could get them safely married.

"I think I'll go out to the farm when I've finished," Beau
said, already halfway out the door. "Might go watch them drill
for a while."

"As if there's anything to see," Alice said. She had come to
hate any mention of the well that grew deeper and deeper each
day without hitting oil.

"We're going to hit oil, Mama," Beau said. "I've been
reading up on it. Where they're drilling is most likely right on
top of a big salt dome, with lots of oil trapped underneath."

"And with lots of it being rescued by Beau Chêne No. 1!"
Alice said. Since the night at the governor's mansion, she had
let these new oil operations become her excuse for hostility.
With every barrel of oil that poured up through the pipe into the
tanks, another pool of anger in Alice was tapped. Anger
against Hélène, whose husband did not want her—but whose
position was nonetheless secure. Hélène had sure entry to
places Alice might not necessarily wish to go, but to which she
wanted the right of refusal. Hélène was one of those people
who "had" money, who had always "had" it, so that the purest
proof of wealth was never to speak of it directly, but only to
surround oneself with it and its pleasures. Anger against
Charles Livaudais, who had insulted her because she did not
have that position, nor the protection it gave. She shuddered,
remembering his voice in her ear. "I'll wait," he'd said, and his
cold eyes had flicked her bodice from her shoulders, her skirt
from her hips. If only we strike oil, she thought. She wanted a
wall of money around her, a wall so thick that even the insolent
eyes and hands of Charles Livaudais could not cross it.

In late May, Enterprise Oil Company made a second strike on
the Beau Chêne property, after having drilled to a depth of

more than three thousand feet. When the well blew, oil gushed thirty feet above the top of the derrick; later, under control and pumping, the well began producing eight hundred barrels a day. The strike so near to their own unsuccessful drilling had a strong effect on Dusty Hawkins' crew; they went about their work with their backs turned to the activity forty feet away, heads bent earthward. "Mr. Langlinais going to feel like keeping on paying us with nothing to show for it?" one of the men asked Dusty the last payday in May.

"Hell, man, we're into limestone now, showing traces of sulfur." His chin jutted out, a reflection of Claude's own stubbornness. "We'll make it, man. We'll make it." When the crew gathered again on Monday morning, Dusty himself steered the drill pipe when it was lowered from the derrick. "I got me a feeling," he said. "I smell *oil*!"

His spirits reinfected his crew; Claude, out with the foreman of his lumber operation, heard them singing and decided to drift over to the rig, see if there was any special reason for their mood. Dusty saw Claude break through a screen of greening cypress and waved his big gray hat. "Hey, Langlinais! Come up by me, man! My backbone's jumping and my nose is twitching—if we don't hit this morning, you can chop me up and use me for boudin."

Claude clambered up onto the rig and stood watching the rhythmic pace of the drill pipe, the churning of the earth it cut through. His whole world seemed to focus on that small square of earth, which had suddenly become the most important piece of all the land he owned. Then, toward midmorning, when the June sun had climbed high enough to make itself felt on the backs of their necks, the mud used to cool the drill bit began to bubble up. A low roar, coming from deep in the earth, coughed up gobbets of black mud, sending them through the crown block at the top of the derrick like ink marks against the blue skirt of the sky. "Run," Dusty shouted to the crew, grabbing Claude's arm and pulling him along. Covered with mud, they slid to the ground and began running. The roar grew louder, erupting from the earth like the mud, and like the mud, covering all around it. There was only the great sound coming up from the depths of the earth; and the mud, flinging itself high, hung dark against the sky, then fell back to the ground. Claude, his eyes wide to photograph this moment, remember it forever, saw the drilling pipe rise in one great cataclysmic belch, crashing through the top of the tower and then, like a dart thrown by a giant, falling and sticking into the soft ground. There was a strong smell of natural gas, like a breath from hell. And then, spouting high, black oil.

For a moment Claude was sure he was imagining that high dark fountain, so badly did he want it. Then he felt Dusty's arms around him, hugging him, dancing him around in the suddenly darkened air. "Hey, man, hey, man. We've done it—there's your oil, man, there it is!"

The crew was shouting, running forward, letting out in one exuberant moment the pent-up frustration of the previous weeks. Claude hugged Dusty back, feeling the bristle of his beard, the roughness of his shirt. He pounded Dusty's back, and felt his own spirits soar like the oil gushing against the sky. "God damn, Dusty," he said. "God damn. Tonight I'm throwing a party for this crew that will make even this morning sit in the shade."

Dusty picked up his hat, shoved it down on his head, and cocked an eye at the derrick. "First things first," he said, marching toward the rig. "Before we tap your kegs—we got to get this oil pumping into your pipes." He threw a grin over his shoulder. "You can't sell oil to the clouds, Claude."

And by mid-June, Acadiana No. 1 was pumping four hundred barrels a day, with a second derrick going up not far from the first well.

"Won't be able to get between those things to hunt," Claude said.

"You should have seen the Spindletop field," Hawkins said. "We had as many as 150 rigs on five hundred acres."

"Just you leave me room for my dog and me," Claude said.

"We bring in a couple more good wells, you can go hunt those big animals out in Africa, like Teddy Roosevelt," Dusty said.

"Only reason a man has to go to Africa to hunt is he doesn't know about Louisiana," Claude said. "If you're still around come duck season, I'll show you some hunting."

"Best hunting I do is for oil," Dusty said. "As for being around—I'll stay till we hit suitcase rock." He laughed. "That's when there just ain't no more oil. Time to pack your suitcase and move on."

"That bother you any? Moving from place to place like you do?"

Dusty drained his coffee cup, stood up, hitching up his heavy work pants. "Told you I wouldn't be able to get a belt around my britches if I ate much more of your ma's cooking. Mind moving? Listen, Claude, a man who ain't willing to move to where the opportunity is might just as well call his life a dry hole. You know?"

"I know," Claude said. He, too, stood. "You hear what I hear? That Beau Chêne No. 1's slowing down some?"

"Yeah, I heard." Their eyes met, agreed on the question. "Who's to know if our well has anything to do with it? That rig's on their land, our rig's on yours." Dusty tightened his boot laces, retied them. "Like you say—boundary lines don't dam a pool of oil."

"You got any arms out there?"

Dusty stopped in mid-stride, faced Claude. "Now, you've heard something I maybe haven't. You expecting trouble?"

For the first time since he had met Claude Langlinais, Dusty Hawkins saw the measuring smile which meant Claude had assessed a situation and determined its meaning. "I'm not particularly *expecting* trouble," Claude said. "You might just say I don't want it to surprise me. If it should come."

"I got me an old pistol. Don't know about the other boys. Guess they've got something to kill snakes with."

"Find out," Claude said. "I couldn't exactly arm the entire U.S. Army—but I sure can field a few shotguns and rifles."

He watched Dusty march through Geneviève's kitchen garden and on into the fields, almost knee-high now in corn. He knew every foot of the Langlinais land, every inch of it. What the surveyors had tried to take by stealth others might well try to take by force. He'd be damned if he would give up a half-inch to anyone, for any reason. He looked at his watch. He'd have to get a move on if he wanted to drive into New Iberia with Alice to put Beau on the train to New Orleans. He went out on the front porch, where Jumie and Geneviève sat, Geneviève crocheting, Jumie gazing at the fields. "Well, Papa, you and Mama going to do something fancy with all this oil money?"

Jumie smiled. "Claude, when I look out and see the blackberries sweet on the vines and the roses starting to bloom— I've got everything fancy I need."

Claude's eyes met his mother's. "No stronger," hers said. Claude's lips touched her cheek, brushed his father's forehead.

Driving home, he seemed to feel the strands of the family around him—the old ones back at the farm, his sister and her family in New Orleans, his wife, his children. One point of the road took him near enough to the drilling so he could see the tip end of the derrick, dark, solid. He smiled. That tower, and others like it, were making those strands strong, binding. A net of safety for the Langlinaises. A fence to keep others out.

Sheets of summer rain like wet laundry hung across the high July sky; Claude, waking early, turned to Alice. "What's the best way to spend a rainy summer morning?" he asked her. Alice sat up, pulled off her thin batiste gown, and drew him to her. Out in the oil field, the crew also woke to hear the rain. To a man, they pulled their pillows over their heads and slept on.

There was no one to see a pair of men with shovels and axes slip across the line that divided Beau Chêne from the Langlinais farm and begin quietly to rip holes in the wooden-rimmed, earth-dammed storage tanks, filled almost to the brim with oil. It was not until a clap of thunder, violent against the wet silence of the rain, woke one man in the hut housing the Acadiana Oil crew that any notice was taken of the lake of oil that was forming. That man, going outside to relieve himself, scratching his head, yawning at the sky, was brought fully awake by the oily smell of the air. He turned, and saw, pouring from the ruined tanks, a strong flow of oil that wound around the rig, gathered into a pool, filled the space between the derrick and where he stood. "My Gawd!" he took time to say. Then he ran to the door of the hut, shouting against the fear ramming itself down his throat.

The men grabbed shovels, went to the breaks in the tanks, and began trying to bank them. Oil was everywhere; they were saturated with it, human wicks in a great bowl of fuel. Suddenly, from a spot somewhere on the Beau Chêne property line, a brand of fire sailed through the air, fell into a pond of oil, and ignited it. With a great roar, the entire area quickly became a sheet of bright orange flames, with thick black smoke that bellowed up between earth and rain. The human wicks caught, flickered with movement as they tried to run out of a world on fire. Like sparks riding on the explosive air sailing up a chimney, they were flung from the hot heart of the fire to the outer edges, where they flamed, burned, and finally fell to earth, black and charred fragments of bone and dangling strips of flesh.

Marthe, from the gallery of Beau Chêne, saw it first, a bloom of dark against the gray morning. "Berthe!" she cried. "Tell Nat to round up the men—there's a fire!" She could tell the flames were not from her land; running to the telephone, she frantically called Claude. "There's fire—down at your derricks. Claude—it looks bad. I'll meet you there."

"Marthe—"

"Don't argue with me, Claude."

A tremor of fear raced through Claude as he drove to the farm and almost ran the distance to the drilling site. He had never tried to imagine hell before; he had no intention of going there, and would not waste time on its horrors. Seeing the flames, he knew he had no need to, now. A pit of fire consumed itself before him, heat so intense he could see blisters rising on his skin. At the edge of it one creature, not even a man anymore, lay screaming. Marthe de Gravelle knelt beside him, her face tortured. Claude strode to her side.

"There's not a damn thing you can do for him, Marthe. Get back to the house. You're not safe out here."

"Where do you want the backfire started?" she said. Her face was blackened from the thick soot, her eyes wide, staring. But clear with determination.

The screams of the dying man burned into their souls. Claude thought of his pistol, in the drawer next to his bed. When the world was flaming, did rules still matter? He shook the thought away. "Over there. On the other side of the pit." He wet his finger, tested the wind. "Thank the Lord, there's enough of breeze to keep the fire from the well. If that catches . . ."

He heard a new, and blessed, silence. He touched Marthe's shoulder. "It's all right, Marthe. He's dead." He helped her rise, saw her cross herself, her lips murmur a prayer. "There'll be no hell for him, whatever he's done." She moved away from the black form on the ground, motioned to Nat and the hands from the plantation to come forward.

"Listen to what Mr. Claude tells you, Nat. He wants you to start a backfire." She turned to Claude. "There must be something else I can do."

"All right. Since you insist on staying. Go get the crew off the Beau Chêne wells. We need every man we can get." A grim smile crossed his face. "They won't come to save my oil—maybe they'll come to save yours."

She vanished into the sparsely wooded strip of land that divided the properties, the bright blue of her dress appearing between the trees like the flash of a darting bird. Lord, he hoped the marsh grass and trees were wet enough so that it would take more than one sailing spark to turn them into torches. He moved toward where Nat and his men were clearing brush away, making a firebreak before setting the backfire. They worked quickly, their machetes moving with the practiced rhythm of old cane-field hands; sooner than Claude could have hoped, a wide strip of almost bare earth served as a barricade, and they were ready to light the fire, which, under their tight control, would help the rampaging demon burn itself out.

He watched the backfire catch, send its own flames like a bright challenge against the tower of fire on the other side of the pit. The two fires seemed to march across the space between them, keeping pace step by furious step. Their heat was engulfing the oxygen in that space, making a vacuum which would first feed the fires as it sucked up hundreds of gallons of oil from the wasted tanks, but which would then turn on them, strangle them by keeping from them the air they needed to breathe. It was a dangerous ploy, but it was the only one they had.

Orange flames were everywhere, turning the whole world into a horrible glowing ball. The ball was set in a frame of black smoke that choked the lungs and clung to the skin and carried death. Claude felt suddenly alone, helpless. The men were separated from him by that smoke, that wall of fire. Hell was here, and he was in it.

Then a puff of wind cleared a space, and he saw Marthe emerge from the woods, alone. She reached him, her breath struggling with the foul smoke. "They won't come," she said. "They said they work for Enterprise Oil, not for me, that they've got their own rigs to protect." Behind her, the flames burned more intensely than ever; there was a beat of stillness, and then the fountain of oil sucked up by the force of the opposing fires exploded. Flames leapt upward; a roar made the entire world one great angry cry. Claude grabbed Marthe, pulled her down to the wet ground, shielding her body with his own. He felt daggers of pain on his back and legs as points of fire hit him. When he peered from behind his arm at the sky, he saw fire falling as though each drop of rain had exploded. Then the roar dropped out of the sky; the furnace of fire flickered, the sky lost its unnatural glow and became a sheen of soft rain. Claude rose to his knees. The main fire was out; there was nothing left but small pools of flame, like candles on a giant's table.

"Go back to the house," he said to Marthe. "Fix food. Coffee. And get a doctor out here. There'll be burns to see to, God knows." He watched her leave, then picked up a shovel and headed toward one of the small candles of fire. An arm came from behind him, grabbed him, spun him around.

"Claude, my Gawd. Claude."

It was Dusty, whole, alive, his face stunned. Claude stared at him, shovel suspended from his hand. "Claude . . . what in the hell . . ." And at Claude's look: "Got up early, saw the rain, knew the crew would sleep in. Took up my pistol, went out to shoot a rabbit for my breakfast." His eyes reflected the devastation he saw. "Heard the roaring—the flames . . . Gawd, Claude."

Claude clasped Dusty, then handed him the shovel. "Over there. Nat needs help. We'll talk later." He found another tool, and worked alongside the men.

By late afternoon, the fire was completely out, but the earth lay in black violation under a white sky. No color anywhere; not the blue that the sun, when it finally found its way past the smother of cloud, would paint in the sky, not the gray of rain. Only the bright white light of a hidden sun, and on the earth, the black of destruction. Eight men had died, and only heaven knew how they would know which was which. As for the oil which had burned—there was no way of ever knowing how much had been consumed. The men from the Langlinais farm and from Beau Chêne had repaired the storage tank near the pump, so that already a layer of oil hid its earth floor. Claude walked over, looked at the thick black flow. He remembered the day they'd found the oil, he and Beau, and how innocently happy he had been. Lagniappe, he'd called it. Something you didn't have to pay for. He looked at the eight charred bodies, lying in a row, waiting for coffins. He looked at the burned land, the black scars on it. There was no lagniappe now.

Before leaving, he glanced across at Beau Chêne No. 1. Her crew had been building a fire line to keep their rig clear of the devastation. They worked silently, backs turned to the bleak landscape so near them. No court of law could ever fix their guilt for this, nor would he even know how to try to prove it. But Claude knew, as surely as he knew his land, that they had set this fire.

By nightfall, armed men were stationed all along the border between Langlinais land and Beau Chêne.

7

The low-pressure area that was bringing rain up from the Gulf, already reaching St. Martinville, had not yet spread over New Orleans. When Beau and his cousin Hal Larroque took the streetcar out to Lake Pontchartrain to sail the Larroques' new star-class sailboat, the air was clear. Beau, on his first holiday in New Orleans without the rest of his family, felt grown-up and ready for anything as they swung off the streetcar at the end of the line and walked the rest of the way to the yacht basin. "What's that?" he asked, pointing to a large white frame building whose many windows offered a fine view of the lake waters lapping close to one wing.

"Southern Yacht Club," Hal said. "Where the really rich guys sail."

Beau cocked an eye at his cousin. "We're pretty rich. How rich do you have to be?"

Hal kicked at the oyster shells that made the path down to the dock where the boat was moored. "It's not just rich, I guess. Certain families, they belong."

Beau felt a quick rise of anger. "Certain families? Not Langlinaises? Not Larroques?"

Hal shrugged. "Langlinaises may be famous down in St. Martinville, Beau. Here?" He shrugged again. "And my papa's respected, sure he is. He's got his own pharmacy—and then there's the money Mama gets from her side . . ." He laughed and slapped Beau's shoulder. "Look, Beau, you can have a good time in New Orleans whether or not you belong to the Southern Yacht Club or Comus or Rex or any of that."

Beau stopped, squared off in front of Hal. "Wait a minute. I don't understand. Who decides all this?" He waved toward the clubhouse. "Who can be in that? Who decides?"

Hal stared back at him. "Beau. You've never been in a club? Never had a few guys you went around with, you wouldn't let other guys in?"

"That's kid stuff."

Hal's black eyes stared at him, boring the meaning of his words deep into Beau's thoughts. "I never said it wasn't. That doesn't make it any less real."

"So—it doesn't bother you?"

Hal took Beau's arm, tugged him on down the path. "Wouldn't change it. Look, Beau, they go their way, I go mine. All right?"

"All right for you, maybe. But me?" Beau clenched a fist, shook it at the white building gleaming in the sun. "Someday they'll beg me to join their club. That and every other damn thing in New Orleans."

Hal laughed. "I hope you'll say no. It can't be all that much fun, sitting around feeling superior to everybody else." Then he pointed to the lake. The brown-gray waters of Lake Pontchartrain, lying in a shallow bowl of earth that stretched from the edge of New Orleans to the open Gulf, shone under the July sun. The light, slanting from just above the horizon, put a sheen on the water's surface that reminded Beau of a bowl of his mother's gumbo. And rocking on the surface, bobbing in the clear light of morning, was the new boat. A little over twenty feet long, it had two triangular sails, the larger one sporting a star near the top, the symbol of the boat's class.

"She's a great little boat," Hal said, leaping down into the hull. "She can sail in less than four feet of water, and believe me, it can handle rough water."

"Can't get much of that here," Beau said, jumping down beside Hal. "Lake looks safe as Bayou Teche."

"Don't you believe it," Hal said, loosening the rope that moored them. "Squalls come up on this lake so fast you hardly know they're coming before you're in the middle of one. High winds, waves over your head . . ." He caressed the side of the boat. "But this little lady can handle it. She's what they call a wet boat in heavy weather, and man, can she race!"

"Wish we could race now," Beau said.

Hal laughed. "This is your first sailing lesson, Beau. I don't think you're ready to race." He sat in the bow, put his hand on the tiller, and began to steer them out toward the open water. "I'll let you take over when we get past the buoys marking the course for the regatta the yacht club's having Saturday. She almost sails herself; you won't have to do much."

"I think I can handle it," Beau said, feeling put out. Then he laughed at himself. Hal, a year younger, had had plenty enough experience letting Beau be the teacher, introducing him to rabbit and squirrel hunting, taking him on his first deer hunt, his first duck hunt. And initiating him into the intricate balance necessary to pole a pirogue through bayou waters made treacherous by floating logs and tangling roots. Fair was fair; he'd let Hal enjoy being captain for once.

They were out past the pier now, heading toward the center of the lake. The breeze off the water touched Beau's hair, ruffling it so the light edges the sun put on it bent in a ripple of gold. "There's another boat new around here," Hal said, pointing back toward the Southern Yacht Club. "It's a twenty-one-foot knockabout sloop—they were brought down here from Massachusetts a couple of years ago. These star-class boats came a little later."

Beau followed Hal's finger to a boat that seemed held out of the water by the three sails that had just begun to fill with wind. A small figure was casting off; as they watched, the boat hesitated, then plunged forward on a course parallel with theirs. "What's that third sail? Looks like a wing."

"It's a balloon spinnaker."

"Does that make it faster than this boat?"

"Not necessarily. But look, you don't need to know all that. Here, come take a turn at the tiller."

"Sure," Beau said. He exchanged seats with Hal, took the tiller in his hand.

"Just keep her pointed due south for a while," Hal said. "Away from that squall line over there." Beau's eyes darted to the far horizon. A long black smear blotted the line between blue July sky and gray water.

"Is it going to storm?"

"Already is, over there. We'll be in before it moves this way, if it does."

The small boat had a distinct life of her own; Beau could feel her pulse in the movement of the tiller. For a moment or two, he gripped too tightly, forcing his will on the spirited craft. Then, with a tiny shudder of surrender, the boat gave herself over to his control and settled on course. Beau leaned back against the side and looked beyond the water to the shore. The morning had the clear and secretive quality of a picture. Buildings, half-hidden by close-growing trees, were held in that clear air as though frozen, with all life inside a state of static being. Across the water, Beau could see other boats—an occasional trawler, sailboats whose leaping canvas pulled their shells through the water, a rowboat with two fishermen. One of the fishermen stood, cast out his line, braced himself against the roll of his boat with locked knees and stiff spine. But he, too, seemed under glass, distant, not real. The silence, the stillness, of the scene captured Beau's thoughts. He sat quietly, hand lightly on the tiller now. The wood beneath him was warm and growing hotter in the strong sun.

He squinted his eyes against the glare off the water and gazed at the dark horizon.

Hal looked past Beau at the sky. "We'd better be getting back. This weather's turning faster than I thought it would—doesn't look good at all."

A shout came from behind them, the words a taunting command. "Get out of the way or get run over!"

They looked to see the sloop they had watched earlier coming over the whitecaps, heading straight for them. A man stood in the bow, hands cupped around his mouth. "You're right in the middle of the course set for Saturday's race. Get out of the way!"

"Well, damn," Beau said. "Isn't this lake big enough they don't have to sail right here?"

Hal moved to the tiller and began to turn the boat. "I wasn't watching the markers." He pointed at the red-and-white floats moored in a wavering line that stretched back to shore and out into the wind-tossed lake. "They're practicing the course and we are in the middle of it."

"If they give prizes for rudeness, the captain of that boat will win in a walk," Beau said.

"Well, they take their racing seriously," Hal said. The sailboat was drawing near, spinnaker bulging, and Beau could see another man and a young woman on board. "Sir Thomas Lipton, that English lord who's always trying to win the America's Cup, was here last summer and the yacht-club members almost went crazy entertaining him."

Beau looked at Hal. "I thought you said all that stuff was just a big bother."

"I've got sisters," Hal said. "They're better than the *Times-Picayune* when it comes to keeping up with things like that."

The second boat closed the space between them and pulled up alongside. The girl in the boat had her back to them, her head hidden by the big collar of her white dress, which had sailed up behind her, caught on a gust of fast wind. "Move it!" the same man shouted.

At the same moment, the collar flapped down and Beau saw a familiar profile, a flow of golden hair. "Caroline Livaudais!" he said, even as she turned and saw him.

"Why, Beau Langlinais!" There was only three feet of water between them; her laugh rang across it, sketching notes in the air. "What in the world are you doing here?"

"Sailing," Beau said. He gestured toward Hal. "This is my first cousin, Hal Larroque." He raised his voice to make himself heard over the rising wind. "I'm visiting him for a while."

"And you haven't even come to see me!" Caroline said.

He thought he had remembered how blue her eyes were— now he decided that no memory would ever be more than a teasing shadow. "We were over at Pass Christian for the Fourth," he said. "I was going to call on you this afternoon."

"Well, I should hope so!"

The man who had shouted at them earlier leaned toward Caroline. "Caroline, this isn't a tea party. I'm trying to time this course."

"Oh, Stu, for heaven's sake."

Beau watched her mouth make a tiny frown, then curve again in laughter. How could he have forgotten how beautiful she was in the few months between her visit to Beau Chêne during Lent and now! He cupped his hands around his mouth, leaned forward. "I'll come around four o'clock, all right?"

Her answer was blown away on the wind, and covered by a shout from the man she had called Stu. "Want to race? If you're not going to get out of my way, you might as well give me a fight."

Beau saw Hal look up from the tiller, take a measuring look at the darkening sky, the rising waves. "No, thanks!" Hal called.

"Hal! Do it," Beau urged. He saw the smile on the sailor's face. It was the kind of smile one wanted to get rid of by slapping it off.

"Don't be crazy, Beau. That's Stuart Favrot. He spends more time sailing than anything else—he'd beat us to smithereens and we'd be out in the middle of the lake in what looks like a bad squall coming up."

"I'll give you a head start," Favrot called. And when Hal smiled and shook his head: "What's the matter? Your boat got more go to her than you do?"

"That does it," Beau said to Hal. "You won't take that from him, will you?" He moved to Hal, sat beside him. "Or are the only sailors with guts members of the Southern Yacht Club?"

"You're crazy, Beau Langlinais," Hal said. But his eyes were angry too, and he lined up his bow with the bow of the other boat and followed its turn as it tacked against the wind. "You're on," he shouted to Stu Favrot.

Now Beau could feel the increased force of the wind. He peered northward, across the waves which were gradually increasing in height as they increased in speed. "It's looking worse," he said. The long black blur seemed closer now. It had more shape, filled more of the distance between lake and sky. Leaning against the side of the boat, he could feel the water piled up against it.

Hal was keeping almost abreast of the other boat, the two craft bouncing like wind-powered corks. Then, as though a monstrous wet sail had been dropped over the sky, the sun disappeared completely behind black clouds. Raindrops blew against their faces, sharp pricks of wind-driven water. "Damn," Hal said. "I am heading back." He fought to turn the boat, take her home.

"Quitting?" came the cry from the other boat. Even against the growing sough of the wind, the word cut through them, its sting bringing color to Beau's cheeks. He held himself steady, seeking the face of the man who challenged them. Caroline, struggling to stand, reached toward Stu, her mouth forming words.

"Caroline, sit down!" Favrot yelled.

As Beau watched, the boat seemed to bounce off a wall of waves, hitting it head-on. There was a flurry of movement, and suddenly a flash of white as Caroline toppled over the boat's side.

"My God! She's overboard!" Beau had one terrified glimpse of Caroline, her hair plastered against her face, before she went under. With barely a moment's hesitation, Beau dove over the side where he had seen her disappear. Water pulled at his canvas shoes and made lead of his light summer pants. He fought his way to the surface, grabbing for air; turning to dive, he saw her come up. Quickly Beau reached out and managed to grasp her shoulder before she could sink again; with two powerful kicks fueled by adrenaline, he pulled her to the cradle of his body, holding her in front of him while his legs scissored against the water. Where are the boats? he thought desperately.

Suddenly something blue and white, tied to a gold rope, sailed past his head, skipping across the water. The life preserver hit slightly behind him; at the other end, a man was holding fast. Beau heard himself murmuring words, making sounds in Caroline's ear. He found the ring, got it over Caroline's head. "Can you hold on?" She nodded yes, raised tentative hands up through the opening in the ring, took hold of the edge of the life preserver. Then she seemed to make a fierce act of will, and thrust her body higher until her head and shoulders rode clear of the threatening waves. Grasping the life preserver tightly in the hook of one arm, Beau began swimming toward the boat.

The rain was coming down faster, long piercing lines that stung his face. The wind seemed to come from all directions at once, and the sailboat seemed to fight to break free. In a burst of power Beau's legs closed the distance between them and the boat. "Pull, dammit!" he yelled at the man holding the rope. He could see Stu battling the tiller, his face white. "Try to lift yourself out of the water," he told Caroline. "Try to use the rope to pull yourself up."

Her dress was sodden, dragging her back. She hung on the side of the boat, before he let go of the rope and reached out to grab her with his hands. For a moment, she was suspended between deck and water, her body leaning backward, her head lifted. Then she slid over the boat's side. The man had the life preserver in his hand, threw it once again. Beau put his head and arms through it, and began to propel himself closer to the boat. Just as the man began to haul Beau in, Caroline stood next to him, her hands reaching for the rope. "Let me help, Robert," Beau heard her say. And then a wave seemed to lift him out of the water, and on its crest, Beau flopped over the side of the boat, a tumble of arms and legs. He lay in the bottom of the sailboat, taking in air that he did not have. When he opened his eyes, Caroline's face was above him. "Oh, Beau," she said. "Are you all right?"

Beau struggled to sit up; he had not realized how completely he had used his strength until he felt the effort needed just to reach a seated position. The man who had hauled them out crouched beside Beau, a hand out. "Robert Livaudais," he said. "Caroline's first cousin. Langlinais, I've a lot to thank you for." Then he looked quickly at the bow, where Stu Favrot battled to keep the boat steady. "I've got to help Stu get us in— you all all right?"

Caroline nodded and Beau smiled. Caroline's eyes plainly told him she thought he was a hero. He felt just fine. He looked toward the lake and saw Hal's boat bouncing along on a parallel course. He raised himself to his knees and waved at Hal until he saw an answering wave. Then he sank back beside Caroline and took her in his arms, feeling her shiver with cold and fear. "It's all right," he said, lips against her temple. "It's all right."

Her eyes were larger than he had ever seen them, dark with sudden terror. "Beau, we both might have drowned. Oh, Beau, it was awful!" He knew she was at the edge of one of those crying jags his sister Francie had sometimes. If he could make her laugh . . . "Caroline, we wouldn't have drowned. Cajuns have webbed feet, didn't you know that?"

The tiniest curve lifted her pale lips, the tiniest tremor of relaxation went through her body. She settled closer to him. "Oh, Beau," she said, but now she did smile, and he knew she would be all right.

But the danger was not yet over. The boats, one after the other, turned away from the battering wind, stood at the tip of a high green-gray wall of water, searching for a path home. The waves chased after them, drenching them rhythmically with their endless force. The wind refused to take a predictable course. It changed, varied, went this way and that, so that the sailing skills of both crews were tested over and over.

"Your cousin's a heck of a good sailor," Robert Livaudais shouted to Beau. The Larroque sailboat darted through the water, seeming to dodge the heavier gusts of wind and higher waves as though by some kind of homing instinct. Hal was an indistinct figure at the tiller, misted by the incessant rain, silenced by the shriek of the wind.

The journey back seemed to go on forever; no matter how hard he looked, Beau could not see the shore. And then suddenly the rain seemed to lighten, the waters to become calmer, and they were inside the shelter of the approach to the Southern Yacht Club dock. When the sloop bumped against the wooden pilings that marked her slip, Robert threw a loop of rope around one of them. Hal docked beside them and climbed out onto the long pier edging the water.

Robert Livaudais vaulted up to the pier and held out his hands toward Caroline. "Here, Beau, hand her up to me, will you?"

Between them, they got her out of the boat. She stood with her cousin's arm supporting her, her face still as white as her dress.

"Let me say thank you again," Robert said, clasping Beau's hand in his. "Don't know what we'd have done if you hadn't been there—Stu was insane to keep on with Caroline on board."

Stu Favrot climbed up from the boat, his face back to its normal color. He was tall and lean, hard-muscled, with the deep tan of a sailor. His blue eyes were hard; his blond hair made a tight cap over his well-shaped head. He was not smiling when he looked at Beau, and Beau knew instantly that no matter what Robert Livaudais said, Stu Favrot felt no gratitude. "She'd have been all right if she hadn't stood up," he said. "She knows better than that. What got into you, Caroline?"

Something in the way Stu said her name made Beau's hackles rise. He thrust out a hand. "Beau Langlinais," he said.

Stu seemed to look at Beau's hand before he took it. Then: "Stu Favrot. Is your father Claude Langlinais? In the legislature?" At Beau's nod he said, "Then our fathers know each other, I imagine too well." A lazy smile formed, taking time to make its easy way across Favrot's face, but still not quite reaching his eyes. "They're on opposite sides of the fence, I believe."

"If people put up fences, that's bound to happen," Beau said. Now Favrot was angry. Beau had come to know that kind of anger already, come to know people who kept anger always in their hearts, letting it burn at a steady, furnacelike pace. Very little fuel was needed to make that kind of anger leap and burn—and destroy. His shoulders shifted in a small, almost hidden shrug. Let Favrot be angry. Let him waste his passion on things like hate and anger and fear. The person who would suffer most would be Favrot.

From behind him on the dock, he heard Hal's voice. "God, Beau, I thought I'd die, watching you in that water." His hand gripped Beau's shoulder. "You all right?"

"I'm all right," Beau said. "Just cold." He looked at Caroline, whose face was pale, washed of color. "You must be freezing, Caroline. Sopping wet in all this wind—"

"You're right," Robert said. "We'll get her to the car, there's a carriage robe there." He put a hand under Caroline's elbow and moved her slowly forward. "We'll have you home and dry in no time."

"Yes," Caroline said. She began to move forward along the pier, Beau on one side, Robert on the other, Favrot and Hal following behind. Favrot looked sulky, angry. He had made a motion as though to replace Beau at Caroline's side, a motion both Beau and Caroline had ignored. Beau could almost feel the heat from those smoldering eyes on his cold neck. Suddenly Caroline halted. Her face seemed to dissolve. "I almost drowned." The look in her eyes reflected compressed terror, remembered panic, and Beau knew the respite from it she had had in the boat was over. "Beau. I almost drowned!" Her voice was higher now, shrill. Her body began to tremble, caught like the slender mast of a boat by the violence within her.

"Caroline!" Beau took her shoulders, pulled her around to face him. "Caroline! Look at me!" Slowly her eyes focused on his. "Now, listen. You were always all right. Do you understand, Caroline? There was nothing to be afraid of. Nothing." His eyes had grown dark, clouded with his intense purpose. His hands moved to her upper arms, began stroking her, soothing her as he soothed the mares on his grandfather's farm after a storm or a birthing. He felt the trembling gather itself up into one long tremor. Then she was still. Her eyes still blazed into his, her lips parted, and the breath coming from them was slower, calmer. She sighed.

"Yes. Yes, that's right." Another sigh, cleansing her of the final shreds of fear. Then she smiled. "I'm being dramatic. Mama says that is a very common fault in unsophisticated young girls."

Robert met Beau's eyes over Caroline's head. "And now I'm going to get you home," he said. "Here, I'll carry you." He picked her up and began striding down the pier. Stu Favrot broke into a trot and ran past Beau and Hal, his face still hard.

Caroline raised her head and looked over Robert's shoulder, past Stu. "Beau!" she called. "Call me tonight." Her eyes were clear again, and beneath their blue surface, Beau could see that he had established something this afternoon, something within her center. There was a way she looked at him now that no one else saw, or knew.

"I will," he said.

Hal's mother, Claudine Langlinais Larroque, heard the tale of the rescue with strongly mixed feelings. "It's good you saved her," she said, cutting Beau a large slice of chocolate pound cake. "Of course, that's very heroic, very brave." She set the plate before him and poured milk. "But, Beau. If you hadn't encouraged Hal to race, everybody would've turned around and gotten home safe." She put her hands on her hips, an unconscious reflection of her mother's posture. "Being a hero in a foolish situation isn't all to the good. You understand what I'm saying?"

Beau swallowed a chunk of cake, washed it down with milk. "Aunt Claudine, I know just what you're saying. But I promise you—Stu Favrot would've kept going no matter what anyone did. It's just a good thing Hal and I were there—"

Claudine laughed. "It's always a good thing a Langlinais is around, Beau." She fixed her gaze on Hal. "But, Hal—the next time, the only racing you do is on your bicycle to the grocery store for your mama, you hear?"

The telephone in the hall began to ring shrilly, and Hal got up to answer it. He stuck his head through the door and said to Beau, "It's for you. It's Caroline."

Caroline's voice spilled over the wire so rapidly that he could barely separate the words. "Oh, Beau! Something's happened, I don't know what, nobody will tell me. Except that it's not about Grandmother. But Papa came home early from the office, and shut himself up in his study, and he's been on the phone, and he won't say one single word. And when I asked Mama, she just gave me that look she has and told me to go pack. We're leaving for our house across the lake." He heard another voice in the background, a high, impatient whine. "All right, Mama. Beau, I have to go now. But I will write. And you—will you write, Beau?"

He tried to put seventeen years of waiting for a girl like Caroline into his answer. "Yes, Caroline. Of course I will."

He stood in the hall, staring at the posts of the staircase railing. Then he lifted the receiver and asked the operator to get him his father's office in St. Martinville. When his father answered the phone, Beau's question spilled out of him with uncontrollable urgency. "What's happening down there, Papa?"

There was such a long pause at the other end that Beau thought the line was dead. Finally he heard Claude's voice. His words were measured. When Beau heard the nightmare of tragedy and death, he felt a river of rage. Guns along their boundaries! Armed men on patrol! Suddenly the war in Europe was very far away, much too far for him to think about. He remembered his grandmother Geneviève, laughing at him. "Beau. If the good God wanted you to fight in this war, He'd have had you born earlier—or waited to start it later. You know?"

"I'm coming home, Papa," he said. "I want to be with you."

His father's sigh, across the wires that stretched from St. Martinville through the swamps to New Orleans, went to Beau's heart. "That's good, Beau. I sure could use you."

"I'll take the first train in the morning," he said.

"I'll tell your mother," Claude said.

Beau put the receiver back, set the telephone in the precise center of the crocheted doily his aunt had placed on top of the table. The hall was tall and cool and dark, curtains and blinds closed against the afternoon. From the kitchen, he could hear his aunt and cousins talking, and the smell of a roast cooking floated out to him. He tried to imagine how the flames had looked back home. And he wondered what other lines had been drawn that he would know nothing about until he tried to cross them.

8

It took a full six weeks to fence the Langlinais land; at the end of that time, three strands of barbed wire stretched between tall, thick cypress posts, making definite the ragged mile that began just below the big house at Beau Chêne and ended at Bayou Teche. "Work with the crew, son," Claude told Beau. "You'll see parts of this land no one has seen since the first Langlinais came here in 1759." And so Beau had walked from Bayou Teche, which the Spanish had used as a convenient boundary for their Attakapas land grants, through the fertile fields near the bayou, high now with corn and cotton and sugarcane, back through pastures where cattle grazed, under the trees of the pecan orchard, and into the denseness of the swamp. In full summer, the swamp was thick with green undergrowth. The branches of the cypress waved their feathery leaves in the barely stirring air; white and blue herons, standing like statues in a small stretch of quiet water, whirred up suddenly in Beau's path, their great wings making shadows in the sky. One morning he came across the ruins of a small cabin, its chimney bricks falling upon themselves like a forgotten tombstone. And he remembered, with a strange feeling of having lived at another time, the tale of an ancestor who fought with Jean Lafitte, and of the pirates who came to store booty here.

Jumie and Geneviève's house slept through the long summer days, sheltered by the live oaks and clumps of pine planted to break the smooth stretch of prairie. Built in 1808, the house was raised on pillars so that the cool air coming up from the earth could help break the terrible heat of an Acadian summer. Wide galleries formed another barrier against the heat, and the high gabled roof yet another. Cypress timbers from the Langlinais swamps formed the frame; the wooden pegs that held them together had been cut from that same tough wood. A wide central hall with doors opening onto galleries at front and back, and windows on a straight line with inside doors and other windows formed natural corridors through which air circulated. "If one small breath of air stirs on the bayou, it makes my parlor curtains wave," Geneviève was fond of saying. And it was true that the house, set on a slight rise, seemed to catch the merest stir of air, and was an oasis on the hottest day.

The only long-term battle Geneviève and Alice had ever had was the one over the furnishings of the house. When it had been built, the rough-hewn armoires and benches and beds from the original cabin had been moved into it. These had been augmented over the years by an assortment of furniture which reflected nothing so much as the current needs and financial abilities of whatever generation of Langlinaises lived there.

"It's a hodgepodge, Mama Geneviève," Alice had said, standing in the center of the parlor, hands on hips. "The house itself is lovely, it's got wonderful lines—except for one or two pieces, you should just throw everything out and start over." Geneviève had been so shocked she could hardly repeat the conversation to Jumie. "Mais, Jumie," she had said, "it was today I reconciled myself to Alice and Claude and their babies moving into town. Because I tell you the truth, Jumie, if Alice got her hands on this house, in two days you wouldn't be able to find your own bed." And so it remained as it had always been. The rocking chair that long ago the first Claude Langlinais had made for his beloved Mathilde when they had finally had a roof over their heads still stood by the kitchen fireplace; the bed Mathilde and then Claude died in was in an upstairs bedroom. "You sleep under a quilt that kept your great-great-grandpapa warm, you may wake up more like him, isn't that so?" Geneviève would say, tucking up a visiting grandchild. Only the oil derricks poking inquisitive heads above the swamps changed the landscape from the way it had looked for more than a hundred and fifty years. Those derricks, responsible for the fence that intruded upon the land, made other intrusions.

Claude, coming home from a final inspection the day the fence was finished, took the bourbon and water Alice handed him and threw himself into his big chair. "I'm not cut out for this," he told her.

"For what?" Alice said. She leaned forward, stroked his hair where it fell across his frown-creased forehead.

"To be an oil baron," he said, and tried to smile.

She pulled his head against her softness. "The fence? That's bothering you? Claude, lots of people have fences!"

"It's not the fence," he said. "It's why we have to have one. Even the foolishness and lies and shenanigans that go on in the legislature aren't like this," he said. "This is home, you know?"

She knew. She remembered her own sense of violation when Claude had told her of the fire. Alice kissed the top of Claude's head and untied her apron. "And you're still boss," she said. "You want a little salad with your gumbo?"

He nodded and watched her set out plates. The bourbon relaxed him, the good smell of gumbo soothed him. But he felt cold. For the first time he was beginning to realize that power did not run just one way.

They hadn't told Jumie about the fence. "Don't lie if he asks you, son," Claude said to Beau. "But we don't want anything to worry him. We're not sure he'd . . . understand."

Beau wasn't sure he understood, either. Some days, walking along that thin wall of wire, he decided it was all a game. Such a fence would stop a wandering cow, but a human being could crawl under it, or between its strands. But then something about the very presence of the fence took hold of him. Since he had been a very little boy, first walking over the fields and into the woods and swamp with his father and grandfather, their land had seemed to stretch to heaven. Now he knew it ended, knew it in a way that made him sad.

For Jumie, taking one of his daily walks, the first sight of the fence, square in the middle of the path he had taken to the back door of Beau Chêne since he could remember, was like the hard fist that, coming out of nowhere, had felled him on New Year's Eve. Not only the blow, the jolt, but the consciousness that came afterward, changing his perception of the world; from the blow, he had learned that his body would betray him. From the fence, he learned that men would.

He left the path, took a stick to hold branches back, and followed the fence. Its shiny wires had an ugly strength; the barbs meant that this fence was not just a boundary marker, but a barrier, meant to keep intruders out. Intruders from where? For how long had these two holdings made almost a kingdom, a place of safety, and peace, and happiness? he thought. There was no foot of this land, and not much of Beau Chêne, that Jumie had not stood upon, looked upon, felt the bond that comes, not from a paper title, but from knowing the land as friend, lover, enemy, mistress, and provider. Back to back, Beau Chêne and the Langlinais land had been the center of all their lives. No matter how far the children went, no matter how thin-spun the thread that wound from that center to the dark reaches of other lands and other lives, still, this was home. For generations upon generations, for Langlinaises and de Clouets, there was more than one place that when you went there, they had to take you in. Now there was a fence between them, and that he would never understand. Nor abide.

With a shout that was half a sob, dredged forth from him with the force of his memories, Jumie leapt toward the nearest post and began pulling at it with his hands. The cypress, sunk deep in its hole, packed now by the settling earth, resisted as though it were a human being whose strength was so much

more than Jumie's that it had no more to do than just stand fast
to defeat him. Jumie bent to his task, choked his hands around
the unyielding wood, then placed his shoulder against it and
heaved. His whole being was focused upon that post, upon the
wires so arrogantly stretched from it to the next one. Something had been brutalized here; trust, love, friendship. The
sound came again, but this time it was a sob. Pain came, too,
the hard black pain he had felt before. There was no breath to
bear the pain with, no breath to sob with. Tears formed in his
eyes, urging him to cry, to release the torture in his chest. But
the pain was stronger, as strong as the post that seemed to grow
larger and taller as his grip slackened, and he fell. As the dark
grew larger, filled all his world, he heard a mockingbird singing, heard its mate answer. Jumie smiled. Some things could
not be fenced out. Some things did not change. Not mating
between mockingbirds, not love between men and women. He
thought of Marthe. And then, because he knew he was dying,
he thought of Geneviève.

Over all Hélène's objections, Caroline went to Beau Chêne to
comfort Marthe. "You have fittings," Hélène said. "A million
things to do before you start Newcomb. It's not as though he's
family."

"I'm going, Mama," Caroline said.

"Caroline—"

"I'm going," Caroline said again. Hélène looked at the
young girl sitting across from her. The deep, dark blue eyes set
beneath perfectly curved brows, the fine complexion, the curling golden hair—all these were the same. But the mind behind
that doll-mask, girl-face, was not the same as the one she had
been ignoring for years. This mind looked out at Hélène with
open challenge. "Stubbornness is never attractive," Hélène
said. She tucked her petit point into its bag and rose. As she
left the room, she heard Caroline's voice. It was low, barely
fueled with breath sufficient to clear Caroline's lips. But the
words were distinct. "Is selfishness?"

Every family in the area made at least one call; those close to
the Langlinaises came often, bearing bowls of gumbo, tiered
cakes, tins of cookies, loaves of fresh bread. But daily, no
matter what else Marthe had to do, she and Caroline tucked
needlework into baskets and went to spend an hour or so with

Geneviève. They could go the old way now. Claude had ordered a gate made in the fence that had barred the path, and though the heat of late August was fierce and strong, the many layers of tree branches that lay between the searching sun and the path kept it, if not cool, a tolerable place to walk.

Throughout the slow afternoons of mourning, time marked by the quiet drip of boiling water through freshly roasted and ground coffee beans to make yet another pot of strong black brew, the history of the families emerged. The stories wove themselves together, their separate colors blended by the western sun that shone through the back windows of the house. Their people, their events, all seemed part of one time, one whole. The scent of roses from Geneviève's garden wrapped itself around the stories; for the rest of her life, when Caroline smelled a rose, whether in a corsage for her shoulder or a bouquet for her boudoir, she would think of this time, and of this place.

Beau became part of that time and place. Whatever strictures Caroline's mother had in New Orleans, there were different rules out here. Geneviève and Marthe welcomed Beau, fussed over and spoiled him. "The image of his grandfather," Marthe would say, giving him a hug. "Now, listen while I tell you about your grandfather, you should be like him," Geneviève would tell Beau, passing him a plate of cookies. And when that part of the afternoon was over, when the women, emptied and wearied by their tales, were ready to settle into a grown-up tête-à-tête, Beau and Caroline were shooed away, sent out into the cooling dusk and told to amuse themselves until time for supper.

"Should we put them so much together?" Marthe asked Geneviève one afternoon. "Encourage them like this?"

Geneviève looked up from the crochet work in her hands. "Zut! Encourage? When do young people need encouragement? Or give up if they don't have it?" She put down the work, pressed Marthe's hands in hers. "Marthe. Isn't it better than the other way?" And she raised their hands and made a fence in the air.

Claude sat in the farm office, feeling its emptiness. He had had an office in town where his constituents could come to him since he was first elected to the legislature five years before.

This office, its log walls still solid, was where the Langlinais family holdings were managed. He pulled the current ledger toward him and opened it.

In the weeks just before his death, Jumie had been spending a few hours every morning in the office. His handwriting was formal, the letters curved and clean. Claude had a sudden image of his father as a young man, learning that a commercial college was opening in New Iberia, and that he was to go there, was to learn to be a businessman. "A businessman! You can imagine how impressed I was by that!" Geneviève would tell him, describing her first meeting with Jumie. Then her smile, the flirtatious curve that still put mischief in her eyes. "But, let me tell you the truth, I was more impressed by his strong arms and his beautiful eyes!"

Claude's own eyes blurred. The emptiness of the room was powerful. It forced itself on him, made him acknowledge that his father was gone, and that nothing would ever, ever bring him back. His head sank forward, supported in his hands. All those afternoons with his father, making coffee, opening, at the end of a long afternoon over the books, a bottle of good red wine. Settling their feet comfortably on the big square desk, they would swap stories, catch up on news. The ledgers on the shelves near the desk were more than just pen-and-ink figures of profit and loss. They were a journal of the family, and of all it had achieved since the first Claude Louis Langlinais and his little family had faced the wilderness here. Claude straightened. Sacrebleu! He was not the first Langlinais to feel he had more than he could carry. He pushed away from the desk, went to the window and looked out upon the fields, trying to see them as they were a hundred and sixty years ago. Wild, grown over with sprawling marsh grass and thick trees. Full of snakes and alligators and possums and raccoons and deer and bears. But, mon Dieu, he'd rather have that morass to clear, that good, clean physical work, than the morass he faced now, faced alone.

Long ago they had talked him into running for the legislature, those men from New Orleans trying to break the Ring's power. Some Langlinaises fought snakes and bears, some fought soldiers. In the legislature, with the constant pushing for position and power, Claude fought greed. And in the business world, where the grasp of those who would snatch the fruits of another man's labor seemed well equal to their reach.

In the parlors and drawing rooms of the people they saw. Eyes measuring the size of a woman's jewels, the cut of a man's coat. Damn! If he didn't have St. Martinville to come home to, he'd chuck the whole damn thing. Become a farmer. Grapple with the land, which might be unyielding, might try to break one's back—but which fought fairly, with no malice, no wicked joy. He stared out at the fields, rich and luxuriant under the late-summer sun. Why in hell not? Why not just chuck it all, come home, and run the farm? Sit in the kitchen and visit with his mama? Ride that big black mare of his papa's over fields he knew as he knew his wife's body. He could feel his shoulders relax, his legs loosen.

The dream closed around him. He could hear the quiet movements of small animals, the soft calls of birds. A breeze sprang up from the bayou and raced across the fields, kicking dust before it. The sky stretched over his land, a tightly fitting awning of blue. A small cluster of clouds, like embroidery on a dress, scattered its way across the blue. The air, heavy-scented with warm clover, filled his lungs. Never to sit in a room thick with smoke. Never to have to dicker and bargain and joke his way through yet another committee, yet another session! There was money enough, God knew. He turned and looked again at the ledgers. And felt his dream vanish into the place where hope lives. Those ledgers could record year after year of improvement, year after year of progress, because Langlinais men before him had turned their eyes away from their own dreams to make the family dreams come true. The oldest son took care of the land, husbanded it well, and divided its yield among all. With the privilege of living upon it came the responsibility of making all secure—and that of matching greed with cunning, rapaciousness with guile. With one last look at the fields, Claude turned and sat again at the desk.

He pulled a letter toward him, reread it. It was from a member of the group in New Orleans that was working still to unseat the Ring. "Ever heard of a man named Huey P. Long? Word from Winn Parish is that he's going to run for Railroad Commissioner. I can hear you laughing, Claude, asking if he doesn't know that election's not until 1918. But the way I hear it, he's going around all the little towns, making friends, neutralizing enemies. Building a base, he is. So keep your eyes and ears open, Claude. We need those Hill parishes."

Long again. A man he'd never seen, upon whom he must

already depend as a possible ally. Merde. That he would never get down his craw without a struggle. People said politics made strange bedfellows, but he had no one in his bed but Alice. What politics did make was strange dinner partners, strange hunting partners. All those men pretending to be friends, when most of them would stab you in the back and then ask you to eat with them, cutting your meat with the knife you took from your own flesh. And their wives. The women were worse than the men, most of them. He hated to throw Alice in among them, hated the glances, the looks to see if she would do. And now the girls were coming up, and they'd go through the same damn thing. He clenched his fists, pounded on the closed ledger. By God, he'd make so damn much money no one would dare judge his women. Not Alice, not Francie, not Marie. He'd make so damn much money that if anyone dared keep them out of a place, he'd buy it and tear it down. He'd make so damn much money that he could settle the hash of every cotton-picking son of a bitch in this state. He'd own the whole goddamned state before he got through, and to hell with everybody.

He took a deep breath. Lord, he'd give himself apoplexy, on top of everything else. Even as he controlled his rage, he took its measure. He knew that never again would he allow himself to think of the life he might have lived, had he not been a Langlinais, and the one to take over from his father. He would never again allow himself to feel such rage, to want to take on the whole world to punish it for denying him the peaceful, easy life on his farm. But knowing the rage was there, knowing its power, he could face the terrible arena that was his life. The last tremor left, and he leaned back in his chair. Lord, had he really told himself he'd own the whole damn state? Claude laughed. Well, maybe not the whole damn state—there were pieces of it even a land-loving Cajun wouldn't want. But a good portion of it. Yes, indeed. By the time he finished, the Langlinaises would own a damn good portion of it. He looked at his watch. Dusty Hawkins would be back at his quarters now, sipping a cold beer, watching the sun go down. He picked up his straw hat, clapped it on his head, and went to meet him.

As he walked through the fields, head-high now with waving blades of green corn or cane, he thought of the great stretch of land he owned, and of all the other land around it. Land that covered, could cover, oil. He thought of the money to be made from that oil. No one would sell their land; he didn't need them to. Just the mineral rights, that was all. Claude smiled, the wolf smile that signaled a coup. Those outsiders, those outlanders, might know more about the oil business than he did. Now. But one thing. They didn't know the people. Claude's people. And if the choice were between leasing mineral rights to Claude and doing business with some Eastern company, for the people of St. Martin Parish there was no choice at all.

"Reached suitcase rock yet?" he said when he reached Dusty's hut.

"Not quite. Those wells have slowed down, though. Slowed considerable. One thing, this field's no Spindletop."

"Something I want you to do," Claude said.

Dusty rolled a cigarette, stuck it in his mouth. "All right."

"Want you to go around and about. Look at land. Talk to people, but quiet. Then come tell me what I should get some leases on."

Dusty grinned. "You fixing to take on them Rockefellers after all?"

"You ever heard tell of people who don't fish and don't swim but put a fence around their pond to make sure no one else does?" Claude gestured, pointing beyond the derricks towering over his land. "Lots of ponds out there, Dusty. I might not be ready to fish in them yet. I want to make damn sure no one else does."

"You're going to sew this parish up tight, that it?"

"Tight as me and a high-priced lawyer can make it."

"I'll start tomorrow," Dusty said. "You want me to talk money?"

Claude smiled, the smile Dusty had seen when Claude was about to clobber him at bourrée. "No, you leave the money talk to me. You just sniff out the oil." He stood, looked at the low sun. "Time to do a little pole-fishing before supper. Want to come?" And as Dusty fell into step beside him: "Tell you what. I'll get that lawyer to draw up a partnership. You and me, for starters. Okay by you?"

"I don't need no paper to do business with you, Claude."

"Nor I. But from here on out, everything I do's going to be legal." The wolf smile creased his face. "Leastways, as legal as a lawyer thinks it needs to be."

Dusty slapped Claude on the back. "Better tell that boy of

yours to hurry up and get on down to lawyer school. Save
yourself a heap of money, having a lawyer in the family."

"He starts LSU in September. If he doesn't make a fool of
himself over that little Livaudais girl first."

"She's a purty thing."

"If that were all," Claude said. "If only that were all."

9

Marthe decided to have a party for Caroline the last night of her
visit. "It's time we brought some youth into this old house,"
she told Caroline. She reached out and caught Caroline's hand,
held it tightly. "I wonder—will this house just settle down with
its ghosts when I'm gone?"

"Grandmama!" Caroline said, kissing Marthe's cheek.
"Don't talk like that."

"No one lives forever," Marthe said briskly. "I've no intention of departing anytime soon, but when I do—when I do,
Caroline, who will love Beau Chêne?"

They were sitting in the parlor near open French doors that
brought in a soft bayou breeze. The room was rich with old
wood and fine brocade, carved marble and heavy rugs. Caroline looked around her. "Who wouldn't love Beau Chêne,
Grandmama?"

"Your mother," Marthe said. She had grown close to Caroline these past weeks, closer than she had ever been to
Hélène. The genes skipped a step, she thought to herself,
watching the way Caroline slipped into the life at Beau Chêne
as though she had been born there. Then, laughing at herself:
Raising thoroughbred horses is a heck of a lot more dependable
than raising children.

Caroline bent over her embroidery. "She . . . Mama likes
. . . well, a lot of parties. Like that."

"Oh, I know we're too dull for her," Marthe said. She rose
and stood in the open doorway. "But, Caroline. This house has

stood here for more than one hundred years. It can't just slip away from us!"

Caroline put her work down and went to Marthe, held her. "But why would it, Grandmama? I don't understand."

"Someone has to inherit," Marthe said. "Before, there was always someone who wanted it—usually the eldest son. The other children got other property." She brushed a wave of gold-gray hair from her cheek. "If René even remembers what Beau Chêne looks like, I'd be very much surprised. Your Aunt Nanette certainly doesn't want it. And I doubt very much if your mother does, either."

"I do. I want Beau Chêne," Caroline said.

Marthe looked into the blue eyes so very like her own. "Yes, I believe you do. I believe you really do."

"Then give it to me, Grandmama. If Mama and Aunt Nanette and Uncle René really don't want it."

Marthe laughed. "It's not that simple, darling. The law says they inherit it—and they'll just have to decide who will take care of it. Though I think there's no question that will be your mother—she's the only one close enough to do it."

"And then she'll give it to me?" The blue eyes were dark, fixed intently on Marthe's face.

"Goodness, darling, I should certainly think so." Marthe laughed again. "Though the way she complains about this old house, we'd better hope she doesn't just get rid of it."

The effect of her lightly spoken words on Caroline shocked her. Caroline's hand closed over Marthe's arm, gripping it tightly. "Oh, Grandmama! She couldn't, could she? Sell Beau Chêne? It could never be *for sale*?"

"Darling, of course not, I was just teasing!" Marthe put her arm around Caroline and drew her close. "Your mother would never sell this house, no matter how much she complains about it. Why, it's our home place, Caroline. Hélène may not have much of a head for business, but surely she has a heart for family feeling!"

"All right then," Caroline said, her face happy again. "But one thing you can be sure of. When it's my turn to have Beau Chêne, you won't have to worry about it being loved and taken care of." She kissed Marthe's cheek. "It'll be as safe as—as safe as houses!"

"All right," Marthe said. "I won't. Now, we'd better get

busy and invite your guests, or we'll be dancing all by ourselves."

Young people were coming from St. Martinville, from New Iberia, and even from as far as Franklin. "The Langlinaises are coming, aren't they?" Caroline made sure.

"Alice says she's not so sure she should let the youngest girl, Francie, come." Marthe touched Caroline's curls. "She says Francie has already given her more gray hairs than Beau and Marie put together. Is she really so . . . so old for her age?"

"Beau says she just likes to make people think she's . . . well, a little wild, I guess. But he says he keeps an eye on her, and if Beau is keeping an eye on her, she'll behave herself."

I wonder if she knows how much the way she says his name tells me? Marthe thought, taking out the peach undercloths and lace cloths for the tables Nat would set out on the long upstairs gallery. I wonder if she knows that when she looks at him, her eyes seem to say they will never really see anyone or anything else? She sighed, remembering her fears about throwing Beau and Caroline so much together. Well, soon enough she would be at Newcomb and he would be in Baton Rouge at Louisiana State University. And though the road between New Orleans and Baton Rouge was not that long, the course already set for Caroline that winter was. She would make her debut, beginning with a large evening reception her parents would hold Thanksgiving week. And from then until the last waltz was danced at the Comus ball on Mardi Gras night, Caroline's engagement book would be filled with luncheons, teas, tea dances, theater parties, dinners, galas, balls. Marthe smiled. To be culminated when she was crowned with the most elegant, prestigious crown of all, as Queen of Comus. No, there was not much room in that schedule for Beau Langlinais, whose parents had achieved an amazingly wide range of acquaintance, but who had not yet done more than stand outside the formidable wall of New Orleans society.

As she arranged peach roses in silver vases, Marthe made herself face her own feelings toward that society. Oh, outwardly she laughed at it, enjoyed plaguing Hélène by making fun of some of its most sacred cows. But be honest, she told herself. If you didn't belong to it, if you didn't enjoy the lovely luxury of being included in everything you wish to do—you'd hate it. Her honesty cheered her. At least, she thought, smiling, you know you're a hypocrite. "Come see the tables," she

called to Caroline. When her granddaughter appeared, already
dressed for the party, Marthe's breath caught in her throat.
Caroline's dress was white, with a deep lace hem and a lace
panel down the front. The sleeves made soft bells of lace,
coming just to her elbows. Around her slender waist was a blue
sash the color of Caroline's eyes. Marthe thought again of the
way Caroline looked whenever Beau Langlinais was around.
But over five hundred years of careful breeding had produced
Caroline. Did that tip the scales, so that love didn't matter at
all? Marthe shrugged. Thank God, that was not her problem.
There would be all sorts of young men thronging around Caroline this winter. Closed in by that crowd, she would forget
Beau. So let them have tonight, let them have a memory. She
went forward and handed Caroline the rose corsage she had
made her. As the years went on, it became more and more
clear that good memories were all one had.

The party was one to make good memories. The small dance
band had set up in the parlor, and the music flowed through the
French doors, the sweet sounds swelling out onto the long
gallery where dancing figures swayed. The young men were in
white or light gray or pale blue suits. In the veiled light of the
candles, they all were handsome. The girls wore cool pastels,
ribboned, sashed, lacy—and all seemed beautiful. If it could
always be just this way, Marthe thought, sitting in a low
wicker chair, one foot tapping in time to the music. Sweet
music and young beauty. Peace and joy. Love. And no social
distinctions? that voice inside chided her.

But her heart was more insistent than her head. She watched
Beau and Caroline dance past her, his head bent toward hers,
his eyes intent. She thought of Jumie. In all the years they had
known each other, worked together, lived side by side, she had
never admitted to herself that she loved him. A friend, she told
herself. The brother I lost. The father who is no longer here.
But a memory flew at her, beating its wings against her face,
making her remember. An October day, not too many years
ago. She'd had Berthe pack a picnic, fled to the woods behind
the house. Jumie had found her there. And stayed to eat, to
visit. Nothing had happened, nothing they could not put on the
front page of the *Times-Picayune*. And yet there had been a
feeling, a feeling that surrounded the small clearing in which
they sat, joining with the golden October leaves to make of that
day an amulet. But they are not you and Jumie, her head said to

her heart. Or rather, they are. And just as you and Jumie could cross every bridge but one . . .

She watched Beau pull Caroline out of the crowd, stand her in the shelter of one of the columns. I'm going to let what will be, be, she thought. I'm too old and too tired. With Jumie gone, I have to do it all myself. And I am too tired to take on another fight. My heart can wish with all its might they find a way around the barriers. But my head is too tired to help them find it. She picked up her needlework, settled back in her chair. Beau had gotten punch, he and Caroline stood sipping it while the band began another song. It was Jerome Kern's "Till the Clouds Roll By." Beau and Caroline's heads were close, the space between them small. The single notes of the clarinet, spilling one after the other, seemed to hold the moment suspended in time.

"You look beautiful," Beau said, touching the blue bow at Caroline's waist. His hand drifted up to a strand of hair that teased her neck. "I like your hair up."

"I'm practicing," Caroline said. "For this winter when I'll be all grown-up and wear it this way all the time." She looked out past the gallery rail, to the front lawn where the great oaks marched silently under the moon. "But I'm going to miss Beau Chêne dreadfully. I've spent more time here this year than I ever have before—it's like home."

He took one of her hands. "And me? Will you miss me?"

"Oh, Beau! Yes." Her eyes expressed the emotions of her heart. Looking into them, Beau felt a love so strong that his tongue lost the power of speech. Suddenly he wanted to reach out and take the long pins from Caroline's hair, to see it fall upon her shoulders. Desire surged through his body, though he himself did not recognize the nature of his passion until he knew he wanted to remove her clothes, wanted nothing between him and the sight of her naked beauty. Then reality intruded; such thoughts were unthinkable! He blinked his eyes to rid his mind of the image.

"What train are you taking tomorrow?" he asked.

She, too, seemed to be coming back from some other world. She made a small movement with her head, as though shaking herself back to the gallery, to the summer night. "The noon train. Will you come see me off?"

"I'll do better than that. I'll ride with you," he said. His voice was his own again, gay, teasing, leading her into passages of promise.

"Ride with me?" Her eyes grew large, filled with happiness. "To New Orleans, do you mean?"

"Sure," he said. Another feeling held him now, one he did not recognize, as he had not quite recognized the other. He felt easy, confident, pleased with a world in which a simple gesture like traveling with your best girl to New Orleans could bring so much delight. "I have to be measured for some suits," he said. "Now that I'm all 'grown-up,' I'm having them made by Papa's tailor in New Orleans."

Marthe watched the way Beau held Caroline's hand, the way their lips moved so softly, making words that made bonds, bonds that meant commitment. She sighed. Her heart made a wish—after all these years, a de Clouet and a Langlinais, married. The land married in one great holding, a fortress against the world. But her head did not believe in wishes. The battle between heart and head was heated—but the stalemate at the end left Marthe suddenly chill.

Claude had watched the increasing closeness between Beau and Caroline with a helpless feeling that his political and economic battles were about to be swept up into an intensely personal cause. The truce he and Charles Livaudais had made outside Jumie's hospital room had held—but then, so far, they had met only that night at Pleasant's dinner party, where the formal strictures of the occasion had set forth the behavior required. He did not think that Hélène had ever apologized to Alice, by word or deed. But to believe that Alice had forgotten the feel of Hélène's hand on her cheek, or the tone of voice in which Hélène had drawled—"It looks like a lady . . ."—was to be far more naive than Claude had ever been. Alice had buried her wounds deep; when they met the Livaudaises in Baton Rouge, she had been proper, civil. But Claude had seen her eyes. Those eyes had been cold, unforgetting—and unforgiving.

He sighed. Too bad to bring Beau back to earth. But this had all gone too far, much too far. "You should have seen Beau mooning over Caroline at the party last night," Francie had said at breakfast. "And she was just as bad. Did you kiss her, Beau?" she had teased.

"That's enough, Francie," Alice had said automatically, but her worried eyes had been on Beau, who had continued to eat his grits and eggs calmly.

"No, but I might today," he'd said, winking at Claude. "I'm going to take the noon train to New Orleans with her." He had looked at Claude again. "I guess your tailor won't care if I come a few days early."

"Guess he won't," Claude had said, keeping his voice deliberately noncommittal. "Say, if you have a little time before the train goes, drop by my office, will you? Alice, you going to be able to drive him in?"

"Yes," she had replied. Her normally full lips were thin, and he knew she was biting words back, depending on him to set Beau straight.

Which he was about to do. He could hear Beau in the outer office, talking with Claude's secretary. Then he was in the doorway, his square shoulders almost filling it. He looked happy, relaxed, eager—as why would he not, Claude thought. About to be with his girl—young, full of vinegar. Remembering the form that vinegar could take in hotheaded, full-blooded young men, Claude sighed again. Keeping sons steering clear between the good girls and the willing ones was a task nothing, not hours of business dealings, not weeks in the legislature, could ever prepare a man for.

"Sit down, son," he said. "There's something I need to . . . to talk to you about."

Beau sat opposite Claude, one leg cocked over the other, hands resting easily on the arms of the chair.

"So what's all this with you and Caroline Livaudais?" Claude said. "Sounds like you're getting pretty involved there, Beau."

"Sure am," Beau said.

Claude raised an eyebrow. "Meaning?"

"Meaning I'm courting her," Beau said, grinning.

Claude looked at the paneled walls of his town office, out the linen-draped windows at the street. Anywhere but at that young, happy face. "I'm not sure that's the smartest thing you've ever done, Beau," he said, still looking away.

"Why not?" Beau said. Claude looked at him then. His posture was still easy, relaxed, but something in the tone of Beau's voice, something in the strong anger at the back of Beau's eyes, warned Claude that the Langlinais male before him had his back up and his temper just barely held in check.

"Her people don't think you're good enough for her, Beau." The words fell between them as though they were leaden coins, separated from the gold and silver ones that had value.

"So? I'm not marrying them." The words were out, the declaration made. Claude's mind called up the front-page picture in his morning paper—boys, not a hell of a lot older than Beau, fighting on the fields of France. War was hell, no question about that. Those boys would lose limbs, eyes, faces—lives. But Beau had just declared war, too. Another kind of war, where, when disfigurement or death came, it came to the spirit.

Claude's hand reached out, touched Beau's arm. "Now, son. Aren't you rushing it just a bit? You and Caroline, you're how old? Not eighteen yet, either one of you. Little early to be thinking about marriage—"

"I will never love anyone but Caroline." Beau's arm under Claude's hand was rigid, tensed with the force of his passion. Then Beau lifted his face to his father, and Claude saw behind the anger to the pain that waited there.

"Love isn't always enough, Beau." Claude's two hands came up in a helpless gesture that mirrored the way he felt.

"You mean because our blood isn't blue enough, something like that?" Beau's voice was scornful, but it held a touch of fear, too.

"Something like that."

"Mr. Livaudais is a canaille who hits old men and Mrs. Livaudais is a fool," Beau said. "So how are they better than you and Mama are?"

"They're not, really," Claude said. He surveyed the room, the office Alice was so pleased with. Paneled mahogany walls, heavy linen draperies, big leather chairs, antique brass fire-dogs—hell, the room was so damn rich Claude felt he had to wear a coat and tie in it even when he was working alone. But didn't it fit him, and he it?

"It can't be money," Beau said, warming to his argument. "We've never had to sell off land, the way Mrs. de Gravelle did."

"It's not money."

"All right. What is it, then?"

Claude shrugged. "Mrs. de Gravelle traces her ancestry back to Louis XVI's court. So did her husband. While we . . ." He shrugged again. "We trace ours back to peasant farmers from Nova Scotia, who themselves descended from peasant farmers in France."

Beau stood up, eyes blazing. "What the hell does that have to do with anything?" His voice boomed against the walls, echoed out through the open door. Claude's secretary stuck her head in.

"Sir?"

"Nothing," Claude said, waving her away. "Wait—could you go to the café, bring us two coffees?"

"Sure," she said. Claude waited until he heard the outer door close.

"It shouldn't have anything to do with anything," he said. He stood, too, so he could face Beau squarely. "But it does. No matter how much money we have . . ." He thought of the maps Dusty was drawing that showed where oil deposits probably sat. "Or will have . . . no matter how much. Your sisters will never be asked to be in the court of any New Orleans ball that counts. Nor will you ever be asked to be in any of the oldest, the most respected, krewes."

"Papa, for God's sake! That's playing, that's nothing—"

"It's everything," Claude said. He sat down again. The outer door opened, closed, and the secretary came in with two demitasses. She handed them each one and went out, closing the door softly behind her. "It's everything," Claude said again, sipping his coffee, looking over the rim at his son's face.

"Hal said something about that, the day we sailed at Lake Pontchartrain," Beau said in an almost conversational tone. "How only certain people could join the Southern Yacht Club. How we couldn't." Beau looked at Claude; there was more pain than anger now in his gray eyes. "I didn't really believe him. I thought about you, and about how it seemed to me that anything you set out to do, you did do, and I thought: Hal doesn't know what he's talking about. My papa just never wanted to join that club. But I guess you couldn't, could you? No matter how bad you wanted it."

At the sound of his son's voice, Claude's arms went out and he drew Beau to him. "Maybe I've learned to want only those things I can have," he said.

Beau sighed. For a moment, he seemed to be looking down a long corridor, a corridor that stretched back to his childhood. His father was walking along that corridor, moving in that confident way he had of entering a space and taking it over. It had been a long time before Beau was old enough to see what he had always thought of as his father's self-confidence was, in truth, power. And if all that power could not bring happiness, what then? Was it worth even having?

He pulled back. "Is that true?" he asked. "That you just pretend you don't want things you can't have?"

Claude pulled back, too. Reaching for his cup, he drained the last of the coffee. "Maybe. I don't know." He threw his hands up. "Beau. What it comes down to. You do the best you can with what you've got. A man's got to hope, he's got to dream." He shook his head. "How to hope, dream—and not let it kill you if they don't work out—well, hell, Beau, I guess that's what being a man's all about."

He could see Beau's anger become resolve, and knew that Beau's own path was set. Nothing Claude or anyone else could say would change that. Maybe it was better that way, after all. "That's what it is to be a Langlinais," Beau said. He stared out the window, his eyes on some inner view. "I went out to the farm early. It's . . . it's beautiful, you know? I'll miss it, this fall." He thought of the farm. Soon it would be harvest, and then the earth would be buttoned down with brown heaps of fallow dirt, to be covered against the onslaught of winter. Then 'Tit Nonc would be out in the fields early, directing the work of the field hands from the back of Jumie's big black mare. Grandmama Geneviève would be sorting through the preserves in her large pantry, putting the last of the old to the front to be eaten, putting the newly canned jars to the back. Ducks, holding themselves high on anxious wings, would be starting the long flight down the Mississippi flyway. Beau's hands twitched; the feel of a long, clean gun muzzle, the smooth, heavy stock, was in them. He could almost hear Duke's short bark, see his pluming tail held stiff, the broad face raised to the sky. To have all this fussing over, to bring Caroline out to the farm, to live there, work there, have children there! "I'm going to live there someday, Papa. See if I don't. With Caroline."

"In the meantime, son, there's work to do. Work for me and work for you." Claude lit a cigarette, was quiet for a moment, pulling smoke deep into his lungs. When the smoke emerged, pale blue-gray, blurring the air between them, his words seemed caught in it. "Your work is to learn to be a lawyer. Way things are going, I want everyone, my lawyer included, to be as near blood kin as I can make it."

"So what's going on? It's always politics as usual, isn't it?"

"Not anymore," Claude said. "The stakes have changed. They're higher. What we've got now is a war. Right here in Louisiana. Right here in St. Martin Parish."

Beau's face was hidden in the shadows cast by the high wings of his chair, but his voice showed his interest. "War? Like the one in Europe?"

"Like the things that made that war happen," Claude said. "Men wanting what by rights belongs to someone else. Land. Resources." He paused, let the word sink in. "Oil."

"Oil? But we've got oil."

"Not like we're going to have." Rapidly Claude sketched his plan. "Dusty's been going around looking for likely places to drill. We'll start picking up leases, me and Dusty and a couple of men who are in this little venture with me. Quiet-like, so the big oil companies won't know what we're doing until we've got the best part of this parish sewed up. Tight."

Claude crushed his cigarette out in the big glass ashtray on the bronze stand next to his chair. "That New Orleans machine could run a damn long time on oil, the money it brings. And, son, don't forget it. If we don't beat that machine, a lot of work the men you and I are named for will be down the drain."

"I don't understand. And how can my being a lawyer help?"

"I need someone on my team who knows the law inside and out—knows how to use it as a friend and defeat it as an enemy." Claude lit another cigarette; its smoke rose lazily in the air, in contrast to the force behind his words. "Another thing—you'll get to know people at LSU, people from all over the state. You'll be making contacts, discovering people who feel the way we do—who will be allies." He leaned forward and waved his cigarette in the air. "And you'll be identifying enemies. Knowing who your enemies are is a hell of a lot more important than knowing who your friends are."

"But what can the New Orleans machine do? To us?"

"Standard Oil's made a beachhead in Baton Rouge that gives it a good place to shoot at the rest of the state," Claude said. "They're buying and hauling independent producers' oil now, sending it through their pipeline along with their own. But when that war is over . . ." Claude shrugged. "No telling. If the New Orleans machine gangs up with big oil companies like Standard Oil, they can keep that pipeline for Standard's products only—leave the rest of us damn near out in the cold." Claude stood up, his body straight, taut. "To beat them, we're going to have to take our fight out of the fields and bayous into the courts and legislature." His wolf grin was in place, challenging Beau. "For now, I'll hold down the legislature. I need you to take on the courts."

Beau stood. The faintest shadow of his father's smile was on his face, its grimness born of the pain he'd felt that day. "All right, Papa. I understand." His back grew tall, his spine locked. "Charles Livaudais is part of that machine. And if I didn't like him before, I hate him now. So I'm going to be the best damn lawyer this state has ever seen. I'm going to be so damn good that those fancy society people will beg me to take care of them. I'm going to be so damn good I can make my own laws." He looked at his father proudly. "And damn well punish anyone who breaks them."

There was a note in Beau's voice Claude had not heard before. It expressed a lust for power, and it echoed the way Claude himself had felt, just a few short weeks ago. Still felt, if it came to that. Hearing that note, Claude felt saddened. If he ever began adding up all the kinds of ways in which they paid for their land, he might lose the will to hold it.

10

Beau stood on the sidewalk watching the Livaudais house. It was situated deep in the Garden District, a two-story, rather square structure, with rectangular wings jutting on either side at the back of the central section. Square wooden columns, laced with ironwork, supported both the upper gallery and the roof above it, with two dormers protruding above the upper gallery like watchdogs surveying the lawn. One great live oak dominated the area between house and sidewalk, strewing shadows that were patterned like iron lacework across the gleaming, closed facade. The grass was clipped and smooth, the low shrubs that edged the brick walk to the house were neat, close-cut and shaped, and even the ivy filling the urns that flanked the steps up to the lower gallery seemed to have been first traced, then scissored, from some glossy green paper and then carefully pasted into place.

"I'm here to see Miss Livaudais," Beau told the maid who answered the door. And then, as she waited: "Beau Langlinais." His name seemed to echo down the high hall behind the girl, to be caught there somewhere in the shadows, to be lost.

"I'll announce you," the maid said. She stepped back so that Beau could enter the hall. Before he had time to really see the Persian rugs scattered over the floors, the chandelier that hung from a chain two stories long, the statues, the paintings, the French settees and the pier mirror filling an alcove near the stairs, Caroline was coming toward him, hands held out.

"Beau! I'm so glad to see you!" She swept past the maid, whose hand was still outstretched for Beau's straw hat. He felt Caroline's hands take his, saw the smile that filled her eyes curve her lips. "We're going to sit in the study, Maddy," she said. "Bring us some lemonade there, will you? And tell Tante to fix a plate of those cookies she made, you hear?" She was leading him down the hall, past open double doors that, like half-raised curtains, gave glimpses of luxurious and theatrical settings. She saw the look on his face. "That's why we're going to sit in the study. It's the only comfortable room down here. Mama is forever redecorating, but there's so much stuff she can't get rid of, either because it's inherited or it's too valuable, even if it is horrid and ugly, that I feel like I'm living in a curio shop—or a warehouse!"

The study overlooked a garden, where a few roses put up a gallant struggle against the August heat. Zinnias and marigolds blazed among them, but even that deep color browned in the oven of summer. Caroline let the drapery she had pulled fall back. "It's so hot in the city! I wish I were back at Beau Chêne."

"But then you'd miss all those parties this winter," Beau said. "All that fun."

"Bother the parties! As for fun—would you think it was fun to have to be dressed up all the time, do all that shopping, go to all those fittings?" Her voice seemed as unable to bear the burden ahead of her as the flowers outdoors were unable to bear the hot burden of summer. She sat down in a low chair, back straight against its upholstered frame. Her blond hair, that when flying loose around her face was like a film of gold, was up; it could have been carved from solid metal and placed on her fragile head to further weight her. The tucks in her bodice, the gathers in her skirt, could be thin bands of steel, caging her, binding her.

"Then don't do it," Beau said.

"If only I didn't have to!" she said. Maddy came through the open door carrying a silver tray with tall crystal glasses and a matching pitcher filled with lemonade. Beau saw the carefully ironed and folded linen napkins, the doily placed under the cookies on the silver cake plate. The case around Caroline was made of those things, of this house, of that elaborate social calendar already made for her. Made of more than five hundred years of breeding, if it came to that. And against all that, he could offer what? Himself? The Langlinais name? The Langlinais fortunes?

"Thank you, Maddy, that will be all," Caroline said. She poured lemonade into their glasses, wrapped one in a napkin, and handed it to Beau. She watched while he drank. "Is it all right?" She looked as though it really mattered, and he smiled.

"It's fine." He leaned back in his own chair. Across the ocean, a war to "make the world safe for democracy" was going on. And the descendants of those same proud aristocrats who were contemporaries of Caroline's own ancestors were happy enough to have American peasants come fight for them. Merde. They couldn't have it both ways. They couldn't say you were good enough to fight at their sides, trade with them, all that—and yet still were not good enough to marry their daughters. If his kind of blood could be shed to save people with Caroline's kind of blood—then it was all the same, no matter what airs people like Mrs. Livaudais put on.

"But really, Caroline, why are you going to make your debut, do all that, if you don't want to?"

Her eyes widened as though he had just said he was leaving that afternoon for Mars. "But, Beau. I couldn't just not do it." She laughed. "It's something you do, that's all."

"But why? Look, you're going to college, doing that because it's something you want to do. Won't all this other stuff get in the way of studying, classes?"

"Well, of course it will, Beau!" She still looked surprised, as though she did not understand how he could ask her these questions. "But it's not as if Mama wanted me to go to college. *She* doesn't care whether parties and things interfere with it or not."

Beau shook his head. "It's beyond me. Maybe you better start from the beginning, explain this whole system to me." He tried to sound only amused; underneath, he felt that cold finger of fear. He remembered his father's voice, when Beau had said none of this society business meant anything, that it was nothing. "It's everything," Claude had said. And meant it.

"Well, Beau. It's simple enough. Girls my age 'come out,' that's what it's called." She smiled, then laughed. "I know you well enough to know you'll laugh at what I say next. The truth is, Beau, you 'come out' so people will know you're old enough to be married."

"Married!"

"Don't look so outraged, Beau." She reached a hand toward him. "It doesn't mean girls get married right away. It just means you're old enough to be included in grown-up society— old enough to be courted."

His hands were clenched tightly, his lips taut against his growing temper. "So you'll be courted this winter, lots of men hanging around you, sending you flowers and candy?" He stood up, his blood steaming. "Fat chance you'll have of passing even one course, with all that foolishness going on!"

"Beau Langlinais. Are you jealous?" Her eyes would never let him lie.

"Yes," he said. He dropped to one knee, knelt before her, and took one of her hands. "Yes, I am jealous. There I'll be at LSU in Baton Rouge, slaving away, and here you'll be, the belle of every party. How could I not be jealous?"

"You needn't be," she said. Then, with an air of having just thought of it: "Anyway, there'll be a lot of girls at LSU, Beau." Her lashes, long, thick, drooped over her eyes. Then they lifted, allowing a flash of light to hit him. "Pretty girls, I've heard."

He turned her hand over and put his lips against the palm. "Caroline. Are you flirting with me? Because you perfectly well know that I will never look at another girl the rest of my life." He dared to kiss her palm again, then looked into her eyes. "You do know that, don't you?"

Her hand moved in his, and her fingers curled around his flesh. The stillness of the afternoon, the heated silence, stopped time, thought. Beau leaned closer; she did not move. Was she even leaning toward him, closing ever so slightly the small space between them? His lips touched hers. Her mouth was soft, still. He put his arms around her and drew her to him, his mouth closing over hers. Then he felt her nestle against him, felt her kissing him. His heart seemed too big for his chest, he knew she would hear it beating. Then a clock struck outside in the hall, tolling five times. Caroline jumped, a quick jerk away from him. "Mama will be home soon. She's been at a card party."

"I'd better go, then," he said. It was a question—did her mother know he was coming?

"Yes, I guess so," she said. Her unspoken answer pleased him. As he walked toward St. Charles Avenue to catch the streetcar, he thought about the afternoon. He knew two important things he had not known before. That blue blood could be just as passionate as the ordinary kind. And that Caroline was willing to risk her parents' displeasure to see him. Whistling happily, he swung upon the streetcar and let it bear him through the gathering dusk.

He called Caroline the next day with no success. Each time he called, a polite voice told him Miss Caroline was out, with no expected time of return. On the day after that, he went to the house and left a note. Maddy answered the door again, her face a formal mask. "Miss Caroline's not in," she said. Something seemed to be working behind that mask; she reached deep into a pocket in her black skirt, pulled out a small square envelope, and handed it to Beau. "Miss Caroline, she say if you come, I'm to give you this."

"Maddy, is she really out? I've been calling and calling—"

The woman's hand came out toward him. "Chile. They say I'm to tell you she's not in." She turned suddenly at some sound in the dark hall behind her. "Mr. Charles, he's just finished his lunch. You don't want him to find you here." She stepped back and closed the door, a wall of solid green. Beau's hand lifted. He would beat on that door until Charles Livaudais himself came to answer it, and he would demand to know by what right he was kept from seeing Caroline. Rage surged through him; how dare these people keep him standing at their door, a beggar, a tramp who would not be admitted? Then he became aware of the envelope in his hand. It was smooth, like the memory of Caroline's skin. His hand fell. Turning, he went back down the walk and swiftly up the street until he reached St. Charles Avenue. He sat on one of the benches at the streetcar stop and ran his thumb under the flap, then removed the letter inside.

"Dear Beau," it read. "Mama came home early, and saw you on the street. When she asked me if you had been here, I couldn't lie. I told her yes, at my invitation. She was angry, Beau, so angry! She tried to pretend it was because I had had a young man visit me when no proper chaperone was here, and that she feared for my reputation. Oh, Beau, it's so silly! I'd laugh except I'm afraid. What I'm afraid of is that she was angry because my visitor was you." Beau stared at the dusty shrubs set around the green bench. He could see the streetcar approaching, see people filling it. He wondered if by looking at him they could tell that each line of the letter he held in his hand was a knife cut in his soul. His eyes scanned the rest. "She never mentioned your name. She didn't have to. But the servants are under orders to screen my callers, my mail, and my phone calls. Oh, Beau! I want to be back at Beau Chêne. I don't know what's going on here, it doesn't feel like home." The letter ended, her name scrawled at the bottom. The streetcar stopped and Beau boarded it. Funny, the things money and power couldn't do. They could change the boundaries of voting districts, but they couldn't change one silly woman's mind. They could breach prison walls, but they couldn't breach a private fortress on Fourth Street. They could merge companies and land, marry money with money. But they couldn't merge lives.

He thought of his speech to his father. He still would become that damn fine lawyer. But now he knew that that would not be enough. The Livaudaises had other weapons, weapons both above and beyond the law. The money and power his family had now could not match those weapons—he would find out how much would. And then, he thought, pulling the cord for his stop, he would get it.

By the time Beau went down to Baton Rouge to begin his freshman year at Louisiana State University, he had decided on his campaign against Charles and Hélène Livaudais. He gave himself two weeks to settle in; when he knew his way around the oak-studded campus that ran alongside the Mississippi River, the main buildings forming a pentagon around an open space of grass, he got a ride with a boy going home to New Orleans for the weekend, and opened the first segment of what might be the longest siege in romantic history. He was prepared for his task to be long, to be difficult. He was not prepared to lose.

"It's like this, Hal," he said to his cousin. They were in Hal's room, windows open, curtains pushed back to let in any breath of air that might stir the September heat. "She cares for me and I care for her. But she's well-brought-up, she's not going to defy her parents openly. But I know she'll see me if I can find a safe place."

Hal put a finger in the textbook he was holding and looked doubtfully at Beau. He was studying dentistry at Loyola, he was already courting seriously a girl who had lived down the street from the Larroques since Hal was three years old, and he was well on his way to becoming a steady, stolid man who would never divert from that serious path because he would never think of it.

"I don't know, Beau." Hal sighed. Somehow, when Beau was around, life got awfully complicated. "Can't you just settle on another girl? I mean, gee, aren't there lots of pretty girls, nice girls, at LSU?"

"But I love Caroline!"

Hal sighed again. He loved Suzanne. He would marry Suzanne, and would, he was sure, be quite happy. But he knew that he did not mean by "love" what his cousin Beau meant, he knew that if you felt about a girl the way Beau did, all this trouble, all this conspiracy, was well worth it. "All right, Beau. Tell me what you want me to do."

"I'm staying over Monday," Beau said. "I'll take the train back."

"You're missing *classes*?"

Beau fixed Hal with an awful glare. "Hal. Have you heard a word I've said? Until I get some way to see Caroline, I don't give a good damn about classes or anything else." He waited until Hal's face was once more acquiescent. "All right. So then on Monday I'm going to hang around the Newcomb campus until I see her. When I do see her, I'm going to tell her to think of a place where we can meet—not a public place, I won't risk her reputation and I won't risk her being caught." Hal heard the protective note in Beau's voice and wondered at the logic a man had when he put a girl in jeopardy and then tried to save her from the consequences. He shook his head, but Beau fixed him with another glare and went on. "Then, when she knows where it is, and when she can meet me, she's to call you."

"Me?" Hal looked around the room as though there must be another person there whom Beau meant.

"Of course you," Beau said crossly. "What do you think?"

"That might be hard to explain," Hal said.

"You help out at the pharmacy, don't you?" Beau said. "On Tuesdays and Thursdays and Saturdays?" Hal nodded. "All right. She'll call you there. She'll use some code phrase, something, so you'll know it's her."

Beau sounded excited, caught up in his elaborate scheme, and Hal wondered, not for the first time, if his cousin did not enjoy the sport more than the kill, the battle more than the victory. Caroline had sure better be worth all this.

"Then, when she calls you, you'll let me know." Beau sighed. "And I'll come. And I'll see her."

Hal opened his mouth. There must be something he could say. But not one single word came to his mind. "All right, Beau," he said, opening his textbook. "All right."

Beau stood near the streetcar stop on St. Charles Avenue on the outskirts of the Newcomb campus. It was almost eleven-thirty; if Caroline were going home for lunch, she would surely be coming any moment. He had been gazing at girls for the past hour and a half. He did not think he had ever seen so many girls gathered at one place, at one time, who were not Caroline! Then a familiar figure came out of a building and stood at the top of the steps hesitantly. Caroline wore a light blue middy blouse and skirt, and her hair was caught back with a big blue bow. She looks about thirteen, Beau thought. He wanted to rush across the space between them, catch her up in his arms, carry her off to the train station, get on the train and stay on it until they were safe in New Iberia. Then, he thought, moving forward, I'd call Papa and say . . . But she was coming toward him, walking slowly through the clusters of girls that drifted across the sidewalk, calling a greeting to one, stopping to speak to another. She carried three books on one arm; the free hand moved quickly, punctuating and underlining her speech. Then she saw him. He knew the exact moment when her eyes found him, and registered who he was. He could almost hear her intake of breath, almost feel her heart skip a beat. Then she broke off the conversation she was having and began walking rapidly down the walk, her eyes fixed on him. He knew he must not betray his feeling, knew that too many eyes could watch them, too many lips betray them. He waited until she was almost to him before stepping forward. "Why, Caroline Livaudais. What a surprise to see you here," he said in a voice that would carry to bystanders.

She put out a hand and he took it for a brief, formal gesture. "And what brings you to town?" she said. Her voice was steady, but her eyes were leaping with joy.

"I needed to look up a few things in the Tulane Law Library," he said. He gestured to a streetcar approaching them. "That your car?"

She barely glanced at the sign on the front. "Yes," she said, and let him help her aboard.

They sat on one of the wooden-slatted seats, hands clasped beneath the shield of her books. In a low voice Beau told her his plan. Watching her face, he was filled with joy. He didn't need to explain anything to her, didn't need to convince her to meet him—she already knew that being together was the most important thing in the entire world.

"Let me see," she said. "All right. I've got it. I go see my *nainaine*, my godmother, one Saturday a month." Caroline smiled. "Mama doesn't go with me because she thinks Nainaine is a tedious old woman. Actually, she's not tedious at all, she saw through Mama long ago, and simply ignores her. Which makes it perfect. Because she will let you come to see me there, I know she will."

Beau gripped the hand he held more tightly. "Are you sure?"

"As sure as I can be without asking her." She looked out the window and reached up to pull the cord. "That's my stop, Beau, I mustn't be late getting home or my parole officer will want to know where I've been." She rose, her body swaying with the car's movement. "I'll call Hal as soon as I find out." Her eyes met his in a long, long look. "Beau. You're wonderful, do you know that?"

He watched her descend from the car, watched her vanish out of sight as the car rattled on down St. Charles Avenue. He would stay on, let it take him to the train station. By tonight, he would be back in his dormitory room, trying to keep his mind on his books. But all the while, he would be waiting for the telephone to ring, and for Hal to tell him when he could see her again.

The one flaw in the plan was the infrequency with which they met. The first meeting, a meeting that began awkwardly, took place with Beau making conversation with Caroline's god-mother until that lady was satisfied he meant well, and left them alone for all of twenty-five minutes before she returned bearing coffee and sweet cakes. "She'll give us more time next month," Caroline whispered when he left her. Striding down the brick sidewalk that led to the little raised cottage on Calliope Street for their second meeting, Beau hoped so. He had come down with several of his fraternity brothers who were bent on a night of New Orleans jazz, New Orleans saloons—and New Orleans women. They had discovered that Beau had an entrée into legendary Storyville, and had not let him alone until he had agreed to escort them there and introduce them to the madams his father knew.

But before that agreement had been worked out, there had been two black eyes and one bruised chin, badges his fraternity brothers wore as signs that they had dared impugn his father's honor. "You don't understand," he had said when they teased him. "My father doesn't patronize those places himself. But he's in the legislature, he's got people who want to be taken down there—they go upstairs and he sits and has another drink and listens to the music." "Sure," one boy had said, "I'll bet." Beau had driven the cynical look from his eyes by closing them with a well-placed fist. Only one more boy had teased him; he earned a damaged face for his trouble. The rest of the group had agreed that Claude's contacts were useful, and they believed with all their hearts that he never himself took advantage of them.

As a reward, and a pledge of his own acceptance of their apologies, Beau had taken out a copy of the Blue Book, the directory of houses and girls in Storyville. The names of the girls were listed neatly, phrases describing their attractions nearby. "She lets it go as it will," was a frequent comment, as well as other, franker ones.

Beau looked at his watch. He was to meet the group at Arnaud's for dinner before they walked the few blocks to Storyville. But the hours between then and now would be filled with Caroline. He quickened his pace, almost ran up the wide wooden steps to the porch, and knocked on the pale gray door. Caroline opened it immediately, reached out a hand, and drew him inside. "Oh, Beau!" she said. Then she put her arms around his neck and pulled his face to hers and kissed him. His own arms went around her; he felt as though he had walked out of the brilliance of the October day into a dream. "Oh, Beau," she said again, her breath warm on his cheek. "Let's go in here." She took his hand and led him into the small parlor, guided him to a love seat, and pulled him down to sit close beside her. His arm went around her and he held her against him. Then she turned her face against his chest and began to cry, a soft stream of tears that wet his shirt and felt warm against his skin.

"Caroline, what is it?" They've found out, he thought. But they won't keep me from seeing her, no matter how hard they try. I'll take her away from here, I'll marry her, I'll—

"Beau, we're moving to Washington!"

She lifted her head and looked at him. Tears covered her eyes, like old glass on a portrait.

"Washington! But, Caroline—what about New Orleans, your debut—Caroline, what in hell is going on?" The word was out before he thought. He started over. "Sorry. Caroline, tell me."

She nestled closer, as though his arms could protect her from her own truths. "There's not going to be a season. Well, not much of one. They've canceled Mardi Gras next spring—because of the war." She smiled. "I'm not sorry about that, it does seem terrible to be playing at royalty when people are fighting and dying. Mama's having a fit, though—you'd think the Germans declared war just to keep me from being Queen of Comus." She sighed. "Then Papa got some kind of appointment in Washington, I don't know just what. A Mr. Herbert Hoover is heading up something . . ." She brushed a hand wearily across her forehead. "Food for Europe, I don't know."

"What the devil does your father know about food?"

She shrugged. "Governor Pleasant got him appointed. I don't know. Papa seems pleased, he told Mama there was a lot going on in Washington and it wouldn't hurt him to spend some time there."

"But moving! Caroline, what do you mean? Not forever, you don't mean forever?" He could imagine the house on Fourth Street, its elaborate rooms empty, waiting for the players who never appeared.

"No, of course not forever. Mama wouldn't hear of that." She sighed a long, sorrowful sigh. "But it might as well be. We're leaving next week, Beau. Next week!" He felt the words hit him, as forcefully as his own fists had hit his fraternity brothers.

"We won't come home for Thanksgiving, or for Christmas. We've got relatives on Papa's side in Virginia and New York—we'll visit them. Oh, Beau!" The tears had paused while she talked. Now they began again; he wanted nothing so much as to weep too. His hand stroked her back, gentling her, soothing her.

"I'll see you, Caroline. I'll see you if I have to walk to Washington. See if I don't." He took her face in his hand. "And look. If I send letters here, to your godmother. Will she send them on to you?"

"I think so. I'll ask her."

He held her, his lips brushing her hair. Then he thought of something else. "Caroline, your college! You'll give that up?"

"Give up Newcomb, anyway. I told you, Beau, Mama doesn't care about that."

"Because you could stay, couldn't you?" The new idea excited him. "Caroline, couldn't you?" He held her away, took both hands in his. "Live with your godmother? Go to college?"

For a moment, she stared at him. Then she began to sob, not just the quiet flow of tears, but hard sobs that shook her body. "I didn't want to tell you, Beau. I didn't." She couldn't speak around the sobs, and he held her, thinking that if he could not find an outlet for the anger building in him against the people who made her so miserable, he would explode. "Beau, I suggested that. I told them how much sense it made." She gulped, swallowed hard. "Mama told me there was only one way I could stay in New Orleans. If I decided to marry Stu Favrot."

"Marry Stu Favrot! Caroline, what—"

She put her fingers against his lips. "Stu's seven years older than I am, Beau, already established in his father's brokerage firm." She shrugged. "He's from an old family, he's rich—"

"He's a canaille," Beau said. "Caroline, you're too young . . . Caroline, you're going to marry me." He pulled her to him and kissed her, the passion in him channeled into the meeting of lips. He felt her shaking, trembling, felt her struggle against him. He let her go. "I'm sorry. I . . . I didn't mean to frighten you."

She sat a little away from him, breathing fast. "You didn't . . . frighten me." He wanted her so badly then he was not sure he could bear not having her. "Beau, I'm not going to marry

Stu. I'm not even going to be engaged to him." She held out her hands, palms up, vulnerable. "But, Beau—there's nothing I can do."

Nor I, he thought. Elope? His allowance was generous, but a man didn't support a wife on his allowance from his father. Not if he were honorable. "All right, Caroline. Go on to Washington." He put his arms around her, careful to be gentle. "But, Caroline, I'm telling you, if you go looking at any of those Yankees, I'm going to have a voodoo woman put a hex on you!"

It had rained during the day, and pools of rainwater collected in the uneven brick sidewalk glared at Beau and his friends like indignant eyes as they walked down Iberville Street. They had had a good dinner at Antoine's, had listened to jazz at one of the saloons that filled Bourbon Street. When the bourbon in their heads and the beat of jazz in their blood had reached a sufficient level, they had headed toward Storyville, joking, laughing, keeping up a running stream of bawdy comments as they passed the "cribs," the single rooms opening onto the street with the girls sitting in the windows, the "parlors," a little more elaborate, with two rooms and perhaps a servant to open the door, and approached the area where the last of the great houses stood.

"Place sure has fallen on hard times," one of the group said, surveying the Arlington, closed now, where the renowned Josie Arlington had reigned supreme for so long.

"Sounds like you know what you're talking about," another jeered. "What did you do, go to kindergarten here?"

"I've got big brothers," the speaker said.

"Come on," Beau said. "If we're going, let's go and get it over with."

"Now, what kind of attitude is that?" someone said, slapping his back. "You're the one with the entrée, man, we're counting on you to show us how to have a good time."

Beau looked at him levelly. "I'll take you to Mahogany Hall and I'll introduce you to Lulu White. After that, you are strictly on your own." He put an even emphasis on each of the final words.

"Sure, Beau, sure." They winked and laughed and followed him down the street.

He was not at all sure why he was here. All through dinner, he had wanted to bolt, to go to Fourth Street, to charge through that solid green door, to defy Charles and Hélène Livaudais, dare them to take Caroline from him. Only the firm knowledge that such a course would be the worst thing he could do kept him seated, kept him poking at the trout amandine, sipping at the Chablis. But the need for action was strong in him; he felt tense, taut with suppressed energy and passion.

"Wow!" someone said when they stood in front of Mahogany Hall. The building had four stories, and the veiled light from the upper floors excited them more than if they had been gazing through the windows into the rooms themselves. Beau went up the steps and knocked on the door. A woman opened it, a woman dressed in bright green brocade, with diamonds at her neck and wrists, and with tall feathers pluming from her head. They filed after Beau into the wide entrance hall, eyes staring, mouths agape. Mahogany Hall was known for its crystal chandeliers, its Oriental rugs, its gold mirrors. Lulu White prided herself on the most elaborate setting and the most compliant girls of any madam in Storyville. "If you're not satisfied at Lulu White's, honey," she was fond of saying, "you're dead and don't know it."

"I'm Claude Langlinais' son," he told the woman. "Are you . . . are you Mrs. White?"

"Well," the woman drawled, linking an arm in Beau's. "I'm Lulu White. Doesn't matter about a title, does it?"

"No, ma'am," Beau said.

Lulu's eyes swept over the boys clustered around Beau. "What you got here, son? A Sunday-school class out to see the devil's work?" She laughed, an easy, friendly laugh that made Beau feel suddenly at home.

"No, ma'am," he said. "They want girls." His words made every one of the four faces in front of him turn fiery red. "You do, don't you?" he challenged them. He felt a sweet sense of power. He alone had been able to give these friends what they wanted, he was the key, the important one. He turned to Lulu White. "I imagine you can fix them up, can't you?"

"I imagine I can," she said. She laughed again. "You boys just follow me," she said. She glanced at Beau. "And you. You, Langlinais. You stay here." She marched up the staircase, the four boys straggling behind her. The last one turned and looked at Beau, as though he hoped Beau would call him back. Beau raised his hand and waved the boy on up the stairs. Then he looked around, found a small velvet settee, and settled down to wait.

Lulu was back in a short while, smiling and humming under her breath. "All right. How about you? You want a girl?"

Beau felt again the tearing passion he'd felt when he held Caroline, just hours ago. "I'm not sure," he said.

"All right. You want a drink?"

He followed her to a small table far enough away from the piano player that they could talk. She beckoned to a waiter, ordered bourbon. She put her elbows on the table and leaned forward. "You like your daddy? Do a little drinking, listen to a lot of piano, while your friends go upstairs?" She shook her head. "Your mother must be some lady." She saw the flicker of anger in Beau's eyes and raised a hand. "Now don't go getting riled up. I mean that as a compliment. She keeps your daddy happy, he doesn't need to go upstairs." She sighed. "I mean really happy. Do you know what I'm talking about?"

Beau smiled. "Probably not." He remembered how he had felt the first time he had come across the Blue Book, and read the descriptions of what the girls listed there would do. He had had a very hard time looking at his mother after that, wondering if women like her, women who looked so calm and cool and chaste, could possibly behave like those descriptions when they were behind closed doors. His father had found out Beau was reading the Blue Book and had a talk with him, setting him straight. "Some women make a man feel dirty when he wants them, even when they're married and have God's blessing." He shrugged. "Your mama's not like that, Beau, thank heaven." He had looked at his son sharply. "I don't know for sure how you can tell—but, Beau . . . be sure you don't marry a woman like that, you hear?" He had flicked a thumb at the Blue Book lying between them. "Places like that, women like that—they're necessary, I guess. For certain times, certain reasons." He had grinned. "Hell, you ever get to the place you can't get your head above your belt, you go on down there and tell Lulu White I sent you." He had leaned forward and taken Beau's hand. "But, son, I sure hope you visit there sowing wild oats, not burying a bad marriage."

The woman laughed, the kind of towering laugh his father had, the kind that swept up to the height of the moment and filled it with lightness. "Probably not," she agreed. "So. You want a girl or not?"

He thought of going upstairs, going into one of those veiled rooms. Of having a girl strip herself, lie down beside him. A girl that was not Caroline. But he would be thinking of Caroline, wanting Caroline. "I think I'll sit this one out," he said, and reached for his drink.

11

As the tides ebb and flow with the whim of the moon, so did Beau Langlinais' moods swing with the rhythm of Caroline's letters. At first, she spoke only of her loneliness, of the strangeness of a city caught up in the European war. Then she began to notice the richness of Washington, to visit its museums and art galleries, to go to concerts and lectures. "There's a different atmosphere here, Beau. It's not just the war. Politics, of course, you can't get away from that. It's worse than Louisiana, if that's possible! But the women are so different! Even girls not much older than I know so much, Beau. I feel tongue-tied and foolish, and aware of how much time I've spent on clothes and parties while other girls *learn* something!" Later, from New York at Christmastime, letters talking about the Metropolitan Opera, the Metropolitan Museum of Art, about visiting great houses on Fifth Avenue, and going to tea dances at the Plaza Hotel. "Damn!" Beau said, tucking her latest letter along with all the others in the leather case he used to save them. "She's certainly not sitting around wasting time missing me!"

The tender paragraphs that closed each letter, hesitant, careful, reassured him. None of the Yankees who seemed so eager to escort her in both Washington and New York had replaced him in her heart. But when she came back, changed by all she'd done, all she'd learned, what then? How would a Cajun from St. Martinville measure up then? In the early weeks of her absence, Beau's studies had suffered as well as his sleep. Now, thinking of Caroline growing, stretching her mind—"stuffing it with enough knowledge to make me as smart as you are," as she said—he began working harder and going to New Orleans more often. There was opera there, too, and there were lectures and concerts and plays. He went to her godmother and asked for advice; what tickets to buy, what books to read. She looked at Beau, a deep, serious look that ended with a pat on his cheek and an approving smile. "Good," she said, taking up pen and paper and writing rapidly. "You will set out to improve yourself in order to please Caroline. The happy result will be that you will end up pleasing yourself."

She was herself a devoted patroness of the arts, this spinster sister of Charles Livaudais. Annette Livaudais had husbanded her share of the family money well; in her small house she lived a widely varied life, and she shared it with Beau. Sunday-afternoon musicales, Saturday lunches, all with a kind of people Beau had not known existed. "They're the local version of bohemians," Annette said, her lips curved in a curious smile. "Charles and Hélène look down those very long, very pinched aristocratic noses at my friends." She shrugged. "I will not tell you our opinion of them."

As winter worked itself into spring, Beau felt his own mind stretching. The first time he wrote to Caroline about a book she had recommended, he felt something else, too. A new kind of intimacy, a new way of being with Caroline. So that when he listened to music, or picked up a new book, or watched the curtain go up on a play, he could tell himself: "Caroline would like this," and see and hear with her soul as well as his.

"I guess you think it's strange that a 'country boy' would care about all this," he said to Annette Livaudais one Sunday late in May, just before school closed for the summer. "I mean, I did start all this . . ." He grinned, laughing at himself. "All this culture so Caroline won't think I'm a country bumpkin when she gets back. But you were right, I have ended up liking it for myself."

Annette sipped the anisette she loved, looking at him over the rim of the tiny crystal glass. "And why should I be surprised? St. Martinville has a heritage of culture. At one time it was known as 'Little Paris,' and it had an opera house before New Orleans."

It pleased him to think a long-ago ancestor might have dozed over opera, surrounded by fields of gently waving cane.

The mood of the country the summer of 1918 was uneasy. The war in Europe seemed to peak and hold, a conflagration that threatened to burn the entire continent before the diplomats and generals between them could find a way to put it out. "Papa has become quite committed to the idea that food is helping win this war," Caroline wrote. "Beau, we really are keeping those countries alive!" While it was true that the massive tonnage of wheat shipped to Belgium and Britain in 1918 fueled the troops and civilians needed to wage the war, it was also true that a strictly domestic war was being fueled, too. In order to send wheat abroad, American consumption had to be cut, and in September 1918 the Agricultural Appropriation Act temporarily prohibited the sale and consumption of intoxicating liquors, on the premise that spirits were distilled from needed foodstuffs. The banner of the Anti-Saloon League, carrying forward a temperance crusade begun a century before, added the star of patriotism; who but a traitor would drink, knowing that each drink deprived some needy soldier, some desperate civilian, of the bread of life?

And Charles Livaudais, walking the corridors of national power, took note of each development on the national scene that might work to his local advantage. He was privy to the federal action that contracted Cuba's entire sugar crop at a price well below the world price; he knew before it was publicly announced that American beet- and cane-sugar planters were to be given special price advantages. And so he was able to invest his capital where it would do the most good, if not for the war effort, then for Charles Livaudais' personal benefit. His trips to New York were not motivated entirely by family feeling and a desire to renew acquaintance with a distant branch of Livaudais relations. The main offices of Standard Oil were in New York City; with a letter of introduction from the head of the plant in Baton Rouge, Charles had no trouble gaining entry. If there was one thing he prided himself on, it was being able to see the way the wind was blowing before anyone else had even wet his finger. The presence of Standard Oil in Baton Rouge, and of its huge refinery there, was giving the company increasing economic, political, and social force, not just locally, but statewide. Its pipelines, now, in wartime, carried oil from Louisiana fields, making money for both the company and local producers. But Charles, who could see the dark side of any transaction, knew that he who controlled those pipelines controlled much of the state. If the day came when he needed to be on a team more powerful than the one run by the Ring, Charles Livaudais would have the private number of its captain in his breast pocket.

The mood in Louisiana was uneasy, too. The midterm elections in November would cast a long shadow, a shadow reaching to the gubernatorial race in 1920. John Parker's supporters intended to hold the line in the sixteen sugar and rice parishes that had gone for him in 1916; they further intended to make strong inroads in the ten parishes outlining French South Louisiana which had given Parker better than thirty-seven percent of their vote that gubernatorial election. And to do that, they would have to put a significant number of local officials sympathetic to the Parker cause in key positions. "Huey P. Long can write the book on how to work those rural parishes," Andrew McShane, the man being groomed to run for mayor of New Orleans in 1920, wrote Claude. "He knows his opponent for the railroad-commissioner spot already has the sheriffs and clerks of court and assessors sewed up—so he's made a list of every police juror, justice of the peace, and constable in the third district, and he's courting them good and proper. Add to that the fact he knows almost every farmer and householder from being a traveling salesman, and you can see he'll give Burk Bridges a tight race."

Long again. They had not yet met, but every story Claude heard strengthened the image of Long as a coming power in state politics. Then Beau came home from a trip upstate to visit a fraternity brother, chuckling over a story of his own. "Will and I were driving out in the country, heading for his family's camp on a lake outside of town. Well, it had rained hard all day, and his father had told us we'd better wait until the road had time to dry, we were sure to get stuck. But Will had it in his head we were going to spend the night at the camp and get up early to fish. Sure enough, at one bad place he skidded off the road and got stuck in the mud on the side. Soon a man driving an old Overland 90 came up. He climbed out and surveyed our situation, and said he'd go find a farmer to pull us out with his mules. He asked Will if he had something to pay the farmer with, and Will said he had a couple of dollars, would that be enough? This man started laughing and went back to his car and pulled out a bottle of whiskey and said we'd better offer the farmer a swig of that, and that if we were planning on doing much traveling on these roads we better take to carrying it regularly, because no matter how 'dry' a farmer swore he was, he could get 'wet' in a hurry." Beau laughed and leaned forward, his eyes filled with the scene he was describing. "So then Will stuck his hand out and said who he was, and the man shook it and said he was Huey P. Long!" Beau looked at Claude and nodded his head. "Sure enough. So I said my name was Claude Louis Langlinais, and he asked if you were my daddy."

"So he knew me?" Claude said.

"Anyone who reads the papers would!" Beau said. "Anyway, he said he'd heard good things about your work in the legislature, and to tell you that when he got to be railroad commissioner, he'd be coming to see you." Beau took out a much-folded piece of paper. "Then he gave me and Will each a bunch of these, and said if we felt like nailing them up, fine, and if we didn't, be sure we threw them out where voters could pick 'em up." He handed Claude the flier. Claude read it quickly, then handed it back.

"If you can believe what this says, Huey P. Long is the savior this state's been waiting for," he said. His voice was dry, noncommittal.

"I don't know, Papa. But there's something about him—I asked him if he just went around politicking all the time and he laughed and said he did a little selling and a little talking every place he went. What does he sell, Papa?"

"Hope," Claude said. Then he ruffled Beau's hair and laughed. "Oil cans, that's the latest, I think. To keep kerosene in." He saw the surprise in Beau's eyes. "Long's not the only one who keeps up with what's going on. If he pulls off this race, beats Burk Bridges—we'll need to go after him, and damn quick."

"I don't even know what the Railroad Commission does," Beau said.

"Not much of anything, when it comes down to it. It's supposed to regulate railroads, steamboats, telephone and telegraph companies, pipelines, things like that. Make sure their rates and the way they do business are fair." He shrugged.

"Most people who run for a spot on it are looking for a place to sleep well and honorably."

"Pipelines?" Beau said. His eyes went past Claude's, toward the direction of the Langlinais oil wells.

"Pipelines," Claude said. "Which are now owned and maintained and controlled by Standard Oil. Makes you think, doesn't it, son?"

"But Standard Oil does buy our crude oil right now."

"Sure." Claude rose and stretched. "Want a beer?" He led the way to the kitchen, took beer from the icebox. They went to the back steps and sat in the cooling evening. "You got a little time, I'll fill you in on what Dusty and I have been doing."

Claude picked up a stick and sketched a pattern in the soft dirt at the edge of the steps. "Now, this is St. Martin Parish," he said. He began making circles inside the larger design. "And these are where Dusty thinks there might be oil." He took up his beer and drank, looking at Beau over the bottle. "What I've been doing is going around and taking leases on that land."

Beau looked doubtfully at the picture on the ground. "Taking people's oil?"

Claude gave Beau a disgusted look. "Hell, no, Beau. Making it possible for them to *have* oil." He pointed to the circles in the dust. "You think the little landowners around here have the money to hire a crew, sink a hole, drill?" He spat, an arc of moisture that spattered against one of the circles. "Hell, no, they don't. If they're going to get anything at all, bonuses on their leases and then royalties if oil is found, someone else will have to take the risk. That means either I do it—or some big company, like Enterprise, operating over on Beau Chêne."

"So you're signing them up, and you'll drill on their land. But if you find oil, they'll share in the profits?"

"Now you got it." He smiled at Beau fondly. "Hell, son, if I tried to steal anything on a man's land or underneath it, I'd be through in this parish forever—or longer. Cajuns have damn good memories."

Beau lifted his beer bottle in a little salute. "You wouldn't, anyway. You're no thief."

There was a pause; then Claude said, "Heard from Caroline lately?" Beau did not need to ask why Claude's next thought after the word "thief" had been Charles Livaudais—and from there, his daughter. Neither of his parents had had much comment when he'd told them the Livaudaises were moving to Washington temporarily. Claude had muttered that he hoped they had the White House bolted down. They had both said they were sorry for Beau's disappointment in missing Caroline. Except for an occasional inquiry, Caroline's existence was ignored. They hope I'll get over her so I won't be hurt, Beau thought, and, in his turn, maintained silence on the subject. Now he said lightly, "Got a letter the other day. They're about ready to leave Maine and go back to Washington."

"Hmm," Claude said. "Get us another beer, will you, son?"

It was good to have an almost grown son to talk with, have a beer with. Good to have a son like Beau, who was managing to grow up without getting into the kind of scrapes so many young men seemed to think was part of the territory. He took the beer Beau handed him. "About to give you a lesson in Louisiana politics, Beau," he said. "We were talking about the Railroad Commission. Now, from what I hear, Huey P. Long's no fool. If he's running for the Railroad Commission, it's because he knows that the right man can turn that agency clear around, make it a dynamo that runs the wheels that move this state."

"You mean he could really have power? If he got elected?"

"Hell, yes. The commission's got the constitutional power to make even the big utility companies sit up and beg for their supper. No one's ever used it, that's all." Claude paused. "Mainly because the commissioners are eating at the same trough as the companies they're meant to regulate, I guess."

"So who's on it now?" Beau looked wide-awake, as though he were memorizing every word Claude said.

Well, Claude thought. Politics has been used for some funny things, I've never known it to cure lovesickness before, but there's a first time for everything. "Shelby Taylor from Baton Rouge and John T. Michel from New Orleans. Neither one is up for reelection—a commissioner has a six-year term." He laughed. "If Long gets in, from what I hear of his methods, they'll have to change the way they do business. Get with him or get out of his way, one or the other."

"So what is Long after, do you think?"

"To get elected," Claude said, finishing his beer.

"But what for? I mean—"

"Hell, son, isn't that enough? Man can't accomplish anything until he does that."

Beau lifted his bottle and drank. He could see the trees, the grass, the backyard, through the curving amber glass; his familiar world distorted, changed, the colors muted and somber. He lowered the bottle and blinked at the brightness. "I always thought men ran for office because there was something they wanted to do—like Abraham Lincoln. Or even Woodrow Wilson."

Claude slapped Beau's back and laughed the big booming laugh that changed the world, too, making it broader, lighter, more open, and easier to get. "Son, that's what I'm telling you. What it looks like is, Huey P. Long's purpose is to get elected. Once he's done that, he'll figure out what to do next."

They stood up and went into the kitchen, where the smell of the figs Alice had put up that day still lingered. "Are you going to support him, Papa? Long, I mean."

"He's not running in this district, Beau."

"But you have friends all over the state. You going to talk to them?"

Claude's eyes looked past Beau, into an arena Beau could not see. Claude remembered his own words to Beau. It's more important to know who your enemies are than to know your friends. Yes. So far, he wasn't sure which Long was. He dipped a piece of cold biscuit into the bowl of preserves on the table and ate it carefully, leaning forward slightly so the syrup wouldn't drip on his shirt. Then he turned to Beau. "I don't know, son. But what I think I'll do is, I think I'll sit this one out."

As summer slouched toward autumn, the weight of dragging heat gradually lifting, goldenrod and asters and Queen Anne's lace beginning to star the dust rising from parched lanes and roads, the spirits of both state and nation rose. The election campaigns were picking up speed, as were the military campaigns across the sea. Then came October. The cane stood tall, making a final waving dance before bending beneath the harvesters' long curved knives. Across the sugar belt, wheels in sugar mills began to turn. Across the ocean, the wheels of the Allied military machine made a final decisive turn, and arrived at Armistice.

Beau called home from LSU. "I've never seen anything like the madness here when we got news the war was officially over," he said. It was early the morning of November 12;

Claude had already been to vote, and was home drinking coffee, surrounded by newspapers proclaiming yesterday's great event. "At one o'clock this morning," Beau went on, "we were still part of a parade bunny-hopping up Third Street, with Toots Johnson and his jazz band heading the march." His voice was exhilarated, and Claude was reminded that the war's end also meant the end of wartime appointments. Caroline Livaudais would be coming home.

"There'll be a lot of excitement today, too, when the returns start coming in," he said. "Think your friend Long's going to win?"

"Gosh, I haven't even thought of the election," Beau said. "It is today, isn't it?"

"I've already voted in our parish elections," Claude said.

"Does it make Mama mad she can't vote?" Beau said. "Caroline wrote a couple of times about meeting ladies in Washington who want women to vote. She sounded all fired up about it."

Claude looked at Alice, who was reading the *Times-Picayune* across the table from him. "Don't know why they can't," Claude said. He laughed and said, loud enough for Alice to know she was meant to hear, "They make all the decisions anyway, might as well go on record as doing it." He listened another moment and then handed the instrument to Alice. "Say hello to your son before he falls asleep standing up."

He went back to his papers, musing. Funny the way history could put events right next to each other. The war in Europe over and a new war begun right here in Louisiana. He read a statement Huey P. Long had made on election eve. The statement had all Long's hallmarks: confidence, cockiness, and an overriding theme—that the game of life was brutally and cruelly unfair, with the dice loaded so that riches fell to a few, poverty to many. What the game needed was a new judge, a new referee—a new rule-maker. Reviewing what he knew of Long, Claude wondered: Would Long's game be any less unfair? He shrugged. That would depend, he supposed, on who rolled the dice. And on who loaded them.

Beau ripped into the letter he received from Caroline, his eyes running rapidly over the words. "And so we won't be home for Thanksgiving, but we will be home by Christmas!!!!" He need read no more. The waiting was almost over, the test almost passed. They had been separated over a year, and their love was stronger than ever. He walked back to his dormitory room, the letter in his hand a talisman of hope.

He went through the rest of November in a daze, began to count the days until Christmas as though he were a small boy waiting for Père Noël. And then came the letter giving the day, the hour, of her arrival. "I can't go to Nainaine's the minute I get home, Beau. But I can go on that Saturday, which is only forty-eight hours later. Oh, Beau! Can I stand being in the same state with you, and not see you for forty-eight whole hours?"

The same city, Beau resolved. He would be at the train station, he would watch her arrive. He would be in New Orleans each of those forty-eight hours, and when the moment came, he would be at Annette Livaudais' cottage with flowers and chocolates, waiting arms and a devoted heart.

When the train did come in, smoke puffing up around the shining brass fittings of the engine, he could barely remain concealed behind the post that hid him. He watched Caroline stand on the train steps, waiting for the porter to help her descend. Her traveling hat had a veil that was close around her face; her hair was up, and the suit she wore had a stylish look, a grown-up look, that went well with the poised way she held herself, the graceful way she moved. Then he heard her laugh ring out at something the porter said, heard her cry, "Oh, it's so good to hear a voice from home!" and knew that Caroline had changed, but not in any way that mattered.

Not until Charles had bustled Hélène and Caroline away, leading them to the waiting car, did Beau leave the station. He looked at his watch. Only forty-six hours and twenty-nine minutes before he saw her.

"If that rug wasn't already so old nothing could harm it, you'd have worn a path in it," Annette Livaudais said to Beau.

"Sorry," he said, throwing himself down in a chair. "I can't seem to stay still."

"I'd be worried if you could," Annette said. "Of course Hélène and Charles would kill me by the slowest torture they could think of if they knew I encourage you and Caroline like this."

"I've wondered why you do," Beau said. "I know you don't

like her parents—but you are a Livaudais." He smiled dryly. "One of the New Orleans aristocrats."

Annette snorted. "Humph. I've told you what I think of all that foolishness." She fumbled with a small gold-and-onyx locket on a chain around her neck, an ornament Beau had never seen her without. "Foolishness like that ruined my life, because I let it. I wouldn't want to see that happen to Caroline." She opened the locket and motioned to Beau to look at the picture inside. "My fiancé. A very fine young man whom I loved very much and who loved me far more than I deserved." She snapped the locket closed. "Only he had the misfortune to own a grocery store, several of them in fact. And to have a name with the wrong sound."

"So you didn't marry him."

"I didn't marry him. My parents stormed, and I stormed, and when it came down to it, I couldn't do it. I couldn't bear never to see them, or any other member of the family, again." She looked at Beau, and he could see behind the cynical, worldly mask she wore. "He married someone else, and now owns several businesses, lives in a big house not far from my dear brother's, and though he does not and will not ever belong to the 'right' clubs and krewes, that does not seem to have prevented his children from having brilliant academic careers or him and his wife from doing a great deal of good in this city."

"Well," said Beau. "Caroline—" The sentence remained unfinished. He had heard light, quick footsteps on the porch, heard the rapid beat of the door knocker. Without another glance at Annette, he dashed out of the parlor, through the small front hall, and tore open the door. For one long moment they stood staring at each other. Then she was in his arms, and he was kissing all the days of separation away.

"We must go inside," she whispered breathlessly.

"Yes," he said, and led her through the hall into the empty parlor.

"Isn't Nainaine here?" Caroline said, looking around.

"Somewhere," Beau said, lifting her face again. They settled on one of the love seats that flanked the fireplace, and in one-quarter of an hour, closed all the gaps the year had made.

"Coffee coming," Annette's voice came. She entered, bearing a silver tray with small porcelain cups and a tray of cakes.

"Oh, Nainaine!" Caroline said. Annette put the tray on a table in front of them and took Caroline in her arms, holding her close. "What would we do without you?"

"Die of broken hearts, I imagine," Annette said with her dry laugh. She handed them coffee. "This is a mighty interesting young man you've got hold of. We've had some good times together, Beau and I."

"I'm so glad," Caroline said.

"So. You've come back changed, I hope," Annette said. "Some of your mama's silly ideas routed. Not that you ever paid them much attention, anyway."

Caroline laughed. "Heavens, no. Of course, Mama thinks I've changed for the worse. I heard her telling a friend on the telephone this morning that I have become 'serious,' and you know what an awful label that is!"

"Indeed I do," Annette said. She turned to Beau. "In case you don't know, the very worst thing that can be said about a young woman out in New Orleans society—one whose reputation is above reproach, I mean—is that she is serious." Annette shrugged. "No longer . . . amusante."

"It made Mama furious how much time I spent with girls and women I met in the East. People who were interested in things, working for causes. She told me once, as if she were telling me I was doomed to perdition, that I was turning into a regular bluestocking."

"Yes, she wrote me that she was afraid Stu Favrot would not like the way you were changing," Annette said. The words fell around them like a wire snare.

"Stu Favrot?" Beau looked at Caroline.

"From what your mother wrote, I assumed that when you returned, Favrot would have entrée de la maison." She looked at Beau and Caroline. "Am I mistaken?"

Caroline's color had fled. She twisted her fingers and stared into the fire. "No. No, you're not. Mama is still throwing Stu Favrot at me every time I turn around. There was a huge bouquet of roses from him the day I got home, and a bunch more came today." She looked miserable; Annette or no Annette, Beau could not keep from taking her in his arms and comforting her.

"Caroline. Look at me. You don't have to see him, do you? You can say no?"

"Oh, of course I can say no. But he'll be everywhere I'll be, all winter. Now the war's over, people are planning all kinds of parties. Mama's having a huge one Christmas night. I'm considered 'out' now, you know." Her eyes filled with tears. "I know Stu. Once he gets an idea in his head, he's the stubbornest

man on earth. He'll just hound me and hound me. Oh, it's
awful!"

Beau thought of the last time he had seen Stu Favrot, after the
race on the lake. Angry eyes, thrust-out jaw. Contemptuous
tongue. He hugged Caroline, then let her go. "You haven't seen
stubborn until you've seen a Cajun with his mind made up," he
said. "Don't worry about Stu Favrot." His eyes went to the
locket around Annette's neck; she caught his glance and nodded.

Caroline took out a handkerchief and wiped her eyes. "I hate
to, but I've got to go home now. Mama and Papa are taking me
to the opera tonight." She sighed. "To show me off to everyone, let them see my new dress from Worth."

"When will I see you?"

She thought a moment. "I know—I'll go to St. Louis Cathedral for early Mass tomorrow morning. Mama can't ever get up
before ten, she always goes to late Mass at Holy Name."

"I'll be there," Beau said.

He and Annette stood in the door watching her walk down
the brick path. "Stu Favrot," Beau said. "I'd hoped he'd found
someone else to marry."

"Trouble is," Annette said, fingering the locket. "He's not a
grocer. And his name doesn't have the wrong kind of sound."

"I know," Beau said. Then he laughed, an echo of Claude.
"Mrs. Livaudais can plot. Stu Favrot can hound Caroline all he
wants. But it's like we say at home: 'Quelquefois vous plantez
des haricots rouges, et ce sont des haricots blancs qui pous-
sent'—Sometimes you sow red beans, and white beans grow."

"Good," Annette said, kissing his cheek. "I can think of no
better harvest."

12

Long before the Angelus rang in dawn the next morning, Beau
knew he must ask Caroline to marry him, must protect her
against Stu Favrot and everyone like him with a ring of gold.

We won't be able to marry right away, he thought, striding
through the damp mist that caught in the branches of the trees
like puffs of frozen breath. But we can be engaged. He walked
quickly toward St. Louis Cathedral, looming ahead of him
from its veil of fog. Winter's damp hung on like an old cough;
warmed by his thoughts, Beau hardly noticed it. He tipped his
hat to two nuns passing him, urging a column of little girls,
orphans from the home they managed, ahead of them. An old
woman dressed in black began to climb the broad steps, cane
held tightly in gnarled fingers. Beau moved forward, put a
hand under her elbow, and guided her. The eyes that peered up
at him from behind her wispy veil were filmed, their brightness
dulled as the rising sun was filmed and dulled by the mists from
the river. "Très beau," she said, and her aged lips curved in a
smile. "Très, très, beau."

His name, used in that context, startled him. Her face frightened him; incomprehensible as it might seem, she had once
been young, even as he was, with dreams, hopes—she must
even have loved. He held the tall carved door open for her and
watched her move across the stone floor. In a rush of feeling,
he hoped that there had been flowers along the path that led her
to this place, and that she had had time to smell them. Depression settled over him, brushed him even as the smoky air
brushed his skin, his hair. He knew that he would love Caroline Livaudais all of his life, that if he lived to the same
wrecked age as that old woman, his heart would either be torn
by her memory—or blessed.

"Beau! Beau!" The lovely urgency in Caroline's voice
pushed depression away and made room once more for hope.

He turned. She was coming up the stairs toward him, her
hands outstretched and her eyes beneath her veil speaking to
him as urgently as had her voice. He met her in mid-step, first
took her hands, and then circled her in his arms and held her.
He felt her head rest against him, felt her gloved hand reach up
and touch his face. "Beau." Now his name was breathed on a
sigh, and he knew at least one other heart had kept watch each
long minute of the night. "We mustn't be late," she said,
raising her head and looking at the church behind them. She
put her hand on his arm and moved with him into the cathedral,
down the long central aisle and into a pew.

Beau knelt beside her, his eyes on the altar before him, his
thoughts filled with Caroline. In this huge church, vaulting

hundreds of feet in the air, his thoughts seemed to compress themselves. While his family would not put up a hand to stop their marrying, they could not aid it, either. The Livaudaises were against him, and while he believed that Marthe de Gravelle would welcome him into the family, he did not think she would help him get there. Which left him. Incense sailed out in long gray puffs as the altar boy swung the censer at the Consecration of the Bread and Wine. He breathed in the sweet smell. He felt Caroline move beside him, saw her take a small silver rosary from her reticule and begin to tell the beads. He was not sure how he would manage this great enterprise, how he would make her his. He only knew that in St. Martin was a great stretch of land, which he loved second only to the girl at his side. He knew only that he would never be happy until he lived on one, with the other beside him all his days. He rose, stepped into the aisle, and let Caroline precede him for Communion. As he watched her walk toward the altar, he let his dreams bloom. Before too many months had passed, she would walk down an aisle to him.

"Let's have coffee," he said when they emerged from the cathedral into the quickening life of the French Quarter. He steered her to a coffee stall, ordered café au lait and calas. She remained quiet, keeping her eyes steadily on his face as though she had no other way to speak to him. He took her hand. "Well," he said. "And how was the opera?"

"The music was lovely, though the soprano was a very plump Madame Butterfly." She giggled. "Someone said she looked like Madame Butterball, so then every time I heard her sing I had to close my eyes to keep from laughing out loud." Then she frowned. "But, Beau, Mama had asked Stu Favrot to join us in our box—of course she didn't tell me, I wouldn't have gone." She looked into Beau's eyes, which mirrored her own annoyance. "He was awful; he never let me alone one minute, and during the entr'acte he paraded me around as though I belonged to him."

"Wish I'd been there," Beau said. "I'd have given him something for his trouble." He clenched his fingers tightly on the handle of his coffee cup. "Can't you just tell him he's wasting his time, to go make some other girl miserable?"

"Oh, Beau, he hasn't said anything yet. I can't just refuse him when he hasn't asked a question, can I?" She stirred sugar into her coffee and sipped, eyes staring into the distance. From across the square, the call of a vegetable man came. "Greens. Fresh greens. Yellow onions. Potatoes." The syllables were a chant, the voice rising in a bell-like call. At the final sound, there was a pause, and then, like a mockingbird practicing his repertoire, the chant began again. "Greens. Fresh greens. Yellow onions. Potatoes."

"Well," Beau said, keeping his voice calm. "What if you were engaged to someone else? Wouldn't he have to let you alone then?"

Her eyes flew to meet his, large with hope. "Of course he would. Everyone would."

"Then become engaged." He put down his cup so he could take both her hands in his. "To me."

Her eyes grew larger still, as though to take in every little bit of the world around them. Then a smile teased her lips. "Beau Langlinais, are you asking me to marry you?"

He burst out laughing. He kept forgetting how direct she was, how he could always say exactly what it was he needed to say, straight out, no beating around the bush, no pretending. "I am asking you to marry me," he said.

Her smile was wider, chasing any memory of Stu Favrot's attentions far away. "Because you want to relieve me of the unpleasantness of putting up with Stu Favrot?"

His hands gripped hers more tightly, squeezing them so that her bones became his, her flesh his. His voice was suddenly hoarse. "Because I love you. Because I love you more than anything else in the entire world, more than I ever thought I could love." He bent and kissed her quickly. "Because I love you."

"Beau," she said. "Beau, let's get out of here."

They found a small green bench sheltered by a great azalea bush and sat, bodies close, hands entwined. "You haven't said yes," he reminded her.

"Yes," she said. She laughed, the happy sound that had echoed in his mind all the long months of separation. To think of hearing that laugh every day of his life!

"I'll need to speak with your father," he said. "He's not going to like this."

"I don't care," Caroline said. She drew herself up in a gesture exactly like that of Marthe when she "put a poker down her spine." "Women in the East, they're different, Beau. They have ideas I'd never have heard of if I'd just stayed here." She laughed, and Beau could hear the woman that waited beyond the girl. "While Mama played bridge and angled for dinner invitations to Embassy Row, I kept my eyes and ears open—and I found out that no matter how hard Papa and Mama try to pretend, this really is not the Dark Ages, and I really am not a serf."

"If they say no . . ."

Caroline shrugged. "They can't stop me from marrying you, Beau." She put her hand against his cheek, making him feel as though he had been marked. "It's not as though you can't take care of me, is it?"

"I can take care of you," he said. His eyes were fixed on hers, his whole being locked to her.

She looked at her watch. "Heavens, look at the time. I've got to fly." She stood. "There's no question it would be nicer if Papa and Mama give their blessings. But with them or without them—I am going to marry you."

Beau stared at the slender girl at his side. Her pale gray skirt bloomed around her, just touching the tops of her gray kid boots. Her hat was of gray velvet, with great silk roses caught on its crown, and a gray veil covering her face. She was the picture of elegance and ease, wealth and grace. She looked as though she thought no further than the next tea dance, or luncheon, or theater party. But she had just made a declaration that, if it stood, would be like that first salvo at Fort Sumter, which had begun a war, and ended a way of life.

The golden glow of the candelabra on the cathedral altar seemed to hang in the air the rest of that Sunday; Caroline moved through what she felt was a softer, richer atmosphere, as though the joyous heights to which she had been carried really existed, as though she had truly entered an entirely different world. Catching sight of herself later in the long pier glass in the downstairs hall, she was startled. The mirrored girl was familiar, yes—but there was something about her which was different. Caroline swung around and faced her image, measuring it, looking it up and down. Finally, frowning, she turned away. Girls in love always think they are different, she told herself. That afternoon, however, Caroline was. At nineteen, she was neither girl nor woman, child nor grown-up. The intensity of her response to Beau, and the depth of her trust that their love would indeed be blessed, sprang as much from the careless enthusiasm of the child as from the new passion of the woman. Carried on the forward thrust of the joined force of both, Caroline drew her battle lines, marshaled her artillery, and threw her entire forces on the outcome of only one encounter. Had she been any age but nineteen, she might have known better.

She waited until midafternoon, when Charles was deep in the financial pages and Hélène had finished dissecting Society, before approaching her parents with her decision. The Sunday callers would arrive soon; Caroline told herself that only her anxiety that an early caller would interrupt made her tremble. "I saw Beau Langlinais this morning," she said.

Charles looked up in surprise.

"We want to be married."

Even in his shock, Charles had to admire her coolness. Damn, he thought. She's got courage all right. No beating around the bush for her. Of course, that's not always the way to win. Hélène's mouth had dropped open, the expression on her face still on its way from boredom to anger. Then her eyes finished the journey. "You said you were going to Mass!"

"I did," Caroline said. "We met at church."

"And where else have you been meeting?" Hélène said.

Caroline stared down at her. "At Nainaine's," she said.

"At Annette's!" Charles said.

"She always did have a penchant for peasants," Hélène said. There was a shrillness at the end of the last word that warned Charles to intervene before Hélène had them embarked on one of those tirades with which she relieved the frustration and rage she daily swallowed along with her morning café au lait and her evening wine.

"Hush, Hélène," he said. He moved forward, blocking slightly the direct sight line between mother and daughter. "Caroline. You know very well your mother and I will not give you permission to marry Beau Langlinais." His own voice was easy, calm. And though he felt an extremely rare and extremely small twinge of conscience at using his manipulative skills against his only child, he had always known it would finally come to this.

"Why won't you, Papa?" she asked.

"That should be obvious." He felt that Hélène was about to burst out and gestured her to be silent.

"But it isn't," Caroline said. "It isn't obvious at all."

"We don't have to give you a reason," Charles said. Now he let some of his sureness in victory show in his voice—there was absolutely no point in prolonging this miserable business by letting Caroline think she had a chance of prevailing.

"And I don't have to listen to you," Caroline said. She walked across the room and sank into a tall-backed velvet upholstered chair. "I would like to have your permission. Better, I would like to have your good wishes, your blessings." One small foot began to swing slowly, the only sign that her calm was held by force. "But if I have none of those, I will marry Beau without them."

The look on Caroline's face when she said those words pulled Hélène onto her feet and propelled her between Charles and Caroline. The years of being treated by her husband as though she had no body and by her daughter as though she had no mind moved her into one moment of violence.

"There is something else you won't have if you marry Beau Langlinais," she said.

For the first time since entering the room, Caroline looked at her mother. "What, Mother?"

Hélène took one more step forward. "Beau Chêne," she said, hurling the words at Caroline.

Even as the rage burned purely through her, she saw the sureness in Caroline's eyes begin to fade, and a sweet sense of power filled her. "I'll sell it. I'll put it on the market the minute Mama dies." Her head tossed. "God knows, the others won't care. Nanette always needs money for her natives and René always needs money for . . . whatever it is René always needs money for."

"Sell Beau Chêne!"

Charles had moved aside when Hélène had confronted Caroline; now, hearing the deep anguish in Caroline's voice, he almost wanted to warn her, to tell her not to so plainly put her pain in her adversary's hands. Then he froze. There were no clean outcomes in dirty fights; he had always known that. He turned slightly away and thrust his hands into his pockets.

Caroline went to Hélène, reached out to her. "Mama! Sell Beau Chêne! But why, why would you do something so awful, so mean—"

"Mean, is it?" Hélène said. "Mean, is that what you call it?" Hélène laughed. "Well, missy, if you are so madly in love with that . . . that farmer, so besotted you've lost all sense of what's right, I haven't." She paused, picked up a cigarette from a small porcelain urn, and lit it.

My God, Charles thought. If I had known how vicious she can be, I'd have let her make more of my bargains for me.

Caroline watched the thin blue smoke trail from her mother's nostrils; the smoke seemed like the air she breathed, a different kind of air, meant for a different kind of being. "I don't want the de Clouet heritage handed over to those peasants along with your body, Caroline. Let him breed on you if he must—but he won't lay a hand on Beau Chêne. That I promise you."

I wonder if I've missed something after all, Charles thought, staring at Hélène. Under that meanness, that sexual jealousy—was there still passion? Caroline, too, stared at her mother, but her eyes were dark with fear and her mouth made a small O of shocked surprise. "Mama . . . Mama . . . don't sell Beau Chêne. Don't sell it, Mama."

"Then don't you marry that Langlinais," Hélène said. "It really doesn't matter to me one way or the other, Caroline. You may have one or the other, but not both." She looked at her diamond-set watch. "I'm going to freshen up. We'll have callers anytime now." She crushed out her cigarette, swept from the room. She doesn't even need a parting shot, Charles thought. She had stormed Caroline's fortress, slaughtered its garrison, and left it in complete disarray.

"Papa . . ." She sounded so lost, so frightened, that he almost melted. "Papa." Her arm was on his sleeve, and then both her arms were around his neck and she was crying, huge heaving sobs that racked them both. "Stop her, Papa. Oh, Papa. Stop her."

"I can't," he said. And knew it was true. Any bargains he might have made with Hélène had ended long, long ago when the one he wanted most was made—she would not ask him where he spent certain hours, and he would be discreet enough so that no one could ever tell her. "I can't," he said again.

She pulled away. "You don't want to, you mean."

"I can't," he said. He put his hands on her shoulders and felt the gentle trembling of her body. "Caroline. If I ever had any . . . power over your mother—of any kind—I have it no longer." Looking up at his face, she saw his eyes reflect the stark reaches of the barren landscape in which he lived.

"Power, Papa?" Her hand brushed his face. "What happened to . . . love?"

"When two people bring out the worst in each other, there's very little of that," he said. He turned and went to the cellarette in the corner of the study. "I'm going to have some brandy. Would you like some too?"

"No—I . . . I've got to think. I've got to talk to Beau."

He swung around, the glass in his hand. "What are you going to tell him?" The agony in his daughter's eyes made him blink.

"That I can't marry him." Even as she said the words, Caroline still did not quite believe them.

"Does Beau Chêne mean that much to you?" Charles asked softly. Seeing his own daughter in such emotional devastation made him suddenly aware of the enormous amount of human pain a number of his meaner actions had caused, and he felt a small surge of repentance.

"I don't know." She moved, as though trying to push her way out of an enclosure. "How can I know what Beau Chêne means? I only know I can't be the one to lose it for everyone else." She raised her eyes so that he could see them fully. There was no child left in those eyes. The child had fled to the green reaches of memory, where hope blooms and prospers. "Mama knew. I could give Beau Chêne up if it were only me." She moved again. She was like the small animals Charles came across in field hunting, that scurry and run and dart and hide, only prolonging the time before the jaws of the hounds close on their necks. "But it isn't." She blinked and looked away, and he knew she was about to cry. "What makes the whole thing so terrible is that she's bargaining with something that isn't yet hers—and will never really belong to anyone. You know?" Then, feeling her tears to be a form of self-betrayal to be hidden from other eyes, she turned and ran from the room.

They had arranged to meet at Holy Name Church at noon on Monday. Beau, standing at the low wall that bounded the church grounds, saw Caroline walking toward him, hands thrust in a big fur muff, head bent before the wind. Watching her, he knew something was wrong. She was to have told her parents yesterday of their decision to marry. Suddenly, with a sick feeling he knew it was not going to work out after all.

"What happened?" he asked when she reached him. He was almost afraid to voice the question. Then, rapidly, trying not to flinch: "You're not going to marry me, are you?"

"How do you know?" she said. Her eyes were shielded by her veil, but he could see tears glistening behind the lacy mesh.

He pulled her out of the path of people on the walk. "Because I love you," he said. "I know because I love you." He put a hand beneath her chin and turned her face up to his. "And you love me. So why won't you marry me?"

"Mama has threatened to sell Beau Chêne if I marry you." She paused. "Beau, she means it."

"Christ!" He felt as though the entire mass of the land, his, Beau Chêne, all of it, had settled over him and was forcing him to his knees. It had a presence, it breathed and moved and sighed and laughed in his ear, it came between him and everything else, it pulled at him, stood behind him—as it did her. "Christ!" he said again. Her face in the wintry light was pale, a small white bloom that had been a promise of spring yesterday morning, but was now fading before winter's angry blast.

"What will you do?"

"I'm going back East," she said. "I decided this morning. I have to get out of New Orleans, Beau."

He caught at her hand, an absurd relief flooding him. "I thought she might have made you promise to marry Stu Favrot, too."

"I'll be gone before she thinks of that," Caroline said. "I'm going to stay with our cousins in New York, and I'm going to sit in on lectures at Columbia, and look at paintings until my eyes fall out—I'm going to the opera, and I'll haunt the theaters—I'm going to try to keep my mind busy every single moment I can, Beau, because if I don't, I'll surely go stark raving mad. I surely will."

He took her in his arms, oblivious of passersby. "Caroline. Caroline, you won't go mad. You'll want to, we both will." He kissed her pale forehead, her cheeks wet with tears, then released her. "But we won't, Caroline. You won't, I won't. We're the strong ones, and we're just beginning to find out how awful that is." He leaned back slightly so she could see his face. "Because the strong pay for and carry the weak, Caroline. As we are paying for your mother's weakness. For your father's. With our lives, Caroline. With our lives." His voice broke on the last words. There can be nothing worse than this, she thought. If there is, dear God, please don't ever let me know it.

"I'll have to marry, of course," she said, trembling. Her voice came from some dark place inside her she had not known about before. "I can't ever really live in that house again—and I want a family, Beau."

"Don't marry Favrot, Caroline. Please. I couldn't stand it if you did that."

"Favrot!" She laughed, a piercing slice of sound against the increasing cold. "And repeat my parents' history?"

"Then who?"

"I don't know. Someone kind, Beau. Someone I can trust. And respect. Because I won't love him. I won't." The dark place inside her was the grave each person carries, the grave that knowledge opens when illusions must be buried. "And you must marry, too, Beau."

"Why?" His eyes blinked in a sudden shaft of sun shimmering through a cloud that fell full on Caroline. He knew he would never forget this moment.

"Because you need someone to take care of you, Beau." She put a hand on either side of his face. "You rush into things, you don't look out for danger—people who live at the edge need someone to keep them from falling off."

"That's what you are, Caroline. And always will be." He stared down the avenue. It seemed to stretch into eternity. Looking into that implacable length, Beau thought wearily of all the minutes and hours he had to get through without Caroline at his side. There would be other women, he knew that. And he knew she was right, that he would have to marry. Still, he had that long march to make alone, and it did not seem fair, somehow, to ask someone to watch him make it when he did not really want her along.

"When are you leaving?" he said.

"The day after Christmas. I want to have Christmas with Grandmama. If it weren't for that, I'd leave tomorrow."

"Then we can see each other. I'll stay in New Orleans until you leave—"

She held out her hand. "No, Beau. I'm not going to see you again, I can't put myself through that." She looked at him. "I don't know how I'm going to manage . . . losing you, but I guess I will." The sight of her face as she tried to smile finished his destruction.

"You haven't lost me, Caroline. You couldn't lose me if you changed your name and dyed your hair and moved to Africa. I'll always know where you are, and what you're doing—and if you ever need me, Caroline, I'll be there so fast you won't have time to even worry."

"I know, Beau. I know. Isn't it terrible that we won't either of us ever be able to forget?"

She came into his arms then, stood in their strong circle, and pressed her body against his until she thought she had an indelible memory of how it felt to be held by the person you love the most in the entire world. It was a memory she would keep forever, until her own long march was over, and she could be put to rest at Beau Chêne.

13

Caroline left New Orleans the day after Christmas, heading for New York, where she could bury grief in an avalanche of new experiences. Beau somehow got through Christmas, through the New Year's fete, and endured a long and dismal spring at LSU. "Don't let them ruin your life completely," Annette Livaudais warned him when he crept to her for comfort. "Don't stop studying, stop making your grades." She grasped his chin almost roughly, turned his face to hers. Her lips curved in her familiar, cynical smile. "No way losing Caroline won't scar you. Don't let it maim you, too." Those few words had helped him keep going, but it was an exhausting business, and when summer finally came, he returned home to St. Martinville ready to plunge himself into the Langlinais world, ready to try to forget the painful memories he could not seem to let go. Ready for some peace and quiet, he promised himself. He soon learned there was little of either in a household that contained a volatile adolescent girl, as did his parents. "Watch out for Francie" was a new chore, one that fell to him as the protective big brother. At first, Beau thought her pranks amusing, a distraction from his sorrow. Then it became a chore.

One evening late in June, Claude came in for supper, seersucker coat slung over his shoulder, shirt sticking wetly to his back. "Rather plow three fields than listen to bankers hassle," he said. He sat at the table, reached into the pile of boiled shrimp, selected one and peeled it. Then he looked at the two empty places. "Say, where is everybody? Where's Francie? And Beau?"

He saw Marie's head jerk toward her mother, saw their eyes meet. Alice put sugar in her iced tea and stirred it carefully, her eyes now on the leaves of mint swirling around the silver spoon.

"I'm not sure where Francie is," she said. Her voice seemed to have caught the chill of the ice in her glass, and its fragility. "She should have been home two hours ago. I sent Beau to look for her."

"Damn." He heard the force in his voice, saw it hit Alice, shatter her calm. "Alice . . ." He got up and went to her, turning her sideways in her chair so he could hold her against him. "Alice, what is it?"

She was not crying, but her voice was muffled, threatened by the barely held-back tears. "She said she was going over to Barbara Landry's. When she wasn't home by five, I called over there. She . . . she hadn't been there." Her voice stopped. There must be more, Claude thought. From behind him, he heard Marie.

"I told Mama I thought she might have gone to New Iberia. There's a picture show she wanted to see."

Now Claude felt pinned between Alice's silence and Marie's words, words that spoke of things about Francie he didn't know. He looked at his elder daughter. Her eyes were large and calm, like her mother's. He saw no worry in them, no concern. Something else. Disgust? "Why in the hell would she pull a stunt like this, scare your mama, to see a show? Doesn't she get to see damn near everything that comes along?"

"Not this one," Marie said. She had peeled a dozen or so shrimp, arranging them neatly on her plate. Now she began to eat, dipping each one into the sauce in a small bowl in front of her. She raised her eyes to Claude's face, a catsup-tipped shrimp poised in front of her mouth. "It's got that vamp in it. That Theda Bara."

"But are you sure that's where she is?"

Marie shrugged. "I heard her on the telephone to Barbara, trying to talk her into something—and I heard her say, 'But, Barbara! It's got Theda Bara! And you know what that means.'"

Claude kissed Alice and went back to his chair. "What does that mean?"

Marie blushed, her cheeks suddenly blazing against her pale olive skin. "There'll be . . . love scenes, Papa."

"Oh, Lord," Claude said. He looked down at his plate. "Pass me the potato salad, will you, Marie? I'll tell you both one damn thing. She better have been at that picture show. Her brother had better have found her. Because she's caused just about as much trouble for her mama as I will allow." He could feel blood pulsing in his throat, knew his face was red, heavy lines creasing his forehead.

"Now, Claude," Alice said. "Now, Claude."

"Don't tell me 'now, Claude,'" he said. "Don't think I don't see how Francie gets around you. Gets around everyone. Well, she won't get around me."

The sound of an automobile motor throbbed through the open windows, and headlights made a slow arc of light and shadow as the automobile swung around the corner of the house and headed to the garage in the back.

"That's Beau," Alice said, rising.

"Sit down, Alice," Claude said. "I'll handle this. Go on eating, both of you. I'll not give her the satisfaction of having made a scene."

The door between the dining room and the pantry opened and Francie came through, her brother's big hand on her shoulder. "She was there, just like we thought," Beau said. He looked flushed and angry; along with the anger, Claude saw a trace of the look in Marie's eyes when she told him about the show Francie had gone to see. Francie's head was up, her chin high. Her eyes stared straight into Claude's, and for a moment he was caught by her courage, her grace under fire, even when she had started the skirmish, and with a sneak attack at that.

"Gosh, that looks good," Francie said. "And I'm starved. Don't send me to bed without my supper, will you, Papa?" She was already slipping into her seat, unfolding her napkin, quickly crossing herself and murmuring the blessing.

"Is that what you think I should do, send you to bed without your supper?" Claude said. He saw Beau take his seat and begin to spoon salad onto his plate. Beau looked relieved, a man whose job was finished. Claude looked again at Francie. "That's how babies are punished, Francie. Are you a baby? Is that what you're saying?"

"Do I look like a baby?" she said. Her voice seemed to have dropped, to have taken on a low, husky quality. Her eyes held him; when he finally looked away, he had seen Francie for the first time, seen that she was indeed not a baby, not a girl. Dammit, fifteen and the body of a woman—and apparently the appetites of one, too.

"You behave like one. Running off, telling lies . . ." The enormity of that struck him. "Do you know what happens to people who tell lies? They lose the trust of everyone around them. No one believes them, ever again. Is that what you want to happen? Your mama and me not to trust you?"

Francie had been eating, peeling shrimp, putting them in her mouth, chewing them placidly and with clear pleasure. Now she stopped eating, rested her head on one raised arm, and stared at her father. "I don't understand about that," she said.

"About what?"

"What you said. About lies. And trust. I don't understand."

"For God's sake, Francie! You lied to your mama, didn't you? You said you were going to Barbara Landry's and you went to New Iberia—" A new thought hit him. "How in the hell did you get to New Iberia?"

"I got a ride."

"With whom?" He saw her lips begin to form around words and knew that he did not want to hear the answer. "Never mind. Never mind. About the lies, Francie. If you keep telling lies, your mama and I won't trust you. Now, don't you see that?"

"I understand that. What you mean. But you see, Papa, I don't understand what difference it makes. If you trust me or not, I mean."

Claude could almost feel the silence cover the table, stealing from the four corners of the room with a heavy veil that quieted even the clatter of forks against plates. Then Francie spoke again, her voice still low, husky, not so much breaking the silence as entering it. "You and Mama wouldn't let me do things I want to do, a lot of times, if I told you about them. Isn't it better if you think I'm doing something you approve of, so you won't worry all the time?" Her eyes flicked across his face; he could almost feel their touch. "Because I don't think other people always know what's right for somebody else."

"Parents do, Francie. Parents do. My God, are you listening to yourself? You really think your mama and I would rather be lied to, you really think that will make us feel better?"

She gave him a final look, a look she might bestow on a curiosity in a museum. "It's all I've been able to work out so far, Papa. Maybe I'll think of something better. I hope so. Because you see, I am going to live the way I want to. I am." She stretched her arms over her head and yawned. The cloth of her dress pulled tightly across her breasts; the nipples stood out against it, two small points that made Francie seem naked, bare.

He looked down the table at Alice. Her eyes were on Francie, too. They were dark with fear; they made Alice look helpless and vulnerable. "Well, you're not going to break the rules of this house as long as you live in it, Francie," Claude said angrily. "You're fifteen years old. Fifteen. I think you'd better prepare yourself for a few more years of living in chains." He felt old, defeated. His enemies in the legislature, his opponents in deals, at least fought with weapons he knew, even if they were underhanded. But he did not recognize the weapons Francie used, had not known they would ever be brought into his tight kingdom. "Go to your room, Francie. I'll talk this over with your mama. And then I'll tell you what your punishment will be."

They all watched Francie rise, pull her napkin through the initialed ring, and turn to walk away. At the doorway to the hall, she turned. "It was an awfully good picture, Papa. No matter what you come up with, it's probably going to be worth it." Then she disappeared into the dimness, hips swaying slightly, head high.

"Now she's going to act it all out," Marie said. Her plate was clean, hardly a smear of catsup on it. "She'll rig up a costume and do the whole picture show in front of her mirror." Her voice was suddenly disordered, as though the tangled emotions of the day had finally found a way to disturb her calm. "It's disgusting. You should see some of the things she wears when she's acting. They're . . . they're not decent."

"You mean she asks you to watch?" Beau said.

"No. But she doesn't always close her door. Not all the way, anyway. And she leaves the shades up. Anyone passing by can see her. It's disgusting. You should do something."

"Marie, aren't you going to be late?" Alice said. "It's almost eight o'clock. Do you want Beau to drive you?"

"Paul and Helen Laborde are picking me up. But I'd better freshen up."

"She's going to a party at the La Fleurs'," Alice said. "Beau, weren't you invited?"

"I guess," Beau said.

"Well, aren't you going?"

"I don't think I will," Beau said. "I . . . I don't much feel like it."

Claude heard the anxiety in Alice's voice and sighed. She was worried about Beau—so was he, for that matter. Ever since Caroline Livaudais had gone back East, Beau had gone around tight-lipped and sad-eyed, walking like he was in quicksand all the time, just about to be pulled under for good. Claude sighed again. Damn! When the children were small, and there'd been the constant stream of measles and chicken-pox and broken arms and skinned knees, he'd consoled himself by thinking that someday they'd be grown up and he could stop worrying. Well, if that hadn't been a damn-fool thing to think. Here was Francie so far down her own path he wasn't sure he could even follow her to bring her back. And then there was Marie, getting set in her ways, beginning to think the road she walked was the only one for everybody else, too. People said she was like her great-grandmother, Françoise, who had damn sure run life with two iron hands. But Marie was too young for iron. What young man courting a girl wanted to hold an iron hand? As for Beau—

From the doorway, Marie spoke. "I hate Caroline Livaudais," she said. Her voice was low, but the intensity was as hot as the steam from the big kettle of shrimp, fueled by a deep vein of resentment and dislike.

"Marie!" Alice half-rose, gesturing Marie to silence.

"I do," Marie said. She came forward, stood by her brother, whose eyes were on his plate, head low, a sweep of light hair falling over his forehead. "She's hurt Beau, you know she has. Thinks she's too good for him!" Marie's eyes were not on Beau, nor on either parent. They blazed at some target only she could see, the passion that fired her bent on destruction. "Thinks just because she's a Livaudais and descended from the de Clouets and will own Beau Chêne someday . . ."

Then Claude heard the jealousy, and the envious rage, and understood. Next year Marie would be old enough to attend Carnival balls in New Orleans, old enough to be in their courts. Invitations to those courts would be going out very soon now; Marie would certainly be included in some, but how those would stand in the hierarchy of New Orleans royalty was another matter. Whereas Caroline de Clouet de Gravelle Livaudais, had the war not intervened, would have reigned as queen of the most prestigious of all courts, the privileged consort of Comus himself. "That's enough, Marie," Claude said, and made a mental note to get in touch with some of his New Orleans contacts. Hell, a man had no pride where his women were concerned. "That's enough, Marie." His voice was kind; he smiled at her and watched her anger fade. At the other end of the table, Alice relaxed, and Claude felt relieved. After all, his family was a fraction the size of the legislature; he could handle it. "Run on to your party, honey. Maybe Beau will look in later."

Beau's head lifted and his eyes met Claude's. For a long time, since he and Caroline had said good-bye, his eyes had lost all light; they stared out at the world like two gray ponds under a still, blank sky. For a moment, Claude lost heart. Already, too much energy had been consumed fighting the raging pyre of Beau's illusions. What would using more do? But if you don't try, you'll never know if you could have helped him. He could almost hear his father talking to him, hear him telling him it wasn't what you had that mattered, it was what you did with it. All right. He had a fine son, a son who'd had a big blow before his shoulders were quite ready to carry it. Well, dammit, there was not a thing wrong with Claude's shoulders, and if his son needed to borrow them for a while, all right, all right, that was fine with him. "Got some coffee, Alice? Beau, something kind of interesting's coming up, something you might want to take a look at." He took the cup Alice handed him, spooned in sugar. "There's a big rally up in Hot Wells on the Fourth of July. I don't usually poke my nose up that far, but this governor's race is pretty important— thought I might get an early sight on it. How about coming along?"

"Thanks, Papa." Against the kindness in his father's voice, Beau's own fragile shield of courage had no strength. Tears were suddenly in his eyes; he blinked and looked away. "I don't know—that's a week away. I don't know. Maybe."

Claude drained his cup, held it out to Alice. "You remember a little conversation you and I had, oh, a couple of summers ago, son? About the kind of war we got going in this state?"

Something broke the smooth surface of Beau's eyes, a ripple of memory. "I remember."

"Son, this election coming up—it's not just a skirmish, you understand what I'm saying? It's one of those monumental kind of battles, like Waterloo. Borodin. Gettysburg. You following me?"

"Yes, sir." Claude saw Beau's shoulders straighten, saw the ripples go deeper, something stir in the back of Beau's eyes.

Claude's voice dropped, became soft, confidential. "Well, now, Beau, I want you to be my aide-de-camp, see?" He laughed. "Son, I am venturing up into territory where they're not sure if Langlinais is a name or a cuss word." His hand crossed the space between him and Beau, touched Beau's arm. "I need you with me."

Then he saw it happen, saw the old, old dedication to family, to clan, take hold of Beau. "Well, Papa. Sure. Sure I'll go." There was pride in Beau's eyes now, pride and a beginning of confidence.

Claude tested his victory and risked that it had the strength to carry one more compromise. "Beau. Your mama would rest easier if you went by the La Fleurs' awhile." He glanced at Alice and saw that she was smiling. "Funny things make the ladies happy, Beau. How about it?"

Beau took in a large breath of air and then released it in a rushing sigh. "All right, Papa. All right." He stood up and suddenly grinned. "Anyway, Mrs. La Fleur makes the best fig ice cream of anybody, and there's bound to be a couple of freezers full." He went to Alice and kissed her forehead. "'Night, Mama." Across his mother's head, his eyes met Claude's. "'Night, Papa. And, Papa—thanks."

They waited until he had gone upstairs, looking at each other in silence. "What do you think, Alice?"

She shrugged. "It's a start. Progress." She shrugged again. "At least you've got him interested in something again. Even if it is politics!"

"Politics is life, Alice. Leastways, it is in this state." He rose and stretched. "Damn, since when does a family supper damn near wear a man out?"

Alice came to him, lips soft on his. "Not totally worn out, I hope," she said, as her arms held him.

Claude laughed. "Not totally," he said. He felt her quicken, press against him. "Never totally," he said. Then: "Alice. Make Francie wear a what-do-you-call-it? A camisole."

Claude pushed through the gathering crowd, beckoning to Beau to stay close. "The speeches won't tell us nearly as much as the audience will," he said. He waved to a man several feet away, nodded to another. "Damn near every political leader in the state's here in Hot Wells today, Beau."

Beau took off his hat and began fanning his sweat-grimed face. "All these pine trees make this place look cool—wish it felt that way."

"If the speeches are any good, you'll forget the heat," Claude said.

But the speeches were dull. Four of the candidates in the gubernatorial race had accepted the invitation to speak at the Hot Wells rally; the first three routinely condemned the Old Regular machine, knowing full well they had no hope of winning the Ring's vital support in the coming election anyway. The fourth speaker, who thought he might be the Ring's man, found other things to denounce, but neither the subjects of the denunciations nor the denunciations themselves could make the crowd forget the heat, nor the discomfort it caused them.

"There's Huey Long," Beau said to Claude at one point, nudging him. "See him?" He pointed to a man slouched against a bench. Claude looked where Beau pointed. Though Long's posture was relaxed, his right arm was moving, slapping against his thigh in a rhythmic motion. He was not large enough to be impressive by size alone, and his face, full, with a bulbous nose and a cleft chin, was not handsome. And yet . . . and yet there was something there, they could both see that. "He looks like he's scouting a field for birds," Beau said. "He hasn't kept his eyes on the man he's talking to yet."

"Man like Huey Long can't afford to work at only one thing at a time," Claude said. "Nervous son of a gun. The only time that man will ever be still is when he's in his coffin." They watched while Long shifted from the bench and moved toward the chairman of the rally, covering the short distance with a movement somewhere between a walk and a run. "Now what's he up to?" Claude said. The chairman listened, then nodded, then mounted the platform. The crowd was not only hot, it was bored. And its boredom was minutes away from dispersing them—they had come all this way to stand around in the July heat only to hear the same old political stew served up that they'd been fed over and over again, without even the compliment of new seasoning or a fancier plate. But when the chairman introduced Huey Long, stating that the railroad commissioner, while not a candidate for governor, wanted to talk about what was going on in the state, the crowd seemed to sniff the possibility of a new dish being prepared. Everyone seemed to settle down, gazing expectantly at the raw young man who got up on the platform and stood gazing back at them.

"What's he up to?" Claude wondered aloud. He, along with the huge throng at Long's feet, quickly found out. With no more than one fast slap at the Ring, Long suddenly trumpeted the announcement of a new enemy, Standard Oil. He systematically began attacking it on every front. "You all know I've been trying to get a lasso around that beast since I got elected to the commission," he began. His voice was clear, carrying easily over the crowd. "And you know I had drawn up a law, a good one, a pipeline law that would've made pipeline companies public utilities, so they couldn't keep freezing everybody else out." Now his voice rose, becoming almost raucous, almost like the cries of the crows that sheltered from the heat in the high limbs of the pines. "And you know what our good Governor Pleasant did to that law. He wouldn't call the legislature into session, even after I'd gotten my fellow commissioners to go along with the law." Long laughed, rocking back and forth on his heels, gripping the podium and rocking it, too. "And let me tell you, after what I went through to get Taylor and Michel to agree with me, that legislature'd have been a piece of my wife Rose's angel food cake." A sudden change, a gust of power, and phrase after phrase, heavy and black as the crude oil Standard Oil carried through its pipelines, gushed from Long's mouth. "Standard Oil carries crude oil all right, but it comes not from the independent producers of Louisiana, not from the people who pay the taxes in this state, but from Mexican tankers. Why, I've seen those tankers chug up the Mississippi and dock at the Baton Rouge refinery under the very noses of the people whose investments are being ruined with each barrel of foreign crude pumped."

"That's smart," Claude reflected. "A lot of the men here got stung when Standard Oil refused to carry their crude once the war was over—Long was one of them, and got hurt pretty badly—but what better bonds to hold people together than hating a common enemy."

"He's going after them all right," Beau said. Claude heard the admiration in Beau's voice and shot a look at him.

"Son—" But Long's voice, higher, louder, silenced him.

"Standard Oil is an octopus," he cried. "And the men who run it are among the nation's most notorious and leading criminals." A stir, like a breeze across the tops of the pine trees, surged through the crowd. "As for Governor Pleasant—he is the agent of the octopus. He proved that when he refused to call a special session to pass that pipeline law—proved what arm makes him dance!" The crowd was no longer bored, nor did it feel the heat.

"Say, who the hell is that?" Claude heard a man ask his neighbor.

"Railroad commissioner, didn't they say?"

"But, man, who the hell *is* he?"

The admiration in the man's voice was like that in Beau's. Then Long's voice rose again, filled the space above the crowd, lit a fire in the air. "Pleasant, it will take you forty years and forty barfly appointees to live this down!" The crowd's own voices reached up, blew away the sultry atmosphere, charged it with lightning.

"Guess I'll have to stand in line to talk to Huey, after this," Claude said, turning to Beau. He saw, for the first time since Christmas, light in Beau's face.

"Let's talk to him, Papa," Beau said. His fists were curled at his side, his body taut. "He looks like a fighter, doesn't he? Worth standing around for." Without waiting for Claude, Beau began pushing his way through the crowd. Following him, Claude wondered at the effect of his own prescription, that had wrought such sudden transformation in his son, who for weeks had been dragging himself around like a man condemned to death. Then all at once he understood. Huey Long's speech was stirring, without a doubt. But even more stirring, Claude realized, was that one of the arms of the Standard Oil octopus Long had railed against ended in Charles Livaudais' well-lined pocket. Politics, in this case, was a passenger in a wagon marked Revenge.

Layers of brown leaves, the top crisp, rustling underfoot, the deeper ones rotted from brown to the color of the damp black earth they covered, had drifted across the woodland paths, sifting against the exposed roots of giant oaks, catching in the space between low brush and ground. "Pretty country you have up here, John," Claude said to gubernatorial candidate John Parker. "I could walk from one end of my land to the other and never see anything higher than an anthill."

"We like it," John Parker said. "Question is, though, will

you get as good hunting up here in the Felicianas as you do at home?"

Claude grinned. "You promised me wild turkey for Thanksgiving," he said.

"And that's the easiest promise a gubernatorial candidate could ever make," Parker answered. "If you don't have a brace of turkeys, and some quail to boot, I'll concede right now."

Later, sitting over bourbon and a steady fire, feeling the good pull of well-worked muscles, Claude surveyed the political backers Parker had gathered at his plantation for the weekend of hunting. These men are not so much for Parker as against the Ring and its candidate, he thought.

"Never thought I'd see the day when I was hunting John Parker's land and drinking his bourbon," the man next to Claude said. He represented Governor Ruffin Pleasant himself, who, restricted by law to one term, had decided to make a complete about-face. He had fired hundreds of state employees in New Orleans who worked for the Ring, and now spoke at Parker rallies.

"You think we can make inroads in New Orleans?" Claude asked. "If we can't, Parker's finished. You can't get elected in this state without a big New Orleans vote." Over a fifth of Louisiana's population lived in and around New Orleans, and a sufficient number of that voting block marked ballots any way the Ring told them to. The Ring doled out jobs, distributed Christmas baskets and election advice; its boss, Martin Behrman, bragged that he could swing twenty-five thousand votes the very night before an election to any candidate he chose.

"That's right. But the Ring can't elect a man either, not without the country vote. So if Parker can hold those sixteen parishes he carried in 1916, take the ten in South Louisiana, and pick up some in the Hill country—we can get enough city votes to win."

"My group plans to deliver a hell of a lot of city votes," a man from the Orleans Democratic Association said. The group had split from the Old Regulars; it hoped to cut the Ring off and claim the election spoils for itself. He laughed. "We've learned how to deliver votes from the masters. It'll be fun to beat them at their own game."

A man lounging in front of the fireplace spoke up. "The Good Government League's hung on long enough without making any real progress. Hell, Parker organized the League in

1912, and we haven't elected a governor yet. This has got to be our year."

"Maybe you've finally found the right bed partners," the first man said, laughing. Then he looked around. "How come Huey Long's not here? Company too rich for his blood?" someone asked.

"That wouldn't hold him back," Claude said. "Not from what I've seen of him. He makes the occasion, and everyone else fits in. If he's not here it's because he's out stumping, making deals, pulling those strings he's got around those Hill parish voters. He pulled an organization his brother Julius put together right into his fold—one Julius had meant to deliver to Stubbs, at that."

"What do you think the Ring sees in Frank Stubbs?" someone said.

Claude held up a hand and began counting off on his fingers. "One, he's from an upstate country town; two, he fought in France, ended up a colonel of the First Louisiana Infantry, so he's a war hero; third, he looks dignified, the way a governor ought to look." He laughed. "What else does he need?"

"He needs Huey Long, that's what he needs. I still can't figure out why Long's working so hard for Parker—you wouldn't think he'd like one thing about him."

"He gets those Hill parishes for us, I don't care about anything else," John Parker said, coming in the door. "The cook tells me dinner is served, gentlemen."

Claude rose and followed the rest of the men out the door. Some of the game they'd shot that day would be on the table, and some of Parker's best Bordeaux would flow along with the hunting stories, the easy laughter. Parker's skills might be more subtle than Long's, but they were effective. By the time the dinner was ended, this unlikely group would have lost some of its hard edges that bumped and cut and ground. It would begin to fit together, to mesh. And by the time election day came around in January, he hoped it would roll across the state like a finely wrought machine, carrying the remnants of the New Orleans Ring with it.

Driving home in the hard clear air of late November, his promised turkeys bulging in his game bag, Claude felt optimistic. He had never really believed, when men opposing the New Orleans Ring had first approached him to run for the House of Representatives in 1912, that he or any other man could make much difference in Louisiana politics. He had remembered too well the flirtatious dance in which the Bourbon Democrats led first the Farmers' League and then the Populists. That dance had ended with the country bumpkin fleeing back to his fields and the city belle laughing behind her fan. There was no real reason to think that this time was any different. The coalition Parker had put together could win— but would it make a difference, when more than half the politicians supporting him did not support his platform? In fact, anyone following the campaign would hardly realize that Parker had a well-thought-out ten-point program for solving the economic and social problems plaguing the state; the thrust of the Parker message to voters was that the Ring rules New Orleans, and that rule is bad. If the voters were so foolish as to let the Ring elect another governor, the Ring would rule the state with the same bad result. Thus, a vote for Parker was a vote against the Ring. Parker was counting on sufficient people being fed up with the amount of the pie the Ring kept for itself before doling out the rest according to its own rules. Whether the votes against the Ring could be translated into support for Parker's reform program was something no one knew—or seemed to worry about.

Except me, Claude thought, as he turned into his own driveway. Except me. I know I'm not like the others. For them— well, the game is worth the candle. He caught sight of Alice standing in the door and waving. But for me—hell, the candle's got to shine pretty bright to keep me playing. As he ran up the steps to Alice, he breathed a quick prayer. "Please, God. Let my son find this. Please, God."

From the window of his room, Beau saw his father head toward the front steps where his mother waited. It was dark in his room, the shadows falling from the tops of the oak trees. A newspaper lay across Beau's knees, opened to a page with a picture of a smiling girl. A headline was followed by a story whose length attested to the Livaudaises' prominence. He did not need to look at the picture, nor read the story. The gas lamps marking the edge of darkness cast small flares against the coming night; Beau still remembered the words, every one of them. "Mr. and Mrs. Charles Stanford Livaudais announced the engagement of their daughter, Caroline de Clouet de Gravelle Livaudais, at an elaborate reception held last evening at their home on Fourth Street. Miss Livaudais will marry Dr. Raoul Marcus Hamilton, son of . . ." But what was the point of going on? It had been useless to warn himself that she would marry. Useless to tell himself that he had recovered from the pain. He remembered his own words to her. "We won't go mad, Caroline. We're too strong." He was tired of being strong. He had spent the day in his room, telling his mother he was clearing out the armoire where his stamp collection and all the other paraphernalia of growing up were stored. He had taken the *Picayune* with him. His family would find out, of course. Mrs. de Gravelle would have been at the party, would be full of the news when she came home. But by that time, he'd have found a face he could wear, a face that would never, never betray him.

A gust of wind rattled the windowpanes. The cold front he'd smelled earlier was coming in; tomorrow frost would silver the marsh grass, edge the ponds with mist. Good hunting weather. A good excuse to avoid his family one more day. He thought about the farm, about walking over it. The land would be hard under his boots, and Duke's fur thick under his hand. He could feel the long gun buck against his shoulder, its steady fire plucking ducks from the black air. Geneviève would cook breakfast for him, fussing over him, teasing him, loving him. He got up and turned on the lamp behind him. He needed a face to wear. His grandfather's face. That had always faced whatever it had to, when it had to.

From downstairs, he heard voices. Papa's voice boomed over the voices of his mother and sisters, telling them stories, making them laugh. Good. At supper, there would be all the talk of what had happened at John Parker's plantation. He could lose himself in that. Because what was good for John Parker was bad for Charles Livaudais. He must never, never forget that. Maybe not now, maybe not next year, even, but someday. Someday he would have Charles Livaudais where he wanted him. And before he broke that proud neck, he would give himself the sweet pleasure of watching Livaudais squirm.

14

White camellias banked the altar of Holy Name Church. They
also formed the bouquet Caroline held in her hands, the deep
green of their shiny leaves separating their color from the white
silk of her dress. The weight of the train seemed to hold her
back as she made the slow, deliberate steps down the aisle
toward Raoul. She felt the crush of people in the pews, heard
the sighs of admiration as she passed each one, her silk-shod
feet stepping on the rose petals the flower girl scattered before
her. She tried to focus on Raoul, think about marrying him;
otherwise, the setting seemed too much like a Carnival ball,
where the play ended and the royal robes were removed. She
knew that her decision to marry had baffled everyone—including Raoul. "I never thought you'd say yes," he had told her.
"Do you want to take your proposal back?" she had said,
allowing herself to tease this serious young doctor just a little.
"No." He had smiled. "Why shouldn't I have said yes?" she
had asked. And though she had not explained herself to him,
she knew very well the reasons for marrying Raoul Hamilton:
friends since kindergarten, they had been in the same dancing
classes, gone to the same tea dances, the same sailing parties,
the same balls. She liked his parents, felt close to at least one
of his sisters—and knew that Raoul Hamilton would never do
anything that would not bear the light of day. A very good
man, she had told her grandmother, referring to Raoul. I can
trust him. And she could.

She saw Raoul waiting at the end of the aisle by the altar.
She tried to memorize his face, to make it the one she saw in
her dreams. It's a nice face, she thought. Quiet, fine. But
somehow the quiet features blurred, the fine serious eyes
dimmed, and a laughing, bold face looked back at her, gazing
with love. Go away, Beau, she told herself, turning to kiss her
father at the end of the aisle. Go away. Then, with a deter-

mined step and eyes firmly fixed on Raoul, she went up the low steps to the high altar to become his wife.

Standing in the receiving line in her parents' drawing room following the ceremony, smiling and being smiled at, kissing and being kissed, Caroline longed for it all to be over. For these hundreds of people to finish pouring in the double front doors, for all the sandwiches to be eaten, for all the champagne to be drunk, for the cake to be cut, and for them to be gone away from here. Behind her, a small orchestra began to play. The crowd's voices rose over the music; all the sounds blended together and rose up against the ceiling, making the air feel solid and close around her. "Trust Charles to have the best champagne," she heard someone say. "Lucky thing Prohibition's not in effect yet. Weddings will be pretty dull affairs then, let me tell you." Another guest laughed. "Don't believe it for a minute. People are putting in private stocks to last a lifetime—if you're not, you're the only one."

The last of the guests had arrived, and the receiving line was breaking up, her attendants waltzing away in the arms of their groomsmen. Raoul held out his arms to her. She picked up her train and went into them, telling herself again that she loved him.

Stu Favrot stood against a wall, staring at her. She felt a small breath of relief and turned her face to Raoul's. He bent forward and kissed her cheek. "I love you, Caroline," he said. "I love you." Then he put his lips close to her ear. "Enough for both of us." The music seemed to become louder, to become a shield of shining notes that separated them from the other dancers, and put them in a close and private place. For the first time since she had accepted his proposal, she knew, not just with her mind but with her heart, that the place he made for them would be good for her.

Marthe saw Caroline slip away and knew it was time to help her change into her traveling suit. She made her way through the throng, hoping that Hélène would forgo pretending to be the devoted mother, and would let her and Caroline have this last piece of time alone. How good that Caroline would live in Lafayette, where Raoul was taking over his uncle's practice. She knocked on Caroline's door, entered, and took Caroline in her arms. "Oh, Caroline, when I think you're going to be so close to me!"

"Yes, it's wonderful, isn't it?" Caroline held something in her hand, a small, finely chased silver bud vase.

"You are happy?" Marthe said, trying to see into Caroline's eyes.

"Of course," Caroline said, but she did not meet Marthe's gaze.

Marthe picked up the jacket of Caroline's suit and began smoothing the blue velvet collar. She had been surprised when Caroline had called her one night in November and said she was marrying Raoul Hamilton. Caroline had been back in New Orleans . . . what? Three months then? "It seems very fast," Marthe had said. Caroline had laughed and said when you had known someone since you were four, there was no such word as fast. "And why are you marrying so soon? Late January— what kind of month is that to be married in? Wait until spring," Marthe had urged. "Be married here, here at Beau Chêne." "No!" Caroline had cried, and for the first time, Marthe heard passion in her voice. Then, more quietly: "Raoul's uncle died in October, Raoul is to take over his practice." There had been a small pause. "I'm not really interested in a lot of parties, anyway."

"Well," said Marthe now, "you were absolutely the most beautiful bride I have ever seen. You and Raoul make a very handsome couple."

"Not nearly as handsome as she and that farmer," came Hélène's voice. Marthe and Caroline spun at the same instant and saw Hélène standing in the doorway, a champagne glass clutched in her hand. She came slowly into the room and shut the door behind her. "She thought she was going to marry that Langlinais boy. Beau, they call him." Hélène felt their attention lock on her, and a small happy pulse beat inside her. "Told us she was going to, Mama. Oh, you'd have been proud of her. Fancied herself to be just like you, I imagine, with that famous strength we all very well knew only Jumie Langlinais could give you." Hélène lifted the glass and drank, her eyes glittering over its edge.

She really is a monster, Marthe thought. She really, truly is. She looked at Caroline and saw that she still held that small silver vase, her knuckles white with tension.

"But I fixed that," Hélène said. "I may not be the credit to the family you wish I were, Mama, but I'm not completely stupid." She lurched forward. How lovely to have them both staring at her, to know she could anger them, make them weep. How lovely. "I told her, fine, marry him. But you'll not have Beau Chêne if you do." She heard Caroline's low moan, saw the fear fill her mother's face. Advancing toward them, her champagne-laden breath encasing each word in false sweetness, she said, "I told her I'd sell Beau Chêne the minute I inherited it if she married him." The look on her mother's face almost frightened her, almost stopped her. Then all the days of Marthe's faint disapproval, all the nights of Marthe's disappointment in her, closed around her and she saw neither of them. "And I would have, too." She drank from her glass, finishing the last of the champagne. She set the empty glass down and stared at her mother. "Isn't it strange that a young girl like Caroline would prefer land to . . . her lover?"

In the heartbeat of silence that followed, Hélène wondered what would happen now. Would either of her listeners break, perhaps pick up a hairbrush or a mirror and hurl it at her? Would either of them break the senseless boredom of her days? Then Caroline spoke. "Raoul will be waiting. Will you help me with my jacket, Grandmama?" She picked up the garment and crossed to Marthe. Then she handed the silver vase she still held to her grandmother. "Beau Langlinais gave me this, Grandmama. He has wonderful taste, don't you think?" She allowed herself one proud look at her mother. "I wonder if you would take it home with you, keep it for me until I can come for it? I . . . I don't want to leave it here."

"Caroline—" Marthe's arms went out, but the plea in Caroline's eyes stopped her. She can't hold out much longer, Marthe thought. She helped Caroline into the jacket, watched while she settled the small blue hat on her golden hair. "Goodbye, Grandmama," Caroline said, kissing Marthe's cheek. She squeezed her hand. "I'll be down to see you at Beau Chêne very soon." One last look, one last brave lift of her chin, and Caroline was gone.

"That was terrible, Hélène," Marthe said. "Terrible." The fear that had shaken her had quieted, the shock had lessened, and she was looking more like the old Marthe, capable of facing anything down. "You know of course she will never forget what you just did?" Nor I, she thought. She remembered the evening of the party for Caroline, herself making it so clear that Beau Chêne was larger than all their dreams, more important than all their hopes. And she remembered watching Beau and Caroline together, knowing their feelings, empathizing in her heart—while her foolish old mind had allowed her to play the lady watcher and not become involved. Maybe Jumie was

my conscience, she thought, and in that moment, admitted she
was old.

"I really don't care whether she does or not, Mama. I really
don't." Hélène heard Marthe leave the room, heard the faint
slide of her shoes on the polished hall floor. She toyed with the
empty glass and smiled. Whatever they thought of her, she had
done it. Caroline had not married Beau Langlinais. Raoul was
a nice young man. Hélène lit a cigarette and stared into the
bedroom fire. But a girl like Caroline would not be happy in
bed with a nice young man. A small smile, delicate and half-
formed as the drift of smoke from her cigarette, spread across
Hélène's mouth. Good. Let Miss Caroline find out what it's
like to be in bed with a man who does not suit one. She rose
and tossed the cigarette into the fire. Thinking of the hours
ahead of her daughter, she felt finally satisfied.

Beau Langlinais, also in New Orleans that day, deliberately
avoided Holy Name Church, avoided any place that might
remind him that today was Caroline's wedding. He wandered
aimlessly awhile, and then took out a slip of paper upon which
was written a certain address, a small pretty house where, he
had been told, champagne was always on ice and the lady
always exactly the opposite. "One of my best girls," Lulu
White had said. Storyville had been closed down over a year
before, and its women had scattered, finding nests in which
they could continue their trade. "Go see her, and tell her I sent
you." He hailed a cab to the Quarter, screwed up his courage,
and knocked on the bright pink door.

"Chéri, you're going to get yourself drunk," the lady said
after he had emptied two glasses of champagne in less than half
an hour.

"Exactly what I came here to do," he said.

She shrugged. "Well, in that case . . ." and opened another
bottle. The next morning, having made him drink something
she said would cure his head, even if it did nothing for his
heart, she saw him off. "Come back when you don't want to
get drunk," she said. "And when your lady hasn't just married
somebody else."

Through the slow beats of pain in his head, he remembered.
They had gone to bed, the woman soft against him—and nothing had happened. Every time he looked at her, he knew that at

that moment Raoul was looking at Caroline. When he touched her, he knew that Raoul was touching Caroline. Something in him had turned to stone, and he found himself a leaden weight next to that warm, round body. He knew then it would a long time before he tried to have a woman again.

Three weeks later, Claude and Alice Langlinais arrived in New Orleans for a round of Carnival parties and balls. Their names were on a significant number of lists now; Governor John Parker did not forget those who had helped him, and his aristocratic friends had opened a number of doors that had formerly seemed stuck shut. Dressing for the first ball, Alice was happy. Her new dress was perfect, the scarlet satin setting off her dark beauty, the scalloped edge of the neckline showing off the smooth swell of her breasts. Miss Inez did a beautiful job, she thought, fingering the shimmering fabric. She thought of the dress Miss Inez had made for Francie, the awful way Francie had acted, stamping her foot and saying she hated dresses that made her look like a sweet little girl, that she wanted a dress like her mother's. Miss Inez had set her lips tightly over the pins in her mouth and taken up her scissors. "Stand still, miss," she had said to Francie. "I can fix it. Not like your mama's. But enough maybe so you can stand to wear it for your birthday dance." Miss Inez' eyes had been cold, and Alice knew Francie would never regain the ground she had lost with her that morning. She looked into the hotel-room mirror. Dark hair drawn back in a low French knot, with two waves curving deeply over her smooth forehead. Ruby earrings matching the sparkle in her large gray eyes, smooth line of cheek, throat, breast. She sighed. A wonderful new world Claude had conquered for them, one she couldn't wait to enter. But thinking of Francie, she sighed again. Thank God he did keep conquering new worlds. Francie ran through the old ones so quickly.

"Who's the brunette dancing with Favrot?" the man standing next to Charles Livaudais said. "Our call-out list has improved—look at that figure, would you?"

Charles, vision constrained by the mask he wore, followed the man's gesture to where a dark-haired woman in a vivid red dress waltzed with a costumed krewe member. Just before the pair turned and he saw her face, he knew it was Alice Langlinais. "That's Claude Langlinais' wife," he said. "I guess when John Parker swept into office he swept all the riffraff he'd picked up in with him."

"Riffraff? You don't have eyes, Livaudais. I'm going to see if I can exchange my next call-out. She makes even getting rigged up like this worth it." The man moved off, the satin bag holding his favors dangling from his arm. Charles moved back against the wall, standing clear of the people surging around him. His mouth had the sour, used taste that would get older and older until Mardi Gras night itself, when the season would end. He had drunk so much champagne at so many kings' and queens' suppers that he could almost wish the Prohibition that went into effect January 17 was effective; all it had achieved so far was that immense private stocks, purchased in the months between the Volstead Act's passage in November and the beginning of Prohibition in January, had been accumulated and hidden by those who could afford them, himself among them. His eyes, once having found Alice, had not left her. God, but she could dance! He remembered the feel of her in his arms at Ruffin Pleasant's dinner party. The way her eyes looked up at him when he teased her—the way her body had been pressed against his. A smile crossed his face for the first time that evening. She must be staying in town; surely it would not be difficult to find out where. And to call upon her. Feeling more alive, more interested in the scene before him, Charles took out the card upon which were written the names of his call-outs. Then, his step once more firm with purpose, he found his partner and entered the dance.

Claude had taken a suite at the Monteleone Hotel; it was foolish, he told Alice, to do anything but stay in New Orleans when the balls followed so closely on one another's heels. He could go up to Baton Rouge when he had to, and between parties, she could shop, meet friends for lunch, have a good time. He left for Baton Rouge early the morning after the ball at which Charles had seen Alice, planning to return in time for that evening's festivities. Alice, filled with the pleasant weariness of having danced well and often, lingered over yet another pot of coffee, her chair pulled up in front of double windows looking out onto Royal Street, idly watching people pass, holding umbrellas as shields against the piercing February rain. A day to stay inside and write letters and mend gloves, she thought. She settled herself at the writing desk, put a stack of engraved stationery on one side and a stack of letters and invitations to be answered on the other, and went to work. For a long time, only the sound of her pen scratching across the heavy paper competed with the low hiss of the coal fire, the quick beat of the rain on the windowpanes. Lulled by the rich quiet, the distance from her usual world, Alice slipped into a kind of cocooned existence where there was neither time nor place; when a knock came at the door, she went to it without thinking, her mind still encased by the morning's peace.

Charles Livaudais stood before her, a bouquet of yellow roses in his hand. Before she could close the door, he was inside and had closed it himself, his eyes never leaving her face.

"Mr. Livaudais! What on earth? Do you want Claude? He's not here, he—" She clutched at the lace that edged her morning gown, holding it closed over her bare throat.

"I have nothing to say to Claude," Charles said. His gamble had paid off, and that first success made his blood race—coming over to the Monteleone, he had told himself that if she were out, if he did not gain entrance immediately, he would abandon this whole idea. But this was success beyond anything he could have hoped. Alice in, and in déshabille that said clearly very little stood between him and his goal. "Nothing whatsoever." He moved a step nearer, holding out the flowers. "I hope you like yellow roses."

"I must ask you to leave, Mr. Livaudais," Alice said. She stood calmly, only the tension in the hand holding her robe closed showing her fear. But her mind moved rapidly, thinking of a way out. The suite had already been done, no hope that the maid would appear. And they were in a corner, down a short passage with a door that barred it from the main hall of the floor. Even if she screamed, who would hear her? And if they came, what would she say? That Charles Livaudais had attacked her? So far, he was only standing there, the roses between them like a shield. But her one quick glance at his eyes had been more than enough to frighten her. She had seen that look in men's eyes before, a combination of desire and laxness, of selfishness and power that turned everyone into an object with no feelings to regard, no dignity to respect.

He moved past her, stood in the door of the bedroom, and looked inside. "Very nice," he said, turning back to her.

"Claude does well for himself." For a moment, they stood in stillness. The sound of the rain seemed stronger, the hiss from the grate louder. Then he tossed the roses aside. Alice saw a fall of yellow as they splayed out against the deep blue carpet; there was another movement, something dark, something white, something silken, gray-striped. Livaudais was holding her, his arms clamping her against her sides, his lips searching her face. She twisted her head, held it back from him, tried to move in that circle of steel. "Keep fighting me," he said. "I like women who fight. It makes the . . . conquest all the more exciting." He shifted her position so that one arm was bound against his body, the other held by his hand. His free hand moved to her gown, found the tie around the waist, and loosened it. She could feel the silk being dragged from her shoulders, could feel it slide down her body. And then his hand slipped the small straps of her nightdress down, and it fell around her waist. His mouth came down over her breast, and as she tried to arch away from him, in the mirror over the mantel she saw a picture that would never leave her—herself, naked from the waist up, with Charles Livaudais bent over her, making her his.

If she were very still, if she were very quiet, let him think she would not struggle, could she get him off guard? He held her away from him and shoved the nightdress lower on her body, pushing it just past her hips so that only its own clinging fabric held it to her. She saw his eyes as he tugged the garment down and let it drop at her feet. They were no longer only lustful, they were angry, pierced with rage. "Damn! So this is what Langlinais has in his bed!" He grasped her and began pushing her to the floor, kneeling over her as she lay there pinned by his powerful legs. She could not believe this was really happening, could not believe that Charles Livaudais was really going to rape her. Claude would kill him, he would shoot him and tell any judge who questioned him the truth. Her mind beat against the hold Charles's eyes had on it. She could not tell Claude. She could never tell Claude. He would kill Charles, of course he would, and then the violence that was now contained in this quiet, rich room would spill out into all their lives, where it would poison them forever.

Charles was loosening his trousers now, those eyes still furiously on her face. Alice, with an act of will, forced fear back into its corner. Suddenly an idea came to her, an avenue of escape. She began to laugh, a light, clear sound that slid through the thickness of her throat and made a small opening in the blackness that surrounded her. She saw something flicker at the back of Livaudais' eyes and took courage. She laughed again, opening her mouth and laughing with her whole face.

"Are you hysterical?" He sounded more than angry, and for a moment she almost stopped. It's the only hope, she thought, and breathed deep, and laughed again.

"You look so funny," she said. "If you could see yourself. You look so funny." She forced herself to look at his open trousers. "Compared to Claude . . ." And she laughed again.

He will either kill me or be unable to do anything at all, she thought. The sound of the rain, and of the fire, filled her mind. She would not think of the man before her, or of what he could do. Then she felt his weight shift, felt him get off her. She rolled away, found her robe, and pulled it on. He was buttoning his trousers, his back turned to her. Don't say anything, she told herself. Stay absolutely still. She watched him go to the door, open it, pass out into the hall. Then she ran to it, locked and bolted it, leaning against it as though with her body to add to its strength. She saw the roses, still spread across the floor. And then she began to shake, and to cry with great tearing sobs that seemed capable of ripping out her throat. She stumbled across the room, fell on a chaise longue, and let her fear and horror and disgust surge through her. When it was over, when the last tears had washed her clean, she got up and went to the bath, where she drew a tub full of steaming hot water, scented with the new bath oil she'd bought at a French Quarter perfumery the day before. She lay in the bath a long, long time, forcing herself to look at her body until she could see her breasts without his lips, her waist and hips without his hands. She would not tell Claude, no, she would not do that. She would throw the roses away and have a good walk and a nice lunch and a long nap. When Claude got back from Baton Rouge, she would put on another beautiful gown and then he would take her to dinner at Arnaud's, and then they would go to tonight's ball, where she would hold her head high and dance as gaily as she ever had. But from this moment, starting right now, she would be looking for ways to pay Charles Livaudais back for the way he had looked at her when he had made her naked. To pay him back for what she saw in his eyes. Because what she could not forget or wash away was that for

one small moment, a moment she refused to believe in, she had
wanted him, too. And he had known it.

15

The Volstead Act took effect on January 17, 1920—the nation
was constitutionally "dry," but most of its citizens were still
"wets." It was no longer possible to legally buy liquor, wine,
or beer—but it was possible to drink. Both private citizens and
farsighted bootleggers had laid aside a huge quantity of liquor
before Prohibition went into effect. And the U.S. government
guarded millions of gallons more in some eight hundred warehouses; the liquor was owned by the distillers, but its use was
regulated by law. Representative James R. Mann, in a speech
in Congress on January 30, 1920, summed up well the difficult
position these distillers were in: "The man who owns liquor in
a bonded warehouse is between the devil and the deep sea. He
cannot sell it for beverage purposes. He cannot withdraw it for
beverage purposes. He cannot destroy it without paying the
government tax on it. He cannot make use of it in any way
except to let it remain in the warehouse at his own risk, not the
risk of the government."

By law, some liquor was released for use in the manufacture
of a few food products; rum was used in tobacco manufacture,
brandy to fortify sacramental wine. A great deal more was
released to wholesalers, who in turn sold it to druggists, who
dispensed it according to the dictates of an astonishingly large
number of prescriptions to relieve or cure ailments by the
judicious use of liquor or wine.

But the largest amount was "released" by bootleggers, who
took the distribution and sale of liquor into their own well-
armed hands. They raided government-watched warehouses,
bought from ships at sea, and had a steady source of supply in
the hundreds of thousands of moonshine stills which sprang up
all over the country, ranging from those making only five

gallons a day to those producing two thousand gallons of high-proof alcohol every twenty-four hours. This booze would fuel a decade-long party just getting under way; it would also fuel the big gangs and corrupt politics of major American cities.

No part of the nation was immune. Claude Langlinais discovered soon enough that if he were going to continue a lifestyle that included highballs before dinner and wine with meals, not to mention the requirements of the large amount of social, business, and political entertaining he and Alice did, he would have to find a dependable bootlegger. He found him in a former trapper known to all as 'Tit Jacques, a wiry, tough Cajun who boasted that he teethed on an alligator's hide and was weaned from his mother's breast to gnaw on duck and venison. 'Tit Jacques and his middle son ran their boat out to the Gulf of Mexico, meeting vessels bringing liquor in from southern ports.

Beau first learned of 'Tit Jacques's new business when Claude sent him to pick up a case of liquor one wild March afternoon. The wildness of the sky, wind-tossed, with ragged clouds like strings of hair blowing across a woman's face, matched Beau's mood. He felt wild most of the time now, wild and restless. Increasingly, it took a higher and higher pitch of excitement to release the tautness of his nerves. Caroline still dominated his thoughts. She had settled less than twenty-five miles away, in the town of Lafayette, in a big square white house on St. John Street, within walking distance of St. John Church. He had never seen her there. He did not know the color of the parlor draperies, or whether her front hall had wallpaper or paint. He tried hard to put her out of his mind. But still she haunted him, golden hair glinting at the edge of his dreams, silver laughter teasing in his ears. To rid himself of that image and that sound, he would do almost anything.

So when 'Tit Jacques mentioned, as they were putting the liquor in the back of the big Buick, that he would have a hard run that night, because his middle son was down with a bad ear, Beau leapt at the chance to test himself against the open waters of the Gulf, against the dark and unknown sky, against the danger of bootlegging. He would exhaust himself with excitement.

"I'll come," he said. "Let me."

"Your papa, he'd kill me," 'Tit Jacques said, but his eyes were measuring Beau.

"Not if he didn't know," Beau said.

'Tit Jacques shrugged. It was nothing to him, what went on between Beau and his papa. "So. All right. Be back at eight-thirty. Dress warm."

Beau got through supper, then went to his room to dress. He pulled a thick gray sweater over his head, tugged it down over the flannel shirt beneath it, then surveyed himself in the mirror. He set his shoulders, jammed his hands in his trouser pockets, and made a narrow line with his mouth. I need a cap, he thought. It'll be cold out on the water. He also knew that all rumrunners wore caps pulled over their faces so no one could see who they were. His excitement had been rising all after-noon, ever since 'Tit Jacques had agreed he could go. He knew such runs were just work to 'Tit Jacques, a man who had lived by his wits and his gun all his life. But the smell of danger, the element of risk—Beau smiled at his image, and took a tougher stance.

"You look like a thug," a voice behind him said. "Where are you going?"

Francie stood in the open doorway, giving him a look that seemed to say she knew every secret he had and some he didn't yet know.

"Nowhere," Beau lied. "Don't you ever knock?"

"Afraid I might see you without your clothes on?" she re-torted, coming into the room and picking up a cigarette. "Where're the matches?"

"Cut that out, Francie," Beau said, his hand coming down on hers.

"Oh, Beau, why can't I have just one little cigarette?" When Francie pouted, her lips became even fuller, her eyes larger.

"Because you look like a tramp," he said, pulling on leather gloves.

"Tramps have a better time than good girls," Francie teased. "I'll bet you'd rather be with a tramp than a good girl, Beau. I bet that's the kind of girl who gives you the best time."

"What are you talking about?" he said, feeling his face telling her more than the words he was saying.

"'Guilty conscience needs no accuser,'" Francie said. "Does the name Bootsie mean anything to you?" She laughed and darted away from his reaching hand.

"What do you know about . . .?" Beau said, and then broke off. He turned away to hide his reddening cheeks. Damn! How had Francie found out about *that?* "You're crazy," he said, trying to sound bored.

"You're the one who's crazy," Francie said. "Papa and Mama'd kill you if they found out you were going to see that whore."

The word entered the room and shattered Beau's calm. He whirled around and grabbed Francie's arm. "Don't use that word, Francie!"

Her gray eyes were steady on his. "It's what she is," she said. She shrugged. "It's nothing to me, I don't blame you at all." She laughed, and the knowledge in it chilled her brother. "Sometimes I wish there were men whores." She stared at him, unblinking. "But if you don't give me these cigarettes, I'll tell."

"Jesus, Francie," Beau said. He looked at his watch. "You're a silly girl. There's not a damn thing to tell and no one to tell it to. If you want to smoke and have Mama come down on you like a ton of bricks and probably get sent off to boarding school or something, all right. Fine. But get out of my room. I'm in a hurry."

"I'll just bet you are," she said, tucking the cigarettes down the front of her dress. "Have a . . . good time, Beau."

He found a wool cap, put it on, took up a flashlight, and went down the stairs. He thought of what Francie had said, that sometimes she wished there were men whores. Jesus. Where did she get ideas like that? Then he shook his thoughts away. She would never tell his parents he was one of the boys who visited Bootsie in her little house on the far edge of the town. Because she would never want them to know how much of the dark side she knew, nor how much it interested her. Thank God she's under Mama's eyes, he thought, and then gave himself over to the excitement ahead.

Darkness seemed to gather itself like a cloak around him as he drove his little coupe out to 'Tit Jacques's place. The moon was in the last quarter, a thin curved strip of light against the black, black sky. The cloud cover that had made the day a wintry gray from dawn until dusk hid the stars, with only a few of the brighter ones finding their way through the thick vaporous mass. When he opened the window to toss a cigarette away, he could hear an owl calling, the repetitive cry echoing down the sky. There was a tension in the night, a tension that matched the feeling inside him, so that he felt a part of it. He parked the automobile and made his way onto the low wooden dock, where 'Tit Jacques was busy in his boat. The wind that whipped across Vermilion Bay made a line of chill at the edge of his cap and around his neck. "So, Beau. You ready?"

"Sure," Beau said. He let himself down into the boat and saw the guns lying on its bottom. "What are we shooting?" he asked.

'Tit Jacques looked up. "This is serious business, yes," he said. His teeth flashed in a sharp-edged smile. "The law, it doesn't like what we're doing, Beau."

"Hell, nobody patrols out there. Papa says with the amount of liquor being made, sold, and drunk in this country, the Volstead Act was probably drawn up by bootleggers, they're making so damn much money."

'Tit Jacques grinned again. "Mais, your papa's right. It's a stupid law." He loosened the rope that tied the boat to the dock piling. "Stupid. Mais, you can't tell people they can't make a fête. And they can't make a fête without liquor, no." He moved to the tiller, his small, wiry figure moving with a kind of tensile grace. "Anyhow. You think I'm scared of agents?" He squatted over the motor, cranking it slowly. "Not me, no. But listen. Other men, they want that liquor, too. And if they wait, if they sit in their boats and wait, they think they can take it from me when I come back in." He turned and looked at Beau. "That's when this business gets very serious, Beau."

The excitement that was filling him rose higher, like a breeze ripping off the bay's waters. "Let them try," he said. "Let them just try." He picked up one of the guns and fingered its smooth stock. The boat motor was running now, its sound pulsing against the dark. 'Tit Jacques sat at the wheel, steering them clear of the reeds that clustered at the water's edge, heading out for the stillness that stretched before them down to the Gulf of Mexico, and to the boats that hovered just beyond the three-mile limit.

"Okay, Beau, it's all right by me, you're a man now, you can call your own shots. But, Beau. Don't leave anybody to talk. If we run into something. You know?"

Now the breeze was colder. It must be, Beau thought, feeling a cold chill run along his spine. "I can handle a gun," he said. His hand closed more tightly against the one he held.

"That's loaded; don't blow your foot off." 'Tit Jacques laughed. He sat at the wheel, one hand curved over its top, eyes fastened on the black water. His body was easy, relaxed. They might be setting out traps, or heading for a duck blind; Beau's own tension seemed out of place.

"In a few weeks, it begins to get light earlier and earlier," 'Tit Jacques said. "Then these runs—they not so easy."

"Still feels like winter out here," Beau said.

"Well, March," 'Tit Jacques said. "Like a woman. Cold one minute, hot the next. You know?" Beau heard the sly knowledge in 'Tit Jacques's voice. He thought of Bootsie. Hot all the time, because she was paid to be. Being with her relieved his body's tension; it did nothing for the pain in his heart. He was getting tired of her, tired of her sameness, her predictability. His hand ran down the gun. The feel of metal, the smoothness of the wooden grips, the quick slide of the action, the tautness of the trigger, barely squeezed to gauge its resistance, calmed him. "'Tit Jacques. If somebody does . . . try to stop us. Do we shoot across the bow?" Now he wanted to laugh. Words he'd read, words he'd imagined: Stop or I'll shoot.

"Mais, Beau. You didn't listen to what I said? You don't shoot across no bow. You shoot to hit. Beau, this is no game."

"Okay, 'Tit Jacques." He measured the flutter in his belly and decided it was excitement. "That's fine by me."

'Tit Jacques took a cigarette from a crumpled pack, sheltered it against the wind, and lit it. "Men who do that, take another man's haul, they're scum anyway, Beau. Scum."

Beau could imagine the rush of sulfured smoke in 'Tit Jacques's lungs. It had the same acrid taste as did fear. Suddenly he wanted a fight. He wanted another boat to loom out of the dark, wanted to feel the gun leap in his hands. Wanted to work out some of the rage and grief and loneliness that emptied him. Anything to assuage the deadness within him.

"We got a long trip, Beau. Sleep if you want—they don't mess with a boat going out."

"I'm okay." The motor was a lullaby, the waves rocking the boat a woman's hand. He was lulled, suspended between sleep and pain. There was no time, no space.

Suddenly, as he opened his eyes again, there was a shape, a low, dark bulk just ahead of them.

"Beau. You awake?"

"Yes."

"That's them. Be ready to be quick, yes!"

Men appeared on the launch's deck. They lowered a rope

ladder, offered hands to help Beau up. 'Tit Jacques threw a rope up and one of the men made it fast, tying it in rapid loops over the deck rail. Boxes stood on the deck, half-hidden under the burlap. Beau saw 'Tit Jacques take a small pouch from inside his shirt and pass it quickly over. The men's caps were low on their faces; they seemed faceless, bodies whose sole purpose was to pass the boxes from the launch to 'Tit Jacques's boat.

In less than a quarter of an hour Beau and 'Tit Jacques were heading home. All had gone according to some unspoken plan. Beau, watching 'Tit Jacques, knew he had seen another dimension of power, one that operated by its own law.

"Anna, she made some sandwiches," 'Tit Jacques said. "In a bag next to the guns." Beau found the sandwiches, thick slabs of bread filled with ham and cheese, and handed one to 'Tit Jacques.

"We wash them down with some beer," 'Tit Jacques said. He reached under the wheel and pulled up a canvas bag. Beau heard the faint clink of glass; then 'Tit Jacques motioned to him to take the bag and open it. "It won't be cold," 'Tit Jacques said. "But it's wet."

Beau removed two bottles and knocked the caps off against the side of the boat. He handed one to 'Tit Jacques and drank from the other. A bitter, remembered taste, a forgotten smell. "God, 'Tit Jacques. Where'd you get this?" He drank again, then wiped foam from his mouth. "This isn't any of that damn cereal beer."

'Tit Jacques jerked a thumb toward the boxes balanced in the center of the boat. "Same place I got that, I know where to get all the real stuff—liquor, beer, wine—champagne, Beau, real champagne, not that poison with the alcohol needled in." Before long, 'Tit Jacques reached for another beer. Beau took one too, and another sandwich. He felt good, being here with 'Tit Jacques. The food and beer had quickened him, brought him back to the edge of the world; he was ready to enter it, ready to meet anything it might have for him.

"You did good, Beau," 'Tit Jacques said when they reached the home dock. The bow bumped against the pilings, a thick clump of sound in the silently rising dawn.

"Not much to do," Beau said, stretching.

'Tit Jacques flashed his sharp smile. "You sorry we didn't have no trouble?" He slapped Beau's back. "Wait till you're old like me, Beau, you'll be glad it's easy."

They unloaded the boxes, storing them in a small shack near the pier. "What happens now?" Beau said as 'Tit Jacques slammed the door and set the lock. A large hound lumbered over and settled in front of the door, eyes watchful and mouth showing a row of teeth.

"I sell it," 'Tit Jacques said. "Hell, Beau, every one of those boxes got a name on it already." He laughed. "Your papa, too. You want to take it to him?"

"Not likely," Beau said, laughing too.

"Come back day after tomorrow," 'Tit Jacques said. "I pay you then."

"I don't want your money," Beau said. The look in 'Tit Jacques's eyes surprised him. It was dark, a look almost of contempt.

"Hell, Beau. The work was good enough for you. The money should be, too." 'Tit Jacques's eyes narrowed. "You take the money, Beau. That way, I know you don't talk." He thrust out a hand. "Come back day after tomorrow."

Driving home, Beau felt weariness overcome him. Damn, was there any other way to get sleep but in the arms of Bootsie or by exhausting himself courting danger? This, he thought, is a hell of a way to live.

But by the time he went back for his money, the wild mood was on him again, and he told 'Tit Jacques he wanted to make another run.

"My boy's ear is fine, Beau. He goes with me tonight."

"Can't three go?"

'Tit Jacques shook his head. "Don't take more men than you need, Beau. Loads the boat, makes more targets."

"If your son says I can go in his place—then can I?"

"Mais, Beau, I tell you the truth—I don't understand you at all. You come home for Mardi Gras weekend, you spend all of it running around in the Gulf in a boat, trying to get yourself killed. Why don't you go to parties like the other college boys?"

"Because I want to go with you." He continued talking, quietly, evenly, but not giving up until his determination had worn 'Tit Jacques down.

"So all right. My boy goes off to the fais-do-do, you go with me." 'Tit Jacques gave Beau a fierce look. "But no more, Beau. No more."

"I go back to college tomorrow anyway," Beau said.

"Good," 'Tit Jacques said. "And listen. You get yourself a girl, you hear me? A reason to stay home nights, yes."

It was raining when Beau and 'Tit Jacques set out, a steady pouring rain that obliterated their vision and made it impossible to separate sea from sky. "What are you steering by?" Beau asked, trying to peer through the sheets of rain.

"Guts," 'Tit Jacques said.

It seemed forever before they saw lights twinkling dimly ahead of them, small circles of gold in the wet dark. "Are you sure it's the right boat?" Beau asked. He felt nervous, not just excited, but nervous. His clothes were damp even under the protection of his slicker, and his face had been washed over and over again by the beating rain. Nothing was familiar, all was dark, strange—and frightening.

"Who else would it be?" 'Tit Jacques said. He took out a lantern and bent over it, shielding it with his body so he could light the wick. He waved it slowly through the air, three arcs of silver. An answering signal from the boat assured them of their welcome; they moved nearer, and saw the crew waiting.

"You're late," one of the men said as they loaded the crates onto 'Tit Jacques's boat.

"The weather. The Gulf, she don't want to behave herself."

"Don't get drowned going home," the man said. "Hate to have all that good liquor end up on the bottom of the ocean."

The miles between this boat and the safety of shore seemed suddenly immense. What the hell was he doing here? He thought of the party he had been invited to, of his sister Marie dancing and laughing with their friends while he made a damn fool of himself in the middle of the Gulf. He put his back into the task of loading the boxes, willing everything to go easily on the way back.

They broke out of the rain, coming suddenly into still, black air, leaving behind them the heavy clouds that bent over the water. "Rain's moving west," 'Tit Jacques said. He squinted toward the horizon, where bands of light were laid across the dark horizon. "It'll be day soon. I don't like to go home by light, no."

Beau roused himself. It was still night on the water, and though he could distinguish between sea and sky, could see the sides of the boat, he could not see much further.

"Maybe the rain kept everyone else in," he said.

"Maybe." 'Tit Jacques began to hum, a droning sound that made a curious counterpoint to the drum of the motor. The miles of Gulf water slipped away behind the frothing stern of

the boat as the moon lowered in the sky. They would be home
with the dawn, he thought, and his tension slipped away,
slipped into the moonglow on the water, slipped into restless
sleep.

The loud crack snapping the air above his head caught at him
as though it were a wire, looping itself around his neck and
jerking his head up. "Get down, Beau!" 'Tit Jacques yelled. As
Beau ducked, he felt the swerve of the boat as 'Tit Jacques
twisted the wheel hard to the starboard. Another loud crack
sounded, and suddenly a steady rattling sound filled the night
with dread. Beau heard 'Tit Jacques curse, and felt the boat
strain forward, trying to overcome the weight of the boxes, the
speed of the powerboat behind them.

"Machine gun," 'Tit Jacques swore. He crouched at the
wheel, his head down, hands gripping the wheel. "Like those
Chicago gangsters."

Beneath his hand, Beau felt the smooth stock of the rifle he
had checked on the first trip out. For a moment, the rattling
sound, the fear that emptied him, had made him forget that 'Tit
Jacques kept guns aboard. Then he thought, as he touched the
cold length of the barrel: One bullet, well-placed, could kill as
well as many bullets. He picked up the rifle and, for the first
time, turned to see what chased them.

The pursuing gunboat was low in the water, coming at them
with such speed that he was almost mesmerized by the graceful
power of it. A man stood brazenly in the bow, holding a
submachine gun that never seemed to go dry. Bullets hit the
boat as the gunman found his range, and Beau could hear the
soft thud as they entered the wooden sides, cutting small
chunks into the wood. He crept to where the boxes were, and
pulling his cap low over his forehead, made a quick gauge of
the distance between him and the gunman, the speed of the two
boats, and the angle. I am in a duck blind with Papa, he told
himself. Papa and I have made a bet. If I don't get this one, I
lose. His mind filled with the familiar image of marsh grass,
and the sound of beating wings. When he rose up and fired, he
was almost surprised not to hear the small plop the duck made
when it fell into the water, nor to see Duke leap forward to
retrieve it.

Suddenly the machine gun was silent. Beau looked up again
at the boat behind them. No one stood in the bow. The man at
the wheel jumped forward, bent over a shape in the bottom of

the boat. "God damn, I think you got the bastard," 'Tit Jacques said. "But let's not hang around to say the rosary, no." He turned the boat hard to port, got back on course, and kept the throttle on high. Beau clung to the sides of the lurching boat, his eyes on the rapidly vanishing vessel behind them. He saw the man kneeling bend over, struggle to his feet, and push something heavy over the side of the boat. The thing fell forward, entering the water, the only mark the circular ripples in the fading moonlight. All at once, as though each one of the spent bullets from the machine gun had hit home, something slammed against Beau's chest, sent him to the gunwale of the boat, where he vomited the food he'd eaten that night in a sour stream into the water.

For a long time he knelt there, heaving until there was nothing more to heave. His face was cold, and sweat like Gulf spray bathed its features. He fell back with his eyes closed to wipe out the sight of that form sliding into the water. Beau had killed the man with the machine gun. He could never pretend otherwise. He tried to remember how 'Tit Jacques had sounded the other night when he said any man who would steal another man's load of liquor was scum. He tried to understand that if a man were scum, and particularly if he were scum armed with a machine gun, Beau had no choice but to shoot him. To kill him. But the thought was larger than he, or his stomach, could hold. He lay in the boat and watched the sun break through the clouds.

It was not until they reached the dock that 'Tit Jacques spoke. "So, Beau," he said, giving Beau a hand up. "Maybe tonight was more than you bargained for."

Beau looked at the dark, wiry man in front of him. 'Tit Jacques was calm, relaxed. He would, Beau knew, never give another thought to the man who even now drifted in the currents of the Gulf. It would make no difference had 'Tit Jacques pulled the trigger himself. Beau did not know whether 'Tit Jacques was tougher than he was, or braver—or maybe just more foolish. All he knew was that something else had entered his dreams, a dark shape with a gun that spat fire and metal, a dark shape that fell at Beau's command.

"Maybe," he said. He looked at the boxes stacked high. Inside lay bottle after bottle of bourbon, real bourbon, not the rotgut people made in stills in their backyards or out in the woods or the swamps. 'Tit Jacques would give him a case of it, and Beau would hand it around to his friends, saying casually, "I ran out to one of the boats in the Gulf and picked some up." He had been thinking about that moment since the first run, thinking of going back to LSU with the boot of his car laden, thinking about the startled admiration on his fraternity brothers' faces—the amazed eyes of the girls.

The edge of one box was nicked, a narrow gash against the weathered wood. Was it worth it? Beau heard again the insistent rattle of the machine gun, felt the fear that had made him doubt his strength and himself. No. He realized how foolish he'd been to risk his life, to risk all that his family had labored to build for him and for the Langlinais clan, for one night's excitement. For a few moments of distraction from Caroline. He sighed. At least, though, he'd learned about one thing. He'd learned about fear, and the things it was all right to be afraid of. And he'd learned how to stop the fear.

He hefted a case to his shoulder, put out a hand. "Yes," he said. "I guess I did." It was not yet a statement; was, perhaps, a prediction.

As he drove home, the need for sleep ready to overpower him, the earlier realization that he had risked his life hardened into a complete awareness that he certainly could have been killed. One of those bullets could have entered his flesh, shattered the bone behind it, ended his life. Was meant to do just that. Behind him the case of liquor sat, a blanket thrown over it. Twelve bottles of bonded bourbon against the rest of his life. Damn! He stopped the car, and waited while everything inside him seemed to stop, too. He looked at his watch. Almost eight o'clock. Caroline would have seen Raoul off on his rounds, would be doing whatever young married women did in the morning. Behaving with grace and great good sense. Getting on with her life, even if that life did not have Beau in it. Damn! Sitting alone in his car on a deserted country road, he could feel blood flood his cheeks. If Caroline knew how he had been behaving . . . God, he was lucky. He started the motor again and drove toward home. He'd have a big breakfast, he decided, lots of eggs and yellow grits and a hunk of boudin and about a dozen biscuits. Then he'd sleep. And when he woke up, the world would be new, and he with it. He would be ready to go out again, to live again. Perhaps even to find a girl. He was Beau Langlinais, heir to the Langlinais lands, the Langlinais enterprises. For the first time, he realized that carried a duty with it, a duty to provide heirs in his turn. He began to whistle. Then he laughed. Damn it, providing heirs was one thing even a Langlinais could not take care of alone.

16

Lent moved gently through spring, toward the week-long break from classes Easter would bring. Though the solemnity of the season cut down on formal parties, Beau found plenty of gaiety at LSU—and plenty of girls. All of a sudden the world seemed full of them. They were in his classes, sat sipping sweet confections at the soda fountain, made clover chains from the flowers growing thickly in the spring-green grass. With other young men, Beau took girls on a ride around the streetcar line that encircled Baton Rouge, running from Main Street south on Lafayette and St. Louis, turning east on Government Street, north on Dufrocq, and then west on Main, bringing them finally to their original stop. He went to the Paramount Theater, drank coffee at the Old City Market on North Boulevard, listening to politicians who gathered there to gossip. His heart, that for so long had taken far more than its natural space in his body, began to hurt just a little bit less. He could almost feel it healing, and though he knew he still carried a scar, he could write to Annette Livaudais and tell her that he was not maimed.

By the time he drove to St. Martinville for the Easter holidays, he was ready for every kind of fun available, so long as it included girls. His spirits inspired Alice. "Let's have a party," she said. "You don't go back until Tuesday—how about a picnic at the farm Monday afternoon?" Beau got on the phone, calling his friends. At the sound of his voice, happy, enthusiastic, Alice almost wept. "Please God," she prayed during one of the Holy Week services, "let Beau meet a nice girl. Someone he can love, who will love him back."

The weather on that Easter Monday was perfect, the sky a soft April blue, the clouds delicate scallops of white, far too well-behaved to think of rain. The pink and white dogwood blossoms were being crowded out by their leaves, but wisteria still hung in lavender and white clusters from the vines on Geneviève's front porch, scenting the air with sweetness. Alice had driven to the farm earlier, and by the time the party arrived, wide tables covered with bright cloths had been set out on the long gallery, platters and bowls crowding every inch.

Beau spent the first hour of the party catching up with friends who went to other colleges, exchanging notes about classes, finding out that a surprising number of them were already engaged.

"Must be something in the air," Beau said, when yet another friend had announced his approaching marriage.

"It's our age," the boy said. "Time to settle down, get to work."

Beau picked up a piece of his grandmother's fried chicken and began to eat it. "Not me. I've got to finish law school, I've got years to go."

"Do like my cousin did. He read with a lawyer, then took the bar exam and passed it." The boy followed Beau's lead and started in on a drumstick. "Hell, Beau, what you want to spend all that time in school for?"

"I don't know," Beau said. "Never thought of not doing it, I guess." His eyes drifted over the people lounging up and down the steps, playing croquet on the lawn, and sitting at small tables eating. The afternoon sun was pleasant, softly warm. The air was heavy with the smells of new-cut grass and sun-heated roses. The girls' dresses, pale blues and pinks and yellows, blended with the flowers blooming in Geneviève's well-kept beds. Someone had brought a mandolin and was playing a tune; voices picked up the words, and soon they were all singing: "'A pretty girl is like a melody, that haunts you night and day . . .'"

Beau smiled. Yes, as Caroline had haunted him. But he had learned, he hoped, that haunts didn't keep you company, didn't hold your hand, didn't hug and kiss you. Caroline would always be in a special place in his heart, a place sealed over, so that none of the memories could leak out and dilute his life. He began humming, moving down the steps to greet his fraternity brother Hugh Abadie, who was just arriving. "'A pretty girl is like a melody . . .'" he sang. God, what a stunner Hugh had brought! He stood a moment, watching the couple approach.

The girl was small, with auburn hair that curled around her face and seemed to pull all the sunlight into a halo of glory. As they came closer, Beau could see that her eyes were golden-brown, almost exactly the color of the deepest part of Duke's coat. Though she was tiny, her figure was well-proportioned, and she moved with a grace uncommon in girls that short. Beau moved forward, hand outstretched.

"Well, Hugh! Glad to see you, so happy you could make it." He turned to the girl and bowed. "Beau Langlinais," he said.

"This is my sister, Louise," Hugh said. "She didn't want to come without an invitation, but I told her you wouldn't care."

"I guess I don't," Beau said. He offered an arm to Louise. "Hugh mentioned he had a sister, but I promise you, if he'd shown me a picture, I'd have been over to see him like a shot."

"Beau Langlinais is a terrible flirt," Hugh said, winking at Beau. "I want you to promise me you won't listen to a word he says."

Beau watched the way her mouth gathered into a small pink bud before she opened it to speak. "But of course I won't," she said. She looked up at Beau. "I've already been warned to watch out for Beau Langlinais, and I came here well prepared not to be impressed."

"Ouch!" Hugh said. He laughed and clapped Beau on the back. "I'm going to find some of the famous Langlinais food you promised," he said. "I think Louise can take care of herself."

The sunlight on Louise's hair seemed to glow around both of them, a tent of light for the two of them to stand in. "I have no intention of trying to impress you," Beau said, moving them toward the porch.

"Oh?" she said, looking up at him again. Her eyes had a light at the back that made them seem almost like chips of the sun. He wondered what they looked like when she laughed, and determined to find out.

"Cross my heart," he said. "I am going to be perfectly serious, and perfectly mannerly. In fact," he said, "I am going to behave so well that you will be bored to death."

She did laugh, a little tinkling laugh that made her lips curve up and wrinkled her lightly freckled nose. The light in her eyes did not change; maybe it was a little brighter. "I would hate to be bored to death," she said in a falsely solemn voice. "That seems to be a very . . . unpleasant way to die."

"Then don't," he said. He took her hand, held it for a quick moment. "Live dangerously. Don't listen to a word Hugh says about me—let me impress you."

She seemed to measure him with those golden-brown eyes, settling finally on his face. "Do you think you can?" she said. Her voice was low, husky. "Impress me, I mean."

A surge of feeling overwhelmed him. "I will or go down trying," he said. Then, "We're all way ahead of you," he said, leading her to the serving tables. "Except me. I've been so busy visiting, I haven't eaten a thing but one little old piece of chicken." He looked down at Louise. She wore a pale green dress of some flimsy material that swayed with the slight movement of her body. Her hair blazed even in the shade of the porch; he was right, she was a stunner. He felt suddenly shy, as though he had not been flirting with girls since he was fourteen. "May I . . . may I eat with you?"

"I don't know anyone else here," she said. She was looking at him when she said it, her eyes clear, almost blank. When he looked at her, startled at her answer, she blinked, and then smiled. "Of course," she said, "of course. I'd love it."

Now, that was funny, he thought. Awkward. Well, he chided himself, do you think all girls are born flirts? Some of them tell the truth. He settled them at a small table, eating and talking with equal gusto while Louise quietly forked food into her mouth, or meditatively chewed on a piece of chicken, her eyes always on his face.

"Say, do you like to dance?" he asked when they had eaten. "Hugh's one of the best dancers in the fraternity—I guess with a brother like that, you know how to dance, all right."

"I didn't have to learn from Hugh," Louise said. She patted her mouth with her napkin and then crumpled it next to her plate. "I guess I was clever enough to learn from old Miss Sarah Le Beau, same as everyone else in Abbeville."

Now, you have just got to get the hang of the way she talks, Beau said. He laughed. "So long as you like to dance, I don't care who taught you." He went inside and pulled the Victrola nearer the open parlor windows. He looked through the stack of records on the shelf, his hand pausing when he came to a recording of Kern's "Till the Clouds Roll By." Another party, another porch, another girl. He put the record on the bottom of the stack and found another Jerome Kern song, a new one, "Look for the Silver Lining." Taking her in his arms, he thought perhaps the glow from Louise's hair was a sign that there would be a silver lining for him after all.

The first shock of that small body in his arms almost made him lose the rhythm of the music. He found a way to make his body curve over hers so they could keep step. Her hair was just beneath his chin, wavy tendrils of it escaping and brushing his skin. Another surge of emotion—hell, he didn't care if she did think he was just trying to impress her. He waited a moment, praying his old skills would work. "You have the loveliest red hair I've ever seen," he said. "It's like . . . it's like . . ." He smiled down at her. "Well, it's beautiful." He held her closer, whispering against that glowing hair, "And so are you."

Louise did dance well, making up for her short height by moving lightly, always in perfect step with Beau. He waited for the space between them to close a little, for her hand on his shoulder to place itself more firmly. But still she danced with the slightest suggestion of formality, her head held carefully away from his chest, her body held carefully away from his. That small distance seemed unbridgeable; Beau wanted nothing so much as to bridge it.

"Is Louise . . . seeing anyone?" he asked Hugh when they stood in the front yard having a cigarette.

Hugh shot a look at Beau. "Seeing anyone? You mean a man?"

"Well, sure, Hugh." Beau laughed.

"I don't think so." Hugh tossed his cigarette to the ground, crushed it out. "But, Beau . . ."

"What?" Beau could see Louise standing on the porch, a space around her separating her from the other guests. "What, Hugh?" he said again, turning to his friend.

Hugh was looking at Louise, too. "Nothing," he said. "Never mind." He looked at the twilit sky. "Guess we better be heading back to Abbeville. See you at LSU."

Beau fell into step beside him. "What about Louise? She go to college anywhere?"

"Nope. Went to SLI for a semester or two, but now she stays home and . . ." Hugh lifted his hands in a gesture of male confusion. "Hell, I don't know. Embroiders little things, plays the piano. Does church work. That kind of thing. Girls' stuff."

Beau's spirits were suddenly high. Not seeing anyone special, not committed to college, or a job—he smiled. Whether Louise Abadie knew it or not, a campaign to impress her with Beau Langlinais had just begun.

He walked her to the car, lingering a little behind Hugh's faster pace. "May I write to you?" he asked.

"If you feel like it," she said. Then she laughed. "Oh, Beau, I shouldn't tease you, it's probably a sin, but it's so tempting! You look so shocked when a girl doesn't seem ready to fall all over you."

"I don't!" He stood stock-still, staring down at her.

She tapped him with the silk fan that matched her light green dress. "Never mind. Of course you may write." She laughed again. "I may even answer."

"She's an ornery kind of critter," Hugh said, turning.

"I'm beginning to find that out," Beau said. He helped Louise into the automobile and watched the Abadies drive off. Feisty little somebody, wasn't she? Went with that hair, he guessed. He thought of her, of the small, light body, the huge golden-brown eyes, the shining hair. She was pretty, and she had lots of pep. But something else, too. Something that made him vow he would write to her this very night, mail it in the morning before he went back to school.

"How was the party?" Alice said when he went inside to help her clean up.

"Fine," he said. "It was fine. Thanks for thinking of it."

She looked at him and saw something like happiness in his face. "You sound as though it really was," she said carefully.

"It was." He bent over and kissed her. "Hugh Abadie brought his sister. Did you meet her?"

"The pretty girl with the auburn hair?" Alice nodded. "I spoke with her a minute." She looked down at the basket of food she was packing. "Is she . . . is she nice?"

"Yes," Beau said.

The air in the room seemed to become quieter. Bless her, Beau thought. Her and Papa. It had been hard on them, too, his broken romance with Caroline. It would make them feel a lot better if he were seeing someone, were beginning to look around for a girl to court. He put a cloth over the basket and hefted it onto his arm. He didn't want to think about the future, not anything farther off than this summer. Classes would be out in a few weeks, he'd have the summer for getting to know Louise. He smiled. There was something about her, something about the way her small mouth moved so quickly when she spoke, that caught his fancy. He noticed that if she caught herself laughing with her mouth open wide, she quickly cut off the laughter, pulling her lips back into their small, neat bud. Looking at her mouth this evening, Beau had thought of ways to make it open, ways to make her laugh so that she would want her mouth open wide.

"Yes," he said, and he swept his mother up in a bear hug. "Yes, Louise Abadie is very, very nice."

Driving to Baton Rouge the next morning, Beau was thinking of Louise, and on the inexplicable fact of nature that the most down-to-earth, forthright men in the world could have mysteriously attractive little sisters. Claude, following that same road, was thinking of another fact of nature. That politicians would band together to get a man elected, and then not do one thing to help him put his platform in effect.

The current session of the legislature, to which he was returning, was a case in point. A pipeline law that would make pipelines common carriers, force them to carry all crude oil produced in the state, was the price Huey P. Long had asked for delivering the Hill parishes to John Parker in the January election. Parker's method of fulfilling that promise was the first in a long series of lessons he was to administer concerning the chaos a gentleman's code of conduct could create in the quagmire of Louisiana politics.

Claude found a message from Long at the desk of the Heidelberg Hotel when he checked in. "So what's going on, Commissioner?" he asked Long when the operator put him through.

"Not much I can approve of," Long said. "Meet me for lunch and I'll fill you in."

The dining room of the Heidelberg was filled to capacity, but Long had no trouble in getting a choice table. "It's this way," he told Claude. "Turns out Parker really is a gentleman through and through, and we've got trouble."

"Fill me in," Claude said.

"Problem is, Parker thinks everyone's as pure and moral as he is—can't imagine anybody saying something just because it strengthens their view." He took a sharp survey of the room. "Now, you and I both know, Claude, that if the men in this room voted from pure principle, Standard Oil couldn't get away with running this state. But they don't. Their principles are kept in their pocketbooks, and since the war's over, and Standard won't carry independent producers' crude anymore, a lot of those pocketbooks are mighty thin."

Claude fought the smile that wanted to greet this statement. Long himself had been hurt, and badly, when Standard Oil stopped carrying crude from the Pine Island field up in Caddo Parish, a field Long had considerable interest in. But it was true that Standard Oil had independent producers, Claude included, over the proverbial barrel. Except, Claude thought wryly, we can't even barrel the stuff and ship it that way.

"I'd think the independent producers would be united against Standard tooth and nail."

"Not hardly." Long sighed. "They'll compromise, be glad enough to let Standard Oil bake and cut the cake, so long as they get to lick the pot."

"What exactly does it come down to?" Claude asked.

Long pulled a piece of paper from his coat pocket and handed it to Claude. "This is my bill, the one I want in return for all those upstate votes that got Parker elected. It makes pipelines common carriers, pure and simple, completely divorced from producing companies. Hell, Claude, this bill is our only hope. Any other way, the big oil companies can slap on an embargo and freeze the independents out." He looked at Claude, his eyes shrewd. "Affect you, wouldn't it, Claude?"

"Some," Claude said. He played his oil interests close to his chest, never referred to them, and changed the subject when it was brought up. The war being fought over this valuable new resource would be a long one—but he was well-prepared to hold out. Between them, he and Dusty had sewed up St. Martin Parish, and Claude had expanded into Iberia Parish, joining with investors there. The leases were being signed, one by one. He had enough money to pay the yearly rent on those leases if they didn't bring in a well for five years. "Some," he said again. He handed the draft of Long's bill back to him. "Huey, this will never pass."

"That mean you won't support it?"

"I'll support it." Claude shook his head. "But I'm afraid I'll have damn few with me."

Huey's eyes became suddenly fierce. He fixed them on Claude. "If you knew how damn sick and tired I get of having to pussyfoot around all these yellow-bellied men who jump any old way anyone pays them to." His voice was low, intense. "Day's gonna come, Claude, when I don't have to do that anymore."

"Even a governor has to deal with the legislature, the courts," Claude said.

Long laughed. "You say," he said. "Come on, Claude, let's get out of here. Being in a room with so many spineless, sniveling excuses for human beings is making my dinner sit funny."

"They're the kind of people a politician has to deal with, Huey—you ought to know that by now," Claude said, following him from the dining room.

Long paused for a moment in the doorway. "Yeah. I guess you do." He smiled at Claude, a smile absolutely without humor. "At least I know they have a price. All I got to do is bargain 'em down a little and . . ." His hands made a sweeping gesture, one that took in the dining room, the hotel, the city of Baton Rouge, the state of Louisiana.

They walked through the lobby, pausing at the shoeshine stand to get their shoes cleaned. "How you making out, King?" Long said to the black shoeshine boy.

"Doin' all right, I guess," the man said. No boy, he was old, hair gray, eyes filmed with age. "One thing, I got work," he said, slapping his rag across Long's shoes.

Claude opened a newspaper, turned to the editorial page, half-listening to Long banter with the black man. He scanned the ten-point program Parker had taken into office with him, a program that seemed further from being implemented than if Parker had not won. A severance tax on gas and oil . . . good roads . . . labor legislation . . . conservation and reforestation . . . encouraging new businesses to come to Louisiana— something for just about everybody, Claude thought. The shoeshine man moved over in front of him, began rubbing polish into Claude's shoes. Except him. At least, as he said, he had work. Across the lines of newsprint before him, Claude saw the face of the black man who had come by the house in St. Martinville just days before, looking for work: a walk to sweep or a chimney to clean or wood to cut in return for a meal. He'd gotten work, of course, and the promise of more. No matter how often Claude told himself that there would always be such people who somehow could not find work to take care of them and their families, still, he had to help each one. But it's not enough, it's never enough, he thought. He watched the black man, who, although working on Claude's shoes, was still talking to Huey P. Long. I wonder, Claude thought, when men like that will be important enough for some politician to notice them? He shifted his eyes to Long's face. It was interested, warm. Then another face rose before his eyes, a face that bellowed against a hot summer sky, screaming against the monster that was Standard Oil. He knew then that the black man's long time of waiting was probably just about over. His and all the poor people like him. That should make me feel better, Claude thought. But thinking about Huey, about what he'd said at lunch that day, he didn't feel better at all.

Negotiations over the pipeline bill dragged on; Claude, making a path between St. Martinville and Baton Rouge that busy spring, thought wearily that if every point of Parker's program took this long to deal with, the firm hand of a governor who brooked no opposition would begin to look very attractive. Hell, he thought angrily, the man makes up a program and then won't do what it takes to get it passed. What it would take was swallowing some of Parker's ideas about gentlemanly conduct, ideas peculiarly inappropriate in that legislative setting. All right to have principles, Claude thought. Long as you understand reality. He felt soiled, abused, that he had carried Parker's unsullied banner into the field and was still covered with the same old political mud, while Parker sat on a high white horse and rose above it all. As the session wore on, Claude's spirits wore low, and the road between home and capital seemed longer and longer each time he drove it.

The road between Baton Rouge and home that year seemed long to Beau, too. Letters between him and Louise made a path his thoughts could travel, and as summer drew near, his body ached to travel it, too. Louise's letters were quiet chronicles of a quiet life: choir practice on Tuesdays after novena, hours at the piano, more at the sewing machine, with occasional mention of a luncheon or morning coffee to break the routine. She needs some jollying up, Beau thought, knowing he was just the man to do it. He began to imagine her as she went about her day, her hands busy at their tasks while that hair flamed and burned. By the time LSU let out for the summer, he felt he knew how she spent every hour of the day; each letter from Louise made collegiate life less attractive, the pull of domesticity stronger. The summer beckoned as a time for change, for ending this drift from adolescence to manhood. He loaded his coupe the final day of the semester with an odd feeling that he might never come back.

He told Louise about it his first night home, sitting on the swing on the Abadies' porch, a glass of lemonade in his hand. "It was the funniest thing," he said, watching the way her small foot pushed against the floor to keep them swinging, the slight resistance of the wood tensing her small muscles and enhancing the delicate line of her ankle. "I went back and forth from the dormitory to my car, a path I've taken I guess a million times, and it was like I didn't know the place. I was a stranger, and the funny thing is, I didn't care at all."

"That's not so strange," Louise said, sipping her lemonade. "I got the same feeling when I was at SLI. I was sitting in an English class one day, listening to the professor discuss a poem by Shelley, and all of a sudden I said to myself: 'What are you doing here?'" She looked at Beau, and one small hand touched one of his. It was like the quick brush of a bird's wing, light, almost accidental. "So I closed my book and picked up my things and I got up and walked out."

Beau was fascinated. "You didn't even wait for class to end?"

"No," she said, her voice calm and slow. "I knew I didn't belong there. What reason was there to stay another minute? So I went back to my room and I packed my clothes, and then I went to the office and I called Papa to come get me." She set the swing into motion again. "And I've never been sorry the least little bit."

"Well, aren't you *something*!" Beau said. He leaned closer. "I can't figure you out, Louise Abadie. But I've got all the time in the world to try."

She smiled, the small, closed smile that teased him. "You've got as much as I'll let you have," she said.

"Isn't that something? Just leaving college that way?" Beau said, relating Louise's story to his family at supper the next evening.

"Sounds crazy to me," Francie said, her mouth full of fresh corn.

"Don't talk with your mouth full, and don't call people crazy," Alice said automatically. "Well, but, it does seem a little sudden," she said to Beau. "A little . . . well, a little impulsive."

"I like impulsive people," Beau said. "Who wants to be around an old stick-in-the-mud? Pass the gravy, would you please, Marie? Say, Mama, I surely have missed this kind of cooking in Baton Rouge." He looked at his father. "Tell you the truth, I'm getting kind of tired of Baton Rouge."

"Well, you have the summer to get over that," Alice said briskly. "By the time college starts again, you'll be raring to go back. You always are."

Beau looked at his father again. "I was thinking," he said. "I've had three years at LSU. I wouldn't have to keep on there to be a lawyer."

Claude's eyebrows raised, and he put his fork down. "What's all this, Beau?"

"Well," Beau said, rushing the words out so he wouldn't leave any of the rehearsed arguments out. "Lots of people don't go to law school, they just read with a lawyer. Take the bar exam and do just as well as if they'd spent all that time and money at a university."

"That's true," Claude said.

"You know plenty of lawyers—there must be someone around here who would let me read with him."

"Why don't you want to go back to school, Beau?" Alice's voice allowed no evasion.

Beau faced her. "Well, Mama, it's kind of hard to court a girl when she's in one place and you're in another."

"Louise, you mean?" Alice said.

"Well, sure."

"You haven't known her long," Alice said.

"How long did you know Papa?" He saw his father grinning and knew he had won that point.

Claude blew a kiss to Alice. "Your mama and me knew we were going to get married when we'd known each other a week," he said. "It just took longer for the rest of the world to find out."

"Well, then," Beau said.

Claude put down his napkin. "Let's think about this thing,

son. I'm not saying I'm hell-bent for you to finish LSU. Wouldn't hurt a bit for you to be practicing law a little earlier, if it comes to that. I'll ask around, see if maybe someone could put up with you in his office."

"Thanks, Papa!"

Claude raised his hand. "Now, don't go thanking me yet. I haven't said we'll do it. I've said we'd look at it."

"Mama, you wouldn't mind having me home, would you?" He rose, went to Alice, and kissed her. "You're always saying you never see me anymore."

"I won't see much more of you if you're off courting Louise," Alice said. She was smiling, but Beau could see that her heart wasn't in it. Mothers! Not happy if you were suffering a broken heart, not happy if you were trying to mend it with someone else. He went upstairs to phone Louise. Be fair, he told himself as he waited for the operator to connect them. He knew he was considered a catch, and that his mother worried that girls were after him for his father's money and position, not because they loved him. He had seen the way the mothers of all those eligible young girls looked at him, with a yearning that told him just how happy they would be to see a daughter well-married to the heir of all that. But Louise wasn't like that, not one little bit. He heard her come on the line and pulled the mouthpiece closer to his lips. "I'm sending you a kiss," he said, feeling bold. "Can you feel it?"

There was a little pause. Then she said, "No, I can't." She began talking of other things, a hayride later in the week, a new book she was reading. When they finally hung up, Beau said good night, but he did not offer to seal it with a kiss.

Downstairs, Claude settled down with the evening newspaper and Alice picked up a batiste blouse she was smocking for Marie. "Claude?" He looked up. There were small lines of worry across her forehead; Francie had put most of them there, he thought grimly. They were talking seriously of sending her to boarding school; his sister, Claudine, said the Ursulines would educate Francie and keep her out of trouble, and while it grated on Claude to have to ask someone else to help him rear one of his children, he was damned if Francie didn't have them just about stumped, always trying to do things she had no business even knowing about. He sighed. More about Francie?

"Claude, are you really considering letting Beau leave LSU?"

Claude put down the paper. "Alice, I was fool enough to
think that once we got John Parker elected, some of my political battles would ease up a little. Well, they haven't, not one
damn bit. God knows how long this pipeline thing will drag
on." He shook his head. "If I've got to be protecting our
interests down in Baton Rouge, somebody's got to be minding
the store here."

"But what he really wants is to court Louise."

"All right. He's got to court somebody. The Abadies are
good people, I've known her father, Bob Abadie, a couple of
years now—"

"Claude. I've heard . . . well, I've heard that Louise is very
. . . pious."

"Most girls are, aren't they?" Claude laughed, thinking of
all the times he had thanked the good God that women could
kneel for hours, could tell hundreds of decades of beads, could
light one candle after the other, for sons, husbands, brothers,
fathers, whose love of God better showed itself in fields well-
tilled, animals well-tended. Laws well-made.

"Well, yes. I suppose so." She bent over her work. "But,
Claude . . . Lucille Comeaux, she lives just down the street
from the Abadies—she thinks maybe Louise . . . well, maybe
that's all she really thinks about."

"What, God? Well, Alice—"

"Not God," Alice said. She held the blouse up to see the
evenness of the stitches, stared at Claude through the thin veil
it made. "The Church. And, Claude—that's not the same
thing, no!"

Claude picked up the newspaper again. "Alice. If Beau decides to marry Louise Abadie, there will be only one thing to
say. And you know what that is."

"Yes," she said, getting up and going to him. "That we're
very happy. For both of them."

"Yes," he said. Then, hating to even ask: "Where's Francie?"

"In her room." Alice caught his swift questioning glance.
"Beau promised to keep an ear open, catch her if she tried to
sneak out again." Alice stared out into the night as though it
held some answer to Francie. "She was smoking again this
afternoon, sitting at her dressing table putting the most awful
purple polish on her nails and smoking. The door was open,
she didn't give a fig if I saw her or not."

Claude shook the paper, a signal he needed to be finished with this. "That settles it. I've told her time and again—I'll call Claudine tomorrow, ask her to speak to the Ursulines."

"I wonder about the wisdom of sending Francie to boarding school in New Orleans," Alice said. "So many more things to tempt her—"

"The nuns will keep her well locked up," Claude said. "Besides, sometime back, a Langlinais was an Ursuline—it's a family tradition."

"Somehow," Alice said, trying to smile, "I don't think that will matter a whole lot to Francie."

17

Early in July, the pipeline issue boiled over. The big oil companies, realizing they could not force their will in the usual way, asked Governor Parker to call a conference at which all sides could express their views, and a compromise possibly be effected. Huey P. Long, furious that the bill he was fighting to get through the legislature was being so violently opposed, mimeographed a statement condemning the conference and put a copy of it on every legislator's desk, as well as sending one to Parker himself. The statement, in the mode of Long's campaign oratory, said that Standard Oil was about to be part of the legislative machinery of Louisiana, and pointed out that whether the Ring or its opponents sat in power, it was apparent to him that the same "plunderbunding politicians" decided the course of Louisiana's fate.

Having denounced the conference, he refused to take part in it, attending it only to criticize the independent oil producers, who had, in his view, sold out—and sold themselves down the river. For the compromise bill was, like many compromises, suited to everyone and no one. Pipelines were not automatically common carriers, even if they transported oil from a producer other than the one that owned them. But the courts could declare a pipeline a common carrier if it carried other producers' oil with any regularity. "Now all the poor sods have to do is get the pipelines to carry them in the first place," Long told Claude. For a man who had just lost a huge battle, he seemed strangely cheerful; Claude realized that while the battle had been lost, the issue had not been. Standard Oil had not heard the last of Huey Long.

And early in July, Claude decided to let Beau stay home. "Come by the office around eleven tomorrow," he told Beau one evening. "We're having lunch with Mr. Walter Burke in New Iberia."

"Mr. Walter Burke?"

Claude grinned. "The lawyer who said he wouldn't mind too much having you clutter up his office for a while."

"Papa! I can do it? Stay and read law?"

Claude looked away from the light in Beau's eyes. God, he hoped Louise could keep it going. "We'll see how it goes. But one thing—you can learn all you need to know about law from Walter Burke. He was in the Senate when I first went to the House. He helped me a lot."

He drove to Abbeville to pick up Louise, whistling happily. "Everything's falling into place," he told Louise, helping her into the car. "I'm having lunch with Papa and Mr. Burke tomorrow, then I'll start reading law."

"That's nice," Louise said. She tied the long ends of a chiffon scarf over her hair; the breeze rising up from the fields teased at them, whipping them across her face. She sat primly, hands calm in her lap, eyes looking straight ahead.

"Louise, don't you understand what that means?" he said. "I won't be going back to LSU, I'll be here."

"Well, of course you will," she said. He waited for her to say something more, but she was staring out at the cane fields on either side of the road.

He waited for what seemed a very long time and then said, "What are you thinking about?" He expected her to turn to him, her big eyes glowing with that golden light, expected her to tell him how happy she was that he would not be leaving her.

She turned toward him. Her eyes seemed to come back from some distant place. "About the organ at church." She smiled. "It needs tuning, I think."

He felt the shock of her words go through him like the bounce of the car over the mud-tracked road. His shock made him laugh, a great shout that roared above the noise of the engine, into the falling night. He saw the confusion on Louise's face and reached over to take her hand. "Louise. I'm sorry. But you're so . . . I don't know. Most girls, if a fellow had told them he was going to be around all the time, would have . . . well, I don't know, blushed and giggled, and carried on, and finally said they were mighty glad to hear it." He paused and looked at her face. "If they were glad, that is."

She looked down at his hand holding hers and moved hers, just enough so that he let go. "I didn't know it mattered, what I thought, Beau." She looked at him. "You're not being a lawyer for me, are you?"

"Well, no, but . . ."

Louise nodded her head. "I didn't think so."

He waited, but she said no more. They drove on into New Iberia, to a dance at the Frederick Hotel. She was soft and small in his arms; dancing with her, he forgot everything else. Her body tantalized him, its smallness, its lightness, the quick way it got away from him. She let him hold her hand all through the movies they went to, though when the lights came up she quickly drew it away. And when he stopped the automobile in the shadow of a huge oak tree, rather than in front of her house where the streetlamp lit up the night, she let him hold her for a moment and kiss her once or twice before she pulled away. Her face in the lamplight was beautiful, with the mysterious quality he had yet to understand. Something different, something unique—whatever it was, it held him to her. He did not visit Bootsie anymore, had stopped two weeks after he got home for the summer. He did not want to go to Louise from Bootsie's arms; he told himself proudly he respected Louise too much for that. He told himself that if things worked out the way he was beginning to think they would, he would not need Bootsie, or anyone like her, ever again.

Beau was back at the Frederick Hotel with his father the next day, meeting Mr. Burke for the first time. Mr. Burke was mild-mannered, with gentle speech, but from the way his father deferred to him, Beau knew that Walter Burke was someone well worth listening to.

"Kind of a mess down in Baton Rouge, isn't it?" Burke said to Claude. "Looks like the people who got John Parker elected don't give one iota about getting his program passed."

"His behavior's not much help, Walter. He certainly let the big oil companies dictate a lot of that pipeline law."

"Think he'll let them run him the way they did Pleasant?" Burke asked.

Claude shrugged. "Hard to say. John Parker's rich, and he's a gentleman. Meaning he doesn't need Standard Oil's money, and he's not one to do anything unethical. But I'm afraid Huey Long's right about him—Parker thinks everyone is as nice as he is, and that is a big mistake."

"You and Long get along all right?" Walter Burke's eyes were mild, but the look he gave Claude was sharp.

"I don't know. One thing, Huey's a damn fine lawyer." Claude laughed. "Someone said he must have learned law from Old Nick himself, the way he can twist it to suit him."

Mr. Burke turned to Beau. "That the kind of lawyer you want to be, son?"

Beau felt grown-up, sitting here between his father and Mr. Burke, making arrangements to read law, talking about the future of the state as though they could arrange that, too. "I want to be the kind of lawyer who remembers what the law is for," he said. "To administer justice fairly, to treat every man as equal before it." He was suddenly embarrassed, and looked at his plate.

"Fine boy you've got here," Mr. Burke said to Claude. "It'll be a pleasure to have him with us." He turned to Beau. "My brother Porteus practices with me." He laughed and winked at Claude. "Your papa will tell you I'm the salt of the practice and Porteus is the pepper. Between us, I guess we'll teach you what it's all about." He looked at his watch. "I've got a client coming, don't want to keep him waiting. You come around in the morning, Beau, about nine."

Beau looked around him. Sitting here in the hotel dining room with his father, surrounded by men who, like his father, knew all the inner workings of the business and politics of the area, he felt good.

"You're sure you won't miss LSU?" his father said, signaling the waiter to bring their check.

"LSU?" The campus in Baton Rouge belonged to another period in his life, one that was over and done with. "Hell, no, I won't miss LSU." He grinned. "Everything I want is within a twenty-five-mile radius of St. Martinville. I don't need to go any further than that." He paused, then tested this feeling of being as old as his father. "I heard Francie yelling at Mama this morning. What was all that about?"

"She had just been told that she will be at the Ursuline

convent starting in September, and that for the first semester, at least, she will have no weekend privileges." Claude grimaced. "She was yelling at me, too."

"Gosh! You mean she'll spend every weekend at the school?"

Claude shrugged. "Actually, if she behaves herself, she can visit Claudine and her family once in a while. But she'll have to change a lot to earn even that privilege."

Beau felt a wrench, something inside that lurched out of its accustomed place. "Everything's changing so fast, Papa. Marie off to the normal school to be a teacher, Francie to boarding school in New Orleans, me staying here . . ." He shook his head.

Claude laughed, his hand reaching out to clap Beau's shoulder. "Son, I think you have just made a big discovery—that if there is one thing certain in life, it's that it will not stay still." He became serious. "And one other. It won't always move in the direction you want it to."

But at that moment, standing in the paneled dining room, the sound of polite talk and mannerly eating making a background to his thoughts, Beau Langlinais felt that his life was moving exactly where he wanted it to go. "Say, Papa," he said, turning to Claude. "How much money were you making when you and Mama got married?"

Walter Burke's office was in a narrow brick building on Main Street in New Iberia. The high, shuttered windows and fourteen-foot ceilings, combined with the sheltering oaks and breeze from the bayou a hundred feet behind it, kept out the July heat and made a place of dim calm. There was a large cypress table in the library, and it was here that Beau worked, reading one of the leather books that filled the tall shelves, making notes to go over with Burke later. Mr. Burke, he found, venerated the law as Justice's handmaiden, and treated it with awed respect. Coming into the library, his white linen coat damp, the smoke from his Havana cigar wreathing his head, he would pull up a chair and go over Beau's notes, explaining in his gentle voice a fine point of law in one case, illuminating the line of argument in another.

"There are things the law can do, Beau," he said one day, clipping the end of a pale cigar and lighting it, the flame blue against his face. "It can ferret out the statutes that apply, research the case law—make an argument, and find the evidence to back it up." He shook out the match and drew deeply on the cigar. The aroma floated up between them, joining the summer smells that came in the open windows. "But what it can't do is determine the truth." He sighed. "And that, Beau, is both our challenge and our cross."

"But there must be one side that's more right than the other," Beau said.

Burke smiled. "Surely. Trouble is, which side appears more right can change, depending on who's in the jury, who is the judge. Sometimes, it can change depending on the competence of the lawyers."

"Papa says the poor don't get much of a shake in the courts."

"Don't if they can't afford a decent lawyer," Burke said. He eyed Beau. "Lots of work for a man to do in this state, Beau. You going to be one of those who join the battle?"

Beau smiled. This had been the right decision, he was sure of it. "That's what I'm here for." He looked around him, at the sheen of leather books, the stacks of files, the shadowy afternoon world outside. "To learn how to get into the battle—and win."

The days of July and August slipped by one after the other as easily and smoothly as Beau's grandmother's rosary beads slipped through her hands. The days had a pattern now; every morning at nine o'clock to the Burke law office on Main Street, every evening to Abbeville to court Louise. When September came, it was taken as a matter of course that Louise Abadie was Beau Langlinais' girl; if no more formal commitment than that was made, it was because that too would come in time, the harvest of all the love seeds he had sown. September brought Francie's departure, a Francie seemingly resigned, seemingly aware that her parents really had her best interests at heart.

"You know people in New Orleans, don't you?" she asked Beau her last day at home.

"Well, sure. People I went to school with—they're too old for you, Francie."

"Now, don't go jumping on me," she said, her lips quivering and her eyes tearful. "I'm going to be good, I promise I am, Beau. I never thought Mama and Papa really meant they'd send me off. If I had, I'd have—" She bit her lip. "Well, never mind. I'm stuck and I'm going to make the best of it." She went closer to Beau. "Wasn't there that aunt of Caroline Livaudais' you liked so much?"

"Annette? Goodness, Francie, she's old! What would you want to know her for?"

Francie tossed her dark head. "Well, she may be old, but she did sound like she had a little . . . go to her. A little pep. Won't you write to her, Beau? Ask her to take me out sometime?"

"Papa said you had to stay at the convent every weekend," Beau said.

"But if I'm very good, and the sisters say so, he'll let me go out a little." She drew herself up and her eyes flashed. "And I intend to be good, Beau. I really do."

He relented. Poor little girl, they had come down on her mighty hard. In his own happiness, he could forget the trouble she had caused. He tweaked one of her curls and kissed her cheek. "All right, Francie. You behave yourself and I will. I'll write to Annette and ask her to look you up."

"Oh, Beau, you're the best brother in the world!" Francie said, hugging him.

Marie, going down the hall with a stack of blouses for her own trunk, looked at them and frowned. "You'll never learn, will you, Beau?" she said. "Francie hasn't changed, she never will."

Beau patted Francie's shoulder and turned to follow Marie. "Don't be so mean, Marie. Give her a chance."

"She's had more than I'd ever give her as it is," Marie said. She put the blouses in an open drawer of her trunk and patted them. "Well, it's not my problem. I'm off to do what I want for a change, let someone else watch Miss Francie."

He went slowly to his room. Things had changed more than he knew. Marie didn't even talk like she belonged to the family anymore. The house, which for as long as he could remember had been filled with the sounds of life and laughter—and bickering, too, he had to admit—was quiet. It would be this quiet from now on, he thought, and shivered. And went to phone Louise.

The fires of October, burning the stubble left in the fields after harvest, blew smoke over the land, great lazy rings of it that curled into the low ground, hazing it, blurring the cut-over fields and browning pasture. The three of them, Claude and Alice and Beau, gathered at a supper table that was suddenly shrunken, and welcomed the occasions when Geneviève could be persuaded to come in from the farm and fill up the empty places.

She came one afternoon, bearing fresh ham and thick pork chops, boudin and cracklings from the boucherie. "You have news from the girls?"

"Marie has made an A on every test since school started and Francie hasn't risen above a C," Alice said.

Geneviève shrugged. "Well, Marie wants to teach, she has to be smart. But Francie . . ." She looked at Alice. "Francie will marry, she doesn't need to make A's for that."

"Speaking of weddings," Beau said, his eyes teasing her, "I'm going to be in one. Not mine," he said quickly, when she looked at him sharply. "Not yet, anyway. A fraternity brother of mine is getting married in New Orleans this weekend—I'm supposed to usher."

"So many young people getting married," Geneviève said. "Such a hurry they're in." She buttered a biscuit and looked at Beau. "Your mama and I met Mrs. Abadie this morning, Beau."

He waited for her to say something else. "She's very nice," Alice said quickly, filling the gap. "Very . . . very interested in . . . well, in what you're doing, Beau." She seemed to realize the implications of her words and stopped.

"I had an idea she had you all picked out for Louise," Geneviève said.

"Now, Grandmama—"

"Well, for heaven's sake, why shouldn't she?" Alice said. "She and every other mother for miles around. And I don't blame them. When it comes time for Francie and Marie to marry, I'd be very satisfied with a young man just like Beau."

"I imagine Beau can decide all that for himself," Claude said, and changed the topic.

Beau heard the swell of talk around him, and let it slide into the background of his thoughts. He pictured Louise, the way her small hands seemed to draw together all the pieces of his life to make a whole that would surround him and become his world. There were times, leaving the law office in New Iberia, scuffling leaves as he walked to his automobile, that that world seemed inexplicably, achingly desirable, a beautiful illusion almost within his grasp. Questions of politics and business faded and disappeared when she was near. He would go to his fraternity brother's wedding—and he would take notes.

Beau had gotten out of the habit of looking for her, was no longer accustomed to scanning a people-filled room with eyes that saw her image and nothing else. When he saw her at the wedding reception in New Orleans that weekend, it was with the shocked recognition that he had not thought of Caroline in weeks. He saw her lift her chin in the familiar tilt, heard the familiar laughter silver the air, and pushed his way through the crowd to test this hard-found objectivity. He stood at her side, waiting for her to notice him. She turned her head toward him, her eyes polite. Then she saw him—saw him, he knew, with her heart. His own heart lurched, and he knew he could be objective only so long, and so far. "Why, Beau! Beau Langlinais!" Her lips closed tightly over what else she might have been going to say; she formed them in a smile and offered her hand. The couple she had been talking to moved away, leaving them caught in a flow of people that rippled through the reception rooms like strands of many-colored silk.

"How are you, Caroline?" he asked. He heard the low intimacy in his voice, saw its reflection in her eyes, and cleared his throat. In a louder voice he asked, "What have you been up to?"

"Let's sit over there a minute, can we, Beau?" Caroline said. "I tried to cram three days into one, I'm afraid, and I'm all tuckered out." Her words were clear, the tone carrying. Beau followed her to a small sofa in an alcove, smiling. She hadn't changed one bit. She still had that charming way of arranging the world in a better order, a more pleasing situation. He took two glasses of champagne from a passing waiter's tray, handed her one, and seated himself beside her, engraving the soft lines of her blue dress, and the way her hair curved around her forehead, in that sealed place where her memory lived.

"You won't ever guess what I have been doing, Beau," she said. Her blue eyes were clear, happy, filled with the mischief he remembered so well.

"I wouldn't be so foolish as to even *try* to guess what you might set your mind on, Caroline," he said. Comfort covered him like one of Geneviève's quilts. He had forgotten how easy she was to be with, how ideas seemed to dance across the space between them without words at all. "What have you been doing?"

"Trying to get the women in Lafayette to register to vote." She laughed. "You do know that women are allowed to vote now, don't you, Beau?"

"Sure," he said. "Word does penetrate to the outback. All that time in the East—I guess you did hear a lot about women's suffrage."

"I more than heard about it. I went to meetings and addressed envelopes and even had tea with Mrs. Carrie Catt, the main force behind the whole movement. Beau, I wish you could meet her, she's so wonderful!" Her eyes glowed in a new way, the passion behind them a passion for ideas, for causes. He was suddenly sad. He had thought to see that burning in her eyes for him, had thought himself to be the only one who could cause that glow, or know the passion behind it.

"She's supposed to be effective, all right. Worked miracles getting the amendment passed."

"I went up to Nashville, Beau. For the vote in the Tennessee legislature."

"You did!"

"Oh, Beau, what a lesson in politics it was!" She was animated, filled with excitement; her words bubbled like the champagne in her glass, and made her light-headed. "I can't tell you what pressure everybody was under—the rumors on all sides, the efforts the opposition made to get representatives on our side out of town. Why, Beau, one representative on our side was halfway home to see about his baby, who was ill, when we got him back to the session by arranging a special train to take him home later that day!"

"Didn't you have to fight over again, even when they passed it?"

She had reached out to touch him, one light hand unconsciously holding his arm. "Beau, it was awful! The very minute most of the legislature had gone home, the opposition came in a body and voted to suspend the ratification." She lifted her chin in that way the de Clouets had; he had to smile when he thought of that rowdy Tennessee legislature being subjected to that proud stare. "Of course, that wasn't legal, they couldn't really do that, but Mrs. Catt was afraid we'd lose the whole amendment, so all kinds of pressure was put on the Connecticut legislature, and thank goodness, they passed it, so it didn't matter what Tennessee did after all."

"So now you're stirring up the ladies, putting all kinds of ideas in their heads," he laughed. His voice reached back to the days they had walked together, and talked, teased, played, and dreamed together.

Her smile broke. "Oh, Beau. Not ideas. Freedom." Her voice was ready to break, too, and he spoke quickly to cover the chasm, give her a bridge to composure.

"Caroline. If there'd been any hope of passing that amendment down here, you know Papa'd have led the fight." He shrugged. "But there wasn't."

"He had his hands full anyway, didn't he? With that pipeline bill?" At the question in his eyes she said, "Oh, I keep up with . . . what's going on."

"Women have made progress, Caroline. I guess you take a lot of pleasure in that."

He heard the scorn that burned the edges of her voice as she thought about politics and women. "Certainly! Why, in most states, married women now own their own clothes, Beau! They're even considered fit guardians for their children—and can sign their own wills." Her eyes dropped all pretense and looked at him, naked except for the wisp of sorrow that blurred them. "But they still don't own their lives. They still don't own that."

Some inner clock warned him: This has gone on long enough. He rose, offered her a hand. "I know, Caroline. But they will. And, Caroline. If I can help . . ." He laughed. "The Langlinaises know a little something about politics!"

"I want you to meet Raoul," she said. "My . . . husband."

"I want to," Beau said.

She paused and looked at him. "What are you doing, Beau?"

"Reading law with Mr. Walter Burke in New Iberia."

"Not at LSU anymore?" Her eyes were steady, as though she could measure his heart.

"No." He led her to the next room, where a small group of musicians played Strauss waltzes. A restlessness he hadn't felt for months seized him. "Wonder if they can heat that music up a little," he said. "If they can, would you dance with me?"

Days of quiet, hours of loss, minutes of resignation, gathered in her eyes. "Yes," she said.

She waited while Beau walked over to the band and spoke to the leader. The man smiled, cut off the waltz, and signaled to his pianist.

"Come on," Beau said, reaching for her. He felt her feet find the rhythm of the music, and his own. He held her carefully, a polite distance spacing their bodies. But electricity leapt across that space. He remembered the feel of her with every step, and the scent of her perfume threw a veil of enchantment around them. He thought briefly of Louise. He had been waiting for the moment to come when he knew beyond all doubt that he wanted to marry her. Looking at Caroline, he knew that moment would never come. He saw a man standing in the double doorway watching them, and knew it was Raoul Hamilton. He began steering Caroline that way, so that they would be with Raoul when the music ended.

And on the dying coda of the music, he heard Caroline say: "Beau. Being married doesn't make you forget. But it . . . takes up the days. Beau. Marry."

She turned to her husband, hands outstretched. "Raoul, isn't this fun? Beau Langlinais is here, you remember me talking about Beau? My grandmother just thinks the world turns around Beau's family. We practically grew up together."

Raoul was gentle, his eyes kind. As Beau talked with him, his heart eased. At least she was loved, loved and respected. His eyes went again to Caroline. Her eyes were careful, watching each word, controlling each glance. He knew then that there were two Carolines. One belonged to Raoul Hamilton, and to causes. The other one belonged to him. Later, he thought over what she had said. That being married did help. He would never be any surer that he wanted to marry Louise than he was right now. He might as well ask her, put the whole matter in her careful hands.

So sure was he of her answer that he decided to stay over in New Orleans an extra day. It was a day spent largely with one of the jewelers at Adler's, who helped him select the diamond and the setting for Louise's ring. "This is rather large," the jeweler said. "But I assure you it is in perfectly good taste."

Beau looked at the stone, glittering on the deep blue velvet behind it. He wondered what he was doing here, what he meant by asking Louise to marry him. He blinked his eyes, looked out the glass front door at the traffic on Canal Street. All those people, scurrying about their lives—they probably didn't know why, either. He shrugged and picked up the stone. "It's fine," he said. "I'll take it."

One other thing was accomplished that weekend: Beau made good on his promise to introduce Francie to Annette Livaudais. Alice had given him a letter to the mother superior, asking that Francie be allowed to spend Sunday afternoon with her brother. They left the big gray-blue building, Francie shedding the restraint of convent walls as soon as they had turned the corner. She chattered away, telling him about the other boarders, about how maddening it was to watch from behind the Ursulines' high iron fence as free people strolled the streets of the Quarter. "It's like being out of prison," she said as they crossed Jackson Square to the coffee shop where they were to meet Annette.

"Learn to behave yourself like the lady you're meant to be and you'll enjoy being out more often," Beau said. Then he caught sight of Annette, sitting at a small round table with a number of other people. She wore a scarlet hat that curved low over her cheeks, and smoke from a cigarette in a long carved ivory holder swirled around her.

"Is that Miss Livaudais?" Francie said, her voice full of excited interest. "You didn't tell me she was so exotic-looking, Beau!"

"Guess I didn't really think about it," he said.

"Are those some of her friends? They look wonderful!"

Beau steered Francie through the crowd, thinking that perhaps this had not been a good idea. Francie tried to act grown-up, but under her veneer, she was a little country girl with no experience and less sense. Annette's friends, the artists, writers, actors, and dancers who had opened new worlds for him, would be just as willing to open them to Francie. "You wouldn't like them," he said, making Francie's curiosity about Annette Livaudais' friends soar. "They're interesting, all right, but now that I come to think of it, they're very different from the kind of people we've always known." He turned and made her meet his eyes. "Not our sort, Francie, not really."

Francie smiled and nodded. But as Beau turned away, she murmured to herself, "But then, neither am I."

18

"I'll go out to the farm and get some holly," Alice said to Claude. "I love holly piled in a silver bowl, don't you?"

"You love everything about a party, Alice. That's good, chère, that's good." Claude looked at his watch. "I'll get 'Tit Jacques to send the liquor over midafternoon. You need anything else?"

"Just for the weather to hold," Alice said, looking out the window at the bright December day. "Practically everybody in St. Martinville and some of New Iberia will be here to meet Louise and her parents tonight—I don't need rain."

"So I'll call the nuns, ask they should pray," Claude said, and laughed. "It won't rain, Alice. Everything's going to be fine." Claude put on his coat and went to the office. The party that evening would have to wait.

Driving out to the farm, the cold December wind seeming to push the automobile along the rutted road, Alice prayed that everything would be fine. Not just the party, but this forthcoming marriage. Don't be such a worrier, she told herself. Louise is a lovely girl, she certainly loves Beau. But that's just it, Alice thought. Does she? She had found herself watching Louise and Beau, who had spent more time with the family after they became engaged. Alice had tried to measure the depth of Louise's feelings. And very frankly, unless Alice had lost her ability to size up her own sex, whatever Louise did feel for Beau, it was not the kind of all-encompassing passion she had felt—and still felt, thank God!—for Claude. She had said so to Claude, once only. "Alice," he had said. "Leave it alone. Leave it alone, chère. There is more than one way to love. Most of the time, for most people, it's something less than what we have." But for Beau to have to settle for less than the best! Somewhere in Alice's heart, a small tender place began to rankle.

But tonight was a party, and she and her house had to be at their brilliant best. Leaving the car in the driveway at the farm, Alice took off, through a small stand of bamboo, toward the pond that lay like a sheet of dark metal under the December sky. The sky was tall, deep blue, alive with the steady breeze that had heralded last night's cold front. Setting the basket she carried on the spongy ground, she began to cut the holly that grew near the water's edge. She worked quickly, the sound of the heavy shears clipping the thick stems a counterpoint to the energetic calls of a pair of cardinals in the woods behind her. Then, something else entered the morning, a kind of stillness, a quality of silence in the sudden cessation of bird call, that weighted the bright fresh air and made her turn swiftly, body rigid.

Charles Livaudais stood not fifteen feet from her, a cap pulled low over his forehead and a shotgun balanced in his hand. He was so silent, so still, that she could almost convince herself he was not there, until he moved a half-step toward her, the familiar smile cut across his face. "Good morning, Alice. Nice morning, isn't it?"

"What are you doing here?" Her voice was sharp like the increasing bite in the chill air; sharp, but small against the vast reaches of silence, emptiness, between her and Mama Geneviève's kitchen.

"Why, doing a little hunting," he said, coming closer. "Caroline wrote that she is . . . to bear a child. So of course her mama had to run right down to Lafayette." He took another step. "I understand your family has something to celebrate, too. A wedding."

Alice stepped to firmer ground, holding the holly like a bouquet. "You seem to have the same problem you've had before, Mr. Livaudais. Knowing where you've a right to be." She took one more step away from him and plunged one hand deep into the pocket of her khaki pants. "This is Langlinais land, Mr. Livaudais. And you're not welcome here."

"Now, just how intimate does a man have to be with you before you call him by his name, Alice?" He made something different of her name, it was a new word, a new sound, one she did not like. "I've seen you naked, Alice. Naked and ready." He was still moving slowly, taking his time, closing the distance between them with slow steady steps. "Last spring in New Orleans? Did you have some lady friend coming—afraid we wouldn't have time?" She stared at him, her eyes on the red mouth that produced words that dirtied the morning. "But out here—why, time doesn't exist out here, does it, Alice? Claude's safe in his office in St. Martinville, and here we are, you and I, with the day before us. Now, isn't that pleasant to contemplate?"

He was but a few feet away. Alice dropped the holly and pulled the hidden hand from her pocket. A small pearl-handled revolver was clutched in it, and her finger was on the trigger. "Don't come any closer, Mr. Livaudais."

His eyes went from the gun to her face. He stopped moving, went still. Then, in a slow easy voice: "You're telling me you'd use that thing? Why, I could get it away from you before you made up your mind to shoot."

"Don't count on that," she said, and moved back two long steps until her back was at the stand of bamboo and there was a clear six feet between them. "You're on my land, Mr. Livaudais. That's trespassing, down here."

"You don't shoot a man for trespassing," he said, and made a quick rush forward. A bullet exploded at his feet, dusting his boots with dirt. "Dammit! Watch that thing, Alice—"

"You watch, Mr. Livaudais. I won't tell you again. Now, get going."

He stood watching her, eyes beneath the shade of the cap narrowed. "You might shoot at my feet. You might even try to wing me. But you wouldn't shoot to kill—hell, Alice, that's murder, I don't care if this is your land or not."

For the first time since she had turned and seen him standing there, the hot look of his face thrown at her like a challenge, she smiled. "You forget, Mr. Livaudais, where you are. In St. Martin Parish. Which my husband has in his back pocket. You're wrong, Mr. Livaudais. I will shoot to kill. I came out to get holly and I have it. I've got to get back to town—I've got several hundred people coming tonight. So I don't have time to stand around here arguing with you." She held the gun so that the sun picked up the silvery sheen of its barrel, traced a line of light along it. "If you don't turn around and get the hell out of here, I will shoot you, Mr. Livaudais. And you'd better hope I shoot to kill. 'Cause if all I do is disable you, it'll be a long, slow death out here. Do you get my meaning, Mr. Livaudais?"

"I don't believe you. Back pocket or not, you're talking about murder." The sun was high, beginning to be warm on his back, but the breeze still tickled his neck. The woman before him was breathing hard, her flannel shirt under her leather jacket rising and falling over breasts that taunted him. The khaki pants skimmed her hips, held at her waist with a wide leather belt. Lust rose in him. The woman was a fool, she'd never shoot to kill, no matter what she said. But Lord, how her anger would work for him, once she gave in. He lunged for her. Something sharp bit at his shoulder and stopped him. He touched the torn cloth; it was already wet with blood.

He looked up at Alice. She held the gun still pointed at him, her face set, hard.

"I thought about Caroline," she said. "And that baby she's

going to have. So I aimed higher than I originally intended."
She watched him as though he were a new kind of swamp
creature, something she had never seen before, and had but
mild interest in. "I imagine if you take your handkerchief and
hold it tight against the wound you can make it back to Beau
Chêne all right." Now she laughed, a laugh filled with triumph
and relief. "I've seen you undressed, too, Mr. Livaudais. So I
know how very hard your muscles are, what a shield they made
for you." She sounded as though she was taunting him with her
memory of his body; he wanted to kill her. "Your son-in-law
should be able to fix that little flesh wound up in no time. Now,
get."

"I'll bring charges. I'll have you arrested. You can't just—"
The world was suddenly spinning around him, and he had the
terrible conviction that he was going to be sick at Alice's feet.

"I wouldn't try, Mr. Livaudais," Alice said. She moved to
where the holly lay, and stooped to pick it up, the gun still held
on him. She rose with an easy grace, dropping the branches in
her basket. Looping the basket over her arm, she faced him
once again. "You have no witnesses, nothing but your word.
And, Mr. Livaudais, as far as the people around here are
concerned, if it's your word against mine—why, you'd be
lucky if they believed your name. Comprenez-vous?"

His face caved in—he knew she was right. He turned somehow, defeated, and stumbled off toward the woods. His bag
was there, he remembered, with a flask filled with good bourbon. Behind him, he heard Alice Langlinais laughing, her
laugh as tall and wide as the December sky, as brisk and chill
as the breeze which filled it.

Alice waited until he had disappeared into the trees before
walking swiftly toward the path that would take her back to the
farm. She moved almost at a run, sending quick glances over
her shoulder, brushing aside the branches that pulled at her
hair, tried to twine around her legs. She slowed only when she
reached the edge of the pasture. The sight of 'Tit Nonc on
Jumie's big mare reassured her. Leaning against the fence,
breathing slowly, she forced herself to take even, deep breaths.
The gun was a weight in her pocket, the barrel still warm—so
warm she could imagine it burning a scar into her flesh. She
shut her eyes against the meadow's brightness and saw Charles
Livaudais' face. It was large, looming against every other
image, blotting them out. She had thought that when his face

was contorted with that hot lust, he could not possibly look worse. But when he had finally turned away, when she had finally defeated him, the look in his face then had indeed been worse.

I wish I could tell Claude, she thought. She wanted to crawl into Claude's arms, to feel those strong barriers that shut the world away, made her safe. She began to tremble. I want to fall apart, she thought. I want to go to Mama Geneviève and have her tuck me up in her big bed and bring me some hot tea and hold my hand. She stood and took one more calming breath, then looked at her watch. In less than eight hours she would stand in her big square foyer receiving guests. She picked up the basket of holly and went to her automobile. The basket made a filigreed shadow against the ground, under cirrus clouds filigreed against the sky.

Charles Livaudais, sitting against a big cypress tree, drank more liquor as he heard the roar of Alice's car down the road. He felt stronger now. The flow of blood had slowed and the wound was beginning to clot. He'd be damned if he'd ask Raoul to bandage him back home. No, he'd stop at that woman's place down the road, the one where men sent girls to be fixed up. He tipped the flask to his mouth again, thinking hot, dark thoughts. That was twice she'd gotten the better of him. There would not be a third time.

"Look, Mama Geneviève, there's Huey Long!" Alice cried. "Well, for heaven's sake, I didn't expect him here!"

Geneviève followed Alice's gesture. "Humph," she said. "His wife must be picking out his clothes now. He looks better—not like he just climbed out of the rag barrel."

Rain had poured throughout the night before Beau's wedding, obscuring the sky. The day of the ceremony guests drove to the church in Abbeville huddled into coats, wrapped up in mufflers, herding into the building under glistening umbrellas. The church was cold; even the candles on the altar seemed to glow with a diminished flame.

"I hate to keep my coat on," Alice said to Geneviève. "But I'm freezing!"

"Everyone is," Geneviève said. "But, Alice, look how many people came!"

Alice turned in the pew and gazed around the large church.

The groom's side was filled, overflowing, and some of the Langlinais' guests were being escorted into the pews on the bride's side. Her eyes went over the faces and put names to them. Every important politician in the state seemed to be present, except the governor. But the magnificent silver soup tureen he had sent carried his presence with it.

"Oh, they're coming," Alice said. Across the aisle, she saw Mrs. Abadie turn, too. Their eyes met, held for a moment before they smiled and turned again to the aisle.

On the altar, Beau Langlinais, the formal morning clothes accentuating his good looks, stood with his father. "You have the ring, Papa?"

"Yes," Claude said. He found he was having trouble talking, having trouble getting the words past the constricted place in his throat. His hand fell briefly on his son's shoulder. Claude sighed and looked out over the church. His sister and her family, down from New Orleans for the wedding, filled the pew behind Alice and his mother. Behind them, row after row of people he had grown up with, or did business with, or had political alliances with, filled the other pews. Claude felt a kind of coming together of everything that was important in his life, and tightened his hold on Beau's shoulder.

The bride's attendants—Marie, Francie, Louise's sister, two cousins—were on the altar. Beau saw Louise coming down the aisle, floating on her father's arm, clad in a white velvet dress which clung to her body and swirled from the hips in a heavy cloud. She looked almost unbearably beautiful, with the delicacy of a porcelain figure. Beau fixed his eyes on her hair, blazing under the Chantilly lace veil. He saw her lips brush her father's cheek, and felt her small hand come into his. His eyes left her for one moment and found those of his mother. Alice made a smile. He smiled back, and took his bride to the altar. Almost before he knew it, they came to the part of the Nuptial Mass where the marriage ceremony occurred, and he found himself gazing into Louise's clear amber eyes, repeating the vows, and slipping the ring upon her waiting finger.

"Thank God for champagne," Claudine Langlinais Larroque said to her brother at the reception. "I'm getting warm for the first time today." Claudine sipped appreciatively. "This is the real thing, not that cider pumped with air with a little alcohol needled in. Where in the world did you get it, Claude?" Then she laughed. "Never mind. I don't want to know. God, this Prohibition's giving my husband fits. People come into the pharmacy insisting they need liquor for 'medicinal' purposes—lots of pharmacists just sell it to them. For a price, of course. But he won't. Makes them have a prescription." She shrugged. "Which most of them can get with no problem." She sipped again. "Claude, what do you and Alice think of this girl? Louise?"

"She's very nice," Claude said. His voice carried perhaps a bit more optimism than conviction. Claudine looked at her brother. His eyes were on the crowd that filled the Abadie home, flitting from one face to the other, making mental notes of what he was to say to each.

"Which means you hope it works out," Claudine said. "Claude. I wanted to say . . . I'm impressed."

"By what?"

"By you. By what you've done. The farm, our businesses, our holdings, your contacts and accomplishments in the legislature. I just sit comfortably in New Orleans and leave it all to you, and put the money in the bank when it comes." She looked around the room again, settling her gaze on the bridal couple standing with the Abadies and the attendants in the receiving line. "He has a big place to fill, Beau does. When the time comes." Claudine drained her glass and held it out to a waiter for more. "Maybe that's what I wonder about Louise. If she understands what being a Langlinais means."

Claude took his filled glass and touched it against Claudine's. "To being a Langlinais," he said. The dark suits of the men, the multicolored dresses of the women, seemed to whirl around him like a kaleidoscope, shards of bright and dark ever-shifting and changing. The air in the room seemed suddenly close, the heat from the fireplace roaring in his ears. "But I'll tell you the truth, Claudine. Sometimes when I think of all the work ahead, all the confrontations—I want to tell Alice to pack up and get on a train to New Orleans, and New York, and go all the way to Europe; just go around from place to place until we get good and tired of it and are ready to come home again."

"Why don't you, Claude? Why don't you? God knows you can afford it," Claudine said.

"I can afford it in money," Claude said. "But not in any other way, Claudine. Parker's called a constitutional convention to try to put this state's house in a little better order, you know that. Hell, it starts in about ten days. A week from now I'll be in Baton Rouge getting ready for it."

"You work too hard," Claudine said, kissing him quickly.

"Comes with the territory. I wasn't about to let the constitution be reorganized and not put my oar in, so I ran to be a delegate."

"And of course won," Claudine said fondly. "Will the convention really accomplish anything, Claude? Or will politics as usual create the same old stalemates?"

"Parker hopes to clean up the patchwork constitution we've got now, make it compact and more workable." He saw Alice pushing through the crowd and beckoned to her. "Whether he can make his hopes a reality is anybody's guess. I'll help all I can . . ." He shrugged and drank the last of the champagne in his glass. "Who knows?"

"It's going well, don't you think?" Alice said when she reached them.

"Now, Alice," Claude said, slipping an arm around her waist. "Relax and be a guest. For once someone else can worry about the party." He kissed her cheek. "Come on, let's show these young folks something about dancing."

Claudine watched them head toward the long back hall where a small orchestra was playing. Her eyes surveyed the reception rooms. She had spotted each piece of Langlinais silver that had been brought over to flesh out what Mrs. Abadie had. She knew Claude had sent the champagne, had filled in any gap that might exist between what the wedding should be and what it would be if he did not help. I wonder if they minded, the Abadies? she thought, going off to find her own husband. Her eyes went to Louise, who stood talking with a guest, cheeks pink and eyes bright. I hope she's up to all this, Claudine thought. She spotted her husband and moved toward him, joining the revelry of the other guests. And I hope, she told herself, this wedding is one of those worth celebrating.

"Are you warm enough?" Beau said. He had taken the lap robe from its rope across the back seat and spread it over Louise's legs, tucking the fringed ends around the green wool of her traveling suit. Her face rose above the white fox collar draped around her shoulders; it looked carved, still, with the glow of the morning fading. They were spending their wedding night in the Frederick Hotel in New Iberia; Claude would have Beau's automobile picked up from the train station, from which they would take the train to New Orleans later.

"I'm fine," she said. He waited for her smile, or the movement of her gloved hand from the silver fox muff to close over his. But her hands remained thrust deeply into the muff, and her lips remained quiet. Beau found himself filling the miles between St. Martinville and New Iberia with talk, just talk, comments on people at the wedding, information about the various politicians and businessmen who had thronged to Abbeville for the event.

"I realize how important your family is," Louise said at one point, and then quickly smiled as though she were teasing him. By the time they reached the Frederick Hotel, Beau was tense and almost angry. He fought his emotions with wine at dinner and a large brandy afterward; by the time they went back to their suite, he was feeling happy again. The bridal suite was in a corner of the hotel; it was large, with a fire burning in both the parlor and the bedroom fireplaces; heavy green velveteen draperies were pulled against the deep February darkness. Beau sat smoking in front of the parlor fire, waiting for Louise to finish undressing. His fears about how to behave with her were quieted. After all, she would not really know whether he was experienced or not; how could she know he had learned his sureness, his ease, in the bed of a woman like Bootsie—a woman she would call a "consort of the devil"? Louise's fierceness on such topics was funny. More than once, thinking of the way Louise denounced human weakness and frailty, he had found himself laughing—she was such a perfect mouthpiece of all the nuns who had taught her. But of course, even the convent did not follow a girl around when she became a woman; women knew what girls did not, that God could wink when he had to.

He heard Louise close the door between the dressing room and the bedroom and entered the dressing room from the parlor side. Her suit was hanging neatly on a hanger, her shoes neatly standing beneath it. There was no trace a woman had been there, not a drift of powder or a reminder of perfume. He undressed quickly, pulling on the silk pajamas and wool robe, thrusting his feet into leather slippers. He emerged from the dressing room to find Louise already in bed, covers pulled up to her chin, eyes closed. He had never had to approach a woman who wasn't already naked; he wondered—did he undress her or would she do it herself? For a moment, he stood looking down at her. The creamy linen sheets were heavily embroidered and edged with deep lace; Mama Geneviève had sent her best linens to New Iberia for their wedding night, telling Beau that if the hotel were not as good as being at home, why travel at all? Against the cream lace and satin-stitched roses, Louise's hair fell in one long braid. Her face was almost the same color as the pillowcase. Beau was seized with a sudden desire to excite her, to bring pink and crimson to her cheeks. He slid into bed, and began kissing her forehead and her cheeks before he moved to her lips. "Beau," she said, and he could see her golden eyes open and look up at him. They were so calm, so clear, that for a moment he felt held back. You've just kissed her, he thought to himself. Give her time. His hand touched her face, then moved slowly down her throat and found her breast. In the stillness, he could hear the small French clock on the mantel ticking, seeming to pace the way he moved. He cupped his hand over her breast, kissing her harder. Then his fingers found the buttons that held her gown closed and began unbuttoning them. When he pulled the cloth aside and reached inside to hold her bare breast, he felt a sudden tautness, a quick resistance. He took both hands and pulled the gown from her shoulders, tugging it down so that her arms were held to her sides and her upper body exposed. He began kissing one breast while stroking the other, waiting for the wildness Bootsie had accustomed him to to lash out in her, and to meet his.

"Beau!" It was almost a scream. He lifted his hand. She was staring at him in terror, her eyes glazed with fright. "Beau!" The husky voice was harsh, strangled. "What are you doing?"

He sat up. Louise struggled to get her gown up again; he reached down and pulled it over her. "Louise. I'm . . . I'm making love to you."

She clutched the covers now, held them close against her white face. "Making love? Beau, what is that? What were you doing?"

"Louise. Surely your mother talked to you . . ." The terror was fading, but her eyes were still cloudy, confused. "About what . . . what men and women . . . husbands and wives . . . do?"

"My mother never talked about anything like what you were doing," she said. Her voice was flat now, flat and defiant.

Anger rushed over him. "Where in the hell do you think babies come from, Louise? Come on, Abbeville's not such a big city you've never seen dogs mate—or been on a farm."

He saw the force of his anger hit her, saw the words bring her to the edge of knowledge, and regretted he had ever said them. "Dogs? Beau, what do dogs have to do with . . .?" Then she knew. For five ticks of the French clock, she stared at him, fear fighting disgust. Then she pulled the covers over her head and turned from him, clinging to the edge of the bed.

He looked down on her small form, hardly making a sound under the comforter. How could her mother have been so stupid? How could her mother have let Louise marry without knowing what would happen? Compassion overtook his anger. Well, there was time. Before they left New Orleans to take the *Crescent* to New York, he would ask Aunt Claudine to talk to Louise. It was a long train ride to New York, there would be time to win her, gently. He patted her back. "It's all right, Louise. I'm sorry. I thought . . . It's all right."

She turned then, pulling the covers from her face. She was crying, the silent tears creeping over her flushed face. "No, Beau. I'm sorry. Sorry I . . . screamed at you. It's just . . ." He knew that if she really began crying, the fatigue and tension of the last weeks before the wedding—all the parties, the gifts to be opened, the excitement of which she was the center— would demand release. She could become hysterical, and he needed her to be calm, to forget this bad beginning, to sleep.

"It's really all right, Louise. You'll see." He smoothed the covers. "Now. You go to sleep. I . . . I'm going to sit in the parlor, have a cigarette."

"All right, Beau." He knew that she wanted him gone, wanted to go to sleep alone in bed as though she were still at home, and safe from a husband who so brutally assaulted her. He pulled on his robe and went into the other room, adding coal to the fire.

For a long time, Beau sat and smoked and stared into the embers, trying to think what to do. Then, with a sigh, he knew that tomorrow night he would settle Louise in bed at the Pontchartrain Hotel, and that he would then go back to a pretty little house in the Quarter, where the champagne was iced and the owner was not. Sitting there thinking that, he began to laugh. He had used women to help him forget Caroline. But he had never, not in his worst nightmare, thought he would have to use them to forget his wife.

Their honeymoon was dichotomized clearly into day and night. During the day, they roamed New York, experimenting with strange new foods, wandering down little foreign streets. Beau's knowledge of music, and art, and theater, acquired under Annette's tutelage to match Caroline's sophistication, proved a source of pleasure to him, even as Annette had predicted. And Louise was an eager student, listening to him talk about an opera before they heard it, intensely reading the libretto so she would understand the story line. She was an amusing companion, with sharply insightful comments on the people around them in a theater, or seated at a nearby table. Every morning he fell in love with her all over again. Seeing her head bob alongside his as she tried to match her short strides to his longer ones as they walked up Fifth Avenue to the Metropolitan Museum, he was seized with such love for her that he wanted to hug her and kiss her right there in the middle of the sidewalk.

But in the evenings, when they had exhausted themselves with yet another late night, following a theater or opera performance with an hour or so in a nightclub where they could listen to the New York version of jazz, a change seemed to come over Louise. Her movements would become quick, mechanical, as she went about the business of getting herself ready for bed. She avoided looking at him, answering his remarks with one-syllable replies or with silence. He knew she feared another encounter such as that of their wedding night; Aunt Claudine had spoken with Louise, but whether anything even a kind woman said could erase the memory of Beau grabbing at her, Beau did not know. He had been gentle, considerate, ever since.

Louise liked to be held, she curled herself against him, his arms around her, and went instantly into a deep sleep. He had done nothing more in New Orleans or on the train. Only when they had been in New York two nights did he whisper that he wanted her. She had turned in his arms and looked up at him. He couldn't read the expression he saw in her eyes—it was not fear, not anger, but neither, did he think, was it passion. "All right," she said. Then she lay quietly while Beau made love to her. At first, carried by his own rising passion, he ignored the stillness of the woman beneath him. But when he entered her, and her body still lay quiet, he felt suddenly awkward, awkward and as though he had taken advantage of her. He held her afterward, feeling her body stir in his arms as Louise found her favorite position close to him.

The next night, when he whispered once again that he wanted her, thinking that surely with time she would become more responsive, she had not only looked at him with those unfathomable eyes but also spoken. "Beau. So soon? Wasn't last night enough for a while?"

The question shocked him. Enough? But there was no "enough" when you were a young man in love with your equally young bride! He found himself unable to pursue an answer to her question, or, for that matter, his original desire.

After that, he watched her carefully, trying to determine by subtle signs that this night was a night when Louise would welcome him. The joy in life she showed during the day still gave him hope that she would eventually find in sex something of what he did. With the resilience of youth, he woke each morning with that hope.

19

The quiet February sun glanced across the surface of the Mississippi River; the high banks, bare and exposed, before long would be near to overflowing when snows of winter farther north began to melt. Claude Langlinais, standing in the window of his room in the Heidelberg Hotel, looked out over the placid river, stretched, and sighed. A nice Sunday morning. What the hell was he doing here in Baton Rouge? he wondered. A knock at the door announced his coffee; when he opened it, the waiter handed him the *Sunday Advocate*, already open and folded to one black headline.

The waiter set the tray down on a small table and began lifting covers. "Your eggs. Ham. Lots of biscuits. Honey and strawberry preserves." A clatter of covers being replaced; then the man came to stand beside him. "Heard the news yet, Mr. Langlinais?"

Claude put on his glasses and reached for the newspaper, his eyes rapidly taking in the subheadlines and the lead paragraph of the story. "What the hell!"

"Everybody's talking about it. That Railroad Commission letting Cumberland Telephone raise rates like that. Twenty percent. That's a lot of money."

Claude poured coffee, let the first black jolt go through him. "A hell of a lot. Especially without any real supporting data." He reread the article more slowly. "If only Long had been there. God, he's been opposing this increase since Cumberland brought it up last October."

"Mr. Long, he probably thought he could count on at least one of them men to see the right and do it," the waiter said. He paused in the doorway, looked at Claude. "Mr. Langlinais. Me and the other people in the hotel—we sure think a lot of you. You and Mr. Long. He's a real gentleman to us, just like you are." The passive cheerfulness of the professional servant broke and Claude saw the man behind it. "Just wanted to thank you. For what y'all try to do." The door closed abruptly behind him, its solid panels smooth and blank.

And that's why I'm here, Claude thought, pouring more coffee and tucking into his eggs. To try to see to it that when the Constitutional Convention convenes on Tuesday, that waiter and others like him get some share of the pie. He began a methodical reading of the newspaper, circling certain articles with a blue pencil, memorizing statistics and figures for later use. His eyes returned more than once to the article reporting the rate increase. The whole thing appeared to be underhanded. The commission had met on Saturday to hear Cumberland's reasoning behind their requested rate increase, and in a matter of hours, the decision had been made.

Buttering the last biscuit, Claude thumbed through the remaining sections of the paper. There was little national news of importance: Warren G. Harding, having ridden into the presidency on a slogan of "Less government in business, more business in government!" had made a speech on the theory of running government as though it were a business. Trouble with that is, Claude said to himself, pouring the last of the coffee into his cup, is that business is supposed to make a profit—and government should do no more than break even. All right to make government businesslike. But it mustn't ever lose sight of men who might be counted a loss on a ledger statement but who nonetheless were human beings of worth, value. Papa, you shouldn't have taught me to be an idealist, Claude thought. Then he laughed. His papa was the first one to say ideals were something you kept quiet while you worked hard to make them come true. "If you've got ideals, you don't have to talk about them—they'll show." It was something he'd often repeated to Beau. Suddenly he reached for the telephone.

"That you, Jennie?" he said when the telephone operator came on. "Get me Commissioner Huey Long, up in Winnfield, will you?" Claude laughed. "No, I don't have the number. Isn't he important enough you've got it written down somewhere?" He laughed again. "Thought so." While he waited for the call to go through, he watched the river. One thing, with Huey P. Long loose in this state, life would never be dull. Long must be furious; he'd been fighting Cumberland's request for a rate increase since last fall, when their attorneys had presented the request with no supporting data at all. Their arrogance had fueled Long's passion; he had demanded statistics, reasons, evidence, that the company could not indeed survive without a hefty raise in rates. Cumberland had come back with a scant amount of backup, only to be sent back to its kennel like an ill-trained dog, ordered to produce a better performance next time. Yesterday's meeting of the commission was to review that better performance—but there was no way, simply no way at all, that the commission could have held a lengthy hearing all day and gotten the kind of opinion printed in the paper that night.

A booming voice, resonant, full, interrupted Claude's thoughts. "Representative Langlinais. What can I do for you this Sunday morning?"

"Hope I'm not keeping you from church, Huey. Being a Catholic, I forget you Protestants don't have a whole mess of services to pick from."

"Not keeping me from a thing in the world." The voice sharpened. "You been reading the paper?"

"I have." There was a silence on the line, a testing.

"And?"

"Stinks to high heaven, doesn't it, Huey?"

Claude could hear a small rush of let-out breath. "It does."

Long's voice lowered, became confidential. "Listen, I thought sure Taylor'd stick by his guns. I knew ahead of time those sons of bitches at Cumberland couldn't justify that kind of rate raise, no matter what kind of data they brought in. Wrote my opinion up and sent it in." Long snorted. Claude could just see him, shirt collar unbuttoned, sleeves rolled up, jowly cheeks red with his anger. "Knew I couldn't count on Michel, 'course not, the man's the tool of one of Cumberland's attorneys, no way he was going against the hand that keeps him. But Taylor'd promised, and damn, Claude, you've got to trust a man's promise sometimes, you know what I'm saying?"

"When you've been in politics as long as I have, Huey, you'll know to get those promises witnessed—better yet, in writing," Claude said. "You think Taylor sold out?"

"What else could it have been? Man's set on being firm, won't let Cumberland raise their rates no way—then turns around and decides so fast it isn't hardly out of their mouths before the girls are finished typing it." A pause. "You know Barrow, the commission's attorney, handed out the typed decision at midnight. Think about it, Claude."

Claude's eyes glanced out over the river again. At home, Alice would be lying in bed drinking coffee and reading the *Picayune*. Soft, cushiony, her skin rosy and ripe. Damn! "Were you offered anything, Huey?"

The answer came quickly, surely. "Damn right I was. Legal business, plenty of it—with plenty of rich clients, too."

"You think that's what they offered Taylor?"

"He'll say I'm a liar. Because who in the hell can prove he was bought?" Now Claude heard a new note in Long's voice, a note he recognized because it was one his own voice had when he was making a pronouncement. "But, Claude, I want to tell you something, and I want you to mark it down. Sure as I am sitting here in my kitchen on Sunday morning, sure as I am talking to you, I am going to take this Cumberland decision, which affects sixty-six thousand telephone subscribers in this great state, and I am going to ram it down their throats. Again and again and again. And after I have done that, if I have to, I will walk on their backs, the backs of those responsible for it, right smack into the governorship of this state."

"There's a good piece of road between where you are and the governor's chair," Claude said carefully. "Long and twisted."

Huey laughed, the confident, eager laugh of one almost excited that a fight was to begin. Claude grew wary, as though he were out hunting and had seen signs of a big cat lurking somewhere behind him.

"You know what the Bible says, don't you, Claude? Or does a good fish-eater like you know the Bible? Well, I'll tell you what it says, Claude. It says that the crooked ways shall be made straight and the rough roads smooth." The same power Claude had heard in Long's voice at that Hot Wells rally so long ago came pouring down the telephone wire. "And I am going to make the crooked ways straight for the people of this state. I am going to see to it that Standard Oil and Cumberland Telephone and all those other big boys who eat up the little people don't keep on doing it. And I am going to make the rough roads smooth, Claude. I am." The sun seemed to hold the room in a golden bowl of light, the air a perfect balance of light and warmth from the roaring heater.

"Well, all right, Huey," Claude said. "All right." It was not until he had hung up the telephone and finished dressing for Mass at St. Joseph's Church that Claude realized Huey had not bothered to ask for his help.

Beau Langlinais returned from his wedding trip to learn that Caroline had had a son while he and Louise were traveling. He found himself involuntarily counting back—she had been three months pregnant with another man's child when he had held her, danced with her. The knowledge gave him a claim on her, somehow; even bearing Raoul's child had not completely separated her from him. He went to an antique dealer in New Orleans his next trip into the city and bought a baby present, a beautifully designed silver stirrup cup.

His resilient hope was wearing thin; if all he had wanted from Louise was companionship, he would not have married her. While she was still amusing, bright, making their days together interesting and pleasant, the shadow of her resistance to sex still darkened their life. He felt himself withdrawing, too, so that the intimacy he had hoped for in marriage was more distant than if they had not wed. He felt a gradual waning of emotional loyalty to Louise. The carefully spaced lovemaking she allowed him still brought forth no response in her at all. And now, more than a month after their wedding, he did not think there ever would be. But there was something else that bothered him even more than her passiveness—after all, a man could beget a son on even the most passive wife, and if he needed excitement, that, as he well knew, could be found elsewhere. No, what bothered him was the way Louise looked when he touched her, when his hands and body touched hers. Something glittered at the back of her eyes, something distant that seemed to stand aside and . . . what? Judge? He could not tell what it was, that expression that slid over her great golden eyes, that tension that made her lips small. He only knew that he did not like it. He felt her changing, becoming a woman he did not know.

"I've got a meeting in Lafayette," he told Louise one bright March morning. "It will last late, and I may not be home for dinner."

"It's novena tonight anyway," Louise said. "I'll leave something warming for you."

All day at Mr. Burke's office, while Beau looked up citations, made entries in the notes he was compiling in preparation for the bar examination in June, he looked forward to the moment this afternoon when he would see Caroline. He had phoned her the day before, saying he had a gift for the baby. Could he come by around four o'clock? "That's perfect," she had said. "Perfect." The sound of her voice had put an added brightness to the day; when he pulled up in front of the big white house at exactly four o'clock, the brightness had become a fever.

"Miz Hamilton's around back," the large black woman said, holding the screen door open. "Her and the baby. Come on in, I'll call her."

"I'll find her," Beau said, shifting his package to the other hand. "Can I just walk around the house?"

"Sure can." He went down the brick steps and followed a brick path through a gate in the low fence. Coming around the house, he saw Caroline sitting in a large wicker rocker with her face half-turned, singing to the infant that lay in her lap. For a long moment he stood motionless. The early-spring sun already had the strength to turn her hair to golden blond. She wore a pale blue dress with a lace bertha, and a light ivory shawl half-covered her shoulders. Looking at her, he knew there was no more beautiful woman in the world. He stepped forward, feet quiet on the moss-cushioned brick. Before he could speak, she looked up and saw him.

"Beau!" He saw the instinctive effort to rise, saw her catch at the baby and settle back in the chair, one hand stretched toward him. "Beau, how lovely to see you! I've been looking forward to it all day."

He brought her hand to his lips, bending over it. "I'm sorry I haven't come to see you sooner." He looked at the baby. "Why, if I'd waited much longer, he'd have been ready to use this."

He handed her the package and watched her open it. Caroline held the curving silver stirrup cup up to the sunlight, watching the beams pick out its intricate chased design. "Beau! It's wonderful!"

Beau pulled a chair closer to hers and sat down. "Maybe he can use it to drink milk from. Until he's old enough to hunt."

"Here, Beau, look at him. Isn't he a marvel? Of course, he's named Raoul Marcus, for his father." She looked up and their eyes met over the baby's head. In that brief look, he saw the same thoughts in her eyes that he knew she must see in his. His hand moved to the baby's blanket, lifted it so he could see the firm little body, the fine length of him.

"Yes, he is, Caroline." He let the blanket fall and turned his head away. He had thought long and hard before he had decided to put himself through this. And seeing Caroline with another man's baby was even more difficult than he had imagined. Still, if he were to see her at all, if the loneliness of his days was to be abated even a little, he had to take this opportunity, this very natural occasion for calling upon her, and for establishing, with any luck at all, the basis for a friendship that would work.

"I . . . I had a note from . . . your wife this morning," Caroline said. Her eyes were on the baby in her lap. "Thanking me for the silver bowl." She laughed, the confident throaty laugh he so well remembered. "She said she was sorry I hadn't been able to be at the wedding—she had looked forward to meeting me." Her eyes flashed at Beau. "I guess she didn't remember I wasn't in any condition to go anywhere around that time."

"She might not have known you were . . . waiting for a child," Beau said. He held out a finger to the baby, who grasped it solidly. "I . . . no one might have mentioned it to her."

There was a silence. Then Caroline picked up a small bell that sat on the table next to her and rang it. "I don't want him to get chilled. But let's sit out here awhile yet, shall we? Do you have time for coffee?"

For anything, he wanted to say. For everything. A slender young black woman came down the path and picked up the baby, crooning under her breath. "Time for this baby to go in. Yessir, time for Bea's baby to have some loving," she said.

"Beatrice, ask Luella to bring us some coffee, hear? And maybe a little of that fig cake, if there's any left." She watched the girl carry the baby away and leaned toward Beau. "Oh, Beau, it's so good to see you! It's like going home, almost. To Beau Chêne, I mean." She frowned. "I guess that sounds strange. I have a home of my own now, I know that. But still . . . I don't know." She laughed, the free, open laugh that still haunted his dreams. "But Beau, I swear, with Luella and Beatrice both, and with a man to keep up the yard and do the floors and the silver—why, this house takes care of itself. Raoul's gone so much—of course, a doctor has to be. Even the baby doesn't take up much time. I don't know." Her mood changed again, her smile faded, and her eyes grew dark. "There's too much time to . . . miss Beau Chêne."

"But surely you go there to visit your grandmother?"

"Yes, I do that. Have you seen Grandmama lately, Beau?" When he shook his head, she reached out and took one of his hands. "She's failing, Beau. I never thought I'd use that word about Grandmama. But Uncle René's death took a lot out of her."

"René? Your mother's brother? Who lives in Europe? I hadn't heard that."

Her hand was holding his tightly, squeezing it hard as though she had forgotten who he was, or how dangerous her touch was. "They didn't really tell anyone, Beau. I mean, it wasn't even in the papers. He died in a . . . a rather unpleasant way. Some man he was . . . living with, killed him." The color was dark in her cheeks, and her eyes shifted away from his. She rushed on: "Grandmama was just devastated, but Mama was so afraid people would find out that she just shut it all up, wouldn't let on a thing. Beau, she even went to a big party the night she found out he was dead! Her own brother!"

His own free hand covered hers. He could stay here forever in this quiet green place, where pink and white and lavender azaleas made a rainbowed border behind them, feeling the March sun on his back, seeing the warmth in Caroline's face. "People do strange things in a crisis, Caroline."

"One thing you can count on. Whatever Mama does, it won't help." She put the gentlest pressure against his hand and then pulled her own free. "Well, enough of that. Tell me about you, Beau. How do you like reading law with Mr. Burke? You must be about ready to take the bar exam, aren't you?"

"In June," he said, leaning back in his chair. If he could learn to live a moment at a time, not worry about whether he would feel worse after he left her than if he had never seen her at all, he could manage these little visits, could drop in from time to time, could . . . pretend. "I do like it." He looked at her. "I'm not sure being married fills up the time," he said, deliberately quoting her. "But studying the law, looking after the oil leases, learning the business—that does."

Luella set a tray down on the table and handed Caroline a glass of milk. "I brought you milk 'stead of coffee, Miz Hamilton. Nursing that baby and all, you need milk, not coffee that just makes you nervous!"

"Now, don't boss me around," Caroline said, but she sipped from the glass while Luella poured Beau's coffee.

"Doctor'll have my hide if I don't take care of you," the woman said. She turned to Beau. "Don't you stay so long you tire Miz Hamilton out, you hear me? She needs to lie down before Doctor gets home."

Beau watched her march back to the house, white uniform stiff with starch, turbaned head high. "Luella worked for Raoul's uncle," Caroline said. "The one whose practice Raoul took over. And we moved into his house, too, so of course she thinks she can run all of it—me included!"

"Last time I saw you—last fall? . . . has it been that long?—you told me you were getting women to vote."

Caroline finished her milk and set the glass down. "The women behind the suffrage movement have started another organization—the League of Women Voters. Now that the baby is here, I'm going to get involved in that." She stretched both arms over her head, pulling the soft fabric of her dress gently against her full breasts. He forced his eyes from them, forced his thoughts from imagining the way they must look now, milk-filled, with droplets of milk forming on each nipple.

"I'd . . . I'd better go," he said, rising. "Don't want to get on Luella's bad side."

Caroline rose too. "You'll come back, won't you, Beau?" She stood close to him, touched his sleeve. "You told me you'd help me, remember, Beau? With politics?"

Her blue eyes were so huge, her face so near—swiftly he kissed her cheek. "I remember, Caroline." Then he took her hand. "And I'm ready to help you, anytime you say." He made her look at him, made her acknowledge what was in his eyes. "What do you need?"

"Some names," she said earnestly. "Ladies who might be interested in the League. Or men who might not want to drive us out of town on a rail!" She shivered. "Oh, that reminds me of that awful Ku Klux Klan! Beau, have you ever in your life heard of such terrible things? Has everyone gone completely mad?"

"I don't know, Caroline. I know Papa's getting so disgusted with what goes on in Baton Rouge I wouldn't be a bit surprised if he resigned his seat."

"I thought of your papa when that Cumberland decision came down." She moved away from him, put a distance between them that could not be crossed by a kiss or a handclasp. "I knew he'd be thinking of what that rate increase would mean to everyone."

"He didn't like it. Neither did Huey Long," Beau said. He looked at her face, watched it carefully. "By the way, what does your father think of Huey Long?"

"Hates him through and through," Caroline said. She laughed. "Does that surprise you?"

"Not a bit," Beau said.

"I don't talk politics with him, though," Caroline said. "As a matter of fact, I don't talk to him about anything that really matters." She came a step closer, one hand half-outstretched. "How about you, Beau? What do you think of him?" Her voice was soft, and he knew what she was thinking. That Huey Long was a bitter—and effective—enemy of her father, and of everything he stood for.

"I'm not sure. I know one thing, though. So far, a lot of Mr. Huey P. Long's interests match up with certain interests of mine just fine. And so long as that's the case, I can overlook those that don't."

"I wonder if I could," Caroline said. Then, her voice even softer, a breath of sound: "If he could get back at them—I wonder if I could."

Beau looked at the blank face of the house, crossed the space between them, and took her in his arms. "God, Caroline. To get back at your parents—isn't that reason enough?" He could feel the warm length of her against him, feel her fit into the circle of his arms.

Then she whispered, the words all but smothered against his chest. "Beau. Beau, I want to see you. But you mustn't try to make love to me, Beau." She looked up at him, and he saw the fear in her eyes. "Please, Beau, promise me you won't."

He let her go, let the safe space come between them. "I'll promise, Caroline. On one condition. That you tell me it isn't because you don't want to."

He saw her stand tall, saw her head lift in that way all the de Clouets had when put under fire. "Oh, Beau. You know why. Because I'm afraid that I will."

He felt the nights of lying by Louise's side gather into a burst of smoke and disappear as he gazed into Caroline's eyes. He thought treacherously of the tight look on Louise's face when he took her, the narrow line of her lips, the narrow line her eyes made as she squeezed them tightly shut. He had yet to see Louise naked. They made love under the covers, with Louise's gown pulled up only far enough to allow him to penetrate her. He could touch her bare breasts, but she would not let him pull her nightdress down, would not let him kiss and caress them. Night after night of release without love, companionship without passion. New Orleans and Tess and her chilled champagne had proved too far; Beau had returned to Bootsie, who took in gentlemen's laundry and their frustrations as well. It's doing a lot of people good, he had told himself, driving home after an hour in Bootsie's bed. I won't hate Louise, and Bootsie makes a good living.

He pulled himself back to the present. "All right," he said. "All right, Caroline. I promise I won't try to make love to you. But I won't promise I won't ever ask if you've changed your mind."

The way back to St. Martinville seemed longer and darker and colder than it ever had before; though the tires moved across the gravel road, carrying him closer to home with every revolution, he felt as though he were in a mire, sinking more and more deeply every moment. He stopped the car and leaned over the wheel. The weight of the promise he had made to Caroline that afternoon only now struck home. He would never be able to forget that he would have to spend the rest of his days wanting Caroline—and not having her. He sat there for a long time, so long a time that the moon rose and tipped the tallest trees with silver before he started the motor and headed home once more.

Louise met him at the door, the light at her back throwing her shadow ahead of her. Who is that woman? he wondered as he came up the steps. For though he knew she was Louise, knew he had married her, he knew, too, that he would never be able to think of her as his wife, never be able to know her as his wife, never be able to love her as his wife.

"Your supper's in the oven," she said. "Must be all dried out by now."

"That's all right," he said. He opened the hall closet, carefully hung up his hat and overcoat, keeping his face averted. If only he could get through the next few minutes without somehow making her angry . . . Behind him, he heard her voice, the first querulous note sounding the alarm.

"Father Adrian came by after novena for cake and coffee. Of course, I . . . we both thought you'd be here." She moved so that when Beau turned from the closet she was facing him, confronting him. "He didn't say so, but I could tell he thought it was peculiar you weren't home."

"I told you I had a meeting in Lafayette, Louise. That I would be late." He tried to step past her, moving slowly as though he were only going to the kitchen for his supper, not trying to escape his wife. But she caught hold of his arm.

"Men so newly married don't have late meetings, Beau. They don't."

"Did Father Adrian say that, Louise?" he said.

The rapidity with which Louise's face could change, could go from irritation to rage, still shocked him. Her voice came, a low hiss of anger. "He didn't have to say it. I could just tell he thought it was . . . funny."

"I doubt if he thought a thing of it, Louise. Unless you went on about it." He was hungry, tired, emotionally exhausted. He wanted a drink. And a woman. A woman who would take her clothes off and pull down the covers and laugh up at him and tell him he kept her warm, she was never cold with him. "Anyway, you're the one he comes to see, not me."

Louise's voice rose, a thin stream of anger against the blue shadows of the hall. "That's an awful thing to say, Beau. You take that back right now. Now, Beau."

"What? Take what back?"

"About . . . about Father Adrian. Wanting to . . . talk to me."

Now she astonished him. Did she really think he was hinting that the priest was interested in her? Attracted to her? He looked at her. The small, fragile features that had seemed so doll-like, so vulnerable, before he married her, were already, in six short weeks, changing, becoming narrow and pinched. She's like a nun, Beau thought. Not a woman. There was that look in her eyes again, that kind of glitter they got sometimes when they were in bed. He looked at her more closely. Did she think about Father Adrian that way? Sit there talking about religion and wanting to take him to bed?

"You're the religious expert around here, Louise. As for being alone—Susu was here, wasn't she?" He moved away from her toward the kitchen. "So you and your priest were well-chaperoned, Louise. If that's what's bothering you." He let the door swing shut behind him and stood breathing the familiar smells in the kitchen, the faint aroma of roasted coffee beans that was renewed daily, the smell of garlic and onions from the strings hanging in the window, the spicy scents from the rows of jars on a shelf near the stove.

The kitchen smelled the way a kitchen should. For that matter, this whole house, with its fresh new paint and brand-new furnishings, looked the way a home should. Two blocks away from his parents', Beau had thought the house a perfect place for them to begin their life together. Later, there would be time to think about the farm. He shook his head. Funny how lonely a man could be in a place that had everything a home was supposed to have. Including a wife.

"I'll serve up your plate, Mr. Beau," a voice said. Susu got up from her chair near the stove and began to stir the pots sitting on its surface. "You want to eat it in the dining room? Or your study?"

"I'll eat in here, Susu," he said. He watched her serve up steaming stew, heap vegetables on the plate. "Miz Louise said you'd put my plate in the oven—I was all set for some mighty dried-out food."

Susu set the plate before him, went to the oven for corn-bread. "That ain't no way to feed a man, Mr. Beau. No more trouble to keep it all hot for you."

The stew was good, seasoned well, the way his mother

cooked. Susu set a glass of red wine at his elbow. "I'll just start on these pots while you eat, Mr. Beau. I got sweet-potato pie when you've done with that."

"You're here mighty late, aren't you?"

"Miz Louise, she was kind of . . . nervous. I didn't want to leave her."

"I'll have to arrange for someone to live on the place, I guess," he said. "If she's going to carry on—if she's going to be nervous being alone." He wiped up the good stew gravy with a thick slab of cornbread. "Because we can't have you not getting home when you need to." He thought of Bootsie. "And I sure as hell can't guarantee I'll be home all the time."

"No, sir," Susu said. "Yes, sir. I got an aunt, she don't have nobody, she might want to live here." Susu looked at Beau, a dark, knowing look. "She's good with babies, too. When Miz Louise has her some."

Beau laughed, a dry sound that echoed around the wooden walls of the room. "Those talents might not be needed, Susu. But talk to her. Send her to see me." He pulled out his watch. Louise had gone up to bed, was probably going to sleep as fast as she could so that he would not even be able to touch her breasts, kiss her once. Well, Bootsie's house was just past where Susu lived. "I'll take you home, Susu," he said. "And talk to your aunt right away." Let Louise have someone else to vent her moods on, someone else to dog her heels, placate her. The hell with it.

Louise heard the back door slam, heard her spaniel turn itself around on the rug three times and then settle down. That had been ugly of Beau to say that about Father Adrian, she thought darkly. As if he noticed whether she were a woman or not. Priests weren't really men; you could talk to them and feel comfortable. She punched her pillow down and shifted her position. Priests were pure, they weren't undressing you with their eyes all the time. She shivered. Sometimes when Beau looked at her like that, she thought she'd die. Not that he insisted. After that first night, he had been very polite. She let him do what he did because it was her wifely duty, it would be a sin not to. But all the while, she knew what he really wanted. He wanted to take all her clothes off and see her in the light. She burrowed deeper into the pillow, putting that thought from her mind. She would have to go to confession tomorrow, would have to kneel in the little dark place and whisper in a voice she hoped that Father Adrian wouldn't recognize that she had had unpure thoughts. Thinking of how clean she would feel when he absolved her, thinking of how lightly she would leave the little box, her penance on her lips and grace once more in her soul, Louise slept.

Later, across town in a small frame house, her husband slept, too.

Beau Langlinais stood beside his father and Walter Burke, the voices of the men clustered on the front porch of the governor's mansion ebbing and flowing around him. He had driven into Baton Rouge late the previous evening, suddenly tired of St. Martinville, tired of the routine of business, tired of cramming for the bar exam scheduled for mid-June in this year of 1921. The small breeze created by the man next to him, fanning the warm May air rhythmically with his soft straw hat, lifted Beau's light hair from his forehead and cooled his cheek. The porch stretched across the front of the two-story mansion, an upper gallery throwing shade over the men who had walked from the state capitol building a few blocks down North Boulevard to the governor's mansion, there to try one more time to effect a compromise on the severance tax.

"What are you hoping for?" Beau asked Claude.

"A two-and-a-half-percent severance tax, with the half-percent going to the oil parishes where the tax is collected," Claude said. He looked at his son. Beau looked a little better this morning, his lean face not quite so drawn, his dark eyes not quite so haunted. Hell, a man should look like that because he needed to get home, not because he'd just left it.

"Nice for St. Martin and Iberia parishes if that works out," Beau said. "Won't Parker go along with it?"

"Don't know," Burke said. "From the beginning of all this, he's reminded us he promised the oil companies the severance tax would never be more than two percent while he was governor."

"But, good Lord, that was nothing but a verbal agreement!" Beau looked at the governor, who stood in the center of the men clustered around him, listening patiently to their arguments. "How can Parker think that could be binding on a state convention, one with a mandate from the people who elected it?"

Burke smiled. "Parker's theory seems a distortion of democracy as we have always known it—that the word of one man, even that of a governor and a gentleman, can bind an entire body." He shook his head. "If it were anyone but John Parker, he would probably back down."

"Should back down," Beau said. "The man will throw away every gain he made in this last election if he lets the oil companies dictate this convention!"

"Now you sound like our friend Huey Long," Claude said, watching Beau's face come suddenly alive, the haunted shadows fleeing before the forceful sun of his passion.

"Worse men to sound like," Beau said. "Wait, what's Parker saying?"

In slow, deliberate, aristocratic cadences they overheard the governor saying, "Now, gentlemen, I'm not saying I can't live with a two-and-a-half-percent tax. But if you will just be patient a few minutes longer, let me make a phone call—perhaps we can get this whole issue settled today." He waited for a sign of assent from the men, then disappeared into the mansion, the screen door closing softly behind him.

"What now?" Claude said. He looked at Walter Burke, who shook his head.

"God knows." Mr. Burke took out a large linen handkerchief, mopped his brow. "Surprised you came in to all this heat, Beau. Unseasonable for May. Cooler out in the country."

"I needed a break," Beau said. He stood, hands thrust in the pockets of his white linen suit, light straw hat cocked over his brow. "Needed some time to . . . think."

Burke's hand fell lightly on Beau's shoulder. "Not a bad idea. You can check out some sources in the law library while you're here—that exam's not that far away." Burke moved away to talk to a delegate farther down the porch; Claude was deep in conversation with former Governor Pleasant, whose denunciations of the oil trust over the past few weeks had been so vehement that it was rumored he was a new disciple of Huey P. Long. The delegates had broken their tight cluster, were dispersed over the porch in little knots; they were smoking, joking, a respite from the hard business of the day. Beau was still tense, his eyes lost in darkness. What he needed to think about was Louise, and about his marriage. He had talked, finally, to a friend recently out of medical school, a man who read extensively the writings of an Austrian named Sigmund

Freud. "She sounds . . . well, not quite . . . normal," his friend had said. "Whatever that means. A certain shyness is to be expected—but from what you tell me . . ." The man's eyes had been compassionate. "There are some doctors in the East you could take her to." Beau had left that conference sure of only one thing—the way Louise made him feel, the way she looked at him, were, if not wrong, not right. He had also talked with a Jesuit at Holy Name, a wise confessor who knew Beau well. The priest had listened, hands clasped beneath his chin, eyes intent on Beau's face. "Complex," he had said. "Very complex. For a man to find satisfaction out of marriage is a serious sin, Beau. You know that. Yet, from what you tell me, I wonder if your wife is . . . is able to be a wife. Able to understand what that requires of her." There had been no mention of an annulment. But before he had returned home, Beau had researched the Diocese of New Orleans archives, and had learned by heart the grounds for requesting such a procedure.

"Hell of a long phone call," the man next to Beau on the porch said, taking out his watch. A stir in the crowd nearest the steps, a break in the groupings of men to make a passage, signaled that Parker had emerged from the mansion. The governor moved forward to greet a man who was just coming up the steps. "I think some of you know Mr. Gordon," Parker said, his hand on the newcomer's arm. "He's treasurer for Standard Oil, and I just called him and asked him if he would join with us, tell us what Standard Oil's position might be on that two and a half percent you all are talking about."

"We don't like it," Gordon said. He faced the men, his posture defiant. "John Parker promised us there would never be more than a two-percent severance tax, and we expect to hold him to it."

"I can't believe it!" Beau exclaimed. "If any proof were needed who still runs this state . . ." He turned and began to push through the crowd.

"Where are you going?" Claude said, catching up with him.

"Home," Beau said. He pulled his father aside, leaned toward him so that he could not be overheard. "You watch, Papa. Huey Long's going to take what was done here today and make damn sure that every voter in the state not only knows Parker doesn't move without Standard Oil's permission—but doesn't ever forget it." Beau looked at the men around him, whose first astonishment had settled into resentment against one more intrusion of Parker's personal code into public business. "I want to help him, Papa." Anger welled up in Beau, an anger that had many parts, one of which he could concentrate upon. "When I think what that half-percent share of the severance tax, the share Parker's willing to drop, would mean to the people of our parish—well, I want to get behind somebody who remembers people not as well off as he is."

"It's why I'm here, Beau." Claude felt something new in Beau; he had crossed a line this morning, and the feel of the new territory was in his voice, the way he held himself. He was no longer just interested in what happened in his state—he was bound to it, committed to it, dedicated to it.

Beau took his father's hand. "I know, Papa." His voice was softer, some of the anger diminished. "And when my turn comes, it's why I'll be here, too. In Baton Rouge. In the legislature." He straightened up and looked deep into his father's eyes. "But until that day comes, I'm going to work with other people who have the same ideals." Behind them they could hear A. K. Gordon speaking, explaining all the reasons why Standard Oil was against a two-and-a-half-percent severance tax. "I'm going to work with men who are against the kind of thing that happened here this morning, Papa. When one man and one big company can frustrate the will of the people—it's not right."

"No, it's not right," Claude began. "So you're getting on Long's wagon."

"Yes." Claude saw the challenge in his son's eyes. A weariness came over him—the state convention to amend the constitution had convened on March 1, had dragged itself through that capricious month, had spent April in session, was well into May, and would never get finished if they couldn't reach an agreement on this confounded severance tax. He sighed. "Hell, son, I'm so tired I'm almost ready to forget what's right or what's wrong if they'll just let us go home."

"Will it bother you? Me working with Long? For him?"

This was not just his son standing beside him. This was a man, a man with a secret life, with thoughts that belonged to himself alone. "Not my place to be bothered, Beau." Claude's hand clapped onto Beau's shoulder. "Your mama and I—we were finished telling you what to do the day you married Louise and took over your own life."

"I know, Papa. I know. But I don't want to do anything you . . . you wouldn't approve of."

Claude laughed. "Oh, Lord, Beau. Oh, Lord. Now, listen, son. I'll be damn near anything. But I damn sure will not be your conscience." He looked at his son. "Not in politics—or in anything else."

"All right, Papa," he said, and smiled. "Reckon I can take that on too." He turned and went down the steps, walking swiftly to the street. The May breeze skipped over Mrs. Parker's roses, bringing a sweet scent to tease him. At the moment, he knew what it was he had to do. No matter what the cost, no matter how long it took, he must somehow get out of his marriage to Louise. He was twenty-one, he had all his life before him—and he could not, would not, spend it with a woman who made him feel dirty every time he touched her, made him feel like a degenerate every time he forced his way between her tightly closed legs. He swung off down the walk, letting the buzz of voices from the porch blend with the sounds of late spring. He slowed to a walk, strolled back toward the river under the massive oaks that shaded the boulevard. It would not be easy, dissolving his marriage. People would be upset. Some would be more than upset—they would be angry, ready to censure him. He took a deep breath, and the delicious fragrance of sweet olive filled him. There was a large sweet olive growing at the far corner of the Hamiltons' back porch; his last visit to Caroline, just a few days ago, they had sat and had lemonade and lazed an afternoon away, the smell of sweet olive holding them in a contented trance. She was not free, he did not expect that she ever would be. But there were other women, women more like Caroline, women not at all like the . . . whatever she was he had married. He paused at the foot of the Confederate memorial, impulsively took off his hat, and saluted the bronze soldier who stood timelessly and mutely, a reminder that men will fight even lost causes well. Some things are worth fighting for, Beau said to himself. No matter what the cost. He went to the hotel to pack, whistling a tune that at first he did not recognize. Then he whistled it again, listening. It was "Whispering," the song Paul Whiteman had recorded the year before. Caroline had been playing it on the Victrola when he'd arrived the other day; he had danced her around the room for a few spinning, golden moments before the song had ended and the record had stopped. He felt his heart break loose, felt it getting free of the ropes that held it in such dark bondage. There was a whole world out there, filled with pretty girls and sweet music, cold champagne and hot jazz. Huey

Long and tough, good fights. By the time he was on the road for home, Beau was holding fortune in both his hands, feeling as though, this time, he owned her.

"Miz Louise is lying down," Becca said when he bounded up the back steps and opened the kitchen door. "Seems like she's feeling poorly."

"I won't disturb her, then," Beau said. But as he put his clothes away in his dressing room, he heard Louise's voice from their bedroom next door. "Beau, is that you?"

It won't be much longer, he thought, squaring his shoulders and going through the connecting door. He stood in the door-way, looking at Louise. She lay in their big bed, the mosquito net looped high in filmy folds of whiteness on the tall mahog-any posts. She wore a tucked and embroidered batiste gown, fastened close around her neck with tiny buttons that impeded a man's thick, hasty fingers, taunting him with their slippery smallness. Well, never mind. He would not bother her again, would not thrust himself against the cold white columns of her legs, nor try to keep his hand from crushing her breasts. "What is it, Louise?"

Her eyes glittered at him through the dimness of the twilit room. "Can you come closer, Beau?"

"I haven't finished unpacking," he said, maintaining his stance by the door. There was a daybed in his dressing room; it was narrow, but by God, it would be better than any bed he shared with her.

"I went to see Dr. Jaubert this morning," she said, and now the glitter in her eyes dominated the room, seemed to make it grow light with a harsh brilliance that burned into him. "He said I . . . I'm to have a child, Beau."

The glitter in her eyes and the silken coils of her voice spun around him, over him, pulling him back from the bright world of the morning. He looked at her, lying surrounded by the lace-and-beribboned pillows she could make barriers of. The rib-bons were like strands of a net; she was in the center of it, she was pulling him slowly back to her, back to the world of darkness and anger.

"Aren't you going to say anything, Beau?" Her voice was rising now; soon she would be screaming, the solid walls of the house barely containing her shrillness.

"When?" he said. He fought the passion that consumed him, tried to remember that this was his child, too, someone he should welcome.

"The end of November."

"Well," he said. "We'll have a very special Thanksgiving this year, Louise." He could say no more. Turning, he went back into the dressing room and closed the door. He finished putting his clothes away, laid out his silver brushes on his dresser, keeping his mind still, his thoughts on the simple tasks he was performing. Then he stood in the window, open to the garden below him. There was sweet olive blooming there, too, that same sweet scent. Its softness probed his wounds, opening them afresh. There is a world out there, he told himself. A world I must make mine, no matter what.

He thought of the woman who lay in the room behind him, and of the child she carried. His child. And he felt the last bright hope of the morning fade. Tears came; he muffled his face in the muslin curtains that framed the window and silently cried. And as he stood there, feeling his morning dreams dissolve in the tears of evening, he knew that while he cried for himself, he cried, too, for the child who was to come, whose life was being purchased with so heavy a forfeit.

20

"Liar!" The word thundered against the walls of the House chamber and echoed out through the open windows onto the green lawns that stretched toward the Mississippi River. "Liar!" Shelby Taylor repeated, pointing at Huey Long. Claude Langlinais, seated at his desk, glanced at Long, who sat calmly in the witness chair, a smile creasing his face.

"This thing's getting out of hand," Claude whispered to his neighbor, Harney Bogan of Caddo Parish.

Bogan, eyes on the tense figure who stood confronting Long, shrugged. "Maybe it's getting out of the House's hands. Doubt it's getting out of Huey's." He looked at Claude. "I've known Huey since he was knee-high to a hound-dog pup, Claude. Been telling you all along, these shenanigans are for one thing and one thing only—to get attention. If y'all had listened to me, we'd have just ignored the whole damn thing."

Long's angry fellow railroad commissioner had subsided into his chair, where he sat conferring with James Henriques, Cumberland Telephone and Telegraph's lead attorney. Long's testimony concerning his charges that Shelby Taylor had been suborned by Cumberland to support their request for higher rates continued. Claude picked up a small sheaf of papers from his desk, formed a tight roll with them, and tapped it softly against his desk. "Man shouldn't print charges like these just to get attention."

"Hell, Claude," Bogan said, grinning. "You know good and well Huey picks the biggest damn target he can. Papers pay more attention that way."

"All the same, these allegations are serious. To tie up the entire House just to get attention—that's a little too high-handed, if you ask me," Claude said. Bogan shrugged. Huey Pierce Long made his own rules, and if those rules were not what other men, gentlemen, were accustomed to following— well, either they would learn them, or they would get out of the game.

Claude unrolled the three pieces of paper and spread them out on his desk in the order in which Long had printed them. Copies had been run off so that each member of the House of Representatives would be sure to have the "evidence" of Standard Oil's control over Governor Parker and his entire administration. And though evidence that would stand up in a court of law might be in short supply, accusations of a damning nature were not—that Parker had made the son of Standard Oil's chief counsel the superintendent of the state-owned Charity Hospital in New Orleans; that Parker had sent the proposed oil-severance-tax bill to Standard Oil's New York office for approval before he submitted it to the legislature; that the legislators of Louisiana were allowing their laws to be written by the New York attorneys who worked for the Standard Oil empire that controlled their state. The effect was electric, the message unmistakable.

"Liar!" the cry went up again, as Long again accused Shelby Taylor of collusion with Cumberland Telephone and Telegraph. Now James Henriques and Shelby Taylor both jumped to their feet, hands clenched into fists, their faces stained with anger. A hubbub of sound rose around their cry. Long's supporters surged from their desks, joined by others who had stood against the rear wall of the House waiting for Long to finish his testimony. The speaker of the house rapped his gavel, but the sound was lost in the opposing waves of angry taunts each side directed against the other.

Claude rose, too, and stood for a moment, hesitating. He couldn't much blame Shelby Taylor for being angry—Long had no real proof Taylor had sold out and made a deal with Cumberland to approve the rate increase Cumberland wanted. Claude's thoughts went back to the conversation he'd had with Huey Long the morning after the rate increase had been granted: "And I will make the crooked roads straight—and I will walk that straightened road right into the governor's chair."

Claude began stuffing papers into his briefcase. No, it wouldn't much matter to Long whether Taylor had or hadn't sold out, as long as he could make enough people believe Taylor had. As for James Henriques, Cumberland's attorney—Long knew damn well Henriques was paid to take care of his client's interests. If Henriques had an opportunity to influence the rates his client was allowed to charge, he would certainly take it. And if Governor Parker consulted with Henriques, Parker should know whose interests Henriques would look after. Parker—there was the real culprit. The lock snapped shut, a small click of finality. Parker should know better; he shouldn't have his head stuck in such idealistic clouds that he forgot, if he ever knew, how the real world worked.

"You leaving, Claude?" someone asked as he pushed his way through the crowd.

Claude paused, surveyed the crowded chamber. The hearing into the integrity of the Railroad Commission was a farce, as Long had known all along it would be. The House had called the hearing to investigate Long—but it couldn't attack him without also implicating Shelby Taylor and John Michel. Already, Long's cohorts had asked for any number of solutions to the problem, the most popular of which was that all three of the commissioners be asked to resign and stand for reelection. That had been quickly abandoned when the House realized that of the three, only Long was sure of winning.

"I'll come back when we get back to what we're supposed to be here for, which is to work out a severance-tax bill," Claude said. He stood for a moment surveying the room. Long sat in the witness chair, his large body resting comfortably against the wooden chair back, one leg cocked up over the other, hands splayed against the top of the stand. He looked at ease, comfortable. Happy. By damn, the man looked happy. Claude turned his back on him and pushed his way toward the chamber door.

A moment later, he stood on the capitol steps, breathing the cool air. It was scented with burning leaves; the aroma filled his nostrils and was heavy on his tongue. The sky was clear, blue; even this first week into October, there was a bite, like the small new claws of a kitten, in the air. Feeling better, Claude shifted his briefcase to his other hand and strode down the steps. A reporter from one of the New Orleans papers, the stub of a cigar jammed in his mouth, slouched forward and barred Claude's path. "Hey, Representative Langlinais—is the hearing over?"

"For me it is," Claude said.

"So what's going on?" The man had pad ready, pencil poised.

Claude jerked his head back toward the House. "In there? A circus. There's a new force in there that just may sweep Louisiana—a force named Huey Long." The reporter saw the intense emotion in Claude's face. "The people don't know who Huey Long is. They never saw him and wouldn't know him if he stepped off the train at their station." Claude reached out and gripped the reporter's arm. "But they know him in name and you can't make them believe he is not their defender."

"Isn't he?" the reporter asked.

Claude looked back at the capitol, its turrets gray against the clear sky. "I think he's a chameleon," he said. "A chameleon who hasn't found a spot yet he couldn't change to accommodate to."

"Should he be stopped?"

Claude stared down at the man in front of him. Behind that one face, he saw the faces of thousands of Louisianians whose lives were lived on the margin of poverty and despair. For many years, the mouths of those faces had been shut, clamped tightly over bitterness and fear. They had a champion now, those mouths, a voice to lead them, a voice to teach them new slogans and new demands. "I don't know. But I don't think he can be," Claude said slowly.

Beau put down the *Times-Picayune* and yawned. Lord, Papa must be going crazy down in Baton Rouge, having to spend time listening to a bunch of fools and liars. Deliver me from that, Beau thought. He glanced across the porch at Louise, who sat in a big wicker rocker knitting. No one seeing her sitting in the rocker, gold-red hair curling from the French knot, her eyes fixed on the baby sacque in her hands, her blue gown covering her mounding stomach, would dream of the way she had looked a few hours ago, when Beau had criticized her for making Father Adrian bring her Communion. All because she wouldn't show herself in church.

Her surprising outburst, flooding out of control, still filled his ears. "I won't go out, I won't let people see me! You don't understand, all you think of is what you can get—what you want. I won't, I won't, I won't!" Becca had finally taken Louise upstairs and put her to bed.

"Some womens, they gets like that, Mr. Beau," Becca had said. "When the baby gets here, she be better."

He had been too tired to lie. "I wish I thought so," he had replied. Then he had tucked a five-dollar bill into Becca's hand. "Sometimes I think we don't pay you enough, Becca," he said, and tried to smile.

And yet here was Louise, hours later, calm as you please, the picture of impending motherhood. If only she were in reality the wife she pretended to be to the outside world. God, he was bored. He suddenly felt the need for someone to talk to. Weren't the Landrys having a party tonight? Of course Louise had refused. He stood up and paced across the long porch, counting the wide gray-painted boards that made its floor.

"Goodness, you're restless, Beau!" Louise said. "Can't you find something to do?"

Plenty, he wanted to answer. But everything I can think of requires a concerned and loving wife. He kept silent, pacing past her, turning and starting the other way.

"Beau, really, you're making me crazy." The warning whine came back into her voice. Suddenly he didn't care. Let her go off into another tirade. He just didn't care. He heard the telephone ring inside and moved to the door just as Susu stuck her head out.

"Telephone for you, Mr. Beau. It's your mama." Thank God, he thought. Anything to break the emptiness of an afternoon with Louise.

"Beau? I don't know how to tell you this," Alice said. "Beau, Marthe's dead." Beau caught his breath with a gasp.

He stared at the telephone in his hand as though his mother had just spoken an incomprehensible language. "Beau? Beau, I'm sorry—I shouldn't have sprung it on you like that. It's just—we're all so shocked."

"When did it happen?" he asked. He thought of Marthe, of Beau Chêne, of all the days he'd spent there with Caroline. He felt tears filling his eyes.

"Mama Geneviève just called. Berthe got worried when Marthe didn't come down from her nap at the usual time—she went and found her." There was a long moment of silence, broken only by Alice's quickly caught breath. "She went in her sleep, Beau—it's a blessing."

"Does Caroline know?"

"I want you to tell her, Beau. Marthe meant so much to her—"

"Yes," he said. "Yes, I'll go right away." He returned the receiver to its hook and set the telephone back in its cubbyhole. It was only four o'clock, but already the approaching shadows of autumn were cutting the days short and making the hall dim, its colors muted. He saw a figure looming at the back of the hall.

"Susu?"

The figure moved toward him. "Yassuh?"

"Mrs. de Gravelle died this afternoon. I'm going over to Lafayette to break the news to Mrs. Hamilton. I . . . I don't think I'll be home for supper."

"All right, Mr. Beau." Susu came to him and put a hand on his shoulder. "She was a fine lady, Mrs. de Gravelle. Not one person ever had nothing bad to say about her."

"Her granddaughter's the same way," he said, and heard the fierce longing in his voice.

The road to Lafayette was like a road back into time; scenes from the past seemed to float up to him, pass before his eyes. Christmas Eve—was it really only five years ago?—when he had spied Caroline in the de Gravelle pew, standing next to her grandmother. The spring Caroline spent with Marthe at Beau Chêne. Her visit the summer after Jumie died.

But as he drove into the town, he forced his own memories down. No one knew better than he what Marthe's death would mean to Caroline. She had lost her parents, by any standard that mattered, on the Sunday afternoon when they had made her choose between him and Beau Chêne. Now, sadly, the forfeit would be paid; that great white house with its small circle of land would be one generation closer to her care.

When he arrived, Luella answered the door, peering out at Beau suspiciously, and then smiling and opening it wide. "What you doing in Lafayette on a Sunday evening, Mr. Beau? Miz Hamilton wasn't expecting you, was she?"

"Her grandmother died this afternoon," Beau said, his voice hushed.

Luella's eyes widened and one hand flew to her face. "Lord, Mr. Beau. Miz Hamilton, she's going to feel terrible. She was mighty attached to her grandmama."

"That's why I came in person, Luella. Is she here?"

"She's with the baby. But he don't need her, he done already had his dinner. You go sit down and I'll get her."

"Don't tell her," Beau warned.

Luella shot a look at him. "No, sir. Ain't nobody she should hear that from but you, Mr. Beau."

He made his way back to the room Caroline called her "morning room" and took a chair near the door. Lowering his head into his hands, he thought of Marthe, and Beau Chêne, and all the promise life seemed to hold for him only a few years ago. Suddenly it seemed so far away—

"Beau?" He felt Caroline's hand on his shoulder and looked up. Her hair was loose around her face, and she wore a long tea gown with lace ruching making a deep V neckline. Beau felt a rush of desire. "Is anything the matter?"

He stood up and drew her to him. "Caroline—your grandmother died this afternoon."

"Oh, no! Beau . . ." She fell against him, sobbing. Beau held her tightly, overwhelmed by a mixture of compassion and unutterable longing. Her sobs racked his heart. He wanted to take her to the couch that sat in the bay window and lay her down upon it, hold her, kiss her, make love to her, until all her tears had stopped. He felt her tears soaking through his coat, and softly stroked her hair. As her sobs ceased, he took her face in his hands and kissed her on the forehead, on each tear-filled eye, on each cheek, and finally on her lips. For one beat of time, her lips under his were still. Then they stirred, responded. In one miraculous moment her arms came around his neck and pulled him closer to her. That moment seemed to go on forever. Finally, slowly, she drew back.

"Beau." Her voice was soft, steady, quiet now. "They say

time stops when there's a death. For a while, anyway." A small smile, a glimmer of her old humor. "When I kissed you just now, it was because time had stopped." She reached out a hand to him. "Oh, Beau. Whatever will I do without her?"

His eyes met hers, and his hand closed over Caroline's. "Sometimes," he said, "people we think we've lost seem . . . closer than people we see every day." Their eyes met, and Caroline let out a long breath.

"Yes," she said.

A door banged at the back of the house, and they heard voices from the kitchen. "Raoul's home," Caroline said, going toward the door. "He's been at the hospital for hours. Beau, he works entirely too hard."

Her voice sounded normal again, ordinary, the concerned wife for the overworked doctor husband. But even though she stood in the doorway waiting to greet another man, Beau felt a moment of peace. Her lips had told him, during that long, sweet kiss, what he had begun to doubt—that part of her was his, now and forever.

"Grandmama died this afternoon, Raoul," Caroline said as Raoul entered the room. "Beau came to tell me."

Beau saw Raoul's eyes fasten on Caroline's face, saw the caring there, the quiet affection. For one moment he envied Caroline the tranquillity of her marriage; if she did not have passion, at least she did not have raw pain. Raoul set his bag down and kissed Caroline gently. "Are you all right?"

"Yes," she said. "I haven't taken it in yet—I . . . I think I don't really believe it yet."

"How did she die?" Raoul asked. When Caroline looked blank, he turned to Beau. "She wasn't sick . . ."

"I don't know," Beau said. He lifted his hands, shrugged. "Mama said Berthe found her. She . . . she died in her sleep, apparently."

"Her heart, probably," Raoul said. "They'll have called Jaubert." He reached out and took Beau's hand. "It was awfully good of you to come tell us, Beau. A thing like this shouldn't be broken to someone over the telephone."

"He knew—he knew I needed to be with someone who loved her too when I heard," Caroline said. She looked startled, raised a hand to Raoul's cheek. "Oh, Raoul, I didn't mean you didn't love her—"

"Of course," Raoul said. He moved to the door and picked

up his bag. "But you all practically grew up together, you're bound to share a lot of . . . feelings about this death." There was a small silence; then Raoul looked at his watch. "Caroline, I feel terrible not to be able to stay with you, but I've got a patient in labor and I'm already dead on my feet. I'd hoped to catch a few winks before I have to go back to the hospital."

"Of course, Raoul," Caroline said. "But you have to eat, too. I'll have Luella bring a tray up—and don't worry about me, Raoul. I'm fine. Beau has been very kind, you mustn't think about this." She straightened her back and smiled. "After all, there's nothing you can do about Grandmama now." Her eyes filled with tears and she slumped into a low rocker near the hearth. The two men looked at each other, each face mirroring the helplessness the other felt.

"Caroline . . ." Raoul went and knelt beside her. "Look, I'll see if Dr. LeBlanc can deliver this baby—"

She sat up as though shot. "No! I won't hear of it! I'm fine, I really am." She rose and pushed him toward the door. "Now, you go rest so you'll be fresh to deliver that baby."

"But you need someone with you . . ." He looked at Beau.

"I can stay," Beau said.

Raoul seemed to measure Beau, his eyes moving over Beau's face. Then he nodded. "Good." He bent and kissed Caroline's cheek and vanished down the hall. They heard his footsteps as he mounted the stairs.

"He . . . he doesn't seem to mind my . . . well, filling in for him," Beau said.

"He doesn't," Caroline said. "Raoul isn't jealous of you. It wouldn't even occur to him to be." She crossed the space between them and took Beau's hands. "I don't think he even misses the part of me that went away somewhere to die—that lived only in memory after you and I . . ." Her lower lip trembled, and she bit it. Then she lifted her face to his; the light from the chandelier fell full on it, caressing her fine skin, lighting her deep blue eyes. "He doesn't know that part of me, Beau. I'm not sure he could."

"It hasn't died," he said, his voice urgent. "It doesn't live just in memory. You kissed me just now, Caroline. A very live, present kiss."

"A kiss because time had stopped, Beau." Her chin tilted in that old familiar way. "You promised. You promised you wouldn't make love to me."

He stood squarely in front of her, facing her down. "I didn't promise I wouldn't ask you again."

Then she crumpled, half-falling into the low chair behind her, her face turned against its brocade back. "Don't ask me now, Beau. Please don't ask me now."

A faint cry came to his ears, the wail of an infant. A feeling of guilt washed over him. And frustration. All the other lives forever complicating theirs. Then he thought of Louise's mounding stomach, of the way he felt when she allowed him to feel the baby inside her kick. He shook himself, hard. "All right, Caroline," he said. His voice was calm, gentle. "I won't."

She stirred and looked at him. The baby cried again, louder, and she stood up. "That's the baby, I'd better go to him."

"I'll wait," Beau said. "You're probably going to want to go to Beau Chêne tonight. I can drive you." He smiled. "And the baby and Luella. And all the traps women can't seem to go twenty-four hours without."

"Now, don't go comparing me to other women," Caroline said, smiling and teasing him back.

"I never do," he said, but he said it lightly, laughing while he said it.

Hélène was tired, she was cross, and she wanted a drink. A week after her mother's death, four days after the funeral, and the stream of visitors paying condolence calls had not let up. "Mama's popularity is exhausting me," she said to Charles. "If I have to listen to one more dear old lady tell me how much Mama will be missed, I think I will scream."

Charles, standing in one of the French windows leading out from the parlor to the upper gallery, laughed. The harsh sound held no mirth. "I suppose you think it's been better for me? Everywhere I look, I see either Claude Langlinais or that son of his. Giving me those cold, civil bows . . ." His voice changed, descended into darkness. "I'd like to break their necks for them."

Hélène looked up. The viciousness in Charles's tone intrigued her. Was there something she didn't know? "Why, Charles. You sound as though you really would."

He laughed again, the same harsh noise. Remembering the bullet wound in his shoulder from Alice's gun, and the greater wound still rankling his pride, he said, "Oh, I would. Believe me, I would." He reached into his pocket, withdrew his gold cigarette case, and selected a cigarette. As he brought the flame of the gold lighter to its tip, his hand stopped in midair at the sound of an automobile coming down the driveway. Pushing aside the blue velvet draperies, he leaned forward to better see the two women who had just gotten out and were approaching the house. That couldn't be Alice Langlinais! She had been carefully courteous to both him and Hélène at the funeral, but when she had come to call, it had been when only Caroline was receiving. No, he did not think Alice Langlinais would put herself near him again. Then who?

"You're going to burn the house down," Hélène said. "What on earth are you looking at?"

"Nothing," Charles said. He lit his cigarette and turned from the window just as Nat came into the room.

"Miz Jumie Langlinais and Miss Francie Langlinais are here, Miz Hélène," he said. "You receivin'?"

Hélène looked heavenward, her pale blue eyes rolling expressively at Charles. "Can I not receive Mrs. Langlinais, Nat? Good Lord, Mama would leave her grave and haunt me the rest of my life if I were rude to her precious Jumie's wife!" The servant's face registered one moment of shock before resuming a neutral expression. "Excuse me, Nat. I'm a little undone. Yes, of course, show them up."

"It's a little embarrassing when the servants' manners are better than yours, Hélène," Charles said. His spirits had lifted considerably. So the woman he had thought was Alice was her daughter. Charles smiled. There was no end to the opportunities life presented if one were open to them.

When Geneviève and Francie entered the drawing room, Charles smiled more broadly still. If ever a daughter were her mother's image, he thought, his eyes going swiftly from the dark hair to the cheeks flushed with youth to the liquid gray eyes, Francie was it. Francie's gaze fell upon him, and he saw her eyes suddenly change, the gray deepening almost to black. Something at the back of those eyes heartened him and made his blood race. He allowed his own eyes to meet hers, and then travel deliberately over Francie's rich figure, clothed in a scarlet wool dress with a closely fitting bodice whose severe neckline belied the fullness of the breasts it covered. "Mrs.

Langlinais," he said, going forward and bowing over Geneviève's hand. "It's good of you to come."

"Francie drove me," Geneviève said. "I was going to walk, but she wouldn't hear of it."

"Well, for goodness' sake, Grandmama, you were loaded down!" Francie looked up at Charles, her great gray eyes wide open. "A big devil's food cake and two loaves of bread and a jar of wild plum jam. Now, really!" She lifted her hands helplessly and laughed, her mouth open and her slim neck arched.

God, I could eat her up, Charles thought. "You shouldn't have brought us a thing, Mrs. Langlinais," he said. "I'm taking longer and longer walks already to work off this food, but I think I'm fighting a losing battle."

"I'll put you on starvation rations when we get home," Hélène said brittlely from behind them. She rose from her chair and approached Geneviève slowly. Her eyes shifted toward Charles and gave him a long, cold, disdainful look.

"My usual fare in New Orleans," he replied. His mind worked rapidly; how could he get Francie out of this room?

"This is the most wonderful house!" he heard her saying. "Oh, Mrs. Livaudais, don't you think this is the most beautiful house in the world?"

"Well," Hélène said, her voice as dry as two thin sheets of tissue paper slipping across each other, "I think it's all right."

"All right!" Francie spun around, her scarlet wool skirt flaring out around her slender ankles. "All right! Well, I think it's just splendid!" She came to a stop directly in front of Hélène. "Would it be awfully rude to ask to see it?"

"Now, Francie, don't bother Mrs. Livau—" Geneviève began.

"Not at all," Charles said, stepping forward. "I'll be glad to show it to you." He glanced at Hélène. "After all, your grandmother came to see Mrs. Livaudais. They can have a nice visit and you can look at the house to your heart's content." He eased Francie to the door as he spoke. In another moment they stood in the doorway, ready to embark on the tour.

"That's very kind of Charles," Geneviève said.

"Yes, isn't it?" Hélène said. He heard the fury that lay banked behind the dead fire in her voice. There'd be hell to pay later. But so what? There always was.

"Now," he said, tucking Francie's arm through his. "What do you want to see first?"

"I think the library," Francie said. "I've heard more stories about that room! Did you know one of my ancestors was raped there?" Her eyes were full on his face when she pronounced the word "raped," and he recognized the signal she was sending.

Well, he thought, tucking her arm more firmly under his. Well, now. He thought of Alice, gun pointed at him, that scornful smile on her lips. Thought of the way she had looked on the floor of her room at the Monteleone Hotel, her eyes filled with fear—and, for the briefest possible moment, lust. He looked into the eyes of the young girl beside him. Open, eager. His gaze drifted downward, over the full breasts, the narrow waist, the promising hips. Everything about her was eager. Well, how nice. How very, very nice.

"And what do you do, when you're not driving your grandmother about?" he said.

"Go to school in New Orleans." Her eyes were still on his face, and he saw her pleased look at his question.

"New Orleans? Really?" He smiled. "Now, do you mean to tell me that a charming young friend of the family has been at school in New Orleans and no one asked us to entertain her?"

"Oh, but your family has entertained me," Francie said. "Your sister is very good to me."

"My sister? Annette?" He felt as though he had opened the door to an entirely different time and place. What in hell else went on that he didn't know about? "How do you know Annette?"

They had reached the library on the ground floor and stood surrounded by the towering shelves of books, the family pictures crowding the mantelpiece, the shelves of Marthe's trophies from the days when Beau Chêne's racing stables had provided some of the most formidable challengers at the New Orleans Fairgrounds. Francie perched herself on the great mahogany plantation desk, one leg swinging slowly. "My brother introduced me to her."

Charles shook his head. "I'm not following this. Somehow or other your brother met my sister and then he introduced you to her."

"Miss Annette used to help Beau and Caroline see each other," Francie said. Her eyes were laughing at him, though her face remained serious, polite. "That was before you fixed it so they couldn't marry."

"I didn't—"

"You didn't stop your wife," Francie cut in. "That's the same as if you did it, where I come from."

"You Langlinaises think you can dictate morals to the whole damn world, don't you?" he said. God, just like her mother!

"Morals?" Francie leaned back, her body supported by her two arms braced on the surface of the desk. The late-afternoon sunlight, coming in from the window opposite the desk, fell on her, making the scarlet of her dress glow brightly. Her pose emphasized the curves of her body—a pose Charles knew was completely deliberate. She held the pose, then sat straight. "Morals?" she said again. She began laughing, a laugh that grew until it became almost wild. "I don't know what 'morals' means, Mr. Livaudais. Now, don't get me wrong. I know what rules are. They're what other people want you to do—for your own good, they say, but I've noticed whose convenience is served. And it's hardly ever mine. But whether or not rules are morals, I don't know. And to tell you the truth, I don't much care."

He waited, testing her mood. A wild young girl, playing a game? A tease, like her mother, whiling away a dull afternoon? "Those are mighty bold words, Miss Francie." He let his eyes rove over her body. "Someone might just take you up on them sometime."

"I'm beginning to doubt it," she said.

And then he knew it was going to be all right. His body relaxed, and he smiled. "So. You see my sister very often?"

"About once a month. Sometimes more. Usually I go on the Saturday she has a musicale." Francie laughed; the sound was different, surer, an exchange with a confederate. "She's trying to improve my taste."

"She's got a nerve," Charles said. "She's got some pretty strange tastes herself, from what I hear."

"I mean my musical taste," Francie said. She walked over to one of the bookshelves, selected a book, and opened it. "As a matter of fact, she's having a musicale next Saturday."

"Is she," Charles said.

"This is a fascinating book. Printed in 1672—it must be worth a lot, don't you think?"

"My taste doesn't run to rare books," Charles said.

Francie put the book back and flashed a glance at him from under her lashes. "What does your taste run to?"

"Come out with me next week and find out," he said.

"But I'm going to Miss Annette's," she said. She sat on the window seat, knees bent, arms clasped around them. She laid her head sideways on her knees; a cloud of black hair almost covered her face, taunting him, daring him to lift it. "Are you going to be there?"

"With that bunch of . . . No," he said. "I'm not."

Francie lifted her head and tossed her hair back. "Well, I suppose I could slip out early . . ."

"Yes," he said.

"And you'll be waiting?"

"Yes."

She sprang up. "All right. Fine. Luckily, I figured out pretty fast that if I didn't keep the little rules the nuns made, I'd never have a chance to break the big ones they don't find out about." She stopped in front of Charles and brushed his jacket collar. "You have tobacco on your lapel," she said seductively. Her body was close, only inches away, her red lips before him.

"You're a little devil, Francie Langlinais," he said.

"Yes," she said, and laughed. "Yes, I surely am."

"Well," Hélène said when they were alone again. "Did Francie Langlinais find the house up to her expectations?" She held a cocktail glass in one hand, a cigarette in the other; she drained the glass and handed it to him. "Pour me a dividend, will you?" When he gave it to her, she prodded him again. "Well?"

"She's a very . . . intelligent young girl. Quick to catch on," he said, refilling his own glass.

"Oh, I'll bet she is," Hélène said. She sipped her drink and took a long drag on her cigarette. The blue-gray smoke swirled around her, veiling the discontent in her face. "She's barely seventeen, Charles."

"So?" He turned and faced his wife. Two more cocktails, which she would drink very quickly to get her quota in before dinner was served, and she would be incoherent, slurring her words, remembering nothing she or anyone else said. He stood over her, looking down at the wreck of the woman he had married. "You gave up the right to criticize me a long time ago, remember, Hélène?"

"I don't—"

He leaned down and took her wrist, squeezing it tightly between his strong fingers. "Don't you? An exchange was made, remember? You wouldn't ask me what I did, or talk to me about it—so long as I made sure no one else would. And in return—in return, my dear wife . . ." Her face was pulling itself together, the pain from her wrist penetrating the cloud that surrounded her mind. She opened her mouth again, struggling forward in the chair. But he was stronger, and pushed her back. "And in return, my dear wife, I would make love to you only when you asked me—how you wanted me to—and never ask anything back." He felt her body go limp, saw the slackness in her face. "So you do remember. I thought so." He let her go and went to the bombé chest that held the cocktail tray. "Do you want another, Hélène? I believe there's time before dinner . . ."

She nodded and held out her glass. She would not look at him, but he knew that inside she was raging, a rage that would vent itself at some other time and in some other place—a time and place that, if he were lucky, he could avoid.

He heard the door behind him open, and turned, expecting an announcement of dinner. Instead it was Caroline, her baby in her arms. "I brought little Raoul in to say good night," she said. Suddenly the tension in the room hit her. "Is there . . . is something wrong?"

"Not at all," Charles said. He put his glass down and went to her, arms out to take his grandson.

"As a matter of fact, there is something wrong," Hélène said querulously from her chair. The cocktails were in full control now. Here we go, Charles thought. He moved toward the door, intending to tell Nat to begin serving dinner. "Charles, don't you want to hear what's wrong?"

"You can tell me at dinner," he said.

"It hasn't been announced," Hélène said.

"Mama, whatever it is, will you please just leave me out of it? I've had quite enough for a while." Caroline looked at her father. "I'm going to take the baby back to my room. I'll see you at dinner."

"I've decided to sell Beau Chêne," Hélène announced. The words slurred, the syllables falling against each other, some of them losing all shape in the collision. But her voice was firm, and Charles, watching Caroline's face, knew that Caroline believed her.

"Mama! You can't!" She clutched the baby more tightly against her, as though even the tiny strength her son now had could help her.

"Of course I can," Hélène said. "It's mine." For a moment her face looked almost happy. "You heard what the lawyers said. Nanette gets her share in stocks and bonds—I get mine in Beau Chêne." She laughed. "This house is too expensive to keep up."

"You've got stocks and bonds, too, Mama," Caroline said. "And oil."

"I hate the country. I don't care if I ever see it again. Why shouldn't I sell it?"

Something struggled in Charles's soul. He could make it right now. He could step in, tell Hélène to shut up. . . . He hesitated. Habit is not stronger than virtue, only easier. He settled into a wing chair, neutralizing himself.

"You promised that you wouldn't, Mama. That's why you can't sell it." Caroline was as outwardly calm, as though they were discussing buying white muslin or blue for the baby's room. Something about her reminded Charles of himself. Himself at that age when he still believed that the law was the same thing as justice, and that justice always triumphed. He shifted in his chair. God, would Nat never come?

"Verbal agreements have no force," Hélène said. There was no slurring. Each syllable was clear and perfectly formed, as though she had rehearsed the statement over and over again until she could recite it with no mistakes.

Caroline gave her mother a long look of disbelief, of scorn, before walking quickly to the desk where the telephone stood. She picked up the receiver, hugging the baby against her shoulder. "Give me the residence of Mr. Beau Langlinais, please." She looked at neither of them while waiting for the connection to be made. "Beau? It's Caroline. Beau, Mama has just said she's going to sell Beau Chêne. . . . What? . . . Yes, I reminded her of that. . . . You will? . . . All right. Beau . . . thank you." She set the telephone back into place and turned to them. "He's coming over, Mama. He has something to say to you."

"Well, he can say anything he wants to, but I am going to sell Beau Chêne."

Caroline left the room, sending word to the kitchen that she would have dinner in her room and asking Nat to notify her the minute Mr. Beau Langlinais arrived.

Nat had not yet cleared the plates when they heard a car door slam, and then, very quickly, a rapid knocking at the front door.

"Lochinvar comes to the damsel's rescue," Hélène said. She had stopped drinking, and although she was far from sober, she was at least not as drunk as she normally was. "I can't imagine why we're allowing ourselves to be put through this."

"Probably because we can't stop it," Charles said. He felt totally uninvolved, a spectator at what promised to be an interesting encounter.

When Caroline entered the dining room accompanied by Beau, Charles was instantly sorry they had not somehow prevented his coming. This was not the somewhat unsure, lovesick young country boy he remembered. The man who stood before them wore a suit whose cut was as elegant and as expensive as Charles's own. He carried himself easily, gracefully, with a rare sense of assurance and confidence. If a stranger had come into the room and been asked to choose the master of the house, there was no question it would have been Beau.

"Caroline tells me you're planning to sell Beau Chêne, Mrs. Livaudais," Beau said. He took the coffee Caroline handed him and settled himself in a chair across from Hélène's.

"That's right," Hélène said. Her voice betrayed her anger. Charles saw Beau take note of just how angry she was, and just exactly how much angrier he could make her.

"Well, now, I surely do wish you luck, Mrs. Livaudais. Because I think you're going to need it." Beau's voice was even, calm. But there was an edge behind it, a cutting edge, and Charles knew that whatever cards Beau held, they were higher than Hélène's.

"I don't need luck. Why, I know people who will jump at the chance to buy Beau Chêne." Hélène picked up her wineglass and drank, eyes watching Beau over the rim. "And there's not one thing you or anyone else can do about it, Mr. Beau Langlinais." She set the glass down and leaned over the table toward him. "Your grandfather used to work miracles for my mother. But I don't think you're going to be able to pull one off for Caroline. No matter how much you love her."

Neither Beau nor Caroline seemed to have heard Hélène's last remark; Caroline refilled Beau's coffee cup, then sipped from her own, her eyes never leaving his face.

"That's where you're wrong, Mrs. Livaudais. Very, very wrong. Because you see, Beau Chêne is in St. Martin Parish. I am on the police jury of St. Martin Parish, Mrs. Livaudais.

And you might say that there is not an elected or appointed official in this entire parish who does not owe something to me. Or to my papa." He smiled, a smile that echoed Claude's wolfish grin. "Or to my miracle-making grandfather."

"I don't—" Hélène began.

"You don't understand? Let me explain it to you." Beau looked down the table at Charles. "I could let Mr. Livaudais explain it—I see by the look on his face that he already understands—but perhaps you'll listen better if I tell you." Beau stood up slowly. "You see, to sell Beau Chêne, you'll have to provide a clear title to it. And have it surveyed."

"That won't be a problem, we've owned it since . . . my God, it was a Spanish grant!" Hélène said.

"But you'll still have to have a proper title." Beau was next to Hélène now, looking down at her, forcing her to look up to meet his eyes. "And it's funny how inefficient these little rural courthouses can be sometimes—things get lost, you'd be surprised how often that happens." He overrode the first protesting sound from Hélène. "And then there's the matter of the survey. That sometimes uncovers some real problems." His voice had softened; he sounded as though he were telling them a story, a familiar and oft-repeated story, one to which they all knew the outcome. "And then sometimes the police jury decides to change the way a road runs—might want it to go right through Beau Chêne . . . or might abandon the one running alongside it now." He shifted position so that his body curved over Hélène, screening her from the others. "You see, Mrs. Livaudais, all kinds of things can happen. So while no one can stop you from putting Beau Chêne on the market . . . somehow, I have an idea that all kinds of things will keep it from being sold."

"That's not legal!" Hélène snapped.

It was then that Charles broke his self-imposed silence. His laughter exploded in the room, making them all look at him. "Legal!" he said, when he had breath to speak. "Legal! Hélène, for God's sake, what does legality have to do with any of this?"

"I'm glad you understand that, Mr. Livaudais," Beau said. He reached out a hand to Caroline. "Walk me to my car?"

"Yes," she said. She rose swiftly, took his hand, and they left the room. The outer door closed behind them. Hélène slumped in her chair.

"You're not going to let him get away with that?"

Charles stretched, his arms reaching high, pulling the kinks of the day from his back. "My dear Hélène. If you did not destroy your brain with alcohol, you would know that neither I nor anyone else can keep him from getting away with that. You try to sell Beau Chêne and you will find yourself in the middle of the biggest mess you can ever imagine." He finished stretching and stood up. "A mess they will manage to prolong, my sweet, until the day you are laid in the tomb next to your sainted mother." His eyes glittered at her.

"I'll find some way," she said. "Some way to get back."

Nat, coming in to bring Charles his brandy, thought Miss Hélène must have said something funny. As he set the decanter down, Charles, looking at Hélène, laughed. "Never mind, Hélène. I already have."

21

The last note died softly; there was a long silence and then a burst of applause from the audience seated in Annette Livaudais' music room. Francie Langlinais sighed and peeked at her watch. Slowly, moving with youthful grace, she rose and made her way across the room to Annette.

"I hate to leave," she said, taking Annette's hand. "But I'm having a dress and bonnet made for Louise's baby and I want to pick them up today. The baby's due in two weeks, and I want her to have it." She looked at the soprano who had just finished singing and sighed. "But the music is so wonderful, I hate to miss even a minute of it."

Annette's lips curved into her dry, somewhat cynical smile. "I expect you'll live," she said. Her eyes followed Francie's to the singer, who was now surrounded by enthusiastic listeners. "She's not bad. I'll have her again."

"Oh, good!" Francie said. "Please remember to invite me." Her lips brushed against Annette's cheek. "Thank you for today, Miss Livaudais." Color glowed in her cheeks. "I have a feeling I'll remember this afternoon always." She squeezed Annette's hand, turned, and walked swiftly from the room. The maid put her coat around her and handed Francie her hat. Francie settled it on her head, pulled on her gloves, and tried to keep her steps sedate as she walked through the door. A large black car, curtains drawn over its rear windows, stood at the curb at the corner of the block. Francie walked toward it, her pace quickening to match the quickening of her heartbeat. He was really there!

There was a moment when the hugeness of the automobile, the darkness of the black windows, the deepening shadows of the October afternoon seemed to pervade her soul and make her pause. She hesitated beneath the giant live oak that marked the border of Annette's yard. Sheltered by its great branches, she knew Charles could not see her. She could turn, go the other way, catch the streetcar to the Quarter, pick up the baby dress and bonnet, and be safe in the convent in less than an hour. But the word "safe," entering her thoughts like a chaperone coming into the parlor, made her decision. Safe might be sure, but it was also no fun.

As she approached the automobile, the rear door nearest her swung open. Like a magic coach, she thought; jumping inside, she pulled it quickly closed.

"Well," Charles Livaudais said, leaning toward her from the driver's seat and smiling. "So here you are."

"Yes," Francie said.

He smiled again and put the automobile into gear. As they rolled away from the curb, he said over his shoulder, "Soon as we get out of this neighborhood you can sit up here with me."

Francie took off her hat and opened her purse, removing a box of hairpins and a mirror. Swiftly she began putting her hair up; when she had finished, she looked at Charles and smiled. "There, now. All grown-up." She reached into her purse again. "And when I put this on . . ." She held up a cachepot of rouge. "You'll think I'm almost your age."

Charles almost laughed aloud. Any worries he had had about this little adventure were finally, and forever, settled. Where had the little minx learned these tricks? It was of no consequence. What mattered was that she apparently was well able to handle her part of their meeting—and he was damn well able to handle his.

Francie pinned a veil to her simple schoolgirl hat; that, with the sophisticated hairstyle and rouged lips, made her look so much like her mother that Charles's satisfaction in his scheme was complete. He took his eyes off the road and allowed them to drift over her face, down to the creamy throat that showed above her white silk collar, down to the curving breasts revealed by her open coat.

Francie leaned forward, arms resting on the top of the seat, chin settled on them. "I don't think anyone would recognize me, do you?"

"They'll recognize you as a beautiful woman," he said. His voice was hoarse, strained by the passion that was overtaking him. He saw something in her eyes he had not seen before; was it fear? Be careful, he told himself. She likes to flirt and pretend to be wild; but if you go too quickly, she's liable to turn into a child again and run home to Mama. And wouldn't that tear it! Alice might keep her mouth shut about what went on between him and her, but if she knew he put one hand on her daughter, there'd be hell to pay. He thought of Beau standing over Hélène last week, dictating to her the rules of the game as it was played in St. Martin Parish. He had an instant of fear himself—was even this delectable young girl, who would delight his senses while providing his revenge, worth it? Another look at those glowing eyes, that curving body, and he knew the answer. Yes. Besides, this was not St. Martin. They were on his turf now, surrounded by his allies. He stepped on the accelerator as they turned onto St. Charles Avenue. "I'll pull over and you can hop up here," he said to Francie.

As the car stopped, Francie moved to the front seat and settled beside him, eyes looking up at him sideways, one hand provocatively near his leg. "Where are we going?"

"Thought we might hear a little music," he said. He had the feeling he always had when things were going precisely the way he wanted them to. It was a creamy feeling, a feeling almost indescribable, a feeling of complete contentment in every part of his being. And the best was yet to come. By the end of the afternoon, there would be nothing left for him to want.

"I've been listening to music all afternoon," Francie said, her reddened lips making a pout. "Your sister had a soprano who sang the longest songs. She thought she was Adelina Patti." Francie rolled her eyes at Charles. "But I assure you, she wasn't."

Charles laughed. "And what the hell do you know about Adelina Patti?"

Francie shrugged. "You don't have to be so patronizing. I'm not stupid." Her eyes narrowed, and a look of fierceness came over her face. "When I started going to your sister's, I realized fast enough that I'd better know something about what was going on, or she'd see through me in a minute. So when they all kept talking about Patti like she was the Virgin Mary or something, I looked her up." Francie took a deep breath. "And found out she'd really started her career at the old opera house, and had even lived in the Quarter." She let out the rest of the breath, moved her hand until it rested even closer to Charles's leg. "If you're going to do something, you do it as well as you can. Don't you agree?"

"Another of those Langlinais rules?" He moved his leg until it touched her hand.

"Yes," Francie said, lifting her hand and placing it firmly on his thigh. "But I don't think Papa meant it to apply to anything but work and study." She laughed, her eyes meeting his stare.

"We're not thinking about either of those things now," Charles said.

Francie's fingers moved, lightly, delicately, over his leg. She looked out the window. "Where are we going, anyway?"

"There's a little club I belong to," Charles said. His mouth was dry, and he had trouble getting the words out. The routine of seduction stretched out before him, seemingly endless. The necessary chitchat, the hour or so spent listening to jazz, feeding the girl drinks. What he wanted most to do was take Francie straight up to the little room kept for him, and take her to bed. "We can have a few drinks, listen to some jazz. You like jazz?"

Francie shrugged. "At least it's got some life to it. I like the way it makes me feel." Her fingers were still drifting, touching him as though she were trying to remember him.

"How does it make you feel?" They were in the Quarter now, and the little club, one of the former great prostitution houses when the Storyville district was legal and at its height, lay straight ahead.

"Wild," she replied. "Needing a way to let the wildness out." A Negro in livery came out when Charles stopped the car and held the door open for them.

When they were seated inside, a bottle on the table between them, he could see that she meant it. The long, soaring notes of the trumpet seemed to excite her; first her fingers, her arms, then her whole body became absorbed into the hard rhythms of the music. She seemed to be in a trance, moving to the music as though she were part of each piece.

They'd been inside less than half an hour when Charles could stand it no longer. "Let's go upstairs," he said. She turned and looked at him. Her eyes were wide, dark with a passion that seemed different from the passion that filled him. Her lips were parted so that he could see the moist inside of her mouth. A small pulse beat at the base of her throat. Fascinated, Charles watched the artery move. He reached out and touched her at just that place; her blood leapt beneath his fingers. Standing up, Charles reached out a hand to her. She took it, allowing herself to be drawn up, to be drawn to him. In the curve of his arm, she walked with him up the stairs.

He took a small brass key from his watch pocket and unlocked the thick-paneled mahogany door, his eyes never leaving her face. Opening the door, he watched Francie survey the room, her eyes faltering once at the high four-poster bed. "Well," she said, turning to him and looking into his eyes, "aren't you going to close the door?" Then, without waiting, she walked to the dresser and carefully removed her hat, setting it on one of the carved posts that held a swinging mirror. She stripped off her gloves, tossed them on the rose marble dresser top, and shrugged out of her coat. Sitting on a chair near the bed, she bent over and began to take off her shoes. Charles, standing by the door, saw the smooth curve of her neck as she bent away from him, and was lost. He went to her and leaned to kiss the white skin, moving his lips up to the hairline, breathing the scent of lilacs that perfumed her skin and hair.

Francie stood up, shorter now in her stocking feet. She lifted her hands to her neckline. With one hand on the top button, she looked at him and smiled. "Aren't you going to undress too?"

"Yes," he said hoarsely.

He undressed automatically, his eyes never leaving Francie's. Her buttons undone, Francie pulled the dress away from her shoulders and let it fall to the floor, where it lay in a pool of lavender challis. Her camisole was heavily embroidered, the petticoat beneath it tucked and trimmed with lace. "You look like a French confection," he teased. Something about the dark intensity of her eyes made him want to put this back on the same plane as all his previous encounters in this small, hidden room. But when she unbuttoned her petticoat and let it fall, when she pulled the camisole over her head and finally pulled her knickers down, and, clad now only in silk stockings, came into his arms, he knew with a shock of sadness that Francie was not the same, and that he had perhaps a great deal more on his hands than he had bargained for.

"Carry me to bed," she whispered.

He picked her up, feeling the silken smoothness of her stockinged legs, her white breasts, the round nipples that stood now taut and firm. He laid her on the coverlet, then carefully removed first one stocking, then the other. She was completely naked now. She lay back against the pillows, watching him. "Well?" she said. He suddenly felt as though everything that had ever happened to him had been but a prelude to this moment.

His hands took the pins that held her long black hair and pulled them gently away, until her curls tumbled about her face and over her bare shoulders.

"Will I do?" Her arms reached up, came around his neck, and pulled him toward her. Her eyes, large and solemn, looked into his, and he felt again that shock of sadness.

"Yes," he said. "Oh, yes." He came down upon her, kissing her face, her throat, her bare breasts. Then he felt her move beneath him, her hands on his back, stroking, pulling him closer to her. Caught together in a rising wave of passion, they lost themselves in each other. And Charles knew that at last he had found in Francie a partner whose darkness and passion matched his own.

Later, when he could speak again, he looked down into the great gray eyes that burned up at him from her flushed face and said, the delight he found in her still in his voice, "Were you born doing this?"

"No," she whispered. Her lips closed on the flesh of his arm, and he felt the sharp bite of her teeth before he felt her kiss. "Born to do it."

As they were leaving, Francie, remembering her excuse for leaving Annette's, looked down the street and said, "The woman who has the baby things I ordered isn't far from here—run me by there, will you?"

"Baby things?"

"I had her make a gown and bonnet for Louise's baby," she

said. With her clothes on and her hair up, Francie looked like a respectable young woman on an outing with her father or a favorite uncle. Her voice was calm, friendly; had it not been for the pulse in her throat that still beat with a faster rhythm, Charles would not have guessed her voice could hold the excitement of a half-hour before. Francie laughed, and he heard a hint of her older voice as she said, "I don't know how in the world Louise has managed to have a baby. If any woman is frigid, she is." She leaned back against the seat and ran her fingers across the distance between them. "Poor Beau, I hope he's found someone else."

"I find myself not terribly interested in your brother's marriage, if you don't mind," Charles said.

"That's all right," Francie said. "To tell you the truth, neither am I." She looked out the window. "Pull up right here," she directed. "I'll say good-bye here—I'll walk back to school." She took off her hat, removed the pins that held her hair, and let her curls fall to her shoulders. Quickly tying it back with a navy ribbon, she tucked the veil from her hat in her purse, spit on her handkerchief and rubbed the rouge from her cheeks. "Voilà," she said, laughing up at him. "The innocent schoolgirl returns."

"Let's hope there are no mind readers in that convent," he said. He reached out and held her arm. "When will I see you again?"

"Your sister has a musicale again next month," Francie said, a small smile teasing about her mouth.

"You know damn well I'm not waiting until next month," Charles said. He felt aroused again, alive in every nerve of his body.

"I suppose I could figure something out," she said. Then she sat up straight and faced him. "But, look, I'm not going to continue going to that dreary room—you might as well get that straight right away."

"What do you have in mind?" Did this child think he could take her to the Pontchartrain Hotel? Or to his room at home?

"We could run over to the Gulf Coast sometime—hardly anyone goes there this time of year. We could have our meals sent up . . . take walks along the sea wall. . . ." Her mouth formed a pout. "Wouldn't that be a lot better than an awful old room right here in New Orleans?"

"For God's sake, Francie, if you have a hard time getting

away for an afternoon, how the hell are you going to manage a weekend?"

"My roommate will cover for me," Francie said. "Her mother is dead and her father no more knows what she does than he can fly to the moon. She can invite me up to their place in St. Francisville for a weekend. She'll go home and I'll go with you."

Charles studied her a moment. He admired people who took risks, who could face danger down. But to embrace it, to almost seek out disaster . . . Francie's plan was typical of a schoolgirl's, filled with so many holes he could hardly begin to point them all out.

"I don't know," he said. "If we were caught . . ."

She pulled on her gloves and put a hand on the door latch. "Think it over, Mr. Livaudais. When you decide, give me a call. Say you're my dentist, that I need to make an appointment." She climbed out of the automobile and slammed the door. Leaning in the open window, she said, the confidence she felt in him making her eyes bright, "Be sure to leave your telephone number." She raised one hand to her mouth, then blew him a kiss. "Good-bye." Then she smiled and he knew again that he was lost. "And thank you for a very nice afternoon. I really had a lovely time." She turned and went into the small shop, slamming its door behind her. Damn if she didn't mean it! She either got her weekend on the coast or she'd never see him again. He drove homeward, his mind spinning over possibilities. There must be something else he could offer her instead. But her father could buy her anything she wanted; this wasn't some little waif who would be satisfied with a cheap coat and a ring with more sparkle than value. He slapped the steering wheel in frustration. He would be a fool to take Francie Langlinais away for a weekend; if they were discovered— and there was every possibility they would be—that would be the end of him in every way that mattered.

But by the time evening had arrived, and he sat opposite Hélène at yet another dull dinner party, listening to the same people say much the same thing they had been saying for the last twenty years, caution had flown to the winds. The memory of Francie became stronger and stronger until it was more powerful than caution, more compelling than wisdom. He racked his brains until he came upon a plan that he thought, if not foolproof, at least viable. He would call a friend of his who practiced law in Bay St. Louis, create a mythical client with a problem, and inquire as to which hotel might be relied upon for discretion—and great privacy. He let his mind play with the richness of a weekend with Francie. The inherent danger would sharpen both their appetites, bind them into a web of complicity that would make her his for as long as he wanted. He thought of Alice Langlinais, and his rout at the Monteleone—the terrible humiliation when her laughter had emasculated him. This time, there would be no laughter. His decision made, he leaned toward his dinner partner and made himself agreeable.

Hélène watched from across the table. He has a new woman, she thought. A good one, from the way he's practically licking his chops. A shiver of disgust went through her, and she motioned to the footman to refill the wineglasses. I'll go to Adler's tomorrow, she thought. Look at that emerald brooch again. She shot a look at Charles. He won't like it, he'll fuss and say the money could be better invested elsewhere. But when it came right down to it, he would make the same choice he always did. Hélène could have the brooch so long as he could have his woman. Hélène looked at the diamonds sparkling on her wrist. I've gotten some of the nicest jewels that way, she thought, and laughed to think of all the other women who paid their price.

"Waiting for a baby to make up its mind to be born is never easy, son," Claude said. He reached out his hand and caught Beau's arm as Beau made one more turn and started back down the porch. "Come on. Sit down. This could take a long, long time."

Beau flung himself into one of the rockers on his front porch and stared out into the yard. The day was mild, but already there had been two light frosts the first weeks of November, and the browning foliage in the flowerbeds signaled a long and cold winter. "I wish there were something I could do," he said, thrusting his hands deep into his pockets. But he knew Dr. Jaubert was with Louise, two experienced nurses assisting him; and his mother, Geneviève, Louise's mother, and her aunt were all close by. There was no shortage of concerned and caring people—any one of whom, Beau thought bitterly, Louise would be more willing to see than him.

When the first contractions had set in, Louise had seemed to freeze, going into some dark, cold place deep inside herself where he could not follow. She had seemed not to hear him when he asked how she felt. Only by watching the way her eyes narrowed and her lips grew tight and thin could Beau tell when a contraction seized her. He had called Dr. Jaubert, and then, going down the list Louise had prepared previously, everyone else. Then the waiting had begun.

"I don't know why she doesn't want to see me, Papa. I'd like to be with her, to help her . . ." As soon as he had said the words, he wanted to take them back. "Never mind . . ." he began.

Claude reached out and took his son's hand. "Beau, look. Your mama and I—we can't help noticing. Louise—she's . . ." Claude's shoulders lifted, reinforcing the puzzled look on his face. "I don't know, son. She's not what we expected—what you must have expected." He took a breath and plunged on. "Maybe everything between you isn't as . . . good as you want it to be. But, Beau. A baby is a wonderful thing. And a little child, they can love so much!" Claude's hand took his son's chin and raised his face. "Beau. The baby will help you. Believe that."

Something of the strength of his father's feeling for his children entered Beau, and he felt calmer. All this commotion, all these people—gathering to welcome his child into the world, a child Louise had borne. Even if he didn't love Louise, she had a claim on him now that he could never disown. "Papa." Beau stood and put his arms around his father. And in that exchange of love and warmth, Beau felt hope. He would soon hold his child, just as his father held him. He drew a deep breath. "It's worth waiting for, I know. I just wish it would hurry!"

"Maybe this will help pass the time," Claude said, handing Beau a section of the *Times-Picayune*. They sat down, lit cigarettes. Smoke circled over the porch; the quietness of the house behind them seemed unreal. Beau's eyes fell on a headline and his attention focused on the article beneath it. For a moment he lost himself in the sea of words. "Papa, did you read this article about Long?"

"Which one?" Claude said, smiling wryly.

"Where he talks about his victory in the Parker libel suit. He says it's a sign that the people in Louisiana understand what he's doing and believe in him."

"I doubt that Judge Brunot's decision was a victory for anybody," Claude said, taking the paper. "A lot of people feel that when Long was found guilty of libeling Parker, he lost."

"I hardly think a suspended sentence and a one-dollar fine are much of a punishment," Beau said.

A long, wailing scream burst forth from the bedroom upstairs, followed by another, higher one. Beau half-rose from his chair, his hands gripping the arms. "Louise," he said. He stared at Claude. "Does that mean . . . does that mean it will soon be over?"

"No," Claude said. "It just means she's in a harder stage." He watched Beau's tormented face. "I don't understand why childbirth has to be so hard on women," he said. "I've never understood it. After you were born, I told your mother I wouldn't blame her if she never wanted another one." Claude's eyes left Beau and stared out into the distance, seeing again his young wife. "She laughed and told me that giving her babies was my department and having them was hers, and so long as I took care of my end, she would take care of hers." He paused, then murmured, almost too low for Beau to hear, "She's quite a lady, Miss Alice."

Then the cries from upstairs grew stronger, higher still. The shrill sound filled the afternoon. "My God," Beau said. "Can't Jaubert do something?" He stood. "I don't give a damn whether she wants me there or not. I'm going up." He flung open the door and vanished inside. There was nothing Beau, or anyone else, could do, Claude knew. He shook his head and began reading the article Beau had pointed out. The tenor of Long's remarks was clear—that Long's sentence in the libel suit Parker had brought against him proved that Long was right, that even the courts agreed the big corporations ran the state. "The fight is just beginning," Long was quoted as saying.

Was there no stopping Long? Claude wondered. He wasn't sure he should be stopped—much of what Long said was absolutely correct. But the way he went about doing things stuck in Claude's craw. The hearing into the Public Service Commission's integrity, even the libel trial, were evidence, not so much of democratic processes at work, but of how Long could manipulate them to achieve his own ends—spreading his

fame, rallying people to his causes. Long might denounce
Parker for bending the rules, but he seemed blind to how he
trampled over them himself. He wished Beau could see that,
wished the admiration he heard in Beau's voice was tempered
by understanding of Long's methods—not just an enthusiasm
for his goals. He put down the paper and stared out into the
yard. The new baby would fill part of Beau's life, but that
restless energy a good marriage might have absorbed was
going to have to find another channel. As of right now, Claude
would bet a large piece of change that Beau's channel marker
would be Huey Pierce Long. To follow Long because you
believed in him was one thing—to follow Long because you
needed something to do was another. He'd talk to Beau once
more, he thought. Try to make him see that the Langlinaises
followed no star but their own.

A different kind of scream pierced Claude's thoughts,
seemed almost to hang in the air before him, followed quickly
by two more. Then there was silence, and Claude knew that his
grandchild had been born.

Inside, Beau stood beside Louise's bed, his hand clenched in
Alice's. He had arrived in the bedroom just when Louise's
screams made an unending cacophony of sound. He had stood
in the bay window, helpless, dreading the beginning of another
scream just when the last one ended. Then his mother had
come to him. "Beau, it's twins! Two daughters! Two fine little
girls!" she exclaimed, hugging him.

He had moved slowly to where the nurses stood, each holding a baby. He touched each tiny face with a cautious finger,
and felt something he had never felt before. A fierce protec-
tiveness for these two tiny human beings. A swelling of pride
that they were his. "Like rose petals," he said to Alice.

"They're beautiful," Alice said.

Dr. Jaubert came up to them. "I hope you've got some wet
nurses lined up, Beau. Louise isn't going to be able to nurse
them. She's much too weak."

"I've taken care of that," Alice said. She kissed Beau.
"You're totally done in, and so is Louise. Let's go down and
tell your father, and I'll fix you something to eat."

Beau looked at his daughters. They were asleep, their tiny
hands curled into small fists, their foreheads creased as though
already they slept with the cares of the world as companions.
"Are they all right?" he whispered to Becca, who stood guard.

Becca beamed. "Mr. Beau, these babies is fine," she said. "And these babies is going to be fine, 'cause Becca isn't going to let them out of her sight."

"My heaven, Beau, we need another cradle!" Alice said, laughing. "And more gowns—more of everything!" She moved out into the hall, still laughing. "Twins! Well, they run in the family; your grandfather was a twin." She paused, one hand on the stair railing. "What will you name them? Had the two of you thought of something?"

"Louise wanted Émilie if it were a girl. I was partial to Geneviève," Beau said. The sudden realization that he had two daughters overwhelmed him. "Now we have two!" He grinned up at Alice. "We'll name one Geneviève and one Émilie." He put his arms around her. "Oh, Mama . . ." He held her close and kissed her. Letting her go, he said, "There's someone I have to call. You go tell Papa—I'm going to telephone Caroline."

Alice watched him run down the steps and followed more slowly. The older she got, the more she wondered if there were any occasion in life that was all one way—all happy, all sad. Or was part of getting older learning, with your bones, that the line between the two feelings was so thin that just the way you looked at it made the difference? Well, she thought, slipping through the door and going to Claude, today I'm going to look only at the happy side of the line. "You're a grandpapa," she said to Claude, coming out onto the porch. "To two of the sweetest little girls you ever saw in your life."

"Louise had twins?" he roared, embracing Alice. "Mais, Alice, I'm going right home to get some champagne." He paused, one foot poised on the top step. "And Louise? She's all right?"

Their eyes met. "Exhausted, of course," Alice said. "Dr. Jaubert says she's very weak. But he said too that he was surprised at how little damage such hard births had done." She held Claude's gaze, letting her eyes speak. "I mean," she said carefully, "once she's rested again, there isn't any reason why she won't be . . . as good as new."

"Let's hope so," Claude said. "And, Alice, maybe the babies, they'll . . . well, warm her up a little."

"Maybe they will," Alice said.

"Put some ice in that big silver cooler, chère," Claude said, blowing her a kiss. "I'll be back in a minute."

Alice stood on the porch watching the evening star glow in the dark November sky. "I wish I may, I wish I might," she began, "have the wish I wish tonight." She paused, gazing at the sky. "Happiness for my son," she said aloud. And then, fiercely, as though fearing argument, added, "And don't tell me that's selfish." She turned and went into the house.

Beau was just hanging up the receiver. "Caroline was delighted. She said her little boy must be their first dancing partner."

"She's a good friend," Alice said, putting her arm through his and going toward the kitchen.

"A very good friend," Beau said.

Claude arrived with champagne; while he and Beau chilled it, Alice and Mrs. Abadie went up to Louise's bedroom, where Marie sat with Louise. "We'll stay with her for a while," Alice said. "You go on down—the champagne's just about ready."

Louise opened her eyes and looked around her as they seated themselves near the bed. Shadows flickered on the walls, cast by the firelight and the low-burning lamps. "Is the baby here?" she asked her mother.

"Two babies," her mother said, leaning closer and taking her hand. "Two beautiful little girls."

Louise's dry lips made a smile. "Good," she said. She closed her eyes, drifting back into sleep. "I'm glad." She sighed, and Mrs. Abadie and Alice leaned closer. "Little boys are so horrid." And then, as her mother and mother-in-law met each other's eyes, she slept.

22

Francie lifted the pale lavender tissue from the open box and pulled out a negligee of lace and creamy satin. She held it up in front of her, and dancing to a long cheval mirror, she posed, the sleek material draped against her, highlighting her flushed cheeks and brilliant eyes. "It's gorgeous," she said. "It's the

prettiest thing I've ever seen! How wonderful of you!" She ran
to Charles and put her arms around his neck. "We're going to
have the best time," she said.

A warm rush of affection, something he had not felt in a
long, long time, rose in Charles Livaudais' heart, and he
hugged her to him. "You darling," he whispered against her
hair. Then he held her away and laughed. "If I get this kind of
response for a little negligee, what would you do if I gave you
diamonds?"

"I'd rather have this," Francie said. She began undressing,
tossing her traveling suit and silk blouse across a chair, slipping her arms into the negligee's sleeves and tying the ribbon
sash around her waist. She posed again, watching the way the
lace ruffles fell back from her rounded arm when she lifted it,
the way they fell away from her breasts.

"Here's something to go with it," Charles said, taking another box from his suitcase. The gown inside was all lace,
lined with the sheerest silk. Francie held it, her mouth open,
her eyes filled with promises.

"I'm going straight in to bathe and put this on," she said.
"I've wanted something like this forever and I'm not going to
waste one minute before wearing it." She paused in the doorway to the bathroom. "Maybe tomorrow I'll let you bathe with
me," she said. As she closed the door behind her, Charles went
to the commode to fix himself a drink and then went to the fire
and sat down. His friend had come through in fine style. The
hotel was a small one, but it offered both luxury and privacy. It
was owned and managed by an old woman whose desire for
money was greater than her curiosity about the morality of her
guests. Tall and white-columned, it sat on a broad lawn over-
looking the Gulf; from their room they could watch the whitecaps churned up by the brisk November breeze. He sipped his
drink and thought again of the drive over. Francie had really
amused him, made him laugh as he hadn't in years. Watching
her across the table when they stopped for dinner before reaching the hotel, he had congratulated himself. What a rare find—
magnificent in bed and entertaining out of it. He thought of the
way he had felt when she thanked him for the negligee. Now,
watch out, he told himself as he finished his drink and went to
the commode to pour another. Don't complicate this thing
more than it already is.

"Look at me!" Francie cried from behind him. He spun

around and caught his breath. The lace gown clung to her high breasts, her small waist, and swirled away from her hips. "Aren't I wonderful?" she said. She came over to him and took the drink from his hand. "You don't need that," she said, covering his mouth with hers. She took his hand and led him toward the bed.

Lost in a world made up of creamy lace and smooth satin, teasing eyes and tempting lips, Charles needed nothing else.

On Saturday morning, bundled against the stiff wind from the open water, they walked together along the sea wall. "What would you be doing this weekend if you weren't here?" Charles asked.

"I don't know and I don't care," Francie said. She picked up a pine cone and tossed it out over the water, watching it bob on the brown surface. "I'd love to see really pretty water—bright blue and deep green and every other color. I'd love to see natives dancing and hear drums beating and wear one of those pretty skirt things native girls wear . . ." She moved restlessly. "Sometimes I think I was put in exactly the wrong place. Do you ever think that?"

"Many times," he said. He held her gloved hand in his; he lifted it, pulled back the glove, and kissed her palm. "Whenever I'm not with you."

Her eyes clouded. "Don't make pretty speeches," she said. She looked away, out to where the pine cone still bobbed. "It's all right to tell me I'm pretty, because that's true. But don't tell me how you feel about me, because that won't be."

"How do—" he started to say, and then stopped. "All right," he said. He pulled the glove up, closed his hand tightly over hers, and tucked her arm through his. "There's a delightful little place we can go for lunch," he said. "Excellent seafood, good oysters."

"Wonderful," she said. "I'm starved."

Even so, he was astonished at lunch at the amount of food she put away, dipping one oyster after the other into the hot sauce they concocted out of catsup and horseradish, then feasting on broiled mackerel. She ate with a kind of intense relish that reminded him of her response in bed—her response to everything, if it came to that. After lunch, they poked up and down the coast, stopping the automobile at anything that looked interesting. The smallest, most common things seemed to bring her pleasure. "You really don't need diamonds, do you?" he said when she was exclaiming over a ship in a bottle he insisted on buying for her.

She held the shimmering green bottle up to the light and looked at the miniature full-rigged clipper inside. "The only women who need diamonds are those not pretty enough to get people to look at them any other way." She turned and held the bottle toward him. "How do you think they got the ship in there? Do you know?"

He found himself answering all kinds of questions, dredging up bits and pieces of knowledge he'd forgotten he had. "You've quite worn me out," he told her as they climbed the stairs to their room that evening.

"I certainly have not," she said. She leaned against the door, gazing up at him. Her eyes, which had been quick and alive all afternoon, became soft, their color deepening. "But I will."

The rush of affection he had felt before swirled over him, stronger, shocking him with its force. He unlocked the door and pulled her inside. His fingers unbuttoned her coat, tugged at the drawstring at the neck of her wool dress. "You darling," he said.

Later, as he slipped into sleep, he made himself name the way he felt. For the first time in many, many years, he felt happy. Knowing that, he turned his face into the pillow and wept.

"Heavens, it's your wedding all over again," Alice Langlinais said to Louise as they entered St. Martin of Tours Church and saw the crowded pews. "All these people!" It was Louise's first public appearance since the last months of her pregnancy, and the occasion could not have been a happier one—the twins' christening. Everyone seemed to be in a celebratory mood this December 18. By two o'clock, when the ceremony started, the church was filled.

Louise lifted her veil and peered into the church. "I can't imagine what they're all doing here. They weren't all invited."

Alice hugged Gennie closer to her and glanced at Geneviève, who held Émilie. "They're happy for you, Louise. Happy for Beau."

"Well," Louise said, her eyes narrowing as she lowered the veil back over them. "I hope they don't think they're coming to the house afterward. I don't expect anyone I didn't specifically invite." She moved forward, looking to neither the left nor the right as she almost marched to the front pew. She wore pale gray; the only break in the cold, somber lines of her suit was the stark white of her blouse. The veil that covered her face completed the illusion that Louise was removing herself from the common humanity surrounding her.

"She should have waited for Beau," Geneviève said, her eyes following Louise down the aisle. "It doesn't look right, her going in by herself."

"Oh, the hell with it," Alice said. She was tired of Louise's pretensions and airs, tired of the means she used to get her own way. It had not escaped Alice's notice that although Louise was too exhausted to dine with her husband, she was not too exhausted to plan this new suit with her dressmaker. Or to spend long visits with Father Adrian, chatting about God knew what over endless cups of coffee.

The shocked look on Geneviève's face gave way to laughter. "Mais, Alice, be careful what you say in church! But I have to agree—sometimes, it's too much, the way that girl carries on."

A cluster of people surged in behind them, including Beau. He put his arms around Alice and Geneviève, turning them so the two babies could be seen. "Now, Hugh, what do you think?" he said to Louise's brother, who had been appointed Gennie's godfather. "Sweet enough to make even a confirmed bachelor like you think again, aren't they?"

Hugh held his hands out, a finger protruding from each, and watched the two little fists grab hold. "Maybe," he said. He looked around. "Where's Louise?"

"She went in already; she needed to sit down," Alice said. "Here, Beau, carry your children in." She settled a baby in each of his arms and stood back, surveying them. The twins' christening gowns trailed over the dark cloth of Beau's sleeves. The fine batiste material was embroidered and trimmed with Belgian lace; tiny caps covered their heads, with great rosettes for bows. The shawls were of the softest cashmere, edged with deep bands of lace. "There have never been prettier babies in the whole world," Alice said. She looked around, counting heads. "Now, where's Francie? For heaven's sake, that child will be late for her own funeral."

"Here, Mama," Francie said, bursting through the door. "And look who I brought with me." Caroline came in behind her, laughing, her face pink with cold.

"I was at Beau Chêne," she said. "I decided to drive in to pay a few calls and ran into Francie. Of course, I wasn't going to miss this christening!"

"We'll all miss it if we don't go in," Alice said, shooing them in ahead of her.

Louise, hearing the rustle in the pews, the voices greeting Beau and the babies, turned. Caroline Hamilton! Walking alongside Beau and smiling at him as if those two babies were hers! A rage as cold and dark as the deep chill of a December night swelled up in Louise. She gave Beau a furious look as he entered the pew, and then turned her attention to the altar, where Father Adrian waited to receive Geneviève and Émilie and their godparents.

With everyone else in the church, Louise watched the priest baptize her babies, but the sight did not register in her thoughts. In her mind's eye she saw, not the priest pouring water over the twins' bare heads, but Caroline's face, and the way she had looked at Beau when she smiled at him. To flaunt her before me—and in church! she thought furiously. She buried her rage within her, in a hard, cold place she could touch when she needed strength. Beau would be sorry. She would make sure that he was.

"Come to the fête," Beau said to Caroline when the ceremony was over. The twins had been sped home to their wet nurses; everyone else had gathered in the churchyard, visiting. "We're having it at Mama's; Louise isn't up to entertaining yet."

"I've got to get back to Lafayette," Caroline said. "But I do have something for your little girls." She took two small packages from her purse and handed them to him. "I was going to take them by your house today—I'm so glad I happened on their christening. Will you open them, Beau?"

The wrappings fell away and he lifted the lids of the twin boxes. Two gold bracelets shone against a bed of cotton. He picked one up. It was heavy, solid, with a monogram and birthdate traced on its gleaming surface.

"They're beautiful," he said. "Thank you, Caroline. Can't you really come? I never see you anymore!"

"You're busy," Caroline said. "Oh, Beau, there's so much to do at Beau Chêne. You know Mama. She never would have done much about clearing out Grandmama's things anyway, but after you stopped her from selling Beau Chêne, she acts like it doesn't even exist. I go as often as I can, and Berthe helps—but we get to talking about Grandmama, and then we start missing her like everything—and then we just cry on each other's shoulders!" Caroline laughed as she said that, but Beau saw the weariness and sadness in her eyes.

"Let me help you," he said. "One day this week?"

"Wednesday?" she said.

"Perfect. Come on, I'll walk you to your car."

Louise came over and held out her hand. "It was nice of you to come, Mrs. Hamilton."

"She brought these for the girls," Beau said, handing her the bracelets. He saw a look in Louise's eyes he hadn't seen in a long time as she gazed at the bracelets, picking up first one and then the other. It was a measuring look, almost as though she knew to the minutest degree the exact amount of gold and exact value of the workmanship.

"How sweet," Louise said. She met Caroline's eyes and smiled her narrow little smile. "How very thoughtful of you, Mrs. Hamilton. Beau has always told me what excellent taste you have. I see he is quite right." She tucked the bracelets into her muff. "He usually is, isn't he?" Then she turned and walked away. In the dull light of December, her hair was somber, a dull auburn that held no golden tints, cast no brilliance.

"Well," Caroline said, shaking her head as though ridding it of something that clung to it. "I really must go."

"Until Wednesday," Beau said, walking her to her automobile.

"Yes," she said. He watched her drive out of sight and then joined the others on their way to the fête.

At the reception, Louise seemed inspired, welcoming the congratulations heaped on her, enjoying the celebration. She laughed and talked and sipped champagne, and was so much like the girl Beau had courted that he felt the hope that lay quietly in his heart stirring. She stood beside him holding his hand while one guest after the other came up to tell them how beautiful the babies were. At one point, she lifted herself on tiptoe to kiss him. Champagne made him forget caution. He forced down the way she had looked at him in the pew at church, her coldness afterward when she spoke to Caroline.

And so when the evening was over, and they were alone in

their bedroom, he felt confident as he went to her and put his arms around her, bending his head to kiss her. She did not move or resist, but stood mutely in the circle of his arms while his lips moved over her face. He stepped away and looked at her. "Louise?"

"Are you going to ask if you can . . . can have me?" she said. The small warmth of the afternoon was gone, the familiar chill back. "Because don't." She moved to the bed and settled herself against her pillows. "I don't ever intend to let you do that to me again, Beau. Not ever." She reached behind her and changed a pillow's position. "In fact, you might as well move into another room for all the good it will do you to stay here." She picked up a book from the table at her side and opened it. Her eyes moved over the page, her fingers positioned to turn it.

Beau remained motionless, trying to control the anger that rose within him. He saw shadows leap higher against the wall as the fire behind him burned more brightly. It had begun to rain, a soft steady drizzle that struck rhythmically against the tin gutters that edged the roof. From down the hall, he heard a baby cry once, twice, then stop. Louise, in the bed, had not moved except to turn yet another page. At last his patience ended. He strode to her side and snatched the book from her hand. He felt that if he survived this moment without striking her, he could survive any temptation to violence.

"You are not going to drive me from this bed," he said. "Nor from this room."

She smiled. "Would you give me my book, please, Beau? Before you lose my place?"

He turned and hurled the book in one swift motion. It sailed toward the fireplace and fell into the middle of the flames. He turned back to her; for an instant her control left her and her face showed fear. Then she smiled again. "Well, I shall just have to buy another," she said. She settled lower on her pillows and pulled the covers higher. "Thank goodness that wasn't a rare edition, or that little display of temper would have cost you a pretty penny, Beau."

He could not believe the passion to hurt her he felt. He had been in fights: some sober encounters over points of honor, some drunken bouts over nothing at all. But never had he felt so on the edge of violence. He put both hands against the mantel and leaned forward, gripping the solid cypress, willing his blood to quiet.

He made himself walk carefully toward the bed. "I will sleep in this bed, Louise. Tonight and every night. I am your husband, whether you act as my wife or not. I am the father of your children, and you will honor me for that, as I honor you. I pay your bills, allow you your whims—and I will not allow you to make us the subject of gossip. Do you understand me, Louise?"

She slipped lower under the covers. He could see nothing but her eyes, narrowed against the fire's brightness. "All right," she said. "If that's what you want."

"That is hardly what I want," Beau said. "It appears, however, that that is what I have." Again a baby's cry came from down the hall. "Now, if you'll excuse me," he said, "I think I'll go tell my daughters good night."

On Wednesday Beau drove to Beau Chêne, leaving his automobile windows open so he could breathe in the fresh country air. He could feel his lungs expanding; would anything expand his soul? Walls seemed to have closed around him, walls made by the bitterness in Louise's eyes and the vindictiveness in her heart. Only the twins gave him something to look forward to. Helping set up the crèche at the church the afternoon before, he had realized why the most significant effect of the Christmas story was the hope an infant brings.

He looked up at Beau Chêne as he drove down the driveway beneath the huge oaks. The house seemed cold, alien; he noticed that the swags of greenery tied with red bows that used to grace the upper gallery every Christmas season were missing, and that no tall tree glimmered from behind the parlor draperies. It's as though the house has been put to rest too, he thought as he knocked at the front door.

Caroline answered the door herself, reaching out a hand to draw him inside. "I'm so glad you've come, Beau," she said, smiling. "It's a sad task, but having you to help will make it lighter."

"You'll find I'm a devoted and dependable worker, ma'am," he said. "And I hope you have plenty for me to do, because I came ready to work."

"Indeed I do," she said, leading him upstairs to Marthe's room, where they set to work, making bundles of her clothes, burning old papers in the fireplace, rendering the last services to the dead. "There's still the office to tend to," Caroline said when the morning's work was done, "but that's for another day." She sat in Marthe's low rocker, rocking slowly. "I feel so much better having this done—I can let the rest go until after Christmas." She reached a hand around and rubbed her back. "I'm going to have another baby, Beau. That's another reason all this has worn me out so."

"Louise refuses to ever have another," he said. She looked at him, and Beau knew she realized what those words meant.

Caroline stood up and rubbed her back again. "Isn't it lucky you had twins the first time, then?" she said. Her voice sounded formal, almost cool, and he knew she was struggling to keep from saying what she really thought. "Well, they'll have fun growing up together, our children." She went to the window that overlooked the back of the property and pulled back the drapery. "Is it worth it, Beau?" she asked suddenly.

"What?" he said, coming to stand next to her.

She gestured at the room, out over the landscape below them. "This house. The land."

He knew what she was thinking, but he did not want to hear any more. "Caroline—"

She faced him, put one slender hand across his lips. "Shh, Beau, hear me out. A terrible price has been paid for this house, this land. It had better be worth it, to somebody." Her face came closer to his, and he knew he could kiss her. For a moment, he hesitated. To what purpose, a kiss here, an hour's visit there? Wouldn't it be better to break off completely, let Caroline and Raoul and their growing family go one way, and his go another? Then his lips closed over hers. Maybe later, when the twins were older, and could fill some of the emptiness in his life. Maybe later, when the forfeit they both had honored did not seem so light a weight at its end of the scale.

He took a small velvet box from his pocket and handed it to her. "Merry Christmas," he said. His voice held such love that her eyes misted with tears. She opened the box, and the tears fell. It was a miniature of Marthe he had had painted, set in a small gold locket.

"Beau," she said, her arms around him. "Doesn't it seem strange that two people who know each other so well have to spend most of their time with someone else?"

"Not strange," he said. He longed to touch her, feel the life that grew inside her. "Absurd." His hand turned her face to him. "I think about you all the time, Caroline."

She stepped away from him. "I wish you didn't, Beau. I really wish you didn't."

The look on his face showed his surprise.

"Until today," Caroline said, "I had thought you and Louise were like Raoul and I are. Not the love you and I had. But a good strong marriage." Her face clouded. "Now I know you don't have that kind of marriage, Beau. Thinking of me can't make you anything but sad. I . . . I wonder if we shouldn't just . . . not see each other, Beau. It can't make you happy!"

His own thoughts on her lips sounded like a sentence of execution. "Caroline." He made his voice steady, would not allow the anguish he felt at the thought of never seeing her color it. "You've always said you could never repay me—or my family—for all the ways we've helped you. And your grandmother. I never thought I'd ask you to try. I am now. Caroline, don't stop seeing me. Please." He went to her, knelt, and pressed his face against the rough cloth of her apron.

"Oh, Beau!" She lowered herself to the floor and held him against her. Her eyes fell on the miniature around her neck and she thought of what the priest had said at Marthe's funeral: "The only real tragedy in losing this great lady will be if we, in our lives, fail to imitate her." Her chin lifted and her back straightened. She did not know how she could give Beau the love and comfort he needed without making dangerous inroads into the dam she had built to keep her own emotions checked. But somehow, she had to try. "All right, Beau," she said. "All right."

Down in the kitchen, Berthe looked at the clock. Seems like it's taking a long time to get those things cleared out, she thought. She sighed. I tell you the truth, Miss Marthe. I'se glad you're not here to see those two. Seems like the longer they're married to other people, the more they needs each other. She sighed again. If'n the good Lord 'splains that to you, Miss Marthe, I sure does wish you'd tell me. She heard footsteps behind her and turned to see Beau and Caroline in the doorway. Look at those babies, she thought. Their feelings is all over their faces. She bent over the oven, took out a roasted chicken, and put it on the table. "Looks like you done cheered Miss Caroline up some, Mr. Beau."

"I think she did the same for me," Beau said. But the look in Berthe's eyes told him they had no secrets from her, and Beau wondered—how long would it be before there were no secrets left?

23

Beau stood back and looked at the sign Dusty had just nailed over the door that led into a small office down the street from Beau's law office. "Gemini Oil. It has a good ring to it, doesn't it, Dusty?"

"Sure, Beau." Dusty squinted up at the black letters outlined with gold. "What the hell does it mean, though?"

Beau laughed. "I named it for the twins," he said.

"The twins! I don't get it."

"The Gemini is one of the constellations—it's named after mythological twins, Castor and Pollux. I thought . . . well, I thought that name would bring my new oil company good luck."

"Let's go inside and look at those maps," Dusty said. "We've got some damn good leases. You might not need too much luck to make this company take off."

"Hope so," Beau said, opening the door and standing aside to let Dusty enter. He paused to take one more look at the sign, then followed Dusty inside. Ever since he had gone around the countryside signing up land, leasing it against future drilling, he had toyed with the idea of a production company. He and Claude had discussed it for a long time. Claude had been interested, and willing to put up capital. "But, hell, Beau, I don't want to do one damn thing more. I've got more on my plate than I'm comfortable with now. No, you let this be your baby." He had smiled, that wolf-grin challenge. "Let's see if you can make that oil company as profitable as our other enterprises."

That had been all the challenge Beau needed. He had used the long dull months of Louise's pregnancy to set up the company charter, solidify its leasing position, line up drilling equipment and crews. "You're the field-operations boss," he'd told Dusty. "And my oil dowser as well. I want to start four wells after the first of the year, one after the other. You pick the sites, I'll get equipment to them."

Now the drilling equipment had arrived and waited on a siding just beyond the boundaries of the farm. Beau sat in the chair at the desk and propped his booted feet on it. "Okay, Dusty, what sites do you have in mind? Where should we start?"

Dusty looked at the map of St. Martin Parish he had spread over the desk. His callused finger plunged downward, hitting in turn four marks he had drawn with a heavy pencil. "Here," he said. He reared up and looked at Beau. "Close enough not to lose time and money moving equipment. And to hit the same big pool I just about guarantee is under that land."

Beau laughed. The excitement of forming the company had vitalized his days and worn him out sufficiently so that he slept soundly through the nights. He was learning that the cold he lived in at home could be warmed by his enthusiasm for other things. "I've got a feeling, Dusty," Beau said. "A feeling Gemini Oil's going to be a pretty big operation one of these days."

"I hope so," Dusty said. His voice was serious, with no hint of his normal scoffing humor. "You deserve it."

"Well," Beau said, rolling up the map and slipping it back into its case. "When can you get started?"

Dusty walked to the window and cocked an eye at the sky. It had begun to rain again, as it had all month, a slow, steady downpour that would likely go on for hours. "God, look at the rain," Dusty said. "Seems like 1922 hasn't stopped crying since it was born. We'll be stuck in the mud till March. Try to sink a well in this and you'd lose your pipe, your framing—"

"Do what you can. I don't want those crews idle, and I want oil by summer."

"Yes, sir!" Dusty said, making a mock salute. He pulled his lean form together, stood and picked up the map. "Any particular day you want me to strike oil?" he said, grinning.

"Just so when you hit, you hit big," Beau said. The force behind his voice startled Dusty.

"Beau, what's got you so fired up? It's not like you don't have a heap of money already."

"Money?"

"Well, Beau. Oil is money. Leastways, that's why most people drill for it."

Beau's eyes were focused on a distant landscape, a vision crowded with tall derricks that pumped oil, thick black oil that made a river, not just of money, but of influence and power. It was a fine thing to be a Langlinais, to be born to wealth, to have respect handed to him as his due. But dammit, he did not want to coast on the deeds of other men. He wanted to create his own name, and to be respected because in his own right he was someone to be reckoned with.

"Money's part of it, I guess, Dusty," he said slowly. He rose and stood at the desk, his hands resting lightly in front of him. "But it's more than money. It's . . . well, being part of a new thing sweeping the state—finding a place that's mine, I guess." He paused, took a deep breath, and let it out. "I guess it's like anything else you want, Dusty. Until you have it, you're not that sure what it will be like, or what you'll do when you get it. You just want it."

"You mean power," Dusty said, his voice not quite a question.

Beau saw something in Dusty's eyes he could not quite identify—not disapproval, not disappointment—sorrow? He shrugged. "Some of the highest cards are bought with oil," he said.

"Well, I guess I'd better find you some then, Beau," Dusty said.

"I'm counting on you to do just that," Beau said. He pulled on a raincoat, shoved a hat on his head, and plunged out into the rain. A gust of wind blew in the office door as he went out, and Dusty slammed the door shut quickly, the image of Beau's figure, dark against the falling rain, still in his eyes. When he went back to the desk to begin making careful lists of the order of work, he could not rid his mind of the image of Beau leaving, shoulders hunched against the rain, head ducked low. A lone figure struggling through the rain.

Something about Beau's passion for oil wasn't right. He's taking the fun out of it, Dusty thought. That's what it is. Barely twenty-two years old, and he's taking the fun out of it.

"How do you like it?" Charles asked Francie, watching her look over the parlor of the tiny house on Dumaime Street.

"It's pretty," she said. She ran her hand over the carving on the white marble mantel, picked up the porcelain clock and

studied it. "It's got some nice things in it." She shrugged.
"Who lives here?"

"No one," Charles said. He was finding it more difficult than
he had thought to tell her what he had done. The weekend on
the Gulf Coast had been their last meeting; the long Christmas
break had kept Francie in St. Martinville, and business had
kept him in New York until late January. When he had called
her, following their agreed-upon code and saying he was her
dentist, he had found himself unable to think of anything but
Francie until she had called back. She had sounded friendly,
polite—but not very eager to see him.

She turned to him, her eyes demanding an answer. "I don't
understand. What are we doing here? Do you rent this out?"

"I bought it," he said. "For . . . for us."

She looked so vulnerable that he was suddenly frightened.
Then her usual impertinent smile flashed at him. "For us? Wait
a minute—aren't you forgetting something?" She moved toward him, the smile fading. "There isn't any 'us.' You're
married and I'm a schoolgirl. I'd say you wasted your money,
Mr. Livaudais."

"Francie, listen. We can't continue going to the Coast—it
won't work. And you're right, you shouldn't have to go to
that cheap club. I thought if we had a little house, a private
place—"

"Clara says I'm a fool and that I'll get pregnant," Francie cut
in. "She says I'm lucky I haven't already."

"You can't get pregnant, you little silly. Do you think I'd
take a risk like that?"

"Can't? What do you know about it?"

"I'm sterile," he said.

Her quick laughter cut him in a way he thought he could
never be hurt again. It was a harsh, knowing laugh. It hinted of
intimate knowledge, knowledge he knew he had given her. He
wanted to tell her how he felt about her; would that bring her
innocence back?

"What was Caroline?" she asked in a taunting voice. "An
immaculate conception?"

"Apparently she was my one contribution to the human
race," he said. "I can never have another—so my doctor tells
me. So far I haven't proved him wrong."

Something in Francie relaxed, and when she smiled, it was a

younger, fresher smile. "Well, if you had to have only one, you had a good one."

"Francie . . ." He could argue with her no longer. From the day he began hunting for a little house, he had shut reality out and allowed himself to dream. When he had found this one, located on a quiet corner of a quiet street, he had furnished it as though it were a playhouse, waiting only for the doll to complete it.

"Is this really ours?" she said.

He looked up. Francie was walking around the room, stroking the fabric of the upholstery, absorbing the feel of her surroundings. "I mean, no one else lives here and bolts out the back door when you call and say you're coming?"

"God, of course not!"

"Well," she said. "You've got a reputation for being a pretty sharp dealer, Mr. Livaudais. I wasn't sure you would have gone to all this trouble and expense just for . . . just to take me to bed."

"I didn't," he said. He moved into her path and blocked her way. "I went to all this trouble and expense so you and I could be together. So we can have tea together, and lounge around together—"

"And have sex together," Francie said, her mouth laughing, but her eyes large and serious.

"And make love together," he said.

They looked at each other, their bodies held slightly apart, the tension in their eyes making a wire that wound them slowly together. Her arms came around his neck as his closed around her body, and their lips met. He felt her hand stroking his cheek, felt the silk of her hair, breathed in the light violet scent of her cologne.

"How long is this filling going to take, Doctor?" Francie asked.

"What . . .?" Then he remembered their cover story and laughed. "I think it's going to be a very complicated one," he said. He swung her up in his arms and went into the long hall off which the other rooms opened. He felt young, vigorous enough to carry her to the moon. "I'm afraid it's going to take a very long time." He kissed her again. "And it's likely to require any number of follow-up visits."

"How awful," Francie said. "I'll try hard to bear it."

Just as he bent over to lay her on the bed, she pulled him

against her. "Charles. Oh, Charles. I love . . . our little house."

"So do I," he said. "So do I."

As winter melted into spring, Charles's inner life revolved more deeply around the house on Dumaine Street. Though he kept to his usual routine, going each day to his office on Canal Street, entering into the frivolous pace of the Carnival season, a part of him always lived in the cottage he shared with Francie. Hélène noticed the change in him. "Your new friend must be quite a woman," she taunted. "You're almost pleasant to be around these days, and I know I can't take credit for that." But he refused to enter into the old game, refused to be goaded into one of their confrontations that would end with him reaching for his checkbook.

When her weapons proved useless, Hélène tried to find an ally. "I think your father may have . . . well, I have reason to think he's . . . taken up with someone," she confided to Caroline during one of Caroline's visits to the city.

Caroline lifted her teacup to her lips and sipped, her eyes on her mother's face. "Oh?" she said.

Hélène, thinking she had Caroline's interest, leaned forward. "Yes. You're too young to notice such things—I hope you never have reason to look for them—but there are signs that tell a wife when her husband isn't being faithful." She looked at her daughter. "I wouldn't mind so much—but I'm afraid it will get out. And that would make us all look so foolish."

Caroline looked at the face opposite her. She hardly recognized it as belonging to her mother, and she realized that she had stopped looking at her mother long ago. Each line stood out clearly, each sagging bit of skin telling its own story. Caroline thought of the way her grandmother had looked, her skin almost unmarked, her hair not fully gray. It's not age that withers us, she thought. "Why are you telling me this, Mama?"

"I thought if you spoke to him . . ." Unconsciously Hélène licked her lips. Her tongue, running over the thin, dry lips, as if already savoring the success of her strategies, made Caroline shudder. She stood up, drawing her skirt close around her.

"Whatever made you think I would?" she said, staring down at Hélène.

"Why, he's your father, your child's grandfather. Don't you care?"

"No," Caroline said. Her gaze swept the length of the room. "I stopped caring what happened in this house quite a while ago, Mama. I stopped caring, as a matter of fact, the day you and Papa no longer cared about me."

Then Hélène knew that she had no weapons left. She had to watch bitterly as Charles's spirits blossomed with the spring, and took to drinking sherry in the afternoon, her mind seething with revenge. Plans roiled up out of the darkness of her mind, plans that appeared clearly in the light of the amber liquid she drank. But they faded in the drunken haze she slipped into, leaving her mind empty and it all to be done again. And so the spring slipped away.

Gemini Oil's first well came in on April 16, celebrating, Beau claimed, the twins' fifth-month birthday. "I told you they'd bring me luck if I named the company for them," he said to Dusty as they opened champagne.

Dusty filled his glass and sat opposite Beau. "Those wells should be coming in quickly now—I've got three more shafts started. You sure you got the transport worked out for the oil?"

"I'm sure," Beau said. "It'll go through a private pipeline to Standard's big one." The past months had been busy ones; while Dusty drilled and supervised the field operations, Beau had found buyers for the expected oil, signed a contract for moving it, and gotten a thorough initiation into the state's growing oil industry.

"You ain't scared of Standard Oil cutting you off when they feel like it? The way they did those men up at the Pine Island field?"

Beau tipped the champagne bottle over their glasses. "Nope," he said. He smiled at Dusty. "I haven't hung around my papa all these years for nothing. I was standing on the porch of the governor's mansion when Amos Gordon, Standard Oil's lawyer, arrived to read over what John Parker was proposing to the Constitutional Convention. So I presumed on that small circumstance of being under the same roof at the same time and called on him. Talked to him as one lawyer to another and got a pretty near iron-clad contract."

"Good," Dusty said. "I'd sure as hell hate to pump all this stuff out of the ground and have it sit around in storage tanks."

"Don't worry about that," Beau said. "The police juries in Louisiana have a lot more power than people from outside the state might think. We control roads and levees, for one thing. Rights-of-way across parish land." He winked at Dusty. "I guess Mr. Gordon was able to see the advantage of being on my good side."

"You already playing those high cards, aren't you, Beau?" Dusty said, getting up and shoving his broad-brimmed hat down over his ears. "I sure as hell am glad you're playing on my side."

Francie sat in the big wooden swing on the Langlinais front porch, a book open in her lap, her eyes fixed on the rosa-de-montana vine that filled the end of the porch with pink blossoms and thick green leaves. She had been home only four days, but already she saw what a very long summer lay ahead of her. She tossed her head impatiently. You can't be in love with him, it's pointless and dumb. She tried to think of something to make her dislike him. Surely he had been insensitive, uncaring . . . but she came up blank. When she thought of him, she remembered only his kindness, his tenderness, the way he seemed to worship her.

The spring had been magical, as romantic as any novel she had ever read. The tiny patio of their house had been filled with hibiscus and sweet olive and fragrant magnolia frascati. They had read poetry to each other. Charles, hesitant at first, acting as though she might laugh at him, had become bolder, and some of her best memories were of his deep voice reading the *Sonnets from the Portuguese* to her just before they made love.

She slammed the book shut and pushed her foot against the floor to set the swing in hard motion. Damn! She had to find some way to see him. She couldn't just stay in St. Martinville this entire summer, playing tennis and swimming in the bayou as though she were still a schoolgirl.

"Well," Beau said, appearing at the bottom of the porch steps. "You look like you just lost your last friend. What's the matter?"

"Bored, I guess," Francie said.

"Bored! I thought you'd be as happy as a fox in a henhouse

to be home again and free of your wardens, as you so respectfully call the good nuns." He came and sat beside her. "What are you reading?"

"Nothing," Francie said, shoving the book farther from him. "Just some English poetry." It was, in fact, a copy of the *Sonnets from the Portuguese* Charles had given her. The inscription in the front was dangerous, but it was a book she had not been able to bear to leave in the house on Dumaine with the other gifts Charles showered on her. "To my own little Portuguese, who shows me all the ways she loves me each time we meet," Charles had written. Thinking of those ways, Francie smiled. She had to see Charles, and soon. That was all there was to it.

"Beau, you know how boring it can be down here. New Orleans has all kinds of things to do, I'm used to having a lot going on!" Her mind worked furiously. Maybe she could talk Beau into taking her to New Orleans . . . or better yet, the Gulf Coast. She leaned back in the swing, letting the toe of one foot propel it into slow motion. "Don't you ever want to get away from here for a while?"

Beau's own loneliness responded to the longing in Francie's voice. "God, yes," he said.

"Why don't you go, then? You could take Louise and the babies, go to some really fun place like the Gulf Coast—the girls at school say it's wonderful there during the summer. A lot of them have houses there—they sail, and fish off the piers . . . dance at the yacht club."

Moodily Beau lit a cigarette. He saw the question forming on Francie's lips and laughed, handing her one. "Don't guess you'll go to hell over one cigarette."

Her eyes flickered. "Guess not," she said. "About the Coast—why not, Beau? Get the twins to a cooler place—and yourself to a livelier one."

"Catch Louise agreeing to that," he said. "Leave her church meetings that long? I don't think so."

"Let her stay then," Francie said. "*I* could go, help Becca with the babies."

"I can just hear what Louise would say to that," he said.

"Does everyone marry the wrong person, Beau?" she said suddenly. The passion behind her question startled him.

"Everyone? Look at Mama and Papa, they're happy."

"I didn't mean them," Francie said impatiently. "I meant . . . well, you and Louise."

"Well, my God, Francie, I didn't know I was marrying the wrong person!" He immediately regretted his words. "Look, I shouldn't have said that. Forget it, will you?"

"I won't tell anyone, Beau. But do you think I don't know you and Louise aren't happy? Do you ever look in the mirror?"

"Shows, does it?"

Francie took his hand. "Well, it does to me." She gave him another sidewise glance and then said, quickly, as though she wouldn't speak at all if she did not speak it all at once. "Because I know what it is to love someone—and not really be able to have them."

Something in her tone struck a warning note in his head. "Francie, what do you mean? What have you been up to?"

"Nothing," she said, in that same rapid way. "Nothing at all. I just . . . Beau, even if Louise doesn't go, couldn't you and I go to the Coast, even if it was just for a week?" She held both his hands in hers, and her eyes were pleading. "Couldn't we?"

The idea *was* suddenly attractive. He could almost smell the salt-tinged breeze, see the whitecaps dancing on the water. Feel the hot wood of the piers under his feet, the tug of a fish on his line. "We'll see," he said. He felt his sister's arms come around his neck, felt her place a kiss on his cheek. Her body, pressed near his, was that of a woman. And in that moment, Beau was as sure as he could be without her telling him that Francie had a lover.

He shifted slightly away and looked at her. "Any particular reason why you're so hot to get to the Gulf Coast?"

"No," she said, not looking at him.

"Francie. Is there a man?"

"Maybe."

"Do you think I'd take you now I know that?" he demanded.

She laughed and relaxed against the swing, holding her legs straight out in front of her. She lifted her arms high above her head and stretched. Her body made one long line, from the tips of her fingers to the tips of her toes. Her suntanned skin stood out vividly against the pale green of her dress. "Of course you will," she said. "You of all people won't stand in the way of true love."

"My life is complicated enough as it is," Beau said. "Don't make it worse."

She put her arms down, kicked against the porch floor, and begin swinging gently to and fro. "I won't make it worse, I'll make it better. I'll teach you how to have fun again, Beau."

Thinking of the monotony of the routine legal work on his desk made the idea of a trip to the Gulf Coast even more attractive; by the time Beau arrived at his office the next morning, he had determined that he would go. "Oh, Mr. Langlinais," his secretary said when he entered her office. "Mr. Huey Long just called. He wants you to call him as soon as possible. He said it was important."

Now what the hell did Huey Long want him for?

He placed the call, and soon heard Long's booming voice over the line.

"Beau Langlinais—thanks for getting back to me. Hear you're in for congratulations—got another well down there, haven't you?"

"I didn't realize every well I drilled made the papers," Beau said. He felt put off; he did not like a man knowing his business—or was it the fact that Long apparently made it his business that Beau objected to?

Long laughed. "Hell, Langlinais, don't be so touchy. I've had my eye on you Langlinaises for a while now. Didn't think I'd miss a development like Gemini Oil, did you?"

"You haven't said what you want," Beau said. His own turbulent feelings surprised him. He felt flattered—but he also felt wary. There was a fascination in that voice, in its easy roll, that was almost too appealing.

"You," Long said abruptly. He let a silent pause develop, then spoke in a low, confidential tone. "You been following the Cumberland case?"

"What's in the papers," Beau said.

"It's gotten kind of complicated," Long said. "You know we got a rehearing on the rate increase Cumberland got last year. And you must have read that the commission decided this past May that pending a final decision, all the rate increases allowed last year were suspended. Well, that should have done it. I'd called the final hearing for this month, almost a matter of form. But now Cumberland's gotten a federal judge over in the eastern district court to grant an injunction to keep the commission from suspending those increases."

"They don't give up, do they?" Beau said.

"Neither do I," Long said, and Beau heard the grim force in his voice. "We've got a fight in federal courts on our hands, going to have to appeal that injunction. And that's what I want you for."

"I'm not following you." His earlier ambivalence disappeared. The confidence in Long's voice told Beau how much regard Long had for him. That was more than flattering, it was seductive.

"I'm representing the commission as chief counsel, but I've got so much on my plate I'm going to need help." Long's voice became stronger, seemed to fill Beau's mind. "Any man who can take on Amos Gordon and win is a man I want on my team, Beau," said Long.

"So you know about the guarantee I got on pipeline service to transport my oil," Beau said. "You do have big ears."

"Not big. Just a lot of 'em," Long said. "How about it, can you spare the time to do some research for me?"

Working with Long was tempting. On the other hand, it would mean long hours in law libraries, with very little of the fire and glory of the trial falling to him. "I was thinking about going to the Gulf Coast for a while," Beau said.

"Well," Long said, his tone now faintly contemptuous. "That doesn't sound like you—just walking away from everything while the poor folks pay the price."

This time the silence came from Beau's end of the line. He knew he was being taunted, chided into saying yes. He'd been put in a position that he could not defend; while he did not really believe that he was shirking a responsibility to the people of the state, he couldn't help but see Long's viewpoint. He remembered Long's background—sharecropper family, the barefoot walks to a country school. The good opinion of this man became suddenly important.

"I was really going to oblige . . . someone else," he said, thinking of Francie. "There's no reason that trip can't be postponed."

"Good," Long said.

The easy satisfaction in his voice irritated Beau; it was clear that Long had correctly anticipated Beau's reaction. "But you might wish you'd hired a law clerk to do that research," Beau said. "I don't come cheap."

Now Long's voice was hushed and intimate. "Do you think I'd hire you if you did? Besides, if things work out—this is just the beginning."

"Beginning?" Beau asked. It was amazing how Long's most casual reference seemed filled with meaning.

"Of changes in this state," Long said.

"Changes you're going to orchestrate?"

"Damn right," Long said. Then he laughed. "But there'll be plenty of first chairs, Beau, if you take my meaning."

"Let's get past Cumberland before we take on anything else," Beau said. He heard the use of the plural pronouns and knew he had already committed himself to Long's team. Well, there were probably worse ways to spend the summer. "I'll drive down to New Orleans tomorrow."

"Sure thing," Long said. "I'll be looking for you."

Beau hung up the telephone and sat looking at it for a moment. He still wasn't sure how he felt. He had had little time, really, to think. He agreed with Long on the Cumberland issue, always had. Well, he would work on that. And if there came a time when Long asked him to do something else—then he'd see. Feeling satisfied at last, he reached for a brief and began reading, marking changes and questions as he read.

He left for New Orleans without thinking of his casual promise to Francie that he might take her to the Gulf Coast. Francie, learning from her mother that Beau had gone to New Orleans on business, shrugged her disappointment away. If Beau worked hard in New Orleans, he'd want the relaxation the Coast offered all the more. But by early July, Francie knew that her need to get away from St. Martinville was no longer prompted by boredom, but by necessity.

She called Beau at the Monteleone Hotel. "What do you think about my coming down to New Orleans and staying for a few days?" she asked. "It's so dull down here, Beau." She hoped the intensity of her need would somehow be communicated to him, and that he would say yes.

But Beau was caught up in the intricacies of the case. He heard none of Francie's desperation. He heard only a rather inopportune request which, if he agreed to it, would have him tied to the task of chaperoning this unpredictable sister when he wanted to work.

"That's just not possible, Francie," he said. "I'm working down here. I can't be taking you all over New Orleans. Go visit Aunt Claudine, why don't you?"

"She's stricter than Mama is," Francie said. "I could never—" She bit her lip. "All right, Beau."

She sounded so disappointed that his conscience was touched. "I ought to be clear here in a few weeks. Then we'll go to the Coast, Francie. I promise."

"Fine," she said. The emotion was ironed out of her voice, leaving it flat, but he thought he could hear tears behind the words, and hung up wondering what on earth was going on that Francie sounded like that.

In St. Martinville, Francie hung up the receiver and walked slowly upstairs to her room. She closed and locked the door and stood looking around her as though the familiar objects held an answer she had not yet seen. Then she took stationery, filled her pen, and sat staring at the blank paper.

The stationery bore the name Monarch Oil Company and an address in New Iberia. "Just put 'Personal' on each letter; my secretary won't open it," Charles had said when he had given it to her to use when she wrote to him. In return, she had given him stationery with "The Oaks" and a St. Francisville address engraved on the back of each envelope.

His secretary had better not open this one, Francie thought. If only Beau would take her to the Coast; it would have been so much easier if she could have seen Charles in person. Well, there was nothing for it; she had to get this letter written somehow, and if there was no easy way to tell him, she would have to put it in a letter. She began writing. "Caroline is apparently not to be your only contribution to the human race. I'm pregnant, almost two months, as nearly as I can tell. I am also very, very scared, and wish I could talk to you. I just tried to arrange a way to come to New Orleans so I could see you, but it didn't work out. I *must* talk to you. Please let me know when and how I can see you." She reread the letter, went back and underlined "very" several times with thick black strokes of her pen. The letter seemed inadequate, did not convey her growing terror. But she could think of nothing else to write. She slipped the letter into a Monarch Oil envelope, addressed it in a bold block print, and put a stamp on it. I'll mail it now, she thought. So it'll get there as fast as possible. She walked to the post office on the square, put the letter in the slot, and watched it drop out of sight. Walking home again, she felt better. Charles would know what to do. Charles always knew what to do.

In New Orleans a few mornings later Charles took up the letter eagerly. Francie had become important to him to a degree he found almost frightening. What had begun as a piece of neat revenge against Alice Langlinais was in a fair way of becoming a noose around his own neck. How could I have known, he asked himself as he slit the envelope open, that I would fall in love?

He stared at the letter in shock, using the mental discipline he used to commit to memory the complex details of one of his cases to make himself comprehend the words. It can't be, he said to himself, tucking the letter back in its envelope and slipping it inside his coat pocket. He was sterile—his doctor had told him so. Something else had to be causing Francie's symptoms. I'll have to figure some way to get her here and to a discreet doctor who can examine her and tell us what's wrong. He gave his mind the problem to work on and settled down to the rest of the morning's work.

But lunching at his club, he happened to run across Hélène's gynecologist. He beckoned to that gentleman to join him for a drink. "It's lucky I ran into you; I probably would have called you anyway," Charles said, signaling the waiter to bring them a cocktail. "I've got a legal problem. A client of mine who's been sterile for years is ready to divorce his wife because she's turned up pregnant."

The doctor raised his eyebrows. "Seems reasonable."

"Yes. But the wife just isn't the sort that would have had an affair. And don't tell me you can never know."

"You say he's been sterile for years—was there a time when he wasn't?"

"They had one child," Charles said. "Then no more." He knew the doctor probably doubted the existence of the "client" by now, but it was a risk he had to take. Who better than the man at the table with him knew the probability that Charles's sterility was not permanent.

"Is that all your client has to go on? His wife's pregnancy?"

"You mean, is that all the evidence he has of an affair? Yes."

"And he and his wife have continued to have relations?"

"So I'm told."

The doctor rose. "Well, I don't think I'd go to court on her pregnancy alone. Sterility's a funny thing, Charles, particularly in cases where there was no trauma or definable physical cause." He rose and looked at Charles carefully. "Hope that helps you."

"I don't know if it helps," Charles said. "But it tells me where we stand."

Squarely in the hangman's hands, he thought. A wave of

nausea swept over him, and he gripped the edge of the table, trying not to be sick.

"You all right, Mr. Livaudais?" a waiter's voice asked. Then someone was leading him from the dining room back into the rooms where the steam bath and massage tables were located. He found himself lying on a cot with a cold cloth on his forehead, solicitous voices floating over his throbbing head.

"I just need to be quiet awhile," he said, forcing himself to speak. "Awfully hot outside. Drank that damn cocktail too fast."

The voices diminished, fell silent, and he knew he was alone. He waited for the nausea to quiet, and for his head to stop hurting. And he knew, lying there in the back room of his distinguished club, that the pain that lay ahead would be many times worse than what he felt now. If he chose to face it. He could, of course, just not answer her, leave her to solve the problem herself. She could always go to her father; surely the Langlinais resources were sufficient to take care of one small pregnancy. Even as he thought of abandoning her, the memory of Francie's face rose before him. No—he could never abandon her.

He wrote to Francie, asking her to meet him at Beau Chêne. The long, hot drive over dust-veiled roads several days later was like a journey through hell. When he came finally to the great pink house, sitting serenely beneath its oak trees, a sense of unreality overwhelmed him. Francie, coming slowly toward him, seemed part of that unreality. The branches of the trees, cutting through the strong light of the July noon, made a chiaroscuro effect; the alternating light and shadow put Francie's figure now in bold relief, now in obscurity. She wore a scarlet linen sailor dress with a large collar and a navy bow tied at the neck. Her walk was slow, steady; she held her body carefully, as though it were something she had been given to carry.

When she reached him, Francie flung herself into his arms, sobbing against his chest. Just as suddenly, Charles found himself thrust back into reality; he knew that if he were frightened, it was because he had reason to be, and if he felt shame, it was because he had done a great wrong. "It's going to be all right," he whispered over and over again. He didn't know if he were whispering for Francie or for himself. He pulled her to a bench set beneath one of the great oaks. "It's going to be all right."

She turned her face to his. Her body was in shadow, but by a trick of light, her face remained in full sun; it shone with hope. He knew what lay behind that shining look—the same bubblelike dream he had allowed himself for one short hour. He had let himself imagine running away, marrying her, having the baby. Living happily ever after. He knew it was sheer madness. Denying that dream had been the hardest thing he had ever done. He fixed his eyes on her great eyes, still shining with love and hope.

"There's a woman near here," he said, and he shifted his gaze from hers. "She can . . . take care of you."

He saw the shadow move up from Francie's waist to her face, but before it shielded her, he looked back into her eyes and saw hope die. He felt a fist form against his chest. "Kill it, you mean," she said, and turned away.

He wanted to object, to tell her there was no real baby yet. But one look at her straight back, her set shoulders, and he knew he could not. "Yes," he said.

He could not see her face. Only the way her shoulders and back stiffened, and her head came even more erect, told him she was fighting tears. He could see her slender hands clenching, see the nails digging into the soft palms he had so often kissed. "Francie!" He grabbed her shoulders and turned her to him. "Francie, don't you know I hate this almost as much as you do?"

For one long moment her eyes met his. And he saw in them something he had never seen there before—hate. He tried to hold her against his body, but she jerked away from him.

"We'd better get on with it, hadn't we?" she said. She felt caught by the terrible forces Charles had let loose in her life. She could feel them ready to sweep over all the happy memories, all the . . . love. She stood and looked at him, trying to see the man she loved.

Charles felt her scrutiny diminishing him. "She's . . . she's very experienced, I'm told," he said, rising.

"Good," Francie said, putting some of her old bravado in her voice. "Because I'm not."

He looked around. "How did you get out here?"

"I rode one of the farm horses home from Grandmama's yesterday. I rode it back this afternoon." She forced a smile.

"Actually, I kind of hoped all that riding would . . . solve my problem."

"It will all be over before you know it, Francie. And then—"

"Don't give me any 'and thens,'" she said. She looked at him, a long, measuring look that made Charles see just how small he was in her eyes. "You don't seem to be able to live up to them."

She got into the car beside him, head held high. Her courage made Charles despise his own weakness. But what could he do? His mind raced over all the solutions he had thought of and discarded. This one, no matter how terrible, was the only one that would work. Somehow, that only made him feel worse.

He turned the car around and drove in silence to a weed-filled drive that wound back to a small, weathered cabin. Then he stopped the car and took an envelope from his pocket.

"Give this to her," he said.

Her eyes widened. "You're not coming in with me?"

"I . . . I've been here before, Francie. I had . . . a gunshot wound, from hunting. She'd recognize me."

"She'd recognize you?" He felt the heat of her gaze on him, then saw her scornful smile. It was an echo of her mother's. "But it doesn't matter if she recognizes me, is that it?" She almost ripped the envelope from his hand. "All right. When I make myself think rationally, I understand why we can't . . . go away together." She paused a moment, struggling for control. "Even when I understood, I still hoped, stupid as that was." He knew tears were very near the surface, and prayed he would not have to see her cry. "But I don't understand your making me go in there alone." She gave him a long burning look that melted the barriers he had put between himself and the world. "You can't love me, you can't ever have loved me."

He reached toward her. "Francie—"

"Never mind," she said, opening the door. "It's a good thing one of us has guts." She leapt out and ran across the hard-packed dirt yard to the house. He saw a head poke out and Francie disappear inside. He pulled the car under the shelter of a low-hanging camphor tree and waited, hidden by the pulled-down brim of his hat. The silence was terrible; it gave his thoughts no room to hide. They kept going to that ramshackle door, trying to picture what was happening inside. Breathing in the thick dust, suffocating in the heat, Charles Livaudais for

the first time made himself admit that he was not worthy of
Francie's love.

When she came out, she walked slowly, stopping to grasp
one of the square beams that supported the tin roof of the
porch. He threw away the cigarette burning unsmoked in his
fingers and ran to her, picking her up and carrying her, laying
her carefully in the back seat. "Francie . . . Francie, are you all
right?"

Her face was absolutely white, whiter than he had ever
believed flesh could be. When she opened her eyes, they had
lost all light; they were flat, dulled by pain and shock. He
opened the glove compartment and took out a flask and held it
to her lips. "Here, darling, drink this, it will do you good."

She let him put it to her lips and sipped, then pushed it away.
"I'll be all right," she said. "Just take me home." She sank
back and closed her eyes, then roused. "There's an alley that
runs behind the house—you can let me out at the end of it."
She knows I'm afraid of being seen, he thought, and knew she
was right.

"Francie—"

"Shh," she said, touching his shoulder. "There's nothing left
to say, Charles." Then she turned her head and closed her eyes.
He pulled the curtains over the back windows, got in the automobile, and drove slowly over the rutted drive, out to the main
road. He felt every jolt; what were they doing to Francie? The
silence from the back seat terrified him, and he kept turning his
head to check on her. But by the time they entered the outskirts
of St. Martinville, there was a faint flush of color in her
cheeks, and her breathing was more regular. She was going to
be all right, he thought. He found the end of the alley and
stopped the automobile. She opened her eyes.

"Are we there?"

"Yes," he said. "Let me help you—"

"No," she said. "We've gotten away with it so far. Don't
take a chance now." She let herself out of the automobile and
stood beside the open window at his elbow. "Well," she said.
"Good-bye."

He took her hand in his. "Francie, are you all right? You
look . . . so pale."

Her eyes were larger than he had ever seen them, staring out
of that pallid face. Her lips twisted into something that was not
quite a smile. "All right?" she repeated. "Oh, certainly. As all

right as I can be." Her eyes said what her lips did not: As I can be after being betrayed, after being violated. "I'd better go," she said. She turned and walked slowly away. He sat for one moment more, afraid he would never see her again. Then he drove away, waiting until outside of Lafayette to stop and take a steadying swallow of brandy before driving home.

Francie moved slowly down the grassy path beside the alley. The sun felt very hot; she should have remembered to bring her hat. She tried to remember how to work the pump that remained in the backyard, but she could not. She stumbled through the yard, past the beds of flowers, past the rows of herbs, up the back stairs, and into the kitchen. The kitchen was empty, the house quiet. She crept up the stairs that led from the back hall and made her way to her room. Closing the door, she leaned heavily against it. Her legs were giving way, and darkness seemed to be closing down around her. That's funny, she thought, groping toward her bed. It's only about four o'clock; it must be one of those quick storms coming up. She pulled back the spread, but did not have the strength to fold it over the rack that stood near the bed. She fell forward, and was still.

"Go see if Francie is in her room," Alice said to Marie when supper was ready. "I've rung the bell three times; I don't know what that girl's doing. I hope she's not getting into her old ways. She's been so grown-up since she's been back home."

Marie sighed and went upstairs to find her sister. Francie's door was closed. Marie knocked several times. Finally she opened it and peered in. It was dark inside, the curtains drawn.

"Francie?"

She opened the door wider and went into the room. Francie was lying on her bed. "Francie, wake up, supper's ready. Francie?" She moved closer, then saw the deep red stain that surrounded her sister. She stood frozen, terrified. Then she began to scream.

"She was pregnant," Dr. Jaubert said, coming back downstairs after examining Francie's body. "Someone aborted it." He entered Claude's study, waited until Claude and Alice sat down. He could see the shock in their faces. He went to the liquor cabinet and found brandy; pouring two glasses, he handed one to each of them.

"I'll kill whoever is responsible," Claude said quietly. Jaubert knew he meant it.

Alice remained silent, breathing hard, as though she had to work for each lungful of air. But her hand went out to Claude's, restraining him.

"Now, look, Claude," Dr. Jaubert said, making his voice firm. "You can spend a lot of time on a useless hunt for the guilty party—or you can get on with the job of dealing with this. There was only one person who could tell you who Francie's lover was—Francie."

"Dammit, Jaubert!" Claude said. He stood up and lunged forward. Jaubert's arms came around him and held him until Claude began to cry. Over Claude's shoulder, Dr. Jaubert saw Alice's head move, jerking back and forth as though she were trying to throw something off. She seemed to hear the noises Claude was making for the first time. She rose and came to put her arms around Claude, too. "Claude!" He turned to her, and they cried in each other's arms.

They'll be all right now, Jaubert thought, pouring himself a brandy. He thought of the girl upstairs. If he had been asked the one family he thought would escape this particular kind of pain, surely it would have been this one. He shook his head. The gods did not play favorites after all. It was a lesson he saw taught over and over again.

"Look," he said, when their tears had subsided and he could talk to them. "I'm not going to put . . . well, the cause of death is just going to be internal hemorrhage of unknown origin."

"Thank you," Alice said. Her voice was barely audible.

"Are you all right?" Dr. Jaubert asked her.

Alice took a deep breath, let it out slowly. "My heart is broken. But I'm all right."

When Claude and Alice told Beau the terrible news, he stared at them as though he did not believe what they were saying was true. "I'm afraid it is true," Claude said. "Francie had an abortion. It killed her."

"Who did it?" Beau asked, trying to hold on to small details as though they could keep the enormity of Francie's death from overtaking him.

"Jaubert says it's not that hard to find a woman who—"

"The man," Beau said. "Who was it?"

"If I knew that, he'd be dead too," Claude said.

"Yes," Beau said. He thought of Francie, calling him in New Orleans. He remembered his careless assumption that her lover was some puppy, no one to take seriously. Hatred welled up in him. If the hatred were strong enough, he thought he could perhaps ignore his own guilt. Then he saw his mother's face. She looked worn, and frightened by the strength of her men's anger. He forced himself to remember that it was his mother who bore the worst loss of all. "Mama . . ." He folded her in his arms and she cried against his shoulder. But when his eyes met his father's, the message they exchanged was clear: "We will get him. No matter how long it takes."

Somehow they got through the funeral, through the first terrible days. They found themselves comforting each other constantly; they could not pass one another in the hall without touching, a moment of closeness. The stream of visitors paying sympathy calls exhausted them especially, because of the necessity of hiding the truth about Francie's death, and trying to avoid the questions of friends for which there were no answers. Their exhaustion had one good effect. It helped them sleep.

Their wounds were opened again when Alice stumbled into the dining room one evening, where Beau sat with Claude, with a slim book in her hand. She opened the book and put it in front of them, sobbing. Beau read the words: "For my own little Portuguese . . ." He did not believe the pain that surged through him at that moment. Later, he locked the book away in his study safe. Somehow he felt certain the book would provide the key that would lead him to Francie's lover—and the man responsible for her death.

For days after the journey to St. Martinville, Charles jumped whenever the telephone rang, and sorted through the office mail frantically. Surely Francie would find a way to let him know that she was all right; surely she knew he would be frantic with worry. Then, on the fourth day, as he was scanning the obituary page of the *Times-Picayune*, her name leapt out at him. His eyes moved over the words automatically: "Françoise Alicia Langlinais, daughter of Representative and

Mrs. Claude Louis Langlinais of St. Martinville, died on July 16 at the home of her parents."

"It's not possible," he cried out loud. Hélène, sitting opposite him at the breakfast table, looked at him strangely. Suddenly he slumped forward, his cup dropping from his hand and shattering on the polished floor.

When he came to, he was in his own bed, the family doctor standing over him. "Well, Charles," he said. "You gave Hélène quite a scare. You've had a mild heart attack. A warning, if you will." He put his fingers on Charles's pulse and watched the minute hand of his big watch sweep around once. "Pulse is better, and your heart sounds better, too. Racing like a runaway motorboat when I got here." He pulled up a chair and sat by the bed. "Hélène said something you saw in the paper shocked you. She didn't know what it was. You bet on the wrong horse or something?"

"Yes," Charles said. The memory came over him, threatened to overwhelm him again. He turned his face away. "I'm tired," he said. "I'd like to rest now."

"Good," the doctor said. "You need to. I want you to stay in bed for the next few weeks, Charles, to give your heart a rest."

It was not until the next day, when he had the maid bring up the previous morning's paper, that he read the rest of Francie's obituary, and learned about the funeral.

When he recovered several weeks later, Charles went to the house on Dumaine Street. He brought great bouquets of white lilies and roses, filling every vase, scattering them over the bed. He made a pilgrimage through the rooms, sitting at the spinet where Francie had played, taking her books from the shelves, flipping through the pages. He told himself that he was holding up rather well, that there was every indication he could survive this. Then he opened a thin book of poetry by Edna St. Vincent Millay. Francie had gone on about her enthusiastically; he remembered teasing her, telling her she was losing her individuality mimicking this brazen young woman. A blue ribbon marked one page. He opened it and read: "My candle burns at both ends; It will not last the night; But, ah, my foes, and, oh, my friends—It gives a lovely light." The volume fell to the floor and he collapsed on the bed, his head buried in lace-trimmed pillows. The pain in his heart was made worse by the fact that it was not fatal.

24

A cold wind hurled rain against the windows of Beau's automobile as he drove into Lafayette. He had called Caroline that morning, asking if he could come see her. He had to see someone—Francie's death had eaten away at his soul these last months until there was nothing left, only a numbness which seemed to shield him from every feeling but pain and nagging guilt. But as he parked the automobile and ducked his head against the blasts of a November storm, he felt the futility of this visit. Nothing could heal him. Francie was dead. He couldn't change that. What could Caroline do?

"Beau," she said, opening the door wide. She put her arms around him and kissed him. His appearance shocked her. It was not only the weight loss, but the lack of all life in his face, in his eyes. She took him by the hand and led him back to her morning room, where a great fire fought the chill. "Now, you sit right here by the fire while I have Luella bring us some hot chocolate and cake," she said. He sat in the chair as obediently as an old man, and she turned away so he could not see the expression on her face.

Beau leaned back and let the peace of the room fill him. He had forgotten just how peaceful this room was, how a room can hold peace, just as it can hold memories of violence. He watched Caroline take the tray from Luella's hands, set it on a low table, and pour a cup of steaming chocolate from the Haviland pot. The firelight lit her hair. He took in a long, deep breath; he had come here thinking he could pour out his guilt to her, his terrible feeling of responsibility over Francie's death. He had thought he could bring all that pain, all that guilt, and have Caroline touch him and heal him. But sitting there, he knew he could not bring such dark thoughts into this room of light.

"Here, Beau, drink this," she said, handing him the cup. She poured one for herself and sat in the chair next to him, her eyes watching him over the rim of her cup. "What have you been up to?"

He shrugged. "Not much. I . . . I've let a lot of things go these past few months." He lifted a hand, let it fall in an aimless gesture. "I was supposed to work with Long on that Cumberland case—but when Francie died . . ." He was unable to continue, and took refuge in a long swallow of chocolate.

Caroline set her cup down and, leaning forward, put her hand on his arm. "Beau. Beau, I want to say something to you." She took a deep breath. "I want you on your feet and looking at me while I tell you."

An old reflex, stronger than his anguish and guilt, made him stand up. She rose too, and took his hands in hers. "This is what I want to say. There are some things that happen that we just cannot change—and the pain they leave is one we will have to carry the rest of our days. There's no healing, no real relief."

She saw a flicker at the back of his eyes, and knew he heard, that he understood what she was saying.

"In one way, that's an awful thing to know." She sighed. "But in another, Beau, it can be freeing. Because once we know the pain is just going to go on, we don't waste time or strength fighting it. We just . . . well, we just pick it up, put it on our backs . . . and go on." She put one hand on either side of his face. "Beau, you can do that, can't you? Pick up this pain and carry it?"

Beau grasped her by the arms, tears streaming down his face. She was conscious of the hiss of the fire as rain splattered down the chimney and fell on the burning logs. She waited quietly while the rain beat against the windows. Then she saw a new expression in Beau's eyes. She lowered herself into the chair behind her, pulled him down until he sat on the floor, his face in her lap. She stroked his hair, waiting for his tears to melt the hard numbness that enveloped him. He shuddered, and was quiet. When he looked at her, she saw he would be all right. He would hope again, he would live again.

"Guess that was long overdue," he said.

"Yes," she said.

He tested the way he felt: Still sad. Still regretful that he had not been . . . Omniscient? Seen into his sister's heart? But he knew that now he would be able to live with himself again. He brushed at his eyes. "I don't know what you did—but for the first time since last summer, I feel . . . hopeful." He smiled. "Thank you, Caroline."

"Good," she said. "You have all sorts of things to hope for. Your girls, for instance. Think of all the fun you have in store with them."

He thought about the twins, a year old next week. He could not think of them without smiling—two plump little people pulling themselves up on chairs and tables to test unsteady legs, two little faces that lit up like flaring candles whenever he walked into the room. God, he'd love another one! "I want another child," he said, making his wish out loud.

"It's always nice to have another one," Caroline said. She laughed, and mischief danced in her eyes. "I'm going to have another one."

"Good God, Caroline, Henri's not—"

"He'll be thirteen months old when this one comes in June," she said. "Quite old enough."

The longing inside intensified, and he suddenly ached for a baby, a new life that would somehow replace Francie—or if not replace, at least fill the space her death had opened in his heart. "I do want another one," he said. "I really do."

Caroline's eyes were serious, and he saw her hesitate before she spoke. "Will Louise—" She broke off, made an impatient gesture. "I'm sorry. That's none of my business."

"Maybe I can convince her," he said.

"I'll pray for you," Caroline said. She got up, silhouetted against the fire. "Because a baby in the house doesn't leave much time for sadness."

He rose and faced her. "Isn't it funny how a small child can take up such a very large space?" He thought of the twins again and laughed.

Watching Beau come to life as he talked about his little girls, Caroline thought, with an anger that shocked her, that if prayer did not make Louise Langlinais give Beau a baby, she just might ask Luella for a voodoo charm that would.

In the first weeks after Francie's death, Louise had resigned herself to the disruption of routine, the gloom that hung over both houses. She had never really liked Francie; had privately thought her bold and hoydenish; she had no grief of her own to deal with, only the annoyance that someone besides herself was the center of the household's concern. Becca and Susu both fussed over Beau, clearly placing Louise's needs second, and even hinted that she, Louise, could do more to cheer her husband up. But as time went on, and Beau did not "cheer up," she began to wonder. He had no interest in anything; he went to his office daily, but his hours were irregular, and he no longer mentioned cases he was working on. The oil wells still flowed, but he had not ordered others drilled—were they all to founder in this sea of sorrow?

By November, when there was no change, when he was still listless, coming to life only when he was with the twins, her concern was strong enough to make her speak to him. "Is there anything I can do?" she asked one evening when it seemed as though he would never get out of this depression by himself.

Beau looked up from the newspaper, watching her with a look she could not define. "Yes," he said. "As a matter of fact, there is." He waited a moment, assessing whether or not this uncharacteristic interest in his welfare would bear the weight of what he was about to say. "Most people would be thinking about having another child by now."

"But we're not most people, are we?" she said. Then she knew what the look on his face meant. "Are we, Beau?" she repeated.

He came to where she sat in her rocker, sewing in her hand. He knew his face showed his terrible vulnerability, but he didn't care—he had to put himself into Louise's careless hands. "I want a child," he said.

She paused, needle idle. "Beau . . . you know how I feel on that subject." Her voice was firm, but not yet shrewish, and he dared to press her.

"Louise . . . things are different now, aren't they? Francie . . ." He stared over her head until he could control his face. "I keep thinking of the baby that died with her—it's all so damn pointless, Louise. Maybe if another one were coming . . . we'd all have something to look forward to."

"I certainly would," Louise said bitterly.

The familiar anger overwhelmed him. "Good God, Louise, can't you accept one day of pain to bring a new life into the world? Isn't a son or daughter worth that?" He came closer and reached for her hand. "I don't mean to be insensitive to your suffering, Louise, but—"

"But you are," she said. "It's not just the pain." She stared up at him, a glint of darkness shadowing her golden eyes. "It's what I have to let you do."

"Dammit," he said. "I don't understand you, Louise. What the hell did you get married for?" He gestured at the sewing in her hands. "All you think about is sewing for the missions and figuring out ways of getting more money out of me to send to them. You should have been a nun!"

He flung himself back into his chair, hoping that she would at least argue with him, say something that showed she was thinking about what he had said. But Louise ignored him and returned to her sewing, her silence as flat as the garment that lay in her lap. Beau's frustration seemed unbearable. To be married, to have a wife who could bear a child—and to be denied it! Other women might provide sex; they could not provide a child. He sat up, an idea forming in the back of his mind. It was Louise's duty—a duty imposed on her by the Church she was so devoted to. He wrestled with himself. Could he go to Father Adrian, ask him to intervene? He shook the thought away. Expose the failure of the marriage to an outsider's eye? It seemed impossible. But as the evening wore itself away, the idea took hold, until speaking to Father Adrian seemed less a betrayal of their marriage than the only way to hold it together.

He stopped in at the rectory the next morning on the way to his office and spoke with Father Adrian briefly. The priest asked a question or two, but said little while Beau talked. Beau's request might seem bizarre to Beau, but to a priest who had spent years listening to confessions, it was but one more verse in a long epic of human frailty and weakness. "She's . . . misguided," Father Adrian said at last. "It's unfortunate that she was so unprepared for marriage, but still—she knows the purpose of marriage in our church. The procreation and education of children." He shook his head. "I'll speak with her, Beau."

"I'm sorry to involve you in this, Father. I . . . I can't think of anything else to do."

"Louise and I get along well," Father Adrian said. "I imagine she'll listen with an open heart."

But when Father Adrian was seated in the Langlinais parlor, a cup of coffee at his elbow and a plate of pecan pie in his hand, he felt less sure. "I won't go all around Robin Hood's barn to get to what I came to say, Louise," he said. "Beau came to see me. He . . . well, he doesn't understand why you are so adamant against another child."

Louise could not believe what she was hearing. An image of Beau and Father Adrian discussing her in the most private and intimate detail swam before her. Disgust welled in her throat, and she could hardly speak. "He went to see you!"

"Now, Louise, I am a priest," Father Adrian said. "Young girls don't always . . . well, sometimes the duties of the married state come as a shock." He noticed her neck muscles becoming taut, the tight closure of her lips that barely opened to let her words emerge. "Louise, listen to me." His voice was gentle, and he sat very still, using all the authority that his clerical office commanded over her. "Beau is suffering under a heavy burden. His beloved sister is dead. Having a child would help him. Help all of you."

"At my expense," Louise said. Her eyes glittered, and for a moment Father Adrian had a glimpse of the molten fury that raged inside Louise's cold exterior.

"Beau has a right to children, Louise. And you have a duty to provide them. You vowed that."

"I didn't know what it meant," she said. Her control almost slipped; when she saw the astonishment in Father Adrian's eyes, she closed her lips tightly and turned her head.

This is more complicated than I thought, Father Adrian told himself. Much more is going on here than a woman's dislike for marital relations, or reluctance to face the pain of childbirth. She was not married to a brute. She had every luxury, could do what she wished, when she wished. Louise was strong-minded, he knew that. But what could be a virtue when serving good could be a vice when serving only self. Since Beau had come to him, hesitantly telling the story of his marriage, Father Adrian had searched his own soul long and hard for his failure to see when Louise Langlinais' piety had twisted into fanaticism, when she had slipped the restraints of the church and gone off on her own dark spiritual voyage.

"Louise," he said. "You have been, since I have known you, a woman of great Christian charity." He gestured to the work-basket, overflowing with sewing for the missions. "I don't know anyone who more assiduously serves others." He leaned forward and took her hand. "Cannot you think about this child as an act of that same charity? An act of healing for a fellow human being who is suffering very much?"

Something in her eyes shifted as she turned to look at him.

"Before, you said it was something I had to do," she said accusingly. "Now you're saying it's a gift."

He let her hand go and allowed himself a smile. "Louise, no one can force you to have a child. Surely you know that."

"But I could decide to have one," she said. "As a . . . as an example of Christian charity. Is that what you mean?"

Father Adrian wished he had never tried that tactic. Once drawn into the dark snares of her mind, what kind of trap would Louise make of her gift? He rose. "Louise, I've said all I intend to. What you do now is up to you." And to heaven, he thought moments later, gratefully breathing the clear air as he stepped out onto the front porch. Beau sat in the shadows, a cigarette bright against the night.

"I don't know, Beau," Father Adrian said. "She's very complex, isn't she?"

"Yes," Beau said, thinking of the tantrums, the cold silences that followed them.

"Very strong-willed," the priest said. He put a hand on Beau's shoulder. "I imagine it's pretty hard to live with."

"I've learned," Beau said. He tossed his cigarette out into the yard and watched the shower of sparks. "We Langlinaises are pretty strong-willed ourselves."

"You don't worry a baby . . . your children will inherit her will?"

"Father, I hate to say this—but she's just selfish, bone selfish: she prefers it that way. Her famous charity to the missions may fool you, but it doesn't fool me. So long as she's busy working for 'God,' the house can go to rack and ruin and I can't complain. My children can inherit her will, my will— both of 'em. Because wills can be disciplined, people can learn to use their wills to live good lives." He laughed, a sound that was free, light. "I don't worry about what they'll inherit from her. I'll see to it that what they get from me—my guidance, my caring—keeps them steady on course. They'll be fine."

"I believe you," Father Adrian said. He took Beau's hand. "I'll pray for you," he said. "All of you."

Louise sat motionless after Father Adrian left. It was humiliating that the careful picture of herself she had created for Father Adrian had been so brutally destroyed. To think Father Adrian had come here, spoken the way he did! She put a hand to her cheek and felt the warmth of shame. She stirred restlessly. There must be some way she could get back at Beau. Her eyes grew large, fixed. Then the thought came—what if she did have a child? The attention of the family would swing from Beau back to her, where it belonged. Even better, she would have a hostage then. Something—someone—to hold over Beau's head forever. She leaned back in her chair. Yes, it might even be worth getting pregnant for. Thinking of how pliable Beau would be if she gave him what he so badly wanted, she laughed out loud. How marvelous when Christian virtue and her own ends were equally served.

25

The *Sunset Limited* rolled steadily toward New Orleans, the gray smoke pouring from its stack melding with the gray rains of January. Beau, sitting in the club car, was not affected by the threatening skies and tedium of the journey. He was on his way to meet Huey Long, and to be on hand when the final decision in the Cumberland-rate-increase case was made. That decision had assumed new importance: Long expected to be elected governor on January 15, 1924, exactly one year from today. And, as he had said when Beau called to say he wanted to get active again, they couldn't afford to waste one day of that year if they expected to reach their goal. A clear-cut victory over Cumberland would start the campaign off for governor with exactly the right note, presenting Long in his favorite role as defender of the people against the big corporations.

As the train pulled into the New Orleans station, Beau rose and stood impatiently in the train vestibule, feeling suddenly that he could hardly wait to see Long again. He hailed a taxi and directed the driver to the Public Service Commission offices. The unmistakable aroma that defined New Orleans surrounded him. A wet smell came up from the river; mixed with that was the smell of roasting coffee beans and peanuts from street vendors. He heard the cries of peddlers, and a sharp sweet call of a saxophone as they drove past the open door of a jazz club. He soaked up the city's atmosphere and thought about its division from the rest of the state. And as the taxi wound through the narrow streets, Beau saw the cleverness of Long's strategy in using the commission as a base for his higher ambitions. With its office in New Orleans, the New Orleans papers paid a great deal of attention to everything the commission did, and the country papers, willy-nilly, picked it up. The commission was the perfect stage for a performer like Long, Beau thought. He arrived in the hall outside the commission offices to find a group of newspapermen standing outside, pads and pencils ready.

"You fellows look like you expect something to happen this morning," Beau said to one of the men.

"A decision on the Cumberland thing," the man said, licking the soft point of his pencil almost automatically. "You here to sign up on Long's team?"

"I—" Beau began, and then the door in front of them burst open and a stream of people came out, surging against the group of reporters in the hall. Long emerged almost last. There was a broad grin on his face, and his large body seemed to take up more space than usual, as though he knew he had a right to the lion's share of everything.

He held up a hand, commanding silence. "Well, boys, we've done it," he said, nodding to the reporters. "Now, you all just get out your pencils and take down what I'm getting ready to say, and be sure you get these numbers right." He winked at the reporter nearest him and laughed. "Cumberland has bowed to the inevitable will of the people as represented by this commission, and has agreed to refund every last cent of all monies taken in between May 13, 1922, and January 13, 1923." His hand went up again, quieting the murmur of the crowd. "Now, wait until you hear what that means." He paused, and then let the figures roll off his tongue like the promises of a carnival barker. "*Eight*-y *thou*-sand subscribers are going to receive their fair share of a refund amounting to four *hun*-dred for-ty *thou*-sand dollars," he intoned. He waited for the murmur of approval to become louder, leaned forward to hear a reporter's question. "An increase? Well, yes, they're going to get some kind of increase. But mind, we told them they better get going on the construction and expansion program the rate increase is supposed to pay for, or they'll be back in our chambers so fast they won't even have time to call one of their high-priced fancy lawyers—even if they do own the telephones."

"How much is the rate increase?" a reporter called.

"Half what they wanted, more than I wanted. Ten percent." He shrugged, held up both hands. "But like Edmund Burke said . . . 'All government is founded on compromise and barter.' And to tell you the truth, when those subscribers get their money back, I think they'll know who got the sharpest end of the stick." His voice rose. "Now, if you can just spread that good word to some of the unbelievers . . ." He bent his head to answer a reporter's question, and the crowd that had filled the hearing room began to disperse. Beau hesitated. Better go over to the Monteleone and register, he thought. He would try to see Long later. As he turned to go, the booming voice caught him like a metal hook.

"Beau Langlinais! Now, don't run out just when we're winning!" Beau turned. Long had a hand up, beckoning him. "Come on back here. You and me have some palavering to do."

Beau made his way through the stragglers still standing around the hall. Try as he might, he could not ignore the fact that he felt something like the squires at Camelot must have when the king finally took notice of them. He's not that much older than you are, Beau thought. Don't be so impressed.

He felt Long's arm around him. "Let's go get us some lunch," Long said. His big body was warm, the feel of his arm solid. "Nothing works up an appetite like winning, Beau."

"Amen," Beau said. Outside, walking through the rain to the Monteleone Hotel, Beau hardly felt the water that splashed against his shoes when he stepped into a puddle, hardly noticed the rivulets that ran off the edge of his umbrella and soaked through his coat sleeve. Long made a circle of combustion stronger than any weapon January had in her arsenal.

"Here's what I need you to do," Long said when they had ordered. Try as he might, Beau could not suppress his elation at being seated at one of the best tables in the Monteleone's dining room as the guest of the man whose name was in every newspaper's headlines and on the lips of almost every important person in the state. "I don't have an organization right now—and if I'm going to be the next governor of this state, I damn sure need one. Now, here's my plan. You and I both know it's the courthouse crowd that runs every parish. Somebody—usually the sheriff—is the boss of that crowd. And, human nature being what it is, about forty percent of the voters love 'im, about forty percent hate 'im, and the other twenty percent don't give a damn. What I intend to do, I intend to go into a parish and cuss out the boss, whoever the hell he is. I'm going to go around 'em entirely." He leaned back and grinned. "See my strategy?"

"The forty percent who hate him will want to work with you," Beau said. "And the twenty percent who don't give a damn are up for grabs."

"So you *do* do something down there besides hunt and play bourré," Long said, jerking his head in quick approval.

"I'm not my father's son for nothing," Beau said. "How do I fit in?"

"Find out who the bosses are in the parishes down your way. Give me some ammunition to use against them." Long's eyes concentrated on Beau, closing out everything else around him.

"What kind of ammunition?" The look in Long's eyes reminded Beau of 'Tit Jacques, the way he had shrugged and pronounced the death sentence on the scum who stole another man's loot.

Long's voice was soft, but the words were clear. "Whatever it takes to bring 'em out of the tree," he said.

"Might rake up some mud," Beau said.

Long gestured outward, toward the rain that still fell steadily. "You see the condition of our roads? Like gumbo. Hell, this state's been wallowing in the mud for decades. You think a little more is going to hurt?"

I didn't mean that kind of mud, Beau thought. Still, hadn't Parker promised good roads? Beau thought of the number of times he had to dig himself out of the mud in the short trip to the train station in New Iberia. If Long could really change all that, solve some of the rest of the state's problems as he had solved the Cumberland case . . . "I've met a lot of politicians, being a police juror," Beau said. "I imagine I can be of some use to you."

"I know you can," Long said.

"Election's a year off, though. Are you going to begin running this early?"

"Never such a thing as too early for a politician, Beau." He leaned across the table, putting his head close to Beau's. "Got to keep your name in the news. Now this Cumberland issue is settled, I've got another fight ready to bring to the front of the stove."

"Standard Oil?"

"Yep," Long said, and again Beau saw the quick nod of approval. "Don't mind telling you, that's an opponent worth every inch of steel I've got. It's been nip and tuck every bit of the way."

Beau agreed. In early December, Standard Oil, along with all other common-carrier pipelines in the state, had been ordered to show cause why rates for the transportation of oil in Louisiana should not be prescribed by the Public Service Commission. Standard Oil had also been ordered to show why it should treat oil it owned differently in transporting it than oil owned by other companies. With Beau's own Gemini Oil using Standard's pipeline, Beau's interest was far from academic.

"Where does all that stand?"

Long laughed, a raucous bark that made heads turn at the tables around them. "Well, since you deal with them, you're bound to know Standard Oil up and divested itself of its pipelines, and made them a separate company."

"Yes, they redid my contracts with the new name."

"I included Standard Pipe Line in the hearings, too. A skunk can change its name, Beau, but that doesn't affect its stench one bit. They'll have to appear at the hearings early next month, same as all the others."

"Are you going to set their rates then?"

"We're going to begin the process," Long said, signaling the waiter for the check. He winked at Beau. "Though, I expect them to put up a hell of a fight, drag this damn thing on all summer."

Beau laughed. "Keeping your name before the public all the time, right?"

"Right," Long said. "With me wearing my St. George-fighting-the-dragon suit." His eyes looked past Beau, past the dining room filled with men in well-cut suits, past the shining cutlery and smooth linen. He saw something Beau could not guess at, some vision that made his eyes hard. "And there will come a day when all the dragons are slain," Long said softly. "And the people can walk over their land."

Beau's mind for a moment was filled with the landscape he

had passed through on the train that morning—mud-rutted roads, unpainted shacks, slack fences, and slovenly outbuildings. Could even Long bridge such a difference, close the gap between men who were beaten down like their land, and those who sat here so comfortably eating? It seemed so simple, the way Long talked. Break the power of the big companies, and the people will be free. And yet, some people called the Langlinaises "big." He shook his head. That was different—it had been worked for, generation after generation. If their enterprises were big, it was because part of what enriched them also enriched the lives of the people in their region. Steady income for trappers. Jobs in the lumber mill. Better wages than other companies paid. And they gave more to charity, right off the top, than any other family he knew. But so many companies didn't take care of the people. Trampled them.

⁻ He looked at Long. "If you've got an extra sword, I'm a pretty fair dragon slayer myself."

"You're going to need to be," Long said.

Beau's main task, until Long formally announced his candidacy, was to visit the parishes around St. Martin and determine the lay of the land, identifying potential Long supporters, sounding out opponents, estimating the number of people up for grabs. He quickly fell into a pattern: a couple of days a week in his office in St. Martinville working on the family businesses, a couple of days on the road. It was easy enough to find a pretext to go to a parish courthouse—a title to check on, an abstract to look up. Once there, it was also easy to drop in on various officials who, if they did not yet know Beau, certainly knew or had heard of his father or grandfather. Sitting in hard-bottomed, straight-backed wooden chairs, heels hooked over the bottom rung, Beau spent many an hour in seemingly idle chat over endless cups of coffee. Before long, he had a notebook filled with page after page of names, each marked to show whether the man was, as he put it to Long, "a lamb, a sheep, or a goat."

The pattern was interrupted in April, when Louise, who had become pregnant late the previous summer, gave birth to a boy. Beau, calling Alice from the Dauterive Hospital in New Iberia, was ecstatic. "I've decided to nickname him Skye," he said. "Of course we'll christen him Claude Louis—but the initials, C.L., make the French word for 'sky.' What do you think?"

"I think it's fine," Alice said. "Maybe we'll see a little more of you, now you have this boy to look after. All that running around for Huey Long takes you away from us too much." And worried Claude to death, she thought, though she did not tell Beau that. "He's going to make a lot of enemies for himself," Claude had said after Beau told them about his visits to neighboring parishes. "It's one thing to have people against you because of what you believe—hell, a man can hardly get through life in any honorable way without that. But to go around and deliberately stir up one hornet's nest after the other!" Alice had begged Claude not to say anything to Beau; at least, she thought, Beau was interested in something again.

Beau laughed. "Be a while before I can take Skye fishing, Mama. And I have lots of work still to do before the election this fall. I'm running up to Bastrop tomorrow."

"Bastrop! Good heavens, what's up there?"

He laughed again, a strong, confident sound. "It may not be the garden spot of the state, but it's where those Morehouse Klansmen are being tried again."

He heard the quick fear in his mother's voice. "Beau, you're not getting mixed up with the Klan!"

"No, Mama. But you know how many people are accusing Huey of supporting them. I want to listen to the trials, get some facts."

"Don't," Alice said. "Beau, they are terrible, frightening people. I couldn't bear it if they put you on one of their . . . lists." She broke into tears. Hearing her sobs over the phone, Beau knew that the image of violent death would follow her all her days.

"Mama, they won't even know I'm there. But if I'm going to help Long, I've got to understand what's going on. Huey doesn't say much about the Ku Klux Klan, even in private, but I know damn well he has no sympathy for the Klan and what it stands for."

"He should publicly denounce it, then," Alice said.

"It's not that easy, Mama. Huey's from North Louisiana, where the Klan's the strongest. If he comes out against it, he'll lose all kinds of votes where he needs them the most."

"Avoiding denouncing them sounds a little bit like what your father would call selling out.'"

"Now, dammit, Mama, even if Huey did denounce the Klan, it would serve no purpose. Wouldn't hurt them at all, and it would damage him plenty."

"Well," Alice said. "It's been a long time since I went to school, and maybe philosophy has changed since then. But it seems to me that there used to be fairly general agreement that the end does not justify the means."

She hung up, leaving Beau to mull over what she had just said. It was so easy for people to make judgments about what other people should do—so easy for Mama to say Long should denounce the Klan. Beau shrugged. She just didn't understand politics, even if her husband had been in the legislature twelve years. If a man expected to go all ten rounds, he couldn't take himself out of the ring in the first round on a mere technicality. No, Mama didn't understand politics. Not, he amended, Huey Long's politics.

The Ku Klux Klan had been formed during Reconstruction; after dying out in the nineteenth century, it had been revived again eight years before in the summer of 1915. As with many other South Louisiana Catholics, Beau's contempt for the stupidity and ignorance of the Klan precluded his giving the Klan much thought. If there was one part of Louisiana in which it had no strength, it was his own Acadiana. But Long's campaign was forcing him to look at the Klan more closely. On the one occasion Beau had brought the subject up, Huey had thundered, "I detest the so-and-sos! But to come right out and say so from a North Louisiana stump? I might as well take my razor and slit my throat in full view of the voters, Beau."

On the drive up to Bastrop, where the state was trying eighteen Klansmen for the deaths of two Mer Rouge farmers, Beau had plenty of time to think about what his mother had said. The Klan had proved itself a dangerous force: a sinister group of small-minded men who felt putting hoods over their heads and sheets around their bodies gave them the right to commit heinous—and anonymous—crimes. Since last August, when only three men of the five taken to a Klan whipping party had returned alive, the hue and cry over the missing two had gone throughout the state. Already there had been one grand-jury hearing and one trial. At neither had guilt been established, and now the state was playing its last cards. Thirty-one bills of information had been filed against the Klansmen from Morehouse Parish for conspiracy to kidnap, assault with deadly weapons, unlawfully carrying firearms, and a number of other offenses. All were misdemeanors, pertaining to offenses before the two Mer Rouge men disappeared. Although two bodies alleged to be theirs had been found in Lake Lafourche in mid-December, Klan-controlled newspapers suggested no one could tell who they were. Then a belt buckle and a piece of shirt material were discovered and presented as identifying evidence, and the battle raged on.

The country Beau drove through was poor, so poor he was shocked. "Dirt-poor" was an expression he'd heard all his life; for the first time, he understood what it meant. The children who waved from sagging porches as he passed were scrawny, underfed; once, when a little girl ran alongside the automobile, chasing a chicken from his path, he could see her blackened teeth and the blueness of her skin. He had to tie his handkerchief over his face to screen out the thick red dust that roiled up from the clay-bedded road. How can they get any crops from this stuff? he wondered. He thought of the rich black land on his farm; the only way a Cajun farmer could keep things from growing in that fertile soil was not to plant. He was almost to Bastrop when he realized that although he had passed through several towns, he had not seen one Catholic church.

Standing at the back of the courtroom in Bastrop, Beau felt even more an outsider. The men around him were lanky, rawboned, the lines in their faces put there by sun and wind and work, with no room left for laughter. There was an ugly tension in the room that seemed different from that generated in any criminal trial he'd been at before. The trial wouldn't start for a while yet; to escape the men who crowded the benches and stood silently smoking in the hall outside the courtroom, Beau left the building and waited on the courthouse lawn, a cigarette dangling from his lips. Men sat on the courthouse steps, talking in low voices; more drifted in as the hour for the trial to begin drew near. Beau wished he'd left his nice white linen suit at home, worn a pair of the overalls he used out at the farm. He saw eyes shift toward him, sweep him from straw hat to white shoes. Feeling the menace of those stares, Beau turned in the other direction and walked away, moving down the sidewalk as though he knew where he was going, wanting only to find some neutral spot where he could regroup. He saw a café midway down the block and went in. It was dim inside, and when his eyes could make out the interior, he saw that it was empty except for a woman sitting behind the wooden counter, her head propped on her raised arm.

"Are you open?" he asked.

"For what?" the woman said. He could not see her face, but her voice fell strangely on his ears. It was high-pitched, with an unpleasant nasal tone that fit the morning.

"Coffee," Beau said. "Maybe a biscuit or two."

"I got coffee," the woman said. "No biscuits. I can get you a doughnut."

"All right." He sat on a stool at the counter and drank the coffee, a weak liquid he would have teased her about had he not known it would make her angry. The doughnut was heavy, cold and greasy, but he ate it all.

The woman watched him. Finally she asked laconically, "You a reporter?"

"No," he said.

"Somebody with the state?"

"No."

Her harsh laugh jolted him. "Well, you're not a traveling salesman, I can tell that, 'cause traveling salesmen don't wear fine white linen suits and hats made of that kind of straw."

"Actually, I'm on my way to visit an old college friend," Beau lied.

"Would I know him?" The hard suspicion in the woman's voice removed his last feeling of security. The distance between the café and his automobile suddenly seemed enormous; he did not want to speak again, because he knew the soft cadences of his speech betrayed him.

"Brooks Jennings," he said, pulling out the name of an old school acquaintance who lived in the area.

The woman relaxed. "Brooks is a good boy," she said. She went to the stove and held up the black coffeepot. "You want some more?"

"I've had enough," Beau said. "How much do I owe you?" He handed her a bill and waited for his change. The hell with the trial, he thought. He was heading back to his own territory.

"We've got a big trial starting today," the woman said. She was friendly now, chatty, reluctant to let him leave her to the empty morning. "State's trying to tie a couple of murders on some of the Klansmen around here." There was a flicker of something in her eyes as she pronounced the name. Beau bent his head as though he were inspecting the condition of his coat sleeve.

Don't ever let someone see your eyes when you're making your bet, his grandfather used to tell him.

"Thing is," she went on, "just a day or so ago it came out that the doctors said those bodies they drug out of the lake hadn't been in the water more than forty-eight hours, not anywhere near the three months they'd have had to have been." She picked up a rag and began pushing it over the counter in front of Beau. The rag had a sour odor; Beau knew that if the woman were closer to him, she would have that same smell of decay and rot. "Goes to show," she said, "that you can't believe what anybody says." She looked at him. "Can you?"

"Probably not," he said. He looked at his watch. "Got to hit the road," he said, "if I want to get to the Jennings place."

The woman's lips formed a smile. "If'n some men with pillowcases over their heads try to stop you, son—you hit that accelerator and barrel on." She leaned forward, and Beau smelled a strong, rancid odor coming from her lank hair and soiled dress. "See, dressed the way you are, and talking with that kind of Frenchy way of speaking—they just might get it in their heads to take you to a little party. And it's not the kind of party you're dressed for, if you take my meaning."

He made himself walk slowly from the café, slowly down the sidewalk to his automobile. Court had already begun, but there were still men on the courthouse steps, with others standing in clusters about the lawn. Like walking a gauntlet, he thought, and felt an ache in his bladder—a sudden ache that he found himself desperate to relieve. He wouldn't be the first man to wet his pants out of fear, he told himself. He expected someone to call him, stop him, all the way to the car. It took forever to get out of Bastrop, to find a place beside the road where there was no cover of pine or scrub oak for white-hooded men to hide behind. He stood watching the stream of urine make a dark place in the red dust. He lifted his eyes to the horizon. There was a darkness up here, something foreign he didn't understand. A joylessness, an ugliness. Long's people had lived up here for generations; as Beau headed home, he wondered: could you live among these people and not catch whatever disease it was that rotted their humanity and blighted their souls?

Two days after Beau's return from north Louisiana, he received a call from Long. "Got something to tell you, Beau. Hope you'll listen good, because I don't have a lot of time to talk."

Beau listened in shock to Long's next words. "This business with Standard Oil and its pipeline company is taking more time than the law allows. I can't do justice to it and the campaign too. So I'm getting out of the race."

"You're *what?*"

"Come on, Beau, you heard me." Long was irritable, with no effort made to soften what he was saying. "I can't put any time into the campaign. If I can't do my best, I'd rather not do anything at all. So put everything on the back burner, all right?"

Beau thought of the hours, days, taken away from his own businesses to patiently cultivate centers of influence for Long. "Huey, do you have any idea the kind of time and effort I've spent on your campaign? You're making me look like a damn fool—yourself, too, if it comes to that."

"I can't help what you think you look like," Long said, his irritation boiling into hot anger. "I thank you for what you've done, Beau. But I'm out of it." He hung up, leaving Beau holding the silent receiver while his own anger grew. It didn't make sense. There had to be more to the story than what Long had told him. And if anyone would know, he realized, it would be his father.

"I can see how you feel, son," Claude said when Beau called him. "Let down—betrayed, even."

"It doesn't make sense," Beau said.

"See if this makes sense," Claude said. "I've heard rumors that John and Francis Williams, who have a lot of clout with the New Regulars in New Orleans, wanted Huey to state in writing that he would publicly denounce the Klan. If he did, they'd deliver the New Regular votes—a not inconsiderable prize when you realize that without some organized support in New Orleans, he might as well get out of the race. He can't win on Hill-country votes alone." Claude hesitated, then went on. "Obviously, Long refused. Ergo, he quits."

The words from his father's lips were like an indictment. "I know for a fact Long has no use for the Klan," Beau said. "Maybe leaving the race is just some kind of tactic. Maybe after the Mer Rouge thing dies down—"

"Principles aren't supposed to depend on the climate," Claude said harshly. "Man either believes something, day in and day out, or he doesn't, Beau. You know that."

"I know it here, in St. Martin. In parishes like it. But up there? They're a different breed of people, Papa."

Beau didn't have to be able to see Claude's face to know it was filled with scorn. "I don't buy that, Beau, and I don't think you do, either. Long pulled out of the race because he doesn't think he can win. But I'll bet you anything that if a day comes when he thinks he can win, he'll be right back, with no apologies offered."

"He'll offer one to me if he expects me to help him again," Beau said.

In the days following Long's withdrawal, Beau's telephone rang ceaselessly, and his office was cluttered with visits from men he had been bringing into Long's camp. As he tried to explain the unexplainable, his anger and frustration rose. It was with a sense of finally doing something for both that he drove to New Orleans to order new suits and visit a certain house where familiar remedies could be counted upon to calm him.

On the last day of his stay in New Orleans, he went to see Annette Livaudais, whom he had not seen for so long. The house was at once familiar and strange—had it been six years since he and Caroline met here? He shook his head. Thank God we could not know the future. Better it gives us its shocks out of complete darkness.

"Beau, it's good to see you," Annette greeted him, coming into the parlor where her maid had seated him. She drew him toward her, kissed both his cheeks. He looked around, and felt suddenly surrounded by ghosts. Perhaps it was a mistake to come here, he thought. But when the coffee had been brought, and Annette had settled herself companionably near him, ready for a good chat, he felt once again at home.

"Now, tell me everything you've been doing," she commanded. Over the next half-hour he picked his way across the years since he had seen her, telling her about the twins, the new baby, his oil company. "The Rockefellers aren't lying awake at night worrying about me yet," he said, "but Gemini Oil's doing pretty well."

"Glad to hear it," she said. She reached out a hand and put it on his knee. "Beau, I'm very sorry about Francie. My note couldn't say how much." She lifted both hands before her, moved them helplessly. "She was so gay, so lively. When I heard she was dead . . . well, it was as though a light went out."

"That's right—I'd forgotten she used to come here," he said.

"Quite a bit, in fact," Annette said. "She was a nice addition, some youthful freshness in these jaded rooms."

A thought struck him. "Did she . . . did she, well, meet anyone here?"

"Lots of people, everyone who came here."

"I meant anyone in particular," he said carefully.

"A beau?" Annette shook her head. "I don't think so." She laughed. "You've met my friends, Beau. Interesting, a lot of fun. Not, perhaps, interested in a girl like Francie." She peered at him with curious eyes. "Why do you ask? Do you . . . do you think she was involved with someone . . . ?"

"I think so," Beau said. His words were casual, but his voice made Annette look at him more closely still.

"Did this man—did he have something to do with her death?"

"Might have." He saw Annette mull his words over. She nodded briskly.

"How awful." She looked away, not wanting him to see her eyes. Should she tell him her suspicions? About Francie coming more and more frequently, only to slip away almost immediately? For years, she had chosen not to involve herself in other people's lives, to let them do as they pleased. Why change that now? But the pain in Beau's eyes prodded her, and she turned back to him. "There *was* something rather peculiar, Beau. She began coming here more often—but she stayed hardly any time at all."

"I don't see—"

"She might have come here as a cover, Beau. Tell the nuns she was visiting me—and leave to meet someone else."

"As Caroline met me." He smiled sadly. "Funny, it didn't seem so . . . dangerous when we were doing it."

"In your case, it obviously wasn't," Annette said. She looked at her watch. "I've got to dress, Beau. There's a new gallery opening—will you come?"

"Thanks, no," he said. This information she'd given him

wasn't much, but it was more than he had before. The man had to be someone from New Orleans.

On the drive home, he went over and over every scrap of evidence he had. There was something he wasn't seeing, something that would help. All at once he realized that he had never questioned how Francie had gotten to the abortionist that afternoon. He'd never even tracked her movements on that last day.

When he got home, he casually questioned his mother. "Where was Francie off to, the day she . . . the day she died?"

"She'd brought one of the horses home from the farm—she rode him back out there," Alice said. "Why, Beau?"

"I was just curious. I . . . I just realized I . . . I didn't know how she'd spent . . . what she'd done . . ." He couldn't face the question in her eyes and turned away. Later, shut up in his study, he reviewed what he knew. Francie was clearly meeting someone in New Orleans, someone who had known what Francie could not have known—a woman who called herself a midwife and performed other services for pregnant women in St. Martinville as well. Someone who had the money to pay the woman—and the callousness to send Francie to her. Who? He closed his eyes and tried to follow Francie. She rode out to the farm, pastured the horse—and what? A path blazed across the picture in his mind, a path that led to Beau Chêne. She walked to Beau Chêne. Of course! To the man from New Orleans who would know about the woman and who had the money to pay her. A chill settled over Beau; he knew the name of Francie's lover. Charles Livaudais! He knew it as surely as he knew Francie was dead. But how had she met Livaudais? Not at that long-ago New Year's Eve party—Francie had been a baby. At Annette's? But she and Charles rarely saw each other. What other event had brought the families together? Then it hit him. Marthe's death! The Livaudaises had been down; they had stayed at Beau Chêne. Did he remember or was he making it up that Francie had raved about Beau Chêne, what a gorgeous house it was? But who would have taken her there? Not his mother—her aversion to the Livaudaises was as complete as it was somewhat incomprehensible. The rest of them had managed to get over the bumps and maintain civility, but when the name Livaudais was mentioned, she actually turned white. Grandmama! He reached for the telephone. During the course of a long chat with Geneviève, he managed to ask a seemingly offhand question: "I don't remember—did Francie ever get to really see Beau Chêne? She was so crazy about that house . . ."

"Oh, cher, don't worry. She drove me there one day after Marthe died; Hélène and I had a visit and Charles showed her the house." Geneviève's voice rattled on, but he heard nothing more. Charles showed her the house. And made an appointment in New Orleans. He put down the telephone and went to his safe. Removing the book he had placed there months before, he stared at the inscription written in bold black strokes. He knew how to confirm what he was already sure was true, knew what he would find when he went to the courthouse the next day. The next afternoon he examined the documents settling Marthe's estate, flipping them over until he found what he was looking for: the signature of the executor, Charles Livaudais. It was executed in those same bold black strokes. Blood seemed to fill his eyes as the knowledge of what Livaudais had done seared him like a great furnace, driving him to seek revenge.

He could tell no one. His father would go to New Orleans and kill Charles; there was no one else to tell. For the first time, he could not share his thoughts with Caroline. The thought of visiting her with this knowledge weighting him was impossible. And even when Caroline Annette was born a month later, he sent a present rather than delivering it personally. Caroline called to thank him, and to invite him to come see her new baby, but he found excuses, promising vaguely to come sometime soon.

The summer dragged on, its only relief the breeze that blew off the bayou after sundown. There was a stir of excitement in mid-August, when Long got back into the governor's race. Most of his early supporters, including Beau, got back in it with him. "Beau, you ought to have known I was just lying low to see how the wind would go if they thought I was out," Long said when he called Beau to ask for his help.

"You could have told me that," Beau said.

"No, I couldn't," Long answered. "That would have given the game away. You wouldn't have been nearly as convincing telling people I was out if you'd known I really wasn't."

"You can trust me to keep a secret," Beau said. He was still a little angry. If he did join Long again, would the same thing happen?

"Sure I can trust you, Langlinais. That's why I need you. What do you say?"

Beau remembered Long telling him to put the campaign activity on the back burner. Now there was something else he had to put on the back burner: his revenge against Charles Livaudais. In the meantime—in the meantime, helping Long would not only fill a void, but it just might be the beginning of a way to get back at his enemy. "All right," Beau said. "But I'm warning you. Next time you make a move like that, you let me know first."

Beau worked in the campaign grimly, with none of the eagerness that characterized his early efforts in the spring. As he saw it now, every blow struck for Long struck at the power base that supported Charles Livaudais. For a few delirious hours, Beau thought perhaps they had pulled it off. Long would win, and for all of his work, Beau would ask one favor—Charles Livaudais' head.

But although on January 15, 1924, the voters of Louisiana came close to putting Long in the governor's chair, they did not come close enough. When the final votes were tallied, Hewitt Bouanchaud, Parker's handpicked candidate, led with 84,162 votes, followed closely by Henry L. Fuqua with 81,382 votes. Huey Pierce Long, who had been taken seriously by few of the state's leading newspapers, commanded a total vote of 73,985, representing a majority in twenty-one parishes and a plurality in seven. What frightened the conservatives, who knew they would have to fight him again, was that every one of those twenty-eight parishes was full of poor, small farmers. The Louisiana masses had found a leader, and though their rally was not sufficient this time, there would, as Long promised the very day after the election, be a next time.

In the letdown that followed the election, Beau realized he had another cause for his low mood. He had put a terrible distance between himself and Caroline over the last several months. He forced himself to remember the unreturned calls, the unanswered notes. He had excused himself all fall, telling himself that in the rush of campaigning, he had no time for personal life. At Christmas, he had sent her children gifts with a quickly dashed-off letter excusing his neglect on the grounds of Long's campaign. His face burned with shame. He realized he had been punishing Caroline for the simple fact of being her father's daughter.

He sat on for a long time in front of his study fireplace, staring into the coals that glowed and faded into darkness. The effect of Charles's treachery had made itself felt in all their lives. It had turned him from Caroline. It had made him hate. And it made him seek revenge. He shook his head. He had to avenge Francie's death; it was part of a code he could not abandon. He would do it carefully, so that nothing would connect him to Charles's ultimate defeat. It wasn't something he looked forward to.

He sighed. He had the tools, the weapons. His legal practice. His money. His oil company. Each one of those would open doors for him, take him down avenues where he might find a way behind Livaudais' defenses. But what a shame, he thought, rising to build up the fire, that at the end of such a quest lay, not the Holy Grail, but just another dragon. His eye fell on a picture of his three children, taken at Christmastime. He picked it up and gazed at their innocent faces. What a legacy to leave to them.

He put the picture back on his desk, settled into his chair. I wish, he thought wryly, that I were sure the part I'm playing in all this was more like Lancelot and less like Quixote. But whether windmill or real foe, he was committed. He leaned forward, switched on the desk lamp, and pulled a ledger toward him. One thing remained, hot, fiery as the logs in the grate. A hatred of Charles Livaudais and all he stood for. Had Charles Livaudais been able to see the grimness in Beau Langlinais' face, he might have felt something more than the inconsolable loss he lived with. Fear.

PART TWO

26

February 1927

Beau looked down the breakfast table at Louise. She wore a dull gray bathrobe, and her hair was pulled back in an unbecoming, unattractive knot. Her skin was pasty, as though she had spent all of the winter months in some dank cave, emerging only when the skies were overcast or dark. Beau forced back a sigh, changed it into a smile for the sake of the children, whose early-morning chatter at least brightened the day.

"Look what I've got," he said, pulling an envelope from his breast pocket. He waved it enticingly in the air, focusing on Émilie, Gennie, and Skye, knowing Louise would not even lift her eyes from the oatmeal she ate every morning.

"Something nice?" Gennie asked, her gray eyes shining.

"Something for us?" Émilie said.

"Both," Beau answered. He raised his voice. "Your mother and I will have been married six years next Tuesday. And I thought we'd celebrate by going to New Orleans." He had rehearsed that speech over and over while he shaved and dressed, until he no longer heard the hesitation and reluctance to pronounce what seemed to him the term of a prison sentence. Gennie's eyes shifted to Louise.

"Can we go, Mama?" she asked, reaching one small hand out to touch her mother's arm.

"What?" Louise seemed to be coming back from someplace too ethereal for them to imagine; she jerked her head, looked at Gennie as though she had never seen her before, jerked her head again, and then looked at Beau. "What did you say, Beau?"

He allowed himself the slow, deliberate enunciation of each word that would convey to her just how ironic they were. "I was telling the children that I've planned a trip to New Orleans for all of us—to celebrate our sixth wedding anniversary."

"But that's next week!" she said, the dazed look jolted into alertness.

"You do remember," he said softly.

"I can't possibly go anywhere next week," she said. "I've far too much going on here."

"But, Mama—"

Louise overrode Émilie's protest. "However, if you can re-schedule things for the first week of April, there's a conference going on in New Orleans I wanted to look in on anyway." She patted her mouth with her napkin and pulled it through the silver ring next to her plate, then rose and left the room.

"April's forever, isn't it?" Émilie said, pouting.

"Not really," Beau said, smiling at her. "The weather will be better then anyway. We'll spend the time between now and then reading about New Orleans, deciding what you want to see."

But driving to his law office through the soft, steady February rain, he felt again the utter disbelief that overcame him every time he realized that despite his money, his power, he could not make one simple plan involving his wife with any certainty that it would not be vetoed. When his sense of humor rescued him, he could laugh at the sight of the formidable Beau Langlinais being defeated by his high-strung, unpleasant, and thoroughly selfish wife. When his sense of humor deserted him, he had to find quick release from the black mood that descended upon him or be condemned to it for days before he could reassert some degree of optimism.

More and more in the past few years, that quick release came, not from a woman, but from a business or political deal that ended well. The more energy and ingenuity he had to put into pulling such deals off, the more his satisfaction. More than once, after a successful venture, he had told himself ruefully that if he were a happily married man, he would probably be a much poorer one. Not that the word "poor" had any meaning when applied to any material area of Beau Langlinais' life in February 1927. Gemini Oil was one of Louisiana's leading independent producers, and the profits from it had allowed Beau to invest successfully in the stock market. Money making money—the easiest way to grow very, very rich, Beau knew. And he had found, in the years since Long's defeat in 1924, that the power base he built for Long had not really eroded; men who formed it liked and trusted Beau, and so a network had developed, one in which favors exchanged and information traded made the wheels that moved Langlinais enterprises forward turn quickly and well. But even these friends noticed a difference in the way Beau went about doing things. "Man, you take life serious, yes!" more than one associate declared, noting Beau's concentration, his intent purpose. Inevitably that comment was followed by a clap on the back, a firm handgrip, and well-meant advice—"Beau. The good God, He doesn't want us to be miserable, no! Have fun, Beau. Have fun."

Entering his office, Beau smiled. Fun. He did not believe he knew what that word meant. Nor, feeling the well of sadness that waited beneath all this motion to swallow him, did he think he would tempt the gods by trying to remember a time when he did.

"Ooh, Papa," Émilie squealed. "Look at him eat it all up!" She reached up and took another peanut from the bag Beau held out to her and tossed it through the bars to the elephant on the other side.

"He's so big, Papa!" Gennie said, pulling back as the elephant swung his trunk toward the peanut and scooped it into his mouth.

"Someday I'll take you to India and you can ride on one," Beau said, swooping Gennie up into his arms.

"Is India as far as New Orleans?" she asked, fixing her hazel eyes on her father's face.

"A little bit farther," Beau said. He brushed a curl of light brown hair away from Gennie's face, then turned to see what Émilie was doing. "Oh, my God," he said, putting Gennie down and plucking Émilie off the concrete base of the fence around the elephant pen. He stood her up and brushed at her coat. "Émilie, for Pete's sake, you came to see the monkeys, not act like one."

"I'm sorry, Papa," she said. She leaned forward and kissed him, her mouth making a penitent moue. But her gray eyes sparkled, and he knew that in two minutes Émilie would have found yet another temptation she would quite willingly succumb to.

"Let's go get some ice cream," he said, taking each twin by the hand. "Then if we have time, we can go see the fish."

Walking through the zoo on an early April day was almost as

good a remedy for the winter blues as anything he could think of, especially with his two little daughters for company. People filled the paths of Audubon Park, strolling through the Zoological Gardens, or just lazing beneath the oaks, watching the way screens of Spanish moss filtered the spring sunlight.

"It's nice in New Orleans," Gennie said. She walked sedately at Beau's side while Émilie bounced off his opposite arm like a rubber ball on a too-tight string.

"Yes," Beau said. "I'm glad we came." And glad Louise's conference occupied all her time. At least her disapproving presence had not ruined their outings.

The crowd around the ice-cream stand began to thin out as they approached. A woman with two boys and a small girl was ahead of them. Something about the way the woman held her head, something about the way she stood, was familiar to Beau. Then a flash of sunlight struck her hair, and it blazed into a particular shade of gold that he would carry to his grave. "Caroline! Caroline, for heaven's sake, what are you doing here?"

Caroline spun around, a large ice-cream cone in her hand. "Beau! Why, Beau, how wonderful to see you!" She almost ran forward, her free hand outstretched, her face alight with pleasure. Suddenly Caroline stopped. Her face changed, and Beau knew she was remembering his silence and neglect. He moved toward her, trying to think of something to bridge that long gap. Then her hand jerked, and her ice cream fell from the cone, splattering against the ground and leaving a trail of chocolate on Caroline's pale blue skirt. Caroline's daughter Caro took one look at the ice cream on the ground and burst into tears.

Thank God, Beau thought, and set about solving the small crisis that diverted them for the moment from the larger one. He got more ice cream for Caro, cones for his children, and then settled them safely on park benches to eat them.

"Now," he said, sitting beside Caroline. "Let me see if I can make something else right." Her face was turned from him, her eyes on the cone in her hand, but he saw the color begin to flood her cheek. "I owe you . . . well, much more than an apology, Caroline. I . . . I've avoided seeing you these last couple of years."

She shook her head. "People get busy, Beau. You don't have to apologize to me for that." She stopped speaking, and he could see she was close to tears.

"I hurt you, Caroline."

"Why did you?" she burst out, facing him. "I kept waiting and waiting, and hoping you'd call—" She bit her lip and lifted her head. "Never mind. I've no claim on you, there's no reason to carry on."

"You've every claim on me," Beau said. "And that's just it. It . . . it got so painful to see you, Caroline. To realize what it would be like to have your . . . caring all the time." He looked away, remembering all the pain his frenetic activity the last years had buried. "I just couldn't put myself through it anymore."

"So you stayed away—"

"I see how cowardly that was now," he said. "I should have told you."

"I wouldn't have understood," she said. "Not then." She turned and put her free hand against his cheek. "I do now. Because I've learned how empty days can be, Beau. When you were coming so often—I didn't know that." Her eyes were filled with love, and a tenderness he had never thought to see again.

He reached up and caught her hand. "Can you forgive me, Caroline?"

Her laughter told him the answer even before she spoke. "Oh, Beau, of course I can! If you can forgive me the terrible things I thought about you."

"They couldn't be any worse than what I told myself," he said. "But, look, that's over now, isn't it?"

"I should hope so!" she said.

He leaned back against the bench and surveyed her. "You look wonderful," he said. "Whatever you've been up to, it agrees with you. What have you been doing?" He nodded at the children. "Other than bringing up some fine-looking children."

"Oh, the usual. Being a doctor's wife is a career all by itself. Especially in a place like Lafayette. Everywhere I go, someone comes up to me with a message for Raoul. 'Chère, tell Doctor that rash, it went away, I don't need no more ointment!'" She laughed. "And a lot of messages that don't bear repeating!"

"And Raoul? Still working too hard?"

"Always. And, of course, always the last to be paid."

He heard something in her voice that signaled him—did the Hamiltons have money worries? Funny how he'd always thought a de Clouet never had to think about money at all. "But does that present a problem, Caroline?"

She finished her ice cream and ran her tongue around her cream-rimmed lips. "It shouldn't." She sighed. "We don't need that much, and there is other income. But Beau Chêne takes so much, Beau."

"Beau Chêne. Has your mother made it over to you, then?"

Caroline's eyes darkened. "Of course not! But she has left it to me to see that it's kept up—I don't dare ask her to contribute one cent. Even with no one living there, it still needs a lot of maintenance."

"How about the oil wells there? Are they still producing?"

"Some, I guess. But no one seems to take much interest in them, either."

"Your father doesn't?" Beau was astonished, and his face showed it. "My God, with money sitting in the ground, he doesn't do anything to get it out?"

"I don't know," Caroline said. "He doesn't seem interested in much of anything." She shook her head. "He had a mild heart attack a couple of years ago—right after Francie died, as a matter of fact." She saw a black expression in Beau's eyes that frightened her. Now, what had she said? "Maybe that frightened him. I don't know."

"I imagine he's still interested in politics, though," Beau said. "His biggest client is the New Orleans utility system— and it's involved in politics up to its dirty neck."

His tone warned Caroline that Beau's old grievances against her father had been augmented by new ones. Something to do with business or politics, she'd bet. Beau's rising fortunes were carefully cataloged by the local newspapers—she had read enough to know that if he and her father clashed now, the match would be a little more even, and the outcome not quite as predictable. "I don't know, Beau. He doesn't say anything, and to tell you the truth, I don't ask."

"You're visiting them now?"

"For a few days. It's about all I can stand. Of course Mama always thinks it's a wonderful idea to have us here—and then after two days, I have to spend most of my time finding ways to keep the children out of the house." She pulled her watch forward and opened the case. "I'd better get back. Mama's in better condition to deal with them before the cocktail hour."

He let the admission fall between them, a brick that would help build a bridge over the space the years had made. "I'll walk with you. We should get back to the hotel, anyway."

"You're down for a while, then?"

"A week," he said. He made a face. "It was supposed to be a family trip—but there's some religious conference that will apparently fall apart if Louise doesn't watch it. So the children and I amuse ourselves. I left Skye with his nurse—I don't manage the three of them as well as you do yours."

"Oh, Beau," she said, tucking her arm through his. "You always manage everything well." At the touch of her body, he felt the years between them melt away like her spilled ice cream in the warm spring sun.

The children skipped ahead of them, Caro toddling behind the four older ones. Passersby paused to smile at them; the couple walking arm in arm, the five happy children. "A beautiful little family," one woman said as she passed.

Beau saw a quick pink color Caroline's cheeks. "They think these are ours," she said, trying not to laugh. Then the joy of being with Beau filled her, and she turned to him, eyes shining. "Beau," she said. "If you knew how I've missed you."

"Let's meet here tomorrow, shall we?" he said.

"Yes."

A gust of stronger breeze swirled her clothes around her, the loose-fitting jacket blowing away from her body and the scarf at the neck of her blouse sailing back over her shoulders. She grabbed at her knee-length skirt and pulled it down. "Gracious," she said. "You'd think it was still March."

"The new fashions certainly become you," he laughed appreciatively. "You're one of the ladies short skirts were made for."

"Men," she said, turning her face quickly to hide the color that so easily changed her from a dignified young matron to a blushing girl. "You've seen short skirts before."

"Last time I saw you, they were still long," he said. He took her arm again. "I should think you'd feel like a bird out of a cage—young and frivolous." He glanced at her, smiled teasingly. "Caroline the flapper!"

"Well, hardly," she said, but he knew she was pleased.

He put her and her children on their streetcar, then led his children to the one that would take them back to the hotel. Rattling along the tracks to the French Quarter, he leaned out the open window into the soft evening air. The spring twilight suited his mood. For the first time in years, he was in love again. He put out a hand to rescue Émilie, who was hanging out the window at his side. "Did you like Miss Caroline's children?" he asked her.

"They were nice," Émilie said.

"Nice," Gennie echoed.

At dinner, Louise heard all about their day. "We went and saw the animals," Émilie said. "And gave the elephant peanuts."

"And there was a pretty lady with some little children," Gennie said. "We all had ice cream."

"Caroline Hamilton," Beau said, answering the question in his wife's eyes. "She's visiting her parents with her children, and happened to be in the park."

"We're going to play with them tomorrow," Émilie said.

Louise said nothing, but later, when they were alone in their room, she said to Beau, not bothering to lift her eyes from the book in her hand, "I think we should go back tomorrow, Beau. This change in routine is affecting the children, they're getting quite spoiled."

He surveyed her carefully, gauging the risk involved in challenging her. The tightness of the muscles in her throat, the way her eyes had narrowed, the tension around her mouth warned him that this could become a full-scale tantrum, one the whole hotel would hear.

"All right," he said evenly. He went to the telephone and called the Livaudais residence. "Caroline, it's Beau," he said when she came to the telephone. "Louise has decided we should go back tomorrow. I'm sorry the children will miss their visit." He paused, listening. "Yes, we'll do that. We certainly will." He put down the telephone and picked up his hat. "I'm going out, Louise. Don't bother waiting up for me."

27

"MISSISSIPPI RIVER ON RAMPAGE; DELTA FLOODED." The head-lines from the *Times-Picayune* glared at Beau as he took his place at the breakfast table one morning in late April. "My God," he said. His eyes ran quickly over the story. He looked at Louise, sitting opposite him and reading a religious tract while she ate. "Those breaks in the Mississippi River up in Arkansas and Mississippi we heard about last week?" he said to her. He tapped the newspaper. "This article says the whole southern part of the Mississippi Basin better brace itself— we're going to get flooded too."

Louise buttered a piece of the thin toast she favored and looked at him calmly. "The Mississippi's a long way from here, Beau. We don't have anything to worry about."

A familiar anger rose in him; did she never think of anyone else? "Even if you don't care about the thousands of people losing their stock, their fields, everything—we do have cause for worry. A great deal of worry." He put down the *Picayune* and poured himself coffee. "If the Atchafalaya River behind us has to take some of the water the Mississippi's carrying, its levees may not hold."

Her lips closed down on a bite of toast as she returned his gaze. "Well, there's not much you can do about it, is there?" She shrugged. "The water rises every spring, sometimes it runs over—I can't see there's that much to worry about."

"Read the newspaper, Louise, and you'd know what there is to worry about," he said sharply, shoving the paper across the table to her. "Millions of acres have already been flooded, countless head of livestock drowned. My God, we're not talk-ing about some little creek rising!"

She rose, a look of distaste on her face. "Well, Beau, you go on and worry about it all you want to. See if that does much good." She started toward the dining-room door, then turned and looked at him. "But if it will ease your mind a little, I'll pray when I go to church this afternoon."

"Thanks," Beau said. "I always feel so much better when you've told God what you want Him to do."

Now, don't start another fight with Louise, he told himself as her rigid body disappeared into the hall. That won't solve anything. All it will do is give you more to handle at home.

He drove out to the nearest levee on the Atchafalaya to see for himself how high the river stood. Before leaving, he checked the map in the newspaper again to see where the flood had reached; six states were marked off with heavy black flood lines. We're next, Beau thought, imagining the lines creeping around Louisiana, shadowing the top parishes of the state.

A road to the Gemini Oil fields took him close to the levee; he left his car off to the side and walked the rest of the way. Standing on the top of the levee, he watched the rising waters surge past. Men were working unceasingly to strengthen the levees from New Orleans to New Roads in Pointe Coupee Parish, he knew, levees that were usually well up to the task of making even the mighty Mississippi mind its manners and stay within its banks. But what was good for citizens along the Mississippi was bad for the people of St. Martin Parish; if the Mississippi River could not break out between New Roads and New Orleans, it would have to push its way into the waters of the Tensas and Atchafalaya basins, swelling the waters already roiling at his feet. The Atchafalaya, brown with mud and loosened topsoil, was always dangerous, with an undercurrent capable of uprooting small trees even during quieter times. Fed by floodwaters, she could be merciless. Beau saw in his mind the relatively short distance between the Atchafalaya River and the torrent he knew the Mississippi River had become. The floods had been building since March. It will be bad, Beau thought.

The quiet of the fields and swamp behind Beau made the roaring tide of the river seem ominous. The land, nested with animals and birds, was calm, almost deceptively serene. Beyond the swamp lay the Langlinais fields, already plowed and seeded, soon to become lush and green under the warming sun. And beyond the fields lay the road into town, where already people waited anxiously for news of the flood.

Beau leaned over, picked up a stick, and tossed it toward the middle of the river. A whirlpool sucked at it greedily, spun it rapidly before it was swept under by an undercurrent. We should have built a spillway, some kind of safety valve, Beau thought, remembering the arguments the levee boards and police juries of the river parishes had had on the subject. He took one last look at the river and turned away. This, he thought, looking out over the land, will be the safety valve. This and our fields—the whole damn parish. Buttercups, pink and fragile, brushed against his boots as he started back to the car. Early blackberries hung in thick clusters on vines, and wild azaleas waved their last extravagant blooms. Was there any place on earth as beautiful, as good? he thought. An ache filled him. Unless the waters receded, the buttercups, the blackberries, the azaleas, all of it, would be swept up in the rising tide of the river behind him.

He drove to the fork in the road to Geneviève's house and turned in. He found her in the kitchen garden pulling weeds; her blue-and-white-checked sunbonnet, made in the style the first Acadians had brought to Louisiana, sheltered her face. "Why does the good God make weeds grow faster than vegetables?" she asked, getting up and coming to him. "Come sit, we'll have coffee," she said.

"I'm afraid this isn't a social visit, Grandmama," Beau said. "I want you to pack up your things and move into town." He put his arm around her. "The Mississippi River's on a rampage, and there's no telling when all that water pouring into the Atchafalaya will break a levee. Then we're in for it, Grandmama." He waved a hand past the kitchen garden to the pasture where cows grazed. "When that happens, you won't be able to see the fences—or those hedges. There's no telling how bad it could get. I want you out of here and safe under my nose in town."

"Beau!" She backed away from him. "Move into town?" Her eyes darted to the quiet pasture. "You really think there'll be a flood here?"

"I know there will, Grandmama. Our levees can't hold. The ones between Pointe Coupee and Orleans parishes are so strong that ours are the only ones weak enough to break."

Geneviève rubbed her back and stretched. "You're such a baby you wouldn't remember the flood we had, oh, it must have been eighteen eighty-one, eighteen eighty-two. Your papa and aunt were big enough to get scared, pester me to death worrying about it. That was a big flood, Beau, and it didn't get past the west ridge of the Teche." She patted his cheek. "This one won't either. You'll see."

"You don't know that, Grandmama. If it does—if the levee does break, that water's not going to take its time. Grandmama, you haven't seen what it looks like right now, the Atchafalaya. And more water rushing into it every hour. If the levee breaks, and the flood comes, it will be like . . . like . . ." He walked over to the watering can that Geneviève had set near the garden, and tilted it over with his foot. Water rushed over the tin lip, making a small stream in the dirt path. "Like that multiplied a million times, Grandmama. You can't stop it, you can't put it back." He took her in his arms. "And this farm is one of the first things in its path."

"This farm is where I came as a bride," Geneviève said. "This farm is where I birthed my babies. This farm is where I spent the happiest years of my life. I'm not leaving it, Beau."

He released her and stepped back. There was no point in arguing with her when she sounded like that, he knew, when all the soft laughter left her voice and only the firmness was left. "All right, Grandmama, all right. Then I'm moving out here." He saw her open her mouth, and he reached out and put his finger against her lips. "Shhh." He smiled. "I'm as hard-headed as you are, Grandmama, when I have to be. I wonder where I got it?"

Driving home, he felt invigorated, more alive than he'd felt in months. Despite the threat of the flood, he was oddly happy. To have an excuse to get away from Louise, to be out on his land. He'd send Louise and the children to her family in Abbeville, and then move out to the farm. 'Tit Nonc could help him move the livestock to high ground and get the furnishings on the lower floor of the house up to the second story. He'd go out and face that river down.

Louise voiced no opposition when he proposed sending her and the children to her parents'. Obviously, Beau thought, she believed enough in the flood not to risk staying in its way. Nor did she suggest that he accompany them, he noticed.

"It's a punishment from God, you know," she said, looking up as she packed the twins' summer dresses into a big wicker case.

"What did you say?" Beau demanded.

"This flood," she said. Louise's eyes grew large, fixed. "God is sending it to punish us for our sins." She moved closer to Beau, Gennie's little pinafore dangling from her hand. "That's why I'm letting you send me away. I don't have those sins. It's right that I should escape any punishment."

Beau stood up, facing Louise, as though better to see the creature before him as the woman he slept with each night, breakfasted with each morning. "Like so much else, this is your own doctrine, is that it? The flood is sent to punish everyone for their sins. What sins are those, Louise?" His voice was gentle, careful.

Her free hand began plucking at the ribbons in the pinafore, untying the bows, smoothing the ends of the narrow grosgrain. "Sins of drunkenness, Beau. And sins of lying—lying because people say they are obeying the laws, and then they buy liquor anyway." She moved again, stood in the center of the rectangle of light that poured into the room from the tall window that had been bared to the April day. The light touched her at the top of her head, seemingly setting her auburn hair on fire. It spilled down over her small form, glinting against the white of her dress, outlining her in an aureole of gold. "Sins of lust, Beau. It is lust when men beget child after child upon their wives, simply because they cannot contain themselves. Their lust— and their wives' agony."

"You agreed to have Skye," Beau said. "And you can hardly accuse me of bothering you after you conceived him." He really did not believe the figure standing in that column of light would hear him. "You can't accuse me of lust."

"Oh, but I can," she said. She seemed to be speaking from a place she knew Beau would never enter, a place in which she was quite safe. "You do not lust after me—but you do lust." He was readying his protests, readying his denials, when she said, "You lust after Caroline Hamilton." Then she turned and looked at him, her eyes calm and steady. "But it will come to nothing. She is too honorable a woman to violate her marriage vows." For the first time since she had begun speaking, Louise smiled. Beau had forgotten what a violation a smile could be. "I say she is honorable rather than good because very few people are good, Beau."

"But you are, I suppose," he said. His voice was no longer gentle; he didn't care if he upset her.

"I try to be," she said. "Some days I am not entirely without hope that I am." She went back to the pile of clothes waiting to be laid in the case and began to stack them neatly inside.

"Wait a minute," Beau said, crossing to her and taking her by the arm.

She looked at his hand on her arm, looked at his angry face, and then, with a patient look he wished he could slap from her face, turned to him. "What is it, Beau?"

"I don't give one good goddamn where you got the idea that the water coming down the Mississippi from an extremely long and wet winter was thought up by God just to punish people living in this region, when the whole country defies Prohibition. I don't even give a damn about what you said about lust—you've got your own ideas on that subject, little knowledge as you've got to back them up. What I do care about is the intellectual arrogance you've got to stand there and make a pronouncement on the population at large as though you're some kind of prophet or saint. And," he said, bending over her, his eyes blazing, "I care about your defamation of Caroline Hamilton." He found that he could barely speak Caroline's name in Louise's presence without feeling that he was despoiling it. "I do not 'lust' after her," he said, forcing his voice to be calm. "I love her. I've loved her for eleven years—will love her as long as I know what love is." His eyes for the first time showed his vulnerability, the sense of loss which burdened his life. "And I will not allow that love to be debased with the word 'lust.'"

She recoiled from him; her face held an expression of amused contempt, an evil glee at his admission of weakness. "Love!" she said, spitting out the words. "You don't even know what love is. *God* is love. I knew you were infatuated with another woman from the moment we met. That is precisely why you interested me; that's why I married you. I didn't want, really, to marry anyone. I didn't know what men and women did, men and women who were married. But I knew, from lectures on chastity at school, and from scraps of talk, that it was not . . . nice. I married you knowing I could always hold your great love for someone else over your head. I knew that I could control you." She smiled then, that terrible, cruel smile. "If, of course, your own guilt at loving someone else wasn't enough."

The vehemence of her passion, her hatred, staggered him. Suddenly he remembered his doubts before asking her to marry him. Had he known instinctively that it wouldn't work out beforehand? How much of his misery, of this blasphemy of a marriage, had he created? "Finish packing," he said, turning away. "I'll pull up the car." He retreated numbly from the room, the echo of her triumphant laughter following him down the stairs.

Returning from Abbeville, Beau remembered Father Adrian's concern at the time Beau so badly wanted another baby: aren't you afraid the children will inherit Louise's will? he had asked. Beau remembered his confident answer then. Now he wondered if he could keep his children from being contaminated by their mother's terrible sickness. Thinking of the dark soul beneath that bright exterior, he knew as certainly as he knew the floodwaters were coming that Louise's flood-water of hate was held by only the thinnest line of spiritual restraint. Wearily he set his shoulders. He might not be able to keep the Atchafalaya from flooding his ancestral home, but he would keep Louise from engulfing his children. He didn't always understand his life. Unlike Louise, he did not try to be "good," nor did he worry overmuch about punishment. All he could do was go on, with God's help, as best he could; he left it to God to figure it all out. Then he smiled at his own self-deception. He very well knew that what kept him going was not God, but the absurd hope, irrational as it seemed, that someday Caroline Hamilton would be his.

In the weeks ahead, the work of moving livestock to the high ground on Avery Island, and moving the furniture upstairs, took Beau's mind off his domestic worries. The work went well, and he found himself in a much better frame of mind. Indeed, after he attended flood meetings in New Iberia, his hopes rose that they could avoid this flood, after all. By mid-May, the battle between the Mississippi and Atchafalaya rivers and the levee system was even. The men in the towns along the river continued to pile sandbag on top of sandbag to strengthen the levees that stood between them and the swirling river water.

But Beau's brief optimism and the river towns' hopes were shattered when, on May 17, the Atchafalaya River broke a gap in the levee near Melville, opening a two-thousand-foot hole through which an arm of water leapt and rushed, deluging the streets of the town. Hours later, the levee broke again at Cecilia, and then almost immediately at Henderson. Listening to a reporter from the Memphis *Commercial Appeal* describe the flood, Beau remembered his premonitions as he stood on the levee that April day watching the waters of the Atchafalaya roil. The water would not have to go through Bayou Teche. It would come from the Atchafalaya Swamp, from Henderson and Cecilia, rushing over the lowlands that made a great depression of earth which ended at Spanish Lake, just outside of New Iberia. He remembered the chill of fear he had felt, standing on the banks of the Atchafalaya that afternoon. The fear he had felt then was like a quiet trickle of water compared to what engulfed him now.

"I've never seen anything like it," the reporter exclaimed to the men gathered at the meeting in New Iberia. "The torrents and rapids are monstrous—like the rapids at Niagara Falls. It comes from every direction. It's like no flood I've ever seen."

Those words were enough to send Beau hurrying from the meeting, leaving behind the discussion of Red Cross rescue and refugee operations. He drove madly to the farm. Pulling into the quiet farmyard, he stopped the car, leaning on the steering wheel for a moment to marshal his thoughts and calm his fear. The scene was peaceful, the sky serene. It was hard to believe that even now death was rushing toward them.

He found Geneviève in the kitchen making gumbo, humming to herself as she cooked.

"Grandmama, the flood. It's coming. We've got to get out."

Her spoon never missed a beat as she looked at him. "The flood is coming? Is that what you said, Beau?"

"There have been breaks at Melville and Cecilia—they've opened the whole levee system. There's nothing between us and it—nothing that will stop that water." He turned and looked toward the quiet pasture, empty now of all the milk cows he and 'Tit Nonc had moved to Avery Island. He could see the trees that bordered the pasture and constituted the first line in the battalion of cypress and oak marching back through the swamp. Even now he could imagine the water beginning to cover the land. First it would creep forward in small trickles, he knew, that would gradually cover the earth, making a shimmering film over the grass. But then it would become bolder, making way for the great wave the reporter had described, that seemed to come from nowhere and everywhere at once, its power concealed by its silence, a silence which made the awful advance more terrible still.

"Where is it you want us to go, Beau?" Geneviève said. She had already allowed him to have the farmhands carry most of her furnishings to the upper story, and had agreed to humor him by sleeping up there. She put two bowls on the small table they had left in the kitchen and pointed to a chair. "Sit. Eat." She sat down and unfolded her napkin, crossed herself, and blessed the meal.

"Grandmama, there's no time to eat. We've got to get to the Red Cross camp in Lafayette. Or to Aunt Claudine's in New Orleans." He heard her spoon hit her plate as she let it fall.

"A refugee camp?" When he heard the dull firmness in her voice, he knew she would not leave. Geneviève picked up her spoon and began eating again. "I won't leave this place, Beau. The Langlinaises, once they have land, a house to put on it— they don't leave." Her eyes darted around the kitchen, found the fresher places on the walls that marked the positions of the furniture that had stood there—the safe, the big hutch with its drawers and cabinets for flour and sugar and salt and spices, the smooth tracks in the floor near the fireplace where the two big rockers had stood for generations.

Damn, he thought, I shouldn't have told Papa I could handle her. I should have known she'd get her back up.

Beau put a hand over hers. "Grandmama, look." He tried to sound teasing, the beloved grandson whom she adored, for whom she would do anything. "Don't make me worry. Do just this one thing for me." The back of his neck tickled; involuntarily he looked over his shoulder to see if the flood were already here.

Geneviève cleaned her bowl with a bit of bread, ate it, and then sat back in her chair. "Your papa and mama—they're going to that camp?"

"Mama and Marie went to Ville Platte yesterday—they'll stay with her family. Papa and Étienne are between St. Martinville and New Iberia."

Geneviève rose and took her bowl to the sink. She was smiling, the two curved ends of her lips pulling wrinkles of amusement across her cheeks. "You men," she said. "Love nothing better than a big commotion. Meetings here, meetings there. Discussing, talking, making plans." He heard the water running in the sink, splashing over her bowl.

"I'm going to start the automobile," he said. "And then I'm taking you to Lafayette, if I have to hog-tie you." He opened the back door and then stopped in his tracks.

The packed dirt of the backyard path shone with a film of

water. In Geneviève's kitchen garden, the water was already
up to the height of her furrowed rows; in the far pasture, it
stood almost to the bottom fence rail. It must have already been
in the pasture when he came, he realized, hidden by grass and
reeds.

Then he looked at the far edge of the pasture. A wall of
water four feet high hung seemingly suspended in midair. For a
moment Beau clung to the wild hope that the frame would
hold, that the wall of water would stand. Then it broke, crashing over the drainage ditches, leaping toward them, devouring
the pasture in its path. The water in the kitchen garden stirred
to life, swirling, casting up patches of dirty foam like bubbles
on the surface of boiling cane syrup. He heard a quick gasp
behind him and turned. Geneviève stood with a dish towel in
one hand, her clean and gleaming bowl in the other. The bowl
dropped to the floor and Beau heard the china shatter. The
horror in her eyes was old, older than the flood, older even than
the fear of death. Silently Beau swept her into his arms and ran
for the stairs.

As though it were part of a malevolent force, the water from up
and down the Atchafalaya ran across the land, devouring people and livestock before it. The men of St. Martin and New
Iberia parishes began mounting massive rescue operations,
rounding up the region's cattle and driving them to high ground
at Avery Island. Outside of New Iberia, a group of farmers
began damming the culverts that led into Spanish Lake, making small levees across the lower areas in an effort to keep
down the water level in the town.

Claude Langlinais glanced around at the other men grouped
at the table on the upper floor of the New Iberia City Hall.
They all looked exhausted, and Claude knew it was not so
much the hours without rest that wearied them as it was the
grief and loss of the people that poured into the town with the
flood itself. He had let Beau go alone to the farm, remaining at
his post with the rescue operations headquarters in New Iberia.
Reports came in hourly. Freight trains from the Southern Pacific Railroad were coming to the very edge of the flooding
waters, taking on people, animals, and everything the refugees
could carry. The trains rolled across the inundated land to
Lafayette, where the Red Cross was setting up refugee camps,

under the direction of Herbert Hoover. Trucks arrived, driven by men from neighboring towns and parishes, and from places as distant as Beaumont and Houston, Texas, to take the people of St. Martin Parish to safety. Those cattle not already herded elsewhere had been left behind to flounder and drown in the brown sea. Claude promised more than a few devastated farmers stock from his herd when the waters had gone down again. But even this generosity, and that of thousands of Louisianians who sent food, clothing, and household goods to the refugees, could not erase the grief of the women who sat bleak-eyed, hands twisted around worn rosary beads, staring fixedly ahead as though still seeing the linens and pots and tables and chairs that had had to be left behind for the flood to play with and destroy. Children huddled next to their parents, their youthful innocence lost to the roaring river. The Great Derangement, when my people were banished from Nova Scotia, must have been like this, Claude thought. He worked all the harder to assure the refugees that they would rebuild, would recover.

But he could not keep fear for his mother's safety from weighting him like a cross. And that of Beau. He tried to convince himself that his son had reached Geneviève in time. I should have gone myself, he thought, listening to M. W. Fisher, the editor of the New Iberia paper, describe the flood. "A mighty wall of water went across the ridges of the Teche," he exclaimed. "It struck the hills east of Opelousas, Grand Coteau, Carencro, and Lafayette with such force it looked as if it was running uphill. It bounced back with such force that it was thrown back across the Teche at Cecilia and Parks. It filled up the low bottoms between St. Martinville and Broussard. And now it's rushing toward Spanish Lake."

And right over our farm, Claude thought, groaning.

"I don't see how you can look," Geneviève said, huddled in her rocker against the bedroom wall. She had stood beside Beau at the window for one long minute, looking at the water sweeping possessively over their land, and had gone back to her chair and closed herself in its depths, head bowed.

Beau searched his pockets, found cigarettes and matches. He lit a cigarette and tossed the burnt match onto the water below, watching the water grab it, pull it into an eddy, and carry it swiftly away. "Watch you don't drop hot ashes on that bed," Geneviève said when Beau threw himself down on his back, blowing smoke in a steady stream toward the low-beamed ceiling.

He laughed. "I don't think it's fire we have to worry about, Grandmama." His shoes were dirtying the spotless quilt that covered the bed. He knew Geneviève was biting back the words that would have told him to take off his shoes before he lay down. He sat up and pulled them off, letting them fall to the floor with a heavy thud. "I think the house will hold. Thank God, we got just about everything up here," he said. "We won't starve, that's for sure." Geneviève's preserves and jellies, the few jars of tomatoes and snap beans and succotash from last year's canning, were stacked in neat rows on the floor. Smoked hams hung from hooks driven into door frames, and a huge round of cheese sat in one of the linen cupboards.

"Beau, how long do you think it will last?"

"No way of telling, Grandmama." The bed seemed to be alive, wriggling under his body, refusing it rest. He stood up and went back to the window, throwing his cigarette out into the water that now lay just three feet below the sill. "The Coast Guard has boats, surf boats with motors; they've been rescuing people since this damn thing started up in the Mississippi delta. I guess if they can leap crevasses, they can manage to reach us." Suddenly he thought of Beau Chêne. He leaned forward as though that small extra length of body could enable him to see the great house that stood a half-mile away. The sun shimmered on the water's surface; he shielded his eyes with one hand. As far as he could see, there was water, with nothing but the treetops that waved against the soft blue sky, their trunks eight feet deep in the flood. The silence was terrible. Spring was never silent; the land was always alive with animals and birds feeding, mating, making nests, rearing their young. As though his eyes now had some terrible power of divination, Beau pictured bloated, furry bodies that would soon float up and add death and decay to the land's desecration. "Thank God they got Beau Chêne cleared," he said.

Caroline had been at the big house all the previous week, packing things on the lower floor to take to Lafayette and getting the furniture moved upstairs. Beau had spent some time with her; it was odd to think they had been able to laugh and joke and be happy when they were facing yet another crisis, but they had.

"You were a big help to her, cher," Geneviève said. She came and stood next to him, her eyes carefully turned from the scene beyond the window. "Beau, you still love her, don't you?" Her voice was soft, remembering afternoons in her kitchen when her carefree, happy grandson had run in with his string of fish for supper, mornings on the porch when a growing boy had sat and told her about school and what he was learning, evenings by the fire when the grown man shared his dreams.

"Yes," he said. "I believe I always will." He felt Geneviève's silence, her stillness. He turned and faced her. "I've shocked you. I'm sorry. Married men aren't supposed to love someone else. You'll want me to go to confession." He smiled as though he were teasing her, but Geneviève knew him too well to be fooled.

"Confession! Oh, no, Beau, not you. Hélène Livaudais, Charles Livaudais, they should confess. And Louise." Her arms came around his neck. "Beau, something a priest has never been able to explain to me. How is it that the people who commit the worst crimes don't ever seem to let it bother them?"

He was glad her face was hidden against his shoulder, that she could not see the emotion in his face. Even hearing Charles's name mentioned was more than he could bear. "It's because they don't know how terrible they are that they can do such things," he said. "Don't you know people like that think they are the only ones who know what's right?"

"That's wrong, Beau. How can they think bad is good?"

He remembered Louise a few days ago, a tower of rage. "Because they want to, Grandmama," he said. "That way, they can do just as they please."

"Beau—it is God we must please."

"Maybe they think they do," he said. He moved away from the window, overcome by the need to act, to relieve the pressure building in him. Certainly, Louise thinks that when she prays, God snaps to attention.

The day wore on slowly, broken by meals neither had an appetite to eat. Beau watched the water slowly and steadily inch higher until it was only a foot and a half beneath the windowsill. For the first time, it occurred to him that the flood might rise enough to submerge even the second floor. Could he get them onto the roof? He went out into the hall. Though he knew the lower section of the house was underwater, he was shocked to see the dirty brown water lapping at the top step of the staircase. He felt suddenly utterly alone. There was nothing in the world but water, miles and miles of it. They could not walk out of this house, nor could they swim out. If he could not find a way to keep themselves above the water . . . You can't panic now; Grandmama depends on you, he thought. But who would find them? Who would know to come? Claude was in New Iberia; the ten miles that seemed so short by road was an impossible distance now. It was all very well to talk to Geneviève about the Coast Guard and their miraculous surf boats. But with so much destruction, with so many who needed rescue, what were the chances of the boats reaching them? And how could they make their way against the powerful current, past the debris and hidden obstacles? With every landmark gone, perhaps even the Coast Guard could not find them.

He could feel the house trembling as the water moved against it. The house had withstood storms and the weathering effects of time, but it was not an ark. He went back into the bedroom. "The water's still rising," he said. "I think we'd better move up to the attic."

"The attic!"

"If we don't move now, if the water keeps rising into the night . . ." He lifted his hands helplessly. "I wouldn't want to have to scramble up there in the dark."

"I'll begin to put some things together," she said quietly, taking up a split oak basket and packing jars of food in it.

"I'll go take a look up there," Beau said. He smiled, trying to lighten the mood. "Chase the varmints away."

The trapdoor into the attic was in a room at the end of the hall; rough ladder steps had been fastened to the wall beneath it. As Beau pushed open the trap, a rush of humid, musty air filled his lungs. He climbed through the opening, feeling the sticky strands of a spider's web on his cheeks and hands. The latticed gables let in enough light to see mouse droppings and small shapes hanging from the beams. He went to one of the dormer windows set into the rear portion of the roof and opened it. The fresh air smelled good, and he leaned out, breathing deeply and deliberately, looking at the serene May sky, avoiding the brown waters that covered the land. The slope of the roof was not too steep; they could take refuge here if they had to. His eyes measured the water's level—almost to the sill of the second-floor windows. Water would be rising in the house now; he'd better lose no time in getting food and bedding to the attic.

"It could use a good spring cleaning," he said to Geneviève. "But it's high and dry, even if populated by mice and bats."

"They don't bother me, I don't bother them," Geneviève said.

He gathered pitchers from the bedrooms and filled them at the tap in the hall bathroom, then carried them carefully to the attic, covering the open tops with cloth. He watched Geneviève safely up the ladder, then followed her up. For a moment before he closed the trapdoor he took a last view of the room below. To think they had worked so hard, carried so much furniture, so many things, upstairs—only to have them ruined after all. He tried not to think of what some of those things were. Photographs of several generations of Langlinaises. Souvenirs from decades of living. Linens embroidered by Langlinais women long dead, books read by Langlinaises of another century. Damn! He slammed the trapdoor into place and joined Geneviève where she sat on a pallet of quilts before the open window.

"Mais, as soon as this flood is over, this attic is going to get such a cleaning," Geneviève said.

The sun dropped and the world plunged into darkness. No lights shone anywhere, nothing but the glimmer of moonlight on the dark water. They lit a kerosene lamp and sat in its circle of light, crouched near the window. Geneviève's pallet was drawn up close against the wall, and he had ranged crates around it. She slept fitfully, and he suspected that much of the time she was not asleep, but only pretending to make him feel better about her.

As for himself, he did not think he would ever sleep again, although his eyes felt as though they had been burned into his head on the tip of a hot poker. His muscles ached from tension, his nerves seemed unable to settle, his need for action became more intense as the slow hours dragged by. Caught between the mirages of fatigue and the dreams of half-sleep, he would rouse suddenly, his mind filled with an idea of escape, only to be jerked back into reality by the flickering light from the lantern and Geneviève's gentle snores.

When he heard the low roar of a motor, its rhythmic sound pulsing in the coming dawn, he thought at first the sound was but another trick played by an exhausted mind. Until it grew louder, and louder, and he leapt into wakefulness, ran to the window and peered out. There was a boat, a real boat, heading through the murky light toward the house. When it was within hailing distance, a man's voice came: "How many are you?"

"Two," Beau shouted back.

"We're full," the man called. "But we'll have someone out to get you."

Beau watched the boat change its course and head away from the house, vanishing in the mist that rose up from the surface of the water. How did they even know where they were to send a boat back? He lit a cigarette and sat on the windowsill, smoking. The gray light became gradually brighter, though the sky did not have the usual rose and gold and lavender tints of dawn. Beau watched while the sun rose straight up against a pale blue curtain of sky, a blazing orb of orange-gold, already shining harshly on the devastated land. He heard Geneviève behind him.

"Beau, was it a boat?"

"Yes," he said, and saw the terrible fatigue written in her face.

"Good," she said, moving her hands to work the stiffness from her joints. She cut bread and cheese, opened a jar of fig preserves, and they breakfasted picnic-fashion. "I don't mind telling you," she said as she carefully packed the remains away, "I won't be sorry not to have to camp like a gypsy when we get rescued."

No point in telling her she'll be doing just that at a refugee camp, Beau thought. He knew the Red Cross was raising tent cities across the belt of land bordering flooded areas; any shelter was better than none. Still, his grandmother in a tent!

He went to the window and peered into the mist that was gradually being burned away by the sun. Suddenly he saw something moving through it—a long, slender shape. The pirogue broke clear, and the man poling it called, "Hello-o-o!" The pirogue bumped against the house, some six feet below the level of the roof.

Beau climbed out of the window and walked carefully to the edge of the roof, balancing himself against the slope. "God, I've never been so glad to see anyone in my life," he said. "How in the world did you find us?"

"Passed a boat coming out—they told me there were people

here. I've hunted around here since I was a boy—name's Paul Blanchet. I'm from Lafayette—everybody there with any kind of a boat is out picking people up. Some terrible sights, I'll tell you."

"Has the flood crested yet?" Beau asked.

"From what I hear, it has," Blanchet said. "Who else is here?"

"Just my grandmother," Beau said. "I'll help her out." He went back to the window where Geneviève now stood. "Come on, Grandmama, it won't be long now before you're in a dry bed drinking a good cup of coffee."

He almost lifted her through the window and guided her to the edge of the roof. Her eyes went from the pirogue below her to Beau's face. "Beau, how am I going to get down there?"

"I'll lower you," he said. He lay full-length on the roof, his shoulders even with its edge. "Turn your back to the edge and get as close to me as you can," he said. When she was huddled next to him, he grasped her under the arms and said quietly, "Now, go off the edge of the roof, Grandmama. I've got you." He would never forget the way she looked at him, the deep trust that shone in her eyes. She dangled her legs off the roof, then let her body drop. Even her slight weight jolted him, but he steadied himself, and for a moment she swung from his hands before he began edging forward and lowering her to Blanchet's waiting arms.

"Now," he heard Blanchet say. He could not see the boat, could see nothing but the sky ahead as his straining muscles fought the pull of Geneviève's weight. He said a quick prayer and let her go, looking down in time to see Blanchet's arms close safely around her.

"Let me steady the boat," Blanchet called. When it was still again, with Geneviève sitting in the stern, leaving the middle clear, Beau grabbed the edge of the roof, swung over the side, hung for a moment until Blanchet signaled him, and then dropped into the solid bottom of the pirogue. He sat for a moment, breathing hard. The rush of air seemed to be inflating his head, blowing it up like a balloon until it was light, light and dizzy with oxygen.

"Here," Blanchet said, thrusting a flask in his hand. "Drink this."

The liquor steadied him. He wiped his mouth and handed the

flask back. "Thanks," he said. "Now, if you just had a cup of coffee on you—"

"We'll get you some at the camp," Blanchet laughed. He stood in the center of the pirogue, poling it smoothly forward, steering around treetops, heading steadily northwest as though he were reading a map. "There're a couple of Red Cross camps in Lafayette. I'll take you to the one at N. P. Moss School," he said. He looked at Geneviève. "It's not too bad, ma'am. Tents, of course, but people are staying pretty cheerful considering their situation. Someone's always taking out a fiddle and playing."

"Tents?" Geneviève said with a horrified look at Beau. Sitting in the stern of the pirogue, clutching the cypress sides, Geneviève looked small and frightened, and Beau realized how much of a homebody she was, how seldom she left the tranquillity of her orderly kingdom.

"If the trains are running, I'm sending Grandmama to my aunt in New Orleans," Beau said. "Or if I can get her there, to my mother's people in Ville Platte."

"You said your name is Langlinais—are you Claude's son?" At Beau's nod, Blanchet's hand shot out. "Your papa is a good man—we've done a little business together. He says I'm young enough to be his son, but when we make a deal, I'd better be as old as he is." His laughter rang out over the rippling water.

Beau looked up to see a boat just ahead of them, low in the water, laden with a large family with bundles stuffed around them. Refugees. They looked as though they had been on the water all night.

"Y'all all right?" Blanchet yelled as they drew abreast.

The man rowing the boat looked toward them, and Beau saw disaster in his eyes. "We're alive," the man said. "That's all that matters." The story they told was terrible. They had seen water overtake their farm, their livestock, all but one milk cow grazing in the front yard. "When the water came, she began to swim," the man said, shaking his head. "Then she panicked, and when I tried to row the boat past her, she scrambled toward it, ramming it with her head. She was like a pet, the children's cow. But I took my gun and I shot her, 'cause, man, she was coming in this boat, hell or high water. We'd all have been gone." Looking into those eyes, Beau felt that a part of them already was.

Beau took one look at the tent city built on the grounds of N. P. Moss School and shook his head. "Mr. Blanchet, if I have to row her all the way to Ville Platte, my grandmother's not staying here."

Blanchet nodded. "But you need to register with the Red Cross. It's the only way to keep track of where everybody is. You wouldn't believe the people who come in here hunting for husbands, parents, brothers . . ." He clasped a warm hand on Beau's arm. "But it's not all bad. The fiddlers get to playing, and people get to singing—I think these people are converting the Yankee Red Cross workers to Cajun living."

Making their way through the camp to the headquarters in the school, Geneviève saw so many families she knew, in such need of help. She tried to break away to go to their aid. "Beau, only a minute!" she said, seeing a young mother struggling with her small children.

"Grandmama, there's only one thing you're going to do today—get some rest in a good bed and get a good meal."

Paul Blanchet held the door into the office open for them. "You'll be all right now." He held out his hand. "I've got to get back to my boat. There're still plenty people out there."

Beau stretched out his hand and took Blanchet's, feeling the hard edges of calluses, the warm strength. "There's no way I can say thank you," he said.

Blanchet threw back his head and laughed. "Tell your papa to give me an edge in the next deal we make," he said. He tipped his hat to Geneviève, turned, and strode away.

"That's a good man," Geneviève said, watching him walk through the people milling about the school steps. "When I get home—" Beau saw her make her trembling lip behave itself. "When I get home, I'm going to cook him something good."

"You'll get home," Beau said. He guided her through the door, his head bent toward her. The woman at the desk looked up, then caught at her heart and sat as though transfixed. Beau did not see her quickly rise and move toward him, hands outstretched. All at once he felt a soft hand close across his, and heard a familiar voice call his name. "Beau! And Mama Geneviève! I've been so worried!"

"Caroline!" He pulled her to him, and felt her arms come around his neck. His lips touched her hair. Its fresh scent drove away the smell of death that had filled his nostrils and the curve of her body made his blood stir into vigorous life. She lifted her face to his. Her eyes glowed; over and over her lips said the same two words: "Thank God!"

Beside them, Geneviève seemed to suddenly fold, her knees bending and her body sagging. Beau reached for her, holding her steady, while Caroline pulled a chair forward.

"Sit here, Mama Geneviève. I'll get you some coffee, and something to eat."

"I'm all right," Geneviève said. "Just for a moment . . ."

Caroline stuck her head through the office door and spoke to someone outside, ordering coffee and beignets sent in.

"I must say I never thought I'd see you in just this setting," Beau said, waving a hand around the room crowded with a paper-strewn desk, shelves filled with supplies, and a work-table with maps and charts covering its surface. "But you seem to suit it very well."

"When the Red Cross arrived and began setting up the camps, they sent out a call for help." She looked at Beau and laughed. "To tell you the truth, I wanted to help in the field kitchens—or mind the children. But Maude Chambers, one of the nutrition nurses, decided I had 'executive ability.' I help assign refugees to camps and keep track of where we've put who." She put both hands to her temples and pushed back her blond hair. "Beau, I never knew office work could make you ache from head to toe!"

The door opened and a girl bearing a tray came in. "There's another group coming in to be processed, Mrs. Hamilton." She looked at Beau and Geneviève. "Did you want to assign your friends to this camp?"

"No," Caroline said. "They'll be staying at my home." She handed Geneviève a cup of steaming coffee, then poured one for Beau. "Now, sit," she said. She picked up the telephone and placed a call. "Beatrice, I'm sending Mr. Beau and his grandmother to you. They've just come in from St. Martinville in a pirogue and they're dead on their feet. Feed them and get them to bed, please." She paused, listening. "Beatrice, after what they've been through, warmed-up gumbo is fine. And keep the children quiet, Beatrice." She put down the receiver. "She'll be ready for you. I'll get someone to drive you over. I'd take you myself, but you heard what my assistant said— another lot of refugees has arrived to be registered and as-signed."

"Caroline, we don't want to put you to that trouble. We can

stay here today, until I can get Grandmama to Ville Platte or New Orleans."

Caroline went to the window and waved at the row of tents. The schoolyard had been turned into a camp that housed some of the twenty-one thousand refugees pushed into Lafayette ahead of the flood. "She can't stay here, Beau! There's no need for her to. Raoul and I have acres of room—" Her chin lifted and she confronted him. "I've got entirely too much to do to stand here arguing. Just go, will you?"

Beau saw the waiting smile beneath that stern exterior. "Yes, ma'am," he said, saluting her.

"That's better," Caroline laughed.

An authoritative woman in a Red Cross uniform entered the office with a sheaf of papers. "I've made up the menus for the next week," she said to Caroline. "If you'll see about the necessary supplies . . ."

"Oh, Maude, these are some friends of mine—Mr. Beau Langlinais and his grandmother, Mrs. Jumie Langlinais. Maude Chambers, Beau. You heard me mention her just now." Caroline looked at the nurse with respect. "She's a miracle worker, feeding all these people!"

"The miracle is getting them to eat what I can provide," Maude said. "All they want is gumbo—and coffee! And café au lait for the children. I never heard anything like it in my life."

"But you do give them gumbo as much as you can, Maude. Even if it is made from wienies instead of chicken."

"These are wonderful people," Maude said. "I've worked in many refugee camps, but I've never met people like these Cajuns—the most courteous, but the most individualistic people on the face of the globe. And the most appreciative—they reach out and pat me as I pass." She gestured toward Beau and Geneviève. "Will your friends be staying with us?"

"No," Caroline said. "I'm sending them to my home. I was just going to see who could drive them."

"I've got to go to another camp," Maude said. "I can take them."

Beau helped Geneviève to her feet; she leaned heavily on his supporting arm. "I won't say I'm not just a little bit tired," she said. "And the longer I think about it, the longer that bowl of gumbo and a dry bed sound like heaven."

Caroline watched them leave, standing in the window until

they were out of sight. Then she turned and went back to her desk. A long, weary afternoon of work waited for her, but she went at it with a light heart. Beau was safe, and that was all that mattered.

Beau slept the afternoon away, the deep sleep that comes at the end of a long, demanding trial. When he awoke, he went down to find Raoul and Caroline having dinner. "Sit down, Beau," Caroline said, picking up the bell and ringing for Beatrice. "We set a place for you here, but your grandmother let me persuade her to have her supper sent up on a tray."

"You must have the skills of a Clarence Darrow, then," Beau said. He took Raoul's hand. "I can't thank you enough for putting a roof over our heads," he said.

"I'm glad it worked out this way," Raoul said. He poured wine in the glass at Beau's place. Beatrice came in and set a plate before him and stood back smiling. "Mr. Beau, I sure am glad to see you. You didn't have to swim to Lafayette, did you?"

"Thank God we didn't," Beau said fervently.

"You eat all that and I'll bring you some more," Beatrice said. "You must be plumb worn out."

"You don't need to talk me into it," he said. He turned to Raoul. "I'd like to be put to work, Raoul. There must be something I can do to help."

"No question about that," Raoul said. "You get a good night's rest and we'll talk about it in the morning."

"It took a while, but I finally got through to City Hall in New Iberia and left a message for your father that you and Mama Geneviève are with us," Caroline said. "And I spoke with your mother in Ville Platte. She was very relieved."

"That was good of you, Caroline. Thanks," Beau said. "I'll try to get in touch with Louise later. She didn't seem impressed by the flood. She probably doesn't even realize the farm was flooded."

"I won't let myself think about Beau Chêne," Caroline said. "I keep telling myself that when lives are threatened, houses don't matter."

They sat in the morning room after supper. The children came in to say good night, and Beau felt a part of the serene order that marked the Hamilton household. It was impossible not to notice Caroline's solicitude for Raoul, her thorough knowledge of everything that made him comfortable, and her attention to his needs. What must it be, he thought, to be married to such a woman? Fresh flowers filled every vase, the floors gleamed and the windows shone. Everywhere there was order, yet without that rigid neatness which defies attempts to make a house a home. The clear pastels in the draperies and upholstery picked up the tones from the old Kirman rugs that covered the floors. It was a happy house, arranged by a woman who lavished special care on every detail that added comfort and charm.

It won't be easy, staying here, he thought.

Nor did it prove to be. It was, as he realized later, like hanging on a rope swinging between heaven and hell. Heaven when Beau sat over coffee with Caroline before they drove out to the refugee camp, where he worked estimating the losses of the refugees. Hell when he lay in his bed at the opposite end of the long hall from Raoul and Caroline's room, and knew that Raoul lay next to, had possession of, Caroline. He willed himself to take each moment with her as a separate gift, one he could remember later when he needed it.

Then it was over. The rivers receded, slowly withdrawing from the land they had deluged. People returned home and began the massive task of cleanup, shoveling mud from their houses and getting on with their lives. Late crops were put in with prayers that summer would last long enough to bring in a harvest. And Beau returned to Louise and the children, wondering what kind of man he was when even the devastating disruption of a flood was preferable to domestic life with his wife.

Louise seemed oblivious of the ruin the flood had left. While the people of St. Martinville shoveled mud from their houses and carried furniture out to dry, she sat and read or sewed, eyes turned to her own inner world. She had one comment, and one only. When Beau told her that he and Geneviève had stayed at the Hamiltons', she looked at him for a long, silent minute and then laughed. The laugh was unpleasant, chilling. "How nice for you and Caroline," she said. "I suppose Raoul was at the hospital a great deal at night?"

The ugly accusation in her eyes enraged him. But he knew that to deny it would only make matters worse. He forced himself to say nothing, thinking that Louise had vented her anger and would soon forget its cause. After all, he thought, it's not as though she thinks of me often. Daily he was realizing what a blessing that was.

28

The telephone at Beau's elbow rang insistently, finally breaking through his concentration. He put down the report from his stockbroker and picked up the instrument, his attention still on the paper before him. "Hello," he said distractedly.

"Beau, I have to see you. Today." It was Caroline, but her voice sounded strange and frightened.

"Caroline, what's wrong?"

"I can't tell you on the telephone," she said. "Can you meet me? At Beau Chêne?"

"Yes," he said. "I'll leave now."

When he arrived, Caroline was not there yet. Beau Chêne lay serenely under the July sun. The pale pink brick was washed and clean except for a thin line where the floodwater had risen. Like a mark on the soul, Beau thought, his feet crunching on the gravel drive as he paced. An automobile turned into the gates. He ran forward as it stopped, and as she got out, pulled Caroline into his arms.

She drew back so quickly that she almost fell. "Don't touch me!" she cried. And then she burst into tears.

"Caroline, what on earth has happened?" He steered her to a marble bench beneath a huge oak. Her face was stained with tears, her eyes filled with some terrible grief. Was it Raoul? The children? But she would have told him over the telephone. "Caroline, you've got to tell me what's wrong."

She took an envelope from her purse and handed it to him. The letter inside was thick, several sheets of paper folded into a narrow packet. He opened it and smoothed out the paper. "Read it, Beau," Caroline said.

"'Dear Mrs. Hamilton: You don't know me, but I know you, and everything you do . . .'" He stopped reading and looked at Caroline. "What is this?"

"Read it," she said again, and turned her face away.

His eyes went back to the page. The letters were long and rounded, slanting more and more as they went, until, if he only looked at the sheet and did not try to read, they made a pattern that became less and less controlled, losing all continuity by the time it reached the bottom of the page. But he did read, and felt sick. The obscenities on the page at first startled him, then repelled him. Out of what personal darkness did this come? He read on, forcing himself to finish, trying hard not to look at Caroline. At the end of the first page, his own name appeared, linked with Caroline's in activities he found he could not even think about. Mechanically he read through the descriptions. Finished, he folded the papers again and shoved them into his coat pocket.

"It's Louise," he said flatly.

"That's what I thought, too," Caroline said. "Beau, what on earth possessed her?"

"The devil she assigns to everyone else," he said.

"You read what she threatens to do? To send a copy to every newspaper in the state, beginning with the *Times-Picayune*?" She had regained her composure and turned back to him, her face serious. "Beau, what are we going to do? How can we stop her?"

"She's not your problem, Caroline. She's mine."

"I hate it, Beau!" Caroline burst out. "There's nothing wrong in our friendship, there never has been—"

"Don't worry about this letter, Caroline. Louise won't ruin your name. I'll handle her."

"It's not just that, Beau." She stared down the alley of trees hung with long delicate strands of moss. "It's . . . I don't know. I used to think that you and I lived in a separate place from everyone else, whether we were together or not. You know?"

"I know," he said, his heart aching.

"And now something's come into that place. Something hard and ugly—"

He reached out and touched her cheek. "It won't stay, Caroline. Not forever."

"But for a long, long time," she said, getting up. She stretched a hand toward him. "I was just beginning to get over all those years of not seeing you, Beau. And now it's all to do over again."

He got up and put his arms around her, looking down into

her face. "Caroline, Louise is crazy, that's all there is to it. And I'll have to deal with that. But I will. And there will be a time when this is over. You've got to believe that."

"I do, don't I?" she said. She brushed his cheek with her lips, then turned and walked rapidly to her car.

Watching her drive slowly away, Beau thought of her anguished cry. No, there was nothing wrong in their friendship. And he'd be damned if Louise was going to poison it now.

He waited until supper was over and the children were upstairs before he approached Louise. He asked her to come for a drive, in a tone that allowed no refusal. Driving silently through the town, he found a place just beyond the outskirts where he could stop the car.

"Caroline gave this to me today," he said evenly, showing Louise the letter.

"I thought she would," Louise said. Her face had the same satisfied look it did when one of her tantrums was over and she had once again gotten her way.

"You won't write another one, Louise. And you won't send copies to the papers, either."

"Why won't I?" she said.

"Because if you do, I will go to the parish coroner and have him declare you insane, and you will be locked up in a mental hospital the rest of your life." He said the words coldly, as though he were telling her the minor details of a business deal.

"You can't," she said, her voice taut with defiance. But the fear at the back of her eyes told him she knew that he could.

"Try me," he said. "The Langlinaises own this parish." For a long beat of time, they stared at each other. The cold hatred in her eyes sickened Beau, because he knew she saw the same thing in his.

"All right," she said. She gazed out the window, then turned back to him. "If you're prepared to go that far, I'm surprised you don't do it now. That would solve . . . a lot for you." Her smile told him she was in control of herself again, had already accommodated herself to his new assault.

He reached forward and started the motor. "I have some regard for the proprieties, Louise. I would prefer my children's mother not to be in an insane asylum, if that can be avoided. I would prefer the Langlinaises not be exposed to that kind of public disgrace. But please remember that if I have to, I can do it."

They drove home through moonlit fields whose cane was already knee-high with new growth. As they passed in front of the church, Beau's eyes swung toward it. The steeple, narrow, graceful, was outlined against the star-filled sky, a clear guide to heaven. Magnolias in the churchyard filled the air with their lemony scent. It was still, so still. Tranquil. He thought of the altar inside, the lamp burning to signify the presence of Christ. For a moment he felt like going inside.

"What would Father Adrian think if he knew what you had written?"

Louise's tongue moved over her lips, and she slid her gaze toward him. "I don't see Father Adrian anymore," she said.

"What! When did that happen?" he exclaimed.

"He sided with you. When Francie died. He made me have Skye." She licked her lips again, and gave him another of those sly, knowing glances. "He said it was something I should do out of charity. He made it sound good, but I knew he liked what he was saying, he liked to think about what you would do to me. I could tell. He was like all men, after all. Not pure. A hypocrite. A whited sepulcher. So I don't go to him anymore."

Oh, God, he thought. He was sorry he had involved Father Adrian. Now Louise had no moorings to hold her to the everyday world. Perhaps he should send her away, after all. She's the mother of your children, he told himself. You must think of that.

That night Beau stayed in his study, smoking and staring into the garden beyond the windows. The words in Louise's letter had engraved themselves deeply in his mind. When he thought of Caroline, he could not rid himself of the ugly acts Louise had described. Then he knew Louise had won, after all. He was ashamed of the way he felt about Caroline. He did lust after her. Was his love any different from what he felt for Bootsie or his woman in New Orleans? Yes, he told himself. It is. But Louise's poison made him doubt himself. He hid his face in his hands. He had never made love to a woman for any reason but lust after his foolish attempts to make Louise his wife. Perhaps he had lost the ability to love a woman any other way. The bitterness in his throat stifled him, and he went to the cabinet and found brandy, poured a glass, and sank back in his chair. He could not see Caroline for a very long time. He remembered the way her eyes had looked before she left him that morning. Meeting his eyes briefly, she had blushed and looked away. She had felt shame too. If they had both been poisoned, who was left to apply an antidote?

The next day he ordered Becca to move Louise's things into a room at the back of the house. He moved the children closer to his own room; Becca's silent compliance told him how much she knew. Louise watched the comings and goings quietly, her frozen smile never changing. "Well," she said, standing in the door of her new room at the end of the day. "It is better, I suppose, than one with bars on it."

29

By midsummer, Louisianians' attention was focused on the gubernatorial campaign, and on Huey Long's rising power. Beau plunged himself into the thick of it, glad that the foundation work laid in the spring was over, and that he could actively and publicly campaign for Long. The campaign gave him a place to put the energies that would otherwise, like an animal in a small cage, circle around and around, unable to solve the problem central to his life, unable to move forward. He welcomed the long days, the fatiguing trips, and when Claude and Alice took a house at the Gulf Coast through mid-August, taking the twins and Skye with them, he was free to devote his entire life to Long.

As the campaign gained momentum that summer of 1927, Beau realized just how many other people had Long first on their agenda. One after the other, parish bosses fell into Huey's camp. "Not because I know the man, 'cause I don't," a Lafayette parish boss told Beau. "But because the people who put me in office want him." He shrugged. "They're going to get him, whether I help or not. That being the case, I damn well better be on board that train carrying us forward into prosperity." If there was a cynical tinge to the man's voice, Beau ignored it.

This won't be 1924 all over again, Beau mused, driving

home from yet another meeting to firm up Long's support. The twenty percent up for grabs had long since gotten behind Long; the voters on the outs with the old political bosses were in Long's vanguard, and the bosses themselves, except for those too blinded by their own conceptions of how political campaigns should be mounted and run to see the strong and powerful tide that was about to overwhelm them, fell in line because they saw nothing else to do.

Only a few seasoned observers, who should have known better, still believed that Long's two opponents for the governorship, Oramel H. Simpson and Riley Joe Wilson, could, with their combined strength, stop the Long machine in its rustic tracks. They expected a gentlemanly second primary, after which Long would be sent back to his flamboyant, if effective, practice of law.

Had Long been just another country politician, those observers might very well have been right. But he was not. He was Huey Pierce Long; in South Louisiana, they called him Huey "Polycarp" Long, a sure sign of the affection the French Catholics had for him. Grateful for Long's support of their favorite "Cousin Ed" Broussard in his successful bid for the Senate, they had bestowed on Long a saint's name—and he was shrewd enough to know the value that had at the polls. He was shrewd enough, too, to build an organization unique in Louisiana politics. Since its nature was not understood, neither was its strength. Every linchpin in his machine held a number of votes solidly in his hand, votes that would be delivered when they were wanted. And his opponents found that Long had perfected the use of the personal attack. He used it as it suited him, paying no attention to the rules which required a politician to stop at a recognized limit. He could ruin reputations, and he did. But despite the rage of his opposition, despite the confrontations and fisticuffs that that rage triggered, the people to whom he appealed listened. Listened and remembered. For when Long finally got down to the issues, the issues were made of the stuff of their lives. Roads. Bridges. Schools. Hospitals. And free schoolbooks.

By August 3, 1927, when Long announced his formal entry into the race, he had wealthy supporters in every corner of the state. His approach to them was simple. They ruled their own parishes, dispensing favors and privileges as a grand seigneur might have in feudal days. If they supported Long, money for roads and bridges, schools and hospitals, would be made available to their parishes when he was governor. In parish after parish, the rich and powerful learned Long's game and signed on with him.

He seemed to grow in stature as he gained support; Beau, following Long as he campaigned in the parishes of Acadiana, compared this Long with the Long of four years ago and thought: He's never looked better. He now wore expensive and well-tailored suits that made his heavy body seem solid, strong. He carried himself with an easy authority that projected itself from platforms with conviction, and his voice, though still expressive and resonant, no longer became shrill when he got excited.

The improved carriage and dress were for the benefit of the wealthy; to make sure the masses still saw him as a man who could poke holes in the silk purse of aristocratic tradition, Long carried with him another persona. At one elegant luncheon, taking one look at all the cutlery laid in shining rows on either side of his plate, Long swept it to the floor, demanding, "Just give me one knife and one fork—that's all I'm used to using."

Sometimes, watching Long speak, Beau realized how much Long's political technique owed to an inborn sense of the theatrical, of what would effectively mesmerize a crowd and make it his. A consummate actor, Long wrote scripts that both entertained and aroused his audience.

"You see this stack of textbooks?" he would ask in one of his typical set pieces, pointing to a several-foot-high pile beside him. "These are the textbooks your children have to buy, new ones every year, 'cause the state keeps switchin' 'em on you." He would pick up a speller, wave it in the air. "If the state hadn't changed books on you, little sister could use Buddy's book; instead, you're going to have to get her a new one." Thumping the book against his knee, he exclaimed, "And I tell you, I looked through this book, and there ain't been six words inserted in the dictionary since Aswell wrote this speller."

Throughout that long summer, the people of Louisiana left their fields early, hurried with their chores, harnessed mule teams and horses, and made their way across rutted dirt roads to the villages and towns to hear Long speak. Standing in the back of an open automobile, or on the steps of a courthouse, or on a quickly knocked-together platform, looking out over the silent men, their blue workshirts stained with field dust and sweat, their worn-out women slowly fanning themselves with straw-colored palmetto fans, he would begin to speak. A hush would fall, a hush that stole from the fields, from the bayous. It was a hush that Long filled with words, just as he filled their emptiness with hope.

"You ought to hear him," Beau said to Claude on a rare visit home. He was charged with excitement; in town after town, he had seen Long change apathy to hope, anxiety to belief. If he had been cynical at the start of the campaign, had seen it as both a diversion from his home life and a road to power, he saw it now as something else. A way to lead his people out of darkness. A way to assuage the ills that plagued them. "Dammit, Papa, Long can make a difference in our people's lives!"

Claude surveyed his son. There was a different look about Beau. It was hard to put his finger on just what it was—a harder look, a more seasoned one. Claude felt a stirring of jealousy. Some other man was taking a hand in forming Beau; he'd better take that seriously, better take a closer look.

"Speaking tonight, isn't he?" When Beau nodded, Claude said, "Guess I'll walk on over with you, hear what he's got to say."

As they walked toward the square, they felt, despite the heat and dust of summer that still lingered in the air, the quickening that meant autumn was near, making itself felt in a sudden frenzied dance of leaves as a gust of cooler air blew against them. They found themselves part of a growing throng of people who were all moving toward the square next to St. Martin of Tours Church, where the Evangeline Oak, named for the heroine of the Longfellow poem about the Acadian exile, stood. The people were laughing, chatting, exchanging the common interests of their lives. But as they gathered around the platform on which Long stood, a hush fell over them, enveloping their laughter and their chatter, silencing everything but their hearts.

Then Long began to speak, his strong voice carrying easily to the furthermost reaches of the square.

"This oak is an immortal spot, made so by Longfellow's poem, but Evangeline is not the only one who has waited here in disappointment. Where are the schools that you have waited for your children to have, that have never come? Where are the roads and the highways that you send your money to build, that are no nearer now than ever before? Where are the institutions to care for the sick and the disabled? Evangeline wept bitter tears in her disappointment, but it lasted through only one lifetime. Your tears in this country, around this oak, have lasted for generations. Give me the chance to dry the tears of those who still weep here!"

In the heartbeat of silence before the crowd began to roar, Claude looked around him. There were his people, and they did need schools. Roads to take their produce to market. Hospitals for their sick. He could afford those things, he and those fellows in New Orleans and other cities supporting Wilson or Simpson. He thought of John Parker, the promises about good government he had made when he was governor. And the compromise after compromise that had followed, in his administration and in Henry Fuqua's after that. Dammit, if it took someone like Long to open up the lives of his people, who was he to deny him? He looked at Beau, who was watching, not the crowd surging around Long, nor the candidate himself, who continued to speak passionately, but him.

"Well?" Beau said, a question in his eyes.

"Yes," Claude said. "I'll support him."

Beau's hands met his. Then they added their voices to the solid ceiling of sound that covered them.

They came in farm wagons and Buicks, in the old Model T's and in the Model A's that had replaced them. They came over mud-filled, rutted roads that they told themselves Huey Long would pave. They passed schoolhouses, telling themselves Huey Long would send their children there, with books the state of Louisiana paid for. They came out of the Hill parishes, their necks burned a deep, rough-skinned red from the constant sun, their overalls faded white, their eyes sunk in lean, hard faces. They brought their women, wiry, thin, dresses made from printed flour sacks hanging on worn frames, hands gnarled and callused from heavy, wearying work. They brought their children, whose small potbellies and blue-tinged skin spoke clearly of poor nutrition, while lackluster eyes and blackened teeth showed neglect. They came from the French parishes of the southwest, clustered together in wary groups, dark eyes flashing reassurance to one another. They were part of the fifteen thousand people pouring into the little town of

Baton Rouge on the morning of May 21, 1928, to watch the man who promised "EVERY MAN A KING BUT NO ONE WEARS A CROWN" be made their governor.

For the first time since the brief and quickly defeated Populist movement at the end of the last century, a man had stood on their side and had embraced their cause with a fervor they could believe in. For the first time in their memories, someone took their needs seriously and gave their dreams the credence the rich and powerful denied them. These were the people Long believed would make a difference; their presence at his inauguration was proof that they had.

The early returns in the January primary had Long trailing both opponents. But then the country votes had begun to come in. And when the last votes were counted, Long had amassed 126,842, carrying six of the eight congressional districts and forty-seven of the sixty-four parishes. Faced with the inevitable, neither opponent wanted a second primary; the Hill farmers and the Cajuns, in a union as powerful as it was unprecedented, had changed forever the face of Louisiana—and her politics.

Beau, standing in a roped-off enclosure for legislators, watched the bands march by. His restlessness had nothing to do with the blaring beat from the "New Regular Democratic Band" or the rhythms the Standard Oil Refinery Band poured into the air from instruments gleaming in the morning sun. He felt poised on the edge of a great experience, one that would climax months of work.

Claude, standing next to him, was relaxed, joking. "Let's hope the music all these groups make in the legislature is as harmonious as what we're hearing now," he said, watching the Standard Oil Refinery Band march past.

"Long's showed them who's boss," Beau said. "You think he'll have problems with the legislature?"

"Not the way it's gone so far," Claude said. He had been in Baton Rouge over a week; the legislature had convened before the inauguration. "You don't need a program to see who's leading the show. It's Long, all the way." He leaned closer to make himself heard above the music. "He's got Philip Gilbert for president pro tem of the Senate, which is a smart move. Gilbert had that office last term, and he's well liked."

Beau nodded, moving his head to get out of the way of Alice's cartwheel hat. "It's too bad Louise didn't . . . feel up to coming," Alice said. She put one hand to the crown of the crimson straw, holding it tightly against the sudden gust of breeze from the river. "You're one of Long's top supporters, Beau; she'd have been made over like the Queen of Sheba."

"Well," said Beau, his eyes on the parade in front of them, "she doesn't approve of dancing, doesn't approve of Long, and doesn't approve of me. It doesn't surprise me that she prefers to stay home."

From under the protective brim of her hat, Alice shot a look at Claude. This was the first time Beau had openly stated that he and Louise did not get along; over the years, they had played a game, all of them, that Louise and Beau had a marriage that worked. Their silence was broken by a shout, a cry that took shape as it grew louder. "Long! Long! Long!"

"He's coming," Beau said. He felt excited, suddenly overwhelmed by the same hope that shone on the worn faces of the crowd that surrounded them.

A long black car rolled slowly by. Long's body filled the window, his thick torso jammed in the black frame. He waved both arms in answer to the cheers swelling around him, broad, expansive gestures that seemed to draw the people into his circle of power. He looks like a runner still in the middle of a race, Beau thought. The man's energy was amazing; despite the confines of the automobile, Long moved from side to side, vigorously embracing the crowd. His ruddy face was split by his immense grin, and his eyes blazed with contagious excitement. The people caught that excitement, they surged toward the automobile, hands lifted. Something seemed to pass from them to Long, and from him back to them. Beau felt a wild need for action. He tossed his straw hat high in the air, and leapt to catch it, shouting above the crowd, "Every man a king!" At that moment, Long caught his eye and grinned. And Beau felt the magnetism of Long's power all over again.

At lunch, Beau heard from Claude some of the tangible effects of that power. "Way Long got John Fournet elected speaker of the house was something, let me tell you," he said. "Long went in with fewer pledged supporters in the legislature than any governor I can think of. If he hadn't had Harley Bozeman and O. K. Allen go around the state all spring getting people pledged, his plans for this state would dry up on the shelf." Claude surveyed the dining room of the Heidelberg Hotel, crammed full and with tables added to accommodate the crowd. "I can just about tell you the price every man here put on his head when Allen or Bozeman came to call."

"Oh, Claude," Alice said. "Are you saying Long has bought the legislature?"

"Well, not entirely," Claude said. He laughed, but he did not look at Beau. "Some of 'em were smart enough to see the lay of the land and just get on the wagon that's going to be driving over it. Others?" He shrugged. "As Bozeman was heard to say, they didn't all come for free."

"If Long could buy them, so could anyone else," Beau said. "I don't blame him."

"I agree," Claude said. "Man ought to be able to resist temptation. On the other hand—"

"On the other hand," Alice said, "just because people are weak doesn't make it right to use their weaknesses against them." Her hand closed over Claude's. "I hope you told them what they could do when they came to see you."

Again Claude did not look at Beau. "No one came to see me, Alice. Got a call from Long himself. Didn't ask me a thing—said he knew what kind of man I was, knew I had principles to uphold and constituents to serve, and that I'd put both of those ahead of him." Then he did look at Beau. "Ended by saying that when there was something I could support him on, he'd appreciate it if I let him know. I thought that was fair."

"Long is fair, Papa," Beau said. He felt as though his father and mother understood something about the situation that escaped him. He shook his head. "Depending on who's doing the talking, Long's strategies can seem ruthless, almost dishonest. Or the only right thing to do."

"Putting Fournet in as speaker was probably the right thing to do," Claude said. "He's young, of course, a freshman legislator who's got a hell of a lot to learn. But he handles himself well, and he's got a good sense of humor." Claude threw back his head and laughed. "And, by God, if there's one thing you had better have if you're going to be in the Louisiana legislature, it's a sense of humor."

"Oh, Claude!" Alice said. "You make it sound like such a circus."

Claude winked at Beau. "Was, last week," he said. "Long was the lion tamer and the Old Regulars and the conservatives were the beasts that got tamed."

"Well," Alice said, "I agree with Sister Mary Dorothy. If

Long can get free schoolbooks for every child in this state, those in the Catholic schools as well as those in the public ones, I don't care what lions he has to tame to do it." She rose. "I'm going to skip the concerts this afternoon and take a nap." She smiled at them, the crimson hat casting a glow over her face. "After all, as the wife of one of the few legislators who still owns his soul, I want to look my best." She kissed Beau's cheek, then Claude's, and walked through the dining room, pausing to speak to people she knew, totally unaware of the ripple she left in her path.

"She's a beautiful woman, your mama," Claude said. He was not unconscious of the way people, men and women both, still paused in their talk, lifted their heads, to watch her go by. "It's not only the way she looks—it's something people sense about her. I don't know," he said, shaking his head. "I wonder sometimes what I did to deserve her." He was aware of the quality of Beau's silence and could have bitten his tongue clean through. He tried to laugh, act as though his next words were not carefully chosen. " 'Course we none of us really deserve anything. Life just happens, just rolls along."

"Like Ol' Man River in the song," Beau said. His voice was dry, detached from what he was saying.

"Yes, like that song from *Show Boat*," Claude said. Their talk changed, became scattered: bits and pieces of news, observations on the men around them, deciding whether to go to one of the concerts or join friends for a private party. The afternoon passed quickly, as did the evening. Beau, moving through the crowd that thronged the governor's mansion, felt the detachment that had begun at lunch wall him from the others. His earlier excitement seemed to have been put on hold, like an engine left running in low gear, throbbing and pulsing and getting nowhere. He greeted allies from the campaign, listened to the same confident predictions over and over again. At one point during the evening, he stood in an alcove at the end of the ballroom watching the crowd. The men's faces were flushed with liquor, the women's with rouge. Voices rose and bounced against the high ceiling and hard-surfaced walls, making the room like the inside of a drum. He was overcome by the same restlessness that had plagued him all day. Claude, catching sight of him, was haunted by the look in Beau's eyes. Later, back at the hotel, he tried to tell Alice what he thought he had seen. "He looks like he's making himself go through the motions, but doesn't believe in it. Doesn't believe in life."

Alice stretched out her arms. "Come here," she said. She held him against her. "And what else do you expect, Claude? He's miserable, has been for years. We've kept up a pretense, all of us—but for heaven's sake, Claude, we knew long before that he and Louise don't . . . don't have a marriage." She held his face to hers and kissed him. "I go over there every day now. She shuts herself in her room doing heaven knows what." He looked at her and saw the confusion and fear in her face. "She's crazy, Claude, as crazy as she can be."

"The children—"

"I see to the children. But I told Beau the other day he might better think about getting a housekeeper, someone to look after the children, oversee Susu and Becca." She lay back on the pillows and sighed. "I do what I can, Claude, but I can't be there every minute."

He lay back and pulled her close, his hand stroking her. "It's funny, Alice. If ever I thought someone had everything in the world . . ." He shook his head. "Well, do what you can. Let me know if I can help."

She smiled up at him. "There is something you can do," she said. He felt her breast moving beneath his hand, felt the tautness of the nipple. "For me. Right now."

Beau found another private party after the inaugural ball was over, a party that promised to last as long as at least two people could remain on their feet. The celebratory atmosphere was thick with smoke, loud with the jazz pouring from a small band crowded at the edge of the dance floor. The girls were part of the fifteen thousand visitors to Baton Rouge; they had come, not to see Long inaugurated, but because among those who did would be some who would view this day as an excuse to slip under the restraints that usually bound them.

"I bet this place is one dead burg when something like a governor being inaugurated isn't going on," the girl sitting with Beau said. Her eyes were ringed with black mascara. Her lips were scarlet, a wide, wet circle of red that left marks on her cigarettes and on the rim of her glass. The makeup masked rather than highlighted her own beauty; Beau felt she was in costume, with no identity that mattered. She moved closer to Beau, turned her chair so her legs were straight out in front of her. Her skirt was short and tight; when she was seated, it rode above her knees so that Beau could see a black garter high on her smooth, rounded thigh, a rhinestone buckle winking up at him like a great knowing eye. "You from here?"

"No," he said. The restlessness was almost unbearable. The parades, the inauguration itself, the afternoon concert, the reception, the ball—each had been just one more thing to be gotten through, with this feeling of anticipation, waiting for climax, sitting squarely in his center. But the ball was over, the great day finished. And still he had not found release. He looked at the girl—could she give him that release, so he could sleep? His hand closed over her wrist. "Let's dance," he said. Her body was rich, voluptuous; as he pulled her close he could feel her breasts against him, and his hand found nothing but a smooth sweep of fabric as he let it rove over her back. He was suddenly aroused; that thin dress and maybe a thinner step-in were all she wore. He imagined how quickly he could strip her, how quickly he could enter her. His eyes looked into hers. They were blank until she realized he was looking at her; then they came to life, challenging him. Her body twisted under his hand, and her breasts pressed closer.

"I'm very good," she said. She leaned a little away from him. "I'm not cheap, though."

"Neither am I," Beau said. He led her from the dance floor, out to his automobile. He didn't want to take her back to the hotel, to the room adjacent to the one where his parents slept. An idea possessed him, and he laughed.

"What are you laughing about?" she asked.

"You'll see," he said. He drove to the state capitol, parked the automobile, and helped her out.

"What are we doing here?" she said.

"I like a romantic setting," he said. He drew her along with him. The turrets of the Gothic building were dark against the grayness of the sky. All was still, with only the debris of programs left on the grass a sign of the people who had thronged there at noon. He took her to the lawn that faced the Mississippi River, and found a place beneath one of the oaks whose branches swept down to the ground. He flung himself full-length on the grass and stared up at her. "Undress," he said.

He couldn't see the expression on her face, could only the stillness of her body, the tautness with which she held it. "Here?" she said, looking behind her at the capitol.

"There's no one around," he said. "It's three in the morning, everyone's in bed."

She giggled. "I sure do pick 'em," she said. Her hand went to the hem of her dress, and Beau felt his throat tighten. "But this is going to cost you double, you hear?"

"All right," he said.

Her other hand went to the hem, and both pulled upward. He watched the garment rise, revealing her long bare legs, the transparent undergarment beneath. Her dress fell to the grass, and she moved toward him. The moon was not full, but its light was enough for him to see the nipples beneath the thin silk, the dark hair below. "Take that off," he said. She paused, kicked off one pump and then the other, and then lowered the straps of her step-in. It fell with a small rustling noise, making a white blot against the damp grass. "Well?" she said.

"Come here," he said. He unfastened his trousers and pulled them below his hips. "Sit on me," he said.

She stopped, watching him carefully. Then she nodded. "All right." He watched her lower herself over him, felt her take him and guide him inside. Then she began to move, a slow grinding motion that pulled him deeper. He concentrated on her nakedness, on the breasts that swayed above him, on the curve of her waist, the soft belly, the hair that curled around him. Behind him, he could see the capitol building looming. The pressure and excitement of the long day were centered now, focused on this body writhing above him. He felt his tension grow, become almost unbearable. And then he found the release nothing else could bring; he reached up, pulled her body down against his, and exploded inside her.

30

Long's inauguration got the summer off to a satisfyingly high start. It was followed rapidly by the Democratic National Convention in Houston, Texas, in June. Beau went as a delegate; he returned to St. Martinville when the convention was over, feeling that it was going to be difficult to settle into the routine of business after the excitement and challenge of that event.

The summer doldrums set in, bringing boredom with them. So when, sorting the mail one July morning, Beau came across an envelope addressed in Caroline's familiar handwriting, he ripped it open eagerly. "Dear Beau," the letter inside began. "I'm serving as program chairman of the Lafayette League of Women Voters. I wondered if you could come talk to us at our meeting next week about being a delegate to the Democratic National Convention. We're not sure we understand how the delegation was chosen, and, of course, we'd be interested in your observations about the whole convention. We can't pay you, but I can give you lunch. As ever, Caroline."

His spirits rose as he reached for the telephone. It was over a year since he had seen her; not since Louise's ugly letter had made them agree to that separation. Would the sight of her handwriting or the sound of her voice ever stop affecting him? He called her immediately, suddenly not able to bear the distance between them one moment longer. "Caroline, it's Beau," he said. "I can't tell you how glad I was to get your letter. And of course I'll come, you know I will." He laughed happily. "Why so formal? You could have just called me."

She hesitated. "I . . . I wanted to give you a chance to say no. After all, we've been . . . out of touch for quite a while."

He waited a moment to give her an opportunity to be sure of her answer. "Has it been . . . long enough? To get past . . . well, get past all that ugliness?"

He heard her quickly indrawn breath, then, all in a rush, "It has for me, Beau. I hope it has for you, too."

"Well," he said, making his voice matter-of-fact. "Since I think about you constantly, I imagine it has."

"I think about you, too, Beau," she said. He heard something in her voice he had not heard before, and felt suddenly weak with wanting her. "Too much for my own good, maybe." Then, briskly, she said, "I'm glad you'll come. We meet at members' homes; if you come to my house first, we can go together."

He hung up the phone, wondering if the prospect of seeing Caroline in seven days would make the week fly or crawl; either way, he had something to look forward to, to plan for. Whistling, he went upstairs to see if the new white linen suit or the pale gray one was more appropriate. "Do I want to look quietly elegant or charmingly dashing?" he said to himself, laughing at his own vanity, but feeling absurdly happy anyway.

His happiness continued throughout the week. The day of his speech, he drove to Lafayette in a mood that had rarely been brighter.

"You look wonderful," Caroline said when she opened the door. Her hand touched the arm of the gray suit, ran over it briefly. "Even if the ladies don't understand what you're saying, they'll have a treat looking at you." She stepped out onto the porch, pulling the door shut.

"You look pretty wonderful yourself," Beau said. He took both her hands and held her away from him. "I haven't seen you in peach before—you look mouth-watering."

The blush in her cheeks almost matched the soft color of her linen dress. "Well," she said, breaking free and starting down the steps toward the car, "you haven't forgotten how to flirt."

The League of Women Voters proved to be an attentive audience, and Beau's talk went well. "What few people seem to understand is that Long's method of selecting the delegation to the convention is absolutely legal," he said. "Despite the fact that the Democratic State Central Committee has been selecting the slate for a long time using one method, the state constitution allows it to use any method it wants. In other words, according to the constitution, it's not really necessary for the committee to call a state convention where delegates will be voted on." He saw questions forming in the eyes of some of the ladies. "Yes, I can see you wondering if having the committee name the slate itself, with no one else voting, is 'fair.'" He allowed himself a confidential chuckle, the smallest of winks. "Well, ladies, you're not political novices. You know a little more about how democracy works in practice than the average voter, so I think you know, too, that the definition of 'fair' depends on who's using it. Huey Long didn't think it 'fair' for a delegation he didn't think would represent the views of the people of this state to be seated—and the Old Regulars and other opponents didn't think it 'fair' for them not to be. Luckily, as you know, with the support of Franklin Delano Roosevelt from New York, our delegation was recognized and seated in Houston."

A hand shot up in the back of the room. "I've read that many quite knowledgeable men in state politics feel Long steamrollered the delegation through," a woman said. "How do you feel about that?"

"Just glad I wasn't in its way," Beau said, grinning. The women laughed. "Maybe you read what Long had to say about that—he thought it was true, they had been steamrollered. And that the only reason more of them weren't was that there were no more in the way."

"But what does that bode for the future of this state?" the questioner persisted. "Democratic process insists that—"

"That the people be served," Beau said. "Pardon me for interrupting you, ma'am, but while you and I sit and discuss the niceties of the democratic process, children go without education because their parents can't afford to buy them books, farmers can't get their produce to market because they can't drive through the mud ditches we call roads, the poor can't get medical attention because Charity Hospital, large as it is, can't serve all of them." His voice had risen, riding easily over them and filling the room. A hush fell on the women as he spoke. Their hands lay quietly in their laps, their heads fixed squarely to the front of the room, their eyes locked on his face. He dropped his voice, leaned forward. "In view of all that, ma'am, I can't get terribly upset because Huey Long used a perfectly legal means of selecting a delegation to the Democratic convention, one that that body was more than happy to recognize and seat." He looked over the women assembled before him and saw that he had won them. "Any more questions?"

"Yes," another woman said. "Did you meet Mr. Roosevelt? What's he like?"

"An Eastern aristocrat, but a heck of a nice man all the same," Beau said. Other questions followed; Beau, watching Caroline out of the corner of his eye, saw that she was becoming increasingly impatient. Finally she stood up and raised a hand for silence.

"I think we've taken enough of Mr. Langlinais' time," she said. She turned to Beau. "I know I speak for all of us when I thank you for a most stimulating morning. . . ."

"You were wonderful," Caroline said as they drove back to the Hamilton house. "Pull up in the driveway. You can park under the big oak; your car won't get so hot."

"Won't I be in Raoul's way?" Beau asked as he turned into the driveway.

"No," she said. "There's no one here. Raoul and the children are over on the Gulf Coast; I'll take the train tomorrow to join them. I only stayed for the meeting."

He looked over his shoulder at the house behind them. The darkened interior, empty, silent, beckoned. Then he looked back at Caroline. "I see," he said. He got out, went around the car, and lifted her down. He saw the anxious look in her eyes and ran a finger lightly over her nose. "What's for lunch?" he asked, taking her arm and escorting her to the house.

"I thought . . . I thought we'd eat in the morning room. I set a table there," Caroline said. In the kitchen she took bowls and platters from the icebox and fixed their plates. She seemed nervous, on edge about something. She had not met his eyes since she had told him they were alone. Instead she had chattered on about the house they had taken at Pass Christian, about the League and their plans for Al Smith's campaign, about anything except what was most on her mind—Beau Langlinais.

"Caroline," he said when they were seated. "Look at me." She did meet his gaze then, and blushed. His hand moved across the table and took hers. "Caroline, you don't have to . . ." He stopped. Don't have to explain to me what's going on, what all this means? "Never mind," he said. He looked at his plate. "This looks great. Talking to ladies is hungry work; I'm starved."

She smiled and relaxed a little. "Good. Tell me what you've been doing, Beau. Is your automobile agency selling Model A's as fast as you can get them?"

"I guess they are," Beau said. "Last week an old farmer who swore he'd never drive anything but a pair of mules finally came in and bought one, saying his sons wouldn't give him any peace until he did. But guess who was behind the wheel on Sunday when they came in to church!"

By the time they had finished eating and were sitting on the small sofa drinking coffee, Caroline seemed in command of herself and the situation. She set her cup down and turned to face him. "Beau, I asked you to lunch here because I wanted to . . . seduce you."

That word on those lips startled him into laughter. His hand instinctively moved to hers. "Caroline, as if you have to—"

He felt her fingers touching his lips, silencing him. "Beau, I made you promise, a long time ago, that if we kept seeing each other, you wouldn't try to make love to me. And you haven't, Beau, you've been very, very good." She smiled and blushed again. "And now . . . now I find myself, well, lying awake, really. Thinking about you. Wondering . . ." Her head went up, her chin lifted in that defiant tilt. "All right. Wondering how it would be for you to make love to me. Wondering how you manage." She looked at him and smiled again. "You're too much of a gentleman to ask . . . about Raoul." Her face turned from him, and she shrugged. "He works awfully hard, Beau. Has rotten hours. He . . . he doesn't like to wake me when he gets home late." Then she looked into Beau's eyes. "And a lot of the time he's tired."

His spirits had been high since her letter arrived last week; now they soared. He reached out his arms and she came into them, slipped her arms around his neck, nestled against him. He kissed her hair, her temple, moved so that he could kiss her cheek, and then finally, her lips. The passion in her response exhilarated him. Tentatively his hand went to her breast, caressed her. He waited for her to stiffen, to pull back, but her lips opened and he felt her tongue moving inside his mouth. He was conscious of the silence of the house around them, its hot emptiness. White slipcovers hid the dark woods and formal brocades of the furniture, dustcovers were on paintings and mirrors; they were in a house that was suspended in time, a house where nothing that happened would ever exist in any other reality.

As though he stood above a deep dark pool, ready to plunge into a depth of experience that would forever change everything he knew, Beau made himself aware of every pulsebeat, every brush of skin, every probing kiss. "Caroline," he whispered against her hair. "Caroline, I love you."

She drew back, hearing a hesitancy in his voice that had nothing to do with what he had just said. "You don't think we should do this, do you?" she said. Her hair had fallen around her shoulders. She looked as she had looked the winter they still hoped to be wed, and Beau's resolve not to take her wavered. He recognized the state she was in—aroused not just by his presence, but by the danger, the newness of the experience, challenged by that empty, silent house where even witnessing mirrors had been blinded. How easy to take her, then. Easy to undress her, to lay her on the straw matting that replaced the rolled-up Persian rugs. Easy to stroke and caress her until the wildness of her kisses matched his. He knew they both wanted just that—and he knew they couldn't have it. As difficult as it was to give her up, he had to do it, or never face himself again.

"Darling, I'd give anything I own to be able to say I think we should." His eyes darkened as he remembered scenes he wished he could forget. "You said a while back that you wonder how I manage. Well, I have mistresses, Caroline. One in St. Martinville, one in New Orleans. And, I am ashamed to say, I'm not above a casual encounter once in a while." He took her hands. "I can't put you in that class, Caroline. I can't make love to you. It wouldn't be right, for either of us." He paused, made sure she believed him. "I love you too much for that."

She let her hands rest quietly in his, sat staring at her lap, her breathing slowly returning to normal, the color in her cheeks fading. Then she lifted her hands to her hair and raised it toward her neck. "I'm a mess," she said. She got up, went to the mantel, and pulled the cover off the mirror. "Do you see my hairpins anywhere?"

"Here," he said. He picked them up, took them to her. She thrust them into the curls, twisting her hair into a knot that curved against the back of her neck.

"Do you think I should get my hair bobbed?" she said, looking in the mirror. Then she turned, burst into tears, and went into his open arms. He held her gently, wondering how he could be consumed with passion for her one minute and want only to comfort her the next.

"Beau, am I an awful fool?"

"No," he said, kissing her. "A very dear, very adorable woman whom I love very much."

"Thank God for that," she said. She lifted her head and tried to smile. Beau looked worried; seeing the concern in his eyes, she was suddenly aware of how close she had been to the perilous edge of adultery, and how very little she knew about the country that lay on the other side. "Dear Beau," she said, again near tears. "I can always count on you to protect me, even when it's against myself." Color rushed back into her face. "I do feel ridiculous. I can't help it."

"Don't," he said. "You've just paid me the greatest compliment of my life—and there's nothing ridiculous about that."

"Will you come again? The way you used to?" Her eyes were anxious, but her chin was defiant, daring him to say no.

"Will it make it better or worse?" he said. "For you?"

She shrugged. "I don't know." A swift glance from under her lashes. "It's not much fun when I know I won't ever see you at all."

He thought of the long, long days, unbroken by a trip into Lafayette, an hour in the morning room, watching Caroline play with her babies. "No, it's not, is it?"

"So you will come?"

"When you get back from the Pass."

She walked him to the door and stood watching him, waving as he backed down the driveway and drove away. Then she went inside, ran the water in the big tub to the very brim, and took a long bath. She studied her body. No one would guess she had birthed and nursed three children. Of course, she was only twenty-eight. Still young. She remembered Beau's hand on her breast. Even the memory of his touch aroused her, and she thought angrily that it wasn't fair that while Beau could at least get rid of his tension with a mistress, she was stuck with hers. Damn. She reached for the big sponge, squeezed soap over her back. Damn virtue, anyway.

Charles Livaudais walked slowly away from the house on Dumaine Street toward Canal Street and the work that sat neglected in his office. He had just spent an hour, not with a young woman with charms sufficient to make Francie's ghost flee, but with Francie's ghost itself. Her laughter seemed always just ahead of him, the flutter of a curtain in the breeze was her skirt, the sense of fullness in the bedroom they had shared a sign of her constant presence. He went to that house because he could not keep from going. Hélène's irritating voice, her nagging existence, vanished when he closed the door behind him, as did the increasingly tedious details of his legal practice.

He brought a tenuous peace back to his office. It was shattered when he read the messages his secretary had put in the middle of his desk. The general manager of the New Orleans Public Service Incorporated had called three times, at half-hour intervals. "*Urgent!*" the last message read. Charles picked up the phone and placed the call. The general manager barely greeted him before saying: "Long's thrown down the glove, Charles. Three bills were introduced in the Senate yesterday. The main one is a constitutional amendment that will let the city of New Orleans issue enough bonds—up to fifty million— to buy our properties. And before you say the son of a bitch can't do it, let me tell you that the other two bills are enabling acts letting the city either operate the utilities themselves or lease or sell 'em to someone else who will. Now, Charles, the question is—what the hell are we going to do?"

With effort, Charles put his attention on the instrument in his hand. The man on the other end represented his largest client, the bulk of his practice. He cleared his throat, began to make reassuring noises. "Now, hold on. None of this is exactly unexpected. You've had time to think about all this." Suddenly he was tired of dealing with fools. "Long did promise natural gas for the people of New Orleans, and I warned you all along you'd better pay attention and be prepared for it." He heard his voice rising, heard the angry accusation in it. "You know damn well I recommended the utility company and the city council just bite the bullet and bring in natural gas. With all the publicity Long's given the issue, you've left yourself wide open to just this kind of attack by consistently refusing to bring in a cheaper source of fuel."

The silence on the other end told him that this was not what his client had called to hear. He forced a laugh. "All right, so the son of a bitch has lived up to expectations. He hasn't won yet."

"That's better," the NOPSI manager said. But his voice was wary. "So what are you going to do, Charles?"

"I'll call the city attorney, arrange a meeting. Read the text of the bills. I'll take care of it." His anger was still strong, and he couldn't help saying, "Haven't I always, no matter what mess it was you all needed cleaned or covered up?"

"Up until now," the manager said evenly. "See you don't break your record."

As Charles hung up the receiver, he signaled his secretary to come in. "Get the city attorney on the telephone for me, will you?" he said. While his call went through, he waited for the familiar surge of adrenaline, the signal that his body had taken note of the battle, and was ready to join it. But his pulse remained steady, his body quiet. The problems of NOPSI didn't seem important, just as nothing had seemed very important since Francie died. Why shouldn't the bastards use cheaper fuel, when it was so readily available? "Your call, Mr. Livaudais," his secretary said. Charles reached for the telephone, trying to make his voice sound hearty, strong. But most of all, trying to make it sound as though he gave a damn.

"Well," he said to the city attorney. "Long has struck one

hell of a note on this public-utility thing. Guess we better get together, figure out how to shut him off at the starting gate." He listened a moment, his fingers drumming on the walnut desk in front of him. A sudden recollection of the day he had rented this office, had his grandfather's plantation desk sent in to use as his own, came to him. A vision of the simpler life that desk had kept orderly rose before him then, and he felt again the blackness that only a visit to Dumaine Street could lift. "Today at three?" He looked at his watch. "Let's make it four-thirty. I have . . . there's an appointment I can't break."

"Not even for this? Dammit, Livaudais, what's more important than this?"

"I'll see you at four-thirty," he said, and hung up the telephone, knowing he had made a mistake. Where NOPSI and the city council were concerned, there were no other clients, no appointments that could not be broken. He jammed his straw hat over his head. Well, dammit, whether they knew it or not, the world did not rise and fall on their fate alone. Not, at least, in his considered opinion.

In normal circumstances, that hour-and-a-half delay would not have mattered. But these were not normal circumstances. The Senate passed the three bills within a week of their introduction and sent them to the House, which, biding by Long's orders, kept them simmering in the judiciary committee until needed. That tactic gave NOPSI and the city council time to propose the compromise the attorneys had devised—they would bring in natural gas, but, not surprisingly, at rates higher than those Long had in mind.

Perhaps the memories of the NOPSI board and of the city council were too short, or perhaps their behavior was evidence of the human propensity to let hope triumph over experience. No one seemed to recall Long's handling of Cumberland Telephone and Telegraph, and when he called a conference of the city council and NOPSI, they went to it in full belief that a conference meant to Long what it meant to them—an exchange of ideas, a discussion of reasonable alternatives. Of this quaint notion Long quickly disabused them. "A deck has fifty-two cards, and in Baton Rouge, I hold all fifty-two of them and can shuffle and deal as I please."

Those three bills in the judiciary committee were his aces, and they were powerful enough to force the others to throw in their hands. There was a certain amount of stalling, of going through the motions of a fight, but essentially, the battle was over and only the treaty had to be signed. That occurred on July 7, when NOPSI agreed to a rate of ninety cents per thousand cubic feet of natural gas. When the city council and NOPSI reviewed the situation, one thing became clear—from the very beginning, Charles Livaudais had hardly acted with his usual perception, his usual dedication, and his usual brilliance. The fact that he had put some vague appointment ahead of launching NOPSI's counterattack told heavily—that was evidence, they decided, of a negligent attitude they could neither afford nor tolerate. It did not take long for Charles's fate to be sealed.

"Guess a rich man like you doesn't need to practice much law," the general manager of NOPSI said when he talked with Charles shortly afterward. He looked at Charles from under hooded eyes. "Leastways, we don't think you practiced much law in this natural-gas thing."

"Even a very good lawyer can hardly take on the entire legislature and executive branch," Charles said. He had held onto his temper throughout the whole humiliating interview. Dismissal, really! He had not even been given lunch, had been called to their offices as though he were a junior partner or law clerk. He lifted his hat to his head and smiled. That smile was a shadow of the one that had alerted Charles's opponents over the years to guard their property, their wives, and their futures, but the man sitting in front of him remembered its old force and shifted uneasily. "Of course," Charles added, "if I did not agree that the people should have natural gas, I would, perhaps, have told you how to stop him." He turned, moved to the door, conscious that he was leaving the field with his shield, not on it, as had been hoped. He swiveled his head, smiled again. "Now you'll never know how you could have." The door shut behind him, and he walked carefully through the outer offices to the broad marble-floored hall. He got into the elevator, wiping his brow with a large square of white linen. God, it was hot. Hot enough to make you hope your sins weren't damning ones. The anniversary of Francie's death was near. Could he endure it? He fled to the house on Dumaine Street, pulled the blinds against the afternoon sun, stripped, and flung himself across the empty bed. This was one of the days when he believed he could not.

31

Beau paused outside his wife's closed bedroom door before forcing himself to knock. He rarely came to her end of the house anymore. What had originally been a kind of spare room off to itself in an ell had become Louise's retreat from the family. She had begun using the back stairs that led from the back of the hall down into the kitchen hall; Beau had met her slipping down them one day earlier in January and had found the hair rising on his neck before he recognized the thin gray-clad woman in front of him as his wife. "You look like a ghost!" he had said, trying to laugh to ease his real fright.

"Not yet," Louise had answered in a hushed, almost mysterious voice, and had gone past him and out the back door into a dark and blustery winter afternoon.

He could hear a voice from behind the door. Did Louise have company? Then organ music swelled, and he knew the voice he heard was from the radio. His knuckles touched the wood of the door panel in a rapid, staccato beat.

"Who's there?" Louise asked. Her voice came from just the other side of the door. Why in the hell didn't she open it? he wondered. He put his hand on the doorknob and turned it, but it remained locked, unmoving. Now she was locking herself in.

"It's me, Louise," Beau said. When the door did not open, he rattled the knob. "Come on, Louise, open up."

He heard the key enter the lock and turn. Then the door swung open, Louise standing protectively at the threshold, barring the way. From behind her, the woman's voice from the radio filled the room and seemed to take it over, until there was no corner where Beau could feel at home. An odor he could not place drifted forward on the stale, heated air, and he sniffed, head raised like one of his hunting dogs. "What's that funny smell? Is something burning?" He tried to move past her, but her arms went out on either side, grasping the door frame and making a barrier.

"Nothing's burning," she said. "It's the smoke from the medicinal cigarettes I use to help my breathing."

"God," Beau said, sniffing again. The smell was peculiar; it had a sharp, acrid odor with an undercurrent of cloying sweetness. In the close atmosphere of the room, it seemed as pervasive as the compelling voice of the woman. "I'd think your lungs would sit up and behave themselves if you promised never to use that stuff again." He smiled and reached a hand toward her. "May I come in?"

"Why?" Her eyes had lost some of the dark glitter that had so disturbed him; they burned steadily now, with a low intensity that did not seem to alter no matter what Louise did nor to whom she spoke. Beau found it difficult to speak of common things, daily things, with those great light eyes reaching into his soul.

He looked past her into the room, and was startled at the changes in it. The huge walnut bed and matching armoire were gone, as was the elaborate dressing table she had bought with such enthusiasm years before in New Orleans. The headboard of her bed was little more than a pine board. A rough kind of closet had been built into one corner of the room, and a pine table held a black-handled hairbrush and a long-tailed comb. He pushed past Louise and strode into the room.

"Louise—" He made his voice gentle. "Where . . . where is the furniture? Those pretty things you wanted?"

"I sold them," she said. She came in and sat in the one chair in the room, a straight-backed wooden-framed armchair with a caned seat. She sat aligned against it, her bones no less straight than the back of the chair, no less rigid. "I gave the money to the missions." She looked at him, but the light in her eyes did not change. "You stopped giving me money to give them, Beau. I had to get it somewhere."

"You can't be comfortable," he said. Nor was he. Guilt flooded him, and he felt an urgent need to make amends. "Look, Louise, let me send some new things in. And whatever is spent, I'll give you that much for your missions."

For a moment the light in her eyes did burn more brightly. Then it lowered, a steady flame that seemed fueled by her soul.

"I don't want new things, Beau. Not even to get the money."

He struggled against the alien nature of that room. The

curtains were drawn, and he went to the window and pulled them back, letting in the muted light. "All right," he said, making his voice easy. "If you don't want new furniture, fine. But let me give you a check for your missions, anyway, Louise." He felt those eyes swing to his face and looked quickly away. "I . . . I was wrong to keep you from sending money where it was needed. Lord knows there's enough of it." He searched in his coat pocket, found paper and a fountain pen. "Tell me how to make out the check."

Her voice sounded eager, the words falling over each other. "To the International Church of the Foursquare Gospel," she said. Her eyes looked into his, and she gestured toward the radio. "Aimee Semple McPherson's church."

His pen faltered. "McPherson? She's not Catholic!"

Louise laughed—at least, when he had made himself realize what that short bark was, he knew that she had intended to laugh. "Well, no, she's not, Beau." For the first time, he heard a reminder of Louise's old voice. "Does that matter?" she said, a hint of challenge in her tone, her face finally a little pink with life.

"I thought it was the missions that you supported. Our missions," he said. He was risking one of those tantrums; he knew that. But to send good money to that McPherson woman, who used the gullibility and ignorance and fanaticism of her followers to milk them of their money . . .

Louise shrugged, raised her hands in a gesture of dismissal. "But the Catholic missions are managed by men. By priests. And you see, I don't trust men."

A thought hit him. "Louise, have you stopped going to Mass?"

Her eyes did not look away, only burned on, but her lips curved a little in the old, familiar smile. "Yes."

"You told me, when you stopped coming with me and the children, that you were going to the early Mass at five-thirty— it was quieter, you could pray better."

"I lied," she said, and shrugged again. Then, in a voice that was almost totally normal, almost the old Louise, who could explain the reasonableness of her every act, the foolishness of his, she said, "I knew I'd have to listen to a lot of things I didn't want to hear if I told you the truth. So I lied."

"Just so," Beau said. He went to the radio and turned the volume down. "You like Mrs. McPherson, then?"

"She's wonderful," Louise said reverently. She made the words sound, not like praise, but like a statement of fact.

"I realize she has many . . . followers," Beau said. "But she's not always on the up-and-up, do you think, Louise?"

"Of course she is," she said. "Have you ever listened to her?"

"I don't have to," Beau said. "She's an evangelist, a phenomenon who's not entirely religious, all right?" He moved forward a little, made himself stand closer to the still figure sitting before him. "Did you read Lewis' book? *Elmer Gantry?* Don't think Aimee Semple McPherson isn't just like that. She could be a model for Gantry."

Her hands came up over her face, as though he were about to strike her. "Don't say that, Beau."

But his repulsion was greater than any caution. He had listened to Aimee Semple McPherson when she had returned to her congregation following her bizarre disappearance, when she insisted she had been kidnapped. Cynics insisted she'd taken a detour into sordid sex from the high road to salvation she preached and marched on. She was persuasive, she was appealing—but she had not been convincing, at least not to him. He'd felt the way he had when he'd gone up to North Louisiana to see what the Ku Klux Klan was all about. There was a darkness in such people. And dark passions bred dark acts.

"Louise, listen to me. Her own mother doesn't believe her story about her kidnapping. They've split, they're almost enemies now." He went to her, put a hand on her head. "Louise, there's nothing much worse than someone who lies about religion."

She took her hands away from her face and looked at him. "It's all lies." She stood up, and he was shocked to see how thin she was, how the wool dress fell away from her body. "You don't really believe all that they tell you in the Catholic Church, do you, Beau? That you receive the Body and Blood of Christ? Or that Mary could possibly be a virgin after having a baby?" The scorn in her voice seemed practiced. Where had she learned it? he wondered.

"Neither of those things bother me," he said. "Nor do they give me any difficulty. What I need from my church, I get."

"And what is that?" Louise asked. Her hands reached out to

him, thin, knuckles bony. "What do you need from your church?"

"Hope," he said, and heard in his own laugh an echo of Louise's short, bitter bark. "Hope that there is a heaven. Hope for mankind."

She relaxed. "That's all Aimee gives, Beau. Hope. And what she says is so simple, Beau. So easy. Jesus Christ is our savior. Jesus Christ is our baptizer. Jesus Christ is our healer. Jesus Christ is our coming king." Her voice went on by rote; these were words she had heard and repeated many times.

"I'm familiar with her Foursquare Gospel, Louise. Look, I'm not saying she doesn't do some good. I'm just saying she takes in a hell of a lot of money, and I'm not sure building great temples that are more of a monument to Aimee Semple McPherson than to God is the best way to spend it."

"May I go see it?" Louise asked suddenly. She came to him and put her hands over his, and he had to restrain himself from repelling her touch. "May I, Beau?" Her tongue darted out and moved over her lips. "I could go on the train, when spring comes, and the weather's nice."

"To Los Angeles?"

"Yes." For a long time, they looked at one another. And Beau, seeing something at the back of Louise's eyes that was still human, still needing, sighed.

He moved so that her hand fell away from his. "All right, Louise. If that will make you happy." He turned to leave. "I forgot. Your brother Hugh and his wife are coming over— we're going out for supper. Will you come down?"

"I think not," she said. Her voice was back in place now, had none of the wanting it betrayed when she had spoken of her trip. "There's so much I have to do. Will you make my excuses?" She had already gone back to the radio, fixing the volume to her liking. He watched while she took a cigarette from a package on the mantel, struck a match, and lit it. The first swirl of smoke was drawn out into the hall by the air currents, engulfing him.

"I always do," he said, closing the door.

As Beau and the Abadies went down the porch steps that evening, on their way to dinner, ducking their heads against the wind that blew around the corner of the house, Louise stood at the window at the front of the hall, watching. She let the curtain fall and walked down the dark hall toward the square of light her open door made on the black floor. Her step was light; she was happy. Beau had told her she could go to Los Angeles, and one thing about Beau, he did not make promises he did not keep. She got ready for bed and slipped between the sheets, drawing the blankets up over her chin. She was almost never warm now, there was so little flesh to protect her from the cold. But it would be warm in California, and there would be exotic flowers everywhere. Hibiscus and other brilliantly colored blossoms. She would make a huge bouquet of them, and then she would go to the Angelus Temple, where Aimee Semple McPherson waited for her. She would walk inside, would be one with the five thousand people who came there to hear their prophetess and watch her miracles of healing. It would be light inside, and warm. So warm. Louise's fingers relaxed their grasp on the covers. Surrounded by that promise of light and warmth, and of healing, she slept.

Beau fought his way up from sleep at the insistent knocking on the kitchen door. He reached for his wool robe, pulled it around him as his feet found his slippers. A cold March moon shone through the window at the front of the hall. He heard the sound again, the beating of a fist on the back door. He went quickly down the stairs to find a young boy standing at the door, his back hunched against the wind.

"Mr. Beau! Come quick, please! It's 'Tit Jacques, he's hurt, bad!"

Beau pulled the frightened boy inside and closed the door. Turning on the overhead light, he blinked at the sudden brightness. "'Tit Jacques is hurt?" He shook himself, finally coming completely awake. He recognized the boy; he was Jean, who lived with 'Tit Jacques and helped with the trapping and alligator hunting that masked the liquor-running. "What happened, Jean?"

"'Tit Jacques, he made a run, he got hit," the boy said. He was shivering, his body still hunched forward, his eyes large with fright. "He say: Get Mr. Beau."

"Did you get a doctor?" Beau took a heavy jacket from a hook near the back door and put it on over his robe. He looked around the kitchen. Was there anything here that would help? He spotted a stack of neatly folded dish towels and snatched them up.

"No doctor," Jean said, leading the way across the porch. "'Tit Jacques, he don't want no one nosing round where he stay."

Jean had an automobile in the back alley. Beau climbed in, feeling the cold March wind under his coat. "How bad is he, Jean?"

Jean backed out the alley, his hands gripping the wheel tightly, his face set. "Pretty bad, I think." He shrugged, the first movement of his shoulders since Beau had opened the door. "I don't know much about gun wounds. There's a lot of blood."

Blood was still trickling from the wounds in 'Tit Jacques's chest when Beau and Jean reached him. Too much blood. Beau took Jean's knife and cut away the blood-soaked flannel shirt. The size of the wounds shocked him, but he made himself keep talking, joking with 'Tit Jacques as he made pads of the dish towels and pressed them hard against the ragged black holes. "You stood up when you should have ducked, 'Tit Jacques?"

He knows, Beau thought, looking into 'Tit Jacques's eyes. He knows he can't make it.

'Tit Jacques's lips formed a smile. "Hell, Beau, you should have been with me. Remember how you shot that scum that time?" His hand lifted, found Beau's arm. "This one had that kind of gun." His eyes closed. "It's a lot of bullets."

"Yes," Beau said. "It's a lot of bullets." And later, when 'Tit Jacques was dead, and they had roused the family, Beau stood outside smoking while inside the women laid out the body. It was senseless, all of it. The St. Valentine's Massacre had shocked the nation a few weeks before. A lot of bullets. And why? For a few bottles of whiskey. Or a lot of bottles of whiskey. A lot of bullets. A lot of lives. He heard a sound behind him, a murmurous rhythmic sound, and knew the women were saying the rosary for the repose of 'Tit Jacques's soul. "You all right?" he said to Jean.

The boy looked at Beau. "I guess so," he said.

Beau's hand went out and ruffled Jean's hair. "Jean, let 'Tit Jacques's business die."

Jean's eyes shifted. "The trapping? The 'gator hunting?"

"The liquor-running," Beau said flatly.

"It's a lot of money," Jean said, still not looking at Beau.

"It's a lot of death," Beau said.

Jean shrugged. "I take a good shot with me." Then he did

look at Beau. In the shadowed light that came from the kerosene lanterns in the cabin behind them, Beau could see that Jean was smiling. "If I don't run the liquor, Mr. Beau, what will you and your papa, all you rich men, drink?" He laughed, the quick blood of youth stronger than the death behind them. "I can't see you making no gin in your bathtub, no!"

As he drove home in a borrowed automobile, watching the streak of light rising up from the dark edge of the horizon, the words "What will all you rich men drink?" echoed in his mind. Realization of his part in 'Tit Jacques's death stole over him as the dawn stole over the marsh. He turned into the alley, saw lights in his kitchen. Good, Susu was up, making coffee. He parked the car and walked toward the house. A strong house, a solid house. A house that stood for tradition, for family. He opened the back door and let the familiar warmth and the welcoming aroma of coffee surround him.

"Mr. Beau, what you doing out this time of mornin'?" Susu said, surprise clear on her face. "And in your pajamas? Mr. Beau, you'll catch your death!" She bustled around him, pulling a chair for him near the stove, pouring him a big cup of coffee.

He sipped, tasting the strong bitter brew carefully, then almost gulped it down, and held his cup out for more. All the bottles of wine and champagne, all the cases of good bourbon. All the beer. A house that supported and encouraged crime. He saw again 'Tit Jacques laughing from the bow of his boat. "At least you won't blind yourself drinking it."

Across America, people said the same thing. What was wrong with slipping up to Canada, bringing a truckload of liquor back? Meeting ships off the Atlantic coast, and the Pacific? What was wrong with any of it? He roused himself. "Susu, make me a big breakfast, will you? I'm going up to shave and dress, I've got to go right back out. 'Tit Jacques Boudreaux died last night. I need to go to his family."

Susu paused, a big mixing bowl in her hand. "What killed him, Mr. Beau?"

He stood up, remembering those terrible wounds, and the knowledge in 'Tit Jacques's eyes. "As a matter of fact, he was . . . shot."

"Hmmph," Susu said. She poured flour into the bowl, added baking powder and salt, and began to cut chicken fat into the mixture. "You know what the Bible says, Mr. Beau. Who lives by the sword dies by it. That Mr. 'Tit Jacques, he just made his own time run out."

"I don't know," Beau said. "I'm not sure if maybe my hand wasn't doing some of the clock-winding."

Upstairs, he paused in the twins' door. The room was light now, and he could see Gennie and Émilie, curled against each other, only the tips of their noses sticking out of the great down-filled quilts. He could imagine how Skye looked, sprawled over the width of his bed, his hound pup lying at his feet. Beau went quietly to his dressing room and began sharpening his razor on the leather strap. For a long time now, when the world didn't exactly make sense, when what he thought he had to do didn't always jibe with what he had been told was right to do, he had been able to reason it out. So long as he knew what he was doing, and was willing to take the consequences, who could tell him no? But now he couldn't rid himself of the sight of 'Tit Jacques's chest, the rib cage showing bare and white beneath the flowing blood.

As he went down to breakfast, face smoothed, body dressed in a dark suit, he thought: God, if I had to trace every decision through all its consequences, could I ever sleep at night?

Driving back out to 'Tit Jacques's, he made a resolution. He would clear up his calendar and run down to Baton Rouge to look in on the legislature. God knew that agenda would blow the cobwebs from his mind, and all these philosophical speculations, too. If there were anything to take a man's mind off his misery, it was watching Huey P. Long put his legislature through its paces.

But down in Baton Rouge, Huey P. Long was learning that the legislature that had given him everything he wanted his first year in office was not quite as well-trained as he had thought.

This time, certain members clearly had no intention of lying down and letting him roll right over them. Not unless he could flatten them first.

When he convened a special session of the legislature on March 18, 1929, Long expected to be able to re-create certain parts of Louisiana's world in the allotted six days. The announced purpose of the session was to pass laws which would allow individuals and corporations to recover erroneously paid severance tax in the event the tax, at that point being fought out in the courts, was later found unconstitutional.

Actually, Long had only one thing on his mind—and once

he had allowed the legislature to know what it was, any hope of
a short, amicable session, with Huey writing the laws and the
legislature dutifully passing them, was gone. For what Huey
asked the legislature to do on that first morning was to pass an
occupational license tax on the refining of oil, the first such tax
in the history of the state. The price tag in money was five
cents a barrel, but the political price tag was almost more than
Huey could afford to pay. Too many of the state's citizens,
from the eight thousand employees of Standard Oil at the
Baton Rouge refinery to the thousands whose businesses were
aligned with the growing oil industry, would be affected. To
the conservatives, the tax was a declaration of war, and they
rallied, forgetting old scars and old battles to unite against their
common enemy.

Beau found himself watching the early stages of the tax
campaign from St. Martinville. His plans to clear his office
calendar and spend some time in Baton Rouge had been
changed when all three children came down with chicken pox.
By the time the chicken-pox siege wore itself out, the siege
against Huey P. Long had been carried literally to his gates,
and had culminated in a call for impeachment. Huey could no
longer control "his" legislature. The first defeat had come
when Huey realized that a short special session would not give
him time enough to get his oil occupational license tax
through—too many people had broken rank. And so he had
reconvened the legislature on March 18, calling for a new,
longer session to last eighteen days.

Long's opposition, confident now it could do more than
defeat his special bills, searched for a way to destroy Long
himself. They found enough in his administration which bordered on the illegal to make impeachment possible. On the
morning of March 22, the fight spilled from the aristocratic
parlors and corporate offices onto the front page of the Baton
Rouge *Morning Advocate*, with an editorial written by publisher Charles Manship himself. Headlined "THIS, GENTLEMEN,
IS THE WAY YOUR GOVERNOR FIGHTS," the editorial addressed
itself to the legislature and let them know in full and explicit
detail the latest Long ploy. In conversations first with the managing editor of Manship's afternoon paper and then with
Charles Manship himself, Long had threatened, unless Manship stopped opposing him in print, to publish a list of his
enemies who had relatives in East Louisiana Mental Hospital.

Among those names would be Charles Manship, whose brother
Douglas was being treated there. Manship's editorial pointed
to Long's total disregard for all the decencies that ruled even
political fighting. "I might say, however," Manship wrote,
"that my brother Douglas, whom Governor Long has brought
into the discussion, is about the same age as the governor. He
was in France in 1918, wearing the uniform of a United States
soldier, while Governor Long was campaigning for office."

"This stinks," Claude said, upon reading of Long's latest
tactic. Long's first year in office had made Claude more and
more wary; he could fence-sit as long as the next fellow, so
long as the ground on either side looked just about the same.
But the ground on Long's side had suddenly become a quagmire of deceit and bribes and arm-bending, and although the
conservative side had its blind spots, at least, thought Claude,
reaching for the telephone, they believed in the democratic
process.

He was now committed to aid those who would stop Long.
All that remained, as he told the leader of the opposition, was
to find out where he best fit in. There was one other considera-
tion, but that was a private one. What would Beau say? They
had avoided open confrontation, had even shared intense moments of support for Long. But this was one of the times when
loyalties to larger causes had to supersede tolerance of someone else's opinions. Beau would not like it; it might even cause
a temporary distance between them. But if there were anything
Claude had learned, it was that you couldn't expect children to
take roads you weren't willing to follow yourself, and that if he
ever hoped Beau and Marie would have the will to make the
choices their code dictated, he would have to show them that it
was possible to make hard decisions, even those that isolate
you, and still survive.

In St. Martinville, Beau, too, read Manship's editorial. He
could feel anger forming as he read. Why in the hell did Long
have to pull stunts like that? He tossed the paper aside and went
to his study window, looking out at the bleak March day. The
month would go out like a lion if this kept up; day after day of
high winds that seemed to blow down from the top of the sky,
whipping willow trees and driving scraps of paper and autumn's leftover leaves in gusts of litter down the brick street.

The year looked suddenly longer than he could stand. Another spring to be gotten through, the last spring of his twen-

ties. He tried to remember the enthusiasm he'd had when he was driving from one town to the next, campaigning for Long. He tried to remember Long's face, alive with the promises that lit up the hopes of his audiences. He tried to remember the power of that large presence. Then he reached for the telephone and asked for the governor's office.

It took him less time than usual to get through; Huey would of course be happy to talk to a staunch supporter. The sound of that strong voice, almost yelling in his ear, seemed to fill some of the space that had just been yawning before him. Beau listened, let himself be beguiled by Long's version of what he was up against. "Damnedest thing you ever saw. There's a group of men up here call themselves the Dynamite Squad, that's their name, Beau. And they purely do mean to blow me up." The voice became easier, and he could picture Long leaning back in a big chair, placing his feet comfortably on his desk. "Now, Beau, I admit it's not the fairest thing to use a man's relatives against him. But dammit, Beau," Long said, his voice getting raucous, "they started it. Ever since they held my brother George's Klan membership against me back in the '23 race, they've been using my family." Then Long laughed. "Hell of it is, Beau, I can't stand more than a few of my relatives myself."

"Still," Beau said, "you should have known you'd lose a lot more by taking that kind of cheap shot than if you'd come out and fought like a man. Go down to someone else's level, Huey, and you're going to have a hell of a time getting anywhere else."

"You lecturing me on how to run this campaign?" Long said.

"I'm telling you how it looks to me, Huey."

Long's voice became crisp, the words clean and hard. "Well, let me tell you how it looks to me, Beau. What it looks like to me is that the people of this state voted me in because they liked what I said I could do. And last year, they liked it when I started carrying through."

"Many people did," Beau said. "But you made a lot of enemies doing things the way you did."

"Now it comes time to raise some money to pay for some of the things the people of this state say they want," Long said, riding over Beau's interruption. "And I'll tell you, it surely did shock me to find out they still don't understand that roads and schools and hospitals for the insane and help for the deaf and blind don't come free. No, and they don't come out of some Aladdin's lamp. I may be one hell of a governor, but I'm not a damn genie out of a bottle. That five cents a barrel is about the fairest tax I could come up with, and I'll be damned if I'm giving up on it just because a bunch of spoiled politicians can't face up to the fact that somebody's got to pay. I'm trying to see to it that those who can afford it best do it."

"The tax'll be passed on, it always is," Beau said.

"But in proportion to use, Beau. In proportion to use. You think a little old Cajun farmer driving his truck in to market once a week uses as much gasoline as, say, one of those big utility plants?"

"All right," Beau said.

"Now, what the hell does that mean?"

"That means that as soon as my little boy gets over the chicken pox, I'll come on down and see what I can do."

"You do that," Long said. There was a click, then silence. Beau replaced the receiver and picked up the *Morning Advocate* again. Long was right and Manship was right. I wish Huey weren't so whole-hog about everything, Beau thought, going upstairs to read to Skye. I wish he didn't want to remake every last thing in this state without taking time to let some of the rest of us in on the planning. But that would be democratic, he realized. And whatever else Long believes in, democracy is not on the list. Because, Beau admitted, if you believe in democracy, you have to also believe that many opinions, honed into one plan, can be better than one. In other words, you cannot believe in tyranny.

"This isn't a game up here, Beau," Claude said, shoving the paper he'd been reading across the table to his son. "God, I wish it were. I'd hang up my uniform and head for home." He got up and went to the small bar that had been set up in a corner of the living room of his Baton Rouge hotel suite. He poured two drinks, handed one to Beau.

On April 6, the last day of the official session, the House had voted to impeach Long on the first of eight charges—threatening Charles Manship in an effort to silence the press. The other charges were still being processed. The last would be presented tomorrow, the twenty-sixth, and then the Senate would take over, setting a date for trial, and summoning Long to answer the charges against him.

"Why don't you head on home?" Claude said.

"That would be running away, wouldn't it?"

"I don't call it running when a man leaves a fight he's got no business being in in the first place," Claude said. He worked hard to keep his voice even and his temper cool. He had spent countless hours since early April tracking down evidence to support the charges laid at Long's door. As with any other investigation that throws out a large net, a lot of what they had turned up—and had heard in the House chambers—had not strictly pertained to the investigation, but had to do with Long's personal misconduct, his loose use of vulgar language, his indulgence in forms of entertainment that did not bear the light of day. It had been useless to protest that dredging up all that muck did the investigators more harm in the long run than it did Huey. Claude had noticed more than once that men hunting in a pack lost much of their individual restraint. But some of the evidence Claude had dug up was real—and damning.

"Why isn't this fight my business?" Beau said. "I worked for Long's election, I'm still a key man in his organization."

"Listen, anything you can tend to when you feel like it, and put down when you don't, isn't your business, Beau." Claude heard the flatness of his voice, and he knew that the expression on his face was one Beau had seen many times—though never before directed at him.

"You're saying that because I'm not a member of that distinguished body down there, most of whom are waiting to see if the anti-Long forces have as much buying money in their war chest as Long has, I'm not allowed to take an interest in these proceedings?"

"You know damn well I didn't say that, Beau." He wanted another drink, but he would not allow himself to have it. Not when he felt the dirty hands of this mess putting black smudges on him, and on Beau, and on the way they felt about each other.

"What is your point, then?" He had to close his lips tightly to keep the automatic "Papa" from falling from them. The man opposite him did not seem like his father, was not the man who had taught him to swim and to hunt, had told him about girls, and how to behave with them. Dammit, I'm a man, Beau thought. I can damn well make my own decisions without having to be briefed by him first.

"Mainly that your being down here won't matter a hell of a lot in the final outcome of these charges. But it can affect the rest of your life." Claude leaned back in his chair. God, he was tired. "I wish I didn't have to be here myself."

"You could turn your seat over to me," Beau said. "Let me make it my business."

"No," Claude said, snapping each word out. "I don't take pups out to hunt that haven't been weaned yet."

Beau felt slapped; his face tingled with blood, and he could hardly speak around the lump that filled his throat. "Sounds like you don't think much of my . . . ability," he said quietly, but his voice trembled and did not conceal his hurt.

"I didn't say that," Claude said. "I said you weren't weaned yet." He didn't want to look at Beau's face. He began to speak, saying the words he knew had to be said, wondering how much of it Beau would listen to. "Beau, you've got a cross to bear in Louise, a hard and heavy one. But you can't let a sick wife and a love you missed out on be the only things that set your course for you. You dabble in politics, dabble in law. And your marriage—at least you can excuse slipping off to some woman. You have any idea how many married men would like to have that kind of excuse? Are you naive enough to think that everybody but you has a great relationship with his wife? You're stuck with what you've got. And if you let escaping from your life be the main idea in everything you do, your life isn't yours, Beau. Not even one minute of it."

Beau was so angry he could hardly make his tongue form words. "You really think everything I do—the oil company, politics, the law . . . all of it—is to forget Louise? To get over Caroline?"

"Yes," Claude said. It was the most difficult thing he had ever had to say, and, gauging his son's wrath, he felt it was also the most costly.

"It's mighty easy for you to make judgments, sitting in high cotton the way you do," Beau said.

"That the way my life appears to you?"

"Isn't it? You're rich, you've got a good marriage, children, the respect of all who know you . . ." I'm making it sound like a litany of hypocrisy, Beau thought.

"And no cross, is that it? Since I don't carry one, I can't comment on how you bear yours?"

"All right. You lost a . . . a daughter. Lots of people do, not just that way, but . . ." He couldn't drag Francie into this.

"But I do carry something, Beau. Carry it every day I come down here." He moved to the window that looked over the river and pulled the cord that opened the draperies and revealed the night, and the twinkling lights of the barges lined up at the docks. "I can't stand being a politician, Beau, can't stand it so bad sometimes I just have to force myself to get in my car and head it toward Baton Rouge."

"No one's forcing you to do it," Beau said. "Not much of a cross if you can put it down any old time you feel like it." He felt good, throwing Claude's words back in his face. He wanted to hurt Claude, wanted to make his life as small as Beau's life had been made small, and his mind circled, watching for a weakness he could use.

"Something is forcing me," Claude said. He swung around, his body framed by the window behind him. "A sense of duty, maybe. Knowing that the people of our parish need representation, and that I can give them that."

"Now you're sounding like Long," Beau said. He thrust deeper. "Thinking you're the only one with the answers."

"Maybe," Claude said. He felt only fatigue now, and a desire for Beau to leave, so he could sleep. "There is a difference, though. I do what I do in spite of the fact that it takes me from everything I love best. Long does it because it is what he loves best."

Beau stared into the face of the father he suddenly didn't seem to know. "Are you finished?" he said finally.

"Yes," Claude said.

"I'll say good night, then," Beau said, deliberately putting a chill on every word. He walked past Claude's half-extended hand and disappeared into the hall, slamming the door behind him.

It's costing too much, Claude thought. I can give up a lot, but this is too much. Settling into bed, he finished the thought. It appeared as though he had already paid it.

By morning, Beau began to think that the price demanded for loyalty to Huey P. Long might be more than he was willing to pay, too. He sat at the back of the legislature, watching the proceedings with an eye that seemed to have developed a kind of detachment during the long night. By the end of the day, only one fact had emerged from the confusion—that whether Beau liked it or not, Claude was right. Beau was not a member of the House, he had no official business here. His presence could only be construed as moral support for Long—and as an attorney, Beau was well aware that moral support has but one purpose before the law: to lend one person's credibility to another.

He did not join other members of the Long party for dinner. He would not stay, he knew that. Nor would he behave like the pup Claude had called him, turning tail and beating his way home. He lay on his bed staring out at the river. He needed to do something to prove himself; that was obvious. But what? As Claude said, the businesses just rolled along, money piled up on money. Gemini Oil had been a starting point for Beau's own enterprise—but it didn't need him to make it go. He shifted restlessly on the bed and picked up *The Wall Street Journal*, idly turning pages.

A short article on an inside page of the paper caught his eye. New silver mines in Colorado. Silver. He read the story again, slowly. Louise would be leaving soon to go out west. He could go with her, could investigate the silver mines. Sleep on it, he warned himself. Don't go leaping from the frying pan into the fire.

But even in the morning, the idea still attracted him. And what the hell, if it didn't work out, something else would. He packed, feeling better than he had in months.

By the time the Louisiana Senate refused to consider the House impeachment charges against Long, thanks to the maneuvering of Long's Senate leaders, Beau was on the *Sunset Limited* headed west.

Reading about it on the train, he put the paper down and turned to watch the sun blaze the evening sky into graduated layers of red and gold as the *Sunset Limited* sped forward into the darkening prairie. Then he motioned to the porter who stood at the end of the car. He asked for a telegram blank, scrawled Claude's name and address across the top. Then he wrote the message. It was one word: "THANKS."

"It actually feels like fall this morning," Hélène said, pouring coffee into her cup. "When I went out to get the paper, I got chilly." She put down the pot and looked across the table at Charles. "New York is wonderful in October, I can't wait to get there next week." Then she rattled the society section of the

Times-Picayune irritably. "Heavens, Charles, having a meal with you is like being all alone. Maybe you'll at least show a little interest when we go to the Favrots' to hear the Golden Jubilee broadcast. They've gotten up a party, and they have a wonderful new radio that will make us think we're right there."

"All right," Charles said without looking up from his plate.

Hélène leaned forward and studied him closely. "You're not looking well, Charles. Are you ill?"

"Why, how nice, Hélène," Charles said. He mustered a shadow of his old sardonic smile. "You're actually noticing how I look. Thank you, that's very kind."

Ignoring his sarcasm, she said, "Maybe you should go see Maurice before we go to New York. You don't want to get sick and spoil your trip."

"Spoil *your* trip," he said. He took a piece of thin toast and buttered it, then set it down next to his untouched omelet.

"Now, don't be mean," Hélène said. "You know you're looking forward to this trip as much as I am. It's been long enough since we've done anything fun, God knows." She rattled the bracelets on her arm, holding them in front of her face and looking at them critically. "I intend to get some new things from Cartier's while I'm there. I'm tired of these old bangles."

Charles said nothing. He picked up his fork and poked at his omelet, then closed his eyes and made himself swallow the eggs. He could not afford new bangles for Hélène, nor could he afford the New York trip. The loss of his position with NOPSI had initially hurt his pride, but it had since hurt his pocketbook. When he fell out of favor with the city administration, he found that other avenues that normally provided money had closed, too. And although he had cautiously broached a Long man in New Orleans about the possibility of working with the governor, he had been greeted with scorn. "There's a limit, Livaudais," the man had said. "A known turncoat's no good to anybody."

With nowhere to turn, Charles had sold his blue-chip stocks and ventured into the riskier speculative ones. His stockbroker, a member of an old, conservative firm, had not been happy; he had reminded Charles of the steady source of income those blue-chips had provided over the years, and warned him against buying highly speculative stocks on margin. But it had been a bull market for months—he couldn't pass the opportunity by.

He pushed back his chair and automatically looked at his watch. He still went to his office at the same time every day; he had even managed to get a few new clients—nothing big or impressive, but the sense of forward motion steadied him.

"It's a gorgeous day, isn't it, Mr. Livaudais?" his secretary greeted him as he entered the office. "The papers are full of the schedule for the Jubilee. Do you want to see them?"

"All right," he said. He took the bundle she handed him and carried it into his office. She had opened the windows, and the October day poured into the stale confines of the room, clearing away the smell of old cigar smoke and riffling the papers that littered his desk. He listlessly read one exuberant article after the other. God, he thought, to read this you'd think Thomas A. Edison had created a new world when he made the first electric light. He studied the picture of Edison. How must it feel, to know that on the fiftieth anniversary of his great discovery, an entire nation, an entire world, would be celebrating him? Charles felt the emptiness inside him all the more keenly. He looked around the office, let his eyes drift over row after row of lawbooks. His gaze fell, as it always did, to a short span of shelf that held his own personal books, things he kept at the office because he did not trust them to Hélène's unfeeling eye. He did not need to open the thin blue volume at the end of the row to know what it was, or what it said. He almost knew it by heart. Millay's *A Few Figs from Thistles*. He rose, got the book, and opened it. He read "The First Fig," the one that made him think of Francie. And then he read the second one, that made him think of himself. The one about the shining castle, built upon the sand. Finally he snapped the book shut, replaced it, and made himself go back to his desk.

He was deep into a brief when the phone at his elbow rang. His broker's voice jerked Charles back to his own reality: his brokerage account, like every other account, was long overdue. "Look, Charles, we can't carry you anymore. You either make a substantial payment or we'll have to sell your stock."

"Now, just a minute," Charles said. "Those stocks are worth a hell of a lot more than I owe you."

"But it's our money that paid for them, Charles. We're not in the lending business—you pay for that block of stock, and then we'll keep on buying on margin for you. As it stands now—well, we've done all we're willing to do."

Charles's fingers drummed the hard surface of his desk. The cash he had on hand wouldn't make a dent in what he owed the broker—wouldn't make a dent in what he owed everyone from the butcher to Hélène's dressmaker, for that matter. His mind raced over the possibilities. "I'll get back to you," he said.

"By the morning," the broker warned. "That's the outside limit, Charles."

"Right," he said. He stared into space, reviewing salable assets. He could sell the house on Dumaine Street. But even as he formed the thought, he knew that he could not. Dammit, he had to hold onto those stocks. The market had recorded an all-time high just a few weeks ago. It would again, and the stocks he had bought between early September and now would pay everything he owed, and give him a stake again. His fingers drummed restlessly. There had to be something he could sell to pay his broker, shut the man up. Beau Chêne. He could ask Hélène to sell Beau Chêne. He pushed aside a hard fact that cut against the edge of his consciousness: it would kill Caroline. But he could not think of that now.

He went back to his brief, automatically writing. How could he convince Hélène? What reason could he give her? By evening he had decided he must tell her the truth. He let himself into the big house, feeling its quiet settle over him. He would find Hélène in her boudoir, well into the copious amount of sherry she consumed each afternoon. That should make it easier; befogged by liquor, she would hardly know what he said.

Hélène looked up when he entered the room. Her face was caught in the light from the lamp beside her, and he saw the expression that filled it before she put on the carefully civil mask she maintained. Contempt. Contempt and disgust. For him.

He turned and stumbled from the room. She hated him. She thought him a failure. He went down the stairs, out into the street, where the streetlights were making small balloons of light against the autumn night.

Dumaine Street. He had to get to Dumaine Street. He hardly knew how he got there; not until he was safe inside did his heart begin to beat properly, his breath to come evenly instead of in tearing, ragged gasps. He could not ask her to sell Beau Chêne. He could not ask her for anything. His mind turned furiously, searching a way out. And then it came to him. Of course! If he were dead, all his creditors, including his broker, would have to wait while the slow process of settlement went on. Nothing would have to be paid until that was over—by that time, the stocks would have risen even higher. They would be sold, yielding more than enough money to pay everyone. He felt a stirring of pride. Yes, and Hélène would have money. She might hate him—but she would respect him again.

For the first time in a very long time, Charles saw a clear path. Death would solve something else, too. It would solve the awful ache, the wretched loneliness that tracked his days. He would see Francie.

Francie—the girl he had killed? He shook his head, trying to evade the thoughts that crowded in upon him. He did not want to think about his life, about all the dark turnings, the ugly paths. "I loved her," he said into the empty house. "I loved her." Surely that made a difference? That he loved, and had been loved? He remembered the way she had looked at him that last terrible day. The way her eyes had looked. Hadn't she forgiven him? It was all right. She had forgiven him, and he could now forgive himself.

Filled with a great calm, a peace he had not believed existed, he went slowly over the house. The kitchen with its gay flowered curtains, its bright copper pots. The parlor, with the rosewood piano and the pink velvet love seat. The bedroom, where the happiest hours of his life had been spent.

He stood near the bed, suddenly eager to carry out his plan. He took the revolver from the drawer in the table next to the bed and loaded it quickly. Then he lay down, looking at the chinks of light that glittered behind the closed shutters. An occasional street sound came to him, but it was dinnertime, and most people were off the streets. He put the gun in his mouth. The barrel was cold, hard, and he curled his tongue to make room for it. He thought he could smell Francie's perfume, thought he could hear her voice, her laughter.

At the last moment, he did wonder who would find him, and what they would tell Hélène. But by that time, his finger had squeezed the trigger, and in the explosion which followed, it was all left to someone else.

32

"This is mine," Beau said, his hand reaching out to take the check from the waiter. He smiled at the man sitting across from him. "After all, I asked you."

John Porter turned his face and stared out into the lobby of the Frederick Hotel. "If you hadn't, I'd have had a damn poor lunch today, Beau. Certainly wouldn't have eaten here." He tried to smile. "Funny thing. This depression has the whole country scared to death—but it's the little things like not being able to buy your own lunch that really bring it home."

"The sugar company has definitely let you go?" Beau asked.

"Me and a lot of other people. When they hired me last year to come down here and be their chief accountant, my wife and I thought we'd finally hit it big. Nice salary, nice house, nice car." His eyes were suddenly blank, as though he could not allow himself to think of these things he had lost. "Now I couldn't afford the train fare back to Detroit even if there were a job waiting for me."

"How do you feel about Colorado?" Beau said. He gestured to the waiter for more coffee, watched while Porter grasped his filled cup eagerly. In his turn, Beau looked away. To be richer than other men who also had money was one thing. To be almost astronomically wealthy in comparison to others was something he found very, very hard to handle.

"Colorado?" For the first time since they had sat down, the accountant had a look of sharpness about him, a glimmer of the man Beau had met and admired the summer of 1929 when there was no reason to believe that the abundance buoying the American ship of state would ever cease.

"I've some properties out there," Beau said. "Silver mines. I could use a top accountant to keep things straight for me." He smiled again. "Keep me off the train running out there myself all the time."

Porter put down his coffee cup and stared at Beau. "Mines?" His eyes had changed again. He leaned forward. "Let me get this clear. You own some mines out west and you're offering me the job of accountant?"

"More like the general manager," Beau said. "Someone to be my eyes and ears." He laughed. "I've got some partners in Denver; it won't hurt them to have to deal out another hand when decisions are being made." He paused, then named the salary that went with the job. He saw the tears on Porter's face; something in Beau protested against conditions that made competent men cry because someone wanted to hire them and pay them what they were worth. "I can throw in a house," Beau said, bending his head over his pie so that he did not have to watch that face. "If your wife doesn't mind living up from town a little."

"I can't imagine she would mind at all," Porter said. His hand crossed the table and took Beau's. "Look, Beau, you can't know what this means to me."

"It means a hell of a lot to me to get someone out there I can trust," Beau said. "You come on to my office in St. Martinville tomorrow about two o'clock, and I'll go over the operation with you."

"I'll be there," Porter said.

Walking with Beau through the lobby, Porter asked, "How in the world did you get involved in mines?"

"We have a tradition in our family of making sure our eggs are in a lot of baskets, so to speak. And that our hand is on the handle of every one of them." He smiled, remembering again the look on his stockbroker's face when Beau had ordered him to sell everything, just as it was climbing to that record September 3 high. "My father and I—we got out of the stock market late last summer, bought the land out west." He shrugged. "The Langlinaises have always been lucky."

"For other people, too," Porter said. "I'll see you tomorrow, Beau."

Beau looked up and down the quiet street. There was little activity; that could be laid to the fact that it was early afternoon in July, and that the weather was too hot and humid to attract people from darkened houses and cool front porches. But sometimes he could almost feel the slowing down of the economic life of his region, could almost see the shock waves that radiated out from the big urban industrial centers to the north and east, rippling out, engulfing his tranquil parish. The October 1929 stock-market crash had ruined so many businesses, so many individuals. Although so long as a man had land to till, he could hardly be called unemployed, if he had no market for his crops, or an extremely depressed market, he could not be called well-paid, Beau thought.

He walked slowly to his automobile, removing his coat and loosening his tie before getting into its hot interior. He felt uneasy, disturbed. What was bothering him? Then he realized that it was the mention of last summer, the mines, and the crash.

He had been out in Colorado in October, learning about his new investments, reveling in the high, cold air of the mountains, in the roughness of the mining camp. When the stock market crashed, Beau had immediately taken a train home. It was then that he learned someone else's world had crashed as well. Caroline's father had committed suicide just days before the debacle in Wall Street totally wiped out his stock-market investments. He died not even knowing he was leaving his wife a virtual pauper.

Hélène had been pitiful, from all reports, a smashed doll who wandered around in a daze while the auctioneers came to take the furnishings from the house on Fourth Street. It had all gone on the block, the house, too, with Hélène able to salvage only a few things her lawyer could protect. Caroline, Beau knew, had been helpless to assist her mother financially; he knew, too, that among the things being sold were things that had sentimental value to Caroline as well as Hélène.

He had gone to Annette Livaudais. "Tell me the things you think mean the most to the family and I'll buy them," he said. "Through an agent, of course. But I'll buy them and get them back to her somehow."

Annette had lit one of her long Turkish cigarettes, had gazed at him through the mist of smoke. "Mighty decent of you, Beau, after the way Hélène behaved to you." She had waited, as though for an explanation, and when Beau had remained silent, she had shrugged. "I'll see what I can find out from Caroline. Don't worry, I'll be discreet. If you wanted her to know what you're doing, you'd have asked her."

"Yes," Beau said.

Annette had hesitated, then moved to him and put her hand on his arm. "You heard where he was found?"

"Yes," Beau said.

"They found some books there with Francie's name in them."

"Yes," he said again, remembering the pain he had felt, and the hatred. He was thankful that the details had been kept out of the papers, but he would never forget the torment on Caroline's face the day she broke the news to him.

"If only I had gone to him . . . if only I had . . . I don't know, not . . . not judged him," Caroline had said.

He had stood across the hearth from her, feeling his heart rage in a terrible conflict between the hatred he felt for Charles and the love he felt for Caroline. "He didn't deserve you," Beau had told her. "You have nothing to regret."

She had looked at him, her great blue eyes dark with anguish; she had put her hand gently on his face. "Oh, Beau," she said, "isn't that supposed to be the wonderful thing about love? And forgiveness? That we don't have to deserve it?"

He had taken her into his arms then, and she had sobbed against him, his own tears running down his face and glistening in her hair. He had felt, for the first time since Francie's death, a loosening of the grip hatred had put on his heart. And for the first time, he had been able to admit that his sister had loved Charles Livaudais, and that he had loved her.

That compassion resulted in his keeping some of Hélène's things from being sold to strangers; even now, they sat in storage, waiting for the time she could leave Caroline's house and set up on her own again. Though where, and on what, no one was quite sure. He understood from Caroline that Hélène did not want to live at Beau Chêne, which would have been the most sensible solution. But grief had not, unfortunately, made Hélène any more sensible, and for the time being she was firmly entrenched in Caroline's house.

Looking back at the summer and fall of 1929, Beau could see a clear division between the old ways and the new—not only for a nation that went from heady prosperity to desperate poverty in a matter of weeks, but for him. He had realized, those months before the crash, that Claude was right—too much of his life had been a reaction to things outside of it, not nearly enough directed by what he, Beau Langlinais, wanted. He had resolved to take charge of his own life.

Selling his stock and investing in the silver mines had been a first step. That, and Louise's improved state of mind on her return from Los Angeles seemed proof that change was possible: She had been calmer, able to spend an occasional hour with the children without losing either her temper or her head. Then came the crash. And Charles's death. And then the hardest battle of all. Being rich in a land of poverty.

It was then that he had found that the old remedies, whether Bootsie at home or his lady in New Orleans, no longer worked. He had crossed a line, and he could no longer find release in the bed of a woman whose main concern was that he still had the price of her favors. What did work was to spend time at home with his children. They liked to sit on the floor of his study, listening to the radio while they worked jigsaw puzzles or painted in their coloring books. They liked him to read to them—Kipling's *Jungle Books* and Twain's *Tom Sawyer* and *Huckleberry Finn*. They liked to watch while he turned the crank on the ice-cream freezer on Sunday afternoons, while the sound of the New York Philharmonic came from the Columbia Broadcasting System, filling the quiet air with music. In the love and trust of his children, Beau began to find some trust for himself. As he drove homeward, he felt that if he were not really at peace, at least he knew what he had to do to arrive there.

Father Adrian took the papers Beau handed him and read them carefully. When he finished the last page, he said, "This is an overwhelming offer, Beau. A processing location where women are paid to preserve food bought from local producers, food that can be distributed to the needy next winter. It would certainly be the answer to a lot of prayers—but the cost! Are you really prepared to do this?"

"Absolutely," Beau said. "On one condition—that my name be kept out of it."

Father Adrian surveyed Beau's face, then nodded. "All right. Of course, you know people will besiege me with questions as to who's putting up the money for all this."

Beau smiled. "Tell 'em it was set up in the confessional and you're under oath not to breathe a word." He felt light, as though he could sail above the heat that oppressed them this long, arid summer, and survey the world from a cool, high cloud. "I have a suggestion as to someone who could help you in other towns in the area," Beau said. "Mrs. Raoul Hamilton."

Father Adrian picked up his pen, wrote the name and address Beau gave him. "Isn't she Mrs. de Gravelle's granddaughter, used to visit her grandmother at Beau Chêne?"

"Yes," Beau said. "She worked with the Red Cross during the flood. As a doctor's wife, she'll know every hardship case around here. But, Father—please don't mention to Mrs. Hamilton that I suggested her name. She'd guess in a minute I have something to do with this, and that's the last thing I want."

"But you will be on the executive committee?" Father Adrian said.

"Yes. As large as my family looms around here, it would be strange if one of us weren't."

"Where did you plan to set this up?"

"The farm," Beau said. "It's the perfect place. Grandmama could act as overseer; she's great at this kind of thing. I can have a couple more stoves put out there, probably in the open with some kind of shed over them—that would be cooler than the kitchen. God knows there's tons of room to store the jars in the old office—Papa and I have long since moved all the books into our offices here in town. I'll call Grandmama Geneviève right now." Then he looked at his watch. "No, on second thought, I think I'll run out and see her. Haven't been out there in a while. I can check the place over, see how many stoves we can place."

"You certainly don't waste time," Father Adrian said. The admiration in his voice embarrassed Beau—of all the things he wanted, praise was not on the list.

Beau rose. "You'll organize the committee, then?"

Father Adrian nodded. "Right away."

"Good. And I'll get the kitchen set up."

He drove out to the farm, whistling. Pulling up to the wide gravel space at the back of the house, he saw a small, thin figure holding a watering can over pots of fern on the porch. He was startled when she turned and he saw Geneviève's face. My God, she's gotten old, he thought. The afternoon light made her skin seem transparent, as though it were a film so delicate the merest change in the air would dissolve it. When she came to meet him, she moved so slowly that he could almost feel himself growing older, waiting for her.

But the eyes that laughed up at him from beneath her sunbonnet were the same, and when she hugged him, he could feel strength still in her arms.

"I was beginning to think you'd forgotten the way out here," Geneviève said. "You must be working too hard when you don't have time to come drink coffee with me."

"You got some now?"

"Mais, do I ever not?"

Beau followed Geneviève into the big kitchen, sat at the old cypress table, and had coffee and lemon pie she had baked that morning—"Because I woke up early and didn't have anything else to do."

"You want something to do, Grandmama? I can keep you busy the rest of the summer and into harvesttime—if you're up to it." That was all Geneviève needed to hear. Beau had barely finished explaining the idea to her before she was on her feet, pacing off the size of the kitchen, dragging Beau out to a shady spot in the yard where four large oaks made a natural place for their canning shed.

"It'll be cooler with the trees shading the roof. And we're close to the cistern here, we can get water from it to boil the jars."

He was astounded by the vigor with which she moved; the old woman who had greeted him had been replaced by the grandmother he always remembered.

"I'll send supplies out tomorrow," he said. "And Father Adrian will begin hiring the women."

They went into the old office, the building that had begun life in the 1700s as the first home of the Langlinais family. The shelves that had held Claude's father's schoolbooks, and the ledgers that measured the steady progress of the Langlinais fortunes, stood bare. Geneviève turned and looked at her grandson. "So who pays for all this, Beau?" Her hand moved through the thick, hot air. "The pots, the pans, the stoves. The jars. The produce. The wages."

He couldn't look at her and not tell her; he stared out the window instead. "I . . . I'm not at liberty to tell you that, Grandmama."

He felt her come up behind him, put her arms around his chest. "That means it's you. Maybe your papa, too. But your idea. Don't try to tell me I'm wrong."

He turned and lifted her face to his. "You won't tell anyone?"

She shrugged. "Not if you say not to. But, Beau, who else has so much money?" She took the edge of her big apron and automatically moved to the old desk and began dusting its surface. "This Depression everybody talks about—it didn't hurt our businesses?"

The room was settling itself around him; all the hours spent here! He still had a feeling of awe when he thought of all the Langlinais men who had sat at this desk and worked at the books, seeing that this field was earning its keep, that enterprise worth continuing. "We have a lot of things that make money for us, Grandmama. So even if they don't make as much as before—there's still money."

She finished dusting the desk and leaned against it. "You've had to let people go, Beau?"

"No, we haven't. Papa and I, we . . . well, there's always something to be done around a place, even when business is slow." At least, he thought, he had not joined that club of men who had to take from other men their only means of earning bread for their families. Nor would he, no matter how much it took of the reserves that gave their businesses that deep, secure base. When he went to the automobile agency, or to the lumberyard, or out to the warehouse where the furs and hides were stored, he hated the way the employees fawned over him, the knowledge that they would do anything he asked to keep their jobs. He and Claude had written a letter to all their employees, announcing that as far as the Langlinaises were concerned, no one would lose his job because of the Depression. The letter had had two effects. The employees had calmed down. But hundreds of unemployed people had come to Beau and Claude for jobs. "Dammit, Beau, we can't protect the jobs of our people if we take on everyone who's been let go somewhere else," Claude had said. They realized that there were limits to what even the Langlinaises could do, and the idea for the canning operation had come to Beau soon after.

"It'll take care of some bad problems around here now, and when the economy gets itself straightened out, we'll have the basis for a commercial canning operation," he had told his father.

Beau could not believe the Depression would not soon be over. Its cost was too high—one of the highest was the loss of peace and unity. Young adults moved home to rural areas and small towns in droves, devastated by urban unemployment. Those who had no place to go rode the rails west, where the last glimmer of the golden American dream still hung in the sky. Claudine wrote from New Orleans that vagrants came to her back door almost daily, asking for food. She had found a chalk mark on the front gatepost one morning; it was, she learned, a sign vagrants used to mark those houses where food was to be had for the asking. Her husband, Adolphe, insisted she erase it, and he had brought two of his hunting dogs in from his duck camp and posted them on guard. There were simply too many people to feed. Neighbors who were jobless and gradually losing hope seemed hostile toward those still employed; they sat on porches that hot summer of 1930 and gave angry glances to men still fortunate enough to be leaving for work.

Well, Beau thought, looking around the office for one last time, this place will never be the same again. But neither will the world. And neither will I. At least I won't feel as though I go to bed with bags of gold tied around my ankles, weighting me down.

"Let me put up some pie for you to take home," Geneviève said. "And don't tell me no—that cook of yours has no hand for pastry. Her pie crust sits on your stomach for a week, don't tell me it doesn't." He watched her place the pie in a flat-bottomed basket and drape cheesecloth over the top. "Here," she said. She reached up and patted his cheek. "Beau, listen to what your grandmama who loves you says to you. You can't make things well for people all the time. You can't, Beau."

"I don't know what you mean," he said, but he turned his eyes from hers.

"You can't make it up to people because you didn't lose all your money, Beau."

"I know that."

She caught his face and made him look at her. "No, cher, you don't. You think when this canning thing is going, you can sleep better." She shrugged. "Maybe you will. But I don't think so."

"Why not, Grandmama?"

"Because," she said, "you can't really carry anything for anyone else, Beau. You can help them—a lot, even. But there comes a time when whatever it is, they have to carry it alone." She hugged him then, and kissed him firmly. "Cher, I'm old, I'm alone a lot. I think too much. Just don't expect more out of this than it can do, that's all I'm saying."

He made himself smile. "If what we get out of it is a building full of food against the winter and jobs for some people who need them, that's all I ask."

But her words unsettled him; he did not want to drive back into town; what he wanted to do was go down to the bayou and find the deep place they used to swim in and feel the cool muddy water close around him, and lose himself in its placid depths. He walked across the pasture, found the path that, although badly grown over, still led back to the bayou and from there to Beau Chêne. Thinking of Beau Chêne made him curious—how was it faring? I'll just go look it over, he thought. Swim on the way back.

When he broke through the vines choking the path at the edge of Beau Chêne's lawn, he was shocked to see a shutter swinging loose on its hinges, shingles from the roof lying in broken pieces on the weed-filled grass. Nothing's been done out here for months, he thought, circling the house to the front. The shutters were closed tightly, but they afforded little protection against thieves. He thought of the silver, the books, the soft old rugs. Didn't Nat still live out here, look after things? Beau Chêne was going to rack and ruin; it was a disgrace. Then he looked up and saw Caroline rocking slowly in one of the tall wooden rockers on the upper gallery, the small stir of air fluttering her dress. Her eyes were closed, and she looked as though she were locked in some private grief almost past bearing. His heart almost broke. That she should look so sad, so . . . worn.

A squirrel, chattering at Beau from the big camellia bush growing at the side of the drive, caught Caroline's attention. She opened her eyes.

"Beau! What a lovely surprise!" She stood up and waved her hand over the gallery. "Come on up, there's actually a little breeze."

He turned words over in his mind on the way up the stairs. Did he just ask outright why Beau Chêne was such a mess? The sight of peeling paint on the porch floor, of mortar crumbling away from the upper wall, persuaded him. "The place looks like hell, Caroline," he said. "Isn't Nat around to take care of it?"

"When he can, he gets by," she said. She looked away, color stealing into her cheeks. "He has to earn money, and I . . . I can't always pay him." She looked past Beau, staring straight ahead into the branches of the centuries-old oaks that made the alley out to the road. That averted look and the blush in her cheeks told him he was trodding on delicate ground. The de Clouets had their pride, and God help him if he trespassed on it.

"But what about all the stuff inside?" he said, making his voice gentle. "Aren't you afraid of thieves?"

She pushed wearily at her hair. She's only thirty, he thought. What are all those lines doing in her face? "That's why I'm out here. I think I'll have to pack it up and get it moved to Lafayette. God knows where I'll put it there, but I suppose there's someplace."

She sounded exhausted. He went toward her and took her in his arms. "Caroline, wouldn't it be easier to have someone living out here? An uninhabited house . . . in this climate . . . can't your mother move out here?"

"She won't, Beau. She won't do anything but lie around and demand to be waited on. I'm surprised Luella and Bea put up with her. I'm afraid I'll never be rid of her!" She bit her lip and blinked her eyes rapidly. "I'm sorry. I used to wonder how women could say such awful things. I didn't realize they were probably just so tired they didn't even care."

He let her go and settled her back into her rocker, took the one next to it. How could he say what he wanted to without offending her? He rocked slowly. "I suppose Raoul's patients are just as sick—but pay even less than usual now."

"Almost nothing," Caroline said. "He can't not treat them, how could he do that? But we have bills too, Beau." She bit her lip and blinked her eyes again, fighting tears. But she was too tired and the tears too strong. She leaned forward, face in her hands, sobs racking her body. He was out of his chair in an instant, gathered her to him and held her close, saying over and over again, "Caroline, it's going to be all right. It really is."

She lifted her face and tried to smile. "I'm sorry, Beau. I . . . I don't always sleep well. There seems so much to worry about. I guess I've been needing a good cry for a long time."

"You've got to let me help you, Caroline," he said. He couldn't stand seeing worry lines around her eyes, or cheeks pale with loss of sleep.

Her back straightened and her chin lifted defiantly. "Now, Beau, you know very well I won't take money from you."

"I don't want you to take money from me," he said, his mind

racing. "Actually, I need you to help me do someone else a service."

"What kind of service?" she said.

"Father Adrian was telling me just yesterday about a family who needs a place to live. They've got a couple of strong boys who could whip this place into shape—keep some cows, plant vegetables."

"You want me to let them live here?"

"Why not? They could take Nat's old house."

"But what would they live on, Beau?" She gestured out at the ragged lawn, the neglected fields.

He forced himself to meet her eyes. "Well, I'd . . . I'd pay them."

He could see her wavering, see the temptation to just say yes. But her back was still straight, her chin still defiant. "Beau, that's very kind of you, but I really can't—"

The words exploded from him: "My God, what's the use of having money if you can't ease the life of the person you love most?" He took her shoulders, made her face him squarely. "Caroline, listen to me. I've stayed in your life, kept a place in your heart. And I've vowed to myself, Caroline, that whatever I can do to make your life easier, I'm going to do it. You wouldn't be so unkind as to deny me this?" He smiled, tempting her to smile too. "Besides, you wouldn't want it on your conscience that a homeless family doesn't have a roof over their head?"

"Beau Langlinais, you certainly went into the right profession when you became a lawyer," she said, but a smile was near the surface. Then she did smile, the old sweet smile that turned the worry lines into laughter. "Oh, Beau," she said, coming back into his arms and nestling against him. "I'm so glad you don't just give up on me."

She watched him down the stairs, watched him blow a kiss before he disappeared around the side of the house. Then she sat down and sighed. Had pride just lost a battle to necessity? Or, where love was concerned, was there no pride? She began to rock, her head back, her eyes closed again. This was the only place she could get any peace now; her mother gave her far more trouble than the children ever had. As she had admitted to Raoul: "We never had a two-year-old who was as spoiled as Mama is." Hélène's thin, high whine penetrated even to the morning room, and Caroline had come to detest the sight of that complaining figure, clutching a lace-trimmed robe around her, and asking for just one more trip up the stairs, just one more service, one more duty owed.

That's just it, Caroline thought, her eyes staring into the green oak boughs. I don't feel as though I owe her anything—not now, not ever. She could almost feel the house behind her as a living presence, its rooms crowded with de Clouet ghosts. I saved this house, she thought, pushing her foot sharply against the floor and setting the rocker into rapid motion. Saved it for ruin—if it hadn't been for Beau. A memory of the way he had looked just now, the afternoon sun bright behind him, casting a glow around his face, his body, caught at her. Suddenly she saw something heroic in what Beau had just offered to do. To save Beau Chêne. To save the property that had caused him to losé her.

She made herself see this new Beau. Not the boy who had courted her so long ago. Not even the young man who sat in her morning room and lazily told funny stories to make her laugh. Nor was he the easily rich gentleman who didn't dirty his hands at the work that made his money. She sat upright. He's all grown-up, she thought.

She remembered the November afternoon he'd come to her, the autumn after Francie died. What she had said to him about bearing pain. She smiled ruefully. Funny how well her advice had worked for him. How arrogant she had been then! Secure in her good marriage to Raoul, confident in Beau's love—sure that the comfortable world she had been born into would continue forever.

She looked at her watch and got up. Better head back, be on hand to help Luella with supper. Anyone would think she and Raoul were well-off, still having two servants. But the situation was more like those so familiar in Dickens—no matter how poor you were, there was always someone poorer who was glad of a little bit of money and three meals a day.

"It's the governor on the telephone," Beau's secretary said, sticking her head in the half-open door.

"All right," Beau said. He had little doubt what Long wanted. Ever since he had announced that he would run for the U.S. Senate, even before his first term as governor was over, Beau had waited for the call to arms.

The familiar booming voice filled his ears. "You been keeping up with me in the papers, Langlinais?" Long said. He laughed, a short, challenging bark. "Because you sure as hell have been scarce around Baton Rouge."

Beau picked up a pencil and began drawing aimlessly on the legal pad in front of him. "I don't have business in Baton Rouge," he said carefully. "I do have a lot of it here, and out west. Keeps me running, I can tell you."

"Man that busy, he forgets to keep up with his old friends. They might get to feeling . . . well, a little put out. You know what I mean, Beau?"

"Maybe the friends should remember that a man has a right to tend to his own business before he noses around theirs," Beau said. The steadiness of his voice pleased him. If Long was expecting the easy acquiescence of two years ago, he had a surprise coming. Beau almost blushed to remember his eager pursuit of borrowed power. Well, things were a little more even now, and Long would have to do a little horse-trading before Beau decided to take time away from the empire he was building to help Long expand his.

"My business is your business," Long said. "Or don't you think the children of St. Martin Parish learn better when they all have books? And how about the roads? Damn it, my road-construction program's providing thousands of jobs and getting us out of the mud besides—listen, Beau, I don't want to hear this stuff about my business and your business."

"Well," Beau said, his voice still even, "I guess it's in the nature of politics that sometimes you have to hear stuff you'd rather not." He let the pause from the other end go on just long enough, then said, "Look, Huey, I'm not saying you aren't doing a lot of good. I'm saying that you can't just call me up whenever you need something and expect me to drop everything else and rush out to do it for you." He took a breath. "Looks like you'd realize the value of having some support from independent quarters."

"I'll tell you what the point is. The only point. The people who've had the power in this state haven't done one damn thing to take care of the poor—haven't done that good a job taking care of people who aren't poor but just kind of struggle along in the middle. The rich don't need taking care of, Beau. They never have and they never will. Their money buys security. All I'm trying to do is even up the game a little. Now, you going to play or not?"

"Work in your senate campaign?"

"That's right."

"Tell me something, Huey. How are you going to manage entering the Senate—if you're elected—without leaving the governor's seat to Lieutenant Governor Paul Cyr? Or are you going to let him have it?"

"Let that double-crossing, lying so-and-so rule this state? Hell, no, I won't. Listen, Beau, it's simple. I get elected this fall. But I can't take my seat until December of thirty-one—by which time Congress will have adjourned until January of thirty-two. I'll finish my gubernatorial term in May—so I miss four months in Washington." Long laughed. "You think I can't get things done whether I'm there in person or not?"

"So you won't obey the law," Beau said.

"What law is that?"

"That a man can't hold two public offices at the same time."

"Oh, that law," Long said, and laughed again. "Beau, don't get yourself so bogged down in legal technicalities you lose sight of the goal."

"I seem to have done just that," Beau said. "Suppose you remind me just what the goal is."

"Why, Beau. To take my message to the people of this country. To help them see that they don't have to live in darkness and despair. To give them hope."

"And if other people don't quite receive your message in the same way, they can be bought or . . . persuaded?"

"That sounds mighty like an insult, Beau."

Beau stared out into the street. He could see the road that brought politicians and peddlers, salesmen and showmen, to this quiet corner of the world. He thought of the kind of power Huey P. Long held. And realized, for the first time, why Claude left the place and people he loved above all else to keep that power from harming both.

"I asked a question," Beau said. "You're the one said it was an insult."

Time beat away at the silence between them. Then Long said, "Sounds like you are pretty busy, Langlinais. Got a whole lot of important things on your agenda. Well, I understand priorities, Beau. Better than anyone else you deal with, probably. You let me know when I'm back at the top of your list, you hear?" Long laughed, and Beau felt a shiver down his spine. Not apprehension, not that. What? A rabbit running over his grave. Yes, that described it exactly. Then, just before he slammed the receiver down, Long barked: "And I'll let you know if you're even back on mine."

33

Dr. Jaubert motioned to Beau and Alice Langlinais to follow him, and tiptoed out of the twins' bedroom into the hall, pulling the door almost shut behind him. He stood for a moment staring at the floor as though something written there would help him phrase what he had to say. Then he reached out his hand and clasped Beau's shoulder. "It's poliomyelitis, Beau—infantile paralysis."

"No!" Alice said. "But how in the world—she's been nowhere. Are you sure?" Then she looked suddenly terrified. "Émilie—if Gennie is sick—isn't it contagious?"

"Yes," Dr. Jaubert said. "Of course it is." He sighed. "Look, I'm plumb tuckered. I was up helping a new baby decide to make its appearance on Bastille Day, and I need a cup of coffee. Could we talk over that?"

They went down the stairs slowly. Beau disappeared to give Becca orders for coffee and sandwiches; Alice settled the doctor at the dining-room table. Sitting opposite him, her head supported by her hands, she asked, "How bad is it?"

"Hard to say, Alice." He saw Beau coming in through the pantry door. "Wait, let Beau hear this, too."

They wanted far more information than Jaubert had. It did not seem enough to know that this was a disease that began like a summer cold but that quickly attacked the central nervous system, causing paralysis, muscle atrophy, and—if the muscles operating the respiratory system were affected—death.

"But it isn't always that bad, is it?" Alice took the coffee Becca handed her, sipped automatically, and then put the cup down. "Gennie doesn't have to be paralyzed—" Her head bent forward and she began to cry.

"Mama . . ." Beau leaned over her, holding her against

him. Tears were pouring down his face. He wanted to scream to heaven, to beat his chest with his fists. The memory of Gennie's fevered face, the small, slender hands clutching the sheet, the moans that broke the rhythm of her heavy breathing, had nearly broken his heart.

"What can we do?" he said to Dr. Jaubert.

"Damn little, Beau." Jaubert took a sandwich. His hands were shaking with fatigue, his shoulders slumped, bent under the weight of his practice. "Get a nurse in. This illness will wear Becca and Susu and your mother down to nubs if they don't get some help. Then . . . wait and see."

"See what?" Beau said.

Dr. Jaubert pushed his eyeglasses back on the top of his head and rubbed his eyes. "First we see how bad she gets. Then, when the illness is past, we see what we've got."

"If she's paralyzed, you mean," Alice said.

"Yes," he said. He was trying to control his own feelings, trying to make himself numb so that he would not think of Gennie as the little girl he had birthed and watched over and delighted in for almost nine years.

"You're dead on your feet," Beau said finally. "Go into my study and snatch a nap on the couch, why don't you? I'll call you in an hour."

"Think I will, Beau. Getting too old for this, I'll tell you." He went down the hall, and Beau heard the study door close behind him.

"Mama?"

"I'm all right," Alice replied softly. She reached out her hand and Beau searched his pockets, then gave her his big linen handkerchief. "Gennie's not going to want a nurse, Beau. Sick as she is, she needs people she knows."

"The nurse can help," Beau said. "It won't help matters if you and Becca and Susu get sick too." He stood up and rubbed his neck. It had hurt since Gennie's light cold had become much, much worse, and her temperature had climbed to the top of the thermometer. "I'm going to send Émilie and Skye out to the farm," he said. "Get them away from the germs."

"Yes," Alice said. She got up and began putting cups and plates on the tray Becca had left. "Beau . . . does Louise have any idea how ill Gennie is?"

"I don't know," Beau said. "I told her—tried to, anyway. She . . . she just smiled the way she does and said she'd pray."

"There are times when I really get mighty tired of Louise," Alice said.

"You think I don't?"

"Beau, why don't you get a divorce and get it over with?" Alice said. The words burst into the room, exploding through their tension and fatigue.

"A divorce? Come on, Mama. Think what you're saying."

"I hate to see you tied to that woman. I . . . I hate her."

He went to her and held her again, rocking her against him. He knew she was lashing out at Louise because she couldn't lash out at anything else, and if she did not find some target for her anger, she would not be able to go calmly back to Gennie, rub the aching limbs and back, put cool cloths on the hot skin.

"It's not as bad as it used to be, Mama. She's gotten calmer, and I . . . well, I've gotten busier. I . . . I don't seem to notice it as much."

"Still," Alice said, pulling away and straightening her collar in the mirror over the sideboard. "Still, Gennie could certainly use her mother right now."

But for the next week, Gennie did not know who was with her, or where she was. Locked in the delirium of a high fever, her muscles aching, she moved endlessly over the bed, twisting, turning, as though in an effort to escape the illness that besieged her. The sheets were changed almost hourly to keep them dry, and Beau, sitting with her one afternoon, seeing how her skin had lost its summer tan, its healthy glow, made himself realize that there was every possibility that she would not make it. When Alice came to relieve him, he went to Louise's room.

Louise was sitting in the window, sewing yet another of the mysterious garments she made and mailed off to unknown recipients. She seemed almost placid. She had never told him what had occurred when she made her long visit to Los Angeles to the Angelus Temple, but he wondered sometimes if perhaps in putting herself in Aimee Semple McPherson's hands, her faith in the woman's power had not itself done Louise good. He did not really believe she would rouse herself and come to be a mother to Gennie, but he somehow needed to keep trying to get through to her, for all of their sakes.

"Gennie's much worse, Louise," he said.

She looked up. "Oh, Beau, I'm so sorry!" Her words spoke concern, but her voice was detached—and how could it be anything else, for a little girl she hardly knew? "How awful, I must pray harder," she said.

"Yes," he said. He waited for anger to overtake him, the old familiar anger at the arrogance with which Louise left to others all the duties and responsibilities of life while she stayed on that shining road to heaven all by herself. But it did not come. He felt only a great sadness for all the hours of loneliness each of them suffered—the children without a mother, himself without a wife, and Louise without any of them. "Please do, Louise."

He called Father Adrian to ask for prayers for Gennie. "It's not . . . I'm not trying to bargain with God, you can't do that. But if Gennie . . . if Gennie—"

"Hush," Father Adrian said. "If God needed to be paid for his mercy, we could not possibly afford it. Don't worry, Beau. Her name will be in every prayer, and her intentions offered at every Mass. And with your permission, I will publicly ask everyone at the Mass celebrating the first anniversary of the canning operation to pray with me for her."

"Lord, I'd forgotten all about that. Is that this week?"

"Tomorrow," Father Adrian said. "You've got enough on your plate. We can handle it."

"You'll have to," Beau said. "I can't think of a thing on earth that would make me leave Gennie."

The crisis came in the early hours of the morning; Beau called Alice and Claude, and they watched together while Dr. Jaubert worked with Gennie, wrapping her in wet sheets, doing everything possible to break the fever that now threatened her life. Beau was kneeling by her bed when she began to shake, her body rocking from side to side, her hands clutching in front of her empty face. I can't stand it, he thought. The pain that gripped his own heart was more intense than any he had ever felt. Never had he been so torn, not even when he had lost Caroline. He tried to hold Gennie, comfort her, but she pulled away, her body fighting him. Then her back arched, drawn up as though by a string that ran from the top of her head to her toes. She rose above the bed in that dreadful arc, was held in that rigid pose for a long, terrible minute, and then fell back against the pillows, finally and awfully still.

He did cry, then. All the tears he had held back, all the grief. Hearing him, Alice and Claude roused, and came to the bed. He heard Alice gasp, then heard her sobs. Dr. Jaubert pushed past them and lifted Gennie's wrist, then felt her face. He turned and put both arms around Beau. "Beau. It's all right. The fever's broken. She's going to live."

The dawn stole up silently from the marshland, creeping gently over the sleeping town, touching the windows of the Langlinais house. The air was still, as though to muffle the birdsong and the sounds of morning while the vigilants slept. It was late afternoon before Beau woke up; bathed, shaved, and dressed, he went to see his little daughter. She was alive! She would live!

His mother met him at the door, her face still haggard. "Beau . . . she's paralyzed. Dr. Jaubert says she may never walk again."

Beau had been in daily telephone communication with Caroline since the onset of Gennie's illness. He had refused to allow her to come help them. "If you carried these germs back to your own children, I'd never forgive myself," he'd said. But her encouragement, her concern, her love for all of them had buoyed him during those dark days. Listening to her steady voice, he could believe that Gennie would be well and strong again.

When he called Caroline to tell her of the paralysis, he was almost unable to get the words out. He heard a shocked gasp, then her voice, overflowing with sorrow and compassion. "I'm coming right now, Beau. I'll be with you before you know it—and don't tell me not to, nothing on earth could stop me."

He didn't want to stop her. He put down the receiver and paced the floor of his study, staring out at the bright summer sky. Caroline could not make Gennie whole again, but she would make him whole. So that he would have the strength his daughter would need the rest of her life. He lowered himself into his big chair, buried his face in his hands, and allowed himself to weep. Gennie paralyzed! Confined to crutches, a wheelchair. He pounded the arm of the chair. Damn it, he would take her the world over, if he had to. Somewhere there had to be someone who could heal her. He'd set to work on it first thing in the morning. He stood and looked upward, toward the room where Gennie lay. You'll walk again, he vowed. You have to.

He raced to the door when the doorbell rang. Flinging it

open, he swept Caroline into his arms. "I've never been so glad to see anyone in my life!" he said.

"Oh, Beau, I've been with you in spirit this whole awful time, you know I have." Then she pulled away and moved past him into the hall. She seemed charged with tense energy, excited. "Beau, has Dr. Jaubert begun using Sister Kenny's method on Gennie?"

He stared at her. It was as if she had spoken in a language he didn't understand. "What do you mean?"

"She's an Australian nurse. She's developed a treatment for . . . for paralysis. The paralysis caused by polio."

He gripped her shoulders, seized now by the same excitement that filled her. "What? What's that you're saying, Caroline?"

"You apply hot compresses to the affected muscles and exercise them in certain patterns. It . . . she's had some good results, Beau."

"How do you know about this?"

"I . . . I've been ransacking Raoul's medical journals. Reading everything I could get my hands on about polio." Her hand went to her hair, automatically pushing back the wave that fell over her face. "Then I called the Tulane medical-school library and had them send me more material." She opened her purse and pulled out a sheaf of papers. "I typed up the procedure, Beau. There's no guarantee, of course—but it can't hurt to try."

He clutched the papers she handed him and began to read, his eyes racing over the pages. When he had finished, he gave her a desperate, hopeful look. "If this works, Caroline . . . I won't ever be out of your debt."

Her face flushed with a gentle color that seemed to erase the fatigue that still weighted her. "If it works, Beau, it's one small installment for me. Mama's attorney let slip you'd bought all those things from her old house."

"Dammit," he said. "Is there no one in the world who can keep his mouth shut?"

"Her rooms in our house are furnished with her things now," Caroline said. "And I assure you, it gave me the greatest pleasure to tell Mama to whom she owed them."

"I didn't do it for her," Beau said. Their eyes met, and he felt his heart settle back into place. Caroline was here. No, there were no miracles—but there now was hope, and compared to his earlier despair, that was miracle enough.

"I want to help Gennie," Caroline said. "I discussed the therapy with a nurse who has used this method. She was very helpful. If I did some of it, and could teach you all to do it, too . . ."

"Anything you say," Beau said. "Let's go up to Gennie right now. Can we start today?"

Gennie was sitting up in bed, propped on pillows so embroidered and beribboned that Caroline exclaimed, kissing her sallow cheek, "You look like a French pastry, all ruffles and cream!"

"Miss Caroline's come to help us, Gennie," Beau said. No one knew if Gennie understood that her legs were paralyzed. They had told her simply that she must stay in bed awhile longer to overcome the weakness the fever had left. If she realized why there was always someone there to move her, she had not yet said anything. When Beau had asked Dr. Jaubert if she understood that she couldn't walk, Jaubert had replied, "She's been very, very ill. She's just a little girl, and quite worn out. I think it will be some time before she even thinks about asking when she will be well." And that, Beau had thought grimly, will be the final turn of the screw.

"How?" Gennie asked. Her eyes, always large like her grandmother's, stood out from her thin white face like two huge gray jewels.

"You need to build up your strength," Caroline said briskly. "Your legs have gotten all lazy, haven't they?"

"Yes," Gennie said, and looked quickly at the storybook in her lap.

Caroline glanced at Beau, and nodded. She knows, he thought. She knows and she hasn't said anything, has been bearing it all alone. His hands clenched with the effort of holding back his tears. That brave little girl—dammit, he'd make her well if it took every last dime he had. It wasn't right, it wasn't fair. His hands relaxed. No, it wasn't fair. But he couldn't allow self-pity to intrude upon the difficult task of making Gennie well.

"I'm not saying we can get your legs over being lazy all at once," Caroline said. She leaned forward and hugged Gennie, pulling the child against her shoulder. "And, Gennie. They're not going to like being made to work. They may fuss about it. And hurt you."

Gennie moved her head so that she could see Caroline's face. "But you said it would help."

"I think so, darling." There were tears in Caroline's eyes, and Beau felt his own anguish ease in the warmth of her compassion.

Gennie's arms came around Caroline's neck. "If you will be here, I can stand it," she said.

"But, Gennie," Beau said, "Miss Caroline has a family of her own. She can't come here every day."

"Oh, yes, I can," Caroline said. Her chin tilted upward in the old way, and she looked at Beau, blue eyes sparkling with the old confidence. "Don't be telling me I can't, Beau Langlinais."

For the first time in weeks, he heard himself laughing. "Lord, Caroline, I've got enough trouble without crossing you."

"Good," she said. "Now, let's get started."

In the coming days and weeks, everyone had to lend a hand: Susu and Becca, Alice, Caroline, Claude, and Beau. The women stood it better than the men; the first time Claude took his turn at manipulating the little legs, and had watched Gennie grip her doll tightly and bite her lips to keep from crying out, he had to force himself to keep on. Alice told Beau later that Claude had gone out to the farm and chopped wood like a madman until she and Geneviève thought he'd have apoplexy.

Caroline, more like her old self for the first time since her father died, moved her family, except for Raoul, who couldn't leave his patients, out to Beau Chêne until school started. "I can kill a whole flock of birds with one stone," she told Alice. "It's easier to be close by at Beau Chêne, and Luella and I can get that house straight at last."

Skye and Émilie soon discovered the old path to Beau Chêne, and before the summer was over, bare feet had once again worn it smooth. By early September, Gennie was able to stand up all by herself. She was still weak, but the muscles gradually gained strength, and they all believed that Gennie would walk again. Caroline's program seemed to be doing the trick; heartened, Beau and Alice promised to keep faithfully to the routine even after Caroline moved back to Lafayette and could no longer attend Gennie daily.

"There's no way I can ever repay you," Beau said to Caroline as he helped her pack her car for the trip home.

"Isn't it nice you don't have to?" she said, smiling up at him. "Oh, Beau, don't you remember what you said to me, just a little before Gennie got sick? How you do everything you can for me, feel . . . well, committed to doing just that?" She put her hand on his and looked up at him, her love etched in every inch of her face. "Don't you know I feel the same way, Beau?"

He knew then that no matter what, he could warm the cold and empty places in his life with the knowledge that in all the important things, they had never, never failed each other—and never would.

"I don't work miracles, though," he said.

"I haven't yet," Caroline said.

But eventually the treatment did effect what seemed miraculous: on her ninth birthday, Gennie could walk the length of the upper hall. By Christmas, she could manage the stairs. And when the second school term started in January 1931, she was back at her desk, a small limp in her right leg the last sign of her illness. Émilie hovered over her protectively, staying in with her at recess to help her catch up on her work. Most vestiges of the crisis polio had wrought on the family had finally passed, and the Langlinaises appeared able at last to settle down, gratefully, to a dull, uneventful winter. As Alice summed it up, "We would all welcome a long stretch of tedium just about now and would probably not mind at all finding ourselves bored to death." But they were to have no such surcease from crisis. One cold February morning, Beau came back to his office from a trial in Lafayette to find his secretary frantic. "Mr. Langlinais, your mother called—your wife's in a coma. The ambulance has just taken her to the hospital."

Beau's face went white with shock. "Louise?" He stood motionless, his hat still on his head, his overcoat still buttoned, seemingly unable to assimilate what she had said.

"Mr. Langlinais? Are you all right? They need you at the hospital. Dr. Jaubert is waiting for you."

Beau shook his head, trying to clear his thoughts. Louise? Ill? He had gotten so accustomed to that wraithlike figure, the silence from her end of the house— Then his mind began to function again.

"I don't know when I'll be back," he said, heading toward the door. "But there's something you can do for me."

"Anything!" she said.

"Go over to the rectory and ask Father Adrian to come to the hospital as soon as he can. I . . . when she wakes, I think Mrs. Langlinais will want to see him."

He refused to allow himself to imagine Louise not waking up. He must keep clear of that dark thought like a man desperately avoiding an abyss; he was convinced such thoughts signaled a very unchristian desire.

"Damned if it doesn't look like starvation," Dr. Jaubert said when Beau reached the hospital. "Does that make any sense to you?"

Louise's body was so wasted that it barely made a shape under the heavy blankets that covered her. Her hair had no luster; it hung around her face like wisps of straw that had been hastily stuck on either side of a wax face to make it look more finished. He could not remember ever seeing a human form so bereft of substance, as though all hold on life had been abandoned.

"I don't know," he said. He felt that he should go to the side of the bed, take the claw that protruded from the covers. He could not. He sank into a chair, leaned back. "She stopped eating with the family years ago. Becca or Susu brought her trays, but she liked to fix her own food. She hardly ever ate what they sent."

"What did she eat?"

Beau lifted a hand; he barely had the strength to make the gesture, as though the terrible emptiness of Louise's body had entered his. "She used to slip down to the kitchen when no one else was there. I'd hear her sometimes, late at night, when we were all in bed. And she kept things in her room. She had a little chafing dish she'd fix eggs in, things like that." He stared at Dr. Jaubert. "Dammit, Paul, she had a whole pantry stuffed with food. If she didn't want to eat it, I could hardly hold her down and put it down her throat." The anger in his voice was fueled by his own sense of guilt. Was there something he could have done? "She was sick. Mentally ill. But I thought . . . I thought she'd be as well off at home as at a hospital. And she refused to see any doctors."

"She wouldn't have eaten in a hospital, either, Beau," Jaubert said. He put a hand on Beau's shoulder and looked at him compassionately. "I know Louise. They might have force-fed her, but ultimately . . ." He went back to the bed and peered down at Louise. "She fasted a lot, didn't she?"

"That was all part of the religion she'd made up for herself," Beau said. "When Gennie walked again, Louise told me she had worked a miracle—she had healed Gennie with prayers and fasting." He did not think he could ever move from his chair. He did not believe he would ever have the energy to do anything, ever again. "I was so glad Gennie was all right again, I didn't give a thought to Louise."

"Beau, listen to me. What Louise did, she did to herself. I don't want you taking any of the blame, you hear me?"

The smile Beau gave Dr. Jaubert seemed more ghastly than the face of the woman on the bed. "Haven't you learned yet, Paul, that if there is one thing we can't take away from people, it is what they choose to blame themselves for?"

"Still," Jaubert said, gripping Beau's hand, "you'll only make things worse for your children if you blame yourself." He leaned closer, looked deep into Beau's eyes. "Beau," he said gently, "you're all they have. You have to be whole, man."

The thought of his children made every other thought fly. He looked at Louise. "Should they come see her, Paul?"

"Not as long as she's in this state," Jaubert said. "What purpose would be served to have them remember their mother like that?" He gestured to the shape on the bed. "She probably won't come out of that coma, Beau. As for how long she'll hang on like that . . ."

It had been put into words, then. Louise was going to die. Beau said the words out loud, almost wonderingly, as though the possibility had not occurred to him. "You're saying she won't . . . live."

"I see no possibility of her living, Beau," Jaubert said. He turned his head quickly. He did not want to see the expression on Beau Langlinais' face. Poor devil. If the only release from the prison you lived in was gained by the death of another human being—your wife, the mother of your children—what a battle you must fight!

"What . . . what should I tell the children, Paul?"

Jaubert shrugged. "What do we ever tell children about death? How do you explain it to children the ages of yours?" He shrugged again. "They all go to catechism classes, Beau. Tell them their mother is going to heaven, to live with God." He smiled. "It's a thought that comforts me, Beau. When I think of those I have lost."

"Yes," Beau said. But what strange God is she going to? he thought, remembering her harsh indictments, her fervent beliefs. He heard voices in the hall and stepped outside to find Father Adrian, his face heavy with concern.

"It sounded serious, Beau," Father Adrian said. "I brought the things to give her the last sacraments." He held up a small black leather case. "Is she—"

"She's not conscious," Beau said. "Paul doesn't think she will be." His voice sounded abrupt, almost hostile. He took a breath and began again. "I'm sorry, Father. I . . . I seem to have trouble keeping my mind straight. All this brings up so much . . ." He bit back the words. So many years of emptiness, he had been going to say. So many years already of loss. "Can you give her the sacraments anyway? Whether she's conscious or not?"

Father Adrian looked at Beau sharply. More than one soul to be healed, he thought. He nodded. "Not communion, of course. But certainly the last anointing." He paused, stared at Beau. "And absolution. Don't worry about Louise's soul. We must have volition to sin. I don't believe Louise has had volition for a long, long time."

"I'm not presumptuous enough to judge other people's souls," Beau said. "I just—you can bury her from the church, then?"

"I'm not presumptuous enough to judge other people's souls, either," Father Adrian said. "Of course Louise will be buried from the church."

Beau went home, sent by Paul Jaubert to take care of the living. "There's nothing you can do here, Beau. The nurse will call you at any sign of change. Your children need you, Beau."

Later, with them clustered around him, Émilie and Gennie on low chairs, Skye sprawled across the hearth, he tried to tell them in words they could understand, about their mother.

"She's tired, and ill. She's ready to go live with God," he said, feeling, even as he spoke, the futility of the words.

Gennie got up and touched his cheek, then leaned closer and kissed him. "Papa, you won't go away, will you?" She burst into tears, threw her arms around his neck, and collapsed against him. "You won't leave us, will you?"

They all began to cry. Something tore at his heart; not just love for his children, but a sudden awareness of just how much they loved and needed him. All the unease and guilt of the last hours fled. How could he doubt that his life had meaning, in the face of his children's love? He gathered them into his arms, whispering reassurance. He would never leave them, he would always be there. Later, he returned to the hospital, and kept watch beside Louise's bed until, in the early hours of the morning, she died. He watched the nurse draw the sheet up over her face and realized that a period in his life had ended. He could not deal with the way he felt; he was much too weary.

The funeral took place the week that would have marked Beau and Louise's tenth wedding anniversary; many of the same people who had gathered in the church in Abbeville on a cold and rainy February day ten years before were gathered again to pay their last respects. The same bad weather repeated itself, and great sheets of rain drenched people as they made their way from their automobiles to the church.

At the graveside, Beau stood under the awning holding Gennie and Émilie on one side, and Skye on the other. The children still seemed confused. They had not known their mother in the sense that most children know their mothers, nor could they grieve for her as though they had. Their grief will come later, Beau thought, when they are older and realize all the years they lost when she was still alive.

Across the gravesite, Caroline stood with Raoul under another awning. The chaos of her own feelings shocked her. Since Beau had phoned to tell her about Louise, one thought had plagued her: Beau would be free. And she was not.

In the days that followed Louise's death, Caroline could not shake that same fact. Beau was free. She could not seem to hold any honorable feelings. She did not regret Louise's death; her sorrow for Beau had nothing to do with the fact that he had lost his wife. She found herself dwelling on his singleness, resenting his wealth and good looks that would attract women to him, fearful of all those years of denial which would make him susceptible to any woman who seemed warm and loving.

How can you be so base! she asked herself one morning when she had set herself the task of emptying the big armoire of household linen and checking each piece for worn places that needing mending. She sat back on her heels, a pillowcase draped over her arms. The rains had not let up. February was hesitating on the brink of March, but there was no change in the biting chill of the cold that swept across the skies, or in the steady, unrelenting rain that beat upon the winter fields. Do you *ever* think of anyone but yourself, Caroline Hamilton? But the sober judge who usually guided her behavior seemed to have fled to sunnier climes, and she had to follow the thoughts that plagued her.

Her needle moved automatically through the heavy linen sheets as she rewove torn edges and whipped lace back into line. But her thoughts were erratic, darting through visions of Beau with other women. Everyone who knew him who had a sister, a niece, a daughter, a friend who was still single, would be after Beau. If he did not have every eligible woman in the southwestern part of the state thrown at him after a decent interval, she would be very much surprised. And why shouldn't he marry again? she demanded of herself. Why shouldn't Beau be happy at last?

She forced her mind to the work in her hands, but that bland routine offered no relief. By the time the armoire was restored, its contents lined in perfect order on its broad shelves, she had made herself face an awful fact. She was jealous. Jealous of every woman who was free to smile at Beau, and flirt with Beau, and dance with Beau. Jealous of every woman who was free to marry Beau.

She must wish for happiness for Beau. She sighed. All very well to say that. She went to the window, pushed aside the curtain and gazed out at the wet, drab lawn. The house behind her was silent. The children had not yet come home from school, and her own mother kept to her rooms, complaining that they were no duller than the rest of the house. Dull. Of course life was dull. No one had money to entertain, and even if they did, to spend money on fancy foods and expensive wines when all over the country people had nothing to eat seemed almost sinful. Even the children were getting involved in their own lives, and had less time to spend with her. Caro's piano lessons, and Raoul and Henri's Scout meetings. Their friends coming home with them after school, filling the house with talk and laughter—but talk and laughter that excluded her. She was, after all, their mother. And mothers, she was learning, while they had a certain role to perform—be there to supply hot cocoa and cookies, help with arithmetic homework—were expected to disappear discreetly when privacy was wanted. She sighed again. If only Raoul needed her. His own life was so filled with caring for others that it never occurred to him that she could not live the same way. He thought she was as giving as he was, thought that her charities and her works of mercy filled her the way his filled him. How could she tell him that what she wanted, what she needed, was a flesh-and-blood man who would sweep her off to bed and make passionate love to her? She made herself laugh. Now you're behaving like a character in a dime novel, she thought. But it was with the greatest difficulty that she kept one thought from following her to bed that night and many, many others. Someday, a woman would be lying beside Beau Langlinais as his wife. And if she were not that woman, she had no one to blame but herself.

34

Beau parked in front of the People's National Bank in New Iberia and looked at his watch. Waiting to drive the twins to a birthday party had taken just long enough to make him late, but if the other directors didn't agree that family came first, he didn't want to know it. "Sorry I'm late," he said, slipping into a chair next to Claude. He surveyed the circle of faces. "What's the matter? Are we about to go under?"

"No, we're all right," Claude said. "The gloom is caused by a little request we just had from our honorable governor." He shoved a piece of paper toward Beau. "Wants us to lend money to the bank in Franklin. Seems they're not as solvent as we are and need some help to stay open."

Beau studied the figure on the paper. "What will this do to our position?"

One of the other directors shrugged. "Well, if none of our big depositors suddenly need a lot of money . . ." He looked around nervously. "It's no way to do business. On the other hand, if we don't agree, you know damn well the state bank examiner will be here tomorrow to look at our books."

"There's nothing wrong with our books," Beau said.

"No, but I wouldn't count on Long's examiner not finding something," Claude said.

Beau glanced at his father and saw the caution in his eyes. "I'll say what you're thinking, Papa," he said dryly. "Long's ends may be good—this tactic may save that bank, and the deposits of all its customers—but his means, as usual, lack . . . finesse."

"'Finesse' may not be precisely the word I'd have chosen," Claude said. "But, yes, that is what I'm thinking."

"Are we ready to vote?" someone asked.

The vote was unanimous; they really had no other choice. "We ought to feel reassured," one director ventured. "If we're threatened with insolvency, he can rescue us."

"Speaking of rescue, y'all hear what Long did in Lafayette the other day?" The man speaking smiled, admiration all over his face. "He heard that the Guaranty Bank was threatened with a run on deposits that would have flat cleaned it out. Damned if he didn't get hold of his main adviser, Seymour Weiss, and they drove all night to Lafayette, got to the bank around seven in the morning. Pushed their way past a big line of people just waiting for the bank to open to get their money out." The man paused, surveyed the men around him. "Well, sir, Long sat himself down at the president's desk and put Weiss at the cashier's desk and they were ready for business. The doors opened, and the first depositor came in, ready to take out every dollar of the eighteen thousand he had in there. Long explained, as nice as you please, that the state of Louisiana had better than a quarter of a million in that bank, more than all the other deposits in the bank. 'And I was in the bank before you were,' he told the man. He waved a state check right in his face and played his ace. 'I'll agree to leave the state's money in if you'll agree to leave yours.'" The speaker began to laugh. "You have to hand it to Huey. Nobody took money out that day, and by the time they opened up again on Monday, Long had got money from other banks to keep them solvent."

"Well," Claude said, "it's a case of damned if you do and damned if you don't. I don't want to see banks fail. I also don't want to see high-handed tactics win." He shrugged. "But Long holds all the trumps, and I'm too old a bourré player to fight those odds."

"You could swear yourself in as governor, Claude," someone said, and laughed.

"Hell, man, Cyr must have gone plumb crazy, to carry on in that fool way," Claude said disgustedly.

"What else is on our agenda?" Beau said. "I don't want to rush you all, but I've got things to do at home." He knew as well as anyone there what effect the spectacle of Paul Cyr swearing himself in as governor had had across the state. Angered by Long's determination to keep him from serving as governor when Long assumed his seat in the Senate and legally had to vacate the governor's chair, Cyr filed suit in Long's home parish. The suit had said Long was already a U.S. senator, that the governorship was open, and that therefore he, as lieutenant governor, could take the official oath and assume the gubernatorial office. What followed had been so bizarre that Beau still had a difficult time believing it. Long, on hearing the news of Cyr's actions, had the Baton Rouge police surround the mansion to keep Cyr from entering it. Then he had collared his favorite reporter and they had made a mad dash to Baton Rouge from New Orleans, Long himself at the wheel. As the reporter later told it, "We found not just police around the mansion—hell, there was a company of National Guardsmen protecting the whole damn town." Cyr, it was rumored, had raised a private army and would march on the capital. "If he did," the reporter had said, "he'd find machine guns mounted at every road into town."

No one in Louisiana took Cyr's threat seriously. No one in the nation did, either. Public officials from coast to coast were faced with men demanding the oath of office as governor of Louisiana; Long thought the mock swearings-in made a fool of Cyr. Other men thought they made a fool of the state.

The directors dealt with the agenda and adjourned. Beau knew Claude deliberately avoided asking him his opinion of Long nowadays. They walked to their cars in silence. Claude, ready to get into his, turned. "Your mama said to tell you to bring the children for supper tomorrow night. All right?"

"Fine," Beau said. He could, he knew, ignore the question that burned the air between them. He made up his mind and faced Claude. "Look, you probably wonder if my feelings about Long have changed any."

Claude shrugged.

"He did ask me to help him in his Senate campaign," Beau said. "I really didn't know what I was going to do about that. Then Gennie got sick, and I didn't have to." He made himself look into his father's eyes. "I still haven't made myself make a decision about Long, Papa."

"You've had a lot of other things to think about," Claude said.

"But as you so wisely told me once, I can't keep letting crosses get in the way of how I live."

They stood in the stillness of early afternoon. The October sun was warm, summertime warm, and the air drifting up from Bayou Teche a block away was humid. But there was a tension between them. Then Beau's hand gripped Claude's tightly. "I wanted to punch you in the nose when you said that, Papa. But I'm glad you did."

Claude laughed. He felt an easing of the tautness that had held him away from Beau ever since Long's pattern of power had emerged so clearly. "I guess you're learning pretty fast that one of the toughest things about being a parent is letting your children make their own mistakes—and still somehow warning them not to make them."

"Am I ever!" Beau said. "When they were all babies, it was easy. Now?" He shrugged. "Which reminds me, I mustn't be late picking the girls up or I'll have embarrassed them forever."

Claude studied Beau's face. "Of course, it's early days yet—but it would be good if you could find them a mother."

"I'm not ready to even think about that," Beau said.

"But before too long, other people will be thinking for you. When the year of mourning is up, unless I miss my guess, Beau, everyone with an unmarried sister or niece or cousin is going to introduce you to her."

"Oh, God," Beau said. "I hope not."

"You shouldn't be so attractive then," Claude said. "And so rich." He threw his cigarette away, crushed out the fire, and turned to get into his car. "We'll see you all tomorrow, then?"

"Yes," Beau said. Then he laughed. "But if there's an unmarried female anywhere on the premises, I'll bolt."

Driving back to St. Martinville, he thought about what Claude had said. He had been so immersed in his children since Louise died that he had given little thought to his own life. I am only thirty-one, he thought. Certainly not ready to be put out to pasture. What would it be like to go out with a woman, take her to dinner, dance with her? He waited for excitement to rise, to feel a sense of anticipation that life still held promise. But nothing came. I don't know, he thought, pulling up in front of the house where the birthday party was. I'm not old. Maybe I'm just settled.

Listening to the girls chatter on the way home, he felt the same ease come over him that always did when he was with his children. It will take one hell of a woman to disturb this, he thought. At the back of his mind, a face smiled. Caroline. That was one of a kind, no question about that. If it came to that, it would take one hell of a woman to displace her. "Hey," he said, breaking into their talk, "what about seeing if the Hamiltons can come out to the farm for a picnic this weekend? I'll get some pumpkins, you can carve jack-o'-lanterns for Halloween."

"That would be fun," Émilie said. "We can make pumpkin pies. Mama Geneviève taught us to make pastry and she says mine is almost as good as hers."

Maybe in a few months he would have to think about entering the world again, Beau thought. But for now, he was going to stay in this nice, cozy place he had made for his children and enjoy it as much as he could.

"Let's sing," he said. "How about 'Shine On, Harvest Moon'?"

Their voices rose, sailing out of the car windows into the quiet evening air, Beau's the loudest of all.

"It's good, yes," Geneviève said, surveying the rows of jars of food that lined the shelves in the old office. "Plenty food here for the winter. And people with money in their pockets, too. You should be proud, Beau."

Beau stood beside her, wondering why the sight of the concrete results of his idea did not make him feel any more than the quiet satisfaction of a job well done. "It does, I guess," he said. "But . . ." He struggled to put his feeling into words. "It seems such a drop in the bucket, against all the want."

"Mais, Beau, you put the drop in your own bucket. If everyone else would do the same—"

"That's just it, they don't," he said. "And I can't do anything about it."

Geneviève eyed him. "Maybe someday you'll take your papa's seat in the legislature," she said. "Then maybe you could do something, Beau."

"My heavens, Grandmama. You're the last person I'd expect to tell me to go into politics. You know how much Papa hates it."

"But, Beau. You are in politics. I don't just mean the police jury. I mean the power you have. From being a Langlinais. From being rich."

"I know. But I'm not sure I want to do any more than what I do right now, Grandmama." He frowned. "It's not like it's all black and white, you know. No matter what side you take, some of what it says and does will be wrong."

Her laughter shocked him. "But, Beau, of course! So you work with the white and work around the black." She shrugged. "Same as you do in everything else."

Funny, he didn't get angry when Mama Geneviève preached. He pulled her to him. "Grandmama, you should run for governor. I think you understand the way things are a lot better than most of the men running this state."

"Oh, no," she said, laughing up at him. "I don't mind keeping the fires going at home, Beau. But I don't ever want to have to stir the pots. You and your papa do that."

"Papa's not ready to give up," Beau said. "I've got time yet."

But he felt time closing in on him: time when he had to make a stand for or against Long.

The next morning, he got up early and drove out to 'Tit Jacques's place to find Jean. Jean was standing next to a pile of alligator hides, stacking them in a long wooden box. The Catahoula hound at his feet got up and approached Beau, tail held stiffly behind him, ears alert. "It's okay, Tige," Jean said. "That's Mr. Beau, he's a friend." He came toward Beau, a hand held out. "Come drink coffee," he said. "I got a new pot."

They sat on the edge of the wooden porch, legs dangling toward the hard-packed ground. The cypress trees that bounded the clearing where the cabin stood wore their long, slender leaves and their streamers of gray Spanish moss as though they were veils, donned for the dancing breezes that would soon blow through the marshes, bringing cool weather and great flocks of geese and ducks. It was quiet, absolutely still. Marsh birds were silent, rising up from the water on graceful wings. A blue heron stood on one leg in an inlet of water that ran up near the house, staring intently at the shallow water. Its head darted downward, the long bill slicing into the water and emerging with a wriggling fish whose scales glimmered silver-gray in the sunlight. Sipping his coffee from the thick mug, Beau felt the peace of the swamp enter him.

"So, how's it going?" Beau asked.

Jean shrugged. "I sell enough hides, enough skins, to make a pretty good living. 'Tit Jacques, he had a lot of money socked away." Jean grinned at Beau. "Mais, it's a good thing he didn't trust no banks, no. Money's safer here."

"Your sister still in school?"

"She's finished, man. She's teaching over in Golden Meadow. What you think about that?"

"'Tit Jacques would be pleased," Beau said.

"I don't run the booze no more, Mr. Beau," Jean said. "'Tit Jacques, he had a big supply of that, too. I sell it off to his good customers, like you." He shrugged again. "When that's gone—tant pis. It's finished."

Beau leaned back against a post that supported the roof. "The whole thing's just about finished, Jean. Prohibition, I mean. The states are in the process now of ratifying an amendment to repeal it. It'll take a while—but the people seem to think it will pass."

"So it was all for nothing," Jean said.

"What?"

"The killing. The running." He spat into the dark. "Me, I like the swamp. I hunt gators the same, I trap mink the same. Out here, it never changes, you know?"

"I know," Beau said. That was why he was here. He remembered how he and his father used to go into the swamp, taking only a few sandwiches, their guns, and Duke. How good he felt when they returned home, as though the simplicity of that one day had erased all the complexities they'd carried in. "Listen," he said, "I want to go on a gator hunt with you. That all right?"

Jean laughed. "You want to fight something you can see, huh, man? Okay. I go tonight."

"What do I need?" Beau said. The marsh beyond the clearing seemed suddenly darker, as though the night had already cast its shadow.

"A good gun," Jean said. "Thick gloves. I got lights."

Beau worked steadily through the day, taking care of tasks he had put off for weeks as too tedious and too exacting for his mood. Revising the will of a client, reviewing a contract between Langlinais Motors and Ford, looking over the terms of a trust. He could make himself stick to the dry documents, because while he worked, he enjoyed the anticipation rising in him, the itch of his fingers for the stock of his rifle, the tautness of his muscles as they prepared for the night ahead.

"I'm going gator hunting," he told Becca after the children had gone up to bed. "I won't be home until dawn. Don't worry about me."

"Lordy, Mr. Beau, what you want to go after those ugly old things for?" Becca said. "Now all we need is for one of them things to bite a hunk out of you. Fine mess that would be."

"I guess I can take care of myself," Beau said.

"Humph," Becca said. "You mens is all alike. When you don't like the place the good Lord put you, you wiggles out into another one. Ain't never been nobody won a fight with a mad gator, Mr. Beau, not without bringing home a heap of trouble."

"I'll be in a boat," Beau said. "Say, Becca, how about packing up a couple of sandwiches?" He smiled and patted her shoulder. "And put some of that cake in, give me strength to fight that gator."

"Like little boys," he heard her muttering as she went toward the kitchen. "Give mens a swamp and a gun and they's just like little boys."

Jean was baiting the hooks when Beau arrived at the cabin, hanging hunks of rotting liver on the heavy pieces of iron. Beau squatted beside him, his hands working quickly to tie the hooks on the strong lines they would set out throughout the swamp. The flatboat rocked gently at the edge of the inlet, her twenty-foot length disappearing in the dark. The only light came from the kerosene lanterns Jean had set around his work space. They would take these on the boat, shining them across the water until they caught the red glow of a gator's eyes.

"Between what the bait gets and what the light catches, we should do pretty good," Jean said.

By the time the flatboat had glided forward into the cypress-pocked waters of the swamp, Jean standing in the bow and poling it with sure, rhythmic strokes, Beau had forgotten everything but the excitement of the hunt, the exhilaration of the chase. They tied the lines to branches that hung low over the water, or to a spur that protruded from a long-dead cypress stump. When they were floating on one of the many small bayous that ran through the marsh, Jean lit the lantern. Its light glared into the dark, like a moon trapped in one of Jean's snares. A sudden beat of wings told them they had startled a nesting bird; Beau felt the brush of its passing against his cheek.

And then two red circles glowed directly ahead of them, sparks of witch's fire in the night.

"There's one now," Jean said. "You want him, Mr. Beau? Aim right behind his eyes."

Beau stood and aimed carefully, sighting along the rifle until it was lined up directly between the gator's eyes. But as he pulled the trigger, the lantern swerved, and the gator was released from the band of light that held it. The bullet careened off the trunk of a tree, splintering the soft bark. "Damn," Jean said. "My pole hit a trunk under the water. We'll circle around and try him again."

There was no moon, or else its rays could not penetrate the tent of thick-woven leaves that stretched across the swamp for mile after mile, making a space of secrets and mystery that no man entered without reason. An owl hooted from a tree branch high above their heads, and on a small island some yards away, the eyes of two deer glowed in the lantern light. A fish leapt directly in front of the boat, its body hanging in the air for one silver second before it fell back into the water. All time had stopped; there was no movement, only the night's eyes, the feel of steel in Beau's hand. Suddenly the water exploded with the quick lashing of the alligator's tail.

"Damn, Mr. Beau, that thing's twelve feet long if he's an inch," Jean said. "Next bullet better get him; I don't want him after this boat."

The lantern held steady on the red eyes, and Beau aimed again. The bullet hit the gator right behind the eyes; the alligator's scaly head twisted as though to get away from a branch that poked at it from the bank. "Shoot again," Jean said. "Damn, shoot again."

Beau's fingers were already firing off another shot, and the second, too, entered the thrashing head. The beast began to move forward, tail churning the water behind it. "That tail, he's going to keep making trouble long time after the brain dies," Jean said. "We need to chop through the spine to make it still." He leaned over and picked up a hatchet, then eased the flatboat nearer to the dying reptile. The eyes were hooded now, making two blank spaces in the center of the great head. The jaws opened and its tongue lolled out of one side, aimlessly moving over the sides of the mouth. "You hold the boat steady, I'm going to get in and hit him," Jean said. His heavy boots came up well over his knees and they were thick against the curious sampling of water moccasins or rattlesnakes. He jumped into the shallow water. But the gator's tail could still lash Jean backward, putting him squarely in the path of its still-dangerous jaws. Beau held out a hand to stop him.

"Jean, wait! Let's just let him die. We can come back later."

Jean shot a disdainful glance at him. "Mais, Mr. Beau. And have that tail telling every gator in the swamp to go dig in the mud and be still? No, I kill him good!"

He worked his way carefully around the side of the gator's head, calculating when he could get close enough to the spine to sever it. There was one moment when the light caught them, the gator and Jean, silhouetted them against the dark trees and strings of moss. Jean, small, wiry, the hatchet lifted in one arm. The gator, head half-turned, raised its tail for one more terrible slap against the water. Then the hatchet fell and was buried in the scales behind the gator's head. Again Jean raised the hatchet and brought it down. And again. At last the tail was still.

"Now we haul him in," Jean said. He was not even breathing hard as he clambered back in the boat and stationed himself and Beau so they could get leverage on the gator. When at last it lay in the bottom of the boat, Jean surveyed its length happily. "Over twelve feet, Mr. Beau. What you think, Langlinais Fur and Hide pay a bonus on this one?"

"They damn well better," Beau said. He poked at the dead gator with the toe of his boot. "Might just buy it myself."

"Hell of a lot of shoes and ladies' purses in that hide," Jean said. He was poling along the bait lines, where shadowy figures lurked, the hooks sunk deep into their throats. Jean cast a look at Beau. "Mr. Beau. You started looking for a lady to put shoes on yet?"

"No," Beau said. He laughed. "But I tell you what, Jean. I think maybe this gator hunt is as good practice for taking on the ladies as anything I know."

Jean laughed back. The air between them was clear, two workmen making a good night of it. He held out a hand-rolled cigarette to Beau. "Thing is, Mr. Beau, a gator lashes at you, you chop him up. A lady . . ." He shrugged. "They're not always so easy."

Beau laughed again. He felt good. Hell, he felt better than he had in years. "True. But I'm beginning to think the game's worth it, you know?"

Jean's laughter joined his own, soaring above the dark trees to meet the faint light in the sky that announced a new morn. "That's good, Mr. Beau," Jean said. "Because I tell you the truth—if you don't go looking for your own lady, plenty of people are going to look for you."

"That's exactly what my papa says," Beau said. And then the feeling of excitement did come, the promise that life still held completeness, and happiness. "But I think, Jean, I might just steal the march on 'em."

When Beau got home the next morning, Becca said, "Well, you done beat that debbil out there?"

He sat on the back steps and pulled his mud-crusted boots off, let them drop onto the grass. The sun was hot on his back, he stank of the swamp, the hole in his stomach would need at least a half-dozen eggs and about that many biscuits to fill it, but his blood was racing and his mind was alive. *He* was alive. "Sure did," he said. "I sure as hell did."

The women in the Langlinais family noticed a change in Beau and took heart. "I think he may be ready to go out a little," Alice told Claude's sister, Claudine, when they met for lunch in New Orleans. "The year's not up yet, but . . ." Their eyes met. But why keep up total mourning? "Family parties, things like that. Don't you think?"

"Yes," Claudine said emphatically. "I do. If anyone deserves to have a little fun, it's Beau. We're getting up a party for the LSU-Tulane game. I'll ask him to come along."

"Come on, it'll do you good," Claudine said when she phoned Beau to invite him to sit in their box at the game.

"You wouldn't happen to be including a nice single lady in the party, would you?" he teased.

"Of course we are," Claudine said. "You think I'm asking you just to see the game? Will you come?"

"How will it look?" Beau said. "I'm still in mourning—"

"You're not in suttee," Claudine said crisply. "You can certainly go to a football game with your aunt and uncle—and their other guest."

"All right," he said. "Fine."

It was ridiculous to be nervous, he thought as he drove to Baton Rouge to meet Claudine and Adolphe. But, my God, how long had it been since he had even talked to a strange woman? Thank heaven they would be at a football game, with plenty of action to provide topics for conversation. And with Huey Long's shenanigans on the sidelines to provide plenty of entertainment.

By the time the first quarter was over, Beau was feeling in command of himself and the situation. The woman was pretty, assured, and obviously found Beau attractive. The whole time she asked him questions about the game, her eyes told him something else—that the game on the field was incidental to the one being played in the stands. He felt pulled into those tides that take men off their course, change forever the direction of their lives. You have been away from women too long, he warned himself. Don't let your head get turned by the first one who flirts with you.

A surge of sound in front of them provided a welcome distraction. An LSU player had just caught a pass and was dashing toward the Tulane goal line. Matching him almost step for step along the sidelines was Huey P. Long, his heavy torso encased in a violent purple sweater with a huge L emblazoned on it. A roar went up from the LSU fans. Their man was over, and Huey Long was in the end zone with him, hugging the player and then raising both arms over his head in a victory signal.

"Huey runs that team the way he runs the legislature," Beau said. "I don't know why LSU bothers to have a coach."

"Let's don't talk about old Huey Long," his companion said. "I get so tired of that man taking over everything." She moved a little closer to Beau. "What I really want to talk about is you."

And even though he recognized the gambit, knew he was deliberately being drawn out, still, it was pleasant to have a pretty woman smiling at his jokes, watch her eyes widen when he related some exploit. Hell, it was more than pleasant. It was fun.

The football game broke the ice for Beau. The holidays brought parties, parties Alice and Claudine assured Beau he could attend without shocking anyone. He began by going alone. Then hostesses began calling him, asking if he would mind escorting such-and-such a lady. There was safety in numbers, and although Beau Langlinais began to be seen at dinners and dances with a lady on his arm, the identity of the lady changed frequently, and he lulled himself into thinking that he was experiencing now what many men experience in their youth—the carefree pursuit of pleasure with no attendant responsibility.

There was a dinner dance in Lafayette on New Year's Eve; Beau asked Ellen Taylor, who taught Latin at the high school, to go with him. The closer they got to Lafayette, the more his mind focused on one question: was this a party to which the Hamiltons would have been invited? And if so, would they be there? He tried to tell himself he should be no more self-conscious to appear before Caroline with another woman than he was to appear before his relatives and other friends. But when he and Ellen entered the long parlor, and he saw Caroline standing talking to their host, his heart lurched in the old way, and he wanted to take Ellen's arm, turn her around, and march back out into the night.

Then Caroline saw him. Saw them. He saw her eyes go from him to Ellen, then back to Beau. She hesitated one moment, then crossed the room to them, a hand outstretched. She wore blue, a long, rustling taffeta dress with a deep ruffle at the hem and a narrow double ruffle outlining the low V neck. She was the most beautiful woman in the room.

"Beau, how very nice to see you!" she said. She looked questioningly at Ellen.

"Caroline, this is Ellen Taylor. Ellen, Mrs. Raoul Hamilton."

"Caroline, please," Caroline said. Her eyes made a quick sweep over Ellen, from the crown of her black hair to the hem of her rose-colored silk gown. "Isn't this a wonderful party?" She laughed. "Actually Raoul and I go to so few parties that I'm probably not a very good judge." She turned to Ellen. "My husband is a doctor, so his free time is very limited. But thank heaven, two other doctors are on call tonight and tomorrow, and I believe we will actually have the luxury of sleeping late in the morning!"

Beau broke the silence that fell. "Make the most of every minute, then," he said. "The band sounds great—you *will* save me a dance?"

Caroline held out her card. "Here," she said. "Oh, isn't this fun!" Her next partner came up to claim her, and Beau took Ellen into his arms.

"We'll get your dance card when this one is over," he said. "I don't want to waste any of that music."

He found his eyes following Caroline as she circled the room. The light from the chandeliers seemed to fall more brightly on her blond head, her eyes seemed always to be meeting his, and the music each danced to separately seemed still to weave them together in that magic world they had inhabited a long-ago New Year's Eve in his father's home.

He forced his attention back to Ellen. She was pretty, smart, and gentle—she deserved better than a partner who couldn't keep his eyes off someone else. "You're looking wonderful," he said, smiling down at her. "That color becomes you. You should always wear it."

"It's a lovely party," she said. "I'm so glad you asked me to come."

"I'll introduce you around in a minute," he said. "Get your card filled."

There were more dances to be gotten through before he could go to Caroline and say, as though it were only yesterday since they had danced together—"This one is mine, I think."

"What's that song?" she asked, leaning away from him to listen to the tune.

"It's a Cole Porter song," he said. He looked into her eyes. "'You Do Something to Me.'"

"Now, Beau, don't flirt," she said, but her smile gave her away. "I can't help it, when I hear a good band I forget how old and dignified I am and just want to dance and dance forever."

"Which is exactly what you ought to do," he said. Their steps matched perfectly. She followed every dip, every spinning turn, as though they had practiced for hours.

"Remember when we used to dance up and down your living room, learning all the new steps?" he asked.

"Yes," she said softly.

When the music stopped, he let her go reluctantly. "I'm down for one more," he said. "As close as I could get to midnight without taking Raoul's prerogative."

"But that one was taken," she said, looking at the dance card that dangled from a silk cord around her wrist.

"'Was' is the correct word," Beau said. "I pulled rank on the young man who presumed to take a dance your oldest friend wanted."

"Oh, Beau," Caroline said. She was laughing, but there

were tears in her eyes. "It's so wonderful to see you your old self again."

The second dance with Caroline was one he remembered for a long, long time. The band had slipped from jazz into love ballads, slow fox-trots that allowed bodies to blend and heads to bend toward each other. The magic world was solid now, and only he and Caroline moved through it. Just before the music ended, she looked up at him. "Beau, there's something I want to say to you." He saw her look away, give an involuntary glance at Ellen, dancing with the host. Caroline looked back at Beau. "Be happy, Beau. There's no one in the whole world who deserves to be happy more than you do."

He read what she meant to say in her eyes. "You're telling me to marry, is that it?" Before she could answer, he bent closer to her. "You told me that once, Caroline. And I did marry. Not because you told me to, of course. But because it seemed the thing to do." He took a breath. "You said something else that day—that being married at least made time pass." His voice was soft, gentle. "Does it still, Caroline?" Again he did not wait for her answer. "I think it's just life that passes the time. For both of us. We have our children—our duties." He shrugged. "I'm not sure I want anything else."

He saw the sudden blaze of joy in her eyes before she lowered her lids over them. "You will," she said, her face bent so that he could not see her expression. "And of course you should."

But driving home, he could not rid himself of that joy in her eyes, or the memory of how it had felt to be holding her in his arms once again. And he made himself face, in the next few weeks, the consequences of taking the easy way out and escorting Ellen Taylor instead of calling other women he'd met. It's not fair to her, he told himself after leaving her one evening. I've been taking her out almost three months now—she has every right to think I'm getting serious about her. He began to take other women to the dinners that broke the monotony of winter; when he called Ellen one afternoon to ask her to a movie in New Iberia that evening, she had other plans. When she had refused his next two invitations, he knew she had read him correctly. And no matter how much he missed her company, he had to respect a woman who refused to be a pawn in a game. So much respect that he almost decided to court her seriously. No, he told himself angrily one cold March afternoon when the children were all out and he had only his study fire for company. You married one woman loving someone else, and you damn well won't do that again. There seemed one solution—play the field like an established bachelor, and try somehow to get over Caroline Hamilton.

35

The Langlinaises would always remember the spring of 1932 as "the year Mama Geneviève died." She shocked them, literally dropping in her tracks. She had been making a roux for gumbo when the stroke took her: she fell to the kitchen floor, the big spoon still clasped in her hand, and it was only when Susu's daughter Lily, who worked for her, smelled smoke and ran into the room that she was found. Lily had first pulled the cast-iron skillet with the burned roux off the stove, and then she had called Claude, whose grateful prayer all the way out to the farm was that Geneviève had gone swiftly. "There is nothing she would have hated more than a long, lingering illness," he reminded Alice and his sister, Claudine, later.

"No illness would have dared linger around Mama Geneviève," Alice said, hugging him. "She wouldn't have given it house room."

Claudine and Adolphe had arrived from New Orleans the next day, with Hal and his family following. Marie and Étienne, living in Jeanerette, came home with their four children, Marie saying over and over again how glad she was the new baby had arrived in time for Geneviève to see it. It was strange, sitting together in the front parlor of the farm, to think that no matter what happened in their lives, Geneviève would no longer be part of it. "I can't imagine my girls making their Solemn Communions without her making their dresses," Marie said. "I thought she'd go on forever."

"Nothing does," Beau said. "But I know what you mean. Grandmama was so little, but she had such a large life."

They watched the people of the parish come pay their last respects to Geneviève, kneeling on the prie-dieu set before the carved mahogany casket where she lay. Alice had cut dogwood and put it everywhere, in jars at either end of the coffin, and piled in low bowls on the mantels. "I know she used to fuss when I brought things in from the woods," Alice said to Claude, her handkerchief at her eyes, "but I think she'd like this, wouldn't she?"

"Anything you did, she liked, chère," he said.

"Except my pastry," Alice said, laughing. "Remember how she'd pick up one of my biscuits and taste it, telling me, 'Alice, it's good, yes. But maybe you still stir it a little too much after you add the liquid, you think?'" She bent her head and began to cry. "Oh, Claude, I'm going to miss her," she said.

It was hard for Alice to believe that Geneviève was really dead, that never again would she hear that bright, energetic voice in her kitchen or at the other end of the hall. Her own mother had never lived near enough to be part of the small domestic cycles that Geneviève and Alice shared. For so many years they had reported events to one another—a baby's first tooth, the first figs to ripen, the satisfactory outcome of a new crochet pattern. How many years had that cheerful voice, always on the edge of laughter, been a counterpart to the harmony of Alice's days?

As the Langlinaises gathered together in mourning, they were comforted by the outpouring of affection for Geneviève from the people of the town. "Everyone loved your great-grandmother," Beau told his children. "When someone is that loved, we know they have had a beautiful life."

He was proud of the way they behaved, the girls standing on either side of him, Skye next to Gennie, greeting all the people who came, allowing their cheeks to be kissed by old ladies, allowing gentlemen to compliment them. "Mais, even if I didn't see them with you, I'd know they were Langlinaises," an old friend of Geneviève's told Beau. "They have that look, you know?"

"Hard-headedness," Beau said, laughing.

"Pride," the old woman said. "But the right kind, Beau." She looked around the parlor, out into the hall overflowing with people, past them to the porch where more visitors crowded. "You Langlinaises, you've meant a lot to us for a long time, yes." She patted his cheek. "It's good to see you have young ones to carry on, Beau."

"Yes," he said. As she moved away to speak to Claudine, he felt a tension he didn't understand. Something she had said bothered him. Now, what? It was not until they had left the farm and were driving into St. Martinville for the funeral Mass that he realized what it was. She had said it was good Beau had young ones to carry on. But as yet, Claude was still doing all the carrying. None of the real weight of being a Langlinais had yet passed to Beau.

He looked at Claude carefully when they were seated in the church. Of course he looked tired, worn out with grief and all the details of death and burial. But didn't he always look tired? When was the last time he had seen his father really carefree, really having fun? He turned his eyes to his mother. Still pretty, still young-looking. And still forced to give her husband up much of the time to the demands of Louisiana politics. If it weren't for his seat in the House, and the need to be constantly alert for Long's next move, Claude and Alice could go to Europe. Go around the world, if they wanted to. If I ran things, Beau thought. It's not as though anyone has been forcing Papa to run for the House these twenty years.

He turned his attention to Father Adrian, who mounted the pulpit to speak. "There are few people, I think," he said, "who go to meet their God with such a life to show Him. In all the years it was my privilege to know Geneviève Langlinais, I never saw her shirk a duty nor fail a responsibility. The legacy she leaves to her family, and to all of us who count ourselves among her friends, is that example." He hesitated, and Beau saw the effort with which he controlled his voice. "My heart is too full of my own sorrow to speak. I should like to read to you these verses from Chapter Thirty-one of Proverbs, which Jumie Langlinais told me once were the most perfect description of his wife that he had ever heard." The familiar words sounded throughout the church: "'Who can find a virtuous woman? for her price is far above rubies. . . . She will do him good and not evil all the days of her life. . . . She girdeth her loins with strength, and strengtheneth her arms. . . .'"

From all over the church, people began to echo the words. By the time the final verse was reached, Beau's eyes were filled with tears, and his voice was choked, but he lifted it in a promise to his grandmother, and to all the Langlinaises, living and dead, that were his family. "'Give her of the fruit of her hands; and let her own works praise her in the gates.'" He had known for a long time that he had decisions to make. Now he knew he could make them.

Beau waited until Claudine and Adolphe, and Hal and his family had returned to New Orleans, and Marie and Étienne had reluctantly left for Jeanerette before speaking to Claude. He found it difficult to put into words how he felt: though he had long since gotten over his anger and hurt at Claude's contemptuous dismissal of him three years ago, during the impeachment battle, he did not want to risk rejection again. It was one thing to announce that he would like to take over Claude's seat in the House; it was quite another thing to convince Claude that he could safely give it up.

It will be easier out at the farm, he thought. He asked Claude to drive out there with him one Saturday in early May. "To look things over," he had said. "We have to make some decision about the house."

They went through the house together, letting their tour take on the aspect of a journey through their own history—the rocking-chair the first Claude Louis Langlinais had carved for his wife when they finally reached the Attakapas Territory after their exile from Nova Scotia. The bed Claude and Claudine had been born in, and where they had later almost died of diphtheria. The lives of all the Langlinaises seemed to be present, reinforcing Claude and Beau in their conviction to preserve tradition, preserve what generations had built and fought for.

Beau paused before a photograph of Jumie, taken several weeks before he died. He was standing in the yard, his hand on the neck of his favorite black mare. He stared straight at the camera, his eyes steady, his mouth firm, with just the hint of a smile to soften it. "This is as good a place as any to ask you what I really brought you out here to find out, Papa," Beau said. He made himself stand tall, face his father squarely. "I want to run for the legislature, Papa. I want to take over your seat."

Claude's eyes measured Beau's face, then went to his father's face in the photograph. He stared at Jumie for a long time, then turned back to Beau. "What brought that on, son?"

"I've had my field trials," Beau said. "I want a real hunt."

The silence that closed around them came from the empty rooms, the quiet May sunshine, the greening fields. Beau could not define the quality of the silence—was it a barrier? He searched his mind for words to convince Claude that this was right, that he was ready. He felt Claude's hand on his shoulder. "You know what you're getting into?"

"I've got a good idea," Beau said.

"Come here, son," Claude said.

Beau followed him into the dining room and watched while Claude found bourbon and poured two drinks. "Let's sit on the porch and watch the sun go down," Claude said. They sat side by side in the big rockers that lined the porch, smelling the scent of the big sweet olive that bloomed near the porch rail.

"Now tell me," Claude said.

"I have to do this," Beau said. "I've enjoyed what all the Langlinaises before me have done. It's time I went out and did something with it."

"I wouldn't call Gemini Oil, your silver mines, nothing," Claude said. "Pretty impressive achievements for a young man."

"A rich young man," Beau said. "I want to do more than that, Papa." He sipped his drink and stared out at the lawn where Geneviève's favorite climbing rose put out tight new buds. "Grandmama and I had a little talk one day last fall— about drops in the bucket." He saw Claude's questioning look. "I said the canning operation was just a drop in the bucket. She, well, she pointed out there were always bigger buckets." He shifted position, leaned forward in his chair. "Papa, I've got to do this!"

"Plenty other men trying to get to those buckets," Claude said dryly. "You're not going to like a lot of them."

"I don't have to like them," Beau said. "Or even agree with everything men do that are on the same political side as I am. All I have to do is take care of my people." He flushed and turned away. "That sounds grandiose as hell, doesn't it?"

He heard the love in his father's voice and felt Claude's warm hand fall onto his shoulder. "Beau, it doesn't sound grandiose at all. If you didn't feel like that, I'll tell you one thing—when you went to the courthouse to file for election, you'd find me standing in line ahead of you."

He turned in his chair to find his father beside him, arms

open. He rose and felt Claude's arms come around him, felt a swift kiss on each cheek. He knew that he was crying, and that when he could see again, he would see his father crying, too.

"Now, dammit," Claude said, brushing at his eyes with his sleeve, "let's go home and tell your mother to put on her best bib and tucker because we have something to celebrate, sure enough."

"You do," Beau said, laughing. "I'm not so sure I do."

But when he called Caroline the next day, his voice was jubilant. "I've got some good news to tell you. Shall I come over or tell you on the phone?"

"Come over by all means," she said. "It's a quiet Sunday. I'd like nothing better than a visit. Bring the children if they want to come. I'll make ice cream."

Beau piled the children into the car and drove to Lafayette, thinking twelve miles had never seemed so long. "Now, what's your news?" Caroline asked when the six children had settled down in the backyard, Raoul and Henri turning the handle of the freezer while the girls wove clover chains.

"I'm going to run for the legislature," he said. An odd expression glowed in Caroline's eyes. Was it relief?

"Oh, Beau! I thought you were going to tell me you're—" She caught herself. "Congratulations—I guess!"

"What did you think I was going to say?" he asked, catching her hand.

He watched the blush rise in her cheeks, making her look ten years younger. "Nothing. I—"

"You thought I was going to tell you I'm getting married!" he said, and her deepening blush told him he was right.

"Now, Beau, that would be a perfectly natural thing to think," she said crossly. Then she laughed. "I hate blushing—and at my age, too! I can't get away with anything, not even the tiniest fib."

"I'm glad you don't want me to marry," he said.

"I didn't say that," she said. "Now tell me about your campaign. Oh, I wish you were in our district—the League of Women Voters could help you."

"You can still help, if you will," he said.

"But, Beau, you don't seriously expect any opposition, do you? A Langlinais, running in St. Martin?"

"Whether I have any opposition or not, I intend to campaign," Beau said. "I want to hear what the people think. I want them to get to know me—well, a lot of them do know me, of course—but I want them to see me in a different light." He stopped speaking. There were some things he couldn't put into words, even with Caroline. But she understood him.

"You mean that you want them to see that you're ready to represent them, ready to take on their problems, and work for solutions," she said. "You want them to see that you're . . . all grown-up." There were tears in her eyes; he pulled out his handkerchief and gave it to her.

"Caroline?"

"Oh, I'm so sentimental," she said, wiping her eyes vigorously. "I got to thinking of how you'll look up on a platform, your face so serious and earnest. I just want to be able to see you, that's all." She blinked her eyes, then tossed her head as though tossing away a dangerous thought. "I have some good news, too," she said. "Mama's gone to live with a cousin in Virginia. She's a companion, really, getting room and board and a little allowance in return for making a fourth at bridge and helping Cousin Laura with her correspondence. But Mama has a great imagination; she hadn't been up there a week before she elevated herself in her mind to the status of pampered guest." She sighed. "You know Mama."

"Thank God," he said fervently. "It never did seem fair for you to have to put up with her."

"Oh, fair," Caroline said, and shrugged. "Now," she said, her voice full of energy and excitement, "how can I help in your campaign?"

The summer moved faster than any Beau could remember. He did not have an opponent for his father's seat; Long phoned him right after Beau announced and said that he wouldn't waste time putting anyone up against him. If the man who could beat a Langlinais existed, Long didn't know him.

"Now, Beau," Long said, his voice getting the old confident tone, "you going to be for me or against me when you get to Baton Rouge?"

"Reckon I'll be like my papa," Beau said. "He supported you when you could and didn't when you couldn't. You never seemed to have a problem with that."

"He was there first," Long said. "He'd earned his spurs in

the legislature long before I ever tossed my hat in a ring. That makes a difference, Beau."

"I'll earn my spurs, Huey," Beau said. "Don't worry about that."

Long laughed. "You just bet you will, Beau," he said. "And I'll be watching you do it."

But as Beau had told Caroline, he would still campaign, not to defeat an opponent, but to establish a rapport with the people of his district. And so the long, sultry evenings of July found him in small village squares, or standing on courthouse steps, or eating barbecue at some local official's camp, telling one group after the other where he thought their state was going, and what he intended to do about it.

"The people have got to understand that you can have progress without giving up democracy," he told Caroline one evening.

"Are you out-and-out opposing Long, Beau?"

"Not necessarily. But it's the kind of power he represents they need to guard against. That and their laissez-faire attitude toward it. I try to tell them that even the fact that I'm not opposed in the election isn't good—that ideally, there should be several candidates to give them a real choice." Helplessly he began to laugh. "It doesn't seem to sink in. One old man told me just yesterday that I should be glad I was in a one-horse race—there was no doubt who would win."

"It takes time to change people, Beau," she said. She loved having a reason to see him again, loved writing press releases and helping set up meetings with groups around the district. Listening to his enthusiasm, she told him that he behaved as though he were the first man to discover politics and to be infected with its fever. "Which is so typical of you," she said. "Have you ever done anything less than whole-hog?"

"No," he said, his gray eyes suddenly serious. "Everything I've ever loved has been whole-hog."

She picked up a sheaf of papers and handed them to him, keeping her eyes away from his. "Read these over, will you? If they're all right, I'll send them out."

Toward the end of the summer, Caroline had to cut back on her work for Beau's campaign. Raoul had developed a bad summer cold, and he had finally succumbed to her insistence that he stay home in bed. "I need to devote myself to him for a while," she said. "It's almost the end of the campaign, you don't really need me?"

"I always need you," he said. "But of course it's all right. Your place is with Raoul." He hung up, the words echoing in his mind. Her place was with Raoul. And no matter how much he pretended otherwise, it always would be.

He plunged into the last weeks before the election, testing the feelings of voters about the presidential election as well. Long's role in Franklin Delano Roosevelt's campaign for the presidency had snowballed. Late in October, he appeared on the cover of *Time* magazine, hailed as a potential force in the Roosevelt administration if Roosevelt won. Beau put the magazine down with a chill tracing down his spine. If Roosevelt thought he could control Huey P. Long, he needed a lesson in politics. The trouble with that was that Long himself was the only one who could teach it.

On election night, he sat with Claude and Alice, listening to the returns. Early on, it was clear Roosevelt had a commanding lead, even though it would be days before all the votes were counted. "A new era, Papa?" Beau asked, switching off the radio.

"Better be," Claude said. "The country can't stand much more of this Depression. There's got to be some relief."

Gennie came into the room and sat on a stool at Beau's side. "Are you going to have to leave us, now that you've won?"

He put his hand on her hair and smoothed it. "Yes, honey, I'll be going to Baton Rouge to be in the legislature there."

"That's pretty far," she said. "Do you really have to go?" Her eyes darkened as she frowned. "I don't like it when you're not here."

He circled her with his arms and pulled her close. "I don't like it much either, Gennie. It's something I just have to do. But I'm going to miss you and Émilie and Skye like anything."

"Your father's off on a quest," Alice said to lighten Gennie's mood. "Like King Arthur's knights."

Gennie smiled. "Really, Papa? Then I'm going to give you a favor to wear, like the ladies gave the knights."

The day he left for Baton Rouge to be sworn in, she tucked something into his hand. He wore it that day, and on many days after, tucking it carefully into his breast pocket when he dressed. It was a small blue square of linen embroidered with a white rose, with the name "Gennie" worked carefully beneath it. When the world of Louisiana politics was more than he could easily bear, Beau remembered that he wore it. It didn't change what was going on—but it somehow made Beau better able to deal with it.

36

"You've got to stay in bed, Raoul," Caroline protested. "You're not well enough to go out, especially in this weather. It's pouring and it's cold, besides. You'll get worse, you know you will."

"I've been in bed all weekend," Raoul said. "I have to make rounds at the hospital and I have to keep office hours. There's no one else, Caroline." He picked up his shirt wearily and thrust his arms into the sleeves. His face is as white as that shirt, Caroline thought. He looks terrible.

"There won't be anyone else if you kill yourself with pneumonia, either," she said. "It doesn't make sense, Raoul. You're ill—"

"I'm over the worst of it," he said. "After all, Caroline, if I thought I were sick, I would hardly go infect my patients."

"All the same, if I had your symptoms, you'd put me to bed," she said. She had lost the argument; she always did. Nothing would come between Raoul and his duty, not his own illness, not fatigue—not the needs of his wife, an errant thought told her. She brushed that one away. She had learned years since that a doctor's wife must be almost as dedicated.

"Raoul, I know you have to take care of your patients! But you can't blame me for wishing you'd take better care of yourself."

He smiled, the sweet, gentle smile that reassured many a patient that no matter how hard the pain nor how difficult the illness, he would pull them through. "I'll snatch a nap at the office," he said. "And come home early."

"Good," she said, though she knew very well he wouldn't. She stood at the front window watching him dash through the rain to his car. The day was bleak, the skies a source of seemingly endless rain. "I hate February!" she said, dropping the curtain and turning to go upstairs. She had a day of sewing to do, a dress for Caro, shirts to mend for the boys . . . she sighed and tried to be thankful that at least she had a roof over her head. At least she could provide clothes for her children. Think of the people all over this country who would change places with you in two seconds, she told herself, trying to shake her self-pitying mood. Usually her lectures to herself restored her equilibrium and normal cheerfulness, but the combination of a cold, rainy February day, a fractious sewing machine, and the fatigue of worrying about Raoul were strong opponents. By the end of the day, she felt that she wanted nothing more than a cup of tea, a warm bath, and bed.

She heard him come in just as she was settling the children down to their schoolwork. He paused in the hall as though deciding whether to come see them, and then went on up the stairs, his tread heavy and slow. "I'll just go see Papa a minute," she told the children, and hurried upstairs, feeling suddenly that there was something wrong, something Raoul didn't want her to know.

He lay stretched out on the bed, his feet dangling off the edge, his eyes closed. "Raoul, what is it?" she asked, coming closer. All the self-pity of the day flew; his face was still, white.

He opened his eyes and tried to smile. "Caroline . . ." She knew then that he was very, very ill.

"What is it?" she asked steadily. "Whatever it is, Raoul, I can manage it."

His hand tightened on hers. "I know you can, Caroline. I . . . I just hate for you to have to, that's all." She could see him willing himself to speak. "I . . . it seems I have tuberculosis, Caroline." Her shocked face made him grimace; he shook his head. "I know. It seems incredible. But at the hospital today, I had a coughing fit. Dr. LeBlanc insisted on examining me. He sent a specimen to the lab for tests, but the symptoms are pretty conclusive." He turned his head away and stared at the wall.

"But, Raoul, that's . . . that's very serious."

"Yes." He turned back to her. "The worst thing of course is that the treatment is rest. I won't be able to work, Caroline."

"Well, of course you won't be able to work! If you hadn't worked so hard all these years, you'd have never . . ." She bit back the words. There was no point going over all that old ground. It would only make him feel worse.

"Caroline, there's little enough money when I do practice— so few people pay their bills now. What will we live on?"

"Don't worry about that," she said. "Worry about getting well." She put her hand on his forehead, felt the warmth of fever. "Let me help you get undressed. Then I'll let you sleep. Later I'll get you some supper."

"I hate having you wait on me," he said.

"Why? It's what I want to do."

"I meant for you to have a different life, Caroline. I wanted your life to be sunny, bright—"

"Now, Raoul Hamilton, do you really think you married such a little silly that everything has to be perfect all the time or she won't be able to bear it?"

"No," he said. His love for her shone in his eyes, and she felt strength flood back into her. "I know I married a courageous, gallant woman." His eyes misted with tears. "I just wish you didn't have to call on that courage quite so often."

"Hush," she said. "Sleep." She blew him a kiss and went out, closing the door softly behind her. But she sat on the top step, giving herself a minute to think before she went down to the children. What would they live on? Raoul didn't realize that for the past few years, since the Depression had reduced his patients' incomes, and their ability to pay him, she had been selling a piece of jewelry here, a small antique there, to tide them over. And of course Beau Chêne was full of such things—none of which were legally hers, but any of which she would sell without the slightest compunction, if that's what it took to keep them going. Then she realized that she knew very little about tuberculosis, or how to take care of it. She rose and went downstairs to call Dr. LeBlanc.

"I haven't seen the lab results yet," Dr. LeBlanc said. "But I don't need them to know Raoul's a sick man."

"But how do I treat him? I know so little—"

"There's no cure, Caroline," he said. He heard her gasp and hastened to add, "I don't mean people don't get over it. I mean there's no medicine we can give for it." He paused. "The best thing, of course, is to get to a drier climate. The humidity here's the worst thing for him."

"A drier climate?"

"A patient I had two years ago went out to Albuquerque, to a clinic there. Matter of fact, she ended up marrying the doctor and staying out there. I could give you her name."

"Please," Caroline said. "I'll write to her immediately."

She said nothing to Raoul of her plans, knowing he was too ill and too exhausted to be bothered. The household fell into a new routine; the children visited him from a safe distance, and were unnaturally quiet to give him rest. They were so quiet that Caroline's nerves almost broke. It's like living in a tomb, she thought. Then she realized that the children's mood mirrored her own. And so while she waited to hear from New Mexico, she made herself restore a semblance of normalcy to the house: Caro went back to her daily piano practice, and Henri and Raoul once more scuffled in the halls.

When the letter did come, it was both reassuring and unsettling. "We have had excellent results at the clinic," Mrs. Lee wrote. "But Dr. Lee has noticed that patients who are isolated from their families do not do as well as those who have family nearby. If you could make the trip with your husband, his chances for getting well faster would improve." The letter fell to her lap, the rest of it unread. Go to New Mexico! It might as well be the moon. She picked up the letter and read it again. Then she went to her desk and formed her response. "I would like to come with my husband, if I can rent a place large enough for myself and three children. Please advise . . ." Her pen raced across the paper. She had no choice about going with Raoul, she must do everything possible to make him well. Nor was there a choice about taking the children. Where would they go? She put the letter out for the postman with a feeling that she had just changed all of their lives in a way that she could not foresee. But there was no other course.

By late March, arrangements were made and she told Raoul and the children her plans. Raoul listened calmly, his eyes never leaving her face. "I'll never be able to make this up to you," he said.

"Get well, and you will have," she said.

The children were at first excited, then upset. "Not a trip? Go live there?" Henri said.

"For a while," Caroline said, stroking Caro's curls. "Luella will come with us—and maybe you can have a pony."

"Hey, maybe there'll be Indians!" Raoul said, and began whooping up and down the hall.

"How long will we be there?" Henri said.

"Until your father is well," she answered. "Children, we must think of Papa. He has to go New Mexico to get well— and he'll get well faster if he has us close enough to visit him. You understand that, don't you?"

And, as well as they could, they did. Telling the children was easy, Caroline thought, compared to telling Beau. Busy with the legislature, he did not even know Raoul was ill; in their hurried conversations, she had deliberately said nothing. Now it could be put off no longer. She phoned and asked if they could meet at his family's farm. "I need a break," she said. "I'll pack a lunch, and if the weather's awful, we'll picnic inside."

"That's great," he said. He sounded vigorous and young, as though he had enough strength for ten. How good it was to know she could lean on that strong shoulder and cry, if she wanted to!

He was already at the farm when she got there, pacing over the front parlor, his eyes swiftly surveying the room. "I'm thinking of doing some renovations out here," he said when she came in. "Maybe move here at some point. What do you think?"

"I've always loved this house," she said. "It has . . . happy memories."

"So," he said. "What's been going on with you?"

Without warning, Caroline burst into tears. Beau went to her and took her into his arms and listened with growing disbelief as she poured out the whole sad story.

"When do you have to leave?" he asked slowly.

"At the end of April," she said. "The children will just miss a few weeks of school that way—and it'll give me time to close the house."

"Why didn't you let me know?" he demanded.

She shook her head. "I . . . I couldn't talk about it, Beau. For a while, I just didn't believe it. I couldn't. And then, well, if I had told you, I'd have broken down, like I just did." She smiled, the old courageous smile. "I had to wait to break down until I could get over it."

"You're the strongest woman I know, Caroline, but dammit, I don't see why you have to keep on proving it. Is there something I can do?"

"I can't think of anything. Luella will come with us, though somewhat reluctantly. She keeps asking me about 'dem Injuns' as though she expects us all to be scalped. Oh, Beau, it won't be so bad. Think of the adventures I'll have! And to live near mountains after always having to look up to see sea level! We'll be fine, you'll see."

"You would make a picnic of a forced march," he said, and turned away before she could see the tears in his eyes.

"Speaking of picnics," she said, pulling out the food. "Let's have ours."

He waited until they had finished lunch to ask the question he could not get out of his mind. "What will you live on out there, Caroline? Pardon me for asking, but I know Raoul does a large amount of charity work—and when he's not working at all . . ."

"We'll manage," she said. The proud tilt of her chin told him to say nothing else, but he made a mental note to see if there were any way he could help her that she would not find out about.

One other question loomed, but that one he found almost impossible to ask. Finally, when he was helping her into her car, he asked, "How long do you think you'll be gone, Caroline?"

She looked at him then, a long, full look that told him how many nights had been haunted by that same question. "I don't know," she said. "Months, certainly. Perhaps . . . years."

"Years!" He clasped her hands between his, almost imploringly.

"But it could take that long, Beau. No one knows . . ." She shrugged. "However long it is, Beau, there's not much I can do about it, is there?"

"No," he said. "Just as there hasn't been anything either of us could do about a lot of other things." He looked away and shook his head. "Life seems so . . . well, happenstance, sometimes. You know what I mean?" He looked back at her.

"Oh, yes," she said. "Hold me, Beau, will you? Just hold me."

They stood in the slanting spring sunlight, locked in each

other's arms. Caroline believed she drew strength from him. He knew he drew it from her.

Beau and his children put the Hamiltons on the train the day they left for Albuquerque. Gennie and Émilie had made garlands of colored tissue paper to drape over Caroline and Caro, and even Luella stood still while they decorated her. Raoul took the bustle with the quiet smile with which he observed everything. Only once, when Beau looked up after bending over Caroline to tell her something, did he see keenness in Raoul's gaze. Well, he's bound to know I . . . care for Caroline, Beau thought. But he was glad that he could meet Raoul's gaze, that there was nothing in his friendship with Caroline that dishonored either of them.

"Susu just happened to have a ham and a couple of chickens on hand that she didn't seem to know what to do with, so I told her maybe you'd be kind enough to take them off our hands," Beau said to Caroline, beckoning Skye, who was holding a large hamper, forward.

"That's enough food for an army! Beau, you shouldn't—"

"Hush," he said. She looked exhausted after a month of closing the house, as well as nursing Raoul and packing them all up.

Beau had not yet found a way of getting money to her that she would not detect. But he had put, at the bottom of the hamper, a small box tied up with ribbon, with a card addressed to Caroline. Inside was several hundred dollars in gold.

By the time Caroline opened the package, they were traveling across the marshes that lay between the Atchafalaya and Mississippi rivers. When she saw the gold pieces, she picked them up, letting them fall from one hand to the other. Raoul had already gone to sleep in the seat across from her, the three children playing with another family of children down the aisle. The countryside beyond the train windows was still familiar, the cypress, the marsh grasses, the stretches of brackish water. But before too long, she would have left behind everything familiar, would be faced with the vast gray-yellow desert and its alien, empty sky. She reread Beau's note and tucked the gold coins away in a safe place in the depths of her purse. No matter what lay ahead, she felt now as though someone had come to sit beside her, had put strong arms around her and told her that everything would turn out all right.

37

Beau pushed through the jostling crowd and took a place near the speaker's platform. The young man who stood waiting for the crowd to quiet was Ernest Bourgeois, a Standard Oil electrical engineer who had emerged on the public scene shortly after Standard Oil announced, early in January 1935, that it would lay off one thousand employees and perhaps even close the Baton Rouge refinery. That action, Beau knew, was retaliation for the five-cent-per-barrel tax on refined oil the legislature, under the whip of Senator Huey P. Long, had enacted in December 1934. Beau had fought it energetically, joining with other Long foes in a sustained but futile effort. They had gone down to defeat—but so would the state's economy, Beau thought grimly, if something were not done to stop Long.

The mood of the crowd was ugly, and Bourgeois' fiery words did nothing to calm it. "We've got chapters of the Square Deal Association all over the state," Bourgeois roared as the crowd surged forward. "Not just Standard Oil employees have joined, but men and women who are sick of Huey P. Long's control of this state, tired of his brand of politics."

It was not the chill of the January night alone that made Beau's blood cold. These people mean business, he thought. Some of them have a real economic ax to grind. Others are just spoiling for a fight. But not one of them is going to listen to reason. He turned his attention to Bourgeois.

"Now, hear this, and hear it good," Bourgeois said. "Yesterday an illegally appointed police jury fired all two hundred twenty-five employees of the parish of East Baton Rouge, put District Attorney John Fred Odom out of his position as police jury counsel, and took the courthouse away from Sheriff Robert L. Pettit!"

By the time the last words had gone out into the cold night air, the heated voices of the crowd were lifted, yelling, shouting for Long's destruction. "And that's not all!" Bourgeois cried. His face in the torchlight was contorted with rage. "A Square Dealer was arrested last night." Bourgeois' gaze went over the crowd. "Are we going to stand for that? Are we going to take that lying down?"

"Hell, no! We'll take to the streets! We'll show Long who has power!" Beau saw men take guns out of coat pockets and wave them high. "All Square Dealers!" a man shouted, standing on the hood of a car parked on the outskirts of the crowd. "Get your guns and go to the courthouse!"

"Get your guns! Go to the courthouse!" The crowd broke, men and women running in different directions, all shouting, all yelling, until Beau stood in a web of violent motion and sound.

I'd better get over there, he thought. He saw Bourgeois running by and grabbed his arm. "Bourgeois, can I talk to you a minute?"

Stopped by Beau's grip, Bourgeois turned impatiently. "Who the hell are you, man? Come on, I've got work to do."

"I'm Representative Langlinais, from St. Martin," Beau said. "Look, you're not going to get anywhere like this. There's got to be a better way—"

"Let me know when you find it," Bourgeois said. His eyes were contemptuous. "I know you, Langlinais. And I'll admit you fight Long in the legislature. But your way is too little and a damn sight too late. You should have thought of that when you helped get the bastard elected in the first place." He shook off Beau's hand and dashed forward, disappearing in the running crowd headed for the courthouse.

Beau went slowly to his car and got in. There was nothing he could do to prevent the assault on the courthouse. He heard the thud of feet running past him, heard the manic cries that split the dark air. But he couldn't stay away. He was pulled by a kind of fascination with what was happening, as though he had stumbled from one world that he recognized into another that he did not. He started the car and maneuvered it slowly through the crowd, parking it on a side street near the courthouse and going on foot the rest of the way.

The scene was unreal, eerie. Almost a hundred men had gathered around the building, guns evident. They milled about as though uncertain of what to do; men moved from group to group, obviously passing some word. "What did he say?" Beau asked one man. He saw the identifying lapel button in the man's shirt, and knew he spoke to a Square Dealer.

"More people coming in from other parishes," the man said. His eyes burned with excitement, and his mouth worked nervously. "We're going to wait till they get here. Then we'll march."

March! And they had been trained; the men knew the rudiments of military science, were organized in companies along military lines. The women were passing out sandwiches and coffee; the incongruity of that homey touch made the scene even more unreal and unbelievable.

But when the speakers began to harangue the crowd, Beau knew there was nothing homey about it, nor anything sane. Long was denounced over and over again—who did he think he was, arresting one of their members? Who did he think he was, to run roughshod over every law of their state?

The roaring approval of the crowd fueled the speakers' eloquence; by the time the men from outlying parishes arrived, the crowd was hungry for action. A young woman climbed up onto the platform, waving her apron for attention. "My mother was a parish employee for fifteen years!" she cried. "She was fired yesterday. I say we need to take action! There's been too much talk!"

The crowd took up the challenge. Rifles, shotguns, pistols— their barrels gleamed in the lamplight, menacing tools of violence in the hands of angry men. They moved toward the courthouse entrance, brandishing their guns and shouting, "Down with Long! Down with Long!"

From the back of the crowd, someone yelled, "Hang him!" They took up the cry, a great surge of sound that carried them up the steps and past the custodian who cowered there. He was pushed outside, propelled forward through the crowd by one stiff arm after the other. As he stumbled past Beau, Beau saw the terror in the man's eyes and stopped beside him.

"You'll be all right," he said, and taking the man's arm, steered him toward the street beyond the crowd. He heard a voice behind him, the same contemptuous voice he'd heard earlier.

"So you don't support us, after all, Langlinais," Bourgeois said.

Beau turned. "I don't support violence," Beau said.

Bourgeois laughed. "Well, man, there's no place for you in this state."

It soon appeared that he might be right. The easy takeover of the courthouse did little to relieve their pent-up anger; now murmurs ran through the crowd: "Let's take the capitol!" Beau saw men jump onto the courthouse steps to debate the suggestion vigorously. It was nine o'clock, and after five hours the Square Dealers were eager for more. Just when it seemed that those who wanted another target would prevail, a man arrived and announced that the arrested Square Dealer had been released. Men looked at one another, then back to the speaker. What did that mean? "We've accomplished our purpose," Ernest Bourgeois shouted. "You can all go home."

The murmur that rose now was disapproving. Had they driven to Baton Rouge to be sent home with no more action than this? But Bourgeois stood firm. They had proved their point; they must now wait for the next call. Beau watched the crowd break up into small groups of disgruntled men, walking slowly away from the courthouse grounds, turning to peer over their shoulders from time to time. But a few faces showed relief, and Beau knew that Bourgeois' crowd was not as militant as it might appear. There were some here who knew they were risking jail by seizing the courthouse, and they were beginning to wonder if the cause was worth it.

Beau was sitting in the bar of the Heidelberg Hotel when the news of Huey's response to the Square Dealers' impudence came soon after midnight. "Damned if he hasn't imposed martial law in Baton Rouge and the parish, too," a man sitting next to Beau said. Beau grabbed the mimeographed sheet a reporter from the *Morning Advocate* was carrying.

Governor O. K. Allen had signed the proclamation, but that fooled no one—it had been authored by Long. The second proclamation was shocking. It created the First Military District, taking in the city of Baton Rouge and the parish of East Baton Rouge; the district commander, Brigadier General Louis F. Guerre, set forth regulations that were stricter than any Beau could remember in the entire history of martial law in America. No one but city and state police could carry firearms, nor could firearms be sold, exchanged, or even given away in the territory. The press was forbidden to print anything that spoke ill of the state government or state officials. More than two people constituted a crowd—and crowds were forbidden to assemble.

"My God," Beau burst out. "It's tyranny!" He threw down the sheet and strode up to the reporter. "What does your paper have to say about this?"

"Mr. Langlinais, if I was to repeat what my editor said when he read that thing, I'd get arrested—under the new martial law, of course." He looked at the group of men in the bar. "Seems like when old Huey got a taste of being head of the army as well as kingfish of the lodge in New Orleans, he kind of developed an addiction to it. I wouldn't be surprised if he runs that National Guard all over the state anytime somebody doesn't suit him." He tipped his hat. "But nobody heard me say that."

"It's beyond belief," Beau said.

But the situation was to become even more incredible. Before noon the next day, more than eight hundred National Guard troops were stationed on the capitol grounds, armed and ready to shoot.

The courthouse was in the possession of one National Guard squad, and the Baton Rouge City Police Station was held by another. Baton Rougeans were treated to the sight of armed soldiers flooding the grounds of their capitol and courthouse, and not a few stayed behind locked doors and curtained windows, waiting for the next act in this incomprehensible drama to unfold. They did not have long to wait. Huey called in the reporters—and what he told them made everything that had gone before seem small by comparison. "I've discovered a plot against my life," he roared, striding up and down his office, shirt open, tie loose, and face red with rage. "Standard Oil's behind it. They figure if I'm gone, they can get this state back. But they aren't going to do it, not if I have to keep the Guard here till kingdom come!"

"Can you prove that, Senator?" a voice from the back of the room called.

"Prove it? Hell, yes, I can prove it. District Judge Womack's going to hold a hearing later today. Better hang on to your hats, boys, you're going to hear quite a story."

The story lived up to Long's promise. The star witness, a man who had joined the Square Deal Association solely to spy for Long, named seven prominent Baton Rouge men he said had plotted to kill Long; not only that, but the sheriffs of Iberville and West Baton Rouge parishes knew all about it, and could back him up.

Long, who questioned the witnesses, surveyed the room triumphantly. "And did you believe this plot was real?" he asked.

"I knew it was," the witness said. His moment had come. Every eye in the room was on him, every ear turned to hear every word. "There were two plots, Senator. One was to rush your suite at the Heidelberg Hotel. I convinced them they'd never get through your guards. The other was to wait by the road and shoot you on the way to New Orleans—of course you know about that, I came and told you."

"And showed me the weapons," Huey said impressively.

The spy's arrest had been a device to put him in protective custody so that the Square Dealers could be exposed. "But unfortunately," Long boomed, "one of the very conspirators in the plot had him paroled. He was urged to keep his mouth shut until they could get him out of town." Long faced the crowded room, enjoying every moment of the sensation he was causing. "Of course he did not leave town, but came to me— with the names not only of those conspirators against my life, but with a great deal of very useful information about the organization that calls itself the Square Deal Association." He looked around the room, letting his eyes fall first on one face, now another. "I had wanted to examine some of those people today—but most of them are missing, it appears. So I will ask Judge Womack to adjourn this hearing until next Friday." He laughed, the big, wolfish laugh that summed up, Beau thought, Long's confidence in his own power. "Maybe by then those witnesses will be located—and maybe by then they'll have had time to polish off their recollections and their memories."

If I were reading this in the newspaper, Beau thought, I don't think I'd believe it. He watched Long emerge, his stride jaunty, his face smiling. His cohorts thronged around him, laughing, cheering, clearly pleased with their hero's performance. To think I once felt the same way about the man, Beau said to himself. To think I thought a man could seize power and use it only for good—and then give it up before it mastered him. He turned and walked quickly away to avoid a confrontation. Soon he would have to speak up. Soon he would make a stand. But not today. He'd see this farce through first—and then he'd seek out Long.

Late on that Saturday, Baton Rougeans were rocked by yet

another piece of news—more than one hundred armed Square Dealers had organized at the airport. "What in hell do they think they're doing?" Beau stormed. "My God, the town's under martial law—they've played right into Long's hands. He'll have their hides!"

And the next day, he discovered that five hundred armed national guardsmen and state policemen had surrounded the Square Dealers, throwing tear-gas bombs. They were all arrested, though they were later allowed to go home.

"Pure chaos," Beau told a friend in the legislature. "But don't think for a minute Long doesn't have method behind this madness. For one thing, who would take the Square Dealers seriously now? For another, I imagine after all this commotion, Standard Oil might just be willing to bargain a little."

"The oil tax, you mean? You think there'll be a compromise?"

"Long doesn't want that refinery closed, man. Have the loss of all those jobs laid at his door? No, he has something up his sleeve—and I guess we'll find out what it is when he has Allen call a special session to make it official."

"All we do is rubber-stamp what Long wants," the other legislator said.

"Under the goad of a rubber heel," Beau said.

His friend watched Beau's mouth tighten. "Let some of that anger out at him sometimes, Langlinais. Might do some good."

"I better do something with it," Beau said. "Seems I'm angry most of the time when I'm up here."

His anger remained, cold, hard, ready, like the weapons the guardsmen carried. Martial law continued; there were rumors that Huey Long and Standard Oil were trying to work out a compromise. Then on February 26 Governor Allen called the legislature into a session that would last only five days. Beau arrived at the House chambers in a disgruntled mood. Nothing in the call dealt with the oil tax, but if it didn't pop up somewhere, he had missed his guess.

He sat at his desk and read over the bills—nothing but routine matters. Just wait, he told himself. Just wait. With only two days left in the session, Long leaders in both the Senate and the House put a resolution before those bodies that allowed the governor to suspend any portion of the recently passed five-cent-per-barrel oil tax he chose. When Allen immediately suspended four cents of the tax on Louisiana oil, Beau saw just how confident that last brouhaha had made Long. Rumors had been circulating to the effect that Standard Oil wanted a four-cent rebate on the tax. A suspension would achieve the same effect—but only, as everyone in the legislature very well knew, so long as Standard Oil stayed in line.

"Win, place, and show, Huey," Beau said to himself. He tucked his papers into his briefcase and rose, his eyes surveying the legislators around him. He had come into this chamber two years ago awed by the marble walls, the ceiling crowned with carved medallions, the elaborate brass chandeliers. Awed by the responsibility vested in him, and in all who sat here. Now he saw it as a theater, where the play was written, produced, directed, and starred in by one man—Huey P. Long. He's made a mockery of all of it, he thought. And I'm not putting up with it one more day.

He walked out into the lobby to find Long holding court. "Hey, Langlinais, how do you like the way I saved you some money?" Long shouted.

Beau shifted direction and approached Long. "How do you figure that, Huey?" He switched his briefcase to his right hand and let the left one dangle at his side.

Huey ignored the slight. "You produce oil, don't you? Hell, you know the refineries pass everything on—we just saved you a bundle in there."

"I don't much care for the price, Huey," Beau said. "Seems a little bit more than I feel like paying."

"What price would that be?" Long asked. He looked at the men around him. "Y'all know Representative Langlinais, don't you? Man of principle. If you don't believe it, just ask him. Why, Beau here's got principles he ain't used yet. Maybe you could spread 'em around a little, Beau." The taunting face drew nearer. "'Course, a man who's been rich all his life can afford principles." He laughed, that raucous laugh that announced one of his favorite statements. "When I was little, there were two things we couldn't afford. One was shoes and one was principles." He leaned forward and gripped Beau's shoulder. "Principles are what men use to stay out of the thick of things, Beau." He released Beau so quickly that Beau, off-balance, stumbled. "Thing is, I'd have thought Claude Langlinais' son would have a little more to him. A little more interest in the people of this state."

Beau could feel his own anger rising; he wanted nothing so much as to see Long's eyes drop from his, see that wide, laughing mouth for once with nothing to say. "I do care about the people, Long. More than you do, if it comes to that."

"There is nobody who cares for the people more than I do," Long roared, "and don't you ever forget it!"

"You've forgotten it, Huey. You've given them roads, books, hospitals—all right. But you've made them fearful slaves in return." Long moved closer, his mouth open, but Beau kept on talking, raising his voice so that it reached to the high marble walls of the lobby. "You control twenty-five thousand state jobs, Huey. Each one of which can produce at least five votes in any election. You think those 125,000 people vote for you because they like you? Don't any of them vote from fear? Intimidation?" He dropped his briefcase and stood, hands clenched, legs braced. "How many people have lost jobs because they didn't jump fast enough, high enough, or far enough when you told them to? How many of those legislators in there have ever made even one decision that didn't come from your office? Dammit, Huey, how many U.S. senators do you think run back and forth from Washington to make sure no one's done one little independent thing behind their backs?"

"You finished?" Long asked. He had his temper under control, though the veins in his neck bulged and his forehead was flushed a deep angry red. "You don't know what you're talking about, been here a little over two years and ready to tell us how to run the world. Listen, Beau, don't put on those airs with me, act like I invented politics. Government's been bought and sold since the first five minutes it was thought of—the thing is, maybe with someone who cares about the little man doing the price-setting, they're getting a better deal."

"You really believe that, don't you? That everyone can be bought."

"Can't they?" Long challenged, his eyes on fire.

"I can't," Beau said, and made his eyes hold firm on Long's. Long relaxed and laughed. He winked at the men around him. "Hell, son, that's 'cause I ain't tried." He moved a little, closing the space between them, a thick forefinger jabbed against Beau's chest. "Better not get so high and mighty, Langlinais. There's going to come a day when you'll be begging me to buy you. I promise you that."

Beau's hard, cold anger turned quickly hot, making his face flame. He grasped Long's coat, a hand on each lapel. He was aware of men coming toward him, arms outstretched. He concentrated on the face that was now only inches from his own. "I'll see you in hell first," he said. As Long's body-guards pulled at him, forced his hands from Long's coat, he shouted at the top of his lungs: "And from now on, Huey, I'll fight you on every damn issue you bring up! You'll get so tired seeing me stand up in that House—" A heavy hand clamped over his mouth. The bodyguards propelled him to-ward the doors leading out to the broad front steps of the capitol, and he stumbled between them, turning his head for one last look at Long.

Long's face was frozen, each feature rigid with rage. His fist was raised; he made a gesture with it toward Beau, and then took one long stride forward. "Dammit, Langlinais, I won't forget this! And I'll make sure you don't, either!"

Beau burst through the double doors, then stood regaining his breath and his balance. He wiped his forehead, straightened his coat. As he started down the steps, he made a vow. No matter how long it took, or how much effort—he'd see Long removed from power if it was the last thing he did.

38

The clear desert light seemed to hold the landscape in a golden bowl, its rim made of the mountains which cast purple shad-ows across the horizon. The road wound away from Albuquer-que, the houses that clustered on the outskirts of town becoming fewer, until finally Beau found himself traveling through countryside empty of anything but the mesquite bushes and the cacti that held stiff branches like candelabra against the sky.

Then he saw an adobe house ahead of him, surrounded by a low rail fence. A woman sat on the porch; as he drew nearer, he saw that it was Caroline. She had a bowl in her lap, and a basket of beans that she was shelling at her feet. Her eyes were fixed on the mountains in front of her. He pulled up in front of the house and got out of the car, his heart feeling large in his chest, and his throat tight. Caroline got up, shielding her eyes with her hand. Suddenly she leapt up, the bowl of shelled beans falling to the porch as she ran down the steps and into his arms. She was crying as he closed his arms around her. He stood there quietly, waiting for her to force back her tears, to lift that proud head.

"Oh, Beau, I was sitting there just wishing for a friendly face—"

He heard the catch in her voice and hugged her more tightly. "You got my letter, didn't you? Telling you I was coming?"

She took the handkerchief he gave her and wiped her cheeks. "No, I didn't. But it doesn't matter. I'm so glad to see you, I don't know what to do."

"You can sit down and tell me how everyone is," he said. "How is Raoul, Caroline?"

"It's hard to say," she said. "He improved a lot at first. Now . . . But they say he's better."

"And the children? They must be all grown-up—my Lord, you've been out here two years now."

"It seems impossible, doesn't it? If I had known it would be this long . . ." Her voice trailed into silence.

"Well, I've brought you a taste of home. Wait until you see the truck Mama sent out—fig preserves and peach jam and blackberry jelly and coffee beans and I don't know what all. I told her they have grocery stores in New Mexico, but she said they didn't have her fig preserves anywhere, so I shut up."

"You don't mean you hauled all that out here on the train?" She was smiling now, leading the way inside the house. Its starkness shocked him.

"Caroline . . . are you comfortable here?"

"Well, Beau, of course we are." She laughed. "I know it's plain—but unless we wanted to live in town, which is really more expensive, a little place like this is about all that's available. And I like it, Beau, truly I do. I get up every morning and just glory in the mountains."

"Well," he said, "it's amazing how homey you've made

it." He gestured to a bright rug hanging on the wall. "I like that."

"So do I. I traded with one of the Navajos to get it." She began to laugh. "You remember how scared Luella was of Indians? Well, the second day after we moved in, she got her first dose of the wild West. I'd gone into the sanatorium, and when I got back, Luella met me with eyes so big I thought they'd come out of her head. 'Dem Injuns was by here,' she said. 'I jest grabbed my big skillet and waved it and they went away.'" Caroline's laughter was an echo of that young laugh he had thought would never, never leave her. "Can't you just see Luella taking on a bunch of peaceful Navajo Indians with that big black pot? Henri said they had blankets to sell, and when they came back, I bought some, because it was so cold. I'd no idea! The first winter we were here, if we put anything out to dry, it would freeze as stiff as a board and we'd have to thaw it out by the fire."

"You astonish me," Beau said. "You look wonderful, Caroline."

"It's the fresh air and exercise," she said. "There's not a lot to do out here, so I walk into the desert in the evenings. It's so beautiful, Beau. The sunsets are incredible. I never, never tire of looking at the mountains. One day, when we'd not been here very long, there was a big sandstorm, and when we woke up the next morning, the wind had piled tumbleweed all around the house, up to the roof! Oh, Beau, it's not so bad, really."

"Most women I know would have crumbled the first week," he said flatly. "I hope you packed an evening dress or some such thing, because I'm taking you to dinner in Albuquerque tonight and I won't take no for an answer."

"That sounds wonderful," she said. "I haven't done anything like that in . . . oh, a long, long time." She took his arm. "Come on, I'll show you around. I'm really very proud of our little camp."

The room they stood in served as living and dining room both. "And library and study and sewing room and anything else that's needed," Caroline said. "But it's cozy in the evenings. We have a fire, and the children do their lessons, and I read and Luella sits with us awhile. She's been such a treasure, I don't know what I'd have done without her." She looked around at the rough wooden furnishings. "It's been good for the children, I think, to live austerely. Find out that they can."

"Austere" was the right word, Beau thought, following her through the house. The boys shared a small bedroom, with Caro in with her mother. Luella had a room off the kitchen; that, and a small bathroom, comprised the house. The walls and ceilings were whitewashed adobe, eighteen inches thick, and the floor was of wide planks. He thought of the richness of Beau Chêne, the comfort of the Hamilton home in Lafayette, and almost groaned out loud.

"I know it's none of my business, but I'm going to ask you anyway," he said when they were back in the central room. "What are you living on?"

"We rented the house at home when we realized we'd be here . . . indefinitely." She hurried over the word and he let it pass; he did not want to think of its implications. "And Raoul has some investments. They don't yield much, with things the way they are, but it's an income." She shrugged. "And, of course, it doesn't take much to live out here. Why, little Raoul and Henri have learned to hunt. They bring home game."

"I'd like to see Raoul," Beau said. "Does the sanatorium allow visitors?"

"Of course. He'd love to see you," she said. A short while later she walked him to the car the hotel had lent him, and stood waving as he drove into town. Then she ran back into the house and found Luella just coming in from the yard. "Oh, Luella," she said, her eyes shining. "You'll never guess who just appeared right out of the blue."

"If'n I had to guess, I'd say it was Mr. Beau," Luella said. She saw Caroline's surprised look and chuckled. "I'm just teasing you, Miss Caroline. I done saw him from out in the yard, but I thought I'd let you all . . . well, have a little visit to yourselves." But I would have known anyway, Luella thought, starting to fold the clothes she had brought in. The way her eyes is shinin' and the way her cheeks is pink— there's only one person makes her look that way, only just that one.

The landscape had more impact on Beau as he drove into Albuquerque to the sanatorium than it had on the way out; having seen the place where Caroline lived, he could visualize her walking across the desert, her feet silent in the soft leather

Indian boots she had shown him. The clear air, so unlike the
heavy, moist air of Louisiana, brought the distant mountains
closer. What must it be, for a girl accustomed to live oaks and
magnolias, not ever to see a green and leafy tree! He had
always thought Caroline had courage, but driving through the
emptiness in which she now lived, an emptiness broken only
by an occasional adobe house similar to the one in which
Caroline and her family lived, he knew that her courage was of
a rare sort. Caroline Hamilton could not only rise to the crises
of life—but she could sustain a level of courage over a long,
dreary passage of time. Dammit, he thought as he pulled into
the sanatorium driveway, I'm going to find a way to make her
life easier no matter what I have to do.

A nurse led Beau out onto a long porch that faced the mountains and basked in the full afternoon sun. Raoul was lying on a
sofa, a book in his lap. His eyes were closed. When the nurse
gently awakened him, he smiled and held out his hand. "Well,
Beau Langlinais! I'd no idea you were coming. Caroline didn't
tell me—"

"She didn't get my letter. I was something of a surprise,"
Beau said. Raoul's skin seemed transparent. Beau thought he
could see the bones beneath it, as though the sun that poured
into the porch was slowly burning away the flesh.

He took the chair next to the sofa and began to talk, telling
Raoul news of mutual friends in Lafayette, catching him up on
Louisiana's news. "I haven't seen your children yet," he said,
"but Caroline looks grand. And I must say, after seeing how
comfortable an adobe house can be, I'm tempted to see if
bayou mud can duplicate one. Make a great duck camp,
wouldn't it?"

His mild joke made Raoul laugh, a laugh which ended in a
racking cough. Beau waited anxiously until the paroxysm was
over. "Caroline says you're better," he said.

Raoul waved a hand weakly. He was still struggling for
breath, but he managed to speak. "I can't seem to get past the
plateau I'm on now," he said. His eyes met Beau's. "But I'm
sure I will."

"Certainly you will," Beau said. But he thought bleakly of
cases he'd heard of in which people had remained in sana-
toriums for years, living in a kind of limbo between life and
death. The idea of Caroline having to endure that strengthened
his resolve, and he made a decision he hoped he would not

regret. "Raoul, look, I want to ask you something. Please hear me out before you answer."

Raoul gazed at Beau. "I think you've earned the right to ask me anything you want, Beau. Caroline told me about the money you gave her—"

"Hush," Beau said. "Our two families have traded favors for so long nobody even tries to keep up anymore." He leaned forward and gripped one of Raoul's hands. The warmth surprised him. Then he realized that this was the false warmth of fever, that flushed cheeks and warmed blood with signs of vigor all the while it was laying the body waste. "Look, Raoul, Caroline has her hands full and you're certainly in no condition to look after things. I want you to give me power of attorney, a letter from you to your bank or your accountant or whoever has your books. I want to take your investments over, handle them for you." He saw the "No" forming on Raoul's lips and lifted his hand. "You haven't heard me out, Raoul. If there's anything I'm good at, it's making money. Whatever the Langlinaises touch seems to turn to gold. I want to consolidate whatever you've got and invest it in Langlinais enterprises. I can guarantee you'll do better than you are now."

Raoul smiled, a smile that reached his eyes and blotted out the answer that had been there. "I'm sure you can, Beau," he said. He closed his eyes for a moment, letting his hands relax on the throw across his legs. "I'm too tired and too worried about my family's future to say no, Beau. You're not fooling me one bit. I know perfectly well you'll make sure we make money even if it comes out of your pocket. But I can't let pride stand in the way of my family's security."

"Nonsense," Beau said. "You'll make money because the investments will pay well. And before you know it, you'll be back on your feet and in Lafayette practicing again."

"I hope so," Raoul said, his eyes lowered. He clasped Beau's hand. "You've . . . you've been a good friend to both of us." Then he stared into Beau's face. "An honorable one," he said. Beau knew this was as close as Raoul could come to telling Beau he knew of that long struggle to keep the relationship with Caroline just that way.

Beau put his hand over Raoul's. "She's a rare woman," he said.

Raoul's face, illumined by a band of sunlight, seemed

illumined from within, as well. "Yes," he said. "Having been loved by Caroline, a man doesn't really ask for anything else."

"How did you find Raoul?" Caroline asked when Beau got back to the house.

He avoided meeting her eyes. "Pretty cheerful, all things considered," he said. "That inactivity would drive me crazy, but he seems to bear up well."

"Thank heavens he likes to read," Caroline said. She held up a book. "And what a treat I have in store! I've been dying to read *Tender Is the Night* ever since I read the reviews, and here your mother has sent me a copy." She looked at Beau and laughed. "Annette sends me big envelopes stuffed with magazines and clippings of what she calls 'civilized events.' I think she's afraid I'm going to become stunted, living out here."

"How is Annette, anyway? Every time I go to New Orleans I think I'll call her, but somehow, I never do."

"You know Annette. She says she's lived in reduced circumstances for years, so the Depression hasn't seemed to affect her."

"Not much does," Beau said. "I guess as long as she has her books and her artistic friends, she's all right."

"Actually, I guess I would feel intellectually starved if she didn't keep me up with some of what's going on. Getting one of Annette's packets is literally like manna in the desert." She came closer and smiled up at him. "Your visit is, too, Beau. Manna from heaven."

He thought of the new arrangement he and Raoul had made. "Manna from heaven" was exactly what the income she received would be, he would see to it. He felt a sense of relief that Raoul had not protested, but had allowed him to help. "Look, I'll wait while you get dressed, and we'll drive in together. Give me a chance to visit with the children—the girls sent them a box, too."

"Beau, why don't you just take potluck with us?" She looked at him and blushed. "I'm not sure I should go in to dinner . . ."

He felt his heart catch. When she looked at him that way, the years vanished, the room vanished. He was seventeen years old, and in love for the first time. "Caroline—"

Luella came bustling in, a pale blue organdy dress hanging over one arm. "I done got your dress ironed and the water fixed for yo' bath. You run along and dress yourself, you hear, Miz Hamilton?" She turned to Beau, shaking her head. "Mr. Beau, 'bout time this chile had a night out. She's been stuck out on this prairie with nuthin' but dem Injuns and me and the chillun for company, and I swear, I'm so glad you turned up, I'm ready to sing hallelujah."

"Luella—" Caroline began, but then she looked at Beau and laughed. "I give up," she said. She took the dress and headed for the back part of the house. "I'll be ready as fast as I can."

"Take your time," Beau said. "I still want to see the children."

"They comin' in," Luella said. She looked at Beau and shook her head again. "It ain't good out here, Mr. Beau. Miz Hamilton, she'd rip my tongue out my haid if she heard me tell you that, but it's the God's truth. Why, I ain't never thought I'd live in a place like this."

"Things are going to get better, Luella," he said. "Dr. Hamilton and I had a little talk—it's going to be fine, you'll see."

"Won't be fine until I'm away from these heathens and back with churchgoing folks. Miz Hamilton took the chillun up on the mountains to watch dem Injuns dance, but not me, nossir, Mr. Beau. I stayed home and prayed 'em back, so those spirits dem Injuns talk about all the time wouldn't git holt of 'em and keep 'em."

"I'd like to see the spirit that could keep hold of Mrs. Hamilton," Beau said. He heard the children clattering across the porch and went to meet them. "You're the image of your mother," he told Caro, kissing her. "And you boys are nearly as tall as I am! Big enough to get that box on the back seat of the car," he directed. "My children packed up so much stuff, I thought the train would need another engine."

The Hamilton children fell on the box when it had been carried inside, exclaiming over each gift.

"Hey, some new Tom Swifts!" Henri said, holding up two books.

"And candy!" Raoul said.

"That's Émilie's first attempt at fudge," Beau said. "She's practicing for when she goes away to college and lives in the dormitory."

Caro looked up from the letter she was reading. "Skye says he goes over to Beau Chêne whenever he can to see our dogs and remind them not to forget us," she said. Her lip began to tremble, and the blue eyes so like her mother's filled with tears. "He sent a picture, too." She held the snapshot out to her brothers, who passed it silently from one to the other, and then ducked their heads, hiding whatever expression might betray them.

"Well, that was lovely of Skye, wasn't it?" Caroline said. She had come into the room quietly, and when Beau turned, he caught the concern in her face as she watched her children. "What else did they send?" She leaned over the box, exclaiming over each gift, teasing and joking until her children were smiling again. "Be good for Luella," she said, kissing them as she and Beau left.

"They damn near break your heart, don't they?" Beau said when they were heading toward Albuquerque. "Children, I mean. God, I can take anything for myself, but if one of the children hurts—when Gennie had polio, I could hardly bear it. Even now, when all she has is that little limp—I'd give anything I have to make her leg straight."

"Yes," Caroline said.

He watched her face when they walked into the courtyard of the hotel. Lamplight made the white tablecloths stand out against the potted palms and hibiscus like moths in a tropical garden; crystal shone, silver gleamed, and music rose into the cool night air from a trio of musicians playing Viennese waltzes. "I'd forgotten places like this existed," she said. She looked down at her dress. "I hope this is all right—it's so old. It can't be in style."

"You make your own style," he said. He tucked her arm in his as they followed the headwaiter to their table. "I'm the envy of every man here, don't you know that?"

They seemed to agree that this one night was to be theirs, with no talk about anything serious or unpleasant. An evening snatched from time—they would both remember it that way. Caroline was like one of the night-blooming flowers. Each dance, each smile, each easy exchange, softened her, relaxed the worry lines in her face, and made her younger, filled with the gaiety that had always been hers.

"It's so good to see you, Caroline," he said. He reached across the table and took one of her hands. "I miss you."

"I miss you, too," she said. Her other hand covered his. "Oh, Beau. At first, when I allowed myself to think about you so much, I fought it. It seemed . . . disloyal to Raoul." She looked at him, knowing he would understand. "Then, when the whole world seemed to be crumbling around me, you were what I could hang on to. And I knew that I had to have something." He felt her hand tighten on his. "I've always been able to hang on to you, Beau. You've been the one constant thing in my whole life."

"I have?"

"The only one." Her eyes were so large, so blue, so filled with love for him. How could something make him so happy, and at the same time tear his heart? "Even Raoul—I don't know, that changed long ago. He's in a private place where his illness is . . . well, it's like another presence, something to be dealt with. I hide things from him, because he mustn't be upset." She shook her head. "But you? Always there, no matter what!"

He fought the words that rose to his lips. What he wanted to say was: Come home, let me be there for you every day the rest of your life. He knew that no matter how much she wanted to, her loyalty would never allow that. No, she would stay out in this desert until Raoul got well or the world ended, whichever came first. Well, the money he provided her would cushion her against the physical hardships. As for the others—they had both learned to live with those long, long ago. "My turn," he said. He took her hand and began playing with the fingers, letting the cool, smooth touch of her skin enter his memory. "You've been a constant presence in my life, too, Caroline— in more ways than you could know. I . . . I haven't had that many hard things happen, I guess. Certainly not what other people have had to bear."

"I'd say you've had your share," she said.

"Whatever it was, it was the thought of you that got me through," he said.

"Oh, Beau," she said. Her eyes glowed, and he could see nothing but her dear, familiar face. "I love you better than anyone in the whole world."

His hand stopped in mid-motion, and his fingers closed around hers. "Caroline—"

"You deserve to know that, Beau."

"Caroline," he said, rising, "I have to put my arms around you right now or go mad—and the only way I can decently do that is to dance with you."

She came into his arms, nestling there while their feet found the rhythm of the music and their bodies swayed. They both knew it might be another two years before they saw each other again. Or they might never see each other again. But they both had the sense to take every last bit of pleasure from this one night, not letting thoughts of empty tomorrows spoil the gifts of today. There are many men who have never had even this much, Beau thought. Caroline, feeling the luxury of a strong shoulder to lean on, the security of strong arms around her, thought that if she could just keep remembering how that felt, she could make it the rest of the way.

Beau drove back out to the house the next day. They walked out into the desert, and he told her that he now had Raoul's power of attorney and would be handling their investments until "Raoul is himself again."

The breeze from the mountains blew her hair around her face; she reached up a hand to brush back a curl and looked at him, a faintly challenging smile on her lips. "That sounds suspiciously like what your grandfather did for my grandmother when he helped her save Beau Chêne," she said.

"And if it is, does that matter?" he asked. "Caroline, last night you told me I've been the only constant thing in your life. Well, except for a few odds and ends, that's all been . . . pretty intangible. Let me do this, Caroline." He put all the force of his love for her into his voice. "If you won't let me do it for you, let me do it for myself."

"Oh, Beau," she said. "You always know how to get around me! And of course I can't be so selfish as to refuse help that will make life more comfortable for the children." She looked up at him as though wanting to measure his reaction to her next words. "I don't want the scales to get too out of balance, though. There's a limit to what I can accept, giving nothing in return." The next words came slowly, carefully. "I wouldn't want what you're able to do for me to come between us. Do you understand that, Beau?"

He did, though he wished that he didn't. How ridiculous that the thing he could give the most easily was also the most dangerous gift of all. Well, he would go slowly, not let their income increase too much, too quickly.

"You'll let me know if there's ever anything I can do?" he said urgently when it was time for him to leave.

"Besides everything else you've done?" She saw the pleading in his eyes. "All right. I promise. If I ever need you . . ." Her lips stumbled over those words—didn't she need him all the time? "If I ever need you for anything special, I'll call, Beau. I will."

He drove away, keeping that last view of her firmly in his mind. And during all the long miles back home, he saw her still—a straight-backed, golden-haired woman standing slim and tall at the gate in the fence, the purple mountains rising behind her.

39

Beau drove into Baton Rouge on Saturday, September 7, for yet another special session. Though what in hell's left for Huey to take over, I'm damned if I know, he thought. Long's power over the state and every branch of its government was now so complete that Beau had the feeling Long played with men and their lives just for the sheer pleasure of knowing he could. Like his plan for Judge Benjamin Pavy of St. Landry Parish, whose crime was that he did not make his judgments upon Long's law, but upon the constitution of the state of Louisiana. One of the bills for this session would gerrymander Pavy's district, effectively ending his judicial career. Beau thought of Pavy, ruthlessly removed. There is no tool Long won't use, no weapon too terrible. As if his attack on Pavy's career were not enough, Long had spread rumors that Pavy had Negro blood. It's incomprehensible, Beau thought. Long's no racist, he doesn't see color, doesn't really see people, if it comes to that. But if he thinks something will hurt an enemy, send him cowering back into his corner, he'll use it.

The peace he had thought would last for months dissipated quickly as soon as the House was called into session. So confident was Long that his legislature would give him everything he wanted that he had not even appeared in Baton Rouge, staying in New Orleans to play golf with Seymour Weiss. But he won't be able to stay away, Beau thought, watching Long's men run bills through. Their arrogance was insufferable; far worse than Long's. At least Long had the personal dynamism that accounted for his power. These henchmen wore the power they borrowed from him like ill-fitting suits; they strutted around like little boys in a grown man's coat. And they're just as foolish-looking, Beau told himself, gritting his teeth in frustration.

By Sunday evening, Beau was wondering why he had bothered to come at all. What good did it do to vote no, time after time after time? What good did it do to protest voting on bills that had been placed on his desk minutes before the speaker asked for a decision? What the hell did any of it matter?

They were close to adjournment when a stir at the back of the House announced Long's arrival. Beau felt his cheeks flush—the humiliation of sitting in this circus when the ringmaster strode in! He sat straight, his eyes on the papers on his desk, aware of Long moving through the chamber, visiting with his men. At one point Long stood at the desk next to Beau's, his body so close the cloth of his sleeve brushed Beau's face. Beau remained rigid, staring ahead until Long moved on to the speaker's dais, where he sat conferring with Allen Ellender, the speaker of the House.

Long looked over the House with an expression Beau thought must be exactly the way a feudal lord viewed his serfs. He had no need to lift a finger, or even an eyebrow. His bills moved from introduction to passage with an ease ascribed to greased pigs, and Long, bored, left, taking a path that would tour him near the desks of his leaders. His big raucous voice could be heard telling those men that he wanted them to caucus the next day to discuss upcoming legislation. Is that for our benefit? Beau thought. He knows damn well he's going to get everything he wants.

The massive double doors of the House chamber swung shut behind Long, and Beau looked wearily at his watch. Nine-twenty. He would have to do something to get the taste of this session out of his mouth before he could sleep. He looked around the room, thinking that perhaps he and a colleague could go out and get something to eat, have a complaint session that would at least relieve their feelings, even if it did nothing to change the situation.

Suddenly he heard a short bark, an explosion, followed almost immediately by another. He looked at the legislator at the next desk, who was peering intently in the direction of the noise, like a pasture animal who has just sensed danger. "What . . .?" Beau said. And then there was a volley of explosions, sounds so sharp, so clearly defined, that Beau knew at once what they were—gunshots!

Men scrambled to their feet, running toward the chamber exits. Beau thrust himself clear of the men behind him and ran through the rotunda to the hall leading to the governor's office.

A ring of men, more than half of them with guns in their hands, stood circling something that lay on the marble floor. Even before Beau reached them and looked over Justice John Fournet's shoulder, he knew what he would see. Even so, the sight of the body hit him with such violence that it took him a full thirty seconds to realize that the man who lay there was not Huey Pierce Long, but a young man he knew—Dr. Carl Weiss, son-in-law of Judge Benjamin Pavy.

The men standing there broke their positions, running down the steps that led to the basement. Beau, in their midst, was carried forward on a wave of confusion. Ahead of him he saw two figures vanishing through the back door leading from the basement to the parking lot. He managed to burst through the door just as one of the men flagged down a passing car and helped Long into it. The car immediately sped off. Beau heard its tires screaming as it took the turn that would lead it to Our Lady of the Lake Hospital, directly behind the capitol across a small manmade lake. He stood staring at the red taillights which made two bloody spots against the darkness.

"Where'd they take him?" a man asked, roughly grabbing Beau's arm.

"Who?" Beau asked.

Then out of the nightmare the answer came. "The governor. Long. He's been shot."

It was then that the image of Weiss's body on the hall floor really drove into his consciousness. The face, flesh torn from the bones by the cascade of bullets which had scalpeled it like a surgeon's knife. The white linen suit, shredded, blood-soaked. The blood.

Beau turned and moved slowly through the basement door, back up the stairs past panic-stricken men surging down it. He looked at the pool of blood on the marble floor, then went up the hall into the rotunda of the capitol. The Senate and House chambers were empty. Long's men were in cars, converging on the hospital across the lake. His enemies were converging on hotel suites, private homes, there to stand watch, to pose the question that was soon on every lip in the state: Will Long live?

Beau, driving home to St. Martinville through the cool September night, knew as well as anyone else why a man dedicated to preserving lives would offer his own to kill another. He had seen violence boiling up across the state, like the mosquitoes that rose in swarms from the marshes. It had been inevitable that someone would kill Huey. He rolled all the windows down, inhaled the fresh air. He said a silent prayer for Dr. Carl Weiss and his family. And another one for the state.

During the hours following the attack, the attention of the entire state of Louisiana was centered on Our Lady of the Lake Hospital, where Huey Pierce Long fought for his life. People milled about on the lawn, staring up at the window of the hospital room where he lay, as though their prayers could penetrate the brick and mortar, provide magic healing for Long's wound. They spoke in hushed voices, bound by one hope—that the man who was leading them out of darkness would live to lead them still.

In St. Martinville, Beau and Claude kept the death watch together. They said little, but their closeness during that time had a quality both recognized. They were no longer just father and son, caught in the momentous event that was rocking the state. They were two men who had helped shape the government of their state, whose own lives had been forever changed by the life of the man who now lay dying. Two men who must gird themselves for the tasks that lay ahead when Huey Long was no more, and his legacy of power descended to lesser men.

The news of his death came in the early-morning hours of September 10. "He's gone," Claude said, after taking the call. He gripped Beau's shoulder. "He said something right at the end—'God, don't let me die. I have so much to do.'"

For a long moment, their eyes met. They had little doubt but that state government would dissolve in chaos, and that in the scramble for spoils, Long's inner circle would fall out among themselves. Steady men whose vision of government was higher than the next election, broader than material gain, would be needed as never before. Claude sighed. His grip on Beau's shoulder tightened. "Son," he said, "I think you're going to have your work cut out for you."

They drove into Baton Rouge for the funeral. The roads were filled with vehicles, all heading the same way. The mule-drawn wagons, the horse-drawn buggies. Model A's and Buicks. It was a cortege that clogged the miles and miles of paved roads Long had built. It was a march of homage from his people. By the time he was buried on the lawn in front of the capitol, a quarter of a million people had stood by to watch, and the flowers they sent covered two acres.

Beau stood beside Claude, his uncovered head bowed. The fury of emotions that had raged in him since Long's death were quieted. His battles with Long were over. As the coffin was lowered out of sight, Beau lifted his head for one last look. And then sorrow swept over him. Sorrow for the man who had caught his youthful enthusiasm and turned it into a white-hot flame. Sorrow for the big man who loved life, loved his people. He thought of Long's last words, and bowed his head again. Sorrow, finally, for a man whose vision had remained pure, but whose means of realizing it had not.

September dragged to a close, one sultry day after another. Beau had no heart for work, no energy for recreation. He went through the motions, almost as though he were in hibernation. I don't want to think about the legislature now, he thought. The scramble for power, the division of the spoils—the hard battles ahead.

Then in the first week of October he received a call from Caroline. Her voice sounded dull, emotionless, as though she had been drained of feeling, and all that was left was the tired knowledge that she had to go on. "Raoul died last night," she said. "You said to call if I ever needed you . . ." Then the voice stopped, and all he could hear were her soft sobs coming over the miles of wire between them, breaking his heart.

"I'll be out as fast as an airplane can get me there," he said. He packed in a daze, watched the swampland turn to prairie and the prairie turn to desert as the plane flew west, arriving at the adobe house at twilight. The deep shadows of evening made the purple mountains huge blurs against the horizon, with nothing to mark the division between land and sky. The house seemed to crouch against the desert floor, surrounded by the monstrous hulks.

Caroline opened the door, framed in its light for a moment. Then she came into his arms. Past her, he could see the three children sitting rigidly at the table, plates of food before them. In that first instant that he held her, he saw three pairs of eyes turn and look at him. He recognized that look. It was the way his own children had looked after their mother had died. He let his arm slip around Caroline's waist, turned her gently, and moved forward, supporting her. He looked at each child in turn. "It's going to be all right," he promised them.

The details of closing the house, making arrangements to have Raoul sent home, calling ahead to Lafayette and making funeral arrangements there, consumed all the time Beau and Caroline had. They worked almost silently, speaking only of the things that must be done, taking no time for anything else. And then they were on the train heading home. Beau insisted on traveling with them. "This time," he said, "you're going to be comfortable. I want you to get in that bed in that drawing room and not get out of it until we're home."

She let him travel with them, let him pay for their accommodations. But she did not stay in bed. She was with her children every minute of the three days it took to reach Lafayette, balancing her mood with theirs. She comforted their grief, diverted them when she could, poured whatever strength she had left into making them feel that no matter how lost they felt, no matter how frightened, she would not leave them. She would always be there.

The first night out from Albuquerque, Beau stood on the platform of the club car, smoking and staring out into the desert night. He had made himself hold back the consciousness that Raoul's death had set Caroline free until the rush of departure and the first hard grief was past them. Now he stood, smoke rising around him like a puff of mist from the cooling desert. He felt himself come alive as his dreams grew more and more real. He and Caroline, living at the farm. Sleeping in the great bed that had held generations of Langlinaises. And the children, finally blessed with the presence of a mother. He thought of how it would be, to live until the end of his days with the only woman he had ever loved or wanted. He could almost feel her in his arms.

He went to her compartment door, his hand raised to knock. Then he paused. She was exhausted, and she still had not only this long, sad ride home, but the funeral and its aftermath to deal with. He must give her time. And he must give her children time. He could remember too well the months after Louise died, when the loss of even so distant a mother had torn at the children's sleep and disturbed their days. He turned and moved quietly down the hall to his own roomette. No, this certainly was not the time to speak.

He undressed slowly. He was more exhausted than he could ever remember being. He almost fell into bed, then lay watching the stars. Out away from the glow of lights, they stood coldly bright, millions and millions of them. He sought his own familiar constellations. The Big Dipper. The Little Bear. Gemini.

But the sky was alien, the stars not the same. He would wait until Caroline had been on familiar ground, under familiar stars. Until she felt secure again. It was one thing, he thought, for them to love each other all these years when there was no possibility of ever doing anything about it. Now—now all they had dreamed of lay just within their grasp. And to assure having it was surely worth being patient, careful, just a little while longer.

Caroline, too, lay watching the stars. For the first time since Raoul's death, she had time to think quietly. Her call to Beau had been instinctive, and she remembered, with a rush of feeling that made her weak, what she had wanted. For him to come out and make it all right again. For him to sweep her up and hold her and tell her not to worry—not ever, ever again. She felt a tear brush against her cheek and wiped it away angrily. She should be weeping for Raoul. But she had wept for him long ago, when the illness ravaged him and it was clear that he would never get well. Now she wept for Beau, and for herself. For all the years they had lost, all the youth they had missed.

Don't be such a wretch, she told herself. Think of everything you have to be thankful for: the children . . . Something inside her was stronger than that litany of thanks. "You have a right to weep," it said. "A right to mourn." She turned her face into her pillow and let the tears come. What made her grief all the worse was that the one person who could assuage it, whose arms around her made her feel forever safe, was only half a car away. And yet, she thought, it might just as well be the moon.

40

Thin slabs of clouds floated in the cold blue December sky like ice on the surface of a pond. The sharp crack of a gun shattered the silence, and a duck fell earthward, spiraling against the rising sun. "Good shot, Raoul!" Beau said. They stood together, watching the yellow hound sprint forward to retrieve the game. "Won't be long before you're outshooting me."

"Guess so," Raoul said, but his smile told Beau how good he felt about that last shot.

"It's good to have you all at Beau Chêne. When the children and I moved out to the farm, I was afraid they'd be lonesome. But I guess y'all have about worn that path between the houses to a nub."

Raoul took in a breath of the clear, chill air. "I like it out here. And Mama—Mama just loves it."

"Yes," Beau said. He squinted up at the sun. "'Bout time to be heading in," he said. "Christmas Eve and all, there's a lot to do."

"I told Mama I'd bring her a tree," Raoul said. "And some holly."

"There's a nice stand of young pine not far from here," Beau said. "Come on, I'll help you."

They found a tree, cut armloads of holly, and made their way to Beau Chêne. Caroline and Luella were in the kitchen, deep in preparations for Christmas dinner. Caroline looked up when they came in; Beau saw how rested she looked. Her money worries, Beau had assured her, were over. He knew that she did not comprehend that the rapid and sizable return on Raoul's modest investments wasn't possible, and he was thankful for that. Every month, when he sent a check to her bank, he felt the pledge he had made to Raoul to care for his family was being honored. If in order to fulfill that promise, he had to deceive Caroline—well, it couldn't be helped.

"We've brought Christmas," he said, dumping the holly near the door. "The tree needs a stand; we'll go knock one together. Anything else you need?"

"About three more hands," Caroline said. Flour dusted her face, her golden hair curled over cheeks flushed with oven heat, and her hands were sticky with dough. She's never looked prettier, Beau thought. "I wasn't sure I was going to do . . . well, a real Christmas," Caroline said. "And then I thought: Of course I am!"

"Good," Beau said. "I happen to know that there are a few packages at the farm destined for Beau Chêne, and the children will be much happier putting them under a tree." He stuck his finger in the cookie dough and sampled it. "Lord, are these those wonderful cookies your grandmother used to make every Christmas?"

"I looked high and low for the recipe," Caroline said. "Do you think they taste the same?"

"Magnifique," Beau said. Happiness rose in him like the steam from the pots on the stove.

All the way back to the farm, game bag swinging comfortably over his shoulder, he tried to decide how he would ask her the question that would not leave his mind. It's ridiculous, he thought. She knows how I feel. I don't have to say much . . . As the day wore on, he thought up and discarded a dozen different scenarios. Would he just take her hand and slip onto it the ring he'd bought a month ago? Ask her, right out, when they could be married? Nothing he thought of seemed right. Dammit, it's been so long . . . He had to laugh at himself. What did he want, a full-dress parade? All you need to do, he scolded himself, is ask her. That's all.

He dressed for midnight Mass carefully, recombing his hair and changing his tie four times. As he tucked a handkerchief into his breast pocket, he stared at himself in the mirror. Thirty-five years old. Well, almost thirty-six. A good age to start a new life. He squared his shoulders and went out into the hall. "Come on," he called to the children. "If we don't get started, we'll be late."

Gennie and Émilie were already young ladies now, with

grown-up manners and bodies that seemed to change almost daily. They're beauties, he thought. Gennie's limp was barely noticeable; she compensated for it with a slow walk that had its own charm. Her great gray eyes glowed with an inner fire that belied her calm face and sedate movements; when she suddenly looked at Beau, his heart caught and he saw his sister Francie. Émilie was as quick and flirtatious as Gennie was quiet; her hazel eyes missed nothing, and her tongue rarely stopped. They were like two sides of a coin, and when they entered a room, they were the immediate focus of attention, one dispensing charm and the other dispensing laughter. Skye, at twelve, looked so much like his father that when they walked together Beau sometimes had the feeling that he was walking with himself. He put his arms around them as they drew near. "I'm a lucky man," he said, kissing each one in turn. "A very lucky man."

Caroline and her children were already in the pew where Beau Chêne families had sat for generations when the Langlinaises made their way up the aisle of St. Martin of Tours Church a half-hour before midnight. The choir was in the loft, singing carols. Beau, entering the Langlinais pew, caught Alice's eye and grinned. "Remember how Miss Bessie used to sing every Christmas Eve and Papa and Grandpapa would always laugh and make you and Mama Geneviève furious?" he whispered.

"They were a disgrace," Alice said, smiling. She squeezed his hand. "Merry Christmas," she said. "You look as though you're having a happy one."

His gaze turned involuntarily to Caroline's pew across the aisle. "I am," he said.

The music swelled, there was a rustle at the back of the church, and the procession began. The child carrying the Infant placed Him in the straw-filled manger that centered the crèche, and voices rose, heralding the ever-new birth of Christ.

Beau felt an anticipation that had nothing to do with the events celebrated in the Mass, and yet perhaps was a part of their promise. He could remember, as though it were the night before, the midnight Mass in this same church nineteen years ago, when he had watched a slender girl with long golden curls and blue eyes take her place in the Beau Chêne pew next to Marthe de Gravelle. He looked at that young girl now. Others might see a dignified young widow, surrounded by her children. He saw a sixteen-year-old beauty whose silver laughter had haunted his dreams during many a bleak and lonely night. He saw Caroline picking wild violets, saw Caroline running down the steps of Beau Chêne toward him, saw them swaying in each other's arms on the long upper gallery, and felt her settle finally in his heart. He let himself enjoy the luxury of anticipation, because he knew that this time, it would be fulfilled.

"Come have eggnog," Caroline said when they stood in front of the church after Mass. "I used Grandmother's recipe. I think it's a tradition for the families to drink it on Christmas Eve."

They sang all the way out to Beau Chêne, one carol after the other; by the time they gathered in the parlor around the piano, they were all in high spirits, and with Gennie playing, the six children sang. Beau followed Caroline down to the kitchen.

"All I have to do is heat it up and beat the egg whites," she said, taking a big pitcher out of the refrigerator. "Would you cut some fruitcake, please, Beau? And put out some of those cookies?"

Ask her now, he told himself. The box that held the ring felt huge in his pocket; he could think of nothing else, nor could he think of anything to say. I'll wait until we've taken this upstairs, he thought. Get her away from the children and just ask her, flat out.

He followed her up the stairs, carrying a laden tray. He helped get everyone served, sat down with his own warm cup. The tree he and Raoul had cut that morning glowed from a corner, packages piled high under its fresh green branches.

"Looks like Santa came sure enough," he said, looking at the tree.

"He seems to have a workshop at your farm," Caroline said. "At least, I think the largest number of packages came from there." She got up and put her cup down. "But I have a few things still to put under it—would you help me get them, Beau?"

He rose and followed her. His idea of asking her to marry him tonight clearly wasn't going to work—it was late, he should take his children home and get them to bed. Well, tomorrow, then. He thrust his hands into his pockets and felt the small velvet box touch one of them. No, maybe he should take her out to dinner in New Iberia one night after Christmas.

My God, a proposal wasn't a family affair, there should be some romance, some excitement. As there was the first time, he thought, and felt a rush of love for her.

They were in the library; Caroline was standing at the desk, sorting through a small pile of wrapped packages. "Here," she said, holding one out to Beau. "Would you open this one, please?"

He took it, read the card. "It's for you," he said, puzzled. "The card reads: 'To Caroline.'"

"Yes," she said. "It is for me. But I can't have it if you don't . . . want me to." She came and stood beside him. "Open it, Beau."

He untied the thin gold ribbon, let the blue paper fall away. A rectangular leather case, like a folio for photographs. He opened it. A mirror? "What. . . ?" he said.

Gently she raised his hand that held the mirror, until it was opposite his face. "Look," she said. He stared into it and saw his own reflection.

"Well," she said. "May I have it?"

The realization of what she meant came over him, and he opened his arms to her. She came into them, and the years dropped away. All the barriers were gone, all the pain forgotten.

"Oh, Beau," she said. "When I think of that awful day . . ."

He knew what she meant. The dark afternoon when they stood in front of Holy Name Church in New Orleans and turned away from each other, each to begin a long, slow march down separate roads. Now the roads had converged again; there were no more detours, no more obstacles.

He pulled the velvet box from his pocket, opened it, and took out the ring. "I thought you could wear this on your right hand for now," he said. "Until we're married." He watched the ring slip down her finger, watched the fire of sapphires and diamonds catch the light and break into a spectrum of color.

Then he pulled her back against him and stood holding her until a burst of music from upstairs broke into their golden place. Six young voices rose in a hymn as old as love, and as new as its promise. "'O come, all ye faithful, joyful and triumphant,'" the children sang.

Caroline stirred and smiled up at Beau. "Listen to what they're singing," she said. She caught his hand and held it against her face. "Oh, Beau, we are, aren't we?" He felt her skin, smooth, soft. He watched her lips come nearer, watched her eyes become darker. "We have been faithful, both of us. And it came right after all." Her face was close, so close. Filled now with a joy he knew was mirrored in his own. As his lips came down to meet hers, he let the soaring music enter him. Yes. They had been faithful.

Caroline moved away from him. "Let's go tell the children," she said.

Hand in hand, their voices making a counterpoint to the ones above them, they went up the stairs, joyful—and triumphant.

Epilogue

Beau stood on the altar of St. Martin of Tours Church, watching Gennie, Émilie, and Caro walk slowly down the aisle, their pale blue organdy dresses floating around them. "Of course the girls must be in the wedding," Alice had insisted. "They can wear short dresses . . ." Her eyes had lit up with a happy smile. "Beau, you're going to have a real wedding! After all these years . . ."

He watched Caroline walk down the aisle toward him, her ivory dress setting off her fair skin and glowing eyes, the roses she carried matching the color that bloomed in her cheeks. Raoul, Henri, and Skye were already on the altar, serving as groomsmen. Claude, again his son's best man, looked out at Alice in the front pew and smiled. He had no reservations about this wedding. If there had ever been a happier occasion in St. Martinville, he would have to work hard to think of it.

The people of St. Martinville had not been shocked when Beau and Caroline announced they would marry in June. Raoul had been ill a very long time—and Beau and Caroline were home-folks, their own. For a descendant of the de Clouets to marry a Langlinais—what would be better?

Beau found he could hardly make the responses to the priest's questions. He couldn't believe it—he was marrying Caroline! When it was time to slip the wedding ring on the finger that now wore only his engagement ring, his eyes blurred, and he had to catch her hand for a moment before going on. The triumphal passage down the main aisle after the ceremony, with faces beaming from every pew, was something he would never forget. Alice reached out to Caroline from her pew, hugged her, and said, "Welcome to our family." Beau knew that sentiment was echoed in every heart.

"Mrs. Beau Langlinais," he said, testing the words, bending over her as they stood outside the church waiting for the people

498

thronging out after them. "Caroline Langlinais. Don't you think that has a nice ring to it?"

"The very nicest," she said.

The June day matched their spirits: a clear blue sky, cloudless, its blue so deep it seemed painted. The air was scented with magnolias and roses. The reception following the ceremony was held at Beau Chêne, where Luella presided over the kitchen. "Oh, Mr. Beau," she said, bustling out to greet them, "we is having the good old times all over again."

Everywhere there were people, music, and laughter. The twins moved through the guests, introducing Caroline's children as "my brother Raoul" or "my sister Caro" to the people from St. Martinville and New Iberia who might not know them. Claudine served punch, telling everyone: "Isn't it the most romantic thing in the world? Like a fairy tale!" Marie slipped up to Alice and hugged her, whispering in her ear, "Now we don't have to worry about Beau ever again."

The height of the reception came when the band began to play. Beau stepped out onto the upper gallery, his bride in his arms, to dance her the length of it alone before anyone else joined in. A hush fell on the guests gathered on the lawn below, in the house behind them. The first song was "Till the Clouds Roll By"; Beau had asked for it in honor of that dance so long ago: before they had gone half the length of the floor, they were both crying, with Beau leaning forward to kiss her tears away.

Alice turned to Claude, her own handkerchief at her eyes. "Oh, Claude, I never thought I'd see this day!"

"They make a fine couple," he said. "If they make a baby, it'll be a nice one."

Alice laughed, the full, happy laugh he had first heard in their marriage bed. "I don't think there's any 'if' about it," she said.

Following the reception, the children went into town with Claude and Alice, leaving Beau and Caroline to walk over the familiar path to the farm, where they would spend their wedding night. They had decided on a brief wedding trip, before collecting all six children for a European tour. "Every dream of my life coming true, all at once," Caroline had said.

She leaned on Beau's arm on the walk over. "I want to remember every moment of this," she said. "I want to remember walking from de Clouet land to Langlinais land, to feel it beneath my feet and to smell it around me."

The farm was ready, the rooms spotless, flowers in every vase, food in the refrigerator and champagne chilling in a silver cooler. Beau's arms came around her and his lips pressed against her hair. He felt ridiculously nervous, as though he had never made love to a woman before.

She nestled closer to him, and then he heard her giggling. "Beau," she said, her voice muffled against his chest. "Beau, I'm scared to death, isn't that foolish?" She looked up at him. She was laughing, but her eyes were huge and dark. It was all right again, he was Beau and she was Caroline, the Caroline who trusted him and loved him and would never leave him again.

"I am, too, a little," he said. "But don't worry, Caroline, we're going to be just fine."

When she came to him later, the only light from the moon fixed against a starlit sky just outside their bedroom window, he felt as though time had circled back upon itself, and as though all the years had been given back to them both. The scent of a sweet olive tree planted outside that room a hundred years before wafted through the open windows. Caroline slipped off her lace negligee and got into bed beside him, lying on her back with her blond hair silver-gold in the moonlight. Her gown was a Grecian style, the pleated bodice tied with a ribbon just under her breasts. His hand went gently to the ribbon, untied it, and then, seeing in her eyes the look he had imagined for so long, he pushed the gown from her shoulders and buried his face between her breasts.

A long shuddering sigh went through her, and her arms came around him. Then, as though she had been gathering the force of her own passion, she responded to his.

The moon rose higher in the sky, casting the room into deeper shadow. The bayou shimmered as the moon skipped over it, a ribbon of silver tying Beau Chêne and the Langlinais farm into one shining stretch of rich, fertile land. A breeze blowing in from the Gulf found the open window and sailed in. Caroline, asleep in Beau's arms, felt it against her back and nestled closer to him. She did not stir, she did not have to. Whatever winds blew over her, Beau's strong back would protect her.

Beau felt her stir and drowsily pulled her closer. Then he slipped back into sleep, and to dreams that were tonight not of power, but finally, only of love.

Sweeping
Stories
of Captivating
Romance

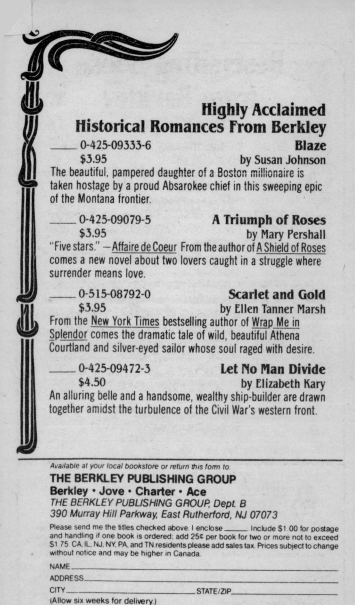

Highly Acclaimed
Historical Romances From Berkley

_____ 0-425-09333-6 **Blaze**
$3.95 by Susan Johnson

The beautiful, pampered daughter of a Boston millionaire is taken hostage by a proud Absarokee chief in this sweeping epic of the Montana frontier.

_____ 0-425-09079-5 **A Triumph of Roses**
$3.95 by Mary Pershall

"Five stars." —Affaire de Coeur From the author of A Shield of Roses comes a new novel about two lovers caught in a struggle where surrender means love.

_____ 0-515-08792-0 **Scarlet and Gold**
$3.95 by Ellen Tanner Marsh

From the New York Times bestselling author of Wrap Me in Splendor comes the dramatic tale of wild, beautiful Athena Courtland and silver-eyed sailor whose soul raged with desire.

_____ 0-425-09472-3 **Let No Man Divide**
$4.50 by Elizabeth Kary

An alluring belle and a handsome, wealthy ship-builder are drawn together amidst the turbulence of the Civil War's western front.

Bestselling Books
from Berkley

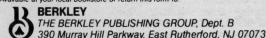